The Long Gainer

Books by WILLIAM MANCHESTER

Fiction

THE CITY OF ANGER

SHADOW OF THE MONSOON

THE LONG GAINER

Biography

DISTURBER OF THE PEACE
The Life of H. L. Mencken

A ROCKEFELLER FAMILY PORTRAIT
From John D. to Nelson

Diversion

BEARD THE LION

The Long Gainer

a novel by

WILLIAM MANCHESTER

LITTLE, BROWN AND COMPANY
BOSTON • TORONTO

LIBRARY OF CONGRESS CATALOG CARD NO. 61-12817

FIRST EDITION

Published simultaneously in Canada
by Little, Brown & Company (Canada) Limited

PRINTED IN THE UNITED STATES OF AMERICA

For J *and* J *and* j

It is a pleasure to acknowledge
the generous support given me
by
The John Simon Guggenheim Memorial Foundation
and
The Wesleyan University Center for Advanced Studies

Times passes on in days innumerable
And brings to light the hidden things, and hides
What once was seen; and nothing is there strange
We may not look for: even sternest oaths
And firm resolves must yield themselves to him.

— Sophocles, *Ajax*, 646-650

. . . the *Interpreter* took him again by the hand, and led him into a pleasant place, where was builded a stately Palace, beautiful to behold; at the sight of which, *Christian* was greatly delighted; he saw also upon the top thereof, certain Persons walked, who were cloathed all in gold. Then said *Christian*, May we go in thither? Then the *Interpreter* took him, and led him up toward the door of the Palace; and behold, at the door, stood a great company of men, as desirous to go in, but durst not. There also sat a Man, at a little distance from the door, at a Table-side, with a Book, and his Inkhorn before him, to take the Name of him that should enter therein: He saw also that in the doorway, stood many Men in Armour to keep it, being resolved to do to the Man that would enter, what hurt and mischief they could. Now was *Christian* somwhat in a muse; at last, when every Man started back for fear of the Armed Men; *Christian* saw a man of a very stout countenance come up to the Man that sat there to write; saying, *Set down my Name Sir;* the which when he had done, he saw the Man draw his Sword, and put an Helmet upon his Head, and rush toward the door upon the Armed Men, who laid upon him with deadly force; but the Man, not at all discouraged, fell to cutting and hacking most fiercely; so after he had received and given many wounds to those that attempted to keep him out, he cut his way through them all, and pressed forward into the Palace; at which there was a pleasant voice heard from those that were within, even of the Three that walked upon the top of the Palace, saying,

Come in, Come in;
Eternal Glory thou shalt win.

So he went in, and was cloathed with such Garments as they.

— John Bunyan, *The Pilgrim's Progress from this World to That which is to Come*

Note

Because the illusion persists that contemporary novels are *romans à clef*, it is necessary to point out that what follows is entirely a work of fiction. The author has been enrolled in or employed by four colleges and universities (two privately endowed and two public). None of them served as a prototype for either of the institutions in this story. Similarly, the author has worked for various newspapers as a reporter, foreign correspondent, and editor, but he created the Birmingham *Star* out of whole cloth. The same is true of the imaginary New England state in which all the action takes place — careful readers will note that it has the attributes of *several* states — and of the imaginary people who live there. In America at least two athletes have become presidents of their universities and later entered politics. Neither was in New England and neither, to the best of the author's knowledge, resembled Doc River in any way. The characters in the novel exist only in these pages. None is based on any living person except the novelist himself, who is the model for all of them.

The Players

Adam R. "Doc" River, B.A. State '29, LL.D. (hon.) Michigan State '51, President of State
Sarah River, B.S. State '29, his invalid wife
Hiram A. "Ham" Markham, B.A. State '46, a journalist
Catherine "Kit" Ryan O'Donnell, B.A. State '46, a sorority housemother
Newton V. Albert, chairman, Democratic State Central Committee
Roger Justice Davies, A.B. Yale '09, LL.B. Harvard '12, Federal jurist

W. Denton Tate, Ed.D. Columbia '36, Provost of State
Sam Theanapolis, B.A. State '30, chairman of State's board of trustees; president, Associate Alumni
Harry Osborne Mikel, B.S. State '16, Ph.D. Harvard '23, LL.D. (hon.) Harvard '32, D. Litt. (hon.) Peabody '36, *honoris causa* Oxford '46, Professor of History
Eric Lutz, Ph.D. Luitpold Gymnasium (Munich) '30, Professor of Physics
Elsie Shoemaker, A.A. Stephens '31, Dean of Women
Thomas A. Yablonski, U.C.L.A. '37, Professor of Physical Education
Gertrude E. "Hotflash" Hatch, Phi Delta Pi, Wingate School of Dramatic Arts '47, Assistant Professor of Physical Education
Solomon Feinblatt, A.B. Cornell '54, Ph.D. Cornell '58, Instructor in English

Governor Norman R. Blandford
Stuart Hathaway Plimpton Witty, A.B. Peabody College '22, LL.B. Harvard '25, LL.D. (hon.) Williams '56, a corporation lawyer
Clare Hewitt, A.B. Peabody '37, chairman, Republican State Central Committee
Hallam Caulkin, A.B. Peabody '24, General Managing Editor of the Birmingham *Star*
Charles Smathers, Chief Librarian of the *Star*
Frank C. "Frosty" Warren, IV, A.B. Dartmouth '49, a journalist
Alvin Swinton, another journalist
Peter N. Healy, a retired journalist
Peter "Geek" Minton, a *Sly* photographer

Robert Budge, S.B. Notre Dame '32, Ph.D. Minnesota '35, a visiting academician
Paul Bauer, B.S. State '38, a State trustee
John Winkler, State '51, director of university public relations
Jacob Russo, B.S. State '39, director of university agricultural services

William Shaw, B.A. State '38, director of university scholarship aid
Joe Massicotte, B.S. State '40, administrator of Haven Square Hospital
William Wallace Whipple, A.B. Peabody '07, Ph.D. Princeton '12, Victor Lionel Hubbard Professor of Classics at Peabody

Richard "Red" Stacy, State '62, a halfback
Daphne "Daffy" Dix, State '61, a Titanette
Jerry Dix, B.S. State '55, her husband, a graduate student
Jill Sanders, State '62, a Statette
Jack Sanders, State '60, a Business Administration major
Trudy Viggiantti, State '60, a Journalism major
Sam Theanapolis, Jr., State '63, a tuba player

* * * * *

Dancy Abigail Davies Markham, A.B. Stoddard College for Women '45, absent in India with her son
George E. "Spook" Duschene, ex State '44, killed in action in Belgium, December 25, 1944

ONE

Saturday's Hero

HAM MARKHAM sprawled across a Victorian couch in his father-in-law's downtown apartment, a study in immobility. His long legs dangled. Even his crisp hair lay flat. Idly he explored his senses, feeling the perspiration gather on his muscular arms, watching the brassy rays of the noon sun wink along the gilt spines of the judge's law books, smelling the room's fragrance of worn leather and ancient must and tobacco. If only he could sleep. He squeezed his eyes shut, but the lids sprang open, and yawning listlessly he stared once more toward the foot of the sofa, where, folded and propped by a telephone on the marble-topped end table, stood a mint copy of the morning newspaper.

Largest daily circulation in the Northeast	The Birmingham Star	The Weather Fair and Hot

G. O. Promises Kept, Gov. Says on Campaign Eve; Demmies Search for Issue, Mum on Candidate

The Daily Blatter, he thought. The old wind machine. The faithful organ of the G. O. Prominent. Occasionally the paper did run a blurb about someone else, though. Today, for example, the picture of a *Star* employee was puffed on page one, and since this employee was Ham himself, his father-in-law had left the paper on display. Ham regarded it narrowly; his own face always seemed to him the face of a stranger. The photograph suggested a lithe, lantern-jawed man with dark, smoldering eyes. It was only a suggestion. The halftone was over-inked, muddy. And that, he reflected wryly, made it a perfect likeness. It was bleary; so was he. The long flight from New Delhi had been exhausting, and now in the dog-day heat of the New England summer he felt drained. He stretched his lean frame and winced. Lately every trip seemed to tax him. He wondered whether he was working too hard. Well. Maybe. But better that than becoming a heavily handsome drone, the usual fate of the spavined old athlete, which, after all, he was.

— or than rusting away like the typical Overseas Press man, which he was also. Squinting, he made out the caption:

Hiram A. Markham, author and Star *foreign correspondent, returns home today after ten years in India and Southeast Asia. See story, p. 16.*

Ham didn't turn to page sixteen, didn't even rise. He was damned if he'd touch newsprint again until he had to. The paper had promised him a week's holiday, and he meant to spend it on his back, asleep. Now. *Now.* His lids twitched, then drooped, but the refrain sang in his head like a teasing jingle: *Ham Markham is home, Ham-Markham ishome, HamMarkhamishome* . . .

Home, die Heimat, la patrie, ciudad natal, blad, ghar, makán, watan, des — after a decade the word was as familiar in one tongue as another. Home itself was another matter, though. It was the real reason he had been wakeful since touching down at Idlewild yesterday. Being in America excited him more than he had thought possible. His wife Dancy flew back each spring for a month in New York, courtesy of the judge, but Ham himself had been in the city just once during the '50's, for his mother's funeral. In the years since he had first flown to Asia Birmingham had been transformed. Every house had a television antenna, and signs of the gleamy changes he had only read about in the international edition of the *Times* were all around him: tailfins, compacts, filter-tips, Bermudas, split-levels, Bar-B-Q pits, tranquilizers, LP hi-fi's, 3-D Todd-AO wide screens, and the heightened accent on packaging. His curiosity was rapacious. He couldn't wait to explore it all.

Yet he had to wait. His need for rest was urgent and growing. Damn it, he thought, I belong on a psychiatrist's couch, not a judge's. He wondered whether a sleeping pill would help, decided not, yawned again, and was dozing off when the telephone rang.

It was, surprisingly, the *Star*'s general managing editor.

"Caulkin here," he said resonantly. "That you, Hiram?"

"Sure," was all Ham said.

More was expected. Hallam Caulkin was a reserve colonel, and the key to him was that he liked to be called by his title. Ham pictured him sitting at attention in his air-conditioned office, wearing his crisp Peabody College tie and a faultless J. Press suit with a ticket pocket and cuff buttons that buttoned, fingering his big black mustache and glancing up at his situation map of the world. The map had pins wherever *Star* correspondents were. One year Caulkin's Christmas card had been a miniature of it, with Ham stuck in the middle of Patiala and the East Punjab States Union. Ham had gathered that he was supposed to be proud, but when he saw the nearest pin was in Vienna he had only felt lonely.

He felt wary now, for he sensed an imposition. This call had the ring of business.

"Feeling fit?" Caulkin inquired.

"I just woke up," Ham said guardedly.

"Ah. Well. Upward and onward."

Ham flinched. It came back to him now. That had always been a favorite expression of Caulkin's, as though life were a kind of rope climb. Another pet, he remembered, had been "by the bye."

"By the bye, I saw Judge Davies at the Clipper Club this morning. He was just leaving for the station. I told him it was a shame he'd be on his way to Washington when you arrived. You know him. He just gave me that startled, wispy look of his."

He probably wondered who you were, Ham thought. Just because you've belonged to the same club for thirty years, don't expect the judge to recognize you. *I'm* in the family, and *I* don't. Ham liked and admired his eminent father-in-law, but sometimes he wondered whether he should be allowed to cross the street alone.

"I'm not complaining. He didn't leave his chauffeur, but the refrigerator's full of beer."

Caulkin laughed mechanically. "Say, it's too bad Dancy couldn't come."

"I left her in Darjeeling. My son has asthma. I'll miss them, of course, but it's only for three months."

That was meant as a cue. Ham was disturbed because he hadn't been told his *Star* assignment here. He knew only that when this week ended he was due for some local reporting, in keeping with the paper's custom of sending for its correspondents once each decade to do a few Birmingham stories. "Operation rotation," this had been christened by Caulkin, who also called all *Star* vacations furloughs. The colonel never forgot his rank; he was forever drawing up formal travel orders, or issuing commendations to the staff. He liked to be brisk, incisive, precise. It was Ham's hard luck that this time he was vague.

Caulkin's dilemma was, however, understandable. It was easy enough for him to bring home the well-bred fellow Peabody alumni who covered Europe for him. They could always write about Continental flavors in Birmingham cuisines, or the charm of old Yankee houses. Ham was the maverick in the *Star*'s stable of elegant expatriates. He was the slum-boy-made-good, the only correspondent with a degree from the state's shabby land-grant college and the only one who really knew the home town. His career, indeed, had been built on that knowledge. Others had risen through office politics or nepotism. Not Ham. He owed the paper nothing. Because his father had been on the *Star* payroll he had been the paper's campus stringer at State and had been given a police reporting job after graduation, but he would have been left to doze away his life in precincts if he hadn't quit to write *Through Darkest Birmingham.*

He had conceived the book as the study of a metropolis—its history, manners, ghettos, class structure, power foci. He had spent a year taking notes, and when he sat down in this apartment, opened his bride's portable, and unsheathed the reams of copy paper he had cabbaged from the *Star,* the thing had written itself. It had come out the following spring and had made him. By June he had been a local celebrity. The paper had had to take him back. For a few months he had written a daily column, but the contrast between his stuff and the rest of the editorial page had become embarrassing to everyone, so he had been shipped abroad with a boost in salary. In the beginning it had been exciting, and if it had paled since, so had life paled; he was in his mid-thirties now, the age of compromise and insomnia, when the illusions of youth vanish one by one and the dreamer of great books written and social wrongs righted awakens, unrefreshed, to find himself panting on a couch in his father-in-law's study, baked by the slanting sun, with a telephone a few feet away shrilly sounding the tocsin of reality.

"By George, it's good to hear your voice," Caulkin was saying. "I can't wait to get you back in the city room."

"Doing what?" Ham asked instantly.

"Well—every state office comes up in November. I've been thinking of using you in the campaign."

"I see." Ham's face was blank as a plate. "Won't that be pretty cut-and-dried?" Later he was to writhe at the memory of his bored tone, but at the time it seemed right. After all, this state was the one unscalable G. O. Pinnacle in New England — "After all, you can practically count the votes now."

"Perhaps. It depends on the Democrat nominee."

Democrat nominee. Demmies. Ham wondered whether Republicans like Caulkin carried cards.

"They have to file a name by midnight tonight. Of course, there *is* a rumor they won't contest the election."

Ham hoped it was true. The prospect of two alcoholic months aboard the majority party bandwagon depressed him, and the other caravan would be even worse; after a century of defeats the state Democratic organization had fallen into the hands of cranks and gyps.

"Understand, I'm just bouncing that one," Caulkin said quickly. "We'll have a long talk about it after you've settled down."

Obviously nothing had been decided. He trailed off into inquiries about Ham's family and praise for his coverage of a Communist riot in Calcutta. Ham was about to reproach himself for having suspected anything but a courtesy call when he heard a memo crackle in Caulkin's hand.

"Look, we just had a message from Doc River."

"Doc got in touch with *you?*"

It was so improbable. Home couldn't have changed that much. The feud between Doc and the *Star* was irreconcilable. Ham's memory stirred. How many years had it been? Thirteen. Thirteen since he had left the upstate town of Gideon, yet he could still remember the class bitterness between the two colleges there — between ancient, heavily endowed Peabody, half-buried in ivy, and Ham's own, non-U State. The *Star* was the broad-A voice of Peabody alumni, and Doc meant State. Meant? Hell, Doc *was* State. In the 1920's he had been its greatest halfback. During the Depression he had returned as football coach — he had been Ham's coach in the early '40's — and after the war State's adoring trustees had astonished everyone by appointing him president. Ham wondered what kind of sailing his administration had had. Rough, probably. Just before the plane had left for Delhi, he recalled, Doc had demanded expansion money from the legislature, and Peabody graduates, the biggest taxpayers in the state, had screamed foul. Or rather, the *Star* had screamed for them. The *Star* was the tireless champion of what Doc had always called The Interests. It had fought him then; doubtless it was fighting him still. You couldn't patch up a thing like that. If anything, the '50's would have deepened the paper's distrust of Doc.

They had. "River and I don't speak," Caulkin said frigidly. He paused. "Actually he asked for you. Apparently he saw today's paper. He wants to talk to you."

That was better. That made sense. And because Doc had been the hero of Ham's youth, he felt a surge of warmth. "So he thought enough to call."

The memo crackled again. "One of his flunkies made the call."

"Flunkies?" Ham asked edgily.

"Well. Aides," Colonel Caulkin conceded.

Then say aides, Ham thought savagely, but before he could reply he realized that Caulkin was tuning up his mellifluous voice. It had always been an ominous sign.

"The man wouldn't say what it was about, but he insisted you come to Gideon today. I smell a story."

So it was an imposition, after all. Caulkin wanted him to work without sleep. Ham frowned, wondering why. The only State news in his stringer days had been routine 4-H jubilees, livestock judging, Grange conventions.

"Listen, there's always a story if you look for it."

"I know, I know." Caulkin was being suave. Ham could just see him marcelling that Guards mustache. "This could be important, though. River's never left word with us before, and he's become rather a big figure in this state since you were here."

"Big?" It could mean anything. "You mean like the judge?"

"No! I mean sinister. Socialistic." The colonel's suavity receded. Ham had touched a nerve. "I can't begin to tell you how much tax money we've poured into his rat hole. He's boodled and buccaneered and pork-barreled that cow college into an alleged university, and—" Caulkin faltered, remembering that Ham had been one of Doc's boys. "But I suppose that's lese majesty," he finished weakly.

So State was a university! Doc had made time after all. Ham's curiosity quickened. Gideon would be the first stop on his explorations. Still, it could wait a day.

"Any idea whats on his mind?" he asked, delaying.

"Well, I can't give you anything definite. You see, he runs that place pretty much out of his hat. We don't even bother to keep a man on campus any more. Our staffers are poison to him. You understand."

Ham smiled bleakly at the mouthpiece. He understood: the editorial pasting of Doc was costing the *Star* desk hard news, and after nervously straightening their Peabody ties and lowering their wall-to-wall voices the men in the front office had concluded that if there really was a story, and Doc insisted on naming his own reporter, they would have to play ball. Well, that was just too bad. He had news for them. He was on furlough.

. . . Still, this *was* Doc. And then it came back to him with a pang — four years ago he had broken a date with him. A funeral technicality had taken him to the Statehouse, and they had collided in a dingy corridor. Colliding with Doc was like running into a towering rock, except that this rock had arms, arms which had almost crushed Ham's ribs in a bear hug. *You'll have to come up to Gideon before you leave, boy,* Doc had said, flexing his knees with that restless energy he had always had, and Ham had answered, *Sure thing, Coach. I'll be there in the morning.*

At the time he had meant it. All that evening he had coasted on a nostalgic jag, remembering the faraway prewar years when he had been tender inside and hard out and every day had been a 3-D Todd-AO poem — remembering the tide of Tau Rho fraternity brothers surging up Union Street between classes, and how the spire of Archer Chapel stabbed the dark red throat of the dying sky late March afternoons; remembering the masochistic exhilaration of spring training and alcoholic bull sessions with doddering Professor Mikel on the leaven of the arts — remembering most of all that long ago afternoon when he had raced down the sideline through a golden November haze, and Spook had hit him with the rainbow pass on the Peabody two, and he had stumbled into the chill sunlight of the end zone while the stands trembled and a light wind strained through the lurid maples overhead and his coed raced to meet him, her face aglow and poster pink and her shabby saddle shoes freckled with mud and the run-down heels flying.

But there shadows had intervened. Age had lengthened them, there was no crossing that darkness. He couldn't bring himself to revisit the campus. Explanations had seemed pointless. Doc, whose own youth was eternal, wouldn't have understood, so Ham had returned to India for four more years without touching base, or even leaving word, in Gideon.

And now life had turned full circle. Fate was fingering him again.

"Here's one lead," Caulkin said. "I've had the desk do a little quick checking. It seems River's been delegating more and more authority to his provost."

"His what?" It *sounded* big.

"Executive officer. Also, State's Birmingham trustees are all up in Gideon today. It looks like an emergency meeting. I've had the feeling for some time that eventually River's aggressive personality would attract one of those New York outfits. It's just possible he's resigning."

Ham's eyes clouded. Was it really possible? No: Doc would never leave New England. Caulkin's hunch sounded like wistful thinking. Yet Ham couldn't be sure. Only one thing was certain. If State had grown — if it had become the true university of the people they had all yearned for in the tattered days of the Depression — then Doc was needed where he was, driving it ahead with his fantastic vitality.

A pencil stub lay beside the phone. He juggled it.

"His man suggested you meet him in his campus office at half-past two," Caulkin said briskly. As far as he was concerned, it was settled. "A car is waiting for you in the *Star* garage. I'll be out on the Swallow Hills course all afternoon; you can phone your story in to the desk. Got the picture?"

Ham wavered. He felt a rising excitement. Then: "Got it."

"*Good*," Caulkin crooned. "And drop around when you get back. We'll have a drink at the club."

"Sounds fine," Ham muttered, without enthusiasm. He knew why he was being invited. His father-in-law was Judge Davies, and that made him eligible to mingle with men of gentle birth. Well, he wasn't having any. He knew where his side of the tracks was, and he liked it there.

"By the bye, better let me brief you. The day has gone when you could find River by listening for a cowbell. Gideon swarms with his herd these days, including, of course, a great many of the Chosen People. This is the drill. You turn —"

"Look, I spent four years in that place."

"Well, you won't know it now. You turn down Union Street —"

"I know." Ham was busy drafting an explanatory note to the

judge. "I told you," he said impatiently as he hung up. "I've been there before."

At the time he meant that. He really thought he had.

**

Birmingham and Gideon were linked by the G.A.R. Highway, an imperfect road. Like so many New England routes it was largely a series of paved paths winding through dreary factory towns, each with its gas works, sagging tenements, and ugly shops — great dingy pens occupied by men in denim and black work shoes who stared out blankly as Ham crept through the ill-timed green lights and coasted into the maw of Herlihy Tunnel. Beyond that, however, the view improved. The tunnel carried him into what was left of primal New England. Meadows appeared, and also barns. Passing brooks were edged by scarlet cardinal flowers, occasional salt box houses by gardens of tansy, and sometimes windows of pressed glass were tinted lavender with age. Ham leaned back happily. This was swamp Yankee country. It moved him, because like Doc he was of swamp Yankee stock. He had grown up in the alleys of East Birmingham and hadn't seen the country until his first year at State, but his family had farmed stony fields for almost three centuries before that, and the rest of the way to Gideon he lazed along through a Currier and Ives scape of willowy birch clumps, massed huckleberry bushes, frost-buckled fences, and flat pasture rocks glinting in the afternoon heat, the homing instinct growing in him and sustaining him.

It had been so long since he had felt this sense of peace; longer than thirteen years, longer than the war. In retrospect he drifted back to the final years of the Depression, when he had first gone to college as a fatherless boy, with the slum grime still on him. He had needed a strong hand then, and Doc's had been there. Doc had formed him as few men form their own sons, giving him a new life and a light to lead the way. That had been the good time. Everything had been blue sky then. Each day had been an idyl of youth, and it had all coalesced the Saturday of his sideline ballet, the afternoon he saw Spook's fifty-yard pitch sailing along the lip of the horizon and cut in and snagged it and reeled over the hash-marked goal. That had been the peak, that had been *it*. And then, right there, at that very instant, the first shade had crept across his life.

Even now he could hear the warble of that penalty whistle. The play had been called back. The next pass had been knocked down, and then the gun had ended the game and State's great chance. It had been an omen. That winter time ran out on everything. Ham wouldn't have another crack at Peabody. His senior year had been canceled. It was 1942 now, and suddenly the country had urgent need of ruddy, well-nourished young males. Strange passwords were heard — Army ASTP, Navy V-12; the brothers slunk away until Tau Rho was a haunted house echoing to ghostly jazz from the turntable downstairs. Ham's countersign was USMC 3-D, the last to be called. In the week before his orders came he was left with his coed, who gave him his final prewar memory of State. The parting with Kit Ryan had been his most cherished souvenir while he was gone, and it was the agony of his youth that it should have been so quickly tarnished afterward.

Through the red years in the Pacific he had treasured the timid way she had crept pigeon-toed into the seedy College Inne room that last night in those Thom McAn shoes and made a face at the faded reproduction of The Stag at Bay over the bed and turned, wide-eyed and anxious to please, with her long black hair a tidy night, and the street light from the jalousies slanting across her pink cardigan and her short, swinging tweed skirt, and her thin legs red because the Inne's heat was famous for never reaching the second floor.

"Ham, are you a stag?"

"At bay. *What are you doing?*"

"Crying, you jerk. Oh, damn! You got a hankie?"

"Jeepers, yes, but it's . . ."

It was soiled. She had wept into it nevertheless, and miserably he had offered to leave, which would have been no sacrifice then, for he was tormented too and repelled by the chill slatternly room. But they had made a pact, she reminded him between sobs; they had agreed it was right, something to keep through the war though they couldn't marry now — *some little something to remember you by* went the lilting Dinah Shore lyric on the desolate Tau Rho turntable by which they had plighted their troth — so they stayed, and Ham had his keepsake. Until he returned.

He had come back early with a bandage, like a comic opera hero, to a campus divested of friends, inhabited for him only by Doc, a few clumsily sympathetic professors — old Harry Mikel, incredibly, was off in the Merchant Marine as a seaman on the Murmansk run — and by Kit, still awkward, with her angular, boyish figure and pigeon-toed walk and the same saddle shoes. The same Kit, yet subtly altered as Ham had been by the strain of the years between and by something else, which in the turbulence of the time might have escaped him, except that he heard about it and rashly faced her down.

"Oh, Ham . . . Does it matter really?"

"Does it *matter!*"

"Ham, you don't know. He *needed* me so."

"Between the sheets. *I* know."

"Don't say it like that. He was on leave and hurt and . . ."

"It was always Spook, wasn't it? Never me."

"Oh Goddamn you, you don't even try. I can't cope. *Oh, Ham . . .*"

But this time he had no handkerchief, and he turned away trembling. And that had been the last of State for him. The shadows had intervened irrevocably between him and Spook's great pass and all that lost innocence. He had quickly graduated and left for another love and another life. Alumni appeals — anything with a Gideon postmark — were automatically discarded, unread, as reminders of his grief. He couldn't bear to face the ruined past, and that was why he had disappointed Doc four years ago.

Now he was going back, voluntarily; even happily. He wondered why. It was, he supposed, because even as America had been changing in the Eisenhower era, so had he. His bonfire with Kit had blazed high and died hard; long after his marriage he had still been troubled by recollections of her hippy shuffle and Indian slant eyes, of the husky inflection in her voice and the way she would swear and touch people when she was excited. But now the stars had wheeled. He lived under older skies. The embers of his passion were ash at last, and his thoughts of State were no longer of Kit. They were all of Doc.

Caulkin's light contempt for State had helped. It reminded Ham of the swaggering Peabody boys who had cruised up and down Union Street in open convertibles each fall before the annual game, slowing past the heavily mortgaged frame firetraps that passed for fraternity houses at State and jeering "Hey, rube!" or "Hey, hayseed!" or drunkenly singing "The Farmer in the Dell." Elsewhere this might have been sport, but in Gideon there had been a jagged edge to it. It had been a cry of class warfare, a sign that the jeerers knew land-grant students were starting to get ideas and deciding that although they couldn't afford Peabody tuition they might like city careers after graduation. Nobody had understood that better than Doc. Once he had told Ham that the awakening had started in World War I, when State men found their degrees were just as good as Peabody's in officer training camps. Ham himself had always thought the tensions of the 1930's had a lot to do with it. It was a fine point. The feeling was there, and everybody knew it on those pre-game evenings when State boys stood helplessly on their rickety, peeling porches, staring hotly at the warbling sots in the Packard convoys.

Union Street had been divided by a barricade those autumn nights, and despite Ham's long absence it was still there for him. The bonfire of first love had darkled and died, but this other spark was more viable. In bitter memory he saw the arrogant, carefully trained praetorian teams of Peabody rolling up the score against the despised State rabble each November and carelessly strolling slug-footed off the field in unmussed green jerseys; he remembered Doc's determination that some day State would be strong enough to match them, and heard again Caulkin's disdain of an hour ago. *Cowbell. Herd. Chosen People.* He could just imagine what Doc would have said to that — or Spook, for that matter, or Kit, with her strong State chauvinism and her scorn for pedigree pretensions. Kit would have laced into Caulkin, he thought, stepping on the accelerator. She had always had a quick Irish temper. He wondered idly where she was now.

There wasn't much to the center of Gideon. Back in the '30's the W.P.A. Writers' Program had published a state guidebook; a copy of it had been issued to Ham when he joined the *Star*, and all it had about Gideon was that Peabody and the State College were there. There really wasn't anything else worth mentioning. Like a thousand other New England villages it had a Common, a dozen stores, a tavern, and a weathered statue of a Union soldier on a plain granite base. Some of the buildings were elegant — Peabody students supported a haberdashery, a select liquor store, and an expensive hotel — but that wasn't the sort of thing you would put in a guidebook, especially, Ham thought with a grin, if you were working for the W.P.A., which *The Tartan*, Peabody's student newspaper, had always referred to as The Public Trough.

In his day the highway had skirted Gideon. Now it ran right through it, and he had almost passed Finch's Haberdashery when he saw the Union soldier pointing stolidly to the right with his bile-colored musket, away from the Gideon Arms hotel and the wrought-iron gate on the far side of the Common that led to the Peabody campus. Ham bowed gravely—like many a State student, he had often rolled out of the tavern and taken bearings on the discolored muzzle—and obediently turned down Union Street. The first five blocks were vaguely familiar. He recognized austere St. Mary's Church, and, with a faint twinge, the ramshackle, peeling College Inne opposite, with the root-warped sidewalks between freckled by arabesques of quiet shade, and the fanning elms, a little taller now, lining the broken curbs and meeting above in lacy green chaos. But at the turning, where everything should have become much more familiar, he slowed to a dazed crawl.

He had expected Fraternity Row. On either side rambling clapboard buildings should have stood on deep green lots, each with its Greek flag hanging limply above the porch—a double rank of faded banners leading to the tidy group of whitewashed houses, pretentiously known as The Quad, that had straddled the street and had led, at the street's end, to the brownstone pile of Archer Chapel. But Fraternity Row had vanished. The Quad was gone, bulldozed away. The chapel spire was still there, but he scarcely saw it; too much lay between, and dwarfed it. Union Street ended here at the turning in a crowded parking lot. Where the fraternities had been was an immense lawn, sloping upward. Dead ahead, surrounding the chapel and simmering in the untempered heat, were the towers of over twenty Georgian halls. The whole landscape had altered, Ham thought dizzily. There were hills where none had been, parks where there had been buildings, graded paths lined with new colonial lantern posts where he remembered wild brush. Most startling, however, was the gate beyond the parking lot. State had had no gate before, but now there was a gigantic ornamental work, twice the size of Peabody's, bearing in polished brass a replica of the state seal.

An anomalous little half-timbered Tudor building alongside carried the sign Visitors Please Register. Feeling very much the visitor Ham gave his name to a girl with a fresh bob, a freshly pressed uniform of State blue, and a pocketful of ballpoint pens glittering like cartridges.

"Mr. Markham!" She smiled. Even her teeth looked new. "Administration is expecting you! Dr. *Tate* is here!"

"Who?"

"The provost."

"The executive officer?"

"And your greeter!" called a bald, skeletal man, arising from a deep chair across the room. Tate's voice, like Tate, was high and thin. He scissored over on scarecrow legs and extended a bony hand. "This is a real privilege, Markham. I consider you our most distinguished graduate in media."

"Thanks," said Ham, who didn't consider himself in media at all.

"Though you'll have competition in the future. We've just introduced a four-year Bachelor of Communications Arts course. One of the many innovations since your day. The old order changing — you must have heard that famous slogan. Everything's new, from curricula to clothes." He pointed proudly to the uniformed girl. "This is one of our employed coeds. Statettes, we call them."

The Statette made Ham uncomfortable. She reminded him of a manikin. "Yes, well, I'm a bit lost," he said, turning away. "I'm afraid you'll have to lead me to Doc."

"Delighted," the provost piped. But he didn't sound delighted. "Ah — I hope you won't mind if your appointment is delayed," he said evasively. "We're a bit off schedule. Dr. River and I are about to meet with the trustees."

"*Dr*. River?"

Tate gave him a sly look. "Of course."

"But that's only a nickname."

"Not any more." He appraised Ham and risked a wink. "The president has an honorary degree now."

Ham grinned. His affection for Doc was too strong to be stung by that. "You mean he's a doctor like I'm a major in the French Foreign Legion."

The provost whinnied. The girl said uncertainly, "I hope you enjoy our campus, Major," and Tate whinnied again and led Ham down the graded walks, pointing out buildings like a guide.

Ham asked groggily, "What happened to the fraternities? And the sororities?"

The sororities were on Maiden Lane, where they had always been, Tate said. Then he nodded toward a hill where a squat observatory had replaced a wood Ham had loved. The new Fraternity Park — it was called that — lay beyond there.

"Is there . . ." Ham hesitated. It really didn't matter. "Is there still a Tau Rho? A local."

Tate thought not, though he couldn't be sure. There were so many little clubs here and there. It was hard to keep up with fourteen thousand students.

Fourteen thousand. A tenfold increase, an explosion. Ham lapsed into a numb silence, unbroken until, as they crossed the great portico beneath the marble legend "Administration Hall," he saw a familiar figure.

He rushed forward. "Sam!"

An older man wheeled laboriously in two-toned shoes, presenting an oval profile. "Hey, you long drink of water!" he yelped, waddling over. "How's the boy?"

The provost smiled. "Very fitting. *Two* media celebrities."

Tate was right the second time, Ham thought. Sam was in a true medium. After graduating thirty years ago — he had played center when Doc was ripping off his famous gains — he had become an instantaneous success in public relations. Yet Sam Theanapolis Associates had always been a sideline with him. His heart had never left Gideon; he had been alumni president as long as Ham could remember. A doglike devotion to Doc had also abided. Before the war he had supplemented thin legislative appropriations by quietly furnishing equipment for State players, and despite his business he had made it a point to read the *Star* as little as possible.

"Where'd you get that ice cream suit?" He pommeled Ham's clothes. "What're you, an interne?"

"It's just India duck," said Ham, dodging his soft shoves.

"Say, that's right, you been over with the gooks."

"Gujeratis, Sam."

"Sure, it figures." He stepped back, breathing hard. "Look — you here for the big story?"

"Came halfway around the world for it," said Ham, wondering what it could be.

"But who told you?"

"I heard it on the drums."

"Bull. It's the biggest secret since the Edsel. Still, if you already *know* . . ." He hesitated, then produced a paper which Ham recognized as a Sam Theanapolis Associates release. "This can't be uncorked till five o'clock, but I guess you could have it now."

Tate had suddenly grown uneasy. "All in good time," he said shrilly. "Right now Sam and I are due inside in the Colonial Room."

"Oh, that's right," Sam said. The release slipped back. "We got a powwow, and I'm chairman."

"Chairman of the trustees?" asked Ham. So Sam's long years of fidelity had been rewarded. "Listen, that's great. But try to hurry things up. I want to see Doc."

Tate took Ham's elbow. "You can wait in his office."

"I'll tell him you're around," Sam called, trudging off.

"Oh, he knows," Ham called back. "He asked me up."

"He did?" Sam turned and scratched his untidy gray hair. "Say, that's queer. I had lunch with him, and he didn't mention it."

"This way," Tate said nervously, and propelled Ham into a corridor smelling of varnish and illumined by bewildering neon directional arrows, through a frosted glass door marked "Presidential Suite," around a deserted secretarial desk, and into an impressive room with a big, kidney-shaped desk, a picture window overlooking the campus, and a row of leather chairs facing a gallery of signed photographs.

"The secretary's on vacation," said Tate, retreating rapidly, "but I'll tell the receptionist you're here."

He scissored out. The door swung shut. Ham sank down with a tired sigh. Maybe it was just as well Doc was tied up. A man needed his strength to cope with him, and the meeting would permit a nap. Yet even as he closed his eyes, an inward eye brightened. He wasn't much interested in that release; if Doc really were resigning, Sam would be all broken up. But the transformation of State was exciting. And Sam had been right about one thing. It *was* queer that Doc hadn't said anything to him. Come to think of it, it was odd Doc hadn't been there at the gate. Sending a stranger wasn't like him. And that stranger, that executive officer, that provost had been strangely furtive. It didn't make sense — unless, Ham reflected whimsically, drifting into deep sleep, Doc didn't expect him at all.

**

Down the hall Tate nodded shortly to the waiting trustees, noted that Doc hadn't arrived, and slid into a chair beside Sam.

"Don't say anything about Markham," he whispered.

Sam blinked. He had been daydreaming. His memories of Ham's era at State were all warm; secretly he missed the dependence of those teams on his largess, and the return of their brilliant left end today appealed to his sense of drama.

"Why not?"

"Doc doesn't know he's here. Calling the *Star* was — ah — your friend's idea."

"Oh." Sam nodded sagely. It figured.

"He's going to break it to Doc afterward. He —"

There was no time for more. Outside a familiar voice was booming at a janitor.

"Did you open the windows in there? Good man. Some of those fellows smoke cigarettes. I don't give a hymn or a hallelujah what they do to *their* lungs, but an hour without fresh air and *I'm* ready for the boneyard."

The trustees chuckled, then smiled in greeting as their president ducked under the doorway and took his place at the head of the long conference table. Doc knew how to make an entrance, and he had the presence for it. He had aged some since turning fifty-five and now wore little Pickwickian half-moon reading glasses thrust forward on his aquiline nose, but his blue eyes were vivid, his face glowed pink, and the only creases were in his cheeks, fixed dimples which grew deeper and cheerier with age.

"Well, boys." He took a deep, bracing breath. "I won't horse around any more than's necessary. Fact is, I'm sorry I had to haul you up here at all. It just so happens there's a few dribs and drabs we've got to get out of the way quick." He twinkled. "Most of it's the usual hokum, but there's a mite of a surprise at the end. O.K., Sam." He raised a horny hand in salutation. "You can pound away with that bung mallet."

Amid new chuckles Sam thumped his gavel and bowed toward Tate, who introduced the agenda. It was a routine opening for meetings of the board. Elsewhere Doc himself would have awaited the chairman's recognition, but here that would have been absurd, for everyone in this room knew where the true control lay. They were all Doc's creatures; that, in fact, was why they had been appointed.

Doc's strength was often underestimated by his critics, who liked to think of him as an American Gothic relic, a stolid old maid, a kind of bumbling, athletic Mr. Chips. Even in Gideon men deceived themselves. Faculty myth to the contrary, Doc had never said, "There can't be too many erections on this campus." Nor, despite the *Star*, had he ever asked for "a university State's team can be proud of." Neither remark would have been in character. Doc wouldn't have called it "this campus." To him it was always "*my* campus." He wouldn't have said "team," either. He rarely called it anything but "the squad." All that, however, is beside the point, which is that he was seldom crude. He couldn't have defined the difference between a declension and a conjugation or calculated the height of his stadium flagpole with cosines, but early in his career he had learned the value of tact, and in the past decade he had become one of the most artful manipulators of special power since Alcibiades, whom he had also forgotten. Only Doc's genius could have parlayed winning teams, ardent alumni, and the university's free services into a personal éclat so imposing that the governor not only hadn't dared appoint an anti-Doc man to this board; he had actually resigned his own ex officio privileges on it. Of course, there were individual legislators who sulked, but every year when Doc rode down to Birmingham, sat in the capitol gallery, and checked off their names during the state university budget vote, they answered the roll call like so many humble R.O.T.C. frosh.

The *Star*, his loudest critic, often wondered editorially why this should be. One reason — overlooked by the editorial writers, who had never met him — was his sheer size. A lovely woman does not cow other women, but something in every man defers to a real giant, and despite senescence Doc was still a six-foot-five powerhouse, all trim and lithe and hard. His vigor had, indeed, long been a state-wide legend, and to enlighten rising generations worshipful alumni had erected on the new North Campus an athletic trophy pavilion whose most striking exhibit was a bronze statue of Doc in his playing days, wearing the lumpy moleskins of the Red Grange era. The plaque on the pedestal beneath read:

ADAM R. "DOC" RIVER '29

In the three years he wore No. 17 for the Blue he gained 4,735 yards from scrimmage, scored 387 points, kicked 54 conversions, and set four other New England Conference records: Longest run from scrimmage (107 yards, from behind his own goal line), longest kickoff return (110 yards), longest punt in air (88 yards), longest punt with roll (110 yards).

Varsity Captain, 1928
Director of Athletics, 1932-1944
Director of Admissions, 1944-1947
President of State, 1947-

In the popular impression football heroes are burly, bull-necked, and heavily muscled. Doc didn't conform; as a youth he had been a raw-boned halfback, and regular exercise had kept him spare. Nor was he leonine. He had always had the earnest, angular look of the stage bumpkin, and as a public figure, he seemed to cultivate that awkward role. Despite his barber's protests he still parted his hair in the middle; archaic slang spiced his speech, which was nasal and harsh with the twang of his north county youth; the sleeves of his old-fashioned suits were always a shade too short, his collars had a tendency to turn up at the corners, and summer and winter he wore, straight on his head, a high-crowned, stained brown felt hat with a scalloped brim, touched a hundred times a day in his celebrated two-fingered salute. Sometimes he seemed a deliberate caricature of a rustic. Yet not many men scorned him to his face. His quaint Yankee mannerisms were too obviously a mask. Behind them, and perceptible, were a natural sense of dignity, a lively mind, and an unmistakable authority.

Doc was a dangerous man to cross. If his famous dimples vanished entirely somebody was in trouble, and not many men courted that. During the decade after World War II, when he had used the great tide of GI Bill enrollment to transform State from a freshwater college to an educational leviathan, his only public challengers had been the *Star*'s legislative reporters. At some point in every session one of them would be told to stop him in the Statehouse corridor and ask how much tax money was being used to support his varsity — his "hired Hessians," in the favored *Star* phrase. The interviewer was always discomfited. Doc would stare down for perhaps fifteen seconds, his jaw lengthening and his sinewy hand flashing in the murky Statehouse light, scratching his silvery hair. "Hi-ired He-es-sians?" he would repeat slowly, as though they were words he was learning. The reporter would start to explain. Somehow he never finished. Doc would turn suddenly and move on the nearest legislator with his characteristic rube's gait, knees lifted high, like a farmer crossing a cornfield. "Doggone it, I hate dressing up the obvious," he would say, shaking his head, "but in my view it's clear as the waters of Gitche Gumee that the alumni of a certain other institution are jealous of State's squad. *Mens sana in corpore sano*—a sound mind in a sound body," he would add under his breath if the man looked blank—"is what your state university stands for. Yes sir, on my campus we're for mental and physical fitness—along with clean young minds."

The legislator would make appreciative noises, and not just because the two university scholarships Doc made available to him each year were his only patronage. Doc's easy academic manner had impressed him. Often it would impress even the reporter, who was aware that the only legitimate degree behind it was a B.A. in physical education. Still, Doc knew it was unwise to leave on a solemn note. Wit was always safer. Moving away, his craggy face flushed with a seraphic glow, he would cast the legislator a sly, sidelong glance and murmur, "But I don't mean to sandpaper our young friend here. He has his orders, and it's the only job the poor boy's got. Far be it from me to resent the *Star*'s sanctuary for private school graduates. Even Peabody alumni have to eat."

Yankee vowels can be remarkably effective. You had only to hear Doc's inflection when he said "Peabody" to know how he felt about the other college in Gideon. Mocking a fellow institution might not be seemly for a university president, who according to custom should have limited his participation in collegiate rivalry to pious reminders about sportsmanship, but Doc had his reasons. For over a century Peabody's graduates had included nearly every top-drawer, pin-striped, upperchurch Brahmin in the state, and in his early years Doc had suffered much at the hands of these Forsytes. If it was bad form for him to slight them publicly, only they were outraged; everyone else understood. Besides, academic etiquette didn't mean much to Doc. Playing the game for its own sake, the shibboleth of college athletics, had always seemed hypocritical to him. In his coaching days a sign over his desk had read, "There are no Good Winners and Poor Losers, only Winners and Losers," and he never deceived himself that State-Peabody competition was healthy. It was the hungry against the fat, the ragtag against the swells, Ins against Outs. Peabody men were fat swells, Ins; they owned the *Star* and most of everything else in Birmingham, and Doc was their archenemy, and the rest was pap.

But he was no cynic. Not even the *Star* ever charged him with that. The paper's cartoonist came closest to the truth when he pictured Doc as a gaunt ape advancing on the citadels of culture—

culture being represented by Grecian porticoes carefully labeled Peabody, Harvard, Bowdoin, Dartmouth, and Amherst. He was indeed a throwback, though in a way his Birmingham antagonists would scarcely have understood. Despite his hostility to privilege he was a traditionalist to the bone. In an age of intellectual flux he was a man of faith — not a *religieux*, but a firm believer in the prime values that sophisticates reject or dilute to pale, qualified pastels. Evil was evil to him, and good good; boys should display gumption and girls gentility; soldiers should be courageous, and a man's word was his bond — so it went for Doc, and if anyone suggested these were Boy Scout, 4-H virtues, he saw nothing wrong with that. He was high in the councils of both the Boy Scout and 4-H state organizations and played host to them in Gideon each August.

"We have the usual requests to use the campus after summer school," Tate was saying even now. He read the list: "The Fellowship of New England Camp Executives, the Twenty-sixth Division Reunion, the Youth Club Council, the Scouts, the Dance Educators, the 4-H, the Candy Wholesalers, and the Cretans Association."

"The what?" asked a new trustee.

"Cretans. I think we can work them all in," Tate said smoothly. "And we should. The plant's idle till after Labor Day."

"Like Doc says, there's no point in an empty barn," said Sam. "Besides, it builds a good image."

The motion passed. Then the provost made another. "Speaking of our image, I move the officers of the university be authorized to proceed with the plan for reaccreditation."

"Reaccreditation?" a trustee asked doubtfully.

"Reaccreditation," Tate repeated firmly.

There was some squirming. This had been discussed before. The trustee inquired, "Are we sure we're ready?"

"I got a boy in the freshman class," said Sam. "I'm sure."

Tate, the author of the plan, glanced at him gratefully, but the skeptic remained skeptical.

"Still —"

He bit his lip. Doc was gathering his million muscles and leaning forward. "In my view we'd *better* be ready," he said sharply. "I've already invited the accreditation team. Second the motion."

Every hand went up.

**

Reaccreditation, reaccreditation, reaccreditation . . .

Sounded like a short cheer, Doc thought laconically. Like one of those tomfool yells where the girls yipped a player's name three times and then hopped up hollering *Yay*. In Doc's view short cheers were the silliest part of the autumn ritual. As a boy he'd never noticed the ones for him, and today's squads felt the same.

But reaccreditation wasn't silly. It was bigger than any game State had ever played. Recognition from other universities was his one unrealized goal here. His administration was approaching a climax, and he wanted academic approval now, before the climax passed. There was no legal need for this, no pressure from the capitol, but he was determined to have that sanction, if only to show his new faculty — "those bearded screwballs in the humanities," as he had once called them scornfully — how sorely they had misjudged him.

It was Doc's irony that in recent years his simple values had become a topic of mirth among certain circles on his own campus, and that this had led to the present crisis in his career. For a long time he had been unaware of his faculty critics. Legislative maneuvers and building plans had kept him isolated, and the critics were furtive. He was generous with them and held tight the strings of authority. Yet over the years the snickers had grown. Doc had appointed the most energetic provost he could find and had instructed him to enlist professors distinguished in their disciplines. Tate could not entice the truly eminent, but those who did come moved eagerly in the van of contemporary thought. Engrossed with the irrationalism and mechanism of their time they looked upon Doc as an anachronism, a cultural incubus, or, as one of them had put it, "an inner-directed lag." Increasingly it had become evident that his vast popularity among alumni and the old, prewar faculty had found no mirror in the newcomers. Their condescension had eventually infected a few of the brighter students, and because a clique of these put out the college newspaper, a few biting pieces had appeared there — parodies, bantering editorials, even reprints of *Star* cartoons. There hadn't been many, and other undergraduates had protested, but Doc had seen them, and he had been hurt.

He had also been puzzled. He was shrewd enough to sense that this was more than a student prank. On reflection he realized that State's expansion had its drawbacks. It had been worth it all — he gloried in the great stadium and the towering brick walls, and each morning as he descended the hill from the old presidential Mansion and struck out toward his office he silently congratulated the Department of Landscape Architecture. Still, something was wrong. He had created an empire but had lost touch. In the old days there had been a professorial camaraderie. Department heads would sit around the Mansion parlor with the president and dean over trays prepared by the Department of Home Economics, dreaming of the day the legislature would make Aggie a State College. Now it had become a university, and the parlor was rarely used. The waxing staff had outgrown it. The one dean of ten years ago had been replaced by a staff of deans, supported by vice deans, associate deans, and assistant deans, and behind them the department chairmen loomed in mass formation, like spear carriers. Apart from a few cronies on the old faculty Doc felt close to none. Whenever he approached the new men they were all business, suggesting expanded facilities, new lab space, or additional teaching positions, and if he introduced a social note they lapsed into a respectful silence.

In frustration he had turned peevish. From behind his frosted glass door came nasal shouts; administrivia was driving him to the boneyard; in this conbobberation a man couldn't give anything more than a lick and a promise. Undeniably his burdens were monstrous. In a typical morning he would be asked to review present teaching loads, pass on next semester's selection of the workbooks which graduate students now used to teach freshmen, approve the courses which would be offered over the university's closed circuit television station, and solve the intricate problems of State's medical school in Birmingham. All final decisions were his, and he couldn't bear to leave pet projects alone. Anything affecting football was almost a personal matter. He pampered players like whelps. If another Conference team was enlisting a lineman in South America, he handled the official protest. If a choreographer arrived to run the coed halftime shows, he wanted to interview her. He dipped into his alumni card file daily, asking this or that graduate to help in the recruitment of high school stars, and even samples of rally torches — which were no longer made by students, but ordered in bulk from a Chicago firm — were carried in to him for inspection.

It was too much, he had finally decided; too much skull practice, too many forms in triplicate. Better let up a mite. And so, last month, he had delegated the bulk of his powers to Tate, called in several old-timers for talks about faculty morale — and learned for the first time of the elegant laughter at his expense. It had come as an icy shock. He felt betrayed, subverted. In Birmingham he would have shrugged, but this was the Gideon campus, *his* campus, and he had squirmed in his big swivel chair, itching and not knowing where to scratch. He had considered running over to Camp TD, the squad's summer headquarters, for a few days. It might have calmed him, but at the last minute he had changed his mind.

He had stayed because at this juncture Sam had brought him a curious proposal. One of Sam's agency accounts was the Democratic State Central Committee. The committee chairman, Newt Albert, had checked registration lists and found that Doc was a Democrat. How would Doc feel about campaigning for a gubernatorial nominee? Hooey, Doc had replied scornfully; stuff, applesauce; he carried no man's water dipper. Nevertheless his interest had been aroused. More conversations had followed, more party overtures, repeated refusals from Doc. Suddenly Newt had made a startling new proposition. Doc had shouted No. Then he had hesitated. Then: Maybe. And then: Yes.

Now he had come to the Colonial Room to burn his bridges. The whole thing had taken less than three weeks, he thought wonderingly, and he felt giddy, detached. Doodling absently on his carbon of Tate's agenda, he heard Sam carefully explain their purpose here, heard the trustees burst into applause. Smiling, he nodded benignly as they approved his leave of absence, the stewardship of Tate, and the inevitable details; yet he remained preoccupied. His entire adult life had been spent here. Going on leave was a big step — a step into space, really, because for all his Statehouse skill he was a political innocent. Until today he had always coached himself. Starting this afternoon, he needed help. He needed — reversing the pencil, Doc fiercely erased his doodle and started another — he really needed Newt Albert. There was no escaping it. The campaign ahead was a new game, and Newt knew how to play it. Doc could only hope that he also knew the rules.

"You'll have to excuse me now," he muttered as they rose, scraping chairs. "I have other details."

The board did not resent being called a detail. Nodding sympathetically, it moved in a body toward the room's hatrack, carefully donned identical straw hats, and lingered there briefly in creased Robert Hall worsteds and gabardines, chattering idly before returning to its C.P.A. desks, hardware stores, nurseries, and G.P. practices — the small business, Civitan bastions in which State graduates were entrenched, and from which they wistfully coveted the richer Rotarian offices of Peabody alumni. It was hard to dislike the board, impossible to admire it. Doc thought of his protégés affectionately, as good men he had made. To Sam their unanimity helped State's image. Tate, strolling briskly up to Doc and Sam, had long ago dismissed them as so many ciphers.

"I think I've got everything," he trilled, riffling through a mass of memoranda. "I'll just run these down to the typing pool."

Doc regarded the sheets with vague alarm. It was astounding how much paper the man could cover. Yet he was an able executive. During his six years at State he had completely mastered the administrative machinery.

"Do you have a minute?" Sam asked Tate, sidling up and flourishing a paper of his own. "I'd like to show you this release. I've alerted Western Union, but we can still make changes."

This was Sam in his creative mood, anxiously soliciting praise. The provost had encountered it before. He shied away. "Sorry, I'll have to beg off."

"Oh. O.K." Sam wobbled off disconsolately.

"I hate to disappoint him," Tate told Doc. "It's just that I'm in a terrible bind. I've got faculty reception preparations this afternoon, the Academic Council tomorrow morning, and reaccreditation team details after that." He smirked, pocketing his notes. "And then, of course, I have to get ready for Monday."

"Monday," Doc echoed thoughtfully. On Monday Tate would take over as acting president. The realization gave Doc a twinge. He was reluctant to yield authority, even temporarily. "Say, I'm expecting that team chairman later this afternoon," he said assertively. "You might drop in."

"Check," said Tate, hurrying away. On the threshold he skipped past an arriving visitor. "Nice timing," he whispered to him and was gone, his pate winking in the neon directional lights of the hall.

The arrival was Newt Albert, a gray, gnomish little man with an expression of infinite calm. "You gave them the news?" he asked Doc pleasantly. "Then I got news for *you*." He padded over, holding a *Star* across his chest like a sandwich board. "Sam told me you don't read the local rag, but I think you know this guy."

He was pointing at the halftone of Ham. Doc adjusted his little glasses. His eyes sparkled. "Of course I know him. He was one of my boys."

"Sure, an ace. I saw him once."

"He was Spook Duschene's receiver," Doc said, remembering them together. Together they had sparked State's finest team in the long hiatus between Doc's own undergraduate days and the subsidized juggernauts of the past decade — the only spectacular team of Doc's coaching days, before he became admissions director and introduced athletic scholarships. Once, on a bright day when the wind was right and their timing perfect, they had come within seconds of beating Peabody. The ball had been on the Peabody forty. Doc could still see Spook fading back to midfield and Ham cutting for the sideline and yawing about and . . .

Newt was bearing in. "When did they play?"

"Ah — 1941 and 1942. There was no football the next three years, of course."

"And when did Markham graduate?"

Newt was probing, testing the tie between them. He himself had known Ham slightly during Ham's year of local reporting, before he went abroad for the *Star*. Newt recalled him as shrewd and aggressive, the author of a short, young man's book about Birmingham which had treated all institutions, including Newt and the *Star*, with virulent honesty. Newt bore no grudge. As a politician he feuded only with other politicians. Indeed, for reasons too intricate for Doc to understand, he welcomed Ham's return now. Until today he hadn't appreciated Ham's State background, because it had been without political ramifications. Abruptly that had changed.

"He came back for one semester early in 1946," Doc said. "He'd been hurt in the Pacific."

"That was the last time you saw him?"

"No, I met him in the Statehouse once. He — well, he promised to come see me, but he didn't."

A shadow flickered across Doc's face. He was like a father pondering the thoughtless slight of a son who had outgrown him. Doc felt a tie to all old State players, but Ham Markham was a special case. He had been the greatest end ever to wear State blue — his jersey lay under glass in the trophy pavilion, retired for his lifetime; only Doc's, retired forever, was more honored. Yet after his graduation he had drifted away. Doc hadn't minded his working for the *Star*. It seemed peculiar, but the boy had been bright and had wanted to write. What was troubling was that in the decade since his graduation Ham had shown no interest in the rebuilt campus, had never responded to an alumni appeal, hadn't bothered to notify the university of changes in his mailing address. If only he had married a State girl, Doc thought. He had obliquely suggested as much during their brief meeting four years before, when he had reproved Ham for not keeping in touch. Ham had just grinned crookedly and said, "Same old Coach. State men are supposed to marry their coeds, who knit tiny blue sweaters with the numerals '1972' while the fathers pore over old alumni magazines."

"By golly, that's not a bad idea."

"Well, I let you down. I spliced with a Stoddard College girl."

"Say, that's keen. Funny how things turn out, isn't it?"

It had been darned funny, Doc thought now, because before the war Ham had seemed sure to make a State marriage. He had been stuck on a pretty Catholic coed when he joined up, but during that semester afterward something had gone wrong, and Doc doubted that the something had been religion. Kit Ryan hadn't exactly been what you'd call the Newman Club type.

Kit Ryan. It rang a recent bell . . .

He couldn't remember. Anyhow, Ham's finding a Stoddard girl *was* keen, he thought loyally. It was nice to think of State boys signing up with graduates of those fancy women's colleges. The only trouble was that alumni who married Stoddard, Wellesley, and Smith girls seemed to lose interest in Gideon. Ham, for example, had not only broken his promise to come up that time; even a request for his picture, to hang in the office gallery, had gone unanswered.

Newt said, "You'd like to see him now?"

"Sure I would. But I'll be cussed if I'll call the *Star.*"

"You don't have to. I had it done. He's in your office right now."

"What? No! Say, that was right nice—" Doc broke off. He said suspiciously, "Why did you do it?"

"I'll level with you. Ordinarily I wouldn't risk a *Star* interview, but they do have the biggest circulation in the state, and Markham's bound to be on your side. He can give us a sympathetic story the one place we need it most. I want you to tell him our plans."

Doc spun away. "I'm not going to exploit a friend."

"Who says it's exploitation? You're offering him a break—an exclusive."

"Don't give me that tomfoolishness. You should have consulted me."

"How could I?" Newt was plaintive. "You were tied up."

"Well . . ." The fellow had a point, Doc thought. Anyway, Ham was already here. "You say he's in my office?"

"Looking at his watch and hoping you'll hurry."

Doc clenched a fist, unclenched it. "All right," he muttered, wheeling toward the corridor. "I guess just seeing him won't do any harm."

In the corridor Newt trotted alongside. "Look, that other guy you mentioned—" He fumbled deliberately. "Spook Duschene. Wasn't that his name?" Doc nodded tightly. Newt pounded a fist into a palm. "Sure, I remember now. Duschene—a frog. And a hell of a back. Incidentally, whatever happened to him?"

There was nothing incidental about it. Newt was probing again, looking for another contact. He didn't get it. He didn't even get an answer. Doc, dimpleless, averted his eye and suddenly picked up his stride. It was a swift, inexplicable change of mood, and it should have warned Newt that he had run a rough finger over an old wound. But Newt, usually alert for other men's scars, missed it entirely. He halted, transfixed, and watched Doc hurtle ahead with that incredible gait and vanish in a twinkle of frosted glass.

So *fast*, he thought. No doubt about it, the old man was still a champion. He could tool along like a locomotive. Nonstop and nonstoppable. All gristle and all the gristle moving at once.

Then Newt recovered and smiled a placid smile. Doc had looked like some huge animal crashing into a trap.

And that, as it happened, was just what he was.

**

Doc's Statette receptionist was a flat-heeled, pony-tailed sophomore of nineteen, married and expecting in December, and as he entered the outer office she bounded up.

"Hi! There's a Mr. Markham passed out on one of those funny little chairs inside."

Doc braked and wagged a finger. "I've told you not to jump, Jill. You have two to think of, you know."

"Roger," she said, and sat with a thump.

It was a daily rite with them. In the beginning she had thought it a joke—there were so many funny little campus jokes about pregnancy — but now she put it down to his age. It was like him, she had decided, quaint but nice, which was how she described him to classmates who had never seen him. Beyond that she had few opinions of Doc, and despite the fact that in one subtle way or another he controlled her entire life, that even her child would learn to walk and talk in one of the Psychology Department nurseries, she seldom thought of him.

She had, however, been thinking of him the last few minutes. "Say, Mr. Theanapolis just showed me his release," she said, bounding up again. "Ter*ri*fic!"

"Why — thank you," he said uneasily. He wished Sam had shown more discretion. The girl was such a chatterbox.

"You know, it's terribly thoughtful of you to worry about my condition," she said, opening the inner door and entering blithely ahead of him. "I mean, considering I'm not old enough to vote."

She cut her eyes at him roguishly; he smiled back uncertainly and crossed the threshold just as Ham awoke. Ham had been deep in dreams of the past, and he opened his eyes to see the hero of Then approaching, welcoming him to Now.

"Hello, Ham," Doc said gruffly.

"Hello, Coach." Ham took his hand tremulously.

"You look tuckered, boy."

"Your campus wore me out. I can't get over what you've done. It's fantastic."

In gentle reproach Doc said, "I tried to tell you that last time I saw you."

Ham flinched. "Well, you were right. As always."

Jill chimed in, uninvited. "Going to be around long, Mr. Markham?"

"I'm hoping he can stay for the faculty reception tomorrow," Doc said. "Ham's on the *Star,* but he really belongs to us. He used to wear the blue for me in the old days."

"He did?" She looked at him with respect.

"Say, the squad's just back from camp," Doc said. "You ought to see them work out, boy."

"They're full of beans, *I* hear," said Jill. "Three years without dropping a game and they think they're all Colts, or something."

"Three years!" Ham whistled softly. "And we thought we were good. We never had a perfect season."

"Never?" Respect dwindled visibly.

"Jill!" Doc whacked his hands together. "Get one of the other girls to take your place; after I talk to Mr. Markham I want you to show him the trophy pavilion. And now—" He nodded toward the door. She left reluctantly, and he winked at Ham. "Harum-scarum, but she has a good heart. And I do want you to look at that pavilion. There's a little surprise for you there — your old number in a case."

Ham, touched, murmured his thanks and then listened with growing awe as Doc spun a brief pep talk about the new campus, citing figures, explaining how the Athletic Incentive Program worked and what Camp TD was, describing the stadium that had relegated old Aggie Field to a practice field, pointing out the broad picture window and urging him to visit here and there.

"Sounds tremendous," said Ham, profoundly impressed.

The word lingered, unchallenged; Doc nodded in solemn agreement. Yet each saw the campus differently. To Doc it was a personal achievement — the book he had never written, the bridge he had never built, the son he had never had. But Ham had his own, idealized picture of State, painted here in Gideon long ago. Because Doc had mixed the oils, held the easel, and guided the brush, he assumed it was his picture, too: the image of a great free institution where the poorer classes of the state could shuck off inferiority, and learn, and leave to lead their own. Impulsively he grabbed Doc's hand and pumped it.

"You know, I used to sit in class and dream of the day we'd shame Peabody."

"Jupiter!" Doc snorted. "I could drop Peabody into a corner of the North Campus and nobody'd notice. I mean, we're *huge* now, Ham."

That wasn't quite what Ham had meant, but he was too elated to notice. "I feel like choking over the alma mater," he went on, still pumping. He saw Doc smiling, flushed slightly, and stepped back. "Anyway, when my son's a freshman you can call him in and tell him what a sappy old grad his father turned out to be."

It was the first off note. Doc's face went heavy; he fingered his collar. Jill darted in briefly with a tray — his afternoon buttermilk, lemonade for Ham — and he seized the diversion. "I'll bet you drink lots of hard liquor in the tropics," he said suddenly, sitting beside his tumbler. Ham shrugged, and Doc shook his head. "It's no way to stay in condition."

Ham perched on a facing chair, suppressing a smile. What could he say? That he wasn't a Doc River and didn't mind outgrowing his jersey? It would only be misinterpreted. Instead he asked about Sarah River.

"Sare's not well," Doc muttered.

"Sorry, Coach."

"Golly, it's not your fault," Doc said and looked away.

Ham sensed that further inquiry would be unwise. Whatever her illness, it was obviously embarrassing. He cursed himself for not realizing that Doc's faded, barren wife could never have weathered the years as he had, and in common discomfort they sat silent, struggling to redeem a lost bond.

"Your teams must be sensational," Ham said.

"They always win," Doc said glumly.

"That's great. Say, remember when —"

"I'm running for governor," Doc blurted out.

Ham stared. Doc in politics. It was a stunner, all right. He reached for his glass, faltered, and impulsively drained it.

"You're filing today?"

Doc nodded shortly. "Sam's fixing to tell the whole state this afternoon, and then one of his men's going to pay my candidate's fee and register my name with the secretary of state in Birmingham. We held off till the last minute because I wanted to clear it with my trustees first. You see, there's a vacancy on the board. If the governor'd heard what I was up to, he might've tried to name a troublemaker. Of course, I have something to say about the appointment; I just wanted to duck a dogfight."

"But —"

"How'd the Democrats settle on an old-fashioned white-birch Yankee like me? Well, if you want to split hairs, they haven't yet. Not officially, that is. Their delegate convention doesn't come till Monday. The committee does the real deciding, though, and they're set. Fact is, it was *me* picked *them*. You see, Newt Albert — I expect you knew him?"

Ham nodded gingerly. He had known him, all right, he thought. The way a curator knows a cobra.

"Newt sent Sam Theanapolis up here to ask would I help his ticket. One thing led to another, and — golly, I guess you recollect how I've always felt about that Peabody clique that runs the Statehouse. Well, I got curious. I snooped around and asked who Newt's folks planned to run. Turned out they didn't have anybody.

Not a blamed soul. I grumped off and went back to my chores here, and the next thing I knew there was Newt, camping on my doorstep and jabbering about a draft." Doc sipped his buttermilk. "I thought about it, boy. I thought brain-fever hard. And the long and short of it is I decided I couldn't bring myself to shirk the call."

Ham looked out across the immense green campus. "But what about this?"

"State? Oh, that's done," Doc said harshly.

"It's never done!" Ham leaned forward earnestly. "This is a campaign that's never finished."

"Well, I guess it's time somebody else scrapped a bit."

"Somebody else lead State? Listen, there isn't anybody else. You know that."

Doc removed his glasses. This was turning out to be more difficult than he had expected. He wondered whether other alumni would feel the same way, accuse him of desertion — perhaps even vote against him.

"Ham, you don't understand. We've got a lot of bigwig professors here now. They think I'm, well, an antique. I'm just getting in their way. It's time I skidooed."

Ham remembered Tate's superciliousness. "They're wrong," he said hotly, "and you've got to stay and prove it."

Doc shook his head doggedly. "I can prove it in the Statehouse."

"In that rat race? You're too good for that."

"No, boy." Doc was on his feet, folding his hands behind him. "No man is too good to stand for office in this country."

His dimples had disappeared. He looked like a bluff sea dog braced for a gale. He really believes it, Ham thought wonderingly; he really thinks it works that way. Doc reminded him of all the copybook myths he had learned in the ninth grade and forgotten in the tenth — that in civics men rose through merit, that every statesman was an Alger hero, that any boy could become President. It was astonishing. Doc must have masterminded some Draconian budget deals to get this campus built. Yet now that it had come down to his own candidacy the memory of that was washed away. Clearly the election meant a lot to him. And smiling up hesitantly, Ham realized that it meant something to him, too. Hell, he thought, the least I can do is congratulate him.

"Let me be one of the first, Coach. I wish you luck."

Doc gripped his hand solemnly, replaced his spectacles, and sat down. "Thank you, boy. I appreciate that. Just between you and me, I'll need every well-wisher I can get."

"This just shows how long I've been away. I thought the Democrats would have quit putting up serious opposition to Blandford."

"Oh, I could never beat the governor. He's retiring. They say it's his ticker."

"His liver, they mean. It was a sieve when I left."

"Well." To Doc alcoholism was like syphilis; it wasn't discussed. "Anyway, the Republicans are running Witty."

"Witty." Ham closed his eyes. "Oh, great."

Stuart Witty had been one of his case studies in *Through Darkest Birmingham.* Ham had been looking for someone typical of the city's elite, and he still remembered his sardonic pleasure when he ran across the Bourbon entry in *Who's Who:*

> WITTY, Stuart Hathaway Plimpton; corp. lawyer; b. Birmingham, July 4, 1899; s. Avery Monkton and Grace Langley (Sitton): ed. St. Paul's School (Concord, N.H.); A.B. Peabody, 1922; LL.B Harvard 1925; LL.D (hon.) Williams, 1956; m. Felicia Wasplett 1926; children —Avery Marcy, Stuart Hathaway Plimpton III. Delta Kappa Epsilon. Republican. Episcopalian. Clubs: Clipper, Links, Swallow Hills, Down Town, Ivy, Racquet, Field (Bar Harbor), Knickerbocker (N.Y.C.). Home: 1 East Ridgefield Pkwy. Office: 1111 Osgood Bldg., Birmingham.

"He's not a well-known man in the counties," Doc said thoughtfully, "but he's got a lot behind him."

Ham was torn. In a way his loyalty to Doc ran even deeper than Sam's. Both were devoted to the Galahad image of the great athlete who in leaner years had given everything — even tuition from his own pocket — to boys who wore State blue against Peabody green. Ham, however, saw clearly what Sam only sensed. In Doc he recognized a symbol of his own class, and because he still hated the mossbacked, old guard, Clipper-Links-Racquet Club clique whose sworn enemy Doc had always been, part of him wanted Doc to run and win in a landslide. If Ham had been a stranger to public life it would have been enough. But the instincts of his craft intruded. Intuitively he began going over the ground, looking for tracks, and the first he found were Newt Albert's. Ham would trust Doc anywhere, Newt nowhere. He had come here from the corners of the earth, but he had seen Newt's type a thousand times, in Egypt's Wafd, in India's Congress, in every cabal of little men clamoring for office. The pattern was dismal and familiar: a party in search of a popular candidate and interested in him only as a source of power. The fact that the candidate was close to Ham altered nothing. It only made it more poignant.

So he nursed his doubts. In the end he surrendered to them and thanked Doc for inviting him here, hating himself for the inference, the implied question. Then Doc answered it and he didn't hate himself so much.

"You're wondering why you're here. Well—" Doc peered over his absurd little rims. He was in an impossible position. How could he explain that the invitation hadn't been his? This was Newt's doing, he thought indignantly. But maybe Newt had been right. Ham *was* in the newspaper game. This could be a feather in his cap . . .

"I'll be blunt, boy. The *Star* will fight me editorially. We know that. All we ask is a square shake in the news columns. Your paper will get a copy of Sam's release this evening, of course, but we thought you might interview me here, now, and write the first story. That way I'd at least get a fair start."

He retreated into a flurry of small activities, readjusting his glasses, sipping more buttermilk, plucking at his trouser creases. Ham sat silent. Nobody likes to be used. If this had been anybody else he would have left then. But it wasn't anybody else. For years he had lulled himself to sleep on bad nights thinking how he could have thrown a key block for Doc if he had been his age, on his team. To him Doc was worth a few bruises. And Doc did have a point. Every hatchet in the *Star*'s front office would be on the grindstone, starting tonight.

After all, he had been sent for a story. He took a deep breath.

"I'll have to ask a lot of questions."

"Oh, I know, I know."

"You won't like some of them."

"I know that, too." Doc dimpled deeply. "I've been putting up with *Star* claptrap for years."

Ham chuckled. "O.K. Let's start with campaign organization," he said, producing the judge's pencil stub and an unused immigration form. "Who's going to run it for you?"

"Newt Albert."

The lead was blunt, but Ham broke it. He took a fresh hold and wrote on with the dulled point.

"What about Sam?"

"He's organizing a Citizen's Committee."

"The citizens are alumni?"

"Some of them."

"Would you say most?"

Doc nodded, frowning. He hadn't liked that one. Ham debated pocketing the pencil and remembering answers, a trick he used when people clammed up. He decided against it. Tricks were out with Doc. Maybe the rest of the questions would be easier. He asked about the trustee meeting.

"They gave me a leave of absence — without pay, of course." Doc attempted a smile. "I dasn't tell Sare about that. She's always been a mite nigh, and she'd start drawing on her store of canned fruit in the cellar. You probably remember it." He made a face. "Awful stuff."

Ham hesitated. "You're staying on in the Mansion?"

"Well, yes." Doc was wary. "Golly, Ham, it's my home."

"That'll be your headquarters?"

"In a manner of speaking, yes. Of course, I'll have my office here."

There was a pause while they considered how that sounded. Doc said swiftly, "I'll be paying rent on the house."

"How much?"

"We — the trustees thought eighty a month would be fair."

Ham wrote it down. He recalled that the place had twenty rooms, wrote that down, too, and asked hesitantly, "Will Newt be there with you?"

"Well, when he's in Gideon I thought I'd let him have a corner of the Mansion library. You know it, you've been there. It's that little alcove by the big bay window, on the rhododendron side —" Doc had been scowling at Ham's jiggling pencil. He broke off, reddening. "Look, boy, I'm doing all I can to keep State out of this. Just the other day I told Newt there wasn't going to be any exploitation of scholarships, or county farm agents, or the medical school clinics in Birmingham."

Ham started. "You mean that came up?"

"Yes, Newt raised the question, and I said I wouldn't have it — listen, don't write that down!"

"Coach, I —"

"Never mind!" Doc flashed. "You're stepping out of line, Ham. And I'm not so blamed sure it's the first time you've been offside, either."

For a long moment Ham looked blank. Then it came to him. Seventeen years before, his touchdown against Peabody had been called back because somebody had been offside. The penalty had cost State its first victory over Peabody. No one had known who had jumped. The players themselves couldn't tell; they had all been jitterbugging. The officials had escaped during the goal post fight, State hadn't been able to afford movies of games then, and the Peabody coach wouldn't lend his. But it had to have been somebody on the line. And Ham had been an end. Doc never got over that game, Ham thought in amazement. He had built a big stadium, but he was right back on that Aggie Field sideline, peering at the scrimmage and trying to decide which man to blame.

"Look, what difference does it make now?"

"I said drop it!" Doc's face was the color of old brick. "If we'd known you were going to be this cantankerous we wouldn't have asked you up."

Ham felt a door slam in his face. He repeated feebly, "We?"

"My friends and myself."

The lock had turned. Numbly he lifted his stub to doodle, but Doc saw and misunderstood. "I said stop writing!"

So Ham pocketed the pencil after all, and in mutual embarrassment they turned to campaign clichés — promises, demands, accusations. The interview had disintegrated. Miserably Ham wondered what had gone wrong. Yet under his pain he really knew; to prove his own integrity he had goaded Doc, and Doc, edgy already, had bridled.

Doc also was miserable. Leaning back limply, he recited his election program in a monotone, reflecting bitterly that this was all the *Star*'s fault. If Ham hadn't gone to work for them — if he'd married Kit Ryan and taken some other job — he wouldn't dream of being flippant. Still, he had hurt him now, and he knew it, and he was sorry. He had had no right to accuse him of having been offside, he thought penitently. That had been a fool thing to do. Why if Ham hadn't caught that ball there wouldn't be anything to argue about. Doc was too proud to apologize, but rising at the end he murmured awkwardly, "You think you can remember everything? I mean, it's all right to put — to put *that* down."

"I'll remember," Ham said dryly. He produced the stub and inspected it. "It's dull anyhow." It was. The lead had entirely vanished.

"Well, we can fix that!" In a spasm of nervous activity Doc strutted about, yanking open drawers. Ham realized with dismay that he was looking for a sharpener. "My provost gave me one of those little portable gadgets. Doggone it, it's around here somewhere." But it wasn't. "Say, I'll bet Jill borrowed it." He was stalking her door when it opened of itself, admitting the gray pixie head of Newt Albert. Doc stared at him angrily. "What do you want?" The head receded. "Wait a minute! You got a pencil?"

Newt entered, bowed to Ham, and brandished an Eversharp. That's Newt, Ham thought. The man with the pencil, or the dollar bill, or the topcoat you just have to have. Take it and forget about it; no questions asked. Ham declined the pencil.

"We're all through," he said, exhibiting his abortive notes.

Doc eyed them suspiciously. "Are you sure that's enough?"

"We want to save something for the campaign," Newt said affably.

"That's right." Ham looked around. "Anyway, I've got to dictate this. What I really need is a phone."

Newt had that too; he had spotted an empty office down the hall. He handed Ham a copy of the finished release and was about to escort him out when Doc said quietly from the window, "Don't forget the trophy pavilion, Ham. Jill knows just where your jersey is."

"I'll remember, Coach."

But he knew Doc wasn't thinking of the jersey. He was still harking back to that old penalty, wondering who had crossed the line into Peabody territory before the snap, who had broken all their hearts that radiant Saturday afternoon and why they couldn't have taken that one game, that last big bright chance before the shadows grew together and night came and Spook left.

"After all — I guess State's steamroller flattens Peabody every year now," Ham said indistinctly.

Newt started to speak and checked himself. Doc was squinting at the window with what Ham recognized as his third-down-and-three-to-go coaching expression. It looked odd here; the campus outside was deserted. Then he realized that Doc was studying his own reflection in the glass.

"We never beat them," he was saying. "Peabody gave up football eight years ago."

**

Newt returned, dropped into Ham's deep chair, and flipped open a copy of *Sly*.

"Girlie magazines are banned on this campus," Doc growled across the desk. "I'd rather you looked at the *Star*."

Tate, entering with a carbon of his typed notes, gave Newt a superior look. Superiority was Tate's normal posture, enhanced, on limp days like this, by his uniform of faultless Dacron. It was one of the provost's minor accomplishments that he never perspired.

"I could have told you smut annoys the president," he said and turned archly to Doc. "Or is it too early to say governor?"

No one had called Doc that before. He began a restrained smile, fought to control it, surrendered, and grinned. Newt observed approvingly. The grin was a good sign, a symptom of capitol fever. The worse a candidate's case, the better his chances.

"No, I don't think it's a bit early," Newt said.

"But I haven't even been nominated yet," Doc protested.

Tate flourished a gaunt hand. "A formality."

"A pushover," Newt agreed. He winked at Tate. "Like State games."

The provost smirked wickedly, and Newt put his magazine away. He did not produce his copy of the *Star*, however. He couldn't. He had destroyed it, for a reason which would have startled Doc. Today's invitation to Ham had been more devious than even Ham suspected. It had been a snare for the *Star*, inspired by a promotion box on page sixteen of the morning paper:

> MARKHAM SERIES SLATED!
>
> Hiram A. Markham, never idle, will be assigned to an exciting, colorful story of the state — and will cover it with his usual matchless skill. Watch for his first article, soon to appear on the front page of
>
> THE STAR
>
> Estab. 1828 Circ. over 300,000

There would be no active campaigning for the next two weeks. Political reporters would be writing background stories, forecasts, interpretations, and a friendly *Star* reporter would be a fantastic break. If Newt could get Ham's by-line over this one story he just might force the paper to put him on the election. He rated his chances as fair. The *Star* hadn't an inkling of Doc's candidacy, and on a sunny afternoon like this the general managing editor would be off golfing. Doc himself, of course, never looked inside the paper. The only problem was Markham. If Ham had seen that box —

"By the way, how did things go?" he asked languidly.

Doc busied himself with Tate's carbon. "We gabbed," he answered shortly.

No clue there. If only he weren't so unmanageable, Newt reflected wistfully. If he'd just play ball and follow the suggestions of a seasoned pol. Maybe he'd change later, Newt thought, and he thought grimly, he'd better. They were up against the strongest Republican organization in New England. It was losing its governor, Norman Blandford, but he had been failing for years; for all practical purposes Stuart Witty had been the real power in the Statehouse this past term. Unlike Blandford, Witty was a city man, a handicap in a state whose political power lay in the big rural counties. He was also shrewd, though — far shrewder than the governor — and his campaign chest, already swollen by twelve years of contributions from party patronage lists, would be bursting by November.

Newt's treasury was almost empty. If there had been one wealthy Democrat in the state he would have offered him the nomination, but there wasn't one. Indeed, despite the heavy Democratic registration in the cities and the tantalizing prospect of a popular governor's retirement, as late as July he hadn't had any nominee at all. Every available man had been drab or divorced or tagged with some inconvenient minority label until Sam, lunching with Newt in downtown Birmingham, had brought up Doc's name. Sam hadn't suggested Doc as a candidate. He had merely remarked that he might be helpful to the party, and as they broke up Newt had suggested Sam sound him out. At the time Doc had merely seemed a useful ally. By next day he was very much on Newt's mind, however, and before the end of that week he had set his cap for him.

He was amazed that he hadn't thought of him before. Most college presidents were political poison, but Doc had been a sports page hero. He had other advantages. He was colorful, had been born on a farm, and was close to the legislature. Everyone knew him; he had spoken to every important luncheon club in the state at least once. Then there was State's team. As Sam had pointed out, they would be playing and winning every Saturday during the campaign, and the big Hampshire game would be televised three days before the election. That game was important to a lot of voters, because any resident of the state could join the Alumni Association by purchasing a season ticket, entitling him to seating privileges in the stadium and an automatic subscription to *The Statesman*, the alumni magazine. Newt himself was an alumnus. He hadn't finished high school, but he had gone to three southern bowl games on chartered State trains, wearing a blue beanie and waving a blue pennant.

The team was a big plus. Yet even that wasn't Doc's greatest asset. Newt had thought of one greater. Studying state expenditures was part of his job, and he knew that Doc's authority ranged far beyond Gideon. Each legislative session brought committee wrangles over what the *Star* called Doc's "carnival side shows"—his off-campus services. They touched every corner of the state. Early in his expansion, for example, he had established a College of Education in Gideon and absorbed the five state teachers colleges. He had never relinquished them. They were strategically located and were now used as community centers. Even more important was the university's Birmingham medical school. Its Haven Square Hospital clinics were virtually free; the slum wards were grateful. And elsewhere voters were sensitive to Doc's immense scholarship fund and his network of farm agents. Ostensibly each of these services was independent. Actually the directors were Doc's proconsuls. Together they controlled a phalanx which could be quickly converted into an effective campaign machine.

Newt was a listmaker, and for a month now he had carried in his pocket an audit of Doc's strengths and weaknesses:

Liabilities: (*a*) inexperience; (*b*) stubbornness; (*c*) sick wife; (*d*) weakness of the party; (*e*) G.O.P. bankroll.

Assets: (*a*) popularity; (*b*) aggressive spirit; (*c*) homespun personality; (*d*) team; (*e*) patronage.

By patronage Newt meant the services. Three days ago he had been tactless enough to call them patronage in Doc's presence, and he had been bluntly told that they would have nothing to do with the campaign. Newt was a professional politician, an artist of the possible. He had swiftly changed the subject. He hadn't changed his plans, though. Instead he had called on Tate, suggested that influential forces were at work, and persuaded him to see that the service directors were in Gideon today. Now he was ready to try again. He lit a cigar, waved out the match, and turned to Doc.

"You know, it used to be every bride brought her husband a dowry. It helped the marriage, like. This campaign will be a lot better off if you can give it a little muscle — apart from yourself, I mean."

Doc shot an embarrassed look at Tate and coughed into his fist. "I told you. I have a few war bonds, a mite in the bank. Not much; my salary's set at twelve thousand. It's not right, but the *Star* would kick up a ruckus if I tried to change it, and somehow I've never had the gumption to try." Under his breath he added, "Of course, maybe some of my friends'll want to give."

"Doc has friends all over the state," the provost said cheerily. "We've a file of twenty thousand of them. Whenever the legislature looks obstinate we send out post cards. It always works."

Newt's eyes widened. "Nice to know."

"I wouldn't dream of rattling a tin cup at them for a political race," Doc said quickly, frowning at Tate.

"Well, I wasn't thinking of money anyhow," said Newt. "Naturally it'll come up later; it always does. Right now I got something else on my mind, though."

He gave Tate a meaningful nod, and the provost straightened slightly. Tate knew what Newt was up to, but he also knew that if Doc won in November the balance of campus power would shift dramatically. Newt could be a valuable ally.

"Russo, Shaw, and Massicotte are in my office," he told Doc carelessly. "Want to see them?"

Doc looked blank. Jake Russo should be out managing farm agents, Bill Shaw should be interviewing scholarship applicants, and Joe Massicotte belonged in his office as administrator of Haven Square Hospital.

"What are those boys doing here?"

"Well, they happened to be in town on budgetary matters, and they —"

Doc's dimples began to fade. "The budget's in."

"Of course," Tate said nervously. "That is, if it ever really *is* in. This was a matter of contingency funds —"

"— which I always handle, as you know."

Doc was glowering. He smells it, Newt thought. It was time to intervene. He blew an oval smoke ring and said softly, "The fact is, I told Dr. Tate here I'd like to meet these guys. Anything wrong with that?"

"Jupiter!" Doc scowled out at the campus. "I thought we'd been over this before."

"We touched on it; I don't know that we really went over it, as you say. But while we're on the subject I'd like to point out that a lot of people in this state should be grateful for the things you've done."

"My career's bound to be an issue, isn't it?"

"You bet it is, and I don't have to tell you the *Star* will twist it every way they can. But the voters could be reminded of the truth."

"I don't see —"

Newt leveled his cigar at Doc. "Clinic patients at Haven Square could be jogged. Your farm agents could tell the grangers. You could have an extension service mailing, and you could plaster those old teachers colleges with posters. You must have a file on every kid's ever had a scholarship here. You could canvass them, get them out in the field. Take my word, it would make a lot of difference, maybe *the* difference, and . . ."

His voice trailed off in despair. He had struck out again. Doc's face was rigid.

"Maybe it would, but it won't."

"Listen, you use your scholarships with the legislature," Newt protested, but Doc cut him down with a glance.

"That's for State, not for me."

Doc eyed his provost sadly. The man had meant well, he supposed; he was just naïve, which was understandable, considering that he had spent his entire life on one campus or another.

"Send the boys away," he told him.

"Right," Tate murmured indifferently. "Though I imagine that as long as they're here they'll want to stay over for tomorrow's reception," he said, and added as an afterthought, "Governor."

Doc flushed. He liked that; he couldn't deny it. Then his eye fell icily on the *Sly* protruding from Newt's pocket. "I spoke to you once about that thing, Mr. Albert. Please get rid of it before a Statette comes in."

Tate's thin chuckle was lost in a babble of voices. Sam, still worrying about his release, had just shown it to a lingering group of trustees. They hadn't realized that today was the day; they surged into the presidential suite with outstretched hands to congratulate Doc, and he, grinning again and nodding, went out to meet them and was rapidly surrounded by their bobbing shoulders.

"Really, he ought to wear a laurel," Tate whispered urbanely. He started to follow and paused in the reception room. "You know, I rather thought you'd put up a bigger struggle over our three unexpected guests," he said pettishly, plucking a cigarette from his shirt pocket. "I mean, it *was* a bit trying, getting them here."

Newt held out a match. "Don't get panicky. The election's over two months away. You got plenty of time to dig in."

Their smoke mingled. Tate peered owlishly through it. "*I?*"

"*You.* Next week you'll be acting president, won't you? If Doc's elected, who'll get his job here? Don't tell me you haven't thought of that."

Tate's poise vanished. He turned quickly and raced away on his stilt-thin legs, but his color deepened and spread until his nude head was a single blush. Newt dropped the spent match in a flower vase on Jill's desk. It sizzled angrily and died, staining the water an ugly gray.

**

Back at his desk, alone for the first time that day, Doc brooded over Newt's impertinence. The more he thought about it the redder he grew. The very idea! As though he'd allow a scrap, tag, or splinter of this university to be exploited in any way, shape, or manner. It was sass even to think such a thing. Why, State had grown bigger than men. It was sacred as Scripture. Imagine sending farm agents and Haven Square interns out to politick like ward heelers!

Horsefeathers.

Hokum.

No question about it, that Newt would bear watching. He'd have his uses the next few weeks, but he needed to have a whistle blown on him now and then. He jumped offside a speck too easy. And not because he was jittery, either. No, he was just a slippery customer. Look at the way he'd tricked Tate—an educated man with a doctorate from Columbia Teachers College.

Doc toyed with his copy of Sam's final draft. Maybe it would be a good idea to attend the Academic Council tomorrow morning. Those huddles of State's full professors were dry as widow's dust, but the revised reaccreditation schedule had been mailed to them yesterday, and undoubtedly there would be some discussion of it. Some of the older men were sure to bridle. Tate was all for pushing the thing through, but judging from the way he'd acted with Newt just now he might be wishy-washy. No, Doc thought; Tate couldn't handle it alone. He'd have to go himself. It would be better to let the old duffers fume at him. He'd fix their wagon; he'd just remind them that if he had never moved without their approval State would still be Aggie.

He leaned back. For the first time in memory he felt tired. Too bad he wasn't a prof himself, he thought; those sabbaticals and grants gave a fellow a chance to rest up. Well, at least his afternoon calendar was light. The Council could throw conniption fits in the morning; until then he didn't have to think about it.

In thirty years he had never learned to anticipate Harry Osborne Mikel.

Jill's Statette replacement was buzzing him. He flicked a switch and she said, "Professor Mikel is here, Dr. River."

Doc swore softly and cast about for a way out. The accreditation chairman was due soon — that might do it. "I don't have time, Mary," he said hastily. "I'm expecting that professor from Illinois."

"Oh, that's not for another half-hour," she said brightly, and Mikel shuffled in on sneakered feet, his scrawny bow legs tightly wrapped by bicycle clips and his habitual rumpled Camel dangling from thin colorless lips.

Doc eyed him with distaste. It was impossible to insult openly the one certified genius on campus, but he had stopped feigning friendship for him long ago. He just wished some of his new faculty critics were here now. He'd like to have them see the kind of thing he had to put up with from this intractable old faculty gadfly. Not that any of them would say boo. They had little affection for Mikel — he scorned them publicly — but the older men were wary of his sardonic wit, and despite his seedy clothes and insulting manner all instructors treated him with awe. Mikel was more than chairman of the History Department, more than senior professor of the Council. He possessed what they all coveted: an international reputation. Like Doc, Mikel was an alumnus of State's Aggie era, an earlier alumnus whose return had, indeed, preceded Doc's. Even then he had been that curious phenomenon, the teacher in an obscure college who stands at the top of his discipline. Because of an attachment which he refused to discuss he had declined Ivy offers and remained in Gideon, the only State professor with an honorary degree from Oxford, a Pulitzer citation, a National Book Club Award, and standing invitations from three foundations to quit teaching and putter.

Tossing his bookbag on the floor and himself into a chair, he wheezed, "Where's your regular assistant? I wanted to look at her belly. Someone told me she was expecting a litter."

"Jill is with child," Doc said grittily.

Mikel's mummy mouth twitched. "I assume she and her stud will soon be taking a larger stall in the Warren."

"Close the door, Mary," Doc called sternly, for he heard her out there giggling. He rubbed his eyes. "The Warren. Is that what you call University Village?"

"If you like."

"You know doggone well I don't."

The old man thrust out his scalene triangle of a face. "Do you prefer Realgonesville? That, I'm told, is what its inhabitants call it. Realgonesville." He shook with silent, demonic laughter. "I rather like that. Not that I disapprove of your quarters for married students. How could I? Utopia realized! Hobbes triumphant! Bendixes provided by the Home Economics Department and a child development laboratory that functions as a nursery, freeing wives for courses in home management and husbands for time-and-motion studies in male domestic efficiency!" He made a grotesque face. "But, my dear Prexy, it *is* a warren."

Doc deliberately fingered the release. "Is that what you came to jaw about?"

"Oh, dear me, no." Mikel swung his legs over the chair arm. "Among other things, I wanted to be the first vassal on the fief to proclaim his fealty." He tugged an untidy white forelock. "I'm assuming that we're all expected to be loyal to the baron in the forthcoming plebiscite."

Doc gave the door a baleful look. Did Sam have to blab to everybody? "I guess you saw the announcement." Mikel raised his eyes piously, and Doc sighed. "Well, of course, it's not true. In your case I suppose I'll be lucky not to get a knife in the back."

Mikel cackled. "Marvelous. But really, you know, I'm delighted. Elements appear so rarely in their unalloyed state. It's enchanting to see such a pure lust for power."

"Then you're here to contribute to my campaign?" Doc asked dryly.

"Ah — no. I shall follow it with a historian's zeal, but my professional standards proscribe involvement." Abruptly he uncoiled his legs, killed his cigarette in the wastebasket, and sat up. It was a characteristic gesture, the mercurial change of mood which had made his lectures famous. His mocking pose had vanished. He said soberly, "Actually that's what I'm here to talk about. *Principia, non homines* — that old dreary matter of standards. I mean the college's, of course."

"University's," Doc corrected him, making a small movement of annoyance.

Now it starts, he thought wearily. He never quits. For forty years Mikel had begrudged every student hour spent away from the classroom, boycotting all games, all dances, even glee club concerts. *Standards.* Doc stared resentfully at the old man's burlap suit and wizened, ill-shaved cheek. To him a college graduate was committed to many standards, including appearance. He didn't ask much. Of course, he liked to see State men wearing fitted suits and narrow-brimmed hats and State women in stylish dresses, but he himself was no fashion plate, and in Mikel's case he would have settled for creased trousers. It was humiliating that the only member of the faculty who crossed town to lecture at Peabody should look like a park bench warmer. Why, he thought indignantly, the man didn't ever wear his Phi Beta Kappa key.

"You think my candidacy will hurt State?"

Mikel smiled thinly and ran a hand through his white coxcomb. "No, I believe we can survive that. This is an academic matter."

Doc drummed his fingers on the desk top. "I'll be blunt, Harry. I've got a lot to wind up. Tate's taking over Monday —"

"So I understand."

"From the same informant, I suppose." Doc made a savage mental note to speak to Sam. "Anyhow, he'll have the authority to act. Why not talk to him?"

"I did, a moment ago in the hall. That's why I'm here."

"So you've found I'm not the only scalawag in the administration," Doc said sarcastically.

"I've never had any illusions about Tate, if that's what you mean. He's always reminded me of Balfour's celebrated remark. His conscience is not his guide, it's his accomplice."

"Balfour?" Fraternity pins?

"Or of that vignette of Charles X — he bears on his shoulders the burden of his immense unpopularity."

"Tate unpopular? Applesauce!" But Doc knew it wasn't. He had long suspected it, and he shifted uncomfortably.

"Don't fret. It's probably inevitable. My colleagues resent scholastic authority as much as I do, and this place being what it is Tate bristles with it. He runs the deans, who run the chairmen, who run everything else except your precious gym. Of course, another provost might be a trifle less despised."

"Ah — how?" Doc was really curious.

"Wit would help. Also taste. Tate's uncouth."

"Eh?"

"The man has a mind like a Rexall Drugstore ad."

Doc looked severe. Mikel should know how he despised backbiting. "Have you told him that to his face?"

"Oh, many times. And after he defended the new accreditation plan just now I went farther. I suggested he be committed to an institution. That's precisely what should be done if he goes ahead, because this university will be ruined."

So the plan was behind this call. Mikel had read his mail and come straight here. "Well, you're always saying it's ruined anyhow."

"I don't care to be publicly vindicated."

Doc swiveled impatiently. "But the whole point of this thing is to *raise* prestige! We're struggling along with agricultural college accreditation. It's a handicap, you know that — you voted for the study last winter."

"A study, yes. I did not vote for a formal review. The two are very different. The original idea was that we should undergo a preliminary inquiry, *sub rosa*, to see if we were deficient, and how."

"Tate doesn't believe that's necessary."

"I believe Tate's wrong, and if he is we have to face the stigma of formal rejection by a committee of learned men." He leaned forward accusingly. "An election's not worth the risk."

"Rejection's impossible," Doc snapped, ignoring the charge that this arose from that.

"Is it? Do you know what questions they'll ask? They aren't even interested in how many touchbacks you've scored."

"Touchdowns." The man's ignorance was unbelievable.

"It doesn't matter. They won't know the difference either."

"I suppose *you'll* tell them nothing about football matters."

"Of course I shall. The game has become a monster. It should be destroyed."

Doc snorted. "Every place that's tried that has dropped it clean out of sight. It'll happen to Peabody. Look at the University of Chicago. Who hears of it any more?"

Mikel grimaced. "Accreditors do. Nearly every accreditation team has a man from there."

"How's that?" Come to think of it, there was a Chicago man coming here. But that wasn't what he was talking about. "Do you know how many boys our athletic scholarships help? Have you any idea how badly high schools need top-notch State-trained coaches?"

"No, and I don't care. Nor will the accreditors. And they won't be cowed by this press agent display," Mikel said, nodding at the gallery of framed pictures.

"Listen, some of those people —"

"— are great Americans. *I* know. But the accreditation team won't be interested. Here's the sort of thing they'll want to know." Mikel jabbed the desk top with a nicotine-stained finger. "What proportion of your faculty has been admitted to the National Academy of Sciences? Answer: a handful. How many have tenure? None, really. What's your teaching load? Staggering. Your scholarship policy? Biased. Your general examination policy? *Non est.* How large is your library?"

"Why, Blandford Library —"

"Don't tell me. It's as big as the Louvre. I've been lost in it twice. But when you deduct Blandford's audio-visual studios, projection chambers, and lounge wings, how much stack room have you got left? In a word, my dear man, how many *books* are there? Less than a hundred and fifty thousand, I'm afraid."

Doc rose, frowning, and went to the window. Outside the campus glittered in the topaz sunlight, almost bereft of students and quite denuded of prewar buildings. A few venerable Aggie halls, some dating from the 1860's, still stood beyond the thicket of Georgian cupolas that fenced Doc's view, but he couldn't see them. Here the only reminder of State's past was the sound of the tintinnabula in the distant spire of Archer Chapel, retained because all alumni had sentimental memories of it. From time to time the bells offered a brief concert, and now they were pealing a medley of old State songs —

Hit the line for brave State . . .
As State's backs go tearing by . . .

Behind him Mikel chuckled wickedly. Doc's frown deepened. State's pirated songs, and the failure of the Department of Music to improve upon them, were sore points with him. Then, suddenly, his spirits rose. A couple had appeared from the direction of the Student Union, capering on the barbered lawn and laughing. The sight of youth always stimulated him. Their workbooks disclosed that the girl was taking an airline hostess course and the boy was in the annual ice cream workshop conducted by the extension service, but in their blazers and shined loafers they might have been undergraduates on any Ivy campus. The thought calmed him. State was sound. He believed in it. Besides —

"It's too late to change," he said, turning back. "The team chairman is on his way. In fact, he's due here any moment."

Mikel started. "But we only learned about it today."

"The trustees just met —"

"That tribe! Ten lickspittles! Or nine — the Governor hasn't named the new man yet, has he? Not that it matters. My agents inform me Blandford's been unwise enough to grant you an informal veto even there."

"I wouldn't call it unwise. He did promise, however." Doc paused thoughtfully. "In writing."

"Then what, may I ask, does that claque have to do with this solemn matter?"

"I had to wait until I could tell them," said Doc, hedging.

"You didn't consider asking the Academic Council's opinion first, *in camera?*"

"Well — there were details to be worked out."

"I'm sorry," Mikel said sharply. "I find that vague."

Doc didn't reply. It was vague because he was vague. The truth was that accreditation was a mystery to him, an academic matter. Tate, hired for his pedagogic talents, had assured him that this inspection was desirable — that it would bring State improved status, acceptance by the Association of American Universities, perhaps even an undergraduate Phi Beta Kappa chapter as a panache. The prospect was dazzling, and attainable. Mikel, Doc decided, was just being Mikel.

"As usual, you're exaggerating," he said irritably. "Even if the accreditation team should find against us, its report will be confidential."

Mikel lighted a fresh cigarette. "You think you could keep it away from the *Star?*"

"Why not? I've kept my candidacy quiet."

"Another matter entirely. Apart from the legislature, their reporters haven't been near you for years. You've been treated as a forbidding but extinct volcano. Now you're erupting again. This campus will be watched."

"I plan to take steps with the *Star.*"

Mikel catcalled. "You've been planning that for years."

Doc sat, smiling. "This time I have a friend at court. Ham Markham's back from India." He had already forgotten his row with Ham. Basically the boy was on his side; there was no question of that. "Not two hours ago he sat where you're sitting, and tomorrow he'll have a story about me."

He had scored — temporarily Mikel was silenced — but at some cost. Uneasily he remembered telling Newt earlier that he wouldn't trade on Ham's allegiance. Now he seemed to be suggesting precisely that. It wasn't really that way, he thought defensively, nor was the reaccreditation political. That was the devil of these politicians. They made a fellow feel so all-fired *guilty* about everything. After all, a thing wasn't bad just because it might help a campaign a little on the side. He sat up.

"I mean, of course, that I was glad to see him again. He's been away ten years."

"I know what you mean," said Mikel, nodding absently. "So Ham is home. He's a highly perceptive young man, you know. I'll never understand how he survived the gladiatorial punishment you gave him here, but the fact is he left remarkably alert. His work since suggests that he has matured. I imagine you missed his article on linguistic chauvinism in Kerala."

Doc shook his head indifferently. It sounded steep.

"It was in the last issue of *The Yale Review.*"

"The Yale Review!" Doc sat up. Ham ought to have dropped the alumni office a line. They could have had a little write-up in *The Statesman.* "I didn't know he wrote releases for magazines like that."

"He appears frequently. Believe it or not, he has a considerable following among people who don't even know he used to score touchbacks for State."

"Ham never scored a touchback for State," Doc said testily.

"Oh, really? I understood he was quite good." Mikel puffed rapidly and smirked in the blue fog. "In all events, I think it highly unlikely he'll be useful for your purposes. Ham's no journalistic *nymph du pave*." He added condescendingly, "That's French for whore."

"Never mind!" Doc struggled to control himself. His interviews with Mikel always ended this way. "You're being aggravating, as usual. I didn't suggest that Ham do anything shady. I just wanted to see him and tell him what I was fixing to do."

"I'm inclined to think he'll regard the difference as molecular."

"By golly, Harry, I —"

But he went no further. He couldn't trust himself to keep his voice even, and so he sat, crimson and perspiring, while Mikel leered and enveloped him in a billowing cloud.

The buzzer rescued him.

"Dr. Budge is here from Illinois," the Statette trilled, "with Professor Lutz."

"I'll be right out. It's the accreditation chairman," he barked at Mikel, glancing furiously at his soiled sneakers.

Mikel rose and stretched. "Buck up. Your distinguished guest will see plenty of faculty fops later, and he probably won't mind me half as much as you do."

Doc growled that he didn't mind at all, though he did, and he felt a familiar despair when Mikel, crossing the threshold beside him, lapsed into his clownish role. Mikel ought to have greeted Lutz, a deaf, bullet-headed, shy little scientist who had come to State in the '30's as an Austrian refugee, and whom even he agreed was one of the best of the old faculty. He didn't; he ignored him completely and hooted at Budge, "Physicist, aren't you? Tell me, will you require me to take examinations? Or will you just want to see my diploma?"

The chairman, a short square man with a voice like a frog's, croaked, "That won't be necessary." He turned to Doc with a tolerant smile. "The only historian I've ever known who would even be entitled to debate with Dr. Mikel is the elder Schlesinger."

"*Not* the late Chuck Beard?" Mikel asked with a golliwogg leer.

Budge laughed, Lutz smiled politely and reached for his hearing aid, and Doc, chuckling nasally, steered his visitors toward his office.

As they entered, Archer Chapel's belfry started its final selection of the medley:

Cheer, cheer for State's hallowed name,
Wake up the echoes . . .

"Why, how thoughtful of you," Budge said. "Notre Dame was my school."

"That's keen," Doc said and improvised hastily: "Ah — these pictures might interest you." He waved at the gallery. "A few are sons and daughters of State — even in Illinois you must have heard of some of them."

As he closed the door he saw Mikel outside on his bike, pedaling merrily in cadence to the chimes, and the Statette at her window, watching him with amusement. He might at least watch himself in front of students, Doc thought indignantly. The majority of undergraduates had always considered Mikel odd, but to the new generation he was an outright crackpot. His clothes and his bike were the butts of interfraternity skits, and it was an open secret that he lived simultaneously at several seedy addresses and wrote ridiculous letters to newspapers over fictitious names. Yet despite the university's weak tenure rules it was almost impossible to get rid of him. His scholarly work was a matter of national interest, and there would be no way to placate the ardent band of alumni who had fallen under the spell of his strange witchcraft during their campus years. They were few, but unfortunately they included State's most successful graduates. With a pang Doc remembered that one of the most devoted had been Ham Markham.

**

So it had all been Pyrrhic, Ham thought, mounting the trophy pavilion steps at Jill's side. On the eve of retribution the Peabody coach had picked up his chips and left. Ham felt cheated. Suppose Doc had stacked a few cards — football scholarships, talent scouts, Camp TD. He was only getting back a little of his own, from the old punishing defeats. State could have refused to play Peabody's patricians in those lopsided days. State men weren't quitters, that was all. Yet despite his pride Ham knew there was another reason. They would far rather have lost than not have played at all, because just taking the field against Peabody had been riband for the State flag. Even when they had known they were going to be whipped it was a consolation that Peabody recognized them and the need to beat them. Now the need was gone. Ham thought of Doc, lowering at the window of his glittering new office, and he thought of himself, too, for his salt had also lost his savor.

The sky was turquoise, the air burnished, even Jill's chatter languid. "Did Doc tell you about the election? I think it's dreamy. Though I guess it won't be really. I mean the other man's so rich. Probably it'll turn into an awful rumpus."

"Maybe that's why he's doing it," Ham said thoughtfully. "Maybe a rumpus is what he's been looking for."

She giggled and then hushed. They were entering the pavilion. Flanked by marble colonnades and crowned by an alabaster dome, it had the somber air of an alien temple. On the perimeter of a chaste oval area stood a ring of glass-topped tables bearing memorabilia of famous triumphs: footballs caked with dried mud, splinters from prized goal posts, silver dollars from opening game tosses when State had gone on to win. In that setting they had the look of sacred relics surrounding the central idol — the statue, bathed in the pale glory of an overhead light, of Doc charging a line with his head low and a ball buried in his belly.

"Wish I could have seen him play," Jill sighed. "He must have had heaps of drive. Still has, of course — I guess that's why State's grown so." She shuffled to one side. "You're over here, Mr. Markham."

A large case, higher than the others, held nine retired jerseys, among them Ham's 88 and Spook's 18. Ham glanced at them and at Doc's 17 in the center, with its rips and stains and ancient starred markings; he read the descriptive cards beneath and then leaned over sharply.

"Does Doc know this is on here?"

He was pointing at the last line on Doc's card. Jill read, *His greatest run was 93 yards vs. Peabody College, in the final period on Nov. 24, 1928. Score: State 27, Peabody 24.*

"I guess," she said hazily. "I mean, the alumni put up the pavilion, but they checked everything with him. Is anything wrong?"

"Only the score. We didn't win that game. Peabody did."

She stepped back. It was profanity in the shrine. "Are you *sure?*"

"I couldn't be surer. You see, I *did* see Doc play. In fact, I was there that afternoon."

She stared and then smiled uncertainly — she had decided it must be a joke, that he couldn't have been old enough. And he let it drop. He shrugged and suggested she show him the Student Union next door, and did not blaspheme again. But he hadn't been joking. Ham had only been a child in 1928, on the five-yard line with a gang from the Birmingham Boys Club junior division, but he had seen Doc's run. The card was right to call it his greatest, he thought. Probably it was the greatest in State's history. But it hadn't won that game.

He remembered the day as a photomontage of childhood—flashes of memory, with great voids between. He had stood by the end zone in his sheepskin coat and corduroy knickers and the high-cuts with the jacknife pocket on the side, wondering, even then, at the difference between the teams. Everybody on the Peabody team seemed sleek and cleft-jawed, like Richard Dix; their stands were crowded with Harold Lloyd students in raccoon coats, and during time-outs one in a dashing green sweater would wheel out a glittering aluminum cart with a tank of distilled water for the thirsty squad. State had had no cart, only a dented tin pail and a dipper. The single cheerleader's slip had been showing—that had been Doc's Sarah, Ham realized with a start—and most of the Aggie men had been closer to clowns than players. They threw blocks like pratfalls and straggled on and off the field wearing splayed-out helmets and jerseys with sickly blue stars on the shoulders and thick rings around their socks, like Mamie's in Moon Mullins. There was something fraudulent about them. They didn't seem to belong here with Peabody, and except for Doc Ham would have thought State was a counterfeit, like the Barbers College on Mechanics Street in Birmingham.

Except for Doc. He dominated the field like an ancient Saxon chieftain, half a head taller than the tallest Peabody man. His muscles were slabs, and the State uniform, so grotesque on the others, fitted him perfectly. There wasn't anything he couldn't do. He would poke the ball effortlessly on kickoffs and it would flipflop high against the sky and land far beyond the goal posts. On defense he would skip through, spill the interference, and nail the Peabody runner for a loss. Carrying the ball, he didn't even bother to zigzag. He just ran over tacklers until they ganged up and smothered him.

On any other team he would have swamped Peabody. But his slapstick team kept betraying him. You could see everything from the sidelines: on each State play there was a lineman pulling back his inside foot to get a quick start, or a passer licking his fingers, or a back hitching his pants and kicking his cleats and giving Doc away. So the score leapfrogged until, in the last minute of play, with State three points behind, Doc tried a desperate solo. He called signals for a right end run. His team lurched to the right, and he ran left, alone, without blockers. He waded through the entire Peabody secondary and then took off for the long gainer, staggering into the end zone ninety yards later with two safety men hanging on his heroic shoulders while the raccoon-coated Harold Lloyds shrieked in panic. Before Peabody could receive a gun cracked and the game was Doc's.

Only it wasn't. The score never made the morning papers, nor Doc the gym. Next morning's *Star* carried the details. Its sports editor had recognized him playing professional football in Syracuse the week before under an assumed name; he had brought the evidence along and turned it over to officials while Doc was being carried through Gideon in triumph. Doc was asked for an explanation. He admitted everything but said he had needed the money for tuition fees. The *Star* printed that, together with a deadpan insert reporting that after paying the fees he had been left a surplus and had taken his ready-made State uniform to Finch, the expensive Gideon haberdasher, for fitting. Beside the story was a three-column picture of Doc standing outside the gym in his tailored jersey, now ruined, with his goliath back to the camera and his starry shoulders slumped in defeat. Beneath it was a caption saying that in the scene above he was crying. Above was the stark line, "DISQUALIFIED."

Ham had clipped all that off and saved the picture for a long time. Doc, however, had saved it longer, and he had kept the cruel caption, too. Ham knew because as a coach Doc had carried it in the celluloid window of his wallet. Ham wondered whether it was still there. He had a hunch that in the course of time it had had more to do with winning State this campus than the charging bronze figure in the trophy pavilion. Come to think of it, he reflected, it would have made a better statue.

He asked Jill if she knew Sarah had been a State cheerleader.

"Was she *really*? Mrs. River?" She stiffened at a sudden thought and snapped her fingers. "Oh, damn," she moaned. "We're too late to see the Titanettes drill. They had a run-through this afternoon outside the Student Union. There's supposed to be a cool new number with hula hoops. *Not* very proper, I hear. But, you know. Interesting."

Ham asked who the Titanettes were. She looked at him curiously.

"The cheerleaders, of course. What did they used to call State teams?"

"Aggies, or Farmers. We didn't like it, but there it was."

"They've been Titans for a long time," she said cheerfully, and Ham felt like an aborigine.

In the futuristic pile of the Student Union he felt nervous. The massive lobby was crowded with restless mobiles, the doors were activated by electric eyes — "Department of Engineering," Jill explained — and the soda fountain was tricked out with a staggering list of forty ice cream flavors.

"You have to pick one," she insisted. "Part of the V.I.P. treatment. It's made here from homogenized milk by the ice cream workshop. They call themselves the Homo Club." She tittered and said quickly, "Of course, they aren't really."

"Black coffee, please," Ham said, feeling the need of it. He wandered to a table.

"Forty flavors," she called temptingly.

The other tables were thinly attended, and idly he watched a corner couple, the boy a freckled, redheaded corsair with powerful shoulders and a thick sloping neck above a stretched T shirt, the girl a striking blonde in tight jean shorts. They were lacing fingers and murmuring over empty cups. Ham mourned his own age, and, when Jill arrived, asked who they were. She colored.

"Oh, he's Red Stacy, the dreamboat back," she said, shoving his coffee toward him and spilling it. She spooned her ice cream nervously. "She's Daffy — Daphne Dix."

"A looker."

"Definitely. She was last year's Winter Rani, and maybe she'll be this fall's Gridiron Queen, too."

Jill was trying to be casual, but clearly she wished Ham would forget Red and Daffy. Instead he perked up. Gridiron Queens were new to him, but Kit Ryan had been a Winter Rani, and he studied this one carefully. Her glances invited it — she was aware of every man in the room — and her costume made it possible. Her shorts were incredibly scant, her scarlet blouse was sleeveless, she wore no shoes. Undoubtedly she was lovely, with long tanned legs, doll's features marred only by a heavy, sensual underlip, and sleek corn-colored hair drawn in a cascading pony tail, like Jill's. Yet she seemed older than Jill. She had an air of maturity, voluptuousness, even procacity. There was something shopworn about her.

"She's a cheerleader, too?"

"Uh — yes. Head Titanette."

"It's a shame we missed her in a hula hoop."

"Oh, don't be a D.O.M." Ham looked inquiring, and she explained slyly, "A Dirty Old Man. Next thing you'll ask to meet her."

Instantly she checked herself. Ham was looking reflective. He finished his coffee and said, "No. I want to meet him."

"Him?" Jill looked alarmed.

"Why not?"

"He's an ape!"

"I haven't talked to a State player in years."

"But his manners —"

But Ham was decided. He crossed the room, Jill fluttering after and stammering introductions at the corner table. "Mr. Markham's a *Star* man," she explained uneasily. "He used to play for the Titans."

"Hi, Hambo," Red said carelessly. He took Ham's hand, pretended to weigh it, and dropped it. Daffy's pony tail dipped; she stifled a giggle. Red snickered. "Tell us what it was like in the old days, man."

"Every play was murder," Ham said lightly, "but we were men of iron."

"Men of iron," Red rasped. "I knew it would be something like that." He made a square in the air with his forefingers and then deliberately turned his beefy back.

Jill retreated timidly, explaining she had forgotten her ice cream. Ham stayed. He never let a snub pass. His face was murky.

"It wasn't like today," he said evenly, "with an army of young punks running around in gold jock straps." He faltered, remembering Daffy, and plunged on. "We didn't have a squad of plutocrats sleeping on the long green."

Red looked around slackly and then snickered again. "I like you, Hambo! I really do! You dig this guy, Daff?"

"His strap don't appear to be gold, stranger," she said in a soft, smoky Southern voice. "And what he goes to bed with hereabouts isn't green."

Red burst into wild, choking laughter, gasped that he just had to tell somebody, and swaggered over to Jill, who peered distractedly around him at Ham. Ham stared down at Daffy. She had produced a rhinestone-studded baton from the booth seat and was sighting along it, cocking her head and sizing him up like a bird of prey. He was wondering whether this was the new breed of coed when he saw she wore a wedding band. Jill should have told him, he thought. How was he supposed to know?

"Sorry I butted in," he said hurriedly. He searched for a peace offering. "Sorry I missed your drill, too — I hear you're pretty good."

Her hardihood vanished. She looked up eagerly. "Did you really? I wish I could be sure. Honestly, when I think of that stadium full and me out there I can't rightly breathe."

"I know. Sometimes it's hard to remember it's just a game."

"Game? Are you kidding? Listen, Jill said you worked for the *Star*." She hesitated, twinkling bare toes. "You don't write dramatic criticism? Like a vid column?" He shook his head, and she looked disappointed. "Well, anyway, you're clued in on what publicity means. You know the Hampshire game? It's going to be on TV. I mean nationally. For *real*. Every scout on Broadway will be looking at the new Gridiron Queen."

Obviously she hoped it was she. Broadway ambition seemed odd in a coed bride, but Ham supposed the big autumn spectacles encouraged it. He asked if she were studying theater, and she sighed.

"I'm really a flick major, I guess. Officially PE."

"PE?"

She had to think — it had become a word itself. "Physical Education. Same as Red."

"Nice."

"Not very. He's in the team dorm, see. Oh, I meet him in classes easy enough, but nights they try to coop him up in that awful ape house."

"Sounds inhumane."

"But def! Honestly, after dark on week nights they might as well put barbed wire around that guy. Luckily he's got a friend signs him in. But then I have my problem, too. You married?" Ham looked bewildered and nodded. "First marriage?" she asked. Exasperated, he nodded again. "I'm having my first, too," she sighed, as though it were a first date, and not much fun at that.

"Well — it's nice to start with a football star."

She started. "Oh, I'm not married to *Red!*"

"You're not —"

"Oh, no." She started to laugh, but something in his eyes warned her, and she said quickly, "We're just good friends, see. The thing we've got is completely mad, I know, but when your husband's a grad student off in a lab all the time, what're you going to do?"

Ham had no chance to reply. Red had returned to fetch Daffy and Jill was bounding up anxiously. On a shaven patch of lawn outside the Student Union she groaned incoherently to Ham, "Oh, *dear*, what a *goof*. The ickiest thing on campus, and you a big alumnus — a newspaperman, even. The powers that be aren't going to like me. Why can't Red and Daffy smarten up? Just because they've been getting away with — with *things* at summer school. Oh, I'm just a *goofball*."

Then she recovered and tried to convince him all was innocent. Daffy was just talk — Jill lived right across from her in University Village and *knew*. After all, Daff had a *husband*. Ham was just being a D.O.M.

The more she ran on, the more he suspected.

"Red's, you know, going along for the ride," she said and swallowed. "I — I don't mean that. Men twist things so! It just makes him a big man if they go to blasts and make like she's his rabbit."

"Rabbit." He nodded. "We used to call them pushovers, but I like rabbit better."

"It's just for kicks. *You* know."

"*I* know. I'm copacetic."

"No you aren't — whatever it is," she said furiously. "Daffy never had any fun before. Her real name isn't even Daphne. It's Drusilla, or something gruesome. Her husband met her near Fort Knox down south in the army and brought her back when he started grad school. He put her in the tiniest, dreariest unit in Realgonesville, where we live, and she gets a bang out of horsing around with Red on dates, that's all."

"How much does her husband know about the dates?"

"The mole? I mean, he's an oddball, that's just a funny little name we have for him. Why, if Daffy's picked Gridiron Queen she can get a big job and support his research."

"In other words, he doesn't know a damned thing."

"Not really. That is, not actually. But Daffy'll be famous if she's Queen, and being Red's girl will help."

"His girl!"

"Don't you understand? He can get next to the selection committee, drop a word at the right moment — and she'll be in like Flynn! They'll listen to Red. He's the best man State's got. I mean, he's really *good*."

"Maybe, but he's not being good."

She stamped her foot. "You're deliberately twisting! I mean —"

She meant there were two kinds of good, and she was trying to keep each in its place. A part of Jill deplored Daffy's flagrant intrigue, and in other circumstances she would have ostracized her. But Jill also respected success. She despised Red; still, she was aware that he had a temporary celebrity beyond the reach of her own husband, a faceless Business Administration major, and she knew it could be made to pay off. Jill was shocked by Daffy. But secretly she admired her.

Ham drove his hands into his pockets. "What does Doc think about this?"

"I — I don't think he knows."

"Well, he's going to find out. From me."

"Oh," she said tragically.

"Find out what, Lazarus?" asked a dry voice, and Harry Osborne Mikel cycled out of a grove. He grinned scurfily at Ham. "I understood you were back."

"Back on parole," said Ham, grinning back and wringing the fragile hand.

Jill retreated. Discussing Daffy was difficult with Ham; with the old man it would be impossible. She muttered excuses and fled.

Mikel kicked down his bike stand. "What's the matter with her? She can't still be in heat."

"We had a little argument. I've met the lady that's known as Daffy."

"Ah! Then it was you! I thought Aphrodite looked upset. I just passed her in a garden, heading, I assume, for the Warren. Come here. Down this rather anal little passage between shrubs." He lit a cigarette and fluttered his crooked fingers toward a long low line of wooden buildings crowned by an aluminum thicket of television antennae. "That's where she resides when she's not sleeping with Eros or," he added with a glint, "in the big gray sodality at the end of so-called Maiden Lane."

Ham pulled a doubtful face. The gray house had been Kit's sorority, a place of floral arrangements, Peter Pan collars, and birdlike quartets singing *Aura Lea,* their theme. "You can't be married and belong there."

"She's not actually a member, but after being elected chief strumpet at the winter saturnalia she was given some honorary status." He squinted afar. "Ah. I was wrong. Her legal stud must dine alone. She has veered toward the sisterhood."

Ham shaded his eyes against the blinding sunlight and saw Daffy cruising out from behind a knoll, her bare thighs rubbing aggressively behind a baby carriage. He said under his breath, "So she's a mother, too."

"Of course. The perfect fertility symbol!"

"Is she really as sluttish as she seems?"

"She has a mind like an unmade bed," Mikel chirped. "Let me tell you where she met her lover. She was the only female member of a telephone booth team. It seems their task was to crowd the greatest possible number of people into a confined space. Apparently Daffy — let's be polite, Mrs. Dix — was wedged against the rufous Mr. Stacy. They discovered that they liked it." He cackled, shedding ash on his tie. "Do you know that she actually conducted a write-in campaign to become Miss Rheingold last year?"

"Wonderful," Ham said sourly.

"It is." He dilated: "It *is!*"

"But not here. Can't anything be done about it? Isn't there a dean?"

"If you refer to the late, somewhat fruity Max Aaron, he's an angel, inexpertly strumming a harp, I imagine. We now have a whole syndicate of panjandrums, led by a provost — the Black Gang, if you'll excuse my insubordination. The Gang is not likely to intervene in this matter. Oh, the will is there. As a rule they are implacable toward black sheep. Last term the editor of the campus magazine published an anonymous ode to onanism and was suspended — justifiably, by the way; it was unbelievably bad poetry. But Mrs. Dix is unique."

"Like hell," Ham said grimly.

"Oh, but she is. In the first place, her husband is a bona fide graduate student — highly regarded, Eric Lutz tells me — so expulsion wouldn't banish her. In the second place, any action would implicate her athletic partner, which is unthinkable because, in the third place, the Gang is at least as interested in the success of this year's gladiators as the coaches. Because of the fourth place."

Ham had forgotten how arch Mikel could be. "And that is?"

"Surely you know. We are preparing for a general election. The chances of the noble Doc will be greatly enhanced by a victorious team, and if he, too, is victorious, the Gang will inherit undisputed control of this alleged university."

"Sodom and Gomorrah. Doc would have apoplexy."

"No doubt. Our Prexy takes the traditional attitude toward sexual individualism. But he is shielded."

"Can't anyone tell him? Can't Lutz? Can't you?"

"Lutz, as usual, prefers not to be involved. And my views on campus athletics are notorious. I would not be regarded as a friendly witness, even if I chose to squeal, which I shouldn't. I prefer to reveal a greater dishonor."

Ham darkened. "There's something else?"

"Something far more ominous. You're an apperceptive young man. Surely you've observed that all this absurd architecture houses an expensive kindergarten."

"Oh that." Ham relaxed.

"*That* indeed! It means nothing to you that this has become a never-never land where every Homo sap passes? That nobody cares about the Pythagorean Theorem, let alone Goedel's? Or what quantum mechanics are? Or even whether angle ABC equals BCD?" His voice had risen. The veins in his parchment skin stood out. "I suppose you'll be gratified to learn that a certified Mongolian was graduated last June — attending the ceremony, I'm told, on all fours."

"It's that bad?"

"I assure you, I do not overstate."

But of course he did, Ham thought. He always had — to his students he had described the football squad as savages, Doc as Bwana, and the games as Aurignacian tribal rites. Ham had defied campus scorn to become one of Mikel's undergraduate disciples, yet he knew that by anyone's lights the old man was erratic.

"The few able men on the faculty are barred from classrooms," he was fuming. "I teach a red light. A television eye. *Fiat lux!*" He started a harsh laugh which turned into a hacking cigarette cough and left him hoarse. "It's done with mirrors, or wires — I forget which. You must see my lecture hall. An immaculate cell, all soundproofing and oval little windows."

"I suppose you reach more students that way," Ham said mildly.

"Reach!" Mikel looked jagged. "You're depraved. No — no,

you're a prig and a hypocrite. You're upset because two of our least literate students believe the plural of spouse is spice. You want to make a *cause célèbre* out of this tiniest blot on our scutcheon because it offends the working-class morality of your childhood."

That stung. Ham flared, "Look, I'm no choirboy. This is a straight matter of appearances, and you know it."

"I see." Mikel spat out his cigarette and said brutally, "Did you tell the Lady Catherine that when you bedded her in the College Inne?"

That stung more. "So Kit told you."

"She told me nothing. You forget I had quarters there. I still have. Who could resist the address? Ah, but *plus ça change*. How well I remember the night the lovely Kit outstripped La Dix, so to speak—"

Mikel's voice rose rhapsodically. He hasn't forgotten how to salt a wound, Ham thought bitterly. It would be pointless to argue that the wartime farewell of lovers was different from cynical adultery. Mikel would only explode into guffaws.

"— deflowered her, fled the barnyard, and forgot her, didn't you?"

"No, Harry. I didn't forget her."

"Have you bothered to follow her subsequent career?"

Ham felt curiosity stirring. He wondered again, as he had on the highway, what had become of his coed.

"I haven't. Have you?"

"With great interest. She married one O'Donnell, class of '47. You knew him, I think." Ham said he remembered a slight towhead, an enthusiastic jazz drummer and an indifferent chemist named O'Donnell. Mikel nodded. "That's him. He sired a son and took her to Chicago, where he had employment. Something to do with soap." Mikel, who had little to do with soap, paused reflectively. "There they discovered less and less community of spirit. Despite her Catholicity Kit shucked him for the usual perjured reasons and came home with the child. She's become rather a scold, I'm afraid. Though perhaps that's a requisite in her new position."

Mikel was leading up to something, and Ham watched him narrowly. He was dancing on his frail bandy legs and glancing at green horizons, like Pan.

"And what is her new position?"

"It was difficult to arrange. The dean of women is a Protestant and sympathized, but Prexy gags at divorced Catholics. One of his crafty concessions to the Papist members of the Legislature, I believe. The Church hierarchy may render unto Caesar and quietly regard divorce as legal separation, but the word has a vile ring for the devout. Even the ignorant parish priest thinks instantly of excommunication. And instruction of the young makes the subject doubly sensitive here. Luckily Kit had been delinquent in answering alumni questionnaires — like you, I understand — and so Prexy was unaware of her domestic tangle. *Ergo,* her appointment was slipped through with references from the diffident Lutz, from me, and from one other, who shall be nameless. Since commencement," he said, rubbing his stained hands, "she has been resident in her old sorority. Her title, I believe, is housemother."

Mikel paused, relishing the moment. "The real reason I brought you over here is that the weekly housemothers' meeting is about to break up, and this is a superb place to view the recessional. Ah. There." He squinted. "Back to their broods the matriarchate goes. Or is it coveys? In any event"— the old man pointed a withered hand toward the shimmering distance — "unless I err, that is she."

Ham looked, blinking. In the late afternoon sunlight a lone figure wearing navy blue muslin was emerging from behind the far knoll, striding gracefully where Daffy had sprinted. Kit wore glasses now; her walk had lost that boyish suggestion of the gamin, and her black hair was drawn back from a central parting and gathered in a sedate knot at the nape of her neck. But there was no mistaking that look of the Indian maiden, those gallant shoulders, that proud, lovely head. He raised a shading hand again and squinted, watching her through the lens of time.

"So that's the story of her life now. Teaching what every young girl should know."

"To girls," Mikel chortled, "who mustn't know that the Empress hadn't any clothes on once."

Twice, Ham thought, turning away as Archer's glockenspiel opened another concert with a gentle sprinkle of chimes. He had just recognized the first bars of *Aura Lea* when Mikel screwed up his face, threw back his head, and drowned them in a cacophony of derisive laughter.

**

Catherine Ryan O'Donnell admitted herself to her private apartment, dismissed the baby sitter, and looked in on the cook. The evening meal was progressing. Mrs. Santo exhibited the correct balance of proteins and starches and reported a pleasant surprise — the two girls who were spending the summer in the house had waxed the upstairs floors. In the television den, however, was another surprise, not so pleasant. The cook glanced darkly that way, and Kit stepped to the door and saw the prostrate form of Daffy Dix, watching Mighty Mouse with glazed china blue eyes and toying with her baton while, beside her, her baby whined weakly.

"She's staying for supper?"

"*Si.* She never tells me."

"Bitch," Kit said tonelessly, and returned to her rooms.

Mrs. Santo laughed harshly behind her, but Kit bit her lip. She shouldn't swear in front of the cook. If she didn't watch herself she'd start doing it around the girls. Then one of them would notice that she appeared at table each evening with a cocktail on her breath, and the first thing she knew she'd be talked about. Kit couldn't afford to be talked about. Her position here was precarious. She had been smuggled into this job and could hope to hold it only if she appeared blameless — "like Caesar's wife," the dean of women had reminded her after the housemothers' meeting that afternoon. Dean Shoemaker was a tall woman with gray bangs and a protective feeling toward alumnae. She had bravely assumed the role of chief smuggler, but now she was having anxious second thoughts. "Try to look *virginal,*" she had said an hour before. Kit had looked wry instead, and Miss Shoemaker had stammered, "Of course you can't, with the child, but — try to give that impression."

Kit had been trying since her arrival. In the week before the girls left for their summer vacation she had not only intimated that she was a widow, as Miss Shoemaker had advised; she had also begun to contrive a new public image of herself, aided by drab clothes, a dowagerish coiffure, and spectacles she did not need. These were more than expedients. The job was ideal for a divorcee whose parents had washed their hands of her the day she left her husband, and she meant to stay if she could, but she was also inspired by a reappraisal of herself. Kit had concluded that she was a victim of her education. As a child she had been a devout Catholic, but at State she had majored in psychology, abandoning grace for what her father, a down-state electrician, bitterly called secular ways. She had become indifferent toward the church, evasive on Saturdays and lax on Sundays. When her marriage became impossible a civil divorce had seemed sensible, but afterward, brooding over the wreckage, she had wondered whether she had been wise to be so careless with her faith. She decided that she hadn't. It had been wrong to sin. She had trespassed, and now she was paying.

In this mood she inevitably exaggerated her trespasses. Kit had never stolen, or cheated, or deliberately hurt anyone. Her sexual history, about which she had brooded a great deal, would have dismayed her poor parish parents, Doc River, and perhaps the dean of women, but it would have shocked few of her friends, and the reassurances of the Chicago priest who heard her out had been sincere. Years ago she had slept with a Protestant named Markham she had loved and a Catholic named Duschene she had pitied. Since then there had been no one but her recent husband; no flirting, no furtive kisses at late parties, not even an urge to stray. Nevertheless, she was guilt-ridden. Her life had gone awry, and she needed a scapegoat and chose herself. Moving toward her dressing table, she paused at the nursery door and praised her little Sean's castle of blocks so extravagantly that he looked puzzled.

There, she thought at the mirror. A dash of pale lipstick, nothing more. Once again she studied her delicate oval face and realized, with mixed feelings, that it was no good; with her bun of black hair neat and her glasses prim on her nose, her dark dress buttoned to the throat and crossed by a plain gold crucifix — another recommendation of the dean's — she remained sleek. The devices merely highlighted her beauty. Instead of resembling a leader of the Future Homemakers of America she looked, she thought, like a Goddamn *femme fatale.*

Kit bit her lip again. That's enough of *that,* she thought sternly, and went to mix her daily gin and tonic, regretting the need of it and grateful for its solace.

There were so many traps . . .

Tomorrow she had to see Doc at his annual reception; he might be inquisitive. Somebody might find out about her divorce and tell him anyhow. Some girl in the sorority could get into trouble, forcing Kit, cringing, into the spotlight. One of those prissy women from national headquarters could turn up at the wrong time and make a bad report on Chapter Tone, bringing down the wrath of other alumnae . . .

That could easily happen, she reflected gloomily, doubling the gin. This house had been consistently unlucky. Over the years it had been one of the quietest sororities on Maiden Lane, yet its reputation had always been wild. The Greek letters hadn't helped. When Kit pledged the house it had been Beta Alpha Gamma, a local whose members were known on Fraternity Row as Bags. After the war it had been chartered by Kappa Alpha Theta and alumnae had delightedly rechristened themselves Thetas. It was no use: on campus the girls were still called Bags. Worse, the sorority itself was now the Kat House. Making me, Kit thought sourly, the old Bag, the Madam.

She drank deeply and studied the framed poem on the living room wall, written by an earlier, more sententious housemother.

If you can rule your heart with power
To say a firm, uncompromising "No;"
If you can conquer present midnight hours
Rather than to make a future, greater woe;
If you can love, yet not let affection master
But hold yourself within your common sense
And not let dreaming lead you to disaster
Nor charity, misguided, shame you hence . . .

It continued in that vein, and concluded:

Then naught in Gideon will hurt you —
And — so much more — you'll be a Gamma, dear.

Or a Bag, Kit reflected, bolting her drink and making a face.

So *many* traps . . .

And that Dix person was the worst.

Daffy had been elected an honorary Theta while Kit's predecessor was in her last illness. At that time she hadn't met Red, and Miss Shoemaker had artlessly decided that a young matron might be a serene influence in a sorority with a disabled chaperone. Kit had assessed Daffy's true influence that first week back. In her the girls had an endless source of dirty jokes, tips about men, and bed wisdom. Brazen was a word Kit had thought outdated, but it described Daffy precisely; she freely confessed affairs with other men before her husband and hinted at others since, and she clothed everything with an air of glamour which was dangerously infectious. Since the house had been virtually deserted all summer the girls were ignorant of her relationship with Red, but Kit knew they would hear all about it the day they returned. She wondered how much there was to hear. Some gossip could be discounted, but Daffy was seeing him openly and everywhere, including here. Especially here, if Mrs. Santo was to be believed. According to the cook they had entered the front hall twice while Kit was out and crept upstairs — making this, Kit thought grimly, a real Kat House.

She dismissed the temptation to make another drink. It was time she had a talk with that young lady, and an alarming discovery earlier in the day provided an excuse. She sent her son to the sorority game room in the basement and stepped to the kitchen door. "Daphne. *Daphne!* Would you step in a minute? Mrs. Santo can watch your baby."

Daffy rose reluctantly, not because of the child — she scarcely glanced that way — but because Mighty Mouse was just getting good. She stumbled in sullenly and then instinctively sized Kit up. Kit flushed. She had seen that look daily for three months, yet it still upset her. It was like a man's, up and down, the insolent, calculating glance of a competitor. She's just a *hillbilly,* Kit thought furiously. It was mortifying, she had told the thoughtful Miss Shoemaker that afternoon, that just as State was moving out of the bush league and becoming a major university it should tolerate — even exalt, as head cheerleader — an underbred, hillbilly, low-fi wife.

"Please sit down, Daphne. I want to show you something."

Daffy clasped her baton around a knee as Kit groped in a desk drawer, whirled, and held out two contraceptives. There was a moment of utter stillness. Then Daffy slowly lowered her knee.

"Have you seen these before?" Kit asked quietly.

Obviously Daffy hadn't. "They aren't *mine,* Mrs. O'Donnell. My husband got me fitted."

"I wasn't accusing you," Kit said coldly. "I found them this morning in the room of one of the girls that graduated."

"Who —"

"Never mind. She was engaged, and I'm told she was married right after commencement."

The knee went back up. Daffy shrugged. "Then everything's all right, isn't it?"

"Everything is definitely *not* all right." Kit dropped the contraceptives in the drawer and slammed it shut. "When a pledge is taken into this chapter she's congratulated by all the seniors, wearing white gowns. Those gowns stand for purity, Daphne. Gammas — Thetas — must be pure."

"Oh." But she looked blank.

"There are other reasons. I'd have thought you'd have understood them."

"Listen, a girl wearing a ring can't be a snowy date, Mrs. O'Donnell."

"Snowy date?" Kit repeated uncertainly. So much State slang was new to her.

"You know." Daffy smiled a tight smile. "Like frigid."

"That is precisely what Thetas *must* be," Kit snapped. "You're a married woman, and I expect you to help me see that they are."

She leaned back against the desk, gripping the edge with both hands and feeling righteous. It didn't matter that she had deceived pledges here in her own senior year; you didn't have to be right to know what right was; you didn't have to be good to respect virtue. She had broken the rules and paid with stabs of conscience, but Daffy was guiltier, for she was defending guilt.

Yet that wasn't true, either. Kit raised her spectacles and massaged her eyelids. The complex code that haunted her had no meaning for the girl, she supposed. No; Daffy was defending nothing. She had nothing to defend. From their occasional, strained talks and from overheard conversations among other girls Kit had pieced together Daffy's earlier life. In the eastern Kentucky coal town where she had grown up, mating was simple: when a girl was old enough to make love, she made love, and when a child was imminent she married. In the normal course of events Daffy would have remained home and would, by now, have produced a large family. Events, however, had been diverted by two freaks of nature. She hadn't become pregnant until she met a soldier in her twenty-third year, and then, after the baby's birth, they had moved to Gideon, where her figure had brought her glory. Daffy looked like a campus queen, and she had begun to realize that campus queens, unlike mountain girls, needn't waste their youth nursing babies. Here at State a new hope had begun to stir in her. It had become the strongest thing in her life, and she would fight if it were threatened.

Kit was preparing to threaten it. She paced the floor twice, nursing one elbow and letting her free hand play distractedly over her face.

"I expect you to help me set an example." She looked down beadily at the shorts. "For one thing, I want you to wear more clothes when the girls return."

Daffy smiled lazily. "Today's right warm, Mrs. O'Donnell."

"It's never that warm. You can save the strip tease for the Titanettes, although," she added quietly, "I think you'd be wise to leave cheerleading to others."

That was the threat. Daffy sat erect. "You mean *quit?*"

"I do. Between your classes and your family you should be busy enough."

Daffy's eyes were slits, her mouth unpleasant. "Listen, you can give the orders around here, but —"

"That's exactly what I'm doing. I absolutely forbid you to wear those shorts in here —"

"But there's some things you can't touch. If you think I'm leaving the Titanettes, you're dreaming, see. Married women are having careers these days, in case you haven't heard."

Kit was perplexed. "Careers?"

"That's right, you heard exactly right. I'm aiming to have me a career. I guess you weren't around last year to see me crowned Winter Rani."

"No, and you weren't around my freshman year, when I was crowned." Kit bit her lip — she hadn't meant to mention that — and added starchily, "The difference is, *I* didn't dream of turning pro."

The sarcasm was lost on Daffy. Her eyes were wide; she was examining Kit again, and Kit read her mind. Daffy was intent on one fact: her stuffy housemother had once been a Rani. She was studying her bone structure, speculating what she would look like if she let her hair down and shed her glasses. Hungry for details, she leaned forward, but none were forthcoming. Kit turned the conversation again, and was delicately suggesting that married women who were seen with single men invited gossip — an allusion which made no impression — when several things happened at once. The baby in the television den began to cry, Mrs. Santo shouted that Daffy had a visitor, and the telephone in Kit's bedroom began to ring. Kit lingered at the kitchen door long enough to see Daffy greet Red in the front hall; then, muttering soft oaths, she ran in and snatched up the receiver.

"Hot enough for you?" asked a cheerful voice.

"It's not the heat, it's the humidity," she answered automatically, and sank, suddenly weak with it, to the bed.

Sol Feinblatt chuckled; Doc had inspired in him a passion for bromides, and Kit humored it. Sol was a new friend of hers, an unmarried English instructor, and she had taken to him because he represented the sophisticated values of the new State. Kit was enchanted with the changes in Gideon, and excited by the prospect of more changes still.

"I've got something *really* hot," he said. "Hold on to your hat."

"Haven't got a hat."

"All right, your seat then. I know you've got one of *them*. By the way, have I ever told you what an exquisite seat you have?"

"Often." Kit smiled patiently into the phone. She forgave Sol much. He was a poet and had lectured at Breadloaf. "What have you heard?"

"Roscommon, arise. Old Man River's running for governor."

"That's a rumor."

"Like hell. It's concepted and finalized. I just heard it on the video," he said proudly. Sol's academic affectations included membership in the Gideon Elk's Club and watching television. Kit gasped, and he chuckled. "It looks like we may lose our millstone in November."

"Please don't call Doc a millstone," she said seriously. "Maybe he's not right for State now, but he was marvelous once."

Sol made a rude noise. "He'll be marvelous when he hands the reins over to Tate. That was on the TV eye, too. Now, now — I know you don't like Tate."

"He gives me the creeps." She shuddered.

"He *is* a creep. But at least he's no windbag. He'll make the old joint jump like a good joint should. Speaking of rumor, the grapevine has it that for some time Tate, unknown to Doc, has been holding informal meetings with deans — including your austere Miss Shoemaker. He's been getting ready for something just like this, I guess." Sol's voice dropped and became suggestive. "Say, if you aren't wearing a hat, what else aren't you wearing? I know it's ninety in the shade, but I think it's going to rain and cool off —"

"Thanks for the news, Sol," she said firmly, lowering the receiver. "I'll see you at the reception tomorrow."

She had remembered the couple in the front room. Striding resolutely through the kitchen, den, and hall, she found them on a corner love seat, looking like a tableau of American family life — Daffy feeding the baby, Red chatting easily. Except, she thought, that they weren't husband and wife. She wondered whether she ought to speak to Red and knew, as he bounded up, that she couldn't. Despite his roughness Red had always been courtly with her. He had besides a strong animal charm. Urging him to sit down, Kit was abruptly conscious of the damp places under her clothes, of her dowdy frock and dull coif. Whatever these two have done has been Daffy's fault, she thought, taking a rocker opposite them. He's just a nice, polite boy.

"Would you believe it, the season hasn't even started and we're already talking about cheers," he said, carefully explaining his visit to her. "Things sure have changed from the old days. Why, the way the Titanettes do it, cheerleading's practically a kind of psychological warfare."

"Or something," Daffy said fatuously, and giggled. Kit glanced at her sharply — she preferred to hear Red — and Daffy said more sensibly, "Looks like rain."

It did: Sol had been right. Outside pitching clouds had blemished the faultless sky, and in the distance they could hear muffled thunder. The room was growing dark. Kit turned on a bridge lamp; Red stood again. "I better get back to the dorm. I catch cold easy."

Daffy couldn't resist saying, "Man of iron."

He scowled. "Yeah, wasn't he some square, that oldie?" To Kit he said, "From your time, Mrs. O'Donnell."

"From my time!" Kit said with mock dismay. She rocked back, twisting her wedding ring. "You make me feel ancient!"

"That's right though," said Daffy. "We saw this guy in the Stu Union. He played end once."

Red moved into the hall, snapping his fingers. "What did he say he was? Reporter, or something."

Daffy never forgot a name that might be useful. "A *Star* man. Ham Markham."

"Oh!" said Kit, and stopped rocking.

"Did you know him?" Daffy asked, and Red asked anxiously, "Is anything wrong?"

For she had turned pale, and was touching her crucifix with trembling fingers. She pressed her thin shoulders against the rocker back and waved Red out. "I'm fine. Yes, I knew him. Not very well, though."

But she wasn't fine, and the lie only added to her sense of guilt. *Not very well* — no, only in the Biblical sense, she thought, making it hurt. And that was how it had all started for her. On a single impulse she had turned her life into a long sleigh ride down: from

Ham to Spook—she never would have gone with Spook if there hadn't been a first time—and from there, under parental pressure, to the proper lace curtain nightmare with Alvin O'Donnell, which had left her with a child, scarcely visible means of support, and the need to live furtively here, lighting candles to the prayer that no one find out about her and tell Doc. So now Ham had come back. Well, she thought, setting her lips, she hoped *she* didn't have to see him. Leaning back, she closed her eyes, lighting a little candle to that.

Opening her eyes she saw that Daffy had left her. She had returned the baby to the carriage and was again sprawled in the den. Mighty Mouse was over, but Popeye was just starting. Kit stood stiffly.

"Daphne! *Daphne!* It's been nice having Red here. I'm sorry I won't be seeing him here any more."

"What?" Daffy wished that just once Mrs. O'Donnell would interrupt during a commercial.

"I'm sure you two must have finished your cheerleading talk. There won't be any need for him to come again. Is that clear?"

"Oh. Oh, sure."

It took a moment to sink in. Kit had swept off to help Mrs. Santo close windows, and Bluto had flattened Popeye with a steamroller, before Daffy understood: if Mrs. O'Donnell meant it, this place was out; they would have to find another.

Kit had meant it, and tugging at the last stubborn living room sash she considered going even farther; tomorrow she just might suggest to the dean of women that Daffy be officially warned before the students returned. The sash yielded and she made her decision. She would do it. It was the only way out, and it was her duty. She would call Miss Shoemaker now and make an appointment. Before she could turn from the sill, however, the storm scattered her thoughts. A violent crash rocked the room. Three blocks away lightning had struck the main campus power line. Kit ducked, hugging her ears. Beside her the bridge lamp went dark, and in the other room Popeye, to Daffy's chagrin, shrank away from a bale of spinach, turned into a winking mote of light, and vanished.

**

It was the summer's last storm, the wildest and wettest of the year. High over Gideon the thunderhead swirled thickly, a great gray belly of mist split by crackling flashes. Below, blinding cords of lightning streaked the livid sky and thunderclaps pealed and echoed in huge vacant dormitories. It was a savage, Hans Christian Andersen night out, with gusts moaning in the tortured tree tops and driving rain, and it wasn't all bluff. Bolts had felled two colonial lantern posts on the State campus, and Peabody College had lost a branch from its most ancient elm, before a raw wind whipped the ragged fringe of clouds southward, toward Birmingham.

The thunder barrage rolled away then, but the rain remained—a steady downpour that drummed along the blacktop of the G.A.R. Highway and drenched the Common and ran in rivulets from the Union soldier's musket. Outside the dilapidated College Inne it rattled tinnily on the rusting bike of Harry Osborne Mikel. The three chiefs of State's off-campus services heard it whispering ominously in the chimney of the Gideon Arms taproom as they ordered another round of Manhattans. In the new faculty housing development west of town it lashed the eaves of the big colonial house in which Tate, a bath addict, eased his emaciated hips into his tub for the second time that day, and on the next street it tilted against the modest bedroom panes of Dean Elsie Shoemaker, who tossed her gray bangs in migraine anguish and stared out miserably at the streaming dark.

Gideon center and the development were unaffected by the power failure, but no building in the university plant escaped. Eric Lutz had to complete a paper with the faint aid of Bunsen burners. Kit presided over a dark table. Red read *Sly* magazine's football forecasts in the Athletic Dorm by one flashlight, while in University Village Daffy's husband Jerry fixed a lonely supper of cold cuts by the light of another, much dimmer. Across the Village street Jill was the most relaxed victim of the blackout. She hadn't even a flashlight, but a camper neighbor loaned her husband a spare Coleman lantern, and with it they ate and later studied while she watched the lamp's glowing elements and wondered chimerically whether this was what pioneer life had been like, whether this was what women had gone through in those olden days.

The storm's martyr was Doc. His Mansion was well supplied with kerosene lanterns, a legacy of the past, but because his radio was dead and his television screen blank he was cut off from the state's first response to his candidacy. This was a corker, he raged bitterly to his wife; this was a real humdinger. The first time in a month he'd wanted to hear the news and he couldn't get it. It was enough to drive a man to distraction. Sarah River nodded and smiled tenderly, and he was about to go on when he realized she hadn't been listening. She was intent on her knitting, and with that shiver of uneasiness he had felt increasingly since her stroke he saw her holding in the yellow lantern light a half-finished blue baby bootie. He didn't have to ask who it was for; he knew it wasn't for anybody; it was for a dream. Balling his fists, he strode downstairs. From his study window he could see a distant gleam of street lights. There was power downtown, there were radios there. Yet he didn't dare leave here. He told himself he was hoping for a Birmingham call from Newt. He was. That was only part of it, however. The other, murkier part, was that he didn't dare leave Sarah when she was like this.

Doc had understood the stroke, but this other thing of hers was beyond him. In his view either you were sick or you were well, and no nonsense. He still believed that, although the college physician had flatly told him he was wrong. The modern opinion was that there were degrees of illness. Sarah had recovered from her physical shock. There was little chance of an early recurrence. Yet in some way that Doc couldn't understand and the Doctor couldn't explain, she had become an invalid of the mind, and all she could be given was understanding and rest.

To Doc it was a vague prescription. She had always had understanding, and as far as he could see she wasn't getting anything but rest. She shunned old friends and sat in her room day after day, rocking and knitting and peering through the awning-lidded window at the elms outside. What she really needed, he thought, was company and exercise. He had stopped encouraging visitors after a humiliating evening during which she repeatedly burst into inexplicable laughter and made unintelligible remarks, but he was still trying to persuade her to take walks.

Leaving the silent, lamp-lit study and reclimbing the darkened stairs, he said to her, for the fifth time that week, "Why don't you get out tomorrow, Sare?"

She smoothed her skirt. "Now, Doc. Where on earth would I go?"

It was progress. She hadn't asked for suggestions before. "Well, you might stroll down by the Student Union."

Sarah puckered. "Where's that?"

Doc's knuckles whitened. There she goes again, he thought. Why, she *must* know. She was there the day it was dedicated, sitting up on the platform, looking bright and pleased—well, come to think of it, she hadn't seemed so pleased, but then for some reason she never was as enthusiastic about the new buildings as he was. Just the same, she'd been there that once, and if she hadn't gone back it was her own fault. His knuckles whitened again. He must stop thinking of things as her fault. That was one thing the doctor *had* been clear about.

He smiled encouragingly. "You remember. It's down where the poultry pens used to be."

"Oh yes," she said softly. "Yes, I do remember the pens." And she looked out wistfully to the pens, as though in nostalgia. But that was impossible, Doc thought fiercely. Everyone agreed that the poultry buildings had been an eyesore, and the Union was a classic of modern design.

"It's a nice walk. The Titanettes will be sashaying around just outside, and you could watch them."

Sarah was puckering again. "Titanettes?"

Doc reddened. "The cheerleaders, Sare."

"Oh, of course." She bobbed her head twice. And then looked pensively out into shadowy trees.

Doc turned from her in dismay. If Sarah took an interest in anything at State, it should be the Titanettes; she had been a cheerleader herself. Of course, times had changed. The girls carried batons now instead of megaphones, and wore cowboy boots and leotards. Doc didn't entirely approve—he liked the old styles, and his idea of proper women's dress was Sarah as she was now, rocking in her navy frock and Red Cross shoes, with her light brown hair drawn back in a comb—but the new choreographer insisted stadium crowds wanted fashionable costumes. Yet all that was beside the point. The *idea* of cheerleading hadn't changed. Sarah should try to follow it. He gently said so.

She looked up with an unfamiliar, crafty twinkle. "All right, Doc. First thing in the morning."

He beamed. "Great! I'll tell Mrs. Hodgkins. She can let the breakfast dishes go and—what's the matter?"

Sarah was knitting again, back in dreamland. "I can find the old poultry field without the cook," she said distantly. "I've been here longer than she has."

"It's not that! You haven't been feeling up to par, and you ought to have somebody with you. You know that, Sare."

She smiled at dripping branches. "Yes. Hand me my mints, Doc."

Agitated, he snatched them from a side table. It wasn't that he didn't trust her alone, he thought. At least, she shouldn't look at it that way. If she met a bunch of students and started acting queer, rumors might get started. After all, it was for her protection. He looked down at the mints resentfully. She bought them by the carton. Suppose some kid saw her popping them away, one to the minute? They were harmless enough, or so the doctor said, but it *was* peculiar. Anyway, most people didn't do it. She should think of her position.

Leaning over, he stroked her hair. "I'll be going downstairs for a spell."

She touched his hand. "The faculty reception's tomorrow. Will any of your political friends be coming?"

It was a delicate subject. Newt had been in and out of the house all week. Sarah had seen him from her window, and Doc had been obliged to tell her everything. She hadn't said outright that she didn't want him to run, but he sensed her misgivings. It never occurred to him that she wouldn't want to see him governor. He had simply concluded that she was afraid he might lose. His reassurances hadn't seemed to help, however, and so they had stopped discussing the campaign.

"Mr. Albert will be here. Maybe one or two others."

"I — may feel headachy. Can you explain?"

He sighed and nodded and left, annoyed with her for refusing to come and with himself because he couldn't regret it. Sarah had been his closest ally for thirty years; he couldn't bear to think of her as a mere complication. And yet, as Newt had said the other day, she wasn't going to score many points for the ticket between now and November. Doc flushed once more at the memory of Newt's flipness. Politicians had to be brassy, he supposed, but one of these days he was going to have to jack up that fellow. The man didn't seem to know what common courtesy was. Take now. Newt should be on the line this very minute, filling him in on reactions in the capital and —

The telephone was ringing. He hustled into the study, but it wasn't Newt. Sam had alerted alumni chapter presidents to wire Doc their support; the Western Union office had a batch of congratulatory telegrams. Doc grunted and hung up, and the phone rang again: more telegrams, this time from delegates to Monday's convention, hacks eager to have the head of the ticket know they were behind him. After that there was nothing, and Doc stamped around the gloomy Mansion, feeling the strain. After an hour his pride gave way. He called Newt's office.

Newt purred confidence. Everything was going beautifully. The Republicans were stunned. They hadn't had time to react yet, but despite the rain they were caucusing; every light in the Statehouse was on.

"We don't have any lights here," said Doc, uncomforted. "What do the papers say?"

"Mostly they just ran the release. The *Star*'s an exception, of course. Tomorrow's first edition's out, and Markham has a long story. I've got it right here." He rustled newsprint temptingly.

"Can you — read it?"

Newt read it, and when he was finished Doc wished he hadn't. The story was a disappointment. In several places it seemed almost as irritating as a *Star* editorial. Ham had quoted him in full on virtually every awkward point, including the rental of this house. Doc had expected so much more. The interview had been a mistake, he decided. Ham belonged to the *Star* now. It was hard to think of him as disloyal, but Doc could think of him in no other way, and he said so.

Newt clucked, "It's not that bad. Look, the man's a reporter. You'd get much worse from anybody else on their staff."

"We'll see about that. They'll send their worst scamps after me now."

"Don't be too sure. This story puts them on the spot. You didn't look at today's paper very carefully, and neither did Ham. There's a big box inside telling readers to look for Ham Markham's new assignment. Naturally, with his by-line on this story tomorrow morning, everybody's going to think he's covering the election."

Doc was shocked. "Had *you* seen that this morning?"

"Sure." Newt chuckled softly. "I figured we could put both Ham *and* his bosses in a little box."

"Why, that's a hornswoggle!"

"No. Just a patsy play."

"I won't have anything to do with such goings on."

"You don't have to. That's what I'm for."

"And I'm not going to have Ham bamboozled." Doc's temper was rising. "And his story's all wrong anyway."

"I told you, it's a straight piece, the best you could get." Before Doc could reply, Newt said easily, "Look, I got to get home — the street outside's a river and my ark's in hock. I'll be up tomorrow. We can talk about everything then. O.K.?"

Doc took a breath — and heard the dial tone break evenly. He lowered the instrument to its cradle and stamped through the house again, muttering and shaking his head and impatiently snapping dead light switches. Back at the study window he paused, calmed by the exertion. It was some storm, he thought absently. Here in Gideon the rain was slackening, but the lightning persisted, illuminating the land with a brilliant, intermittent glare.

The view from this hill was magnificent. Shading his eyes, Doc peered through the scrollsaw carpentry of the Mansion's porch and looked down fondly on the plat of the new campus. It was roughly a diamond, anchored at its Union Street gate, the Student Union, the stadium, and the foot of the slope leading up to the Mansion. Within these were the chief buildings of the university, each raising brick and limestone walls above its landscaped dais; outside the diamond lay University Village, the infirmary, Fraternity Park, and the sororities of Maiden Lane. Doc admired it all, cherished it all, and was somehow sustained by the spectacle of his handiwork undaunted by the fury overhead. Let Newt hoot and holler, he thought, turning away. Let Ham go his tomfool way. Let the flannel-mouthed Percies on the *Star* do their darndest. They couldn't touch him, because he was only going on leave. If the worst happened, if the whole campaign went smash — if he lost the brass ring in November and was snowed under by a blizzard of Witty votes, it still wouldn't matter, because whatever the high-and-mighties and politicans and voters did, this would endure. They could disqualify him at the polls, he thought, fingering his old wallet, but he'd still have State.

Doc touched the wallet again, almost with affection, and at that instant the university's power break was repaired. Suddenly the Mansion was ablaze. All the wall switches he had flipped were on, and he crouched hugely by his desk, squinting in the sudden light.

**

Ham had raced the storm to Birmingham and lost. Before the first drops pelted his windshield he had skidded through Herlihy Tunnel and four factory towns, but there, on the outskirts of the capital, he had to slow to a crawl. Even at ten miles an hour his wiper could scarcely keep up with the deluge. The water was piling up in the streets so fast the drains couldn't handle it. Twice he stopped completely, unable to see the curb; once his brakes flooded and forced him into a tree lane. Steering with one hand and wiping the misted glass with another, he crept into the *Star* garage, took a taxi to the judge's apartment, and fell asleep on the couch with an unfinished sandwich in his hand.

Three hours later his phone rang. It was Caulkin's secretary. The general managing editor wanted to see him in his office immediately.

"Im*me*diately?" It was so unlike Caulkin. Except on election nights he was never at the paper after dark.

"That's what he said, Mr. Markham. He called from a party somewhere, but he's going right there. He woke me up to get your number," she added resentfully, and hung up.

The lower floors of the old brownstone *Star* building were dark, the classified counters closed, the business offices locked tight. Apart from the muffled hum of the basement presses, hammering out the last of the final edition, and the top floor glitter of city room lights, it might have been deserted. In a drizzle Ham paid the cabby and wearily pushed aside the rain-slick glass lobby door, feeling a familiar uneasiness. In childhood he had known the *Star* as a name only, the place where Hiram A. Markham, Sr., went each morning in his neat broadcloth suit with the gleaming gold chain dangling on his vest and his preoccupied manner suggesting grave matters ahead—the place from which he returned each evening with tales of political alliances, foreign revolutions, and social change, told solemnly to Ham as the boy perched on his lap and fingered the chain and savored the wisdom of the Great Insider, the Man Who Knew. Ham grew into his teens thinking of his father as a kind of retired Richard Harding Davis, brought him his first painful stories for criticism, watched him reading *Editor and Publisher* in his battered Morris chair and silently worshiped him. It wasn't until Hiram, Sr.'s, coronary, when he lay paralyzed beside the maw of the big press and the boy was led with his mother through the back door—not until Ham saw his square paper hat and inky denim and pleading eyes that he realized his father had been just a pressman, distinguishable from other pressmen only by his devotion to soap at the end of each day, his well-brushed street clothes, and the careful study he gave the paper on the trolley home. Ham had felt crushed. He couldn't face those damp eyes. He had turned his back on them and left, and on each visit to the building since had felt a dread that did not diminish, but grew as the gap widened between the *Star* of his father's dreams and the *Star* he had come to know.

Caulkin hadn't reached his office. The *Star* Ham knew lay, in tomorrow's edition, on an oval mahogany table outside. His own story was the only real news on page one. The paper had once been a forum of dignity, a twin of the old Boston *Transcript;* its Old English mast, the corps of special correspondents overseas, and the Victorian tone of its editorial page were token offerings to the memory of that era. Competition, however, had forced innovations. Caulkin might despise the rabble, but he placated it with pap. Under his leadership the paper published less and less news and more entertainment, more columns, more stunts. Since Ham had left for India the growth of comics alone had been staggering. Yet the circulation figures under the mast proclaimed success. Caulkin's changes were obviously popular. The most recent had been to replace a venerable front page feature known to generations of Birmingham readers as "Thought for Today" with something called "Today's Laff." The latest of these, in a box beside Ham's story, read:

ROBERT: See that shifty runner playing halfback? He'll be our best man next year.
ROBERTA: Oh darling, this is so sudden.

Ham was reading it for the third time, wondering whether anyone in greater Birmingham would really find it laffable, when Caulkin strode in, unbuttoning a Burberry trench coat and revealing a dinner jacket beneath. "I just stopped in the morgue, and the Chief phoned me there again from the Statehouse," he muttered, kneading his mustache. "I've never heard him so mad. He really ought to control —" Caulkin's eye fell balefully on the paper. "So you've seen it."

"You mean the joke?" Ham asked innocently.

Caulkin looked ugly. "What's so funny about it?"

"Nothing. In fact, it's sad. Roberta thinks —"

"What are you reading?" He grabbed the paper. "I mean *this,*" he said, slashing a finger at Ham's story. "The Chief read it to me over the phone an hour ago. I'm still recovering."

Ham had a brief, bad moment. The Chief was Marcus Gray, the octogenarian publisher of the *Star.* As a rule he left details to Caulkin. If he were aroused it must be something important. Ham wondered whether his partiality for Doc could have crept into the piece. Yet he knew he had been careful. And Caulkin, it turned out, wasn't fuming over the story; his nail was on the by-line. "They never should have let it through," he said savagely. "If I'd known in time I'd have replated and bought up the street." He flung his door open. "Come in here. I'll tell you just what your little excursion has cost this paper."

He had already forgotten that the interview was his idea. The nice thing about being general managing editor, Ham thought dourly, is that you learn how easy it is to kill a fact.

Without breaking step, Caulkin marched to the big leather chair behind his desk. "Sit down," he barked and sat himself, jiggling the swivel spring. Immediately he sank into that deep trance known on the desk as the Caulkinsian Stupor. It was supposed to intimidate subordinates, but Ham was beyond that. He suppressed a yawn and looked around for something to read. There was nothing. Caulkin's office expressed him wonderfully. It was vast and bare and purposelessly efficient, like a parade ground. An American flag stood in one corner, the state colors in another. Copies of the *Star* were mounted on standing racks opposite his desk, and souvenirs of World War II lined the top of a bookcase occupied entirely by generals' memoirs. Among the more personal souvenirs was a leather case containing a Bronze Star. Caulkin had carefully created the impression that he had been decorated for valor — Ham was the only *Star* man who had taken the trouble to find out that the medal had actually been awarded for clerical efficiency in the rearest echelon — and a miniature of it lay under Plexiglas on the long steel desk, which otherwise was stark as a vaudeville runway.

Behind the desk hung the map and the pins. Ham saw himself there, still in the Punjab, and idly wished Caulkin would move him.

For over a minute the general managing editor just sat, riding the chair like a saddle. Then he growled, "You and your friends."

"Look," Ham said, rising and pacing, "maybe I bitched, but I don't see how."

"You bitched when you became an author," Caulkin said tumidly, giving his head a significant little nod.

Ham understood. *Through Darkest Birmingham* was unknown outside the city, but here the book sold steadily year after year. His name meant something to the very readers the editors and board members cultivated — the people they, and especially their wives, met socially. His marriage of convenience with the *Star* and its tensions were no secret. There would be a row if he were fired or slighted.

He had drawn up before the paper racks. Caulkin said in an odd voice, "Did you happen to read about yourself in today's paper, Hiram?"

"How could I? You didn't even give me a chance to sleep."

"Look at page sixteen."

Ham turned and absently read the box: ". . . *will be assigned to an exciting, colorful story of the state . . . Watch for his first article, soon to appear on the front page . . .*"

He whirled. "If this means you had wind of Doc's candidacy and expect me to cover it, I want out."

Caulkin was watching him carefully. "So you don't think it's a good idea, either."

"I think it's a rotten idea — Doc running, the whole business." He paused, curious. "What do you mean, 'either'?"

Caulkin snapped, "You don't think we'd cut our own political throat, do you? Sure, I *was* thinking of using you in politics. But River's declaration changes that. It would be impossible, with your background."

Ham flushed. Barricade memories stirred in him. "Wouldn't that be just as true of Peabody graduates, with their background?"

"Naturally. I wouldn't dream of giving this to any man who went to college in Gideon, on either side of the," he hesitated, "town. I'm putting Frosty Warren on the Witty campaign. Swinton will cover River."

"Of course, they'll be fair," Ham said dryly.

"I'll see to it they are."

There was no way to be frank with a man like Caulkin, Ham thought. You couldn't say, let's put our cards on the table, because he'd been stuffing his up his sleeve so long he'd forgotten they were there. Maybe he really thought Warren and Swinton were unprejudiced because they had never been to Gideon and hadn't met Doc or Witty. Ham knew better. Frosty Warren hadn't gone to Peabody — he was just a Dartmouth man. Sending him to Witty was like asking an Aldrich to report on a Rockefeller. And Al Swinton hadn't gone anywhere. Al was a grammar school man, a graduate of Ham's own Mechanics Street neighborhood, though he had taken a different course, studying the alley texts that produce a few strikebreakers in every working class. Al was Caulkin's faithful dog. All he asked was a scent and he'd bring back the meat and lay it humbly on that runway desk. Ham could just see his pug nose picking up Doc's trail, his mongrel tail wagging as Caulkin unleashed him and whispered, *Sick 'em.*

Ham felt the need to sit down. Crossing his legs, he said, "Still, it's going to be hard to explain. You build me up, I write the opening story, and a new team moves in. There'll be questions."

Caulkins chewed his mustache a moment. "Well, you're right, of course," he said gloomily. "Oh, old River is a slick article, I'll give him that. He saw that box, got us to send you up there, and got this" — he stabbed at the story again — "in the paper. Now we're in the impossible position of denying around town that we switched you because we decided to strangle him in the news columns. It was clever, I admit it. But it was also dirty pool."

Ham's stomach knotted. The instant he saw the box he had realized that the *Star*'s embarrassment couldn't be an accident. In politics these things didn't just happen. But Doc wouldn't do this to him; Doc wouldn't wear a gold watch chain yesterday and a paper hat today. Ham knew. He *knew*.

"I don't believe it."

"Ah?" Caulkin's brow arched.

"Oh, he wanted me to write the first story — he told me so."

"Ah!"

"But he'd never stoop to that."

"You're sure."

"I'm positive."

"All right. Explain this." Caulkin leaned forward. "Less than an hour after the final closed, Newt Albert called the Chief, congratulated the *Star* for assigning you to Doc, and said he hoped we didn't change our minds, because so many people would misunderstand."

Newt. Ham felt reprieved. Of course. It *had* to be Newt. Somehow he had slipped this over on Doc. "Sure, *he's* a toad, but —"

"And Doc's his boy."

"That's right. And I'm Doc's."

They glared hotly across the runway desk until the door opened. It was the lobster shift copy boy with a tray of clipping envelopes from the morgue. Caulkin quickly took it from him and ran a thumb over the flaps. "They're all here?"

"I think so, Colonel. I left a note for Mr. Smathers to double-check in the morning."

It was inevitable, Ham thought, shifting his glare to the floor. Charlie Smathers was the paper's chief librarian, the keeper of the clips. He was a scrawny old man with the instincts of a bookkeeper, and most of his work was frankly clerical — alphabetizing, cross-indexing, tabulating the results of the straw votes the *Star* always conducted during local political campaigns. The polls were the closest he ever came to making news himself, but he was poison to *Star* enemies all the same. Every line of print that had appeared in the state was carefully cut and filed by him and his staff, and it was a rare public figure who couldn't be impaled on some long-forgotten stick of type. Doc wasn't exempt; the story of his 1928 disqualification would be there, tidily filed under River, Adam R., and Ham supposed the *Star* would rerun its three-column cut of Doc crying in his torn uniform. He saw a copy of the *Editor and Publisher Yearbook* on the bookcase and remembered they took situation wanted ads from unemployed reporters. Just then Ham wanted a situation, any other situation, so bad he could taste it.

Caulkin's manner had changed. He had spread the envelopes before him and was gloating over them. "You know," he said mellowly, picking one up and dumping its yellowed contents on the desk, "I have an idea."

I'll bet, Ham thought. Like Cain had an idea.

"Believe it or not, I'm sentimental about Gideon, too. I went to old Peabody, you know."

Old Peabody. *I* know.

"That place will always have a soft spot in my heart."

Or your head.

Caulkin was grinning broadly now. Something's tickling him, Ham thought suspiciously, and all he could be sure of was that it wasn't the memory of his madcap Gideon youth.

"Consider the alternatives." Caulkin dropped the evelope and pinched his little finger. "I can't let you cover Doc's campaign. Understand, your integrity's not questioned. When you come right down to it, today's story isn't at all bad. But sooner or later you'd be bound to be biased."

"That's right. Almost as biased as the *Star*."

Caulkin let it pass and grabbed the next finger. "And I can't send you right back to India. It's a matter of record that you're home for local assignment. Giving you furlough until after the election would be almost as bad — we'd be accused of putting you out to pasture. So." Third finger. "There's bound to be great public interest in Stuart Witty, almost certainly our next governor. The public deserves to be informed about the influences in his life. Therefore," — Ham thought Caulkin was going to break that knuckle — "I'm asking you to start by writing a series of articles about Peabody College."

Ham looked blind. Caulkin nodded benignly.

"I want the college's history, what it stands for now — the works. We'll run it through the campaign."

"Listen, you said something about bias. Have you forgotten *my* college?"

"How could I? Of course, I was overseas in the Torch buildup during your athletic exploits, but I did a little homework when you joined the staff." He picked up an envelope, and Ham winced at the typed label — "Markham, Hiram A." Riffling through the sheaf of clippings, Caulkin chose one and droned, "This is my favorite. '. . . Racing forty yards to the Peabody two, the lanky Markham made an unbelievable jumping catch of a mighty rainbow pass from Spook Duschene in the last seven seconds of the game. However, there was a flag on the play, and . . .' " He winked. "You'll forgive me saying it was *so* like State to have been caught on the wrong side of an imaginary line. How fitting that it should have cost them the game!"

"It doesn't cost them games any more," Ham said tonelessly.

"No. No, you're quite right. They are invincible. And that, I should imagine, has entered into the calculations of Newt Albert. In paying for State's team, the taxpayers are also paying for a campaign device." He added thoughtfully, "Let's pray no other university funds are diverted."

"I left my prayer rug in Asia."

"Don't be impertinent. I think —" He thought. "I think we'll print this deathless prose" — he flourished the old sports story — "in a little box beside your first piece. It will lend cachet, having a former State hero covering Peabody."

"Not that I'm interested, but why couldn't you print it beside a political story?"

"This campaign is no football game. We can't play with it. There would always be some people who wouldn't make allowances for your loyalties. On page one that could be fatal."

Ham began to understand. His project was doomed to be buried inside the paper, one of those tedious numbered series that every busy eye flicks over, read only by retired subscribers and Charlie Smathers.

"Besides," Caulkin said thinly, "campaign copy comes in at all hours. I can't sit at the desk around the clock, and I intend to check every word you write. No offense. The Chief's orders. We don't want to be caught again."

"Thanks," Ham said dully. Nothing was right about this — not the assignment, nor the reason for it, nor the campaign. He felt helpless. His emotional investment was great, but the only way he could protect it was to warn Doc against Newt and the campus scandal. He turned toward the door, determined to do that much tomorrow.

"Wait a minute." Caulkin was rereading the clip. "Who was Spook Duschene?"

Ham turned back slowly, wondering how you answer such a question. Caulkin might as well have asked him who his father was, or what his son was like. He paused and said, "He was that shifty runner playing halfback. He would have been our best man next year."

"What year?" Caulkin blinked. "Say! That's Today's Laff!"

"Or yesterday's."

"Goddamn it, Hiram!" He pawed among the envelopes. If Ham wouldn't tell him he'd find out himself. "I told that copy child to bring all State envelopes — here is it." Brittle clips showered fragments like old confetti. The most recent was fifteen years old. Its head read:

Duschene, State
Gridiron Star,
Dies in Bulge

Ham's eyes flickered. Caulkin paled and stammered, "Oh, I didn't know."

"Next year would have been the year after the war."

"Well, yes, of course."

"We were juniors in 1942. There was an interruption then, you recall."

"I'm — sorry."

Ham fingered the doorknob, thinking how Spook, with his tough sense of humor, would have enjoyed Caulkin's discomfort.

"Do you want to requisition a permanent car for me?" he asked flatly.

"You're going back tomorrow?"

"Yes, but not to Peabody. Not right away. I have to see a few people at State first."

Caulkins weighed this. "Well, I can't say I blame you. I guess you were taken today, too."

Let it alone, Ham thought desolately. "Just the regular fall faculty reception. Some old friends."

"Right. By the bye, we'd better settle on your billet. You can't stay on either campus, you know. It wouldn't look right."

"The Gideon Arms?"

"Out of the question. Witty's a major stockholder. Isn't there a rooming house between State and Peabody? Seems to me I remember a place down near the Catholic Church."

And Ham, thinking bleakly how Spook would have relished *this*, said to the knob, "It's called the College Inne."

"That's it. Bivouac there. And make a reservation for Swinton — I'll be sending him along. When will you start filing?"

"Give me a week. I'll try to send something Wednesday," said Ham, going out.

"Upward and onward," Caulkin called cheerily after him.

He was in good humor again, restored by his solution of Ham's assignment. Shooting his French cuffs vigorously, he brushed aside Spook's obituary, scarcely noticing that it came apart in his hand.

**

In Doc's mid-thirties, when he was no longer a gridiron hero nor yet a state institution — while he was still an earnest young coach sitting nights at his scarred desk in the old Union Street gym wearing a T shirt and a stopwatch around his neck, mastering the new six-man line and carefully building up his following of Kiwanians and stadium alumni outside Gideon — in those days when he was awaiting the greater glory Ham, then a worshipful student, had asked him about his last game against Peabody.

"It must have been lonely," he had said, "being the only real man on the team."

Doc had dimpled jocularly. "Don't tell me there's a legend I took the field all by myself! No, Ham, I had a squad."

"Some squad. I was there."

"So. I expect some grandstand quarterback told you the boys weren't giving me the old block and tackle. Don't believe it. Because it just isn't true. Oh, they weren't in the best condition. How could they be? Everybody had an outside job, we practiced when we could. But I'm not apologizing for them. They were champions, Ham. Nobody knew them the way I did. They were *my* squad. And from Sam Theanapolis on down, they were a great squad."

And Ham had realized that Doc had convinced himself of that, for reasons so tangled within him that no one could ever trace them or show them to him. As a varsity idol it had been enough for him to believe in himself, but now he had become a leader, and a leader needs a larger trust. He must have faith in the led, for if they are unworthy, so is he. Only by honoring them can he honor himself, and a canny man, sensing that, suppresses misgivings about his followers and gives them the same uncritical loyalty he hopes to receive.

In that spirit Doc presided over the faculty reception.

It was held in the Mansion's long dark Victorian ballroom. Last night's storm had left the air dry but still hot, which meant discomfort for young instructors. Custom prescribed that those hired during the previous term stand against a dark paneled wall, each with his perspiring wife alongside, while Doc, at the door, welcomed entering members of the regular faculty and their ladies and started them on the line, down which they progressed, after wringing two score damp hands, to the parlor beyond, its yawning French windows, and the tree-dotted lawn outside, which was illuminated, now in the late afternoon, by fading torches of sunlight. Statettes served bland punch; summer gossip was exchanged; another academic year was under way. The event itself was routine, but was animated today by the announcement of Doc's candidacy and reports of an Academic Council wrangle earlier in the day. Doc beamed at any mention of the first and ignored the second entirely. The fight was over; he had won; and hulking over the swarming room he directed incoming traffic like a jovial, rumpled guide.

He was very rumpled. Finer fabrics always suffered on him: he was too active. He wore a cord suit, the jacket and crotch of which were now crisscrossed by great creases, giving him a spent look. It was deceptive. Despite his age he was the most alert man there. He observed everything, and with satisfaction — Sam entertaining three members of Dr. Budge's accreditation team on the lawn, Tate and Newt muzzling Harry Mikel in the parlor, and the new instructors, who, he noted proudly, included three Ivy graduates. The only rub was Sarah's indisposition, and that was really a blessing; this uproar would only have upset her. Compensating for her absence, he turned determinedly to the arriving women, arching over and booming, "You're looking mighty sassy, Gladys!" "That's a scrumptuous dress, Helen!" and "Why, Kit Ryan! You're smart as paint — prettier'n when you left. It was right nice of you to stop in and visit with Sare, but why haven't you been in to see me?" The ladies smirked — Doc's charm was rough but appealing — and in his ardor he forgot the group in the parlor, the Ivy men and Sam, forgot even Sarah and enjoyed his genial role.

The group in the parlor had grown. It now included Dean Elsie Shoemaker and Kit, who was lurking behind the dean and wondering why Harry Mikel was so quiet. Mikel was under fire, and, incredibly, wasn't firing back. At the Council Doc and Tate had inflicted a stinging defeat on him, gaveling down his protests that State wasn't ready for Budge's team; now Tate was baiting him while Newt chuckled appreciatively and marveled that this shabby old man with bicycle clips on his pants should be a professor.

During a lull Mikel whispered to Kit, "You're wondering why I'm taciturn, eh?"

"It's not like you. Don't you feel well?"

"Feel splendid. And as orally fixated as ever. But I've been waiting for Lutz. In his shy way he's smarting from this morning's decision, and I mean to draw him out." He reached for a cigarette and peered around. "Ah. There he is. Eric!" he cried aloud. "It seems I'm a low fellow. I openly defied our muscle-bound Caliph today, and his Lord Chamberlain has been admonishing me."

"Merely chiding you," Tate corrected him shrilly. The provost was a poster of confidence. He had bathed an hour before, and his bald head glittered like buffed marble.

"Nevertheless, I feel censured. Shall I take to sackcloth?"

"It might be an improvement," Tate said quizzically, and Newt snickered. Miss Shoemaker smiled; Kit, who knew her place, remained silent. Lutz was also silent, but he looked troubled.

"Maybe I'm wrong," Mikel said, crouching over a match. He waved it out with a sweeping gesture that embraced ballroom, parlor, lawn. "Maybe these babbling magpies can survive Budge's inquisition."

Tate was looking imperiously at Miss Shoemaker. He had promoted her; he was her immediate superior. She straightened and brayed nervously, "Oh, I'm sure Professor Mikel doesn't believe there's any real cause for alarm. We all know his bark is worse than his bite." Mikel squinted at her as though she were some gigantic insect, and drawing herself up — she wore tailored sharkskin like a uniform — she said defiantly, "Anyway, everyone else agrees with the provost."

Lutz sighed heavily. "Not everyone, Dean. Some of us think the university is taking a real risk."

Tate was undismayed. He had anticipated this. "You have doubts about your department, Eric?"

"We are sound, but —"

"But like many an academician you have doubts about other disciplines, which, of course, you don't understand. Be fair. That's it, isn't it? No? What, then?"

Lutz hated to say it, and it came haltingly. "It is the administration. The policies. The teaching loads. The library."

Mikel grinned triumphantly. Miss Shoemaker shook her silvery bangs indignantly, and Tate looked grave. He said quietly, "May I ask why you didn't speak out this morning?"

It was a cruel question — the little Austrian's timidity was campus lore — and it ended the discussion. Muttering weakly that his hearing aid hadn't been working properly at the meeting, Lutz bowed to the ladies and fled to the lawn. Newt, bored, followed him out. Mikel withdrew from the reception with the blissful expression of an evangelist who has gained a convert, and the provost was left with Miss Shoemaker and Kit, who, he discovered, had business with him.

His manner altered sharply. He was with underlings now. "Yes? What is it?"

"There is a rather delicate situation in the Theta house," Miss

Shoemaker began and stopped. She was always skittish with Tate, and he was glaring at her.

"Really, Dean, must we discuss it here?"

The dean floundered helplessly, and Kit stepped up quickly, introducing herself as the housemother and explaining that the matter needed clearing up before term. "It's about Red Stacy and Daphne Dix. She's —"

"Yes, yes, I know them. He's one of the most promising young men in his class, and Daffy's a lovely girl."

"She's also married. *And* a mother. And she goes everywhere with Red — including Theta bedrooms when I'm out."

Tate puckered. "I know housemothers have to be vigilant, but isn't it possible you're imagining things?"

"Kit's a Theta alumna," Miss Shoemaker said loyally, as though that excluded that.

"Kit," he repeated, tasting it. "You're new here, aren't you, Kit?"

"She came at commencement," said Miss Shoemaker.

"Oh!" Tate sighed, implying that newcomers always panicked.

"I've had to forbid her to bring him in the house," Kit said rapidly, and Miss Shoemaker, feebly parroting Kit's plea of an hour before, asked, "Couldn't we speak to them?"

The provost didn't tell her that precisely that had been on his mind for nearly a month. None of this was new to him. He had the gossip's ear for rumor, and since summer school he had been meaning to give Red a fatherly lecture. Tate had convinced himself the affair couldn't be serious, however. He was conscious that any disciplinary action would be most inconvenient, at least until the Hampshire game was out of the way and preferably until the bowl teams were picked. He couldn't expect these women to understand why; therefore he retreated into evasion.

"If he's not visiting the sorority any more the matter's out of your jurisdiction," he said to Kit, and, to the dean, "I'm sure you can handle anything else that arises. Possibly the girl's a trifle flighty — possibly *we* are. As you say, it's all quite delicate, and we mustn't be rash, must we?" Shaking his head, he slipped off sinuously between prating groups, seizing a hand here, clapping a back there, working his way toward Dr. Budge.

Miss Shoemaker was conscious that she had been inadequate. The exchange hadn't done her justice. She was a competent dean, astute with young girls, but the postwar phenomenon of married coeds bewildered her, and she was aware that this case was complicated by Kit's awkward divorce — more complicated, indeed, than even Kit had at first realized. Kit had known last spring that Lutz and Mikel had written letters for her, but only recently had she learned of a third letter, locked in the dean's safe deposit box and signed by Sarah River. Sarah had remembered Kit warmly and had insisted on writing it when she had heard of her plight from Mikel. It had decided the wavering dean; she had considered it insurance, even though she had doubted she would ever use it. However, there had seemed no reason then why the appointment should excite attention from the men Miss Shoemaker thought of as the university's Higher-Ups. She hadn't foreseen that that wretched Dix woman would throw herself at the one student the Higher-Ups knew best. It confused everything; while every instinct urged her to move relentlessly against Daffy, she knew that under the circumstances that wouldn't do. At the moment nothing would, she thought, pressing knuckles against her forehead and wondering whether she could be having another migraine attack so soon. Perhaps the provost was right. They mustn't be hasty. Better to let things ride. Mumbling that she might have a talk with Daffy one of these days, she made excuses and joined the flight outside, leaving Kit with her unsolved problem.

Kit felt haggard. Now there was no one to appeal to but Doc, and if he investigated the Theta house she would be out of a job. Lifting a punch cup from a tray, she suddenly wished she were home with a real drink. Gin would be comforting, and she wanted to be alone. Listlessly she glanced through the windows and saw Sol Feinblatt in the center of a party by a rhododendron clump. He waved, and she drew some comfort from his dream that Doc might leave State. Another president wouldn't kowtow to legislative prejudice, she thought bitterly; another would hire any housemother he liked and hang the pious prigs.

Doc's future engrossed Sol's party, whose true center, hidden by shrubbery, was Ham. Arriving late, he had been diverted here by Newt, who, spotting the administrator of the medical school's Haven Square Hospital under a distant tree, had then deserted him. Casting about for a familiar face, Ham had seen Eric Lutz. The Austrian had greeted him enthusiastically and introduced him to this group as the author of that morning's *Star* story. Instantly, to Ham's astonishment, they had surrounded him and begun mocking Doc.

"Oh, it's going to be delicious," Sol was saying. "A knock-down, drag-out fight. And our boy's a caveman."

"Did you notice his handshake in the line?" asked a callow man in shirt sleeves. "His fingers are definitely atavistic — almost webbed." A blonde with a beehive hairdo and a maternity smock inquired brightly, "Will he go to the polls in thingamajigs? Shoulder pads?" and a bearded man in bloated seersucker said muzzily, "He'll never get that far. They'll kill him in the campaign."

"I can't see why they'll bother," said the man in shirt sleeves. "He's been dead for years."

"Wrong, wrong, wrong," sighed Sol. "With his get-up-and-go he's a lead-pipe cinch. My fellow Elks —" They hooted him down, and a slatternly young woman whispered, "Is it true he's acey-deucey? Will they bring that out?" "Probably," the beard lisped. "It's people like him that give bisexuality a bad name."

Only Ham, flushing, and Lutz, frowning at the grass, abstained from laughter. "I hear they're offering a letter to any student who'll write his speeches for him," Sol said. The slattern snorted, "As though they could find one who's literate." She turned to Ham. "What was your school, Mr. Markham?"

Lutz looked up. "I imagine you've never been near the trophy pavilion."

"God forbid," she groaned.

"If you had, you'd know Ham is one of our own graduates."

"You went *here?*" she asked Ham in disbelief.

"That's right," he said harshly. "I played football, wearing," he said to the blonde, "thingamajigs. I only wish I had them on now. I feel like throwing a few brush blocks for Doc."

Embarrassment suffused the group. The slattern said feebly that she hadn't known any *Star* writers were State men; the others fidgeted; the beard walked wordlessly away. Sol, however, was irrepressible.

"Then he must have been your coach! Your pigskin mentor! Ah, ivied walls and storied halls. This *is* delicious!"

"It was," Ham said sourly, "and it would be now if the caveman's den weren't infested with vermin."

Lutz remembered obligations, Sol's friends coughed and left, but Sol himself refused the insult. "You don't mean you admire him?" he asked incredulously. Ham nodded vehemently. "As president of

State?" Ham nodded again, and when Sol rolled his eyes he added stoutly, "Doc belongs here — and every State graduate feels the same."

Sol shook his head lugubriously. "Sorry. Not true."

"Well, everybody from the old days."

Still shaking his head, Sol said, "Would you like me to prove how wrong you are? Follow me."

Thus Ham was led, unawares, to the girl of his youth.

**

Kit saw them coming through the French windows, and a stricken look crossed her face. Oh dear, she thought, cradling her punch cup fearfully. Ham was the last person, the very last person she wanted to see and she couldn't possibly escape. Oh *dear*, this *had* been a day. She offered him a fluttering hand and cried faintly, "I can't believe it. I —" She laughed breathlessly. "I just can't."

Sol said cagily, "So you know each other already. Long time no see, eh?"

"Go poison a well somewhere," Ham told him.

"Three's a crowd," said Sol. "I'll take a powder," he said and did, forfeiting his point.

In clumsy silence they smiled over her lifted cup — smiled across time, across the bundling board of the quarrel that had separated them long ago and was now locked in place forever — and then the old warmth worked its magic; Kit forgot her bitterness, Ham his embarrassment, and they both spoke with a rush: "I heard you were back, but I never dreamt you'd come —" "Didn't anybody tell you I was here —" "Go on." "No, you, I insist." "Ham Markham, you haven't changed a bit!"

Nor had she, he thought. Despite her flat Red Cross shoes and absurd crucifix and the Lenten solemnity of her hair she was still Kit, the instinctive flirt, shuffling her toes with a little girl's hesitancy, cutting her slant eyes about. In a moment an impulse would carry her away and she would touch him.

She seized his hands. "Ham, do you realize what year this is? It's your fifteenth! I mean, of your original class, '44. Just everybody'll be back for homecoming — the Wallace game. And they'll spot you right away, because you *haven't* changed. You know, living in all those queer little countries has done things for you. You've put on a little weight, but not much, and you haven't a single gray hair. Turn around. Let me see. No, not one. How do you like this bracelet? I got it in Birmingham."

Her lost look had vanished, and she was preening herself as she had long ago, the frustrations of the years between momentarily effaced. But the years were still there. Ham really had changed, and so had she. Change, in fact, was all around, and because she accepted it uncritically and he saw flaws, there was an issue between them. Kit, in her prattling, stumbled over it.

"Have you *seen* the campus! All of it?" She caught her breath. "Isn't it wonderful? Oh, I know how you felt at first. You missed the old landmarks. It's natural, nothing to be ashamed of."

"I'm not ashamed, I think it's great. At least, it can be. All the raw material's here, though I gather from Harry Mikel there's still a lot to be done."

Kit wrinkled her nose daintily. "Cloud nine. *That's* where Mikel belongs. Ham, don't you see this is what we wanted as kids? A place to be proud of, that *looks* like a college, with a name people respect and" — she groped — "tradition."

Tradition in a decade. Ham was staggered. But she raced on.

"Do you remember how you wanted a literary magazine? There's one now, thick as a telephone book, comes out twice a year. And courses in practically everything — television photography, life insurance, dancing — you name it."

"Kit, you're worse than Mikel. You make it sound like a trade school."

"There's even one on raising children from broken homes." She colored. "I'm going to take it."

Arguments with her, Ham remembered, had always been mysteriously converted into personal issues. He could scarcely denounce her son. Remembering why he had been brought here, he snatched a glass from a passing Statette. "Anyhow, let's drink to Doc."

"And to his abdication," she said crisply, finishing her punch.

"You mean you want him to win?"

"I mean I want him to *go*. Oh, don't think I'm not grateful to him — none of this would have happened without him. But State has outgrown him. Ham, he only has a B.A. in Gym! Some of us don't think that's right."

Us. Then Sol had been right. Ham said grimly, "There are quite a few of you, I've found."

"Oh, just lots. Particularly the new ones, from other places. Everybody thinks Dr. Tate is an absolutely odious personality — me especially — but obviously he's more qualified."

"And that's why you and your new friends from other places hope Doc's elected."

"Yes. It's much the best way. His leave of absence will be permanent then."

So Mikel had been right, too. "Of course, a red-hot football season won't hurt his campaign any."

His rising voice warned her. "Well, no —"

"Led by that solid old campaigner, Red Stacy," he finished bitingly.

Kit shelved her cup. She didn't like his tone. Her girlishness disappeared.

"What do you mean by that?" she demanded, trembling.

"He's another of my finds. Him and his truelove."

"Now wait a minute. If you mean that girl, I couldn't agree more. She's nothing but a free-for-all, and I happen to be one of the people who's trying to do something about her."

"And just how far are you getting?"

"Never mind," she said uncertainly. "I'll work something out. But you mustn't blame Red. She's older, and she's taking advantage of him."

"And you used to complain about the double standard! Don't you know a swordsman when you see one?"

"Ham, I believe you're jealous of him!"

He was taken aback. It was so feminine a thought. Yet there was a spark of truth in it. He was scorched. "Yes, and maybe you're jealous of her."

Another spark: Kit smoldered. "You're just like Mikel! You're worse! Just because State's going somewhere and burying the hick college you knew, you're down on that boy. You're green with envy because you've come back and found we have a winning team, one we don't have to cry over!"

They were both ablaze. Ham's face flamed. He had to strike out at something, and so, inexcusably, he fouled her.

"At least we were worth a few tears," he snapped. "Or didn't you think so? Did you ever cry over me — or Spook?"

He tried to choke it back, too late. It had hit her like a bullwhip. Everything was on her face but the welt. She drew back in a little shrinking motion and slid away, moving off stiffly in her drab shoes, and as she passed his unsteady, outstretched hand she whispered, "Yes, Ham. I did."

She was gone in a bobble of square shoulders. Despising himself, he trailed her blindly through the ballroom crowd, holding his punch cup aloft, and saw her emerge at the far door, pause to touch Doc's hand, and pass gracefully out into the sun. He knew following was pointless, but he couldn't bear staying there. It was in his mind to quit the reception when Doc loomed massively on the threshold.

"Leaving, Ham? I didn't know you'd come."

Doc looked like an angry bird. Ten minutes before, Newt had handed him the afternoon *Star*. As Ham had foreseen, Caulkin had reproduced the 1928 clipping that Doc carried in his wallet. It was the chief attraction in a full-page spread on the candidate's life. Brooding over it, and still smarting from this morning's story, Doc had seen Ham enter the parlor and concluded that Ham didn't dare face him.

"Sorry. I got sidetracked," Ham mumbled, in no mood to talk.

But Doc wanted talk. He wasn't going to pick at the *Star*. He had a better bone. His receptions were supposed to be pleasant affairs, setting the tone for the term, and he had seen the hurt in Kit's eyes.

"Kit left early, too, before I had a chance to say more than hello. Any idea why?"

"We — had an argument."

"Oh? Can't tell you how sorry I am to hear that. It does seem after all this time you two could quit bickering. Same old squabbles, I suppose."

Ham rolled the cup between his palms. This was as good a time as any, he supposed. "Do you know a young back named Stacy?"

Doc was startled, and partly mollified. Nothing pleased him more than an old player taking an interest in the squad. "Why, yes! You must see him, Ham. You know, it's sort of eerie. He runs just like Spook."

Ham spilled his cup. It slipped out of his hands, and before he caught it juice was streaming down one thigh and dripping on the floor. Doc commiserated and produced a handkerchief, but Ham wasn't worrying about small disasters. "I *have* seen him!" he cried. "And if there's one jerk who's *not* like Spook it's that redhead. Listen, don't you know . . ."

He told him what he so obviously didn't know. The dimples faded entirely, and when Ham had finished, gesturing with one hand and squeezing his soggy duck pants with the other, Doc cleared his throat.

"If that's true, he's subject for severe action. So are any people who have shielded him, from the Athletic Dormitory proctors up. As for the girl — is she in a sorority?"

"She just has a casual status in one. She lives with her husband."

"Yes, but what's the house?"

"That's not important, Coach. It's Gamma."

"Theta now." Doc frowned, trying to remember what Kit had told him in the line. He snapped his fingers. "Why, Kit Ryan's the housemother there!" Lowering his voice, he said, "Is that what you two were arguing about?"

"Just that," said Ham, misunderstanding the drift.

"I see." Doc's eyes narrowed. "I — see."

Only he didn't see, Ham realized with dismay. He saw that Ham's former coed was around and had decided that they had taken up quarreling where they had left off thirteen years before, that Red and Daffy were merely pawns in a minor disagreement between old acquaintances. It was irrational, Ham thought, but like him. To him alumni were just older students. He remembered them as they had been here and assumed that what had once been important to them still was — in this case, that old scars between Kit and Ham mattered enough for Ham to slander a girl in her house. Ham wasn't flattered, but he understood. After all, he thought, Doc had never resolved his own student passions. He was still trying to win the game he had lost thirty years ago. The field was different, and he had changed his suit and joined a new team. But it was the same game.

Ham had no better luck arguing against Newt. Doc wouldn't be warned. *He* was in charge of his campaign, he said, and he'd see to it there was no hocus-pocus. Of course, he was sorry there had been some misunderstanding about that box in the *Star* — he had spoken to Newt about it at lunch — though he understood worse things were done in politics. It was regrettable, and he intended to see that his own political career was conducted on a higher plane, but after all, Ham worked for the newspaper; he should have read it before coming here yesterday. The *Star*, Doc felt sure, would consult its own interests anyhow.

"They have," Ham muttered. "I'm going to cover Peabody."

"Well!"

That was all there, but escorting Ham out he couldn't resist adding, with a twinkle that was more of a gleam, that maybe Ham would be a little more at home across town, considering the Fancy Dan life he'd been leading abroad and his marriage to a Stoddard girl — no offense, but a fact was a fact, and State coeds, well, they just moved in a different crowd.

Then, with a sly expression Ham was to remember later, he asked, "What's your father-in-law like?"

"Judge Davies? He's a Republican, of course. *If* he remembers to vote."

"A fair man?"

"One of the incorruptible rich. Several cuts above my boss. Is that what you're driving at?"

"It's close enough. Maybe you should see a little more of him, boy."

Ham had no chance to reply. Doc returned swiftly inside, leaving him alone on the steps with the feeling that he had been convoyed by a bouncer, driven out for flouting rules.

Driven, he thought bitterly an hour later, to a flophouse.

As though on cue the proprietress of the Inne led him straight to the second floor room he had shared with Kit — to the same white iron bedstead, the mildewed Stag at Bay, the chipped Venetian blinds overlooking Union Street. Only the price had changed, from three dollars to five.

"Do you have anything else?" he asked hopefully, trying to remember her name. "I've been in this one."

"Best I got." She patted her white bobbed hair and strutted around in tailored slacks, opening windows, stirring up dust. "The others leak. And believe me, mister, roofs cost plenty."

But lubricating oil doesn't, Ham thought, wincing as the bed spring creaked under his bag and Olivetti case. He supposed it didn't much matter where she put him. All Inne rooms were alike.

"Anybody else staying here?"

She looked wary. "Why?"

"I want to reserve the leakiest ceiling for a *Star* reporter named Swinton."

"He can take his pick. We're empty except for you and a queer old professor. You taking this single?"

"My wife's in India," he said coolly, handing her a week's rent.

"Pity." She glanced slyly at the double bed. "If she shows it's only two bucks extra."

"She won't."

"I'm only saying."

"You haven't been in any of those queer little countries, have you? Because you haven't changed a bit, Mrs. —"

"Prouty," she said kittenishly, and then, more businesslike, "The flush is still down the hall."

Ham wrote his wife briefly, drove downtown for a drugstore sandwich, and was back on the bed with a dozen paperbacks when others began arriving. Harry Mikel was first, stamping up the stairs, sarcastically congratulating Mrs. Prouty on her new elk's head hat rack in the front hall. Ham hurried to the door, but Mikel was already vanishing down the long sinister corridor that led to the rear of the house, and from the slump of his shoulders Ham knew he was exhausted. An hour later Al Swinton checked in. Ham heard him and lay motionless, in vain. Al had checked the register. He burst in without knocking.

"Hi, sweatheart. The old babe said you were here. Some dump the colonel picked, huh?"

Al affected a role. He wore his hat on the back of his head, cultivated an underworld expression, and drank whiskey neat. He was here for a drink now. Ham referred him to the tavern.

"Nice beat you got yesterday," Swinton said enviously, lingering. "You find any dirt on River yet?"

Ham punched a pillow. "I'm leaving that for you."

"I'd hate to get scooped my first day." Despite his swagger Al was a worrier, and he held Ham in secret awe.

"Didn't Caulkin tell you? I'm covering the other side of town."

"Yeah, but you *know* this side."

"Go get drunk," Ham said, and turned a page.

Al returned at midnight, swearing. It was raining again, he reported, thrusting his red face in. Wasn't this the Goddamndest weather? Ham sleepily agreed and turned out his light as Al stumbled off down the corridor, lurching against stained walls, and subsided with a distant thud, bringing the Inne silence.

Ham tossed, listening to the rustle of the rain outside.

And then to rustling voices inside.

Downstairs a couple was registering with Mrs. Prouty. She led them up to the next room, and though they were mumbling discreetly, her own voice came clearly through the thin wall. Apparently they had been caught in the downpour with blankets. She was showing them where to spread them to avoid ceiling drips, explaining that the flush was down the hall, and demanding advance payment for the room — two bucks extra, since they were taking it double.

She left, and their tones grew more distinct.

"I'm all right," a confident rasp was saying. "Koski's got me covered at the ape house. But what about you?"

That was Red, Ham realized, sitting up.

"He'll think I'm at the Kat House," answered a sultry drawl.

And that was Daffy.

Ham groped for a sleeping pill, feeling the need to escape, if only into dreams of the slain past. But Daffy and Red were noisy lovers. They sprang on and off furniture, giggled often, and talked slush audibly. Later there were other effects. Daffy had brought a transistor radio, which she turned to blaring dance music, and their springs were worse than Ham's. After a certain rhythm crept into the squeaking Ham thought they might do without the music. So, apparently, did Red, but when he protested Daffy answered sullenly that she liked it, it made things more romantic. Thus the blare continued and ended when the springs ended, with a snap of the dial and a grunt from Red. Later the rhythmic squeaking started again. Ham was asleep by then, and awoke only afterward, when Daffy gave a sudden cry and leapt up.

"What's wrong?" Red asked drowsily.

"My baton!" she said, turning on lights and fumbling with the blankets. "My baton's not here!"

"Must've left it in the field. Get it tomorrow."

He drifted off, snoring grossly, but Ham could hear her thrashing about in wrinkled sheets, fretting to herself, and despite a second pill he too lay long awake, marveling at the things women remember in the night.

TWO
Between Two Worlds

SEPTEMBER WANED, and the street beneath Ham's window began to hum with sounds of youth. Students arrived daily via the G.A.R. Highway — first a trickle of upperclassmen preparing for Rush Week, then a tide of freshmen escorted by anxious parents, and finally the full flood of undergraduates, lugging trunks from the American Express office downtown, hailing one another across Union Street, tossing plastic saucers back and forth under the elms and curiously eying the frosh, now parentless, who strolled by in self-conscious groups wearing the emblems of their caste — blue dinks for boys, blue berets for girls. Occasionally green Peabody beanies were also seen, though not often; unlike State, Peabody hadn't expanded since the war, and most of its students remained on their side of the Common. Whenever a flash of green flickered below Ham leapt up, awaiting an insult, a blow, an incident, but nothing ever happened; the intruders were ignored, and each time he returned to his typewriter on the bureau with a vague feeling of disappointment.

He sent the *Star* little that week, but wrote India daily.

College Inne
Gideon
Sunday

Dancy darling,

This place is turning into a brothel. No madam presides (though the landlady would make a dandy), and there are scarely any towels, even in the flush. All the same, we have an old pro, squirming in the dark. You've guessed it: Delilah and her stud have been back — *Four times,* in fact. The freakish showers have continued, and finding that the room is cheaper by the week they've taken it that way, shacking up almost nightly. Every tramp trades her favors for a consideration, and this one is after strange coin. Before each tender episode she insists he renew his promise to back her for Gridiron Queen. Big deal. But really. The Queen will be selected by the Alumni Athletic Committee, whose pet he naturally is. As you've probably guessed, I glean this stuff by eavesdropping; i.e., by lying in my own blameless bed. It's not as comfortable as yours (pause) or as warm (longer pause), but I do learn things. Item: you'll be relieved to know that the baton was recovered, each jewel on its phallic tip intact.

How long can they get away with this caper? *I* don't know. In India they'd be quickly found out, but that's a civilized country. Here everything is fouled up by interpersonal relations — I mustn't do this, because he'll do that. Some possible solutions: (1) Delilah's husband will wise up and discover she's not sleeping in the sorority; (2) the athletic dorm proctors will find their ace is A.W.O.L.; (3) I'll blow my stack, break down the wall, and smash their radio; (4) Al Swinton will run into them and get his cherished scoop. So far they've been unobserved, but we're all cosily tucked under the same rotting roof, and Al would have seen them long ago if he hadn't been so busy belting his Remington down the hall. He's *so* conscientious. I know your lovely G.O.P. eyes are shining at the prospect of Doc's defeat, but I don't think you'd want it on the *Star*'s terms. A Swintonism from today's paper: "Although America's two greatest wars were fought during his lifetime, 'Dr.' River managed to avoid service in either. . . ."

If this suggests the race is getting hot, it's wrong. Al's just taking his daily loyalty oath to Caulkin. Otherwise things are pretty slack. Witty and Doc are now the official candidates, endorsed by their conventions, and Charlie Smathers has launched the *Star*'s traditional state-wide straw vote (which won't be fixed, because the paper's reputation is at stake), but that's about it. Every campaign goes through three phases: the approach, the wild trading of punches, and the final haymakers. We're still in phase one. Doc's out shaking a few hands; Witty (it says here in a Frosty Warren story) is in Birmingham "giving tax cut proposals the earnest study that has earned him the nickname 'Mr. Depth.' " In other words, there's no legit copy. Privately Swinton tells me he's amazed at the way Doc picks up names in the field, but even that's not news, at least not to me. I remember the first time I met Doc, in my freshman year. I was hanging around the practice field with Spook (Did I ever tell you about Spook Duschene? No? All right, he was my roommate, among other things) when a loose ball bobbed out to us. Instead of tossing it to the nearest player Spook heaved it fifty yards to Doc, in midfield — a hell of a pitch. Doc grinned and heaved it all the way back, and your showboating husband yanked it down. Well, he'd never seen us before, but the next morning he met us on Union Street and called us by name. Doc's always been sharp that way. When he's trying he's a walking phone book, alumni directory, and *Who's Who* — he even asked me about your father last week — and if Al's amazed now, he'll be bugeyed by November.

All I know about Doc comes from Swinton these days, partly because I have my own chore at Peabody — *not* a great success so far — but also because I'm poison in the Mansion. Al writes libel daily and is forgiven, on the ground that he's a hireling. I write nothing and am blamed for everything, including, apparently, Al's stuff; the only time I've seen Doc since the reception he mentioned, with heavy sarcasm, that Swinton had told him we were both staying in the Inne. I wish I could get Doc to check the rest of the Inne guest list, but no dice. I got my fingers burned once. If I brought it up again probably he'd just walk away anyhow. Somehow — maybe because he hadn't seen me for so long — he got it into his head that I'd come back the same old Ham, ready to drag down any ball he threw. I muffed the first, the interview, and he's sore. But what could I do? The only way I could have kept him happy was to have stayed away forever, and Caulkin fixed that. Not *my* fault. Still, it hurts. I don't expect you to understand why, but you may get a clue to how I feel if I say *I* understand why you quit going to Stoddard reunions after the first one.

No news from your father. Maybe he took the wrong flight from Washington and is settling down somewhere in the jungle, dispensing palm tree justice. Tell Hammy's ayah to be sure he takes that afternoon nap. Hug him for me and whisper he's to keep a stiff upper lip, there's a good chap.

All my love, always,
Ham

College Inne
Gideon
Tuesday

Dancy Abigail DeLaittre Davies Markham, Marm —

A curious development. Peabody College had decided it doesn't *want* me to write about it. All week I've been hanging around, soaking up campus charm and sensing undercover hostility. I wondered if it was my imagination. Well, it wasn't. Today I hammered officially on the college gate, so to speak, and that, so to speak, was as far as I got. The keepers of the keys wouldn't even give me a Band-Aid for my bloody knuckles. The president was tied up. The dean was tied up. The public relations man was untied, but I wish he hadn't been. After clearing his throat and scratching his head he allowed as how they were honored to have a pukka foreign correspondent around, and they'd like me to give a chapel lecture if I could spare the time, but if it was all the same to me, they'd rather stay out of the papers just now. Nothing personal, you understand, they just don't want to get involved in politics. I think nobility is grand. I only wish somebody would privately endow *me*.

Of course, I could break them overnight if I called Caulkin. He'd finger a dozen of their heftiest alumni quick — but he'd never let me forget it, either. Maybe I'll give the lecture, to get a foot in the door, or maybe I'll twist Harry Mikel's arm. He gives courses at Peabody and must have some pull. I'm going to find some way, because I'm piqued, and, funnily enough, I'm growing genuinely curious about Peabody. At first I wasn't at all. I just wanted Out. Peabody green still makes me see red, and sitting in that public relations office watching the plebes outside the whimsical thought crossed my mind that it would be fun to borrow a bike and ride around lifting the beanies off their heads. Some things inside you never grow up. Spook and I pedaled around doing that once, and when the *Star* identified us as "anonymous thieves," we signed our names to the clip and posted it on our fraternity bulletin board. Kid stuff, huh? But I don't really mean it now. The shy-making truth is that I find Peabody enchanting. It's a kind of museum, like the Red Fort in Delhi or Fort St. George in Madras. The rich still send their sons there, but their day (*and* Stoddard's, Love) is passing. The future, good or bad, belongs to places like State.

— Which is no museum. God, it's alive. Brawling, strident, and not much concerned with scholarship as far as I can see, but seething with animal life. Now and then I wander over to the Student Union for coffee and talk to members of the fifty-man accreditation team (their work's hush-hush, but they're amiable), or to the poet Feinblatt, who's amusing. Sometimes Mikel or Lutz drop by and we start a panel. We never get far. The students won't let us. They have a 104-record jukebox blaring all the time, and the only way we can hear each other is to feed it a quarter and select one of the juke's four silent LP's. We pay for silence. And gratefully.

Random notes. . . . My class has a homecoming banquet upcoming, and Sam Theanapolis (the Nizam of alumni) tried to draft me for the committee. I dodged it. . . . Last night's moon was clear, so the room next door was vacant and I slept. . . . Your father's back in Birmingham and actually sent me a note. He seems to know a lot about the campaign. Now that I think of it I let him off easy in my book — when you were a tot the judge was a big Republican wheel, you know, and some people say he started Governor Blandford's career. Must be nice to be a retired statesman, running down to swap yarns with Supreme Court justices. No juke problem *there*.

Your letter was wonderful. Love to you for it, and to Hammy for napping, and tell Dr. Satakopan the American Rugger season is about to start. Or a reasonable facsimile.

Ham

College Inne
Gideon
Friday

Dance dearest,

First big game tomorrow, with Navy, and State's white hope spent last night working out in the Inne gym next door. Not much excitement elsewhere, though placards in the Student Union advertise a big rally tonight — stunts with goats, a pep talk from Doc, etc. There are the usual ridiculous fears about rain. Today, like any other garrulous old grad, I started telling the Student Union coffee panel about a Coast Guard game when it really poured in New London and Spook almost drowned on the five-yard line, and then I saw them yawning and shut up. Why do I keep harking back?

I'm still the leper of Gideon. Yesterday Swinton wrote a dirty piece about low faculty salaries (have it your way, it was true; but he still *wrote* it dirty) and Doc cut me dead on the State campus. No thaw on the other side of town, though I'm lecturing there tomorrow A.M. and hope to get Mikel aside before then. He's sleeping here tonight.

Think I hear him on the stairs now —

Hastily, but lovingly —

H.

P. S. It was a telegram from the judge. He wants me to dine with him tonight at his club, where the elite meet. Probably I'll go and find he forgot.

**

Ham erred. Robert Justice Davies rarely forgot anything. Like everyone else in the state, Ham misunderstood his father-in-law, but that wasn't his fault. At the peak of his career the judge had concluded that the eccentric is granted a license denied others. He had, therefore, deliberately cultivated the image of the impractical widower, the brilliant but irresponsible jurist whose judgment was sound but whose personal habits were chaotic. From the first he had been relieved of minor inconveniences — no one would trust him with a telephone message or an errand — and in time he had been gratified to find himself being tactfully excluded from civic drives, luncheon meetings, directorates, commissions. His triumph had been complete. He had gained much and lost nothing, for his reputation was undiminished — was, if anything, enhanced among those who vaguely felt that anyone so far above the melee must be wise.

And so he had lived at peace, a harmless charlatan unmolested by society.

Until that dank September day when he wired Ham.

Judge Davies always dressed for his part, and that evening he wore an archaic black string tie, hopelessly askew, and an expensive linen suit in disarray. With his slender build and drooping, tobacco-stained white mustache he looked less like a Brahmin justice than a Southern planter down on his luck. Only his voice betrayed him — the prim, precise speech encouraged in New England's private boarding schools and carried by their graduates, like a knight's pennant, throughout life.

"Where have you been, Markham?" he cried challengingly, greeting Ham in the cavernous Clipper Club foyer. Ham explained that he had been driving down from Gideon, and the judge looked confused. "Gideon, Gideon." Biblical references flickered on his tongue; he suppressed them. "Oh, of course. Where my secretary reached you. Been up at Aggie, eh?" State's new status had never been ratified by the judge.

More patient explanations were cut short; he removed his rimless glasses and winked one mild blue eye. "Not another word. I refuse to listen until we've had a — ah — potation."

In the club library, over Martinis, he inquired about his daughter and grandson and then led Ham through an account of the past week in Gideon.

"I gather your paper doesn't smile on Mr. River's ambitions?" he asked innocently.

"No sir." Sirring the judge was instinctive; even fellow club members did it. Ham looked around at the deep rugs, red leather chairs, and potted greenery. "If my boss were here he'd be glad to tell you why."

The judge nodded absently. "I've met him. Man named Gawkin."

"Caulkin." Ham grinned. "But I like it your way."

"Apparently *you* think River would make an able governor."

"I think he's able where he is. I'd rather he didn't run. He's as honest as Witty, though, if that's what you mean."

"It's not quite." Producing a thin black cigar the judge lit it inefficiently, spending three matches. He puffed and sipped and puffed again and said, "I'm not asking whether he burgles houses or picks pockets. I assume he doesn't. But will he do, really do? Is he honorable?"

In that setting the question did not seem odd; yet to Ham, who understood its nuances, it was as revealing as the old man's accent. It sprang from assumptions that men like the judge never challenged — that honor was absolute, and that every man was free to choose the right. By Clipper Club standards, Ham supposed, there were no men of honor in the mean streets of East Birmingham. Everyone on that level of struggle was looking for a corner to cut, as Ham himself had when he exposed the city's society and wrote his way out of the police precincts, as Doc had in seizing upon the GI Bill to transform State. The judge couldn't understand a man on the make because everything had been made for him. Somewhere, generations ago, someone named Davies had seen a main chance and taken it, and now his descendant sat in easy elegance, savoring a cocktail and asking genteelly whether a rougher man was honorable. No, Ham thought, looking back into those pale patrician eyes — his wife's eyes, he thought with a pang, and his son's — in that sense Doc was not honorable. But neither was he dishonorable.

"He's a good Democrat."

The judge waved the mangled end of his cigar. "No answer. Harry Byrd's a good Democrat, and so is Harry Truman."

"Well. Truman is."

"Markham, when will you realize that these tags mean nothing? You belong to one party because you were born into it. My case is identical. My father saw that I registered Republican while I was still an undergraduate in New Haven."

"I wouldn't say we're identical, sir."

"In any event, we both inherited our allegiances."

"And we're stuck with them."

"I at least am trying to shuck mine."

It was a good-humored debate; they had held it before. Unlike Caulkin the judge was no snob. He had received Ham into his family cheerfully and with sincere pleasure, vastly preferring him to the troupe of crew-cutted Yale and Peabody jackstraws who had squired Dancy about before a publicity chairmanship for a Junior League bazaar had taken her to Ham's old desk at the *Star*. Yet today there was an urgency in the judge's tone, and Ham, who had been wondering all afternoon why he was being summoned here, sensed that this was no diversion. The judge was preparing to lay something on the line.

"Are you thinking of supporting Doc?" Ham asked him.

The old man looked pained. "Out of the question. Social suicide at my age — simply impossible. No, I merely want to size him up, if you'll excuse the vulgarism. I need a fair picture of the man, unclouded by prejudice."

"Why?"

"One moment, one moment. Do you think he'll abuse his office in the campaign?"

"Never," said Ham, believing it.

"Hm. Of course *you* have a few prejudices there. I put it to you — you feel some sort of tribal loyalty to the man. Still, you *do* have good judgment. You should know." He seemed to be arguing with himself, taking this side, that side, and as they polished off their drinks he lowered his cigar end, now hopelessly shredded, and quietly confessed why. "I've been asked to join his board of trustees."

Ham gagged on his olive. "No joke?"

"No, no, no. Unfortunately not."

He was irked, though not at Ham. This was the first trusteeship to be pressed upon him in three years, and he didn't see how he could dodge it. The circumstances made evasion virtually impossible.

"Evidently there's been a vacancy for some time, and in his anility Blandford was stupid enough to write River last winter, stipulating that he wouldn't name anyone the rest of the board found unacceptable. Something to do with the budget — River made a concession, and got this in return. It seemed meaningless then. Apparently he's always had his way with appointees. Now his candidacy changes things. After that idiotic letter Blandford can't name a fire-eater, much as he'd like to, but Witty wants to be sure there's at least a watchdog on the board. They sent River a list of names and told him to check one. I wasn't consulted," he grumbled. "I was in Washington, but that's no excuse; they could have called me. Anyhow, I was on the list."

"And you got the nod," said Ham, remembering Doc's crafty look on the Mansion steps.

"You might say I'm being subpoenaed. It's a difficult writ to deny, Markham. My calendar's light, I haven't any other obligations."

Ham had given Doc an accurate estimate of his father-in-law. Despite the chasm of class that lay between them he thought him an admirable choice, and told him so.

"Condolences are premature," the judge quavered. "My mind's not made up. It could be messy — I'd be walking in blind. Why, I don't even know the name of the fool chairman."

"Sam Theanapolis," Ham supplied.

The mustache wiggled, and for a tremulous moment Ham thought he was going to ask if Sam were honorable. But the governor's invitation was a painful subject. He was done with it. In silence he rose, tossing his mutilated stub into a cold fireplace, and over dinner he transferred the conversation to the other side of the world, inquiring intelligently into Ham's travels among remote Himalayan kingdoms. Only after they had reached the sidewalk outside, and had agreed to meet next week at the apartment, did he mention that he was going directly to the Statehouse now.

"Taxi!" he shouted thinly, flailing a hand at what was obviously a police car. He yanked an ancient gold watch from his rumpled suit. "It's almost two o'clock! Impossible, impossible. Why, the damned thing's stopped!" he cried in dismay.

"I've five after seven."

"Then I'm late," the judge said, more cheerfully. "Better wind the works, though, eh?"

They couldn't be wound; he had lost the key. He fumbled in his pants, gave up, returned the watch to another pocket, hailed a department store delivery truck, a Volkswagen Microbus, and another police car, and finally waited, humble and forlorn, while Ham fetched a cab from the corner. As the judge struggled through the low door Ham surrendered to curiosity.

"Have you decided to take the appointment, sir?"

"Eh?" He glanced back, half in and half out, and strived to look judicial. "I — ah — can't say. Have to tell the governor first. Matter of form."

Or of honor, Ham thought, smiling faintly and watching the taxi edge into dense traffic, the judge's head bobbing in the rear window as he frisked himself twice more, once for the key and then, desperately, for the mislaid watch.

**

He found the watch before the cab crunched up the pink granite Statehouse drive, found the key as he mounted the curving shallow steps within. Entering the immense marble office at the stairhead he plucked it from its cache in his wallet, wound the shaft, and shouted triumphantly, "There now. Safe for another eight days!"

The men within exchanged amused glances as he carefully re-pocketed it without setting the hands. They stood in welcome, and the youngest, a portly towhead in his forties, led him to a brocaded wing chair while the oldest watched blankly from his revolving seat of authority behind a gleaming rosewood desk. Governor Blandford had the look of the hopelessly senile politician — the flaccidity, the turkey gobbler's neck, the big sagging belly. Though five years younger than the judge, he was rapidly approaching the grave, speeded by his alcoholic diet. His hands shook incessantly, his voice was an echo.

"Extremely kind of you to come at this rude hour, Roger," he almost whispered. And offering a ghostly joke he said, "We all know how you dislike forgoing your brandy."

They shared a fraternal chuckle. Ham would have been edgy here; the judge was relaxed. These were the kind of men he knew. Their clothes came from the same tailor, their blessings from the same Episcopalian altar, and apart from Blandford they spoke the same clipped speech. The governor was an upstate farm Republican — "a hewer of wood and drawer of water," the party cadre affectionately called him, but even he hadn't worn denim for a generation, and over the years he had acquired honorary status among the Birmingham elect. He prized it highly. As the gentle laughter subsided he smiled around gratefully and withdrew into a trance of age.

The towhead was the last to hush. He said roguishly, "There's some brandy *here*, by the way. Shall we all have a pony?"

Rather too quickly, Blandford agreed. The towhead bounced over to a sideboard, and the judge, following him with a perplexed gaze, murmured to the man in the armchair opposite him, "Never can remember that fellow's name. He's in your firm, isn't he Witty?"

"Hewitt, Clare Hewitt," the judge's third greeter murmured back. "Clare's very forceful, sir. He's been party chairman since I resigned."

Stuart Witty was the most conspicuous of the three, if the least attractive. He was short and muscular, with a high domed forehead, bushy black eyebrows, and a trim little mustache. Until he spoke his coal black eyes held you, and then you were aware of his teasing, almost effeminate voice. Meeting him casually you might have guessed much about his life — that he led his profession, played the violin, and was frequently seen on squash courts. Other aspects of his life were obscure, and would have surprised. A handful of bruised men could testify that he was an expert boxer, a handful of women knew him as a proficient lover. The judge, who had dealt with him often from the bench and read the *Star* more often than he had admitted to Ham, thought Frosty Warren had fortuitously summed him up. "Mr. Depth" was a vulgarism, and distasteful. But Witty *was* deep.

The question was whether depth would be enough. The judge had quit the party committee when he put on robes, but once he had been its brains, and across his mind flashed a political map of the state, a crude rhomboid, white where the party was safe and black where the Democratic strongholds were. All the dark stains were in the cities — Birmingham, in the center of the state, and Dudley, Rockton, and Pawnattuck to the southeast. There, where the immigrant tradition was overwhelming, the Republicans could only fight to keep Doc's majority small. In the counties, however, it was all the other way. Apart from a few descendants of old Populist families the farmers voted the straight ticket from habit. Because the rural areas still held the whiphand in the state, they had always provided a wide margin of victory. Despite the national trend toward the Democratic party, registration remained heavily Republican, and nothing, not even foul weather on election day, had ever threatened Blandford.

Witty, however, was of a different stripe. Doubtless he would make a capable executive — he had, in fact, done all the governor's thinking for him lately — but reaching office was another matter. It was Blandford's great appeal that he seemed to embody the harsh virtues of the dirt farmer. He might wince to be called a man of the soil, but it had given him an edge. It had, indeed, accounted for his rise; twenty years before, when he was still a county feed dealer, his rough manner had attracted the party's chief strategists, among them the judge. Now, the judge realized, that edge was gone. In Doc the Democrats had nominated one of the old Populist heirs, a heroic farm strongboy who had eaten his peck of country dirt and looked it. Against him Witty could only seem to be what he so obviously was — a silkstocking, a big slick from Birmingham's most exclusive suburb.

It was a handicap. Probably it wouldn't defeat him, because the organization was strong and the straight ticket tradition even stronger. Still, there was such a thing as insurance, and Witty, as the most brilliant strategist in the party since the judge's retirement, could be counted upon to take out plenty. Which brought them, the judge thought sourly, to the reason he had been called here.

Witty seemed reluctant to take that up. He had spent a decade masterminding the election of others; now at last he was the candidate, and he took an almost childish pleasure in political gewgaws, which he drew from a briefcase beside him in tedious succession. Campaign buttons were distributed to all but the judge, who demurred, murmuring that men on the bench couldn't be walking billboards. Lurid green and orange automobile bumper strips were displayed; then a stack of blotters bearing Witty's picture; then a box of match covers urging voters to pull the right lever. His briefcase empty, Witty leaned back, sampling his brandy, and questioned Hewitt about television appearances, the first report from the *Star*'s straw vote, now imminent, and key issues — covering virtually every aspect of the shaping campaign except the vacancy on State's board of trustees.

Vexed, the judge finally brought it up himself.

"Clare, you don't seriously mean to publish a comic book biography of me?" Witty was asking playfully.

"The contracts are out, Stu. The artist has been sketching for a week."

Witty appealed whimsically to the judge. "Don't injunctive powers cover that?"

"No statute," the judge said aridly. He drew out his watch and deliberately glanced at the face. Two o'clock. Thrusting it back angrily, he said, "But I believe you have other business with me."

They quieted and looked at the governor. This line was his. He hunched forward. "Roger, we've been hoping — I've been hoping you'd see your way to accept my invitation."

The judge lifted his snifter, observing them through a prism. They were friends, and he anticipated no misunderstandings, but before he committed himself it was best to clarify things.

"I take it you're planning to barbecue Mr. River next month."

It was a popular topic. Witty's dark eyes sparkled, Hewitt flushed with enthusiasm. "We're going to roast him, sir," Witty said. "I may say we've found quite a stack of fuel in his life. His legislative demagoguery is a matter of public record, and goes back some time."

Hewitt said, "The record's longer than that. Did you see the *Star?* As a student he was disqualified from playing for State. For State!"

And Witty chirped, "He was wearing a fitted uniform at the time. He'd actually taken his mail-order suit to a haberdasher. Why, that's even better than Walter Reuther combing his hair in public."

The judge tasted his brandy. "I find it pitiful."

"It is!" they said together.

"And a trifle alarming, in the light of this proposal to me. I'm being asked to climb into the brazier while you grill it. *Not* a pleasant prospect."

"Oh, I don't think the governor has that in mind," said Witty, looking sharply at Blandford, who was draining his glass. He set it down hurriedly and said, "No, not at all. I'd scarcely expect a man of your standing to become involved in the campaign, Roger."

"I'm comforted."

"Of course, there is that matter of the stadium's gate receipts surplus, which is never accounted for," Hewitt began, but Witty stopped him with a look, and he finished lamely, "Though that's something we can handle."

"We can handle all old business," Witty said smoothly.

"Then my offices are not required?"

"Old business," Witty repeated, "is already on the books. I doubt the governor would expect a new trustee to wade through it."

"Certainly not," said Blandford. "Clare, is there anything left in that bottle? Thank you, that's fine, thank you very much."

"The only real concern is whether he's financing his present adventure with taxpayer's money," Witty said.

"A legitimate concern," the judge conceded.

"For example, his board is permitting him to remain in the residence of the university president."

"Well, really, that seems trivial. You can scarcely ask the man to move out for a few weeks."

"I should, sir."

"So should I. But we have means. Is he paying rent?"

"A low rent. Absurdly low."

The judge shook his head, "I'm sorry, Witty. That's too thin. I think the board is quite correct."

There was a glum silence. They had hoped for another response. The governor emptied his snifter again and shuffled over to the sideboard; Hewitt watched the brandy bottle anxiously; Witty watched the judge. Doc had agreed to the appointment. They didn't have anyone else. Yet Witty knew the judge wasn't taking advantage of that. He was merely handing down an impartial opinion. Witty had considered his integrity when he had told the governor to submit his name to Doc. The decision had been made then, and was irrevocable.

"I think we can survive without that issue," he said lightly and turned to the sideboard, "Don't you agree, Governor?"

The governor was caught tippling. He had polished off his third glass and was refilling it. "Oh yes," he said thickly, splashing brandy on the rug. "Certainly. Of course."

They were gentlemen; they decided to ignore him. But he wouldn't be ignored. Drunk now, he stumbled back, holding a full snifter like a chalice, and presided groggily from his revolving chair, grunting assent and nodding vehemently as Witty reviewed the issue without which, he felt, his candidacy could not survive.

"There's not a department in the state government that could match River. If his hospital started politicking he could go out of Birmingham with a majority of a hundred thousand, and his county agents are known on thirty thousand farms. Every vote," he said, measuring his words, "would be bought with taxes."

The judge could only nod. "It would be unscrupulous."

"Then we're agreed."

"Oh, no question," the judge said peevishly, drumming his fingers on the chair arm. He was tired of watching Blandford drink himself into a stupor, tired of Witty's covetous glances at the great governor's desk. Aspiration for office, he knew, was an exhausting passion. His own had been purged in his youth, in a disastrous congressional election whose most memorable moment, after forty years, was the look that had crossed a factory mechanic's face when the judge, after shaking his hand, had absent-mindedly wiped his own palm on a silk handkerchief. Defeat had stung at the time, but he didn't regret it now. Instead he felt for Witty the same pity that touched him when he thought of Doc in that tailored uniform — a compassion faintly tinged with contempt. Democracy needed the yearners, he supposed, but umpires were also necessary, and a man of honor was happier on the bench. As though delivering a formal verdict he repeated, more solemnly, "There's no question whatever. It would be quite outrageous."

Witty's thick eyebrows arched. "Then you accept the appointment?"

The judge's fingers beat a tattoo. Being an umpire, he thought ironically, could also be disagreeable.

Rap, rap.

"It's clear I should use my own judgment?"

"Oh, absolutely."

"And I shan't suffer reproaches, whatever happens?"

"Never. It would be unthinkable."

Rap, rap, rap.

"In that event I have no choice," he said reluctantly. "The answer is affirmative." Hewitt beamed, Blandford smiled stupidly, and Witty sighed. The judge asked, "When is the next meeting? I assume they meet."

Witty sighed again. "I'm afraid it's tomorrow morning."

"Tomorrow? Now that *is* outrageous."

"Apparently they always meet just before the first football game. It may be inconvenient for you."

"It is. Damned inconvenient. But I'll go. Provided"—he was studying his timepiece again with exasperation—"one of you can give me the correct time."

"It's seven-fifty-two," Hewitt said precisely, and at that instant the desk telephone rang.

Blandford answered, opening a small farce which the judge, adjusting hands, watched with cynical amusement. At first the others listened indifferently as the governor spoke in monosyllables. Gradusually it appeared that he was too muddled to take the call, and at last he confessed it. Covering the mouthpiece inefficiently he mumbled to them that he couldn't make head nor tail out of this; it sounded like Hallam Caulkin at the *Star*, but he was talking in numbers. Hewitt and Witty were electrified. Obviously these were straw vote figures. They sprang up, lunging for the phone. Blandford gave a bleat of distress; Hewitt had upset his glass. In the confusion the connection was broken, and Witty had to call back. Reaching Caulkin, he began to jabber excitedly. The judge decided this was an auspicious moment for his exit. He rose quietly and had reached the door when Witty hung up and cried jubilantly, "They've tabulated their first poll — it'll be in the morning paper. I've got sixty-three per cent."

Only the judge withheld congratulations. "*I've* got to go to Gideon," he said calmly. "Need I point out that this will make me feel like a hostage?"

They reassured him; he shook his head, inquired when the next poll report would be, and was told it would be in a week.

"Seven days. How convenient! It will remind me to wind my watch," he said lugubriously and trudged out, leaving their three heads — Witty's dome, Hewitt's flaxen mop, and Blandford's stringy gray fringe — bobbing over the desk in cadence. Together they were dabbing at the spilled brandy, wiping it off before the glossy finish was ruined. The governor's stationary was too slick to be absorbent. They were using Witty's campaign blotters.

**

The *Star* poll stunned Doc. At breakfast next morning he pored over the figures, added each column himself, and mumbled in disbelief, "It's fixed, it's a trick."

Newt Albert deprived him of even that. "No, it's on the level," he contradicted. To underscore his own acceptance of it he added blandly, "You know these eggs are terrific?"

"Poultry Department," Doc said dully.

"Really? You'll have to ship me some. You suppose I could have just one more, Mrs. River?"

Sarah rang for the cook, then excused herself. It was an act of veiled hostility. She wasn't openly rude to Newt; she merely ignored him. He was now a frequent lodger at the Mansion, but though she saw that he was served at meals, she withdrew afterward at the first opportunity, and if the conversation turned to politics she would push away an unfinished plate and leave immediately. Newt, watching her suspiciously, wondered this morning whether she could be a secret drinker; Doc, irked and embarrassed, vowed to restrict himself to small talk at lunch. He had vowed that before, and this was the first time in three days he had slipped. Today the provocation had been too great.

"What in thunderation happened?" he wondered aloud, staring at the paper.

Newt speared his egg. It was pointless to tell Doc that this was exactly what was to have been expected; that rigid principles of politics dictated that the majority party, led by a skilled politician, should open the campaign with a heavy advantage. Like many men seeking high office for the first time Doc had convinced himself that once the state knew he was available a magical transformation would follow — that party labels and special interests would vanish in a ground swell of approval. Doc had no faith in Newt's maxims. He believed in grass roots, believed in himself, believed now that something fantastic had gone wrong.

"Don't get in an uproar, Governor," Newt said. "They never elected anybody with one of those things, and we got over a month."

"A month to do what?" Doc said despairingly.

Newt laid his fork down and recited the classic evasion of his trade: he was glad Doc had asked that question. In fact Newt was glad. All week, indeed, he had been praying that the poll would report an honest estimate of their weakness. In humbling Doc the *Star* had performed Newt a great service. Without it Doc might have built his air castle ever higher, until November brought staggering disaster. Now there was time for a dozen measures, and with the football season opening this afternoon and his rugged image increasingly in the public eye their prospects could only improve. This was the abyss. Starting today the campaign would be all climb.

Newt didn't tell Doc that — he liked him running scared — nor, in the library alcove after breakfast, did he press his demand for use of the university services. He hadn't forgotten them. In the end, he was convinced, they would be decisive. But Newt had been studying his man. He understood him now, and knew the time for final ultimatums hadn't arrived. Doc was still following his Alger instincts. Every day they grew weaker, however. He was a born fighter, and the will to win was growing in him. When it possessed him entirely Newt would play his trump. In the meantime, with Doc's dream of effortless glory demolished, they could clear a few other hurdles.

"I'm glad you asked," he repeated, straightening his hand-painted necktie and settling his gnome's belly behind his makeshift card table desk in the alcove, "because I have a few suggestions. Those poll percentages will change when individual people change their minds, you know, and there are ways to help them. One, I might say, is to let them know you're interested. Voters like to be asked."

Doc had been pacing the room distractedly. He halted and said, "You mean shaking more hands?"

Hurdle one, Newt thought. Until today Doc had barnstormed under protest. "That's part of it. Clambakes and flower shows always help. But there are other ways of asking. Like coming out for the right things."

"I've got a good platform."

"Sure you have," Newt said soothingly. "The only trouble is, Stu Witty's got the same one. *He's* for mothers and pets and a low accident rate, too. I'm talking about things you don't put in platforms. Take, for example, that unemployment pocket around Pawnattuck."

"You know I stand —"

"— against hard times. So does your opponent." Newt's voice turned rougher. "But what's Witty going to do about it?"

"I don't recall his saying."

"He hasn't. And neither have you. But you'd better. Unemployment never hurt a Democrat yet, because Democrats can demand help from Washington and Republicans can't; it offends their backers."

"You mean Washington ought to do something."

"Right. Something *specific*. The government should pump contracts into Lockwood Aircraft's Pawnattuck plant until the town's lousy with dough. Witty can't ask for that because our stingy Republican congressmen have been screaming for federal budget cuts. You *can*."

Doc ruminated. He felt manipulated. But: "I believe you're right."

Hurdle two, Newt thought, and quickly tackled slum clearance, farm roads, and parity — a national problem, but fair game in a rural state. He won commitments on each. Doc was even growing enthusiastic. He had avoided shirt-sleeves politics before, not from conviction but because he felt he should hold himself aloof. He had left that feeling with the crumpled *Star* in the dining room, and rather to his surprise he was enjoying himself.

It didn't last. Newt was bracing himself for a big leap. He wished there were some way he could make it seem smaller, but it was the one issue that defied camouflage. He said bluntly, "Of course, nothing will mean a damn unless we get some more cash."

Doc smiled wanly. "Seems to me this came up before." He sank to a straight chair. "I told you then I was about strapped."

"So you make only twelve grand. Where I come from that's Cadillac money, and you got a house thrown in. With no kids you must've saved something."

Pride stirred in Doc. "Is this necessary?"

"I've put it off as long as I can. The party's credit's not much good, and I've used it up this week. How much can I put you down for?"

Almost sheepishly Doc said, "I have fifteen hundred dollars."

Newt had been poised over a pad. He dropped his pencil. "That's *all?*"

"The whole shebang."

He considered an accounting and decided against it. It would have been mortifying to explain the support given relatives, the bad investments made, the failure of Sarah's brother's plumbing business. Instead he gave a prodigal shrug.

"Well, it's not enough," Newt said. "You got any idea what media cost these days? Television film alone is a hundred bucks a minute, and if you really want to blanket the state, even old-fashioned billboards come to ten thousand every month. We can't afford that kind of coverage. But the opposition can. And will. Look, I know these guys. I can practically tell you the Republican outlay within a dime. Witty's billboard dough, *plus* thirty grand on newspaper ads, *plus* forty for radio and TV, *plus* thirty-five for direct mail, *plus* ten on printing, *plus* general expenses — at least another eighty. Add it up: it's nearly a quarter-million. And even though you can't match him, if you cut costs all down the line, the minimum, the absolute rock bottom you can get away with is fifty G's."

"You should have told me," Doc said weakly.

"I tried. But you were always busy, or interested in something else — or taking off down the hill."

Doc flushed guiltily. It was true. He hadn't been able to stay away from the campus. All week he had haunted his office, Tate's office, squad practice.

"You must have some other sources," he said hopefully. "Why even those fellows in the legislature get contributions."

"We can count on a little," Newt conceded. "I've already started milking the ward clubs. The unions are good for a few checks. And if you come out big for Lockwood Aircraft we can make a touch there." Doc flinched — it didn't seem statesmanlike to scheme so — and Newt said aggressively, "Listen, that's the way these things are done. Believe me, it's never been any other way. Even Daniel Webster wouldn't have cleared first base without his fatcats. And take it from me, they got their money's worth."

"We lack fatcats, it seems."

"And how. We got what I said, that's all. When they've turned their pockets out there'll still be a big gap."

Doc hesitated to ask it. "How big?"

"At least fifteen or twenty G's."

"Thousand," Doc said, wishing Newt would stop using gambler's slang.

"Spell it any way you want, we need cash bad." He retrieved his pencil. "You got any suggestions?"

Obviously there was nothing to say. Doc didn't have the money, didn't know where to get it.

A cunning look crept over Newt's face. "How about that file? Your twenty thousand friends."

"The A List." Doc frowned. "But that's for State."

"They're on your side, aren't they?"

"Well, yes, I suppose so. They're backers of the university."

"What's the difference?"

It was moot. Until this fall Doc and State had been one. Now they were separating, and Doc wasn't sure where the line should be drawn.

"It's not quite the same," he said, looking troubled.

"Let's not quibble. That list could make up the ante."

"Don't call it that!" Doc snapped, springing up and striding to the bay window. The morning sun glinted on his reading glasses, giving him an opaque look. "You make an election sound like a poker game."

Newt thought of politics just that way, but he scented victory; he could spare a sop. "Excuse it. My upbringing. Let's say it's a deficit."

Doc's back was to him, hunched, driven. "I don't like this."

"Who has the list?"

"I'm not even sure it would help."

"If it doesn't, you're cut off to the showers. As of now you got less than forty per cent of the vote. *In* case you've forgotten."

It was meant to be a clincher, and it was. Doc looked back palely. "Sam keeps the address plates in his office. Tell him I said it was —" He swallowed. "Tell him you talked to me."

Newt nodded briskly and used the pencil at last, drawing up his day's schedule. Doc felt dismissed. The trustees were gathering, he remembered, and though Tate would preside he decided to sit in. He had never missed a meeting, and it was a way to escape.

Newt called after him, "Be sure to get a blue shirt. On television you're going to need blue." He bent over his notes, belched loudly, and said, "Key of C. Excuse it please."

Doc glowered and left quickly, though passing the last tiers of books he slowed and glanced curiously at the spines for the first time in years, wondering whether it was really true about Webster.

**

Newt hadn't overstated his case. The party was in straits. Manufacturers of campaign buttons were always willing to take his notes, however, and with the flagrant exception of Judge Davies everyone in the Colonial Room wore a bright disk announcing, "I'm for Doc!" As the man they were for entered they rose, smiling and applauding and remarking in stage whispers that the Statehouse would only be a starter; there was no telling how far Doc could go; maybe in another four or five years the other forty-nine states would be talking about him, cheering him, voting for the tough old varsity captain who never said die.

Doc shuffled toward a vacant corner chair, nodding his seamed face and holding his shabby brown hat in both hands. "Much obliged," he said, waving them back to their seats. "But I know I've got an uphill fight ahead of me — unless maybe fellows like you forgot to vote in the *Star's* little private election."

Their laughter was strident, and faintly uneasy. Except for the judge, everyone there had dutifully clipped a poll coupon and sent it in, and like Doc they were shaken by the results. It was typical of him to make a joke out of it, they thought admiringly. In chorus they reassured him, predicted loudly that the tide would quickly shift, suggested he take his old chair by Sam at their head and refused to sit until he did. Tate, alert to the cue, danced over like a frail monkey, insisting he and Doc switch chairs. Doc declined firmly. It was right nice of them, he said, but he was more comfortable over here, and if he was in the way, why, he'd just skedaddle. The dispute lasted over a minute. When it abated Doc was still in his corner, Tate was back beside Sam, and the only man standing was the buttonless judge.

"I'm Roger Davies," he said pleasantly, holding out his hand to Doc. "I'm the new boy."

Doc struggled up. "Didn't know you were coming today. The governor's appointed you, then. Fine, fine."

The board observed their greeting with beamish approval. They had welcomed the judge nervously, wondering what his appointment meant, but there was no malice in them; they sympathized with him as the underdog here; they were anxious he should like them, and the judge, painfully aware of his naked lapel, had assumed a whimsical air that had won them completely. Even Sam, the most partisan man there, had swung his palm with moist enthusiasm. The judge, restraining an impulse to wipe his hand, had then opened a deceptively casual conversation with the provost about university affairs. The talk had ended as Doc entered, and Tate was just beginning to grasp how deliberate it had all been. It occurred to him that in a quarter hour he had been pumped of every significant entry in his annual report.

Sam called the board to order, and Tate informed them that Alvin Swinton, the *Star* reporter assigned to Doc's campaign, had been waiting outside for two hours, hoping to cover the meeting. The judge made more friends by making the motion of rejection. All bodies such as this, he observed, should meet in executive session. Tate flitted out on his pencil legs to break the news to Swinton, and Sam brought up the first entry on the agenda. There were only two: a sketchy account of the progress of Dr. Budge's accreditation team and a proposal that Doc be provided with clerical help during his leave. Both could have awaited the next regular meeting, but the trustees would have come to Gideon for the game this afternoon anyhow, and this way they could submit expense vouchers later. The judge understood that. It seemed an excusable peccadillo. He recalled how the American Bar Association had conveniently moved its convention from New York to London, with all expenses deductible, and he didn't object. Nor did he protest Doc's clerk. She wasn't even a permanent employee of the university. Offering him the services of a student was harmless enough. To do less, indeed, would be churlish.

Budge's team, however, interested the judge, and he began to ask questions. The board was startled. Interruptions at meetings were a novelty, and seemed almost impertinent.

"These — ah — professors from elsewhere. These visitors, so to speak. I take it their report will be vital to Aggie."

He faced a collective frown. Sam testily corrected State's name, and Tate said flutily, "It's merely diagnostic, sir. Naturally if we have any soft spots we want to know about them."

"Naturally. But would a negative report mean academic Siberia for Aggie — ah — State?"

The provost said carefully, "It would mean that we wouldn't be recognized by the New England Association of Colleges and Universities." He smiled around the table, amused at the absurdity of such a verdict, and the trustees smiled back politely. "In that inconceivable event, the N.E.C.U. would put us on temporary suspension."

"Quietly," Doc said suddenly.

The judge twisted around. "Eh?"

"The results wouldn't be divulged," Doc said. "That, too, would be an executive session."

"Why, I should think so! It's not a matter of public record at all. Or in the public interest."

Doc nodded heavily. "I'm glad you agree."

The judge, however, hadn't finished. Years on the bench had given him a perspective, and in Tate's reassurances and Doc's mood he sensed connivance. Fussing with his string tie, he said casually, "When shall we know the results?"

Sam started to hedge, but Tate's session with the judge had convinced him that would be vain. As casually he replied, "In about five weeks."

He might as well have said that they would know before the election; it was on everyone's mind. The judge, turning it over, inquired, "And suppose the report is laudatory. Will it be published then?"

"Can you think of any reason why it shouldn't be?" Sam asked belligerently.

The judge could think of one. Doc was having it both ways. If State won recognition the fact would be proclaimed, and votes influenced; if State didn't, nothing would be said. A scrappy Republican would cry foul, and with some justice. The judge, however, wasn't here to protect political interests. He had made that point last night. He was a trustee of the university, and toying with his tie he concluded that whatever their motives, these men were right — recognition would help State, loss of recognition would be a wound to be hidden until healed.

"No, I'm satisfied," he said. They sat back. But only briefly. Tugging at a tie end and undoing it he asked instantly, "Are we to have any warning? Any preliminary report?"

Tate and Sam exchanged a long look. The provost shuffled his hands. "Dr. Blunt may talk informally with Mr. Theanapolis and me from time to time. As a matter of fact, we're going to see him immediately after this meeting. But there'll be nothing for the board."

The implication was clear — there mustn't be any leaks. Since the only possible leak there was the judge, he was affronted. It wasn't flattering to be considered a spy. Looking back stonily, he murmured that the procedure seemed irregular to him, and while he didn't like to seem perverse he was obliged to take exception to it.

Tate concentrated on his notes, Sam jerked his shoulders indifferently, and Doc made a decision. He had been watching the judge and thinking of Newt. By tonight the name file would be in Newt's hands, by Monday the appeals for contributions would be posted. Twenty thousand addressees couldn't keep a secret; the judge was certain to hear about the mailing. He might misunderstand — might even make an embarrassing statement to the *Star*. It was best to bell the cat now.

"I have a point, Mr. Chairman."

Sam was grateful for the diversion. The judge was beginning to dominate the meeting. "Sure, Governor. That is, as long as you're not offering odds on the game. We don't allow gambling on official time."

The board enjoyed a relaxing laugh, and Doc described the A List to them. Really he was telling only the judge; the others were familiar with it.

"Gallivanting around the state, I've met a lot of fellows who share my outlook on things, and this is a list of their names. A couple of times I've written them asking if they'd like to let the Statehouse know how they feel about State." He took a breath. "Well, I'm going to give those names to Mr. Albert. He's —"

"I know him," said the judge, who also knew that this explanation was for him.

He was being asked to make a finding. It was difficult, because there were so many imponderables: how the list was gathered, why it had been drawn up; whether, in the end, it was the state's property or Doc's. Again he thought of Witty and again he dismissed him. The campaign was irrelevant; the question was ethical.

Everyone was watching him quietly. He plucked aimlessly at his mustache and asked, "Is there any record of this in Birmingham?"

"None," Doc said.

"Did anybody there ask you to do it?"

Doc chuckled. "Golly, no. It's caused them a passel of trouble."

"Then this wasn't a university project?"

"In my view, no."

Another ten minutes, Doc thought, and the judge would be a ringer for Harry Mikel. His tie hung loose, his mustache was all frizzed up, and he had started to scratch himself under his shirt. Maybe he was also a troublemaker like Mikel. Maybe Ham had been wrong. Well, this was the way to find out. Somewhat alarmed, Doc saw that the judge was shifting his chair so he could look directly at the corner. Gazing steadily into Doc's eyes, he said, "There are other instruments of the university whose title is indisputable. Any use of them in a campaign for office would be a clear abuse. This case, however, is a matter of conscience. If you are satisfied, so am I."

Doc wasn't at all satisfied. The verdict was an awl in his heart, and after the meeting he shifted unhappily from foot to foot as the jovial board crowded around him, led by Sam whispering, "You sure picked him right, Doc. I was afraid Blandford was pitching a curve at us, but no, everything's fine."

"He acts like God almighty," Doc said indignantly. "Did you see him stare at me like I was sitting there buck-naked?"

Tate's tenor sang to them over the trustees' heads, "He wanted to tour the campus, so I turned him over to the delightful Jill."

Doc groaned when Tate added that Blunt awaited them in the presidential suite. "*Another* meeting? Thunder*a*tion! Can't you fellows handle it?"

"Mikel and Lutz are with him," said Sam, whispering still. "Harry wants us to give Budge's team a rain check."

Mikel made a difference. Just then Doc needed a target, something to strike. "All right. I've had just about enough of his sass."

He hadn't known Lutz had become a Mikel ally, and entering his office he was amazed to see the Austrian bound up, prepared to take the floor.

"We are all here?" Lutz asked. They were: Mikel and Budge were already seated beneath the gallery, and Tate, Sam, and Doc joined them, blinking at the prospect of what was evidently to be Lutz's maiden speech on administration. He had spent a sleepless night working himself up for it; his eyes were almost feverish. "Nobody else coming? Good. Then let me say one thing." He took a combative stance and spluttered, "We must stop this evaluation while it can be stopped. I do not say we will fail — I only say there is a chance. We have no right to take that chance. Instead we must take the way out. While there is time."

Exhausted, he sank to a chair and propped his bullet head on one stubby, trembling hand. It took the semicircle of listeners a moment to recover. From Lutz this outburst was momentous. Mikel, who had incited it, examined a toothpaste stain on his tie and murmured, "Clio avenged! But, my dear Eric, you are too kind. Our indictment is uglier than that."

Sam made a rude noise with his lips. Doc also glanced darkly at Mikel, but he found it impossible to be angry with Lutz. Until now he had left this matter to Tate. Intervention at this point was almost impossible; even an excessive display of interest would be discourteous to the provost. Nevertheless he wondered how far things had gone, and turning to Budge he inquired.

The team chairman made a bridge of his hands. "We are moving as quickly as we can. You requested a statement the first week in November, and I'm hopeful we won't let you down."

"Is it even possible for us to withdraw?"

"Just possible — now. Of course, there would be a good many ruffled feelings, but it could be managed."

"And later?"

"After Monday it would be impracticable. The team members begin to draft their appraisals then, and once they start the report must go to your trustees. And, of course, to the N.E.C.U." He dropped his hands to his lap. "It's not merely a matter of procedure, you know. Unless specific findings were made we would be harassed with inquiries from other members of our disciplines, rumors would be uncontrollable — and, of course," he added with feeble humor, "our institutions would feel cheated. We're all on leave at the N.E.C.U.'s request."

There was a note of finality to it. Doc gave Tate a nervous look, and Sam said anxiously, "How are we doing so far?"

Budge was impassive. "I can't tell you. I don't know. There are many of us here, you know, and each man is deep in his own field. Only when we start fitting the pieces together will we have any idea of the picture we're making. Then we'll have to reach a general agreement and translate it into words."

Mikel cleared his throat creakily, and Lutz, who had been furtively watching him, made a gesture of consternation. Until now everyone had been civil, a hopeful sign; Doc was reasonable unless provoked. But Mikel was a confirmed spoiler. He couldn't restrain himself.

"I believe several of your colleagues are studying our admissions office," he said to Budge. "I assume they've discovered that veterans need no high school diplomas to matriculate here."

Tate said quickly, "That's not unique," and Doc snapped, "I started that practice, and I'm proud of it. A boy who has served his country is entitled to consideration."

Mikel lifted his eyes. "I also am a war hero. I have old wounds, and they ache when I consider our patriotic folly — or, for that matter, our examination policy. Others of Blunt's associates have begun poking into it. I wonder whether they have recovered from the fact that in some of our courses there are *no* examinations — that in lieu of a final the students discuss whether the classes have been interesting or vote on the popularity of the teacher."

He gazed mockingly at Tate, who said sharply, "I don't imagine you carry many elections, Harry."

"Unlike our Prexy, I am inept at canvassing," Mikel flared back. "And that, of course, is what this is all about. Is anyone deceived by the request for a report the first week in November — just before the state goes to the polls? I'm amazed, genuinely amazed, that the reputation of this institution should be a pawn in a play for power."

Doc was on his feet, but Mikel hadn't finished. He was crooking a finger at Tate.

"And *you*. You are even more despicable. Oh, I recognize your fine Italian hand. You are quite indifferent to the results of this appalling inquiry. Indeed, I strongly suspect that you hope for a negative finding, so you can rectify everything — as the new Bwana." He looked from Doc to Tate, and laughed gratingly. As though in response, a ripple of applause was heard outside, coming from the direction of the Student Union. Mikel glanced that way and laughed again. "Our rehearsing Titanettes! The weekly leg show! Oh, it's marvelous, so marvelous — flesh and intrigue and you two presiding over it all like villains in a tawdry melodrama!"

The provost sat rigid. Mikel had never gone so far with him, even in private. Out of the corner of his eye he saw Budge sitting motionless, with only a throbbing neck vein betraying emotion, and he went cold around the lips. He couldn't move, couldn't speak; he wasn't a man of action.

But Doc was. In a hard voice he told Mikel, "You're behaving like some bonehead in a police lineup."

"Tarantara!" Mikel sneered.

"Like an old rip."

"*Tu quoque.*"

"Too what?"

"You're another."

Doc loomed over him. "I think you'd better go."

Mikel left slowly, scuffing his sneakers, and paused deliberately on the threshold to light a cigarette. Doc, slamming the door behind him, looked the picture of outrage. It was illusory. Tate felt humiliation, Lutz despair, Sam indignation, and Budge embarrassment, but Doc remained intent on the purpose of their meeting. The possibility of a bad report was alarming. Crossing restlessly to the window he saw Jill on the bright sward outside, leading the judge down a steep green slope. She was springing from step to step and talking gaily; he was rummaging in his pockets, shedding tobacco flakes behind. It struck Doc that the judge was really the key to the evaluation. He knew about Budge's team and would be curious if it left — which was a reason for going ahead. And he was pledged to silence about it — another reason, and the decisive one. Since any critical finding would be restricted to the N.E.C.U. and the trustees, Doc saw no way State could be hurt. Over his shoulder he said, "I'm sorry you've been inconvenienced, Dr. Budge. My view is that you should continue your work." Because he was technically on leave he added, "I take it you agree, Tate?"

Tate did; he rallied and managed a sickly smile of triumph for Lutz, who was too forlorn to notice. Doc touched his forehead in farewell. They filed out, Sam bringing up the rear like an obese straggler, and left him alone, rubbing the knuckles of one hand on the open palm of the other.

He scarcely heard the latch click. The issue had been resolved, but its implications had led him into a bleak reverie. Last month he had convinced himself that he merely wanted to see the accreditation completed before he became governor-elect, and it was true, he thought, impatiently shifting hands; it *was*. Still, he knew that the evaluation would have proceeded more smoothly if he hadn't set a deadline. If he hadn't entered the race there would have been no deadline — and no scene here this morning. This latest incident was part of a series, all dating back to the day he had announced his candidacy. In subtle exchanges he had been thwarted by Ham Markham, Lutz, Mikel — even by Sarah, in his own home. It was as though each episode was a strand spliced to the last, the whole a net caging and thwarting him. The prospect of the campaign should have been invigorating. He had always enjoyed challenges, and his greatest test lay just ahead. Instead he felt confined. Wherever he turned there were people whose wills conflicted with his, and their wills were really one: they didn't want him to run.

Doc thought of Newt Albert and felt a weight on his shoulders, a constriction within. Newt wanted him to run, but he frustrated him most, because he was trying to remake him into a conventional candidate, prepared to sacrifice all dignity in a struggle for public favor. Doc didn't mind struggling. And he had schemed and wheedled before — for State. Now, however, he was being asked to do it for himself, and the difference tormented him. If he had been entirely free of ambition he could have resisted Newt. If possessed by it, he could have submitted. He was neither. He was torn. Newt had judged him rightly in the library. He wanted to be governor more than he had ever wanted anything in his life. But laced into the net restraining him, strengthening it everywhere, was a yearning to be himself. Newt couldn't permit that. He insisted that Doc surrender self and agree that though the voice of the candidate would be Jacob's, the hands must be the hands of Esau.

Conscience, then, was Doc's affliction; that was why he had bristled when the judge had flung the word at him, and that was what kindled him now when he saw the judge halt at the bottom of the grassy slope and smilingly exhibit his gold timepiece to Jill. If that isn't just like a Percy, Doc thought contemptuously. Scoots up from the big city for a few hours, struts around like he owns the place, and now he has to show a little coed what a busy nabob he is. The other trustees can spare an afternoon to root for State, but not *him. He's* too high and mighty.

The judge was in fact preparing to leave before the game, but he hadn't told Jill so. Doc had been too deep in thought to hear Archer's chimes strike the hour. He couldn't know that the old man was merely proud — and a trifle surprised — to find his watch running on time.

**

Earlier that morning, long before Newt Albert polished off his fourth Poultry Husbandry Department egg and Harry Mikel soiled his necktie — even before the judge shuffled out of his Birmingham apartment, crawled into the rear of his old Packard, and gruffly ordered his chauffeur to Gideon — Ham Markham had rolled over on his lumpy College Inne mattress and opened one eye. His own shivering had awakened him. It was cold and just sunrise, he noticed; the ratty carpet beside his bed was bleary with the day's first light, olive and growing but without warmth. The day of the big game dawned crisp and clear, he thought fuzzily, reaching for a blanket and remembering how he and Spook had never been able to sleep Saturday mornings in the autumn. Probably some State players were awake right now, he thought, wide-eyed and twitching and trying to shake off nightmares of fumbles and dropped passes. It was a comforting thought in middle age, and he was dozing off with it when a rattling alarm clock in the next room corroborated him. A halfback was over there, stirring.

Opéra bouffe, Ham thought, burying his face in the pillow. Comic strip stuff. Old Howard slapstick. Red Stacy and Daffy Dix ought to wear baggy pants and grease paint and carry tambourines. Also a lucky horseshoe — especially for Red. His coach was bound to break out the squad before breakfast. Ham wondered how carefully the lovers covered their tracks. From fragments overhead on other nights he gathered Red depended on a conniving teammate; Daffy, on her sorority alibi and the trusting Mr. Dix. That seemed to be about it, apart from elemental precautions entering and leaving here. Two popular students couldn't stroll in and out of the College Inne during the day, so they crept in singly after dark and slipped away early on the clock's signal. Not much good for Red's career,

Ham thought, yawning. A growing boy needs his rest. So does a graduate student, he thought, remembering Daffy's cuckolded husband alone with her baby. And so does a hotshot reporter, especially when he's scheduled to speak before the Peabody chapel in two hours . . .

Ham had been lulling himself back to sleep. The recollection that he had agreed to lecture on India this morning brought him out of bed with a leap. More than rest he needed preparation — notes, an outline, something to say. He had planned to work on that last night, but the judge's summons to Birmingham had sponged it from his mind, and now his mind was a void. If it hadn't been for Red's alarm, he thought wryly, hopping into his trousers, he might have slept through. Now he had been rescued, probably only to make a fool of himself on the Peabody podium, stammering, splitting infinitives, babbling journalistic clichés and generally sustaining Peabody suspicions that any State graduate with literary pretentions must be a fraud.

Sometime in the next two hours he would have to settle on a subject. The best plan was to drive to an all-night G.A.R. Highway diner which Sol Feinblatt, an early riser, had recommended. After several cups of black coffee he could scribble an introduction, and he'd just have to pray the students would strike some spark in him after that. Trembling hard now, because he was both chilled and apprehensive, he buttoned his thin Indian duck coat, snatched up a pad and pencil, and hurried out.

On the landing he collided with Daffy Dix.

"*Oh!*" she gasped, reeling back. "Mr. *Mark*ham!"

"Well, if it isn't Hambo Cornball!" muttered Red, behind her. "You casing this joint, Hambo?"

"I live here," Ham said slowly, trying to look poised.

Poise was difficult on the landing. Leading off the second floor hall, it was a tiny recess bordered on two sides with hideous flowered wallpaper, with descending stairs on the third side and, on the fourth, a little step from the corridor. This step was just outside Ham's door. In the rush of departure he had taken it blindly, and now he, Daffy, and Red were wedged together. It was an awkward meeting, but Ham was too startled to withdraw, and they were waiting for him, saying *your move* with their eyes — Red grinning, Daffy watching vigilantly like a cornered cat. There seemed no way to leave gracefully. They began jabbering about the weather. Hugging her Marseilles sailor pullover to her Bermudas Daffy said, "Gets cold up here sudden."

Ham said, "This house always was an iceberg."

Red said, "I almost froze to my sheet."

Polite conversation at dawn. It was idiotic, and Ham felt a wild impulse to bet them their bed had been warmer than his. Yet his embarrassment, he realized, wasn't general. Red had been taken off guard, but now he was getting a puckish pleasure from all this. There was a kind of hobo insouciance about him. He was playing with his jacket zipper, and his freckled face looked ready to crease in a what-the-hell grin. Daffy was more solemn. Her doll's face was thoughtful, her lovely eyes never left Ham's. She was unruffled, however, and it occurred to him that some girls actually flourish on sin. Daffy had dressed in haste, without lipstick. Her pony tail was uncombed. Nevertheless her skin glowed; she was blooming and vibrant.

The topic of weather was exhausted. Still they lingered, and Ham groped for words. He wanted to scare them, argue with them, plead with them to quit seeing each other or at least to go elsewhere, but he was dumb; Daffy inhibited him, and his mind was fogged with sleep. He was about to give up and wave them on when he heard a slipper shuffle on the bare hall floor behind him, and, glancing back, was horrified to see Al Swinton approaching from the flush in a frazzled gray bathrobe with his razor, toothbrush, and false teeth in hand. Al saw Ham and snapped his teeth in place.

"Hi, Buddy. Cold as a witch's teat, huh?" Daffy came into view, and he ducked his head. "Oh, what I said. Say, I don't believe I've had the pleasure."

Gloomily Ham said, "This is Al Swinton from the *Star*."

"You write drama?" Daffy asked instantly. Ham, grateful for little things, saw she wasn't carrying her baton.

"Or sports?" asked Red.

Al shook his head twice. His little mackerel eyes were glittering with curiosity, and Ham resigned himself to finishing the introduction. "I want you to meet some friends, Al." He took a breath; there was no help for it: "This is Mr. and Mrs —"

"Jonson," Red said quickly. "J-o-n-s-o-n. Some people spell it with an h."

It was an old trick. Al, who had taken girls to motels under the names of Smythe, Lewiss, and Peersun, hoping the clerk would believe no one would be so finicky about the orthography of a false name, saw through it. He looked Daffy over admiringly and reached across the cramped space, pumping Red's hand in congratulation. Red looked pleased; Daffy took it calmly. She even preened herself a little, though that was rote; in his bathrobe Al was unprepossessing.

He was an excuse for the Jonsons to leave, however. On a nod from Red, Daffy murmured farewells and tiptoed down the stairs. Al watched her go with real regret. "You been holding out on me, Buddy," he said after Red had followed. "Look at the way she twitches that tail!" He made a sound like escaping steam. "Is that kid with her in college?"

Daffy, whom Al hadn't even considered college material, left the Inne immediately. Red remained downstairs, waiting in the hall until she had cleared the block. Ham peered down at his unshaven face, the dull eyes and the slack mouth, and said evasively, "No, Mr. Jonson's not being taught anything. I don't think he's seen a textbook in a long time. If ever."

"Town boy, huh?" Al said absently. Something else was on his mind—he had come here to waken Ham. "Say, where'd you go last night?"

"I had to visit a relative."

"You sure you weren't looking for Judge Davies?"

"I was. He's the relative." Ham wondered what Al had heard about him. "He's been offered a place on State's board, if that's what you want to know."

"Offered, hell. He's taken it. The colonel called me last night on that Alexander Graham Bell relic downstairs. Asked me to try to break into their meeting today. Listen, you really related?"

Ham nodded. But he would have to ponder the implications of the judge's acceptance later. Red was opening the front door and reconnoitering the street. He was alone; this was the time to talk to him. Racing down, Ham called back, "Good luck. If you see the judge you can use my name."

"Hey, thanks, buddy," Al said, really thinking it would help.

Once on the sidewalk Red moved fast. Ham barely caught up, and even then Red tried to shake him off. "Look, man, I got problems. I got to get where I'm supposed to be *now*."

Ham had to agree to drive him to the Athletic Dorm. In the car

Red propped his knees against the dash. "Now don't tell me what's on your mind. Just let me guess. You're all shook up about me ruining that poor li'l Southern belle."

"Not exactly."

"Good. Because I could tell you some things about Daff that would curl your hair — your *short* hair, Hambo. She was gash while I was still a Little Leaguer."

"No argument. I believe it. In Bombay they put sexpots like her in cages."

Red crowed. "Daff in a cage! You know, that's not a bad idea."

"As long as you have the key."

"You know it. But just remember — this ball we're having is her idea, not mine."

"And how you hate it."

Red gloated.

"I'm not worried about what happens to her," Ham said evenly. "Or to you."

"Then what's grabbing you?"

"State. And Doc River."

In mock fervor Red hummed a few bars of State's alma mater, a theft from Cornell. He broke off and turned suddenly, like a ferocious cockatoo. "Look, don't give me that jazz. I've had it from the coach up to here. We got to chew up every team on the schedule, run up the score week after week so the man upstairs will win big the first Tuesday in November. O.K. I'm being paid to put out. So I'll deliver. I know my biz. If I don't and I get clobbered this afternoon you can flip — one more reaming won't hurt. But what I do for kicks now and afterward is strictly up to me. So put away your violin. *And* your music."

His voice was meant to be biting, and it bit deep. Ham hadn't known things were this bad. Mikel had warned him, but Mikel's hyperbole was one thing; cynical wisdom from a boy of twenty was worse. Ham concentrated on the road, avoiding Red's glittering eyes. If the coach really had laid it on the line to Red he should be fired. But the coach couldn't be alone. He didn't decide this kind of policy. A word had been passed to him, and he was passing it along. The shocking thing was that it was so open. The strategy of Tate's coalition had been given the dignity of a syllabus. Ham had lied to Al after all. Red really was being educated. And he was apt, *so* apt. In his way Red was as faithful to his catechism as Ham was to his own. Ham had been trained in State's Depression creed: defend the barricade, fight injustice, defy the special privilege behind Peabody's gate. Now State no longer had a barricade. It had acquired a gaudy gate of its own and other motives. Red, belonging to the new time, recited alien watchwords: put out; deliver; know your biz. And, in the writhing night later, reap, ravish, enjoy.

They were approaching the dorm, one of the new State's Georgian piles. Red sat up. "This is my stop, driver. I'll walk from here."

He stepped out, and Ham made a final appeal. "I'm telling you. If that man you just met catches on, he'll crucify you."

"So maybe we'll shack up somewhere else." He made it sound like a favor.

"Listen," Ham said desperately, "if you're so cocky, why do you cover up at all?"

Red slammed the door. "What've you got for a brain, bubble gum? Don't you know you can't clip when the ref's looking, or walk around with your fly open? People expect a show. They make a stink if they don't get it, every time. Exhibit A: the Kat House is out of bounds for me because Daff started making eyes at number one and the housemother got sore."

"Not at you," Ham said with faint bitterness.

"No? You mean she likes me?" He propped his hands on his hips and smiled vainly. "Say, that's right, you know Mrs. O'Donnell. She's not bad, if you get what I mean. I mean, considering. Nice, if she'd quit wearing shrouds."

Ham should have been offended, but he wasn't. Red was merely bowing before the only idols he knew. Preferring his own and pitying him a little, Ham made a little movement of conciliation. "Look. Take care of yourself today. And whatever happens, don't blame Doc. You'd be surprised at the things you know and he doesn't."

Red was already strutting away. "Grow up, cornball. Daddy-O don't know what he don't *want* to know."

The diner's coffee was strong and scalding, but Ham couldn't concentrate on India. Now in the first week of the football season the diner jukebox carried a collegiate selection, and the waitress kept feeding it. She was partial to Gideon's colleges. Her favorites were Peabody's "Tartan Kilt Song"—which reminded Ham of his imminent lecture—and, even worse, his own alma mater. Each time the mechanical needle dropped to that disk he heard in the echo chambers of his mind Red's derisive voice, droning the tune. He stared moodily at his blank pad, wondering which way duty lay. Until now he hadn't told anyone Red and Daffy were using the Inne. Mikel's reminder of his own night there with Kit had singed him; somehow it seemed wrong for him to cast the first stone. But now Al Swinton was involved. The consequences could be ugly unless someone acted, and the only man who knew the truth was himself. He had to make a move somewhere. But where, he wondered, *where* . . .

The "Kilt Song" ended with a male quartet fading away. It was the alma mater's turn. The waitress slipped a dime in the slot.

> *Fair and fairly shall thou always*
> *Be beloved, great*
> *Blue and true through later gray days*
> *Sainted symbol, State!*
> *Ever, always, our eternal*
> *Shrine and temple be* . . .

Someone had switched off the juke. Ham looked up gratefully and saw Sol Feinblatt, ludicrous in a mauve derby, grinning at the indignant waitress. "I hail from Cornell," he explained, depositing a placatory coin on the counter. "That song and yours truly have had it. Well! Mr. Markham!" He took the stool next to Ham. "Didn't know you were an early bird."

"I've got to lecture at Peabody in half an hour," Ham said dully, looking at the diner clock, "and I don't even know what I'm going to talk about."

"Mind's a blank, eh?" He chuckled heartlessly.

Ham examined Sol's hat, carefully knotted tie, and brilliant shoes. "Looks like you're giving some coed a treat."

"No coed. This P.M. I escort Madame O'Donnell to the stadium. You will find us in Section A, wielding pennants."

It was strange to think of Kit with a date, stranger for the date to be Sol. His hair was kinky, his jowls permanently blistered with impetigo. If Kit married a Jew her family would turn her out. But probably they had disowned her after the divorce anyhow, and Sol did have a raffish charm — and a woman in her late thirties, with a child, couldn't be coy.

The waitress, walleyed, flipped the juke back on.

> . . . *Never shall we leave thy altar*
> — *Loyal, faithful, we!*

Sol groaned. "Some days you can't make a dime. Or give one away." He glanced at Ham curiously. "You *like* that slop?"

For Ham was looking muddy again. Kit was the one, he was thinking. Let her cast the stone. She had a stake — she wanted Daffy's neck — and as a professional shepherd of coeds she had an official motive. For a fleeting moment he thought Kit also might be daunted by memories of the Inne, by that sweet, faraway night of pledges and tender murmurs that even now, with the pledges long broken and the murmurs silenced, could evoke remorse. He shook it off. As Dancy had told him a dozen times, women were more practical about these things than men. Kit could take care of herself. And he had worried enough about the Jonsons.

Speaking rapidly and furtively, he told Sol their story.

Sol had a bachelor's worldliness. He had heard the rumors about Red and Daffy, and news that they were renting a room was diverting. When Ham mentioned Al, however, his eyes widened. "My, my. The plot gets positively gooey. You think your fellow minion of the press would share all this with his readers?"

"In railroad type."

"Love nest bared," Sol said softly. "Campus cutie cuts capers."

"Keep it quiet. But tell Kit."

"Why Kit?"

"Daffy's a Bag, isn't she?"

"Please."

"All right, a Theta. She's in and out of the house, and Kit's close to the dean of women. Not much of this will be news to her anyhow. Just the details. The important thing is to move fast — Al's going to be at that game, too. From the press box he's sure to recognize Daffy, and if she goes back to the Inne tonight he'll ambush her with a Rolleiflex. So don't wait. Phone Kit. *Now.*"

"You sound like an ad."

"I mean it."

"O.K., O.K. Only relax; it's nothing to get tense about. Incidentally, why can't you call her? Aren't you two speaking?"

Ham looked aside. "I told you, I've got to lecture. Right away." He slid off his stool.

Under the derby Sol's eyes were shrewd. "Every time I mentioned you to her this week she changed the subject."

"I'm going to talk about Nehru," Ham said impulsively and fled.

Crossing the elmed Peabody lawn, he was too anxious for in-the-enemy-camp feelings. The college's peppery young dean of students greeted him enthusiastically on the chapel steps, and together they entered a long hall with the homely, Spartan look of a New England antique. Stained-glass windows, each donated by a nineteenth century class, shed a rainbow wash of morning light on a bare hall whose benches, blackened with age, were crowded with yawning boys in various stages of undress. Chapel was still compulsory at Peabody, the dean explained, leading him down the center aisle, though Ham mustn't take this to mean there wasn't great interest in his talk; over a score of faculty had come voluntarily. Very unusual, he whispered, pawing at his unruly blond hair. *Most* unusual, and fittingly so. And what would Mr. Markham's topic be? Ah. Splendid. If Mr. Markham would just sit right there, in that pew, that was fine, the Professor of Religion would run through the prayers first.

The prayers were Anglican and brief. Ham had scarcely collected himself when he heard his introduction, also brief. A moment later he stood alone on the simple oak lectern, studying the blur of young faces and thinking, so this is the Peabody elite, this guileless nursery. He considered opening with a joke and realized he hadn't any. A metronome was clicking in his mind. Time was passing, they were waiting.

"Near New Delhi's India Gate a marble statue of King George V gazes stonily across Prince's Park," he began, feeling graven himself. "The scene he observes has changed mightily in the last twelve years. Today George's supreme role is played by Pandit Nehru. India is going to change still more when Nehru dies, too, because the hard fact is that there's no heir to his responsibilities. I doubt that even a committee could be found to do his work. Certainly there's no such committee in the capital. Certainly his cabinet isn't it. No new leader has emerged to take his place, because when the grant of independence ended the conflict between India and Britain, a kindling spark died. India's old targets are down, her battle won, her curtain drawn, and though a new curtain is rising, the setting has shifted, and the actors are confused."

There was a slight catch in his throat. To him it sounded as though he were gagging. He was astonished no one noticed it — that even the drowsiest listeners, indeed, looked rapt.

**

Daffy Dix also had an audience that morning, also rapt. Before each home game State's choreographer rehearsed her nine Titanettes on the Student Union terrace, and these pregame runthroughs, as the choreographer called them, had become part of the football week-end ritual, as important as the Friday night rallies and far better attended. Over a thousand admiring students formed a vast circle within which Daffy, pirouetting faultlessly, led the eight other cheerleaders in marches, countermarches, baton tosses, and locomotives, each executed with a precision that evoked continuing ripples of applause.

It was this applause which Harry Mikel had heard rattling on the windows of Doc's office, and it was variously inspired. Titanette costumes were frank — this year they were tight white turtlenecked sweaters embellished with the letter "S," tighter blue velvet toreador pants, and no shoes — and boys were appreciative. Girls also clapped, however, because the routines were carried off with a professional flair and Daffy's sense of rhythm was superb. She had instinctive stage presence. There was more to her appeal than swinging hips, arching breasts, and spreading thighs. Her figure was conspicuous, but many were more enchanted by the expression on her face — a sly, barely restrained smile, as though she knew a delightful secret and wished she could share it. Curiously, she was quite unconscious of this. Often students had stopped her on campus after drills and complimented her on it, and she had always been puzzled. It was too subtle for her. She knew her body was good, and she believed that was the ultimate for a woman, the only and the one.

"All right, that wraps it up!" bellowed the choreographer, a squat, powerful woman of fifty furtively known as Hotflash. Hotflash had a peremptory manner, carried herself like a coach, and wore a man's sweatsuit and a whistle, which she now blew twice. Her troupe came smartly to attention. "Turn in your suits and meet me in the dressing room at one sharp," she shouted huskily. "Dix! Come over here."

Daffy's slyness had vanished, she had lost her secret. Once more she was the alert, provocative doll, wondering what was up and what was in it for her. Shuffling over through the dissolving crowd, mechanically acknowledging congratulations, she saw a neatly dressed, middle-aged man standing on the Student Union steps beside Hotflash, grinning at her and showing two gold teeth.

"This is Mr. Bauer, one of the university's trustees," Hotflash said importantly. "He caught the end of the show and liked it."

"It was great!" the man said enthusiastically, taking Daffy's hand. "You'll be an inspiration to the team all season, I'm sure."

Paul Bauer was a successful Dudley insurance man with a wife and four daughters, none of whom had ever looked at him as Daffy was looking now. Her lids dropped a fraction, her lips flickered with promise, and leaning toward him she gave his hand a slight, suggestive squeeze — the best she could do under the circumstances, and offered with real enthusiasm, for she knew who Bauer was. He was chairman of the Alumni Athletic Committee, the committee that picked the Gridiron Queen.

"We do our level best," she said in her warmest drawl, "and Miss Hatch" — she briefly turned her adoring eyes on Hotflash, whom she really loathed — "does help us to beat all."

"Well, well!" Bauer's grin widened, exposing a third gold tooth. "I didn't know Miss Dix was from the Southland!"

"*Mrs.* Dix," Hotflash said maliciously, and Daffy could have slit her throat. All Bauer's teeth disappeared.

"What's the matter?" Daffy asked breathlessly, still clinging to him. He glanced doubtfully at her hand, and she jerked it back.

"Why it's nothing, not a thing." He avoided her eyes. "I was merely thinking about a committee I'm on."

"Athletic Committee?" asked Daffy. She couldn't help it. Her heart was pounding.

Hotflash said smugly what Bauer couldn't bring himself to say at all. "Mr. Bauer means that the Gridiron Queen has always been a single girl."

Daffy felt wounded. Argument was hopeless, and she hung her head, ashamed of her marriage. Bauer made a gesture of appeasement. "Of course, it won't be decided for weeks, and we have to get many opinions, including the squad's." And repeating the line that had won him the besotted look, the promise, and the squeeze, he said, "I'm sure you'll be a real fine inspiration to them."

Daffy took some hope from that, and inwardly she brightened when he glanced at his watch and remarked that he'd better run over and see what shape Red Stacy was in. Outwardly she kept her hangdog air, however. It had extorted one concession from him; she decided it was good politics. In a pathetic tone she allowed that whatever happened, she was right glad he'd liked what he'd seen, and it had been mighty nice of him to say so. He patted her hand clumsily. Hotflash impatiently shifted sweat-suited legs. They formed a mournful tableau until Bauer left disconsolately; then Hotflash snapped that Daffy had better hand that suit over pronto, and Daffy, with the hipswitch Al Swinton had admired, trotted off to resume the schedule of her life.

It was a complicated schedule, and expensive. Being a Titanette, mistress, student, wife, and mother — roughly their priorities — cost her a great deal, and her husband still more. She was always on the move within a quadrangle bounded by the women's gym, the Theta house, the College Inne, and University Village. In each of the first three she kept skeleton wardrobes, and though most of her clothes were home there was considerable duplication, chiefly in lingerie. Daffy spent a lot on lingerie. It had a significance for her. Until she met Jerry Dix on a Louisville street corner she had been almost entirely dependent upon her father, a coal crane operator who limited her and her mother to one-piece woolen undergarments for winter. Fancier things were worse than extravagance, he told them sternly; they were useful only to women who showed themselves to strangers, and none of his kin was going to turn into one of them. His daughter, who had turned into one at fourteen, had been wearing her mail order union suit when she showed herself to Jerry in a walkup riverfront hotel room, and he had been rude enough to stare at it. He had been paying ever since. She now had over twenty brassières, seven strapless brassières, pants in seven different shades, an array of black and white satin garter belts, and, though she rarely wore them, a dozen slips. At State Jerry's income, from two campus jobs and a subsidy his pharmacist father really couldn't afford, was two hundred dollars a month. Each month an astonishing sum was invested in gossamer.

He had never complained, but lately he had begun to wonder why he didn't see more of it. Daffy was rarely home. Each night he returned from the lab to find a few scribbled lines on the kitchen memo pad: she was needed at the sorority, the baby was across the street, something was in the refrigerator, love and kisses. It was all very hazy to him, though he didn't dream of doubting her. In his preoccupied way he was proud of her campus success. Everyone else considered her important, so he was sure she must be. Jerry was a myopic, unassuming young man with slender stooped shoulders and an unattractive, untidy cowlick; he thought himself lucky to have a talented wife, and if her activities gave her pleasure he was willing to make sacrifices — willing even to forgo real love and real kisses for promissory notes. Daffy's absences, however, were beginning to tell in other ways. The wives across the street were complaining. They were willing to pick up the Dix baby afternoons when the university's child development laboratory closed, but they wanted some respite later. They had housework to do, suppers to prepare, and more and more they were using the village phone booth to call Jerry's lab — Daffy seemed to be forever in transit, unavailable — and suggest he take little Charlie off their hands. He found himself becoming his wife's baby sitter. His class work suffered, he hadn't touched his dissertation in a week, and he had been forced to cut down on his campus jobs. He was worried. He wanted Daffy to have fun. He wanted to give her plenty of money. He didn't want to annoy her, or inconvenience her in any way, and if it hadn't been for little Charlie he would have said nothing. Jerry loved his son with the rapt devotion of a shy father. He kept a log of his weight and an album of infant pictures, and he enjoyed exchanging progress reports over fences with neighborhood mothers. Lately there had been little to report, however, for the baby hadn't been well. He was listless, ate little, and cried often in the night. His father was convinced he missed his mother.

Jerry was standing at the bathinette, attending him, when Daffy flung open the screen door and bounded in, tossing her baton aside.

"How was the runthrough?" he murmured.

"But sensational!" She kissed his cheek dryly and glanced carelessly at the baby. "How's Charlie?"

Another glance would have told her. The baby had diarrhea. Jerry slipped a clean diaper in place and pinned it carefully. "He misses you."

"Oh, I know, it's this awful race, race, race. Sometimes I wish I'd never said yes. But what can you do? The show must go on."

She was squinting in cupboards, looking for peanut butter and jam. Sandwiches were the family staple when she was home. Irritably she asked where he had put things, and he gave directions, peering at her over his octagonal glasses and screwing up courage to speak. Daffy had always awed him. Before Louisville he had been a virgin, and naïvely he had thought that true of her also. He had never stopped wondering what she had seen in him. He regarded himself as nothing, an apprentice tinker of science. And she was so much — so beautiful and radiant today, he thought, folding back the baby's shirt and wishing he could see her at the game.

"Say, you *ought* to come!" she said when he mentioned it.

"One of us has got to be here," he said gently.

Daffy looked blank. "Um. Guess you're right."

Jerry picked up Charlie in both hands and turned to her, holding the baby against his chest like a shield. "Daffy, does the show have to go on all the time?" he began timidly. 'Can't you cut down a little? I don't want you to give up your career," — he accepted her theatrical ambitions without question — "but couldn't somebody else do the sorority work? You mustn't let them pile things on you. It's not fair to you or," he said, dropping his voice and patting Charlie's back — "to us."

She was spreading peanut butter, and she didn't stop. For an awful moment he thought she wasn't going to answer at all. Then, without glancing up, she said flatly, "Look at this place."

Jerry gazed around, perplexed. The cheap maple furniture, rattan rugs, books, and infant paraphernalia were as she had last left them, crammed between scarred plywood walls. He said ruefully, "Same as always."

"You know it." She seized the jam. "Same cubbyhole, same rat-hole." Now she raised her head. Her eyes were slotted, her mouth was tight as a seam. "You think you're going to keep me locked up in this crazy cell?"

"Daffy, I only suggested — "

"Don't give me that. You like it here so much, you can stay. Me — I got a chance to do something big, and I'm going to do it. So quit whining."

Jerry's shoulders were trembling. It was their first quarrel, and affected him deeply. In a tone almost inaudible he said, "I wish we could afford a better unit here, but I don't see how we can even pay the rent on this if the drain doesn't stop."

"That's your worry." She pointed the bread knife at him. "If a man can't give his wife a real roof *and* a few nice things, he's a nothing, a nobody with no call on her."

Charlie had begun to whimper. Jerry rocked him frantically. "Daffy, please! If you have any feelings, consider the baby!"

Daffy didn't. She didn't know how. She couldn't consider Charlie or him, because she hadn't any real feelings, for them or for anyone else. It was the key to her — an abnormal streak of indifference which had been broadening since her teens, unsuspected because she was cunning and had intuitively adapted to society. She herself was unaware of it. Like her stage smirk, which spectators found so charming and which was really a disturbing symptom, it was hidden from her, because she didn't know what happened inside other people and couldn't compare. She knew how they behaved, and by watching them she had become a skilled mimic. In the College Inne she gave Red convincing performances of elation, but they were counterfeit; she felt nothing. Sex is something shared, and Daffy had never learned to share. Toward the world she was neutral, amoral, and frigid, seeking only to wring from it some trophy that would pacify her, not knowing that she could never take satisfaction anywhere, from anything, because she could never give. Charlie was in tears, Jerry close to them. But of the three Daffy, biting her sandwich vindictively, was the unhappiest.

"You're going on this way?" Jerry asked tremulously. She nodded, her mouth full. He clung to the baby. "Will you be home tonight?"

Daffy swallowed. "Depends." There were so many things to think about: Red, Mr. Bauer, and now Jerry. She wondered whether Jerry would make trouble. He had always been a milksop, but he was queer about Charlie, she thought, and when a quiet man kicked up anything could happen. That would *really* fix me with Bauer, she thought uneasily. Her heart was thumping again.

"Jerr—" She tried propitiation. "I'll make it if I can. I swear it. But aren't you all right here nights? Can't you study, or something?"

"Charlie wakes up," he said spiritlessly and walked into the back yard, comforting him.

"Don't be that way, Jerr—look, you left your lunch."

He didn't reply, and she was about to eat it herself when the front door slammed and Jill raced in breathlessly. "Honestly! Some people! Trudy Viggiantti's just a secretary same as me. Talk about airs!"

The complaint was familiar in the Village. Trudy worked in the office of the dean of women, which gave her a peculiar power over other married coeds. From the office she would phone the community booth, arrogantly demanding that official messages be relayed by whoever happened to answer.

"She wants you! Now! Right away!"

"On Saturday?" Daffy was incredulous. Girls were rarely summoned on week ends. "Listen, Hotflash needs me. If Trudy calls back, be a doll and say I wasn't around."

Jill shook her head. "It won't work, Daffy. She said if you weren't there in fifteen minutes the dean was coming over here. Dean Shoemaker her*self! *Over *here!*"

That was even rarer. No one from the dean's office had visited the Village in six months, and in any case routine matters were handled by Miss Shoemaker's associate and vice deans. Her intervention meant something big. It could be disciplinary, Jill thought, watching Jerry through the window and wondering why nobody bothered to tell the mole he wore horns. The powers that be could be taking official recognition of what everybody else knew, she thought fleetingly, but more likely the call had something to do with the game. She decided it was just another sign of Daffy's eminence, and her eyes shone with admiration.

Daffy's eyes were again narrow. In high fury she flung Jerry's sandwich down and walked wordlessly from the house, dragging her baton like a toy. Jill skipped after, eager to carry the story to her own home. She had nearly finished it when she remembered that Daffy, in her fury, had forgotten to change to a skirt. It gave the tale a nice fillip, because shorts were out in the dean's office. Why there was even a *sign* by Trudy's desk, *saying* so, Jill told her delighted husband, whose name was actually Jack.

**

"No shorts allowed!" Trudy cried indignantly, eying the Bermudas. Daffy flicked her baton tip in the sign of the square, and Trudy's rhinestone-rimmed glasses flashed disapproval. "Just you wait," she said grimly. She heard the dean coming. "Now you'll see."

But Trudy was wrong. Without a reprimand or even a frown Miss Shoemaker held her door for Daffy. "Sit down, my dear," she murmured, slipping behind her little Hepplewhite desk.

"I'm supposed to be at the gym at one o'clock, Miss Shoemaker."

"Oh — really?"

The deadline was disconcerting. If the dean accepted it she would be conceding that Daffy's role in the game took precedence over the gravest issue any dean of women could raise. In fact it did, but she could scarcely admit it. The best solution was to pretend time was of no consequence and still press ahead.

"Oh," she repeated. "I see."

She couldn't think how to begin. Her head was still swimming from a round of telephone calls. Usually Miss Shoemaker's Saturday mornings were spent quietly with tea and women's magazines. She had scarcely arrived here today when Kit had telephoned from the Theta house, almost hysterical with anger. Sol Feinblatt had just called her from the diner with Ham's report on the Jonsons. Kit was too upset to be lucid. She hadn't bothered to take notes from Sol and hadn't many facts; she just kept insisting shrilly that Daphne Dix had to be expelled immediately — from the Theta house, from the university, from Gideon and the state. Miss Shoemaker had quit trying to calm her; she had promised to do what she could and had gone about tracking Sol. After a dozen calls she had reached him in the Student Union. Unlike Kit, the dean meticulously wrote everything down, including a brief biography of Ham, whom she didn't know; then, bristling with data, she had traced Tate. The provost was more elusive than Sol and, when she found him, far hazier. He had been brooding in the library stacks, still convalescing from Mikel's attack. Over the librarian's phone he had agreed reluctantly that some measures must be taken. But it wouldn't do to bring in the dean of men or the coach. The fewer people involved the better. On Monday he himself would talk to Red Stacy — he would do it now, he explained, but he had a trustee luncheon — and he proposed Miss Shoemaker see the girl at once. The suggestion was so hemmed with qualifications, however, that she was at a loss how to proceed. Daffy wasn't to be expelled, or barred from the sorority. Even suspending her from the Titanettes was unthinkable. After all, Tate had said in his most satiny voice, they were dealing with an unconfirmed rumor. And leaving her once more with the impression that he would rather she settle Daffy's case quietly without disturbing him again, he had authorized an informal inquiry.

"How are your studies going, Mrs. Dix?" she began tentatively.

"Fine," said Daffy, and studied her watch.

The dean stiffened for the plunge. "Or perhaps I should call you Mrs. Jonson."

Daffy's face went vacant. Her hands began crawling along her baton like stealthy kittens. "Mrs. who?"

"Isn't that the name you've been using in the College Inne?" The words came slowly and caused her evident distress. "The name under which you occupy a second floor room with Mr. Jonson?" There was no reply, and she added weakly, "That's what I've been given to understand."

It was a crucial slip. Daffy's animal fear subsided, her hands fell back quietly. She had been improvising a frenzied speech on Red's love for her, the drudgery of her home life, and her right to a career. Now she sensed that the dean wasn't sure of herself. She guessed shrewdly that Ham Markham or Al Swinton had turned her in, but that no one had investigated the Inne.

"It's a lie," she lied.

Miss Shoemaker wasn't prepared for that.

"Not true?" she said faintly.

"Not a word of it." Daffy's eyes flashed. Momentarily she forgot how vulnerable she was — how the Inne could still be checked, how easily Kit could expose her to Jerry. "I've never heard of anything so dirty in my life," she flamed. "This is real dirty, really filthy. I just hope my husband doesn't hear it. He's got a terrible temper, and if he cuts loose somebody's going to get hurt. Who is this Jonson guy? I don't know any Jonson. What's his class? Did he tell you this dirty filth?"

It worked. The dean was intimidated. She despised scenes, and her resolve had been weakened by Tate. Doubts crowded upon her. After all, she didn't even know Ham Markham. Clandestinely, as though she were the sinner, she inspected her own watch and saw time was running out. She stood and edged toward the door.

Yet though outmaneuvered, though betrayed by the provost and the Titanettes warmup schedule, Miss Shoemaker was no fool. Something in her distrusted Daffy; she refused to apologize. "Thank you for coming," she said quietly. "You've been very helpful." And in the outside office she vindicated Trudy by adding, "Please wear a skirt next time you come, my dear."

Trudy made a circle with her thumb and forefinger, Daffy shrugged at it, and the dean returned to her desk and called Kit.

"She denies everything."

"Well, she would! Did you ask about Red Stacy?"

The dean considered explaining that Daffy had had to leave for the game and decided that was undignified. She shifted the blame to Tate. "The provost thinks we should still wait."

"*Wait!*" The receiver vibrated with Kit's exasperation. "We can't wait!" There was a pause while she pondered moves. It didn't occur to her that Daffy might be using the Theta house as a blind for Jerry, and she suggested that she visit the Inne.

Miss Shoemaker approved. "Can you do it now?"

Another pause. In the background the dean heard voices — Sol Feinblatt had arrived and was chaffing the Theta cook. "I'll do something now," Kit said finally. "I'll get what I can over the phone."

She hung up and called the Inne. Too late — the line was busy. Daffy, after sauntering out of Trudy's sight, had ducked into a booth in the corridor and begun dropping dimes in the slot, frantically trying to locate Red. She had made three calls, to the Athletic Dorm, the squad dressing room, and Red's fraternity, explaining in each that she must reach him before the game. No one knew where he was. Now, at five minutes past one, she took a deep breath and dialed the Inne. Her twitching finger beat Kit's by seconds.

"Hello? What is it?" barked Mrs. Prouty, who greeted all unknown calls cagily.

"This is Mrs. Jonson. You know. Room twenty. I got this problem, maybe you can help. My husband owes money all over and, well, this is embarrassing, but there's a collector in town. This person might come around and make trouble. I wonder, could you say we aren't there? And just in case he gets real persistent, could you sort of put our things in a box somewhere else in the house so it'll look like the room's not used? We'll call sometime and pick them up."

Mrs. Prouty had dealt with undergraduate couples before and wanted no scandal. Moreover, Red had paid her a week's rent in advance. This way she could use the room for another couple tonight, charging football week-end prices.

"Don't you worry about a thing, Mrs. Jonson. I'll take care of everything nice. If anybody asks I never saw you."

Kit, meanwhile, suspected that she was being foiled. She kept dialing until the line was clear.

"Hello?" came the harsh answer. "What is it?"

Kit remembered that voice. Her sins came back to her; the last time she had spoken to Mrs. Prouty she herself had been registering under an alias. Then she saw herself in the wall mirror opposite. Her hand crept up, disciplining her hair. She squared her slight shoulders.

"I'd like to speak to Mrs. Jonson, please."

Silence from the Inne.

"Or Mr. Jonson, either one."

"We got no party by that name," Mrs. Prouty said in a monotone.

Kit slammed the receiver down, swore, and called Sol in. "Are you sure you got that name right? It wasn't something like Johannsen, or Jenkins, or Taft?"

Sol looked puzzled. "No, but why the Taft?"

"Oh — it's just a name," she said lightly.

Then, crossing to the mirror she remembered: Taft had been her own Inne alias. Disturbed, she felt mingled resentments toward Ham. It was callous of him to be living there. He ought to have called her direct today, or written a note; she hadn't heard a word from him since the reception. But if he had meant this as an overture he was out of luck. She certainly wasn't going to see him again.

"If you spot Ham at the game, check with him. I'd do it myself," she added unnecessarily, "but a housemother chasing a man in public wouldn't *look* right."

Sol tilted his derby over one ear, "You two sure have it in for those kids."

She whirled. "Kids! Daphne has a child!"

"So she likes extra-curricular activities."

"You're vile," she said and smiled. "And you're not being very practical. We *have* to stop that girl, with or without Tate's help."

"I'm practical as a can opener. And believe me, angel, I'm on your side. *I* know what would happen if this got out. Old Man River would burst his levees, and the *Star* would make free love the biggest campaign issue since free silver. But you and Ham are making a crusade out of it."

Kit toyed with her crucifix. "Maybe we are. And maybe we should." Then she realized this was Saturday afternoon. She had done what she could; it was unfair to inflict more on Sol. She brightened and whispered between cupped hands, "Want a drink before the game?"

"A hair of the dog? Don't mind if I do."

"This is a little reckless," she said, mixing, "but all the girls have gone except the baby sitter, and she's outside with Sean. We won't be disturbed."

They had just finished their drink, and were debating another, when they were disturbed by Red. Kit heard him talking to Mrs. Santo in the kitchen and hurriedly hid the glasses in a drawer.

"Well, stranger!" she called cheerfully.

"Aren't you supposed to be at the stadium, Stacy?" Sol asked him.

Red avoided his eyes. "I'm on my way there. Just happened to be passing by, thought I'd see if anybody wanted to walk over."

It was a feeble lie — Maiden Lane was a dead end, on no one's way anywhere — but Kit, astute with Daffy, was taken in. Flushing, she cried, "This is wonderful!" She darted into the yard to kiss her son good-by, darted back, wriggled into a black wool coat, tilted a black pillbox hat jauntily to one side of her head, and led the men out, slipping her arms through theirs. "Isn't this nice of Red, Sol?"

Sol thought not, and if he had been alone with Red he would have grilled or tricked him into the truth. Kit made a difference. Behind his droll façade Sol was a man of tenderness, and she meant more to him than she knew. He saw that her crusade was entirely against Daffy; that her feeling for Red was more complex and could be easily bruised. It wasn't love. A more jealous man than Sol might have mistaken it for that — and so, he thought, frowning inwardly, might a sexual pirate like Red — but it was closer to girlish hero worship. Kit had adopted Red as a symbol of years she had lost forever; to her he was one of the State stars she had known in her teens. In cheering him she was cheering them — was cheering, he thought with a pang of real jealousy, Ham Markham. Red was the campus idol taking a girl to the stadium gate; Kit was the girl, and walking beside him she was transfigured. In that moment she forgot her age and her divorce and became young again. It was a gift, and in her eagerness to grasp it she couldn't challenge Red's motive.

Red's motive was less intricate. Sol made the easy, and correct, guess that he had come here looking for Daffy, though why here, and why now, when the rest of the team was waiting, puzzled Sol. Actually Red himself could have told him little. He too was puzzled. Half an hour earlier he had arrived at his dressing room and received Daffy's message from an assistant trainer, who had grinned, winked, nudged him playfully, and then shouted wildly after him that he couldn't go now; the coach would blow his top. Red, however, hadn't any choice. He and Daffy had agreed that since messages were risky they would be used only in emergencies. Obviously she was in some kind of jam that included him. The trouble was that he didn't know where. He had tried her dressing room first. As it happened she was inside, but Hotflash, seething because she had been late, told him she wasn't. The only other possible place had been the sorority. He couldn't telephone there — Kit might answer, and he would have to ask for Daffy — so he had sprinted down Maiden Lane for a quick look. Mrs. Santo had just told him all the girls were out when Kit heard his voice. Now he had to hurry back and see Daffy on the field, and, meanwhile, string Kit along.

Striding ahead, making her and Sol run to keep up, he marveled at how easy it was. Kit was like a coed — laughing at his jokes, gasping at his crude boasts, and puckering studiously when he told her how to watch plays from the flow of the line.

"It sounds so scientific," she said breathlessly as they moved diagonally across campus.

"It is, Mrs. O'Donnell. Like last night after supper we watched slow motion movies of old State-Navy games for two hours, just studying option plays."

"My! Is Navy good?" she asked anxiously.

"Don't worry, we'll cream them."

"Best them," Sol panted. "Upend them."

Red didn't acknowledge him. He considered junior faculty beneath him, and Sol, conscious of it and amused, fell behind a few steps as they dodged past arriving fans on the vast parking lot.

"Don't you get pooped out there?" Kit asked, tiring now herself. "I used to know some State players, and they always said the equipment weighed tons."

"I don't mind. It makes me feel — like, big."

She giggled. "You're big enough, I think."

"Gee, thanks. But I'm talking about something else. On the field I feel huge, really huge. I'm more alive. More me. I never get beat because I get this feeling I'm in charge, taking over. It's for real, if you get what I mean."

In the distance Sol did, and thought it profound. Kit asked practically, "Will you be a coach later on?"

"No, I want to turn pro. That's my ambition, Mrs. O'Donnell. Getting an outstanding reputation here and signing up with a big pro football club and making it last as long as I can."

"Well, I think that's nice." She glanced back defiantly, expecting a mutinous look from Sol, but he was out of earshot. "I think it would be fine for you and fine for State. We need a few famous graduates."

Red swelled. He didn't tell her he had no intention of graduating — that he was counting on a contract after this season. Like her he cherished the moment and declined to spoil it.

Kit, however, was about to spoil it for him. Sol had become a hopeless straggler, and she said softly, "Of course, if you're going to be really big time you'll have to watch your training more. Especially nights."

"I don't understand." He began to walk faster.

"You can't throw yourself away on a foolish woman. It's a waste, Red. A waste and a drain."

He wondered how much she knew. This must have been why Daffy had tried to reach him, though he couldn't understand it; until today he had avoided the Theta house. Daffy herself hadn't been there much, and the odds against Kit and Jerry Dix meeting to compare notes were enormous. Then, like Kit in Miss Shoemaker's office, he remembered Ham. The muscles in his face hardened. He passed a swift hand along his unshaven chin and headed doggedly for his dressing room.

Kit wouldn't quit. Stumbling alongside, her pillbox hat askew, she cried, "It'll ruin your career! Don't you know you have to stay in condition? The State players I knew never even touched a cigarette. They lived the right life, Red. They *had* to."

She felt dizzy and ridiculous, and overcome. They had reached his door. The assistant trainer was holding it open and urgently beckoning, and Red started in. Then bitterness delayed him. Spinning around, he said, "You mean like Cornball Markham?" Exhausted, she nodded once. He flipped his hands to his hips. "What'd he ever do?"

"He was one of the best men State ever had," she said loyally. "Haven't you been in the trophy pavilion?" He shook his head impatiently. "Well, you just march yourself up there. Why, Ham and another boy I knew almost beat Peabody!"

"Almost! Peabody?" He laughed harshly. "You mean that jerk school across town?"

Stunned, Kit caught her breath and started to explain what Peabody had meant to them, but there was no time. Red went in with the assistant trainer, and she was left alone, talking to a door that closed and then swayed slightly ajar, releasing a faint, rancid odor of sweat.

**

Talking to a chapel congregation now thoroughly awake, Ham had concluded his lecture with the celebrated quotation from Matthew Arnold: "Thus both India and her leader are still 'wandering between two worlds, one dead, the other powerless to be born.' "

Bowing slightly, he stepped away from the lectern. He had been a success and knew it, though as he returned to his pew there was an instant of doubt; the students were snapping their fingers in unison, and he had a jarring thought that it might be a razz. Outside they surged around him eagerly, however, and when they departed reluctantly for classes the hale young dean congratulated him enthusiastically.

"And now you must come to the faculty club for coffee," he said. "It's a custom with chapel guests."

Ham smiled. "Was that snapping business another custom?"

"Oh yes. A very old one. Goes back to the 1840's, when cheering in chapel was forbidden."

The dean had many such stories. He was a fourth generation Peabody graduate, and he waved at odd objects along the way, explaining them. Every stained-glass window, every ivy root below, every drinking fountain and doorway had a significance, and all were honored, even if obsolete. A granite hitching post, useless for over a generation, was carefully tended. A Burmese bell given in 1891 to celebrate football victories over Harvard glittered brilliantly, though the two schools hadn't played since well before World War I and Peabody had now abandoned the game entirely. Outside the faculty club hung a row of polished leather buckets — "for volunteer firemen," the dean said, "although the student fire brigade was disbanded before I was born."

He was chuckling. Yet Ham suspected the dean would fight any move to clear away the clutter. Scratch a Peabody man, he thought, and you find a necromancer. He had expected ancestor worship — the college owed its endowments to fortunes built in the high noon of nineteenth century capitalism — and felt confirmed. The campus atmosphere was more surprising. After the sheen and expanse of the new State it seemed tiny, cramped, almost shabby. The buildings were of decaying graystone, the architecture Victorian. Moss and lichen grew where ivy didn't, brass railings emitted a pale, elderly glow, and over all hung the reverent hush of the graveyard.

The faculty club was a greater surprise; it was all irreverence. Its main hall looked solemn enough, dark and somber and walled with oil portraits of deceased trustees, but the men seated on deacon's benches around the long dark center table were loudly impious. "Go home, Blandy!" they shouted derisively at the dean, and "Why didn't you invite Markham to speak at a sensible hour?" and "Creeping Blandyism! Routing us out at dawn!" The dean withdrew to a corner, smiling wanly, and Ham found himself in the center of a chuckling, winking, quietly dressed quintet of middle-aged men, who steered him to the table head, to a seat beside a gentle old man who introduced himself as Nails Whipple. Nails seemed just the wrong name for him. He was sparse, venerable, wore a bow tie and gold-rimmed pince-nez, and spoke so softly it was several minutes before Ham identified his accent in the din. It was his father-in-law's. Whipple was an unobtrusive version of the judge. Like him he had an undefinable air of eminence, and Ham, drawing on reportorial skills, elicited that he was the college's senior professor and a former dean.

"Thank God I shirked that," he said, twinkling. "Look at poor Blandy—all alone and friendless. It's nothing personal, you understand. Blandy's a perfectly decent chap. He's simply unlucky enough to represent the law among philosophical anarchists."

Anarchy abided in the hall. Every authority was struck down in the general conversation. Doc River was mocked, but before Ham could bristle Peabody's president was jeered; then it was Blandy's turn again. And yet there was no malice. Over his third cup of coffee Ham began to acquire a more profound sense of the group. They were elaborately casual and proud of it—one man delighted the others by telling how, returning in spattered denim from his private art studio the night before, he had been questioned by the Peabody constable—but their urbanity camouflaged a deeper seriousness. Beneath their affected indolence they were intense, committed. They weren't much interested in Peabody College. College chauvinism, once an imperative for Ham and still alive in him, simply did not exist for them. They were interested only in their academic specialties and were bound together by that consecration. The subjects under discussion were the mysticism of an eighteenth century poet, herbal medicines in South America, Constantinople A.D. 1300, prenatal mice, Kirkegaard's decline—angels dancing on pins, most outsiders would have thought, but Ham found them stimulating; abroad he had spent countless such mornings, fondly remembered, with Kashmiri Brahmins and Buddhist priests, and he was pleased to find himself accepted here as a colleague. He too had a discipline. His articles on Asia had been read; he was considered a colleague. Accepting a Turkish cigarette from Whipple, he joined enthusiastically in the obscure, rather schizoid conversation, making and countering points and occasionally peering through the thickening fog of acrid smoke to match voice and speaker.

". . . then I gather Chiang's a kind of Oriental Uncle Tom, Markham . . ."

". . . Osman let his lack of enthusiasm carry him away . . ."

". . . our capacity to generalize from specific example is almost a national trait . . ."

". . . to paraphrase, Giles, you avoid all the little errors as you sweep on toward the grand fallacy . . ."

". . . a sort of rich man's Westbook Pegler . . ."

". . . had an *arming* smile . . ."

". . . delivered platitudes like epigrams . . ."

It was pleasant, exhilarating. Yet even as he fenced with them Ham felt an alien. They thought themselves cosmopolitan, but they bore the stamp of a culture. It was upper class and Anglophilic — this very hall was called the combination room; its broad sills were littered with copies of the *Manchester Guardian* and *Punch* — and for all their independence they were indebted, like the hitching post and the oriental bell outside, to the industrial freebooters of another era. One man was the Charles Boggs Professor of History, another the Elias Simpson Professor of Philosophy. All appeared to have private incomes, broad vowels, conservative tailoring and a hundred other badges of a vanishing caste. Their interests were Ham's, their mood his; he was more at home among them than he had been in Doc's Mansion. Nevertheless, they were apart from him. He was a stranger here. He was an outsider — between two worlds, he thought; one dead, the other powerless to be born.

Dean Blandy had duties elsewhere. Whipple inherited his role as Ham's host. He enjoyed it, and as the group thinned he grew more expansive.

"I believe you went to school across town, Mr. Markham."

His voice was benign; Ham couldn't take exception. "It was somewhat different then."

"Extraordinary man, Adam River. Reminds me of a Visigoth king — Alaric, perhaps. Maligned people, the barbarians, by the way. History has been unjust to them. The Goths were nobler than the

Romans of their time. So were the Huns, if it comes to that. You can't rebuild until you've destroyed, and your first buildings are bound to be a little jerry. I've been trying to tell Harry Mikel that, but he's not persuaded."

To Ham it was more extraordinary that Doc should have a defender on the Peabody faculty. "You've discussed this with Harry?"

"Often. Nearly every Saturday. I wonder where he is today?"

Ham had forgotten that Mikel also had faculty status here. He not only belonged, he was highly regarded; when he entered a half-hour later, poking his shaggy coxcomb around the jamb, the dozen coffee drinkers left hailed him with snapping fingers, and as he shuffled from chair to chair, dispersing dry insults, he was greeted as genially as Ham had been. It was ironic, Ham reflected; both the guest of honor and the popular arrival were State alumni. So the lines blur and we forget our enemies, he thought, and he wondered uneasily how strong the enmity had really been, whether in the despair of the Thirties State students hadn't exaggerated or even invented it, magnifying the differences between class and class, seizing upon the slurs of the *Star* and the worst Peabody snobs as salt for Depression wounds. He felt uncomfortable, as though he were being unfaithful to Doc, to himself — unfaithful even to Spook.

"Sit down, Harry," Whipple said quietly. "Sing Adam's praises to us."

Mikel screwed his face up. "I've just left Janus. *And* his revolting alter ego."

Whipple said gravely, "Worse and worse. Three weeks ago you reported that Tate drywashes his hands."

"He does. Like Uriah Heep. Life imitating again."

"Two weeks ago you called him a lickspittle. And last week he became Adam's procurer."

"That's not bad," said Ham, grinning. "Tate does look like a pimp."

"This morning he was pandering shamelessly," Mikel said. "Between them they will destroy us all before election day." He pointed a dirty nail at Whipple. "And you, I suppose, are ready with your usual defense of demolition."

Whipple parted his hands in a professorial gesture. "Harry, it's not a question of defense. What is, is. As a scholar you should recognize historical forces. Instead you behave like Adam, draping yourself in the State colors."

Mikel was defensive. "Ridiculous! How many times must you be told that I pay homage nowhere?"

"Stop stonewalling. You've had bids from every responsible institution in the country. You could have a chair here tomorrow if you lifted one grimy finger."

Mikel glared. "A man has to fight where the war is. The present rumble is on River's playground."

"And it will be won. In time."

"After how many eons? I lack your serenity, Nails. I simply cannot play the Trappist while every professional standard is being fed into a political bonfire."

"You talk as though State students would be better off home," Ham said. "They must be getting something."

Mikel looked crafty. He swooped inside his tattered coat and drew out a folded paper. "I stopped at my office on the way here, and my secretary handed me this remarkable document. It is my deepest regret that I lacked it in River's office."

"So you've finished your survey," Whipple sighed.

Ham didn't understand. "Survey?"

"Why not?" cried Mikel spreading it on the table. "Cigarette makers have surveys. Deodorant drummers. Manufacturers of sanitary napkins, laxatives, emetics, nylon athletic supporters. *Fas est et ab hoste doceri*, so I," he said, grinning villainously, "have stooped to learn. About learning. Or rather, its absence."

"He's had the History Department give State undergraduates a questionnaire," Whipple explained.

"Not on history," said Mikel. "On facts every red-blooded American should know."

"How many undergraduates?" Ham asked.

Mikel chortled. "We pollsters call it a sampling. It's a very generous sampling, however. Under our enlightened provost the History Department is responsible for a peculiar cultivation called Becoming a Good Citizen. It being a required course, my graduates were able to reach three thousand respondents. Respondents — admirable word. Connoting, in this case correctly, utter Laodiceanism."

He cracked the paper and read triumphantly:

" 'Could identify Preamble to Constitution — thirty-two per cent. Bill of Rights — twenty-six per cent. National debt within fifty billions — twenty-four per cent. Could name three members of Cabinet — fourteen per cent.' Next: 'Recognition of terms and names. Habeas corpus — eighteen per cent. John Quincy Adams — forty-two per cent. Theodore Roosevelt — fifty-nine per cent.' Bully! A majority for T.R.! 'Worth a continental — seven per cent. Vicksburg — twelve per cent.' " Mikel stared incredulously at a footnote. " 'Six students thought Vicksburg was a popular remedy.' "

Ham winced. "They're not going to become very good citizens."

"Not in this generation, no," Whipple conceded. He coughed into his fist. "I take it you plan to publish this."

Mikel tilted his head. "Eh?"

"Why else did you do it?"

Ham felt a growing respect for Whipple. Mikel was cornered. "To drill a hole in River's skull," he growled, "and siphon a little sense in."

"You know how little chance there is that Adam will accept those figures from you. You planned this survey to prove a point. All right. The point's made, in spades. Why keep it a secret? Why not turn it over to the *Star*?"

"No!" Ham cried, so vehemently that Whipple's pince-nez fell to his vest.

"Harry wants to raise State's standards, Mr. Markham," he said, replacing it. "The university belongs to the public, and if the public is jogged something may be done."

Ham struck the table. "Don't you see Witty would use it as a club to beat Doc?"

"Ah," Whipple sighed. "Then the election is the greater issue."

"Certainly not," Mikel snarled, pocketing the paper. "I don't give a rap who wins."

"I do," Whipple said, and to Ham's surprise he said, "I'm for Adam."

Ham glanced at his watch. Another surprise; it was noon. The conversation, like liquor, had sped time. Whipple led them into an adjoining room, and they argued there through lunch. Whipple persisted in his long view. Colleges like Peabody, he declared calmly, were doomed, while public education was rising. He saw Doc as a transitional figure, a kind of heroic scavenger. But reputations were expendable. If scandal would augment the scavenging he welcomed it. Mikel shook his head. Doc's name meant nothing to him; State's did. Though he stubbornly denied it to Whipple, in his way he was devoted to the university. He couldn't bear the thought of its disgrace. That was why he would suppress his survey, why he fought the accreditation plan. Ham, between them, argued with both, though he was conscious he was making little sense. They were chess players, logicians; he was bound by his old attachment to Doc. Like Mikel he was shaken by the poll. It made State seem a parody of the institution he had dreamt of as a boy. Like Whipple he admired Doc and wanted him to win, but unlike Whipple he couldn't dismiss him as expendable. The survey would affect his election; therefore it mustn't be broadcast. Ham didn't put it that baldly, but that was what was in his heart.

He looked at his watch again. It was nearly game time. Mikel saw him and hooted, "As an ex-gladiator I assume you'll be on hand this afternoon, bellowing along with Prexy."

"That's right," Ham said aggressively. "And if there's a goal post fight I'll be in it."

"There won't be. I don't frequent our Colosseum, but I'm informed the posts are rooted in concrete. Like your idol's ears."

On that waspish note they rose. Outside Mikel mounted his decrepit bike and pedaled away beneath elms, shouting back that he had discovered a new rooming house with color television and would room there tonight. Apparently the affair in the Inne had escaped him. Strolling to the Peabody gate with Nails, Ham wondered what Mikel would do if he knew of it. Probably he'd knock on the Jonson door at midnight, and introduce himself as an observer from Indiana University, treating it all as a huge joke. It was strange that he should be so excited about some standards and so indifferent to others. In a way he was a mirror image of Doc. Everything one admired the other scorned. The odd thing was that the scoffing of both was unjust, because the things each believed in were right. Positive thinking, Ham thought sardonically; that's the ticket. He told Whipple, whose eyes sparkled.

"Adam might agree," he said, chuckling, "but Harry would have a stroke."

In four hours Ham had made a conquest of Whipple, and now he won Whipple's consent to a review of college records. It was an achievement, for the faculty patriarch was reticent with strangers, yet this sort of thing happened often to Ham. As a journalist his strength lay in his innate sympathy for others. People, not ideas, won his allegiance, and they felt that and responded. Because he was attuned to them he also sensed moods that eluded others. It gave him a kind of intuition, and at the gate it led him to ask, "By the way, Dr. Whipple, I noticed that you referred to Doc as Adam all morning. I didn't realize you knew him that well."

"Oh, I don't. Haven't seen him for years."

"I see." Ham waited. Obviously there was more.

"But long ago I knew him very well for a brief period."

Still Ham waited. Whipple seemed to be weighing something.

He said, "This is off the record? Good. Because there's a small matter of ethics involved. You see, Adam was an undergraduate when I had Blandy's job."

"But that was here."

"Yes. Adam was here, also."

Ham started violently. "Doc was a student at *Peabody?*"

"It was less than a term, actually. About three months in the fall. And he transferred to State the following year. Let's see— that would have been in 1925." He brightened, pleased with his memory.

"I never heard that," said Ham, flabbergasted. "He couldn't have played on any team."

"Not the varsity, of course, though I believe he was a one-man freshman squad. Football, indeed, was why he was brought here." Whipple clucked. "Ah, the sinful Twenties."

Doc in a green uniform — it wasn't possible. "But the *Star* has always covered Peabody freshman games like Young Republican meetings. There's nothing in our morgue mentioning Doc here."

"No." He smiled faintly. "I'm sure it would have been removed afterward."

"Why? After what?"

Whipple shook his head, "I've really said all I can."

"Does Harry Mikel know?"

"Yes, he's one of a handful who've heard the whole story."

"He never said anything about it."

"No. He was told in confidence."

"Why in confidence?" asked Ham, exasperated. "Doc's attending Peabody is a shocker, but it's no crime."

"No," Whipple said softly, "but expulsion is." Before Ham could react he added hastily, "You mustn't think of it as a stigma. Unquestionably he was a victim of circumstances."

"What circumstances?"

But Whipple had begun to edge away. "I'm afraid I'm keeping you from your game."

"This is more important. I'm not asking you as a reporter — I've given my word."

Again that faint smile. "I'm not concerned about your paper, Mr. Markham. No. I —Never mind. I've said too much already."

Almost plaintively Ham cried, "You can't leave it like this!"

"I'm sorry, I must."

The old man was retreating swiftly, and Ham was stalking him, pleading for more. This was something he had to know — and Whipple, backed against the Burmese bell, saw it at last and relented.

"Come back Monday," he said hesitantly. "I'll see you after chapel. We can go into the college history then, and perhaps afterward . . ." He capitulated: "Very well. I'll show you some things about Adam."

Ham accepted eagerly and, before Whipple could change his mind, hurried out to his car. He had reached the stadium and bought his ticket before he noticed a nagging cramp in his right hand. All across town he had been nervously snapping fingers.

**

Navy's squad was already on the field, dancing on tiptoes, kicking themselves in the chins, and taking falls in neatly rolled human balls. They were cheered only by their brigade of midshipmen. Elsewhere the stadium faithful were silent. As Ham sank into one of the last available end zone seats the spectators around him were fingering their programs, their parking stubs, their return bus tickets to Birmingham, Pawnattuck, Rockton, or Dudley; a few were glancing enviously toward the press box and the "S" Club's big bloc of reserved seats on the fifty-yard line — for both of which, he realized without regret, he was eligible — but most merely waited, fidgeting, for the ritual that opened State's first stadium game each season. It started ten minutes before the kickoff. First Doc stood slowly in his box directly behind the State bench, his old-fashioned topcoat flapping wildly in a sudden gust of wind. Forty-three thousand people caught their breaths. Casually he raised two fingers to his misshapen brown brim. A semicircle of six cameras, five of them from the university's Department of Journalism, temporarily blinded him; then the nine Titanettes darted out from a cavernous entrance to the right and spread cartwheels on the sward before him while the faithful, rising as one, bellowed throatily,

Hit the line for brave State
Fight and do or die . . .

That was a signal. Out of a huge maw opposite came the Titan squad, wearing, in deference to Navy, silver Nylon uniforms with blue numerals. They trotted in cadence behind the coach, ignoring the swelling roar from the elliptical tiers above and deftly juggling glossy yellow balls while the sixty-piece band, three full measures ahead of the voices now, crashed through the chorus:

. . . show the foe they cannot rate
While the true and blue ride high.
Oh, hit the line . . .

The coach also carried a ball. Unlike the others it was black and discolored with ancient scars. Jogging swiftly across the fresh lime markers, he carried it straight to the box and flipped a little shovel pass to Doc, who caught it easily with his free hand, completed his salute, and sat back, looking — as the *Star* would say tomorrow, in a lead which had also become liturgic — like Titus gloating over his sacrificial beasts. Each year that line annoyed Doc more, each September he swore that he'd be doggoned if he'd go through this folderol next season. He always did, partly because Sam, who had first borrowed the ball from the trophy pavilion after a bad season, asked him to, but also because, for all his protests, he enjoyed the little rite. The ball was the one he had carried against Peabody in his last game. Having it beside him restored a sense of participation he had lost after the construction of the stadium made sitting on the bench impractical for him. Sometimes when the team was in trouble he would grip it in his big muscular hands, feeling for a play or two that he was out there whipping the squad on, and though he didn't like to think of himself as superstitious, he had to admit that in the seven years since the first ceremony State hadn't dropped an opener.

"Seven years good luck, Governor," said Sam, alongside.

"Governor or not, I'll be jiggered if I'll do it again," Doc muttered, slipping the ball between them. To the coach he called more cheerfully, "How are the boys, Tom? Are they up?"

"We'll deliver," the coach said evenly, and skipped off.

Carrying the ball to Doc was part of Tom Yablonski's job, and he accepted it stoically. He had no faith in Sam's talk of luck, however. Yablonski was a pro. He left nothing to chance if he could help it. A thickset, fair man in his early forties, with hard, frozen features and wrists so big that they seemed to come out level with his hands, he had spent ten years as a pro passer and another five as a backfield coach in the Big Ten, where he had learned the important thing was not how you played the game but whether you won. Coaches who lost were burned in effigy by the faithful; their homes were stoned after dark and their families threatened by fanatic fans. His predecessor at State had been let off easily with a polite letter from Doc, who had regretted that he was "losing interest," but the record of the teams since had brought big-time football fever to the state. The coach knew that if he fell now he would fall hard, and he took every conceivable step to insure that he kept his feet. The result was known as the Yablonski System. With Doc's help promising high school players were offered the most tempting lures in New England. Those who came to Gideon earned their pay. They were required to major in Physical Education, to attend Camp TD, and to live in the Athletic Dorm. Pre-season training sessions were filmed, and afterward each member of the squad received a thick, typewritten critique of his performance. Because a team bench is the worst place to watch a game. Yablonski had nine skilled spotters high in the stadium, in touch with him by interphone. If a player fumbled or missed a block he was taken out instantly and ordered to the far end of the bench, where the others weren't allowed to talk to him. If anyone protested this was cruel, the coach shrugged and replied that football was a rough game. Like Doc he gave his share of character-building talks at alumni chapters, but unlike him he didn't believe them. Secretly he was convinced that individualism and team play were incompatible. He liked his home unstoned and his family unthreatened, and so, with the help of cameras, interphones, a huge staff, and breaks he made, he had just finished tooling up his eighth flawless, deliberately characterless machine, the chief cog in which was a cocky, bull-necked redhead named Stacy.

"Taken your pill, kid?" he asked in a dry monotone.

"Took two."

"How you feel?"

Red forked his hands to his waist. "Like murdering the fleet."

Yablonski punched his belly, testing muscle. "I'll murder you if you show up here late again."

Red hung his head fleetingly, like a tardy schoolboy. Yablonski was the one man in Gideon he respected; he had played pro ball and could teach a back a lot. Then he grinned. "You know how it is Boss. I had to rip off a quick piece."

"Yeah? Well, keep your fly buttoned the next couple of hours. You never know, I might use you." He slapped him across the buttocks, and Red raced off to join a formation.

"Why, there's Stacy!" breathed a wispy, elderly woman on Ham's right. "Don't he look grand?"

"I guess he gets plenty of exercise," said Ham.

On the forty-yard line Kit was saying worriedly, "See what I mean? It's his attitude. It sticks out all over."

Sol said, "I know. In front of all these people, too."

"He's so cynical. I don't think it's natural."

"Oh, it's natural enough. He's just a high-spirited, red-blooded American boy."

She set her mouth. "Honestly. There's that girl, looking at him."

Daffy had finished cartwheeling and was peering over her shoulder, trying to catch Red's eye. He saw her and trotted toward the sidelines, but before he arrived Hotflash barked from her first row seat, "Break out the hulas, Dix!"

In the press box a *Star* sportswriter saw the blue plastic rings and said between his teeth, "Hot damn! This looks good."

"Who's that blonde?" asked Al Swinton, beside him. "I wish she'd turn this way."

"You and me *both*."

She had seen Al and had been keeping her back to the press box, but now that was no longer possible. Lining up the Titanettes, she took up a central station directly beneath Doc, shouted a command, and slipped her own hoop over her shoulders. Then she threw her head back and spread her bare feet on the grass. Everything else was quickly forgotten. Her hips arched in a quickening rhythm; the crowd stamped in scandalized approval, and Al, recognizing her, whispered "Jesus H. . . ."

"You said it!" cried the jubilant sportswriter.

"Are they supposed to be wearing halos?" the wispy woman asked doubtfully.

"I don't think so," Ham said. "You don't wear halos down there."

"Such a cute girl in the middle. She does it so well."

"I guess she gets exercise, too."

Behind the band Jill said uncertainly, "It's not very nice."
"No, but it's *nice*," Jack said and chuckled wickedly.

On the deans' row, beside the "S" Club, Elsie Shoemaker shook her head. "I think that's going too far. Really, someone should speak to Miss Hatch."

A murmur of agreement rippled along the row and subsided when the provost, on the aisle, held up a reproving hand. "It seems to me the effect is quite artistic," he said. "Remember that old slogan — to the pure everything is pure."

In the trustees box Paul Bauer, who had praised the Titanettes to Tate an hour before, debated with two other members of the athletic committee over whether a wife could be a Gridiron Queen.

Doc scowled at Daffy. He wasn't shocked. The Titanettes' hulas were whirling dizzily, their loins were toiling in hard pelvic thrusts; but like the woman beside Ham Doc innocently thought the hoops were the attraction. He was frowning because cheerleaders reminded him of Sarah. Until her stroke she hadn't missed a home game. She had watched thousands of plays, yet had never really understood football, and explaining it to her had amused them both. An hour ago he had hopefully climbed the hill and found her rocking in the Mansion, knitting a new bootie. She had smiled and whispered her regrets — she felt headachy, she hoped he didn't mind. He minded terribly; a game wasn't a game without her. He could have interpreted Titan strategy to others — Dr. Budge, on his left, had a baffled look — but he left Budge to Newt Albert, and, after Newt left, to Sam. Somehow Doc didn't care whether others understood or not. He picked up his old ball and stood heavily for the *Star Spangled Banner*, running idle fingers along the rotting, crusty lace. Eighty thousand eyes were on him and he felt lonesome.

Navy had won the toss and would receive. State's captain glanced toward the box, another custom; Doc saluted him, and the kick, cruising on a high wind, sailed over the goal and was brought out to Navy's twenty. Immediately the teams were deadlocked, punt following punt. Doc watched with steely blue eyes until, halfway through the second scoreless period, he realized Newt hadn't returned. He craned his neck to look up the aisle and saw a trim Statette usher approaching him. She bore a scribbled note from the stadium manager. The concessionaire outside was protesting. Men were pressing boxes of Democratic campaign buttons on him, insisting they be offered free to hot dog, soft drink, and pennant customers at the half. The manager hated to bother Doc, but this was over his head. What should he do? A yes or no to the girl would take care of it.

Doc crumpled the note. He felt a powerful temptation to have Newt's men put off the grounds, but a month of skirmishes had seasoned him. He knew what would happen. Newt would appear, all reasonableness, and point out that the pins cost the spectators nothing and Republicans didn't have to take them anyhow. If Doc refused to back down Newt would withdraw quietly—and later in the Mansion library Doc would find the incident had been mysteriously transformed into a grievance against him.

"Is Mr. Albert out there?" he asked the Statette.

The girl was bewildered. She didn't know a Mr. Albert.

Doc fumed. He turned to Sam just as Sam leapt from his seat, shaking a fleshy fist at the field.

"Go!" he was screaming. "Go! *Go!*"

Doc heaved up. Red had just faked a Navy end out of position, turned the corner, and outraced the secondary for eighteen yards.

"How about a rackety-ax-co-ax-co-ax?" shouted Sam, who liked the old cheers, and Hotflash squirmed around to glare.

Doc took his arm. "Look, Sam. I want you to find that scamp Albert. He's somewhere in the concessions."

"Oh, no!" Sam's eyes rolled pleadingly. "We're going to score, Governor!"

"He's up to some hanky-panky. The girl will tell you." To her Doc said, "Take Mr. Theanapolis with you."

"Mr. Wolf was hoping for an answer from you," she said uncertainly. The manager had been adamant: he wanted that yes or no.

Doc thought furiously. Then: "After you leave Mr. Theanapolis, see Dr. Tate. He's acting president."

Reluctantly she left with a reluctant Sam. Doc knew he had equivocated, but hang it, he thought, Tate was on the payroll, he should settle Newt's hash. Knitting his brows, he concentrated on the field and watched State's quarterback squander Red's gain with a midfield fumble.

Tate, resourceful, resolved the manager's dilemma. "Are there any Republican pins?" he blandly asked the Statette. She shook her head stupidly. "I expect there will be," he said confidently, "and we should let *both* parties participate. A university ought to encourage everyone to vote for the candidate of his choice, and this is an admirable way to do it. Tell Mr. Wolf to permit the distribution, by all means."

Thus Ham, strolling out his exit for coffee when the second period clock ran out — the quarterback was still alone on the bench end, listening gloomily to boos from the faithful — found the booth flanked by bins of "I'm for Doc!" buttons. Signs invited him to take one, and he did. He was backing away with a steaming cup when he saw Sam on the outskirts of the crowd, peering around anxiously. Beside him, also peering, was a chubby boy wearing a Doc pin and a bursting State bandsman's uniform. His face, under his shako, was a youthful facsimile of Sam's.

"Hi, Ham," Sam said dejectedly. He nodded at Ham's button with vague approval. "Haven't seen Newt around, have you?"

"No. He wouldn't like my seat. You can't see Daffy's crotch from there."

Sam gave him a swift look of warning, jerked his head toward the boy, and hurried through introductions. "This is my son." He glanced proudly at the swollen blue uniform. "Young Sam's a freshman. Plays the tuba."

"I can see all nine crotches from the tuba seat," young Sam said squeakily, and winked.

Sam's discontent deepened. "Cut it out. You wouldn't want your mother to hear that. Say, don't you have to be on the field?"

"We march after the Crotchettes," young Sam squeaked. "After everybody in the stands gets his kicks."

"Cut it *out!*" roared Sam, so loudly that Ham hastily invited the boy to stroll back with him.

As they slipped between button wearers he said pleasantly, "You can *hear* from my seat. The band sounds pretty good."

"It stinks," said young Sam, as doleful as his father.

"Well, the tuba's loud and clear, anyway."

"You kidding? The tuba stinks putrid. Even Dad admits it."

"Oh. But you'll get better."

"I doubt it. I really do doubt it. Ever trying blowing up a hundred balloons? That's what tubas take. Gas. Me, I got big bellows but no gas."

"If you feel that way, why do it?" Ham asked impatiently.

"Because you got to blow something," said young Sam, just as impatient. "I mean, it's the band or a team or rally leader or the paper or some kick. Otherwise what's for the yearbook? What's for the interviewers?"

A roving vendor selling blue feathers had created a block ahead. They leaned against the stadium concrete, waiting. Ham asked, "What interviewers?"

"You *must* be kidding. The gray flannels that come around when you finish here."

"From the Philharmonic?"

"Oh, you comic," young Sam squealed, trying to make himself heard above the shoving mob. "What I'm saying is, you got to make some campus record. The billboard, they call it. Everybody's got to have one, and it starts your first semester. If you don't make something like band or glee club or whatever you don't get in a house. No house, no B.M.O.C. No B.M.O.C., no billboard, no pic for the interviewer, no job. Get it?"

"What about marks?"

Young Sam edged out into the thinning crowd. "I'm not a science maj! I need a billboard!" he screeched, so harshly that Ham flinched and returned to the end zone reflecting that no interviewer would find the glee club in young Sam's pic.

"It's that Goddamn tuba," Hotflash said five minutes later, cocking her ear professionally. "I don't care if his father *is* a trustee, Fatso's got to go."

The Titans were racing back on the field, exhorted by the cheering tiers above. This was Daffy's best chance to warn Red against the Inne. She strolled to the sideline.

"Keep the customers warm," Hotflash called after her. "Get ready for a slow split after the first huddle."

Red had been watching for Daffy. He cut straight for her, braked triumphantly, and then, to her consternation, doffed his helmet.

"No, don't!" she cried, staring fearfully up at the press box.

"What's the matter?" he asked uncertainly.

Too late: Al Swinton had seen the flaming hair. He had borrowed binoculars from the sportswriter and was studying them. Swiftly she told Red what had happened. "Our stuff's out of the room, but we got to stay clear. But *clear*."

He resnapped his helmet buckle and kicked the turf. "Another pad, huh?"

"*No* pad tonight. I got to be home knitting, just in case."

His whole face seemed drawn into a point. "What's the point of winning if I can't be with you?"

She smiled mechanically. "Look at it this way—think how ready we'll be when we find a place."

"When?" he asked instantly, and, "Where? How about the Gideon Arms? Listen, if I can pull this game out I'll be loaded. There's always a few old mooks slip me double sawbucks in the dressing room after I lock one up."

Daffy was also worrying the grass with bare toes, assessing risks, wondering how long a string she could pay off and still keep Red willing to champion her with Bauer. Red, aware of that, was driving the hardest bargain he could. As the tiers beamed down and thought how charming they were, they haggled in whispers.

"Maybe tomorrow night," she said, "outside Archer at ten."

"You'll be there?" he asked, almost menacingly.

"*If* you sink the Navy and win a pot," she said, making her final offer. "It's too cold for fields, friend."

Between them they dominated the stadium in the second half. In the third period the stalemate was resumed, and the spectators, tired of line play and punts, turned to the Titanettes. Daffy led the girls in the slow split, another hula, more cartwheels, and a hip-swinging rhumba while Hotflash indignantly ogled young Sam. Bauer contended with increasing heat that wives shouldn't be penalized, and Doc, watching tackle after savage midshipman tackle, wondered whether Tom Yablonski was losing interest. Sam, who had returned without Newt, spun optimistic patter for Doc and Budge. Navy hadn't the reserves, he said knowingly. They were getting tired. Stacy would break loose any time now, and that would be it.

It was. Five minutes were left in the last period, and the stadium was darkened by the specter of a scoreless tie, when Red ripped out of a high tackle and fled forty yards to the goal. The safety man never had a chance; two burly blockers cut him down. Head high, Red crossed the lime diagonals, veered left, and carelessly dropped the ball to the ground. The scoreboard behind him flashed 6-0. Yablonski relaxed, the faithful whooped, the "S" Club gave Red the sanction of old craftsmen, Doc bayed nasally that the boy was a whizdinger, even Budge emitted an excited croak, and from the Titanettes scampering down the sidelines to prey for the conversion, came a silvery chorus of soprano delight. A moment later Red skipped over for two points. He *did* run like Spook, Ham thought uneasily. Spook had been slighter, but he had carried himself the same way, cleats high, hips swinging, the ball slung low on his hip. Take that space helmet off Red and put him in a 1942 suit, and he'd be a ghost. Ham looked down, troubled, and when he looked up he saw the trembling stadium was white with handkerchiefs, all waved at the Navy bench.

He hadn't a handkerchief. The wispy woman eyed him beadily. "You a sailor or something?" she asked suspiciously. He explained and exhibited his Doc button. Mollified, she resumed flapping a square of lace and cried, "Isn't this fun?"

"Rubbing it in?"

"Yes, You must be new. We started it after Yablonski took over the Titans. It's our way of saying too bad, bye-bye, better luck next week." She smiled, suddenly inspired, and shouted, "Boo hoo! Poor little middies!"

Sol had brought a soiled blue bandanna — "True blue," he told Kit, "so nobody'll bean me with a coke bottle."

"It doesn't seem very nice to the other team," she said. "We never did things like that. But then," she added cheerfully, "we weren't this good. Wasn't Red marvelous? Did you notice the way he held the ball down by his side? Somebody I knew used to do that."

"We're drubbing them," said Sol. "We're taking their measure."

"Don't you wish I could run forty yards?" Jack asked Jill.

She shook her head and squeezed his hand tenderly. "He looks good from here," she said, "but let's face it — he *is* an ape." She glanced around quickly to see whether she had been heard.

Tate's sense of satisfaction was qualified. He remembered that he had to see Red Monday, and this wouldn't make the interview any easier. Abruptly Red made it much harder. Navy had been held, had punted, had held State and, taking a State punt on its thirty, had gone to the air. Two long passes were knocked down. The third hit an end for forty yards, and the fourth arched straight into the cupped fingers of Red, who zigzagged twice, picking up blockers, and then darted deerlike all the way. The contrite quarterback came in to sneak over the extra points. The scoreboard read 16-0, and the Titanettes, chanting shrilly, counted it up.

"Very impressive," Budge said mildly.

Doc, pleased again with Yablonski, said exuberantly, "I'm glad they uncorked for you, Professor. By Golly, there's nothing girly about our squads. They're tough as crackers!"

He felt vindicated. When the final whistle blew he clapped his hands together, turned his old ball over to a waiting Statette, and led Budge out through the crush, forgetting Sarah for the moment and basking in State's glory. It was a shared glory. Only the brigade of midshipmen was glum. Everyone else was restored and buoyant. Even those who wondered about the wisdom of encouraging the Yablonski System were temporarily warmed by the memory of Red's two runs. Red was a lout, Ham thought, and he didn't belong in college, but he was a rare animal. Elsie Shoemaker hoped Red would behave — he was such a fine-looking boy — and Sol, who would be witty tonight about the barbed wire surrounding Camp TD, tilted his derby back and entertained Kit with gay clichés about pigskins, moleskins, pay dirt, and the dauntless blue eleven.

They were the doubters. The others were half drunk with joy. Kit was incredulous that old Aggie could defeat a school with a national reputation. Young Sam Theanapolis gave his hated tuba a triumphant blast, his father jubilantly invited Paul Bauer to help him kill a pint in his car, and Hotflash flung a muscular, comradely arm around Daffy's shoulders. The faithful, the honorary alumni who had never visited a Gideon classroom and never missed a stadium game, were the happiest. Once more they had been vindicated. They surged out to their herringbones of parked buses, cheering, singing fight songs, and wearing their Doc buttons like the badges of a cult.

In State's dressing room Tom Yablonski peeled off his clammy flannel uniform and joined the Titans in a long, relaxing shower. When the *Star* sportswriter arrived with Al Swinton they found the coach draped in a big, thirsty Turkish towel, smiling beatifically at the naked figure of Red, who was crouched over a mirror, completing the shave he had forgotten after his hectic dawn in the Inne. Beside him were four twenty-dollar bills from grateful alumni. A rosin bag served as a paperweight.

"They treat you all right in the press box?" Yablonski asked the sportswriter.

The question wasn't idle. The *Star* held franchises from all news services; only through its columns could today's radiance be spread beyond the state.

"No complaints," the sportswriter said.

"O.K., then," said Red, spitting out lather. "Now you treat *us* right."

No one asked Al anything. Red avoided his eyes, and Yablonski didn't know him. Yet as it turned out, Al had the big story from Gideon that day. He had spotted the button bins and interviewed the sulking concessionaire during the second half, and back at the Inne he wrote two columns, both of which Hallam Caulkin printed on page one.

The sportswriter's copy was handled differently. Caulkin pasted the sheets together, spread the story on his huge desk, and then attacked it with flashing scissors. Red, reaching the Student Union newsstand before breakfast next morning, riffled through the *Sunday Star* sports section three times before he found the result. The story ran a full column, but it was largely devoted to the color of the midshipmen's brigade, and though the score was given, and the scoring plays described, there were no names there — not even his.

**

Monday morning Red was called to Tate's office.

The provost had read Elsie Shoemaker's report on Daffy and filed it with contempt. He had no intention of being hoodwinked so. Rather he planned a quiet chat, a tactful little lecture on the proprieties without names or charges, with nothing in the open, but with a veiled warning that couldn't be mistaken. It was to be one of those discreet interviews on which he prided himself, and he awaited Red confidently. His assurance lasted less than a minute. He had scarcely lit his first cigarette of the morning when his plans were swept aside by a savage complaint involving, not one student, but the entire Department of Physical Education. It was Tate's first crisis as acting president, and he handled it badly.

The department was his blind spot. Skillful at intrigue elsewhere, he had been obliged to leave athletics entirely to Doc, and although he understood the team's importance, he had only the haziest idea of the machinery behind it. Tate dealt with academicians, not the public. He was a shrewd mayor of the palace who never glanced over the balcony at the street mob below. Because the Yablonski System was a mystery to him, he had assumed beating Navy was enough, at least until next Saturday. He didn't realize how vital to the System national publicity was, and he hadn't even bothered to look for the sportswriter's account of Saturday's game.

He couldn't understand why Red was so sullen.

"That was a splendid feat Saturday," he greeted him merrily. "Or rather feats — two really remarkable runs."

Red slumped in one of the three tubular steel chairs facing the desk. "I'm glad somebody heard about them."

"Why, we all *saw* them."

"All that were there."

"Well, yes. But that was over forty thousand people, Red."

He didn't know him well enough to call him that — this was their first meeting — but so great was Red's celebrity that even officers of the administration treated him with that daring familiarity which is really a kind of deference. It was accepted, as forty thousand cheers had been, with regal nonchalance. Red slumped further and yawned. It looked like disdain but wasn't. He was exhausted. With the rest of the Titan squad he had spent yesterday monitoring broadcasts and studying out-of-town- papers, listening and looking for some word about himself. There had been none. Red was an actor who had discovered, as the house lights went up after his opening performance, that all the aisle seats were empty. Tense with frustration, he had registered at the Gideon Arms with Daffy under the alias of George Meier and flung himself upon her before the bellboy was halfway down the hall. Less than an hour later he gripped her again, and then again, heaving each time in a groping frenzy, as though this would resolve that, sponge away that, dissipate that galling disappointment. It hadn't, and now in a gray fatigue he stared at Tate from under puffy lids, his eyes strained and dull.

Tate propped a dainty, loafered foot on the desk blotter. Informality, he believed, was the key to easy relations with students. He never permitted them to sir him, or hold a door for him. We want no Uncle Toms at State, he said each year in his orientation speech for freshmen. We're all students, all equal. Faculty aren't a privileged class, and the best way to show them proper respect is by respecting yourself.

He took a Marlboro and slid the pack toward Red.

"I can't smoke," Red muttered. His lids were very low. He was in danger of falling asleep.

"Excuse me, of course you can't," Tate trilled, toying with an unlit match. "Rules, rules!" He shook his head and smiled sadly at the irony of rules. "But where would we be without them? Suppose men were free to murder? You and I might be dead. I'm sure *I* would be." He snickered, thinking that rather good, and was annoyed to see Red's head sinking toward his chest. "Or suppose," he said quickly, "we were allowed to copulate in public."

"Copulate?" Red repeated sluggishly.

"Make love," Tate translated. He hesitated and added sportively, "Screw."

Red woke up. "Sir?"

Tate let that pass. He said craftily. "I'm thinking of a couple named Jonson, until quite recently residents of the College Inne."

Red had uncrossed his legs in alarm. Now he lazily recrossed them. For one bad moment he had thought Tate knew about the Meiers. The Jonsons were dead, and he felt safe. "Never heard of them."

Tate lit his cigarette and prepared to try another tack. The match was still smoking when his desk buzzer buzzed. Mr. Yablonski, his secretary announced, was outside and anxious to see him.

Actually Yablonski was inside. He had given her his name and kept walking, and he was standing on the threshold, almost filling the doorway with his low, powerful shoulders. His light hair was tousled. He looked worried.

"Tate, I—" He saw Red. "What are you doing here?"

"I asked him over," Tate said, standing jerkily.

"Wait in the hall, Stacy." Yablonski ordered, but before Red could struggle up Tate intervened.

"I think he may as well stay," he said, looking straight at the coach. This was his office, he was the provost, he would give the orders. Tate knew very little about football, but he understood authority, and never permitted his to be subverted. "Suppose you join us."

Yablonski perched doubtfully on a chair. "I think there's some things shouldn't be discussed in front of students."

"I disagree," said Tate, who assumed Yablonski had heard about the Inne and was here to discuss it. "It's been my experience that secrecy always backfires. If this matter's to be settled it will have to be with Red's open cooperation. I had preferred to handle it man-to-man, but now you're here perhaps you can help."

The coach frowned. "What does a halfback know about newspapers?"

"What?"

"I came to talk about coverage."

"Coverage?"

"The *Star*'s blackballing us."

"Screwing us. Copulating us," Red said with a ghostly grin. He was in real trouble now — he could see the suspicion in Yablonski's eyes — but the defiant imp in him was irrepressible.

"What's this man-to-man stuff?" Yablonski demanded.

Tate fluttered a gaunt hand. "Oh, we were just discussing how we must all observe certain regulations."

"What's that got to do with the team? Our bib's clean. And our training table alone has more regulations than the rest of the campus put together. Every man's got to account for every meal."

Tate was nettled. "But not every night, it seems."

"Yeah, every —" Yablonski broke off and turned his poker face to Red. "You been screwing *me*, Stacy?"

"Not you," said Tate, with a nervous little laugh.

"So on top of everything else I got to start running bed checks," the coach said, glaring at Red. "O.K., that's the way it's going to be. You're campused, kid. Starting tonight you sleep alone."

Still the imp, still defiant, Red asked, "And days?"

"Days you can harpoon every broad in Gideon," Yablonski snapped, forgetting the provost.

Officially Tate couldn't agree. He coughed into his hand and said delicately, "The woman in question is a mother."

"No mothers," Yablonski said quickly. "I mean" — he lifted huge, helpless hands — "no anybody."

But the damage had been done, and Red, thoroughly awake, was relishing it. Things weren't going at all as Tate had expected. He decided to change the subject.

"You have some problem with the newspapers?"

It was then Tate's morning began to go hopelessly awry. Red's flouting of the Athletic Dorm curfew annoyed the coach, but it was incidental. The issue of publicity was central. A few minutes ago, he told Tate, he had left a council of war in the gym. The departmental staff had agreed bitterly that they couldn't hope to attract prime out-of-state material if the *Star* blackout continued. The paper had never been generous with the team, but in other years its stories had been adequate. Although buried in the *Star* they had been sent out on national sports wire and displayed elsewhere. This season the Titans were in limbo, and the coach knew why. The *Star*'s sports editor had called last night and told him in confidence. The paper was out to beat Doc, and this was one way to do it. They were going to play down State victories in the hope that readers' pride in the team — and gratitude to Doc — would atrophy.

"A real political football, eh?" the provost said with a feeble smile. Both Yablonski and Red glared angrily, and, feeling in need of reinforcements, Tate buzzed his secretary. "Ring the president's office," he told her. There was no response. He tried the Mansion, but Jill, answering there, said Doc and Newt Albert had left an hour before on an extended campaign tour.

In despair Tate summoned from down the hall John Winkler, the university's public relations director, a bright young protégé of Sam Theanapolis. Sam handled most university releases from his Birmingham office; Winkler was his liaison man here. As an accredited media specialist he should, Tate felt, be able to offer them some expert advice. He took the third chair and, to Tate's horror, immediately began spreading gloom. The *Star* strategy was no news to him. He had just finished a half-hour telephone conference with Birmingham, listening to Sam's caustic appraisal of the football story and Al Swinton's campaign button spread. In Sam's opinion, Winkler reported, the prospect was bleak. Inside the state there were some grounds for optimism — the Rockton, Dudley, and Pawnattuck papers had sent reporters to Saturday's game and had carried proper accounts — but outside there was nothing, because *Star* control of the news services was absolute. Appealing to the services' New York offices would be useless. The newspaper business always closed ranks against complaints, however reasonable, and the rest of State's games would be regional anyhow. If the Titans couldn't hit with Navy, they couldn't hit all season, at least not until the bowl selections.

"What about magazines?" Tate asked helplessly.

"That *Star* reporter, Swinton, tells me *Sly* magazine has a photographer roving around New England. They have a tremendous circulation, but of course they're not exactly legit."

Tate inquired about other magazines. Winkler shook his head forlornly. Most periodicals worked months ahead on sports stories, and Sam had no contacts with the others. The Hampshire game would get some attention through television; the rest of the season's scrapbook would be blank. It wasn't pretty, but there it was. If a newspaper decided to play for keeps it usually won. He sat back wanly, and everyone looked at Tate. The provost couldn't think what else to say, so he said that it certainly was a real problem.

That was enough for Yablonski. He slapped his hands on his thighs and rose. He had made his point. If there were recriminations later, he was on record with the administration.

"It's your problem, Tate. You and Doc got to carry the ball on this one."

Tate was about to explain that Doc was away when his secretary rang him. Al Swinton was on the telephone, asking about Doc's tour. The provost felt too unsettled to deal with Al. He asked Winkler to take the call in his office. Winkler hurried out, and Yablonski, following, asked whether Tate had finished with Red.

"Ah — no." He restored his loafer to the blotter. Perhaps if he were alone again with Red he could reach an agreement with him, salvaging some dignity. "We'll be just a bit longer."

It wasn't a happy decision. Because Tate didn't understand the Yablonski System, he thought Red vulnerable to administration pressure. If he hadn't been so harassed by the coach, he would have sensed that something was wrong, for as Winkler spoke Red's face had grown darker and darker. Yablonski had been indignant; Red was infuriated. There would be other seasons for the coach, but Red had banked on making his reputation this year. By Christmas he had expected to be another Doak Walker, collecting royalties from some manufacturer of children's clothes selling little polo shirts with his name on the front and his jersey number on the back. By spring he had hoped to be in a professional camp, on salary. That hope couldn't survive press oblivion. A rare Johnny Unitas could reach pro ball from the sandlots; everybody else depended on the college all-star spotlight, and the all-star chances of a halfback who couldn't even make his local paper were zero. The *Star*, in a campaign tactic, was destroying Red's dream. He felt persecuted, truculent, mutinous.

Had he been another student this wouldn't have mattered. Tate's authority would have subdued him. He would have lied about his affair, as Daffy had, or mumbled apologies, or promised to behave. But Red had his own authority, and in some ways it exceeded Tate's. He was the indispensable member of a team which had acquired extraordinary significance in the state. To tens of thousands of honorary alumni he was the university's best-known undergraduate, the most successful and the most glamorous. He was a public figure, and Tate wasn't, and Red knew what that meant.

Status was important to Red. Since his sophomore year in Pawnattuck High he had been flattered by older men, awarded silver cups and gold footballs, enriched by worshipful fans, and granted immunities beyond other boys — beyond, often, the most eminent men in the state. In his seventeenth year he had been picked up almost weekly for traffic violations. He had been released every time by doting policemen. The week before his last game for Pawnattuck a fifteen-year-old girl had charged him with statutory rape. He was in jail just five hours. The girl's parents were bribed by a prosperous young real estate man, a State alumnus who had bailed him out and told him to forget it. That Saturday Red had scored five touchdowns, and in the celebration afterward at the Pawnattuck Country Club the real estate man's wife had given herself to him in the rear of a Chrysler station wagon, panting thickly all the while that she shouldn't do this, she couldn't help it, he was so wonderful, they must hurry so no one would miss them and no one would know.

Everyone had known. Red had told them. He bragged about her, about the fixed traffic tickets, had even bragged about the rape fix, because he not only enjoyed his privileges; he also had to flaunt them. Like any outlaw he recognized some limits — he hadn't taunted the cuckold or jeered at the girl's parents, and in Gideon he had observed certain formalities with Daffy — but he made sure people found him out, and he swaggered when they did. He expected to be tolerated. He assumed it as a right. If Tate had accosted him with ironclad evidence of his transgression Red would have been discomfited, because that would have meant the provost's hand was being forced, but he didn't mind Tate knowing. In Pawnattuck he had discovered that as long as he didn't go too far people would continue to suffer him. That sufferance was his ransom from society, the source of the peculiar prestige he needed and took. He meant to continue taking it as long as he could, which was why he had determined to move quickly into a professional league. If bungling administrators were going to keep him in Gideon another year he had no intention of giving an inch to the bunglers.

And so he yielded nothing to Tate. The exasperated provost tried wit, charm, logic, appeals, threats, and even invoked the name of morality. There was no response. Red listened, but didn't reply, and after a hour's harangue Tate had the uneasy impression that he was making himself ridiculous. He felt mocked. In the middle of a sentence he remembered the stolid midshipmen watching the billowing white handkerchiefs and understood, as he hadn't then, their humiliation.

When Red finally spoke it was to make a demand. He watched Tate light a fresh cigarette and said suddenly, "Daffy's in a lousy unit."

Tate was so startled his foot fell off the desk. "I don't understand."

"You know, her place. In Realgonesville."

"Mrs. Dix is dissatisfied with her apartment?" he asked quickly, groping for some excuse to end his dreadful monologue.

"It's real crummy. All jammed up, she says, and the crazy drains get stuck."

"Scandalous. It sounds like a hovel — a place to escape from." Tate leaned forward. "Perhaps she'd be happier with her family if she were located in other quarters."

"One of those corner jobs is what she wants."

"Reasonable, quite reasonable." The provost made a swift memo and stood to escort him out. "I only wish you'd mentioned it before." His monkey face wrinkled in a little smile. "With the Dixes in a more commodious, sanitary home, I'm sure Gideon will have seen the last of the Jonsons."

Red grinned wearily. He had a badminton lab with Daffy at two o'clock. By tonight everybody in University Village would know what pull could do, and he meant to see that they knew whose pull it was.

In the hall Tate made his final error of the day and gained from it an insight. John Winkler was bowed over a water cooler. Tate tapped him playfully on the shoulder and said, "You know, we shouldn't dismiss *Sly* entirely, John. It mayn't be *Harper's*, but it *is* read."

That was the error. Red perked up, and Winkler said under his breath, "I mentioned that to Sam. He told me no dice. Doc would veto anything there."

"How come he gets to veto?" Red cried, furious again. "Didn't he resign or something?"

"Dr. River is on leave," Tate said tautly.

"He'll be back before the season's over," Winkler said.

And that was the insight. As Red shambled off growling, Tate asked Winkler softly, "Is that also Sam's opinion?"

Winkler flushed. It wasn't Sam's. It was his own, and he hadn't meant to blurt it out. Yet having said it, he refused to retreat — refused even to admit that Sam disagreed. Sam, he thought, was turning a blind eye to the inevitable. "I'm just projecting a trend," he explained defensively. "After all, that *Star* poll's on the up and up. It gives Witty a tremendous edge."

Tate had discounted the poll. Insulated from political realities, believing what he wanted to believe, he had convinced himself that Doc would move to Birmingham in three months and leave him in permanent command here. Until now he hadn't even considered an alternative. He was numbed by the thought that a publicity expert should be pessimistic. Tate didn't know that public relations is an inexact science; he believed that experts could judge the public temper with a sure eye. All month a pendulum of trust had been swinging in him, arching faster and higher toward the exhilarating day when Doc would become governor-elect and his provost president-elect of State. Now the pendulum was arrested. The exhilaration was gone. He was at a standstill.

Back in his office he dealt listlessly with his mail, fumbling at memoranda pages as, within, he groped for some way to regain the sense of movement. A note from Newt Albert asked Tate to have his secretary send along the schedules of the university's service directors. He hesitated, then endorsed it and tossed it in her basket. At the bottom of the pile was a copy of Mikel's student survey. An attached note, from the History Department secretary, said Dr. Mikel was most anxious that the enclosed be kept secret. The provost scanned it with contempt. The questions were so typical of the traditionalist, he thought. Fogies like Mikel could never understand that rote memorization of the Bill of Rights meant nothing, that application was everything. He read the footnote and smirked. Vicksburg! What nonsense! The students who had confused it with a remedy had at least shown some grasp of essentials. Far better that they should recognize a few reliable brands — things they could *use* — than the names of ancient battles, lost causes, dead Presidents, and obsolete statutes.

He called his secretary in. "File this. It's not likely I'll want it again, but lock it up. In lay hands it might be misinterpreted."

She had a final memorandum for him. Before leaving in pursuit of Doc Al Swinton had dictated a list of telephone numbers, in the event anyone here should want to reach him. "I told him it wasn't likely," she said, smiling. "Want me to file it, too?"

The pendulum in Tate flickered slightly. It was only a tremor. He did nothing, resolved nothing. Nevertheless he reflected for the first time that while Doc's election was the cleanest way to vacate the presidency, there were others, and that if the next *Star* report showed him still trailing it might be time to leave his bandwagon.

"No, I'll keep it right here." He slipped it under his blotter. "Something might come up."

It was the decision of an opportunist, a shuttlecock. It wasn't evil, and Tate wasn't an evil man. He was — though he would have recoiled at the thought — very like Red Stacy. Like him he was the harvest of a restless seed planted long ago. Tate was a faithful husband and conscientious father, had never raped a child or run a red light, didn't even jaywalk or throw candy wrappers on the ground, and had been, at the age when Red was learning how to use his elbows in a scrimmage, an Eagle Scout. Yet it had really been the same thing. Both had been straining for public approval, yearning for applause and only that, regarding that as triumph and its lack as failure. Red needed sanction for peccancies, Tate for achievements. Red felt larger than life when he saw himself in the distorted carnival mirror the cheering faithful held up to him, and it was the same with the provost. Only through the approbation of others could he admire himself, and since he could settle for nothing less, he would seize any weapon, any plan that would bring him the gilt and braid and sprangles of distinction. It wasn't evil. It was ambition. But there was evil in it.

**

Ham Markham was in the College Inne flush, fencing with the old-fashioned straight razor which had been his father's only legacy while Al Swinton stood by the basin in a dramatic trench coat.

"Everybody plays I got a secret with me," Al was moaning. "Newt Albert just took Doc off in the bush without a word. Wouldn't you think he could dial here just once?"

Ham carved a swath of foam from one cheek. "Maybe he caught his finger in yesterday's *Star*."

"Oh, Cripes, Ham, cut it out. You know I got a job to do."

"Then do it." He rinsed the razor. "But don't count on any help."

Al made setter eyes. "I looked for a little from you."

"Sorry."

"You know, you *could've* told me about them kids shacked up next door to you."

"*So* sorry."

A sudden thought aroused Al. "Say, I'll bet you got them out of here!" Ham toweled his face in silence, and Al puffed indignantly. "How about that! The best story of the campaign and my sweetheart buddy sells me out! If I was a stoolie I'd squeal to the colonel."

"Squeal. Only do it somewhere else, *please*."

Al barged out, making wounded noises. He left the door ajar, and Ham, stepping over to close it, saw him trudging down the hall with his boxy portable in one hand and a big suitcase in the other, looking from the rear like the *Death of a Salesman*. He had worked tirelessly all yesterday afternoon on Daffy and Red, and this morning he had confessed his failure to Ham. Mrs. Prouty had been tight-lipped, the couple worse. At the Athletic Dorm Red hadn't even given him a chance to speak. He had reared up, denounced the *Star*'s Navy game story, and slammed the door. Defeated there, he had traced Daffy to the village and found her sunbathing in her back yard. She had denied ever seeing him before, and, when he pressed her, had threatened to have him arrested as a Peeping Tom. Ham watched Al's plodding figure with pity which turned to self-pity when he saw he was coming back.

"Do me one favor," Al asked, thrusting his gangster face around the jamb. "A friend of mine might come through town. If he noses in here tell him I'll be back the end of the week. Bugger's named Geek Minton. He's a *Sly* photographer."

"A sly what?"

"You know, the magazine. You never saw it in India? It's terrif. I subscribe — there's some copies in my room if you get lonesome. Well, off to the wars."

Ham was startled that Al subscribed to anything. It was too early to see Nails Whipple at Peabody, and he spent a half-hour looking at Al's dog-eared *Slys*. He turned the glossy pages slowly, conscious that his ears were tingling like a boy's. Girlie magazines were an aspect of postwar America the international edition of the *Times* hadn't covered. In Ham's youth the most provocative literature sold in corner drugstores had been *Spicy Adventure Stories*, with lush, formalized passages describing low necklines. *Sly*, a generation later, had turned to graphic arts and dropped the neckline to the hips. Issue after issue revealed young, heavy-breasted women in lace pants or G strings climbing trees, emptying whisky bottles, leapfrogging over one another, or lying lazily on sunlit beaches, caressing themselves. There were girl-of-the-month and party-of-the-month features, instructive articles on seduction techniques, and letters-to-the-editor columns of correspondence from high school boys who described the figures of their steady dates and, occasionally, included confirming snapshots in *Sly* costume. Obscenity charges were apparently dodged with a few departments about manly arts (knife-fighting skills, zip guns); current vogues ("Join the Beat Generation — Buy a Beat Tieclasp"); and spreads on sports. Even here, however, the dominant theme appeared occasionally, and one copy carried a goatish picture sequence, obviously posed, showing a lithe, raven-haired girl in trunks pinning a muscle-bound wrestler to the floor.

He took it to Peabody, wrapped in the morning *Star*.

Entering Whipple's office he had second thoughts. Pornography seemed a jarring note in the rococo graystone library, and the old man's study, on the second floor, was lined with thick leather-bound books and illuminated by leaded casement windows, like a monk's cell. Whipple, however, spotted it bulging between the folds of newsprint. He looked up inquiringly.

"An offering from the outer world," Ham said grandly, laying it on the teak desk.

Whipple glanced through it and tossed it aside. "Amazing how little text they carry."

"You skipped the climax," Ham protested.

Whipple smiled. "I imagine you're thinking of the ill-matched pair grappling on the mat. No, I saw it last month in my copy."

"*You*'re a subscriber?" Ham whispered, gaping.

He leaned back, wheezing with laughter until his face was rose pink. "Forgive me," he said weakly. "I should have explained. I'm a member of the Chicago Group. The outer world is less a mystery to me than you suppose. We're investigating popular culture and I'm afraid this" — he tapped *Sly*'s slick cover — "is very popular. An interesting comment on American immaturity, don't you think?"

Ham said he thought it inflammatory. Whipple nodded thoughtfully.

"Yes, I must say I'm glad the student senate voted to bar the genre here. A responsible decision, most gratifying. Otherwise I don't know what we should have done. The faculty wouldn't have dreamt of interceding, of course. The undergraduates would have screamed censorship with one voice."

"And that would have mattered?"

"Assuredly."

"It wouldn't stop Doc," Ham said, with a touch of pride.

"No. Indeed, it hasn't — Harry Mikel tells me *Sly* is outlawed on the other side of town by administrative fiat."

"The same end, differently reached."

"Yes. But it's an important difference, Mr. Markham. Like State, Peabody has changed over the years. Once it was rigidly authoritarian. Compulsory chapel is a vestige of that era, and almost the only one. Now, so far as is possible, we rule with the consent of the governed."

"Well, that's nice when you can get it —"

"It's more than nice. It's necessary. You're listening to a rather jaded voice of experience. You see, I learned a few things about forbidding exotic fruit during Prohibition." He lit a Turkish cigarette and inhaled deeply. "Which brings us, I believe, to why you're here this morning."

Ham frowned. "It does?"

"You're interested in Adam's expulsion."

Prohibition evoked for Ham a few phantasmal childhood memories — jokes about the bubbling vats in a neighborhood warehouse, recollections of dark men in derbies and fitted black overcoats entering there after dark, a man in the next block who died after drinking melted Sterno strained through bread — but unlike the Depression it was too remote; it hadn't touched him, and he couldn't see what it had to do with Doc.

"Don't tell me he was thrown out for being a lush. I don't believe he's taken anything stronger than buttermilk in his life."

Whipple's smile was ghostlike. "You know, I'd completely forgotten that. You're right, of course. The students called him 'The Buttermilk Bootlegger.' "

"Doc was a bootlegger?" Ham asked incredulously.

"Actually he wasn't that important. Remember, he was only a freshman. He drove a truck between Rockton and Gideon twice a week."

Ham dampened dry lips. "He needed money that bad?"

"He did indeed. His father was poor and had little sympathy with his son's ambition. He resented his absence from the family farm. Adam had to make it all here."

Still, it was hard to think of Doc convoying beer. "Weren't there any other campus jobs?"

"Not for him. You see, football was rather a Caliban here in the Twenties. We were a bit like State today, if you'll pardon me, but worse, because the college had no control over it. We hadn't any football scholarships — we were too pious for that. Instead, we allowed a few zealous alumni to manage everything." He crinkled his eyes; the admission was distasteful. "They brought husky boys here and found them employment. It was a quasi-official system; once you were in it there was no way out, and because one of the most generous alumni was interested in an illicit distillery, there was always a small group earning its keep by defying the Volstead Act. I recall one ingenious quarterback who delivered gin to fraternities on a commission basis and made enough to finance his way through medical school. Adam, however, wasn't so lucky."

"But why, if he only drove a truck?"

Whipple opened a drawer and drew out a slim Manila folder, gray with dust. "I shouldn't show you this," he said, sliding it across the desk, "but as an admirer of Adam's you're privileged. I'm sure you'll be discreet, and in any event it's all history now."

He busied himself with a manuscript as Ham opened the folder, gingerly, like a child pushing aside a door in an abandoned house, half expecting the stiff cardboard to creak and bats to fly out. Whipple had been right the first time, he thought; he shouldn't show him this. It was better to remember Doc the day of his magnificent solo run than to think of him as a jazz age bravo. As Whipple rambled on Ham had conceived an image of an oversized young Edward G. Robinson wearing a baggy Coolidge cap and roaring through the night in a blunt-nosed Mack truck loaded with barrels marked XXX, and it was surprising — almost disappointing — to find that the only picture of Doc inside was a small, quite conventional photograph attached to a Peabody application form. In it Doc was seated squarely before the camera, looking much as he had when Ham first met him — the face blander, perhaps, but hard and driven all the same, and rough with the peculiar crudity of farm boys, as though the features had been whittled from tough wood by a Yankee idler squatting before a north county general store on a chilly autumn evening long ago.

The completed application itself had a curious pathos. An adolescent youth had provided cagey answers to set questions, unaware that he was giving the college archives a glimpse of himself far sharper and more indelible than any photograph could be. Probably Doc had sat in his farmhouse parlor, Ham thought, cramped in a seat too small for him, licking his pencil — the lead scrawl had a licked look — and fretting over each word, hedging every possible bet. But the form was too smart for him. It faithfully disclosed him as River, Adam R., aged 19, height 6′5″, weight 205 lbs., eyes blue, hair brown, with conspicuous identification marks on the right shoulder blade (birthmark), the left thigh (scythe scar), and the left forearm (sickle scar). The roll continued — Church: Congregrational. Education: Walpole County schools. Father's name: Amos River. Mother's name: Elspeth Hickok River. Father's occupation: farmer. Mother's occupation: farmer's wife. Father's college: none. Mother's college: none. Last grade attended by father: 6th. Last grade attended by mother: 4th. Father's income: $900 a year. Siblings, if any: a blank. Letters of recommendation enclosed from: Reverend Bard, Lawyer Wiggins, both of Walpole County, and Bigelow Thayer Carlisle, Osgood Building, Birmingham. Previous employment: helping father on the farm. Hobbies: playing football, touch, baseball, hockey, soccer, track, basketball, wrestling, boxing, swimming, horseshoe-pitching, weight-lifting, and other healthy sports with the fellows.

A high school transcript was attached. It suggested that Doc had been an excellent student, but like most reports from rural schools it was unreliable. Doc's midterm report from Peabody, his only marks there, had been far less impressive. He had been in the 60's in every course but one. The soaring exception was Physical Education, an even 100. Ham turned the page in his lap, thinking how Mikel must have relished that, and glanced down the next form. It was the last, for he was at the end of routine records, and it was from the Dean of Freshmen. Efficient notations established that River, Adam R., '28, lived in Appleton Hall, was advised by Assistant Professor David Young, was a numerals member of the freshman football squad, had attended chapel faithfully, and had been pledged by three social organizations — Green Letter, the Mystical Thirteen, and Beta Theta Pi. Three was a lot. Doc had been a popular freshman. If he had survived his classes he doubtless would have been elected to the student senate, perhaps even to the presidency of his class.

Achievement ended there, however. The next entry was ominous.

Dec. 17, 1924

Peabody College
Office of the Dean of Freshmen

Dean Whipple,

The undersigned requests a conference at your earliest convenience over the status of Adam R. River '28. A grave disciplinary matter has arisen as a consequence of inquiries from the state police, with whom Dave Young, River's adviser, is now in touch.

Victor Smith-Reising,
Dean of Freshmen

CC: The President
Asst Prof. Young

Then a carbon:

Dec. 17, 1924

Peabody College
Office of the Dean

Smith-Reising,

I suggest we convene in my study at 10 P.M. tomorrow, Dec. 18. Please ask Dave Young to send me a full report.

W. W. Whipple
Dean

CC: The President
Asst. Prof. Young

Young's report followed:

Dec. 17, 1924

Peabody College
Department of English

Dean Whipple,

This morning I was visited by one Trooper Riley Walsh of the State Police, who had just returned from investigating the sordid crime last night at the Hi-Di-Hi Funland roadhouse outside Rockton. Trooper Walsh informed me that the entire affair was observed by Adam R.

River, '28, and that River's presence will be required at the trial as a material witness.

Naturally I was appalled. I informed the officer that Peabody men do not frequent such establishments, and that River had no business being there. He corrected me. It seems that River was on the premises in his capacity as driver for a Birmingham firm. It also seems that this firm is illicit and has as its main interest the transporting of contraband spirits landed on the coast by launch.

Before I could recover from my shock, Trooper Walsh said that quite apart from the major arrest arising from the Hi-Di-Hi episode, River is being detained in Rockton on the charge that his lorry, parked outside the roadhouse, contained fifteen crates which, inquiry disclosed, bore milk bottles filled with beverages of high alcoholic content. Apparently the source was Scotland.

I instantly telephoned Edward Illington, '12, a Rockton attorney and classmate of mine, asking him to interview River in his cell. Eddie called me back an hour later and said the boy is guilty as charged and admits it. River became quite agitated under interrogation and made preposterous allegations about a trustee of this College, which I shall not dignify with repetition on College stationery.

Respectfully,
David H. G. M. Young
Assistant Professor

CC: The President
Dean of Freshmen Smith-Reising

After that there was an urgent holograph:

Dec. 17, 1924

Peabody College
Office of the President
Nails,

Move fast on River. No injustice, but if Young's minute stands up—if the boy really has blotted his copybook—we're in grave danger of having a felon enrolled. This is the stickiest possible wicket. Clear up *everything* before the trial.

Thorton

Everything was cleared up in the December 18 meeting. A brief stenographic record noted that after a discussion and review of evidence, Whipple, Smith-Reising, and Young voted for the immediate expulsion of Adam R. River for proscribed conduct. The registrar received a two-line memorandum instructing him to strike the name of River from the 1928 class roster, and a note was sent to Doc. It was written by Whipple, and was kind.

Dec. 18, 1924

Peabody College
Office of the Dean

Dear Adam,

I know this is a hard time for you, and it is my bitter lot to add to what must seem an intolerable burden. This morning the administrative officers of the College decided to remove you from Peabody's rolls. We had no choice, Adam. I'm not as shy of scandal as some of my colleagues, but I am bound by certain College regulations. Is this fair? Perhaps not. I confess I have my doubts. But there it is — I set it down with a sick heart — there it is.

I should count it a personal favor if, when you are free of your present legal difficulties, you would drop in and call on me.

Yours faithfully,
Nails Whipple

There were no other entries, and Ham closed the folder. Whipple looked up from the manuscript line he had been studying for ten minutes.

"Well?" he said gently.

Ham was staring down at the closed folder. "Did he ever come to see you?"

Whipple shook his head. "I scarcely expected him. He naturally regarded all of us as unspeakable hypocrites, and I suppose we were really. In those days Peabody followed the fallible principle that sin lies, not in sinning, but in getting caught. Nearly everyone here knew some players were paying their tuition with tainted money — that dreadful prig Young was an exception, to be fair to him. Some of us had protested, but we hadn't been able to produce any evidence." He crushed his cigarette in a tray. "Not, mind you, that it was wrong to expel Adam. Our error lay in our failure to turn out the whole lot, the adroit quarterback included. But we were powerless."

"Because of that trustee?"

He dodged that one. "The real trouble was the president. We were helpless until old Thornton died after the war. And then, of course, we gave up the game entirely."

Thornton's use of the word felon rankled in Ham. "Was Doc convicted?"

"Convicted, yes — the case was flagrant. The sentence was suspended, however. His testimony in the other case was invaluable, and the Rockton court released him after the trial. He slipped into Appleton Hall, packed his things, and vanished. Even the proctor didn't see him. Mikel claims that Adam worked in a circus that spring, displaying feats of strength and earning enough to enter State in the fall. I don't know where he heard that. A friend in Walpole did tell me that Adam's family helped a little. His father approved of State." The ghostly smile reappeared. "He thought Adam would become a farmer."

And that, Whipple's tone implied, was that. But Ham knew it wasn't. He had heard too many pat stories not to see the holes in this one.

"What was the sordid crime?"

"The what?"

"The other case."

"At Hi-Di-Hi Funland? Oh, some unidentified man was shot. That's really all I recall."

Yet you remember the place, Ham thought. And somehow the Hi-Di-Hi didn't sound like Whipple's cup of tea. He might read *Sly* for the Chicago group now, but as dean he would scarcely have patronized a dive three counties away.

"There's nothing about it in Doc's morgue envelope at the paper," he said mildly.

"I told you Saturday — the *Star* would have winnowed any mention of Adam's Peabody interlude from its files. It was a trying incident for everyone loyal to the college."

"Yet Doc had already been expelled when he went on trial."

Whipple folded his hands.

"The funniest thing," Ham went on, with the same tranquil air, "is that the paper isn't going into it now. They brought up Doc's disqualification at the first crack of the campaign gun, but this is far more telling, and files or no files, the front office must know all about it."

The old man looked down. "I was under the impression that even newspapermen had some ethics."

"O.K." Ham grinned and returned the folder, as though dismissing the whole matter. "You said you'd be good enough to help me with my series on Peabody. Do you suppose I could start today?"

He could; Whipple would be delighted if he would. Springing up, he drew from his vest a glittering brass key. "Come along. The Memorial Room is just down the hall, and I'm sure you'll find everything you want there. If the librarian pokes his meddling head in, refer him to me." He winked foxily. "I'm curator of the collection."

His relief was obvious. The instant Ham dropped the Hi-Di-Hi he had acted like a man reprieved. Evidently when he had agreed to show Ham Doc's Peabody record he had thought the details of Doc's tragic expulsion would be enough. But no tragedy stands alone. He had produced the frayed end of a single cord. Somewhere back there there was a whole net, and, standing alone in the quiet Memorial Room, Ham fell into a reverie, wondering how he could draw it forth.

It was a room for reveries. Between crank-operated French windows were towering shelves crammed with morocco-bound class albums, college histories, sheafs of policy leaflets, old catalogues, and bound volumes of the Peabody *Tartan* dating back to the Civil War. Portraits of bearded men hung in paneled alcoves furnished with antique desks; besides a blackened fireplace stood an enormous Hitchcock chair embellished with an engraved silver plate which announced that it had been built to support William Howard Taft during commencement exercises in 1912. Ham sat in it, feeling skinny, and studied a weathered oak figurehead of a maiden, bolted to a marble-topped center table and taken, according to a plaque below, from the clipper ship *Charity*, with which Isaiah Wigglesworth Browning, Peabody's first great benefactor, had made his fortune in China trade.

So the past touches us all, Ham thought, and not with a dead hand either. Its fingers are clawing and insistent, reminding us that we are because it was. Because there was a Browning, Peabody became. Because Peabody established a prestige of wealth, her sons, barred by Taft's time from the China trade, turned to less romantic industries and in some cases were, during Whipple's deanship, stock swindlers and bootleggers. Because they needed to display the virility of the old school, strongboys like Doc were enlisted — and there, after a century of serenity, the sequence had gone awry. Doc had been cast out and had, in reprisal, devoted his vast energies to hoisting a rival standard. In retrospect his disgrace seemed an ironic act of justice, for Doc hadn't really belonged to

Peabody. The Brahminism of this room had no meaning for him. He had sprung from another strain in the state's past, the lower but tougher line of common seamen, dirt farmers, and struggling urban poor — of men like Ham's father, who had left him a razor and a razor-sharp will to achieve. In begetting State Doc was building for the descendants of that lowly breed what Browning had given the few. Whipple saw that, if Mikel didn't; ahead lay the proper laurel for the children of toiling Yankee generations whose whiskered portraits hung nowhere, whose memories had never been clasped in morocco and on whose shabby trophies were no engraved plates, nor even a legend in the dust to show that they had been here and aspired and gone, leaving only the flesh of their flesh and their dreams of glory to come. The laurel would be grasped, Ham thought, gripping tight the arms of the monstrous chair; the glory would be; and it would come because fate, in a low brawling honky-tonk fouled with blood and spilt drink, had sent Doc back to his own thirty-five years ago.

That had been the crux. That had been the fork, there in a murk so vile even Whipple shrank from it, on that night when Doc witnessed an ignoble killing, was held for questioning, and innocently became a threat that could have exposed the squalor of Peabody athletics. Ham longed to look back down the corridor of years and see who the trustees had been, what fine old state names had been spattered by bootleg Scotch. He had to know, *had* to, he thought, striding from alcove to alcove and rapping absently on the warped, scarred figurehead and the leather book backs and the desks.

There were ways to find out. Whipple had shown more than he knew. Charlie Smathers's morgue envelopes might have been raided, but back issues of the *Star* were on microfilm, and from the folder Ham had taken a date: December 17, 1924.

He also had a name.

In Doc's Peabody application there had been one off-note, his last reference. The first two had been predictable. Probably the Congregationalist minister and the town lawyer had sent off hundreds of recommendations for local boys soliciting appointments and jobs. The third name, however, had been singular. Men with offices in Birmingham's Osgood Building didn't usually write letters for the sons of north county farmers. The Osgood was the most exclusive business address in the state — firms like Sam Theanapolis Associates spent lifetimes trying to rent suites there. There could have been only one explanation for its appearance on Doc's form. It must have been the bridge between Walpole and Gideon, his passport to the Peabody gym — and his license to drive a truck.

Bigelow Thayer Carlisle, Osgood Building, Birmingham.

Ham hunched forward, his chin on his knuckles. In his research for *Through Darkest Birmingham* he had found no Bigelow Thayer Carlisle, but there had been a score of Bigelows, Thayers, and Carlisles; they were three of the oldest, wealthiest, and most conservative families in the state. Maybe the man never existed, he thought. Maybe the reference had been a straw man, a front. Gazing reflectively over his clenched fingers, he saw, on a shelf opposite, a green spine bearing the gold legend *Alumni Directory, Peabody College.* Crossing quickly, he opened the index to C. He caught his breath — there was a whole page of Carlisles — and slumped in disappointment; none was the right one.

Then, as he was sliding the directory back, he saw, on the shelf above, a companion volume, *They Wore Green,* sketches of deceased alumni.

It was there at the top of a left-hand column:

CARLISLE, Bigelow Thayer, '89. Petroleum executive. m. Alice Dubois Otis June 17, 1893. v.p. Carlisle Pipeline Corp. 1889-1899, pres. 1899-1915, ret. 1916. Service home front 1918. Ofc. 5012 Osgood Bldg., Birmingham. Home, 8 West Willow Lane, Birmingham. Clubs: Clipper, Links, Racquet, Pot & Kettle (Bar Harbor). Sigma Nu. Episcopalian. Republican. Died Nov. 1, 1936.

Doubtless wearing, Ham thought grimly, a big Landon sunflower.

**

Ham copied Carlisle's brief biography and, from a tattered old catalogue, the names of Peabody's 1924-1925 trustees. It was all he could do here on Doc, so he started work on his *Star* series, leafing through records in hope of finding a dramatic lead. The hope was faint, for the assignment still seemed deadly, but his luck picked up; on a ledge above the catalogues he discovered an illustrated memoir of the class of 1922, Stuart Witty's, published for its twenty-fifth reunion. The introduction appraised the average '22 man — the size of his family (2.3 children); the number of suits in his closet (8.4), cars in his garage (1.73), and rooms in his house (11.8); and his annual salary ($13,728.49), unearned income ($5,227.51), and savings ($93,-254.11). Even better were two composite photographs formed by superimposing some two hundred negatives over one another. The first used graduation portraits of 1922; the second, pictures taken a quarter century later. Collectively the seniors of the Jazz Age had resembled a blurred Gibson boy, dimple-chinned, Roman-nosed, high-browed, and self-consciously noble. In 1947 everything had changed but the blurring. Heads were hairless and hung sheepishly. The effect was that of a Thurber cartoon, and while it didn't look much like Stuart Witty, in three columns it could be striking.

Ham borrowed the memoir. He doubted Hallam Caulkin was subtle enough to understand the implications of the pictures, but plenty of readers would. The statistics were less likely to pass. Nevertheless they were valuable; Caulkin, hard put to find a reason for killing them, might quit demanding copy. By noon Ham had hammered out the story in the College Inne. It was a good excuse to drive into Birmingham and visit Charlie Smathers's morgue, and he headed there, stopping only for a quick sandwich in the G.A.R. Highway diner. After supervising the reproduction of the photographs in the *Star*'s art department he took the elevator to the top floor. The general managing editor was spending the afternoon on the links — Ham left the pictures and story with his secretary — but Smathers was in the library, surrounded by bundles of poll ballots. He greeted Ham eagerly.

"Gee, Mr. Markham, I haven't seen you since you got back!" Smathers wore an eyeshade and black alpaca coat. He enjoyed the role of the old retainer. "Guess how many envelopes your India specials fill now! Forty-five!"

It was meant as a compliment. Smathers judged all *Star* men by their productivity. Ham bowed. "Maybe I ought to ask for space rates."

"Hey, that's pretty good! Edna! You hear what Mr. Markham said?" A slovenly old woman peered over a filing cabinet and simpered girlishly, and Smathers assumed a businesslike pose. "We made lots of improvements since the last time you was here, Mr. Markham. New equipment, a ready-reference list, and an index, like the *Times*."

"I just want to check some old clips, if you don't mind."

"Mind! Say, that's what I'm here for, and I hope you'll always feel free. What's the name?"

Ham told him, and sat at a little table as Smathers pattered down a file-walled aisle, pattered back with an envelope, and spread before him the neatly scissored scraps that made up Bigelow Thayer Carlisle's *Star* record. There wasn't much. Carlisle had led a pointless, if comfortable life. It was scarcely surprising that Ham hadn't heard of him before. He had lived nearly seventy years as a member of the city's ruling clan without once exciting the readers of the paper, and only a trained eye would have spotted the flaw in his life. Even Ham, looking hard, nearly missed it. The clippings looked so ordinary. A brown, barely legible scrap in six-point type recorded Carlisle's birth, another his graduation from Peabody, and a third, much longer, his wedding at St. Timothy's P.E. Church. After that came a sheaf of dull fragments: "B. T. Carlisles Return from Wedding Trip"; "B. T. Carlisle to Head 1918 'Eat Less' Drive"; "Support Liberty Loan, B. T. Carlisle Urges." Then Ham saw the glimmering, in three brittle paragraphs dated 1921. The first two, from the financial page, announced that Carlisle had filed a bankrupcy petition in early March and withdrawn it a month later. The third, from a September society page, was a glowing item about Mrs. Carlisle, who had "just returned with her husband from their new home in Seal Harbor, Maine, wearing a divine cloche." Ham groped for a pencil. It wasn't much, but it was promising. Carlisle had been broke in the winter, solvent by spring, and flush in the fall. Possibly the divine cloche had had money, but if so, why hadn't she come across before the petition? The alternative was likelier; she hadn't had anything to give, and her husband, cornered, had tapped a rich new vein of cash.

Ham rapidly checked the final stories — an account of Carlisle's appointment as Clipper Club chamberlain in 1928 and his obituary, which was largely devoted to the names of survivors and honorary pallbearers. Then he returned to 1921, reading and rereading until Smathers cleared his throat.

"Anything else, Mr. Markham?"

Ham scraped back his chair and rose. "Yes. You still have that micro machine?"

"Oh, we got a new one." He bustled over to a corner and exhibited it like a salesman, flipping switches and twisting dials. "Any special date?"

Edna was told to bring the 1924 rolls, and Ham sat nervously before the machine's window, toying with its enlargement arm. He was projecting himself into the unknown, and he had a stake there, and as Smathers took from Edna the film for the second half of

December and slipped it on the reel Ham felt an irrational twinge of fear, recoiling from what he had come to find before he had found it.

But he found nothing. The roll was defective.

"*Gee!*" Smathers quickly removed it and held it up to the light, using his thumbs as spools. "Two weeks gone, all gone!"

"Maybe it's only an overexposure," Ham suggested, though he knew better. This was no accident. It had the marks of a thorough, inside job.

The negative confirmed him. It was, a stunned Smathers discovered, a complete blank. Nor was the catastrophe confined to the *Star*. The Birmingham Public Library had destroyed its old files of the paper after receiving its prints of the rolls. There would be no copies to re-photograph. Smathers observed tremulously that this was the worst thing that had ever happened to the morgue. He couldn't understand it. The films had been carefully checked. No one had asked for this roll until today, and only he and the front office had access to the negatives.

"Mr. Caulkin will be fit to be tied," he moaned.

Ham doubted it. Caulkin might, however, wonder what Ham had been looking for in those obliterated weeks, and that could be awkward. This was no time to rock the boat; whatever had been in the *Star* of December 17 must have been high-tension stuff — the front office wouldn't hijack its own microfilm unless the threat had been immense — and Ham shied away when the librarian, anxious to make amends, said that if he would give them some idea of what he had in mind Edna could call an old reporter on the paper's retired list. Ham also recommended that they forget the ruined roll until the election fever had abated, but Smathers would have no part of that. He had to make a full report to Mr. Caulkin in the morning. That didn't give Ham much time. He waved to Edna, pumped Smathers's hand once, and hurried out, shrugging at the librarian's repeated expressions of regret that whatever he had wanted was lost.

Not lost, Ham thought in the descending elevator. Only undiscernible here. The front office could play ducks and drakes with *Star* property, but that particular power of the press ended at the glass lobby door downstairs. *Through Darkest Birmingham* had been more than a trick title. It had suggested a lesson learned by Ham in his first year as a reporter — that no prehistoric quagmire bore such faithful tracks of its inhabitants as the modern city. American society had become so highly organized that no man could drop out of sight overnight without someone ringing the alarm bell, and the most furtive deed left an imprint somewhere. A gunman's gun had a serial number. The bills that an armed robber scooped into his bag were registered in Washington. The kidnaped child was known to officialdom — its fingerprints, its scars, its dental cavities, and X rays of its chest were in the hands of the police before sundown. Everyone was in a hundred ledgers, folders, and photostats recording his I.Q., the consistency of his body tissues, his school record as a child and his annual income since. It was a strange fact that hadn't been shelved somewhere to await the deft hand. The *Star* could hobble Charlie Smathers, but Ham knew there were other paths in the jungle.

The only trouble was that some of them had gates.

He called at the Federal courthouse to find out which would be open to him.

His father-in-law was on the bench, and Ham waited in his chambers, inhaling the odor of old leather and exotic tobacco which seemed to follow Judge Davies everywhere until the massive courtroom door opened and the judge shuffled in, pulling at his mustache.

"Why, Markham! Good to see you, my boy! Ah — is this the day we're to dine?"

"No, sir, that's Thursday. I'm here on something else. I want to ask you about Bigelow Thayer Carlisle."

The judge drew back. Behind his rimless glasses his eyes went distant, as though covered by a film, and in his most clipped voice he said, "I can tell you very little. Biggy Thayer and I scarcely spoke."

It fitted perfectly: Carlisle was the sort of man he would have despised — the mandarin who wasted his life and so betrayed his caste. Ham wondered how much the judge knew about the bootlegging ring, considered asking, and realized that he would share professional confidences with no one.

"It has something to do with Doc."

"Oh. Well. That's another matter entirely. Have a chair. Cigar? No? Then you'll excuse me." He inhaled and held the flaming match. "You know, I rather like Mr. River. There's a certainty of purpose there — definitely impressive. I —" He broke off with a cry of pain; the match had singed his fingers. Nursing them he finished, "I rather look forward to my next Gideon trip."

Ham glanced at the wall clock and quickly told as much of the story as Whipple's terms would allow. His father-in-law sat stock still, chewing his thin cigar, his eyes inscrutable. At the end he lowered the cigar slowly. He was all judge now.

"Precisely what do you want?"

"Just the truth."

"Ah. The ancient defense. And when you have it, what then?"

"Ask me then, sir. I have to know first."

"And why have you come to me?"

Ham grinned. "For legal advice. I'm going to Rockton, and I want to know what I can expect from the courthouse there."

"Well, you can look at the docket, of course. And I suppose —" He studied his injured finger. "How old was River at the time?"

"Nineteen or twenty."

"But not twenty-one."

"No, it's impossible. He was nineteen that spring, when he applied to Peabody."

The judged sighed. "Then you're limited to the docket, I'm afraid. Until 1928 this state regarded everyone who hadn't achieved his majority as a juvenile. The records of their cases weren't privileged. Only a court order could open River's trial to you, and no court," he added dryly, "would regard a quest for truth as adequate justification."

After a pause Ham said doggedly, "O.K., but that's just strike two. The *Star*'s not the only paper in the state. The Rockton *Leader* must have carried something."

The judge groped for a new cigar and rolled it between his palms. He had reached the age when a yearning for peace becomes an almost physical thing. He would face any new issue squarely, but this old scandal seemed extraneous, profitless, irrelevant.

"Markham, I hope you'll be discreet," he said, measuring his words. "Old bones can make a hideous rattle."

"It's all off the record, sir. Look, the last thing I want is to hurt Doc. But I have to find out."

The judge, however, couldn't leave it at that. He escorted Ham out, fidgeting with his unlit cigar. "I had no use whatever for Biggy, and if I knew he'd been mixed up in anything like this I'd curse his memory. But you must remember, my boy — the times were different then. The Volstead era was unlike anything before or since. Why, even the club had a bar!"

Even the club, Ham thought quizzically on the street outside. Even the hushed halls of deep rugs and potted plants where Biggy Carlisle and his peers had shared the sacred ease of the elite. Even there, and even on the venerable campus of Peabody College — as though that were the ultimate test; as though men there were finer and better and therefore forgivable in any exigency. Ham was bemused that his father-in-law, of all men, should be so susceptible to the law of the pack, and it never occurred to him that in the judge's plea for the mood of the Twenties there had been a poignancy very like Ham's own when, arguing with Red Stacy outside the Athletic Dorm, he had recalled memories of the Thirties. The Depression code still guided Ham because that had been the generation of his youth; the decade of bathtub gin, marathon dancing, and flagpole sitting seemed culpable to him because he had come too late, had missed its heyday, and had left none of himself there. Ham thought the judge was calling to him across class lines, when in fact the lines were lines of time.

**

Before leaving Birmingham he called Caulkin's secretary and told her he would spend the night in Rockton's Hotel Metropole. It was risky, but there was a chance Smathers wouldn't report how he had discovered that the roll was missing, and in any event it was unavoidable. Ham belonged to organized society. He wanted no alarm rung for him.

Rockton lay thirty miles from the capital, thirty-five from Gideon. Either way it was a dismal trip. Nothing, not even the sweet cider air of early October, could make Rockton attractive. Downtown was one wide street lined by parking meters and grimy, cluttered, display windows. In the autumn gloaming boys in nail-studed black leather jackets and girls in tight jeans paraded between meters and stores in a slouching route step, slipping off in pairs while men in denim filed in and out of drugstores and taverns or loitered beneath the glaring neon marquee of the only theater. Crumpled copies of that morning's *Leader* scurried in gutters before the first harsh breath of an evening wind as Ham parked before the Metropole's shaggy stone front, paid in advance, and left without inspecting his room. The thick-lipped young clerk scarcely looked up from his copy of *Sly*.

The *Leader* building, in the next block, was a red sandstone freak, all domes and spires and turrets. On the second floor Ham waded through a surf of discarded paper and approached a surly-looking man in the slot of the copy desk horseshoe.

"I'm Ham Markham."

"Yeah?" The slot man wasn't intimidated by big city newspapermen.

"Could you tell me where I'd find the 1924 files of the *Leader*?"

"Sorry, Mac. We lost all our old files in a fire ten years ago."

Ham sagged. It was too much. First the microfilm, then the judge's disclosure that the trial record would be sealed. And now this. He had one chance left.

"Are there any reporters around who were on the *Leader* then?"

The slot man said grudgingly, "Well, there's old Pete Healy. Just what are you looking for?"

"Thanks. I'll wait for Pete."

"You got a long wait, Mac. Pete just answers the phone after hours now. He don't come on till twelve."

"Can you tell me where he lives?"

The man shook his head. "We don't give out that kind of information."

So Ham went back down dirty marble stairs, ate a drugstore ham-on-rye, wrote his wife on Metropole stationery, and returned to the city room as the courthouse clock alongside struck midnight.

The slot man was gone, the paper swept away. On the horseshoe rim, smoking a corncob pipe, sat a wizened little Irishman with neat white hair and bright black mice eyes. Sure, he was Pete Healy. What was the name again? Not Mr. Markham from the *Star!* Well, wasn't this a grand thing to happen to an old man on a quiet night! And hadn't he been reading Mr. Markham's pieces all these years? It was a great pleasure he'd had from them, squatting here and smoking this very same pipe and learning all about those black devils over there. There was nothing he'd like more than to help Mr. Markham any way he could. Of course, 1924 was a long way back. It would be hard to recall any one case—there was lots of booze around in those benighted days. River? No, the only River he'd seen mentioned in the paper then or now was that fine upstanding Democrat from Gideon. But if Mr. Markham had a date it should be simple as rolling off a rain barrel.

"What you need, laddie, is the *Leader*'s 1924 file."

"But it burned up."

"Malarkey. Who told you that? He was taking you up the garden path. Sure, *our* files burned, but the library's got theirs back to the 1880's. You know our library? A grand place—just around the corner from here, opens at nine. And, say" — Ham was retreating, thanking him — "if you find it, give me a call at home. Main 6-6119. I used to cover Rockton courts and police. Maybe a few facts'd tickle my memory."

Ham was waiting at the entrance of the red brick library long before nine the next morning, and in the basement, a dark dank place smelling of mildew and bindery glue, he tugged a filthy file volume from its stack, spread it on the concrete floor, and turned the cumbersome pages by the light of a single naked bulb suspended from the ceiling.

December 17, 1924. Page one. Column eight. Top head.

Hi-Di-Hi Gigolo Shot
Slayer Slays Self
Truck Driver Held

BY PETER N. HEALY

Whipple had been wrong; the killer, not the victim, had been unidentified. There weren't many details about the crime itself. A cabaret dancer named Shoes Lazzano had been murdered in the Hi-Di-Hi parking lot by a well-dressed young man who had saved his last cartridge for himself. But Healy had been a good reporter. He wrote a lot between the lines. Shoes was a bachelor and a fastidious dresser. He had a great many men friends. The well-dressed young man had been seen at the Hi-Di-Hi before, buying drinks for Shoes, and it was understood that Shoes had given him dancing lessons. On one occasion the two men had performed the Charleston on the Hi-Di-Hi floor, and they were believed to have been close. Recently there had been an argument. Shoes had been giving dancing lessons to another man. This, friends of the late dancer believed, was the source of the quarrel which led to last night's tragedy. There were no names in the clothing of the rejected friend — it might as well have read "rejected lover" — but police were investigating.

It wasn't surprising that Doc's name no longer meant anything to Healy. He had disposed of him in two terse sentences:

"Officers are questioning a young driver, Adam River, of no certain address, who was backing his truck away from the service entrance at the time of the shooting. River's cargo has been confiscated and may result in Federal charges against him."

The third sentence — for which Ham silently blessed the garrulous old Irishman — read simply, "The truck bore the license 46-47-60."

Ham had been praying for just such a break. State license numbers were public record, and he knew a clerk in the Department of Motor Vehicles. Back at the Metropole he called Birmingham. It would take only a minute, the clerk said confidently; the 1924 cards were in the next room. Ham sat on his lumpy, unmade bed, watching a late summer fly crawl cautiously up the window's lower pane, and when it reached the top and vanished the man came back on.

He repeated the license number. Then: "That was registered to a corporation, Mr. Markham. Consolidated Enterprises."

Ham wrote it down. "What address?"

"The Osgood Building. That's all, no special office."

Guess again, Ham thought, breathing faster. The odds were a hundred to nothing that that license had been taken out by Biggy Carlisle, or his secretary, or somebody acting on his orders. Ham depressed the receiver briefly and asked the hotel switchboard operator for Main 6-6119.

It took seven rings to rouse Healy. Even then he was still half asleep, and he mumbled incoherently until Ham mentioned Shoes Lazzano.

"Remember? Ah, that I do. It was my finest story that year, laddie. And do you know they never identified that dead boy? With his clothes so grand and his head so bloody. Sad, sad. A sign of the times, the corruption and the sin."

Ham heard a faint rustling and pictured Healy in a nightshirt, crossing himself.

"How about the witness? The truck driver?"

"Oh, he was let off easy. Very cooperative, he was. It was the devil's own mischief that brought him there that night to lug away his hooch. Ten minutes earlier and he'd have been foot-loose and fancy-free, and nobody the wiser."

The license number meant nothing to Healy until Ham reminded him that he hadn't checked it out. The Irishman's pride was stung, his memory stirred. And he had a curious explanation. Until the Thirties his paper had been Democratic. The Republican *Star* had had a monopoly on Statehouse bureaus. *Leader* men could never seem to get anything from them, and Healy, calling that night, had been turned away with a pretext. He remembered it because — and here his voice rose, still indignant after thirty-five years — the *Star* next morning had carried the name of the truck driver's employer.

"*Star* reporters could get anything from those geezers in the capitol," he said bitterly.

"They still can," Ham said. "At least, I just did. The employer was Consolidated Enterprises, Inc."

"Ah, so it was!" A great deal was coming back to him now. "Caught red-handed with their truck full of whiskey, and never a prosecution. Not a word from the Treasury Department in Washington, just a suspended sentence for that poor driver." There was another rustle; this time, Ham guessed, Healy was scratching his head. "But why ask *me* this, Mr. Markham? Your paper knows all about it."

"My paper doesn't tell me everything," Ham said evasively and hung up.

He was getting close to the high-tension wire now, and there were sparks in the air. Clearly the suppression of the microfilm had been necessary because some *Star* reporter, ignorant that the truck driver had highborn superiors, had blundered into print with the name of their firm. It had been a bad show for the nobs in the Osgood Building and the Clipper Club, and all hands had been obliged to sit tight for a few weeks while the big influence peddlers cooed into the right ears in the Treasury Department and Doc took the rap. Then, later, the *Star* story had been destroyed. It had been a classic power play, perfectly executed, with no loose ends.

Nevertheless . . .

Nevertheless it wasn't quite. There was one big black question mark hanging over the whole wretched business, one row of asterisks covering an omitted scene, one jigsaw piece that had been dropped from the card table and kicked under the rug. The paper hadn't started to put issues on microfilm until 1946, ten years after Carlisle's death. That story had lain in Charlie Smathers's morgue for over twenty years, and the front office hadn't twitched a lash. Then, apparently, something had come up; something big and also fragile — so fragile that it could be threatened by this bony old skeleton. What was it? Ham couldn't even guess. When had it happened? He couldn't guess that, either; Smathers had no idea when the film had been ruined. But there was one sure way of finding out: to climb the rest of the ladder and grab that wire. And Ham knew how to do it. The Motor Vehicle clerk said Consolidated Enterprises had been a corporation. All right. Corporations had articles of incorporation, and articles of incorporation had officers. Get the names of those officers, check them out, and he'd come up with the something and the when and why it had been so important. It was a piece of routine investigation, and it led straight back that dreary two-lane road to the Statehouse.

A short afternoon's work.

But he didn't do it that afternoon.

He was still perched on the disheveled bed, rubbing his knees thoughtfully, when the phone rang. It was Hallam Caulkin.

"Good morning, Hiram!" he boomed. "Hope I didn't wake you up!"

Ham's tongue felt thick. Obviously Smathers had mentioned him in his report, and Caulkin's secretary had reported that he was here. There was no way to brazen it out. He had no business in Rockton.

But the general managing editor was diplomatic, almost unctuous. Ham felt sparks again. Nothing could have confirmed his suspicions more. Caulkin didn't inquire what he was doing at the Metropole or even mention Smathers; his only interest was in getting Ham away from his private inquiry, and it was so important to him that he took bitter medicine. He approved Ham's Peabody story.

"It's first rate, Hiram, really terribly good. Of course it makes Peabody men look a bit more plush than we are in these days of the Roman tax, but it has a nice light touch, and the art work is in the right spirit. I'm running it tomorrow." That was the concession. The demand followed swiftly. "By the bye, I'd like another as soon as possible. When can I have it?"

Ham, caught off base, had to agree to hustle back. He glanced at his watch. By early afternoon he could be in Gideon. He promised to send an installment tonight.

"Splendid. And try to keep the stuff coming every day. It's bad to break a series. Subscribers complain. If I have any questions I'll just buzz your billet in the Inne."

It was a clear warning: don't stray again. Ham, however, knew a way around it. Ten years of dealing with Caulkin by cable had taught him high arts of deception. In the trove of the Memorial Room he could easily turn out two stories in one day and slip down to the Statehouse the next morning. If Caulkin discovered him in Birmingham he had an unimpeachable excuse. On Thursday he was to dine with his father-in-law, and the judge was one man the front office respected.

He spent the next day holed up in the Peabody Library, bowed over the memoirs and histories, tracing the growth of the college, making notes on famous professors and trying to sketch a portrait of an institution. By Wednesday night he had finished his fifth story, an account of Witty's undergraduate years. He wasn't happy with it. It was too kind to Witty. Yet he hadn't had any choice. That was the way the record read. If Ham had been narrower he would have clung stubbornly to his prejudices and painted Peabody as the glittering citadel where the sons of privilege lazed away four years learning the mannerisms cherished by the *Star*'s society page. For many it had been that, but others had had a desperate struggle; here and there a *Tartan* issue had carried a revealing item about boys who had held assorted jobs on campus and in the town. Some students, Ham was surprised to discover, had actually worked their way through Peabody, and among them had been several members of old families down on their luck. Witty had been one of these. He had been a grease monkey in a Gideon garage, a soda jerk in a drugstore, an agent for a fraternity pin manufacturer and a book salesman. It wasn't right, it didn't fit, but there it was. It had happened, so Ham had to write it. He pictured Doc reading it and despaired. Doc would be sure he had sold out now; he would never believe that facts, not Ham, had betrayed him.

There was only one way to atone, and that was to find other facts. Early Thursday he was in Birmingham, mounting the Statehouse steps and turning left into the Hall of Records.

The Hall was a busy place. Young lawyers stood shoulder to shoulder before long sloping counters, squinting at muniments; elderly clerks made entries in ponderous journals. Ham had no friends here. *Through Darkest Birmingham* had charged that the Hall was a fraud organized by the state's lawyers, that searching deeds had been made needlessly complex so that every buyer of property would have to hire an attorney and pay him a fee.

It was complex enough. Even articles of incorporation, which rarely interested laymen, were craftily hidden. Logically they should have been filed by title, or at least under the names of their officers, but long ago a Director of Records — appointed, under the state constitution, by the president of the Bar Association — had decided they would be catalogued by date, which meant that normally only lawyers, who had access to the indexes of the Bar Association's annual *Chronicles*, knew where to look for them. Ham today was an exception. He hadn't an exact date, but he had something almost as good.

Just five weeks had lapsed between Carlisle's bankruptcy petition and its cancellation. Articles of corporation were entered in monthly ledgers, and at the chief clerk's window in the rear of the room he filled out a pink slip, ordering the ledgers for March and April, 1921. They were yielded reluctantly — the slit-eyed old man on the other side had never seen him before — but Ham knew his rights; he was a citizen, the records were public, and after several minutes of listening to peevish grumbling he was handed two huge gray cloth-bound volumes stamped in black with the state seal. Taking them to a counter, he thumbed through the April ledger, turning back from the day Carlisle withdrew his petition.

Ten minutes later he found the charter: Consolidated Enterprises, 5012 Osgood Building. It *had* been Carlisle's office, he realized, feeling a whole shower of sparks. He had reached the ladder's top rung and touched the main current. For Consolidated's powers had been astonishingly broad. Somebody in the Statehouse had read its application with a friendly eye. Legally its officers had been authorized to "construct and operate any work or works designed to help, increase, facilitate or develop trade, travel, or the transportation of freight, livestock, passengers or any traffic by land, water or air from or to any part of the United States." Of course, the corporation had been interested in the transportation of only one kind of freight, by water and then by land, but no credential could have specified that under the Eighteenth Amendment, and the cryptic phrasing guaranteed immunity under state laws, whatever the attitude of the Prohibition Unit, Bureau of Internal Revenue, Department of the Treasury. With the license number, the Motor Vehicle registration, and Carlisle's name on Doc's college form, this charter was bonded evidence of an authentic, dark-of-the-moon conspiracy. It was all a fine old Frank Capra-Clifford Odets screen play of the Thirties, with Edward Arnold gloating in the guarded château on the hill, stashing his bundles of greenbacks away in the safe behind the family portrait in the library while down in the town Gary Cooper, the roughhewn man of the people, was being stripped of dignity and flung into a cell for Arnold's crime.

And there was more. In the notarized signatures at the bottom of the charter was the answer to all Ham's questions — the reason the Republicans couldn't use Doc's conviction against him in this campaign, the explanation for the *Star*'s skittishness over the microfilm, the motive for its late suppression. Carlisle had been president of

Consolidated, and the vice president, one James E. Forbes, was on Ham's old trustee list. But the third officer, a startling bonus, was the real prize of the search, justifying the long trek from Whipple's study, through the Peabody Memorial Room, the *Star* morgue, the *Leader* city room, and the filthy Rockton Public Library cellar to this musty, flyblown end of the trail. The name of Consolidated's treasurer had been Stuart Hathaway Plimpton Witty.

**

Al Swinton was given to sulks. Whenever things went wrong with a job, as he called *Star* assignments, he would thrust out his lower lip and glare at the world. He had developed this pettishness during his childhood on East Birmingham's Mechanics Street, where he had successfully bullied smaller boys by glowers and threats. In the thirty years since, he had never quite grasped that what had worked on a slum playground might be just the wrong approach elsewhere. As a result his trip with Doc and Newt had been a failure. Day after day he had pouted outside television offices, excluded from their conferences; they had told him nothing afterward, had declined to comment on rumors that the Democrats were building a war chest through mail solicitation, and had even left him behind on barnstorming trips. By Friday afternoon, when they returned to Gideon, he was disgusted. The week added up to a dead zero for him. To make things worse he found a telegram under his Inne door — a rocket from Caulkin acidly reminding him that the paper needed something with a real jolt for the front page of Sunday's edition. Al was so upset he decided not to submit any expense account for the week, and he was chewing his nails and stewing over his portable when Geek Minton arrived unexpectedly.

Al admired and envied Geek. Roaming the country in a red Thunderbird photographing nude girls was Al's idea of real journalism, and ever since they had met at a Miss Press Photographer's ball in Birmingham three months before he had carefully followed Geek's picture credits in *Sly*, sending him flattering notes from time to time and eagerly suggesting story ideas — two girls soaping each other in a shower, a farmer's daughter caught astraddle a rail fence, a girl measuring her own bosom. His latest suggestion — a close-up of a man standing on his hands and peering up a skirt — had been postmarked here, and Geek had replied with a note, hinting that he might call. Now he was not only here; like Al he was in trouble. His office, he said gloomily, unslinging his flash bulb bag from his shoulder like a weary infantryman lowering his pack, was complaining that his latest batch of prints had been unprintable, *Ladies Home Journal* stuff. Al sympathized but was secretly pleased. His misery had found company. He told Mrs. Prouty to refer any calls for him to the Gideon Arms taproom. He and his old buddy here were going to tie one on.

By early evening each had drained six Martinis. They became loud and gross and worrisome to the bartender, who suffered them because there were no other customers — the Titans were playing away that week end; Peabody students were off at a Stoddard dance — and because he was fascinated by Geek's claims of sexual conquest. It was hard to credit them. Geek was a slender, unappealing, middle-aged bachelor who wore a dark blue double-breasted suit, slicked his straight black hair down flat, and affected a thin calligraphic mustache and dark green glasses. But then, the bartender supposed, girls who posed for a magazine like *Sly* must be easy quarries.

That was only partly true. Geek in fact led the life of a sexual athlete; what he neglected to explain was that he paid for all of it. His occupation, indeed, was bankrupting him. Five years ago he had been hired by *Sly*'s New York studio. From the first his sessions with naked women had driven him into frenzies of desire, and since nearly all the models were part-time prostitutes, they wound up with most of his money. The year before, his salary had been garnished by a loan company in lower Manhattan. His publisher, in reprisal, had sent him out on the road. He had found plenty of subjects there, usually among disappointed beauty contest entrants whom he crowned Miss *Sly* with a sash he carried in his car, but as amateurs they pegged their bed prices high, and New York fumed over his padded expenses. Tonight he was nearly broke. He let Al pay for the drinks and entertained him with story after coarse story, rambling on like a minstrel of depravity.

". . . so I jazzed the redhead first and gave the blonde her kicks after breakfast," he said in an oddly expressionless monotone, finishing an account of his latest — and most expensive — episode.

The rapt bartender almost missed the sound of approaching footsteps. He cleared his throat warningly.

Al looked up and then said sourly to him, "Oh, Cripes, simmer down, it's a friend."

It was, but Al's welcome wasn't friendly. The newcomer, a crew-cutted man in his early thirties, was Frosty Warren, who was covering Stuart Witty's campaign for the *Star*. Al resented Frosty Warren's easy assignment, and he knew why he was here now. Caulkin wasn't satisfied with a telegram. He had sent an emissary.

"Hello, hello, hello," Frosty murmured, shaking his hand limply. He ordered a Scotch and water, flopped into a chair, crumpling his three-button jacket in his lap, and studied Al's florid face with amusement. "Looks like I'm *way* behind you."

"Then in Memphis I run into this Miss Audubon, she called herself the Rosy-breasted Bedthrasher," Geek droned on imperturbably and broke off, puzzled, when the bartender coughed insistently.

"Geek here's a *Sly* staffer," Al said, as though it were a license.

"Pray continue," said Frosty, waving a tolerant hand. "I'm a bird-watcher myself."

Frosty was being affable because, as Al had guessed, he was here on a delicate mission. Actually it was more delicate than Al suspected. Frosty had brought messages for both *Star* men in Gideon. Jogging Al would be easy enough, but Frosty was apprehensive about Ham. Caulkin hadn't been much help. He was satisfied with Ham's stories — they were, he admitted, better than anything he had expected. All he had really said was that Ham had been seen in the Statehouse yesterday and that he wanted him to stay in Gideon and backstop Al. It didn't make any sense; foreign correspondents on home assignment didn't backstop anybody. If the general managing editor wanted to slap Ham in the face he should do it himself, Frosty thought, and he had told Caulkin so. The only reply had been an implacable silence. Frosty hadn't pressed the point, because he had executive ambitions, but he had driven to Gideon with many misgivings, and the note he had poked under Ham's darkened door at the Inne, inviting him to join him at the Gideon Arms, had been carefully worded.

He needn't be so careful with Al. All that was necessary was to deliver Caulkin's orders to Al, and he did that, adding lightly, "You know how it is. Publish or perish."

Al averted his eyes and mumbled, "O.K., O.K. Tell the colonel to keep his jockey shorts dry. I'm working on something."

"Mind letting me in on it?"

"Oh, it's not set up yet," Al said evasively. "It looks pretty good, though."

"Swell. Tell me what you have."

Cornered, Al blurted out his week-old discovery of Red and Daffy. "I got their names," he said defensively, tossing a wad of copy paper on the table. "Richard Stacy — he's Red Stacy, that halfback. And Mrs. Daphne Dix. I clipped her picture in a hula from the college paper." He spread out the clipping. "How's that for a rosy breast, Geek?"

Geek was lighting a cigarette, his hands wavering and clutching at each other. He leaned over. His mustache wiggled slightly. "A bed-thrasher?"

"Got the real rabbit habit."

"That's great," Frosty said. "And you say you have proof?"

"Well —" Al was defensive again. "I will have."

"Fine. Can you give me any idea when?"

Al looked around desperately and saw Ham entering the taproom, his topcoat over his arm. "Hey!" Al shouted. "We're over here!"

Frosty, undiverted, murmured, "I'll tell the office to count on something big Sunday." He rose and gave Ham the limp handshake. "Now here's a man who always turns up with the big yarn," he said suavely. "No oleo, Ham — some of your stuff from India turned me Paris green. In the lodge, now. How do you do it?"

Ham acknowledged Al's introduction of Geek — who stared over stupidly — and signaled for a rye highball. He pretended to think. "It's this way. I have a staff."

"Yeah?" said Al, wide-eyed. He had always suspected Ham had help.

"Sure. Correspondents all along the Ganges. They wear high silk hats and live in trees."

Al grimaced. "Big joke."

"No, big deal. They send me messages by drum. I pay them off in hair straightener."

Frosty laughed with false heartiness and slapped Ham on the back. Ham eyed him mistrustfully. Long ago he had sized up Frosty as the typical Ivy manikin on the make. No writer, no thinker, untalented and lacking any other qualifications, he was nevertheless destined to rise on the *Star* because he had the right pedigree, wore the Brooks uniform, and could recite editorial page doctrine. Already he affected the air of the junior officer among other ranks, jollying them along and keeping his distance. Ham wasn't deceived by his flattery. Frosty respected him now because Frosty was still a reporter. In another ten years his reporting days would be over; he would have a private office, and he would have persuaded himself that he deserved it because he had distinguished himself outside. Even now he wanted his back scratched.

"That profile of Witty's personality gave me a hard time," he said. "I really sweated over it. Did you happen to catch it?"

Ham nodded. "I thought it was the most one-sided story since the Crucifixion."

Frosty colored. He said abruptly, "By the way, the colonel wants you to stand by to cover if Al gets sick."

He had expected Ham to bridle, but it was Al who felt affronted; Al wondered whether the *Star* was searching for an excuse to replace him here, and he said sharply that he never felt better. Ham merely grinned. He knew what this was all about. He had predicted it to Judge Davies last night after the judge told him that someone at a Bar Association luncheon had mentioned his visit to the Statehouse. The patroons of Birmingham lived in a little world. If the bar had heard, the *Star* had heard, too. Well, it was too late. He had everything he wanted.

"I guess that means I ought to stick close to Gideon," he said innocently.

"Why, yes," said Frosty, surprised. "As a matter of fact —"

"As a matter of fact, Caulkin specified just that," Ham said, less innocently. Frosty blinked, and Ham grinned again. "Swell. You can tell him that suits me fine — I'm tired of running around. You can also tell him that the next time the men in the front office put their little pointed heads together in the board room he can make an announcement. I'm thinking of writing a new book. This one's going to be called *Through Darkest Consolidated Enterprises, Incorporated.*"

"I don't get it."

"He will. It's a private joke."

Frosty didn't like Ham's look. He decided to say nothing to Caulkin. Needling reporters in the line of duty was one thing; needling the general managing editor was risky. If the joke was that private, Ham could tell him himself.

It was time Frosty rejoined Witty's caravan. He stood, smoothing his jacket. "Any other messages? I've got to check in with the desk."

There were none. Frosty shook hands, inquired where the nearest phone was, and learned from Geek, who always observed the ladies' powder room with professional interest, that there was a booth near there. His dialing could be heard in the taproom; Ham had quickly emptied his glass and left, and the original drinkers had fallen silent. They listened absently to Frosty's dull conversation and glanced up curiously when he finished it with a little yelp.

He thrust a gleeful face around the doorway. "Good news for my team. Swinton's new poll report is in the first edition. Witty's still got sixty per cent."

Al struggled up, morose. Now Doc would be less approachable than ever. And somehow he had to turn up a page one story on him by tomorrow evening. He saw no way to do it, but at least he could face the bleak day without a hangover. He shoved his notes in one side pocket, the picture of Daffy in the other.

"You want to sack in at the Inne, sweatheart?"

"No, I got to push on tonight," Geek muttered. "The Dudley K of C's picking a Pumpkin Queen tomorrow."

"Drive careful," called Al, watching the blue suit lurch toward the men's room. "And watch the road. I mean, you're kind of stewed."

Al's own vision was blurred. He hadn't noticed how quickly Geek had sobered after Frosty's arrival, nor had he seen him study the clipping of Daffy and then memorize the notes on the copy paper. Geek had plans for that blonde. He intended to return to Gideon within the week with a loaded camera. Even now he was leaning against a toilet booth door, scribbling her address on a match book cover.

His memory was better than he had thought. In the privacy of the booth he also recalled Red's name, and since he had another match book he wrote that down, too, for luck.

**

One look at Saturday's paper was enough: Doc had to talk to Newt. But not in the Mansion. Sarah's manners had grown worse. The office, then — no one would be there but Jill, typing his campaign correspondence. He took Newt's arm, and together they plunged down the steep hill, Doc striding ahead and Newt running to keep up, like a small boy with a preoccupied father. Doc looked preoccupied. Until this morning he had felt a growing confidence. The A List mailing had produced thirty thousand dollars, Lockwood Aircraft had responded with another five thousand, and his problems seemed solved. Now he saw they weren't at all. Just as he had begun to forget last week's poll this one had come along to remind him of the sickening gap between him and victory. He was disheartened, and thought wistfully of the Titans. This afternoon they were playing a teachers college across the state line—a breather, fun to watch. He had hoped to go and return tonight for his first television appearance. Newt, however, had insisted they review what he was going to say. They had been together all week, Doc thought resentfully, but they hadn't been alone long enough to discuss the speech because Al had hounded them incessantly.

"I don't even like that Swinton fellow's face," he said, bounding up the hall steps. "He looks like a common sneak."

Newt answered with a wheeze. His breath was coming in little whistles, his face was scarlet. Yet his eyes were brighter than Doc's. The straw vote report hadn't dismayed him. A gain of three points was quite respectable. And Doc's dejection was encouraging. Everything was going just as Newt had hoped, and after they had disposed of tonight's script he planned to make his demand for the university services.

Doc had just rolled up his sleeves and was just beginning to work up enthusiasm for the speech when Jill tapped at the door and peered in.

"Dr. Tate and Dr. Mikel are outside," she said in a stage whisper. "Do you want to see them?"

Doc didn't, Newt didn't. Nevertheless they were seen; Mikel slithered past her swollen figure and pranced across the rug. "We crave an audience!" he cried. "A matter of the gravest importance has been raised — raised, I confess, by myself."

Tate entered and said more demurely, "Actually there are two matters, Governor, and I'm afraid Harry and I don't see eye to eye on which is grave."

Doc eyed them dourly. "It'd be the Eighth Wonder of the World if you did." He was nettled. Tate ought to have a firm grip on the reins by now. "I've got other fish to fry," he told him. "Can't you settle things?"

"My problem is rather singular," Tate said uncomfortably.

"*L'état, c'est toi,*" Mikel chirped. "Leave or no leave, you still wear the crown."

"All right," Doc said more hospitably. "Let's have it one barrel at a time."

"*Deo gratias*," Mikel murmured. "But first"—he pointed a jerky finger at Newt—"Paul Pry must go. What I have to say is most secret."

Doc signalled Newt. "Better wait outside."

Newt left lowering at Mikel, who leered, sat, and swung a leg over the chair arm. "I don't imagine you've had time to read your mail, Prexy. Therefore I've brought you my copy of this."

He tossed his student survey on the desk top. Doc hulked over it while Tate fingered his tie. The provost would have avoided this if he could. Years ago he had abandoned trying to explain the finer points of his educational philosophy to Doc, and he was afraid he would be shocked by the figures.

It was a groundless fear. Mikel had come at an unfortunate time. Doc had had enough of polls for one day. Glancing rapidly down the page, he decided that the questionnaire was rigged, the results meaningless. He chucked it back without a word.

Mikel hadn't expected that, and didn't pick it up. Entwining his fingers he said uncertainly, "Rather a large worm in the apple, eh?"

Doc gestured at Tate. "You've seen this?"

Tate smiled tolerantly. "Oh, yes. I neglected to bring my copy, but I believe I remember all of it."

"And your opinion?"

"Is that it is without significance."

Mikel almost pounced at him. He went tense, then sucked in a breath and croaked, "So. The flames spring up and the emperor-elect strums his fiddle."

"Easy, Harry," Doc said warningly.

"In my judgment we are listening to a false alarm," Tate purred.

"My view is the same," said Doc. This, he concluded, was just another example of Mikel crying wolf. "I suggest that we keep the hook and ladder in the firehouse. I also suggest," he added incisively, "that if any more bushwah comes along, the acting president's powers be respected."

Mikel snatched the survey back and stood motionless a moment, looking at them steadily, his grotesque figure invested with a quaint dignity.

"Very well. The cock has crowed three times. I consign you to Budge and his jury."

He marched out stiffly. The sound of his squeaking sneakers died away, and Doc shook his head in honest bewilderment. He would never understand that man. He only hoped Budge wasn't getting the wrong impression from him. One fly in the ointment could gum up the whole setup.

Tate, reading his thoughts, remarked that the reaccreditation seemed to be coming along nicely. The departmental reports were being written, committees of team members were meeting daily, and the faculty was behaving admirably. Apart from a few dissidents like Mikel and Erich Lutz — and one other, important exception — Budge was inspecting a happy ship.

He took Mikel's chair. "The exception is Tom Yablonski."

"What?" Doc asked incredulously. Yablonski was the last chairman in the university to complain — the best paid, with the largest budget.

"You saw last Sunday's *Star*."

"No, Newt's had me on the go all week."

Now Tate was incredulous. "You don't know what they did with the Navy game?"

"Clean missed it. What's that?" He squinted down — Tate had slipped the clipping in front of him — and read swiftly. "That was *all*?"

"Yes, and that's going to be all — vague stuff about the other teams and no pictures. Yablonski talked to the paper."

Doc recoiled. It hadn't occurred to him that the *Star* might strike at him through the Titans, and he didn't understand why he hadn't heard about it. He rang Jill. "Ask Mr. Albert to come in." Newt entered briskly, and Doc held out the story. "Did you know about this?"

Newt knew. On Sunday he had intercepted a mournful call from Sam Theanapolis, and Monday's mail had brought terse notes from three Democratic county chairmen in the area of the *Star*'s heaviest circulation. He had withheld all from Doc, saving them for today. The greater the blow to Doc's assurance, the more complete his capitulation would be.

He gave the clipping a moping look.

"I wanted to break it to you easy, Governor," he lied.

"It's the beatingest thing I ever heard of!" Doc raged.

Newt nodded gravely. "It's bad business, all right." He could have consoled him with the observation that the stadium faithful would find State scores elsewhere, but he was playing a different game. "Kind of knocks us into a cocked hat, don't it?"

In anguish Doc thought of the Titans, ignored because of him. "The squad must be just sick."

"They'll be around next year," Newt said ruthlessly, "but you're going to the post just once. When you put this together with today's *Star* report — well, it all adds up, but I can't say it's the kind of arithmetic I like."

Tate's eyes had been flicking between them. He tittered nervously. "You paint a rather dark picture, Mr. Albert."

"What?" Newt, concentrating on Doc, had quite forgotten the provost. "Oh, we'll figure something out."

His tone wasn't encouraging, however. He wanted to leave Doc no escape this time. The instant Tate left he planned to close in. But this wasn't Newt's day. He couldn't seem to get rid of Tate. The provost peppered him with questions, forcing him to repeat his dismal forecasts until Newt had the impression that he was more anxious about the campaign than Doc. And then, when Tate finally did leave, a telephone call disrupted everything.

"Hello?" Doc said impatiently. "Why, yes, Mrs. Hodgkins. Anything wrong?" He leaned forward — the Mansion cook had never called him here— and then caught his breath. "Holy cow. Yes, you sure did do the right thing. I'll be right there." He hung up and leapt across the room, rolling down his sleeves. "Sare's gone out alone," he muttered. "She's not fit, I don't know what she can be thinking of. Wait here."

So Newt was thwarted. He started after him, contemplated the open door, and said deliberately, "Son of a bitch."

It hurt. And yet, he reflected, as the sting began to fade, the moment could be recaptured. At lunch, or this afternoon, or driving to Birmingham at dusk — sometime before tonight's telecast, anyway — he would corner Doc and bring things off. His optimism returned. He had accomplished nothing, but neither, he thought, had he lost anything. He was just where he had been, holding the right cards and certain to win.

Actually Newt had blundered badly. Tate had returned to his office at the other end of the corridor with the conviction that Doc was as good as defeated. He had been wavering all week, had hesitated even when he read the morning's *Star*, but if Newt was ready to throw in the sponge it was as good as over. The campaign would go on only because there were other, smaller races; the head of the ticket could be written off now. Sinking slowly in his swivel chair and closing his eyes, Tate saw a stark future. On November 3 Witty would be swept into the Statehouse, and on November 4 Doc would resume his duties here. He would remain as State's president for the rest of his life, and Tate would continue as provost because there was no other place for him to go. Six years ago he had made his choice; he had come to State and devoted all his energies to its growth. Since then he had written no papers, had delivered no lectures elsewhere, had built no outside reputation. Only a handful of men outside the state would remember him as the bright young professor of education who had forsaken the classroom for the administrative ladder, and none could offer him a position of this eminence. He was chained to Gideon, chained to Doc.

Until this summer he had been reconciled to that. He drew the largest salary on campus, and Doc had given him a free hand to put into practice experimental techniques almost unknown in higher education. Then, with the announcement of Doc's candidacy, he had glimpsed a richer prize. His career, it seemed, was to have a finer cap. Every time he called Doc Governor he had silently thought of himself as President Tate—had seen his name lettered in gilt on the door of the presidential suite, had imagined himself speaking before convocations of students, had pictured his triumphant appearance before educational conventions in Atlantic City, exciting his old friends with descriptions of his pioneer work in Gideon. He would be honored everywhere, toasted as the leader of America's first truly modern university.

But he couldn't lead if Doc stayed. He couldn't even look forward to succeeding him later. Doc grew healthier every year. Barring accidents, he would survive to the age of retirement—and then, Tate thought bitterly, the fawning trustees would probably insist he stay. The man might live to be a hundred, presiding to the end. By the time he quit Tate would be too old for the appointment. Already the national trend was toward young presidents. A man in his late fifties wouldn't stand a chance. This was the time of decision, this year, this fall. Either he made it now or he lost it forever.

He opened his eyes and crashed a puny fist on the desk blotter. He wasn't going to let it slip through his fingers. He would have that recognition if he had to bribe, steal, and cheat for it. After all, he deserved it. Certainly it didn't belong to Doc. The more he thought the more ridiculous it became: an athlete long past his prime, a hayseed and a humbug, masquerading as an educator. All Doc had done was to build a football team and use it to pander to the most ignorant people in the state. Tate had done the real work. He deserved the office, and he meant to have it.

It wasn't just for himself, he thought defensively. It wasn't as though he were a low conniver. He was devoted to a cause—"the goal," he had once written in an administrative memorandum, "of designing a broad-gauge depth education to meet the overriding challenges of Space Age youth." Tate really thought that. He even thought of it that way. He was partial to cant, and if no one else found his spongy prose inspiring, he himself did. He had resolved to make "major breakthroughs" with "large-group instruction in basic marketable skills," replacing classrooms with "studios," lectures with "field trips," textbooks with "workshops," courses with "projects." His objective in Gideon was to invigorate the university with "personalized educative techniques," and he even had a word for this mission. It was "cross-fertilization."

Because he was indifferent to intellect, slogans were enough for him. He couldn't see the historical irony behind them—that the nineteenth century educational philosophy of Francis Parker and G. Stanley Hall, meant to brighten learning's lamp, had dimmed the lamp instead; had been distilled and then distorted until in the hands of such legatees as himself it was foul and corrupt. He was also blind to the tragic logic of this: that after two world wars and a depression, traditional authority had been discredited everywhere, and that his administrative memoranda represented, not a new system of ideas, but the rejection of all ideas. In fact Tate didn't believe in learning at all. He believed that learning had had its day and was to be succeeded by a vague faith in training for citizenship, in homemaking, in the manipulation of men and machines. He despised facts. In their place he exalted social democracy, and the flaw in his faith, the cross he bore, was that the public scorned men like him.

He knew that. It stung, but he was a realist. He was dedicated to his educationist approach and felt sure that Budge and his colleagues would be farsighted enough to approve it; still, he was aware that it would never be popular with the taxpayers. Many of his innovations would shock them—would disturb even the trustees, whose visits to the campus were limited to Administration Hall and the stadium. Officially Doc was responsible for all of them. If he were publicly saddled with them—and a political campaign offered unparalleled opportunities for saddling — he might be discredited as an educator even as he was being snowed under at the polls. A loud outcry against his resumption of the presidency could force his retirement and permit his provost, as his logical successor, to step up. Tate had no illusions. He knew it was a dangerous maneuver. A dozen things could go wrong. He himself might be tarred, all sins might be forgiven in the elation over reaccreditation, an outsider might be brought in to straighten things out and undo all his work. But those were risks he had to take. If he was determined to move into the suite at the other end of the corridor — and his determination had reached the stage of monomania — he had no choice.

On padded feet he crept into his secretary's office, slid his key in her locked file, and removed his folded copy of Mikel's survey. Padding back, he reached under his blotter and drew out the list of Al Swinton's telephone numbers. The top line read, "College Inne, 6-9625." Al would be there now. Unfolding the survey, he glanced through it once more as he asked the university operator for an outside line. He dialed swiftly, using the key.

Mrs. Prouty answered scratchily: "Hello? What is it?"

"Mr. Swinton, please."

There was a long wait, and when Al came on Tate thought there had been some mistake. Al's decision to leave the taproom last night had come too late. His head was hammering. His voice had dropped an octave.

"This is W. Denton Tate," the provost whispered.

"Oh. Yeah."

"May I see you? This afternoon?"

Dodged by Doc and Newt for five days, Al was taken aback. "Want to see *me?*"

Tate hissed, "Yes, yes. Today."

Al's voice rose slightly. "Be right over."

"No, not here! I'll meet you. Shall we say two o'clock? In the Acme Diner on the highway?"

"Okay. Sure. Mind telling me what's up?"

Tate looked down at the survey report and saw the Vicksburg footnote. He smiled. "I want to discuss a popular remedy."

**

Sarah River's thoughts were cottony. It was as though a fog rolled in over her mind, shrouding familiar landmarks and baffling her sense of direction. Some days the blur was worse than others, and now and then she would have a stretch of lucidity lasting nearly a week, with everything in perspective. Doc would brighten and beam on her then, but it made little difference to her. Either way she was unhappy. All her married life she had been fussing over details, picking up after her husband like a fidgety mother, nursing secret anxieties over the startling changes he had made on the campus she had loved as a girl and hesitating to mention them because, like many wives of dominant men, she had been drained of the power to assert herself. Then her stroke had brought the face of death very near. The attack had been a sign that her life would soon fade, that whatever she wanted to do had better be done now. She wanted to strike back, but she didn't know where to strike and wasn't strong enough anyhow, so she had retreated a little from reality. It was only a small, strategic retirement, not a flight, not a capitulation; only a few short steps backward now and then when the scape ahead was too frightening to bear; only the sly, contained revolt of an eccentric. Mrs. Hodgkins told the ladies at Gideon's First Baptist that her mistress had become "just a bit queer," and that described Sarah precisely; she was the whimsical crank who distresses those close to her but never really hurts them — and never helps them to help her shed her fears — because she is too timid to speak out.

Today the fog over her thoughts was scarcely more than a haze. She knew exactly what she was doing. She was making another gesture of rebellion. Like her mints, her treatment of Newt, and her flightiness whenever Doc insisted she leave the solitude of her room and join ceremonial gatherings downstairs, it was a slight, harmless thing. Doc had told her she mustn't take walks alone. Very well; that was just what she was going to do. She had waited patiently for the chance to elude Mrs. Hodgkins, and this morning, while the cook was cleaning out a cellar storeroom, she had wrapped a shawl around her frail shoulders and slipped out the back door. The hill was too steep for her, so she had followed a circuitous route through the Mansion parking lot, along the sloping path that led to Fraternity Park, then back toward the North Campus and the Student Union. She was looking for the old Aggie orchard. East of the Union, where the poultry pens had been, a lovely stand of apple trees filled a grassy dimple, and there, one April afternoon in the late Twenties, Adam River had first courted her. For all the secrecy and the huddling behind a rough trunk they had been scrupulously correct, yet there was still excitement for her in the memory of Doc in his blue letter sweater teetering uncertainly among the falling blossoms and telling her things she had never heard and he had never said before; it was the most treasured page in the album of her heart, and she wanted to turn back to it now. The orchard had survived. Some of the outlying trees had fallen to bulldozers, but Doc had promised her the center of the grove would stay, and there it was, just ahead, looking anachronistic in the shadow of the futuristic Union. Moving rapidly in her homely black shoes she passed within and would have been obscured entirely if the first red leaves hadn't fallen, stripping the lower branches and revealing her there, standing alone by the scarred old bole, daydreaming and shivering despite the shawl.

Ham recognized her instantly.

He was coming out of the Union when he saw her slight figure, and he hurried over, not to rescue her but to greet her. Ham hadn't any idea what was wrong with Sarah; he supposed her appearance here now meant she must be better, and he wanted to congratulate her. It was the best possible approach. Any sign of solicitude would have estranged her. Even so, as he came toward her she shrank away and glanced about for a place to hide.

"Mrs. River, I haven't seen you in—well, I'd hate to say how many years." Ham grinned, misinterpreting her furtive look. "You don't have to apologize for not recognizing me. I've gone to seed, and I know it."

She peered up uncertainly. "Why, it's Ham Markham! Kit Ryan's old beau!"

He flinched. "Now that *was* a long time ago."

"Oh, go on! You boys are worse than the girls, fishing for compliments on how well you look." She inspected his new topcoat. "Well, I'll say this. You do dress smarter than Kit. Have you seen what she does to herself? I declare, she makes herself look like Old Mother Hubbard."

Ham laughed, and she pinked with pleasure. Suddenly her mind was quite clear. She had always liked him. He had been attentive during Doc's Sunday evenings at home with the squad, and anyone who had been close to Kit was dear to her. As a coed Kit had worked under Sarah in the faculty club kitchen. They had been close then, and it was in remembrance of those years that Sarah had written the clandestine recommendation that had swayed Elsie Shoemaker. It was the first time in her life she had intervened in a university matter. She didn't regret it; her only cheerful hours this fall had been spent with Kit, knitting and talking and rocking Kit's child.

And now Ham Markham was here, too. To Sarah that seemed just right.

He told her he had been back a month.

"Well, I never! I hadn't heard a blessed word! Never mind. It's nice to see you just the same."

They were strolling toward the Mansion, dodging branches tossed by a rising wind. Sarah had turned back without thinking; the need to ramble was gone, and she realized she was chilled. Ham idled alongside, listening to her prattle about birds, the weather, her sewing — the trivial enthusiasm of a childless, lonely old woman.

"My, things have changed so," she sighed, hestitating at a path crossing. "I don't know my way around Aggie at all any more. I keep thinking of the old campus, you know. Now *that* was simple as pie."

Ham was here to see Doc, and he wondered how much Sarah knew about his old disgrace. He said casually, "Still, it must have seemed like Times Square in those days to the Coach, coming here right off the farm."

"Ha! You don't know my Doc, young man. Nothing fazed him. His very first day as a freshman you'd have thought he'd lived in Gideon all his life."

So she knew nothing. The secret was that dark. Ham wondered why Doc was so reticent. Doubtless at the time the wound had been almost unbearable, but the scar should have healed long since, and it would make a matchless campaign issue now. By telling the full story Doc would gain far more than he would lose, which was, of course, the reason the Republicans were keeping it quiet. Yet he had said nothing. It didn't make sense.

Ham was speculating whether Doc was still hostile toward him when Doc himself loomed ahead, standing on the Mansion lawn and gazing around with his hands cupped like binoculars. He spotted them and sprinted down the grade.

"Jupiter! Where'd you find her, Ham?"

Sarah stiffened. "Mercy. You'd think I was a runaway."

Doc's concern confused Ham. He mumbled an explanation and hung back as Doc took Sarah's arm and led her toward the house, and there, at the door, Ham had an inkling of what was wrong. Crossing the grass, Sarah had been teasing Doc reminding him that for months he had been urging her to get out. Abruptly she halted and began scuffing her shoes vigorously on the doormat. If the day had been damp that would have been reasonable, but it hadn't rained here for a week. The ground was dry, her soles were unsoiled, yet she kept stamping and scraping and stamping again, reminding Ham eerily of his son demanding a drink of water, a story, a toy — anything to postpone bedtime. Sarah was like a child putting off the inevitable, and when Doc, still cradling her elbow, gently persuaded her that she must go inside, she gave a meaningless little laugh, popped a mint into her mouth, and scurried over the threshold. Doc followed, leaving Ham to pace the lawn. So that was her illness. Probably it wasn't serious — she had been normal enough just now — but he doubted Doc was helping it much; for all his strength he was the last man to comfort a disturbed wife. And then, pivoting by the shrubbery, it occurred to Ham that perhaps that was the answer, that the only way a woman like Sarah could command the attention of a man like Doc was to withdraw into irresponsibility.

Doc heaved out awkwardy. "I'm much obliged, boy. I was about beside myself."

"I guess it isn't an easy thing to live with," Ham said gently.

"No." Doc avoided his eyes. "No, it isn't, and that's a fact. Some things are hard to cipher. Sometimes the only thing to do is to tuck them away in a corner and not look."

Ham was picking his way carefully. "I'm not sure you're right, Coach. I have a hunch that in some cases the best solution is to drag them out in the open."

"In the open! And let the ragtag and bobtail see her?"

"No, no, of course not. I was thinking of the campaign, of facing political facts. That's why I'm here, in fact."

Doc's gratitude began to ebb. "If you're trying to say I ought to pay any mind to that poll your paper's running, you're just rubbing me the wrong way, boy. I aim to stay in this right down to the last whistle."

"I don't mean that, either."

"Well, what in thunderation *is* on your mind?"

Ham toed a dead tuft of crabgrass.. "It's the story of a boy who was conned into playing football for Peabody thirty-five years ago and given the job of driving a bootleggers' truck between Gideon and Rockton."

The only sound there was the chattering of the wind in the lawn trees. Ham kicked the tuft and looked up. Doc's face was curiously lopsided.

"Who told you?"

"Let's say I found out on the other side of town."

"Is this your way of wishing me well?"

"It's the best way I know — giving you some sound advice. Did you know Stuart Witty was one of your bosses then?"

"I knew. But nobody at Peabody did. How did you find out?"

"Finding things in my business," said Ham, trying to smile. "I went to Rockton and checked up on the Hi-Di-Hi."

Doc's odd air grew odder. His lopsided expression was a trick of the light slanting through the descending leaves and the angle of his head, held back and tilted, and his eyes were wide and fanshaped.

"Did Spook — "

He snapped his mouth shut and turned away, and Ham stared at his trembling back. What would Spook have known? And how would he have known it? Spook had never met Whipple. Peabody memorabilia would have been closed to him. He wouldn't have had the faintest notion how to trace a trustee's name, a license number, or the charter of a defunct corporation.

"Did Spook what?"

Doc's voice was sunken. "I said something to him once."

But in a thing like this you didn't say something unless you said everything. Ham felt a stab of resentment. He and Spook had had the same relationship with Doc. Both had been fatherless Birmingham boys; both had grown as close to him as sons. He wouldn't have confided in one and not the other. And yet he had. He had just said he had.

"What did you say?"

Still the averted face. "No, Ham. I don't want to discuss it."

"If Newt knew, he'd discuss it on a state-wide hookup."

Doc whirled back, his face flashing despair. "That's unthinkable."

"Why?"

"It's out of the question."

"But why?"

"I'd quit first."

"Why, Coach? Why?"

"Ham, you've got to give me your word you won't tell Newt about this."

"I wouldn't anyway. Now give me a reason."

Doc lowered his arms. "I can't, boy. It doesn't make sense, I know, but I told you before — you can't cipher everything. Table this. Let it lay. Let the dust pile up. Forget about it, and don't look any farther."

Ham didn't promise that. He was too surprised to speak; until now he didn't know there was anywhere else to look, and he headed down the hill frowning. Maybe Whipple had been wrong. Maybe Doc really had skidded in some way unrecorded on microfilm, or on crumbling newsprint, or in the Hall of Records. Could there have been a real stigma against Doc's name, buried, perhaps, in those sealed Rockton courthouse records, safe even from the legalistic jimmies and crowbars of the Republican States Central Committee? No; it was incredible. Ham snatched at a passing sprig of dark red sumac. And then he remembered, as though from an old print, the image of Hiram A. Markham, Sr., arriving home in his spotless celluloid collar, patting the bobbing little head that had waited eagerly for the creeping trolley and arranging himself in the Morris chair under the bridge lamp with the silhouette of George Washington on the shade — a tender father, warm and inviting with that barbershop smell of toilet water and sweet pomade that he never lost. In painful retrospect Ham pictured the gold chain that sloped so gracefully over the little paunch and heard the deep confident voice rumbling confidently across the canyon of time with its measured analyses of world events — and saw, superimposed on the tableau, the paper hat, the stained denim, the bar of Lava soap which, all unknown to the boy, the expansive analyst had left in the locker room by the *Star* presses downtown. Carriage and steeds had been metamorphosed into pumpkin and mice once for Ham. He had been hoodwinked then. It could happen again.

But he had been only a boy. Every son believes his father to be a hero. Just because he had been betrayed in childhood he needn't be wrong about Doc. Whatever Doc was — mulish, narrow, stolid — he was relentlessly honest, he was open, he was noble.

Yet there was a fear. The moth had been warned, and shied from the flame. Even as he debated where to look next for the telltale file or serial number or ledger or blurred old photostat that would reveal everything in a flash — even as he planned a new search for the key, he knew he wouldn't follow through. He didn't dare. He had to believe in someone, and Doc was the someone he had been given in the autumn of his nineteenth year. Only through his faith in Doc had he won a faith in himself; only by keeping one could he have the other. He was as good as his roots, and Doc had said, *Table this*, and *Let it lay*. And so, though he hadn't pledged it, Ham decided to do just that, not because he loved Doc but because he loved himself and felt threatened.

Dead ahead another scraggy sumac bough swung in the tearing wind. Reaching out irritably, he seized it and thrust it aside, and a dozen slim scarlet leaves came off in his palm. He flailed it to shake them off, but they were stubborn. Despite a week of frosts a trickle of sap had lingered in the skinned branch, and although he shed the leaves that glistening sap remained, prickly and sticky and congealing on his hand.

**

After the Superanahist commercial and the Lestoil Community Sing, John Winkler appeared on the Channel 5 screen wearing a soft buttondown shirt and J. Press suit. Newt Albert and Sam Theanapolis had given a great deal of thought to the choice of Winkler. He was, they had agreed, exactly right: young, urbane, earnest and transparently apolitical. He had what Sam called the right image; young voters and women of all ages would be drawn by his air of artless sincerity. Moreover, he was an excellent foil for Doc. Winkler spoke smoothly from a TelePrompTer, explaining that this time had been purchased by the Citizen's Committee for Doc River, expressing regrets that *Six Gun*, usually seen at this time, would not be programmed, and announcing that the cameras would now pick up the president of State, who would speak extemporaneously from his Birmingham study.

The study was a fake — a cardboard wall of false book spines, surmounted by a row of silver trophy cups Sam had borrowed from the local Masonic Lodge — but Doc really had no script. That, too, was a carefully considered decision. Sam had argued from the first that he would be hopelessly wooden with the TelePrompTer, and a week in the hustings had convinced Newt that his man was a skillful improviser. He balked only at giving him a blank check. Over dinner the three of them had agreed on an outline and approved three budget charts Sam's staff had drawn up. Beyond that, Doc was to have his head.

His blue shirt was his only concession to the medium. To Ham, watching in an anteroom of the Peabody Faculty Club with Nails

Whipple and Harry Mikel, Doc was entirely himself, right down to the shiny old vest, the turned-up collar, and the short sleeves that left his brawny wrists exposed. Ham couldn't know that minutes before the red studio light winked on Winkler, on Sam's orders, had manipulated Doc's clothes to give just that effect. Sam wanted Doc as roughhewn as possible. He had even dismissed his make-up girl, with the consequence that Doc's features appeared crude and stark, reminding Ham of the whittled farmboy face he had seen in the Peabody application photograph.

It was all of a piece, for Doc was completely in character.

"My name's River," he began nasally, leaning forward and laying his foreams clumsily on a little broken-front desk. "Some of you know me, lots don't. I've met quite a passel of you lately while I've been roaming around asking you to pull down the second lever next month, though I expect I have been stiffer than a stake; politicking's new to me, and I admit I'm pretty set in my ways. But one thing I have learned. If I don't get anything else out of this business I'm sure as sin going to wind up with a cauliflower right hand."

He smiled and flexed his fingers, and the camera man, who had been briefed this far, dollied up and focused on them. On the screen the square-cut nails and rough scarred skin suggested rockstrewn country, Lincoln splitting rails and, when Doc made a loose fist, the great and righteous might of an Ethan Allen.

**

"Now why did they take off *Six Gun?*" Harry Mikel complained. "It's one of the few electronic spectacles I enjoy. Last week the hero slew eight men without reloading."

"Hush!" Whipple whispered, making a little pawing motion.

Mikel hushed momentarily and then, just as Doc began reciting figures designed to expose the Republicans as spendthrifts, he cackled harshly. "All eight were harmless bystanders, too! Nietzsche's morality of the master, I suppose."

"Please," said Ham, trying to follow Doc's argument.

"Impressive," Whipple murmured softly. "Adam's animal vigor comes through very well."

"So would an orangutan's," Mikel said, lighting a Camel. "I doubt I should vote for one, however."

Now Doc was producing the charts, bar graphs showing the growth of the state budget. Ham could scarcely see them. The Peabody faculty club television room was tiny and unventilated; Whipple had lit a cigarette from Mikel's, and a pall thickened quickly between them and the set, veiling the chart numbers and almost obscuring Doc.

**

Hallam Caulkin fumed. "This is preposterous!" *We* are being hoisted on *his* petard. He knows damned well he spends more tax money than any two other departments in the administration."

Caulkin glowered at a portable set which had been wheeled in front of the bookcase of generals' memoirs while Al Swinton sat content in a straight chair by the desk. Al felt delivered. This morning he had been a wretched failure, nursing a sick head. Tate's copy of Mikel's student survey had changed all that. Al had thought it important enough to deliver here in person, and Caulkin had not only agreed; he had promised to write a letter of commendation for Al's personnel folder. "A thing like this," he had said warmly, "belongs in your service jacket."

The door opened noiselessly and a copy boy tiptoed in with a bundle of first editions. He laid one on the general managing editor's desk and was quietly leaving when Al, feeling assertive, slipped another from under his arm.

The story was three columns wide, down the middle of page one.

Professor's Survey Shows up State Students;
U.S. History, Constitution, Stop Them Cold

Caulkin beamed, his swivel spring jiggled. "By Harry, he'll have a job explaining *that*."

"Yeah," Al said gloomily.

Caulkin gave him a puzzled look, then glanced back at the paper. "Why, those sad sacks downstairs forgot your by-line!"

Al knew they hadn't forgotten. He had enemies in the composing room. Still, they had hurt him in only one edition. Caulkin was already on the phone, demanding to talk to the make-up editor. Al settled back and listened, with a little twitching smile, to Doc's attack on the *Star*.

**

Daffy Dix was watching television, but not Channel 5. Channel 7 had advertised *A Star Is Born* as its Movie Tonite, and after a hurried supper of beans and dry bread — Jerry, who did the family shopping, had forgotten butter — they had wheeled Charlie to the television lounge in Blandford Library. Jerry would have preferred to study, but Daffy told him not to be a grind, and he was so grateful that his wife actually wanted him along he had dropped everything. Daffy really did want him. In her mind every evening spent with him was a credit, a kind of coupon to be cashed in whenever Red could slip away to the Gideon Arms.

She was in a blithe mood. Yesterday the Dixes had been moved to a corner unit, displacing Trudy Viggiantti, and this afternoon the Titans had crushed Centralia State Teachers. For tonight's sortie she had therefore chosen the most expensive of her casual clothes. Entering the library she wore Madras shorts, an Angora sweater, a short camel's-hair swagger jacket, and glittering new loafers. In the lobby she instantly became the cynosure of a dozen loitering students, none of whom associated her with the seedily dressed young man cradling a swaddled infant in his arms. With many rehearsed little gestures she paraded slowly toward the lounge, encountering on the far side the remnants of a rump session called by the provost to plan a dinner for Dr. Budge. Hotflash Hatch was there, a study in virilism, talking man-to-man with Yablonski. Tate himself had withdrawn into a corner and stood there in pallid concentration, the uneasy conspirator whose die has been cast. Also alone, looking like an aging wallflower, was Dean Elsie Shoemaker; she gave Daffy a remote glance, and then the faculty group moved into one of the larger television cubicles to watch Doc. Daffy took the cubicle farthest from them. Jerry darted in as she closed the door, and presently they were alone in the dim womb of the room, facing the flickering screen. Neither spoke. Jerry, engrossed with his son, held him so close he could feel the little heart beating against his own, and Daffy was transported by the film. Curled up in a deep lounge chair, she lost herself entirely in the Hollywood success story. Her spirit had fled Gideon. Enigmatic smiles played over her lips; her eyes were dark stars.

**

Person-to-person calls to the University Village phone booth always tried operators' tempers. Often the instrument wasn't answered at all; just as often the answerer left the receiver dangling and never returned. Geek Minton had to wait a half-hour before a responsible student came on the line, and by then Daffy had left for the library.

Geek was in his Dudley hotel, feeling low. The Pumpkin Queen contest had been a disaster for him. The girls he had invited to his Thunderbird to discuss terms had shunned him, and one had called a policeman. Geek had been taken to the station and detailed half the afternoon before the chief, a *Sly* reader, decided that freedom of the press was being abridged. By then all the contestants had gone home. Thwarted and mortified, he phoned Daffy, and when that failed he fished out his other match folder and called Red Stacy at the Athletic Dorm.

Red was in. It was a week since he had defied the squad curfew. Yablonski's bed checks had been thorough, and despite today's victory Red was broke; the Titans had been heavy favorites, so there had been no alumni tips. The strain of celibacy had told. This afternoon he had been a savage back, scoring seven touchdowns. Never humble, he assumed Geek was phoning about that.

"From *Sly*, huh? You get any pictures this afternoon?"

Geek hadn't been at the game, hadn't even known State was playing. But he detected the anxious note in Red's voice, and it gave him an idea.

"You'd like us to carry something about you?"

"Could you? On your sports page?" The note was more strident. "The *Star*'s giving me the treatment, see."

"Well, I'll level with you, kid. I was thinking more about that cheerleader you got. Name's Dix."

"Oh, Daff." There was a pause. "Why not both of us, two stories?"

Geek, angling, said he didn't know about that.

"Listen, I can fix you up with Daff. She's a pretty good friend of mine, if you know what I mean."

Geek pretended to deliberate. "Suppose I come around next week, we can talk it over."

"Oh swell, that'd be great. It'll be worth your while, Mr. Minton."

It had been a long time since Geek had heard anyone so eager to appear in the magazine. He wondered about the girl. *Sly* had never had a bona-fide coed in a really exciting pose. Until now he had been thinking in terms of suggestive angle shots, but with Red's cooperation he might be able to bring home some real bacon.

"Tell you what—keep this under your hat. Don't say anything to her till you and me have our little huddle."

"I got you."

No, kid, Geek thought, *I* got *you*.

**

In Hillvilledale Manor, a suburb of Dudley, Paul Bauer, chairman of State's Alumni Athletic Committee, turned suddenly to his large, sloe-eyed wife.

"Do you think a married girl should be Gridiron Queen?"

Mrs. Bauer looked over distractedly. She had been trying to catch Doc's every word. Because of her husband's position she had been invited to speak on Doc before a Hillvilledale League of Women Voters unit, and she hadn't the remotest idea what she was going to say. She had hoped tonight's speech would give her an inkling, but she wasn't very bright, and the charts confused her.

"What's that again, hon?"

"The Gridiron Queen, Mabel. This big decision we got."

"Oh."

"Some of the boys think she should be a virgin."

"That sounds nice," she said vaguely.

"It does?"

"It sounds real nice."

"Because some others think coed wives should get a break."

"Oh."

"It's all in the point of view, I guess."

"Oh. Well — what do *you* think?"

"I say let's have open competition."

"Even Stephen?"

"It's the only fair way."

There was a pause.

Then: "Paul?"

"Uh?"

"You know what I think?"

"Uh?"

"I think you're right."

"Really?"

"Really and truly. Open competition, that's what *I*'m for."

"Well, that's what I say."

"And you say right."

"You're positive, now."

"Absolutely. There's no question in my mind whatsoever."

"Say, that's swell. You know, old Doc sure is in the pink, isn't he?"

"He surely *is*," she said, glad to be off the reef. "He's what in my opinion I call real cute."

**

"He looks like a cardiac to me," said the professor of medicine on Budge's team, "and he's certainly astigmatic. Why doesn't he wear his glasses?"

"Don't be an ass," the professor of government said with a wink. "Whoever heard of a four-eyed Jim Thorpe?"

The group of visiting academicians in Eric Lutz's laboratory laughed lightly. Already they had picked up the new faculty's bantering attitude toward Doc. Because Budge was a friend of Lutz's he had made the Austrian's lab his headquarters, and because it was commodious, with many little chambers that served as makeshift offices, the others trooped over each evening, bringing, to the dismay of their host, the latest Doc jokes.

The English professor, who had a speech affliction, stammered, "At lunch I innocently r-repeated Bob Hutchins r-remark that whenever he feels an urge to take exercise, he lies down and waits for it to pass. M-Miss Hatch denounced me. She told me I should walk a m-mile before breakfast every m-morning. I was sc-scandalized. I told Tate, and he said it was Cr-Cr-Creeping Docism."

Lutz swiftly manipulated his hearing aid dial and waited until the laughter left their faces before turning it up again. He knew the witticisms were harmless, that the visitors would lean over backwards not to let bias affect their evaluations, but as a European he felt authority should be respected. Americans, he thought sadly, would snicker at anything — the flag, the church, the government, their own fathers. The man who took himself seriously was fair game. To Lutz Doc had many weaknesses, but pomposity wasn't among them. The Austrian liked a paternal manner, an iron hand.

"My God, now he's quoting the Scriptures!" cried a chemist.

"The f-familiar passages, you notice. He doesn't know his Bible, but he knows his B-B-Bartlett."

The hearing aid dial went down again. Twisting it back, Lutz was grateful that the only voice in the lab now was Doc's. It had risen commandingly; he was attacking The Interests. The camera man, with a sure sense of drama, had moved close to frame his face. Doc's craggy aspect grew more striking, especially on this hand-tooled homemade set, designed and built by graduate students. Budge's engineering professor was greatly taken with the quality of the picture. He sidled over to Lutz and said so, and the Austrian reflected dryly that Doc's photogenic dimples were doing their bit for reaccreditation.

**

"So that's the *Star*, lock, stock, and barrel," Doc was saying. "If there's a whopper that's too big for them, I'd like to hear it. They've been rubbing furniture polish into my reputation for some twenty years, and now they're getting desperate, cobbling together any lie that suits their fancy. According to them I'm just about the worst candidate to run for office here or anywhere else. They say I don't know any more about government than a cat, that my experience in Gideon doesn't count for a row of crooked pins. And these dribs and drabs aren't enough for them. Do you know what their newest stunt is? If it gives their lordships any satisfaction, I admit it makes me blister mad. The *Star*'s latest chicanery is to insult State's fine squad by ignoring it. This afternoon — I'm telling you right here because you'll have a long look for it tomorrow — this very day the Titans walloped a mighty fine team by the score of *eighty-four to nothing*. I don't know how you feel, but it makes me stand just a little taller to know that there's that much gumption and get-up-and-go in our boys. Is the *Star* proud? Do they give a little dinky rap? Will they give the squad its due? Sure they will — on February thirtieth."

Doc breathed deeply, enjoying every expensive second.

"Of course, it's no secret that they're bound and determined to elect Stuart Hathaway Plimpton Witty as your next governor. Every day they tell you what a smart man he is, and what a regular slap-on-the-back fellow, and all that fudge. They'd like you to believe Stuart Hathaway Plimpton Witty and Governor Blandford are as alike as two buckshot. Well, you can swallow that one if you want. Somehow my gullet just won't take it. I've known Norm Blandford since the days when he was running a little feed store in Four Corners. He's a big-boned hick, same as me, and what either of us has in common with a chicken-boned city slick is more than I can tell. Blandford's a son of the soil, with the barn smell still on him. What's Stuart Hathaway Plimpton Witty? What's he smell of? Well, I'll tell you, straight and square."

He was on a familiar battleground, and in the sponsor's booth Newt and Sam exchanged a congratulatory look. The gamble was paying off. Doc uncoached was far better than any script could be. Newt thought of the tens of thousands of farmhouses to the north, each rearing its television mast over darkened fields of winter wheat. If half of them were tuned to Channel 5 the investment was worth it. Doc was something right out of a farmer's almanac. He couldn't have been more appealing to the counties if he had grown a Seth Thomas goatee and spoken from a tractor seat.

Newt glanced at the studio clock. Twelve minutes to go. He only hoped Doc wouldn't renege on the agreement they had made during the drive from Gideon.

**

The Gideon Elk's Club occupied three rooms over Finch's Haberdashery, and there Sol Feinblatt, hideous in an electric blue suit, lolled against a varnished pine bar while Doc looked down severely from a high corner shelf.

"He's got the stuff, Solly," said a fellow Elk, a wizened man in a Stetson and cowboy boots.

"Oh, he'll make the grade," Sol said. "He has the know-how."

"Boy, you said it."

"And how."

The cowboy was one of Sol's lowbrow cronies. Last month Sol had been grimly amused to overhear him telling the bartender that Solly wasn't a bad guy for a Jew.

"I think he'll make it," said the cowboy.

"In a walk."

"No, it'll be a photo-finish."

"Close as they come, eh?"

"You can say that again."

"Close as they come, eh?"

Irony, diversion; a month ago they would have been enough for Sol. But now he was restless. Suddenly the beer seemed flat, the man alongside odious, his own clownish suit a pale joke. Perhaps it was time to put away childish things. After all, he could scarcely expect anyone else to take him seriously if he didn't himself. He needn't pull a grave face or quit laughing slyly at the world, but on the other hand he needn't be an Elk, either.

The cowboy banged his fist on the bar. "By God, you know what Doc's got? He's got personality-plus!"

This time Sol didn't reply. He was bowed over his six-ounce glass, watching the Schlitz foam bubbles break one by one and wondering where Kit was, and what she was doing, and whether she missed him as he missed her.

**

"Don't you think that's too loud, Kit?" Sarah said tentatively. "I think it's a hair too much. That's the girl. Just a little, now. Maybe a wisp more — fine, that's just fine."

It was Kit's fourth trip to the set, and the sound was now barely audible. Sarah feigned interest. She tried to keep her eyes on Doc's image, tried to be attentive, but it was a pathetic pretence. Each time Kit left to adjust the volume she glanced furtively at her watch, and she spoke up repeatedly with questions about Kit's son. Anything of Sean's — his baby words, his nap habits, the cold that had kept him at home this evening with a Theta sitter — was more important and more interesting to her than her husband's maiden television speech. She didn't say that; she would have become highly agitated if Kit had suggested they turn him off completely; yet her watching was only a matter of form, and it was so little that that his twang, reduced to a dry whisper, scarcely intruded on their conversation.

They would have made a striking pair of cameos. Kit had taken Sarah as her sartorial model. Both women wore plain navy blue dresses and blunt black shoes, both had gathered their hair in back in tortoise shell combs, each sat primly in a straight-backed Mansion library chair with her legs neatly crossed at the ankles and her hands folded tidily in her lap. Nevertheless they were very unlike. Sarah had the neutral dignity of age; Kit, still attractive in her mid-thirties, was like a flower whose petals have just begun to grow heavy. Sarah remembered herself at that age. It had been a bitter time, when she first began to despair of ever having children, and Kit's plight now, her awkward divorce and uncertain future, had made the bond between them stronger.

"Is everything all right at the Gamma house?" It would always be the Gamma house to Sarah.

"Oh — pretty much. Nobody's asked to see my husband's death certificate, if that's what you mean. But that may change. I may have to stir up a fuss."

"Trouble with the girls?"

"One girl. Lately she's been behaving, though. Maybe it'll straighten out."

Sarah reached over and patted her hand. "If it doesn't, you just let me know."

"Oh, I couldn't — you've done too much already."

"Not a word, now. I mean it."

She did. In giving to Kit, Sarah gained a little of the assurance she so desperately needed. The possibility that someone might lean on her was in itself a source of strength, and she gave Kit a kindly smile and for a moment was, as she had been with Ham, her cheerful self.

It was only a moment. She heard the television set mumbling, and her eyes glazed.

"Would you turn that down a mite? It does seem too high."

She meant that, too. To her it was deafening.

**

A hunchbacked Clipper Club attendant gently lowered another oak log to the gleaming old brass andirons, and the jeweled embers beneath sprang to life. Sharp crackling could be heard in the farthest corners of the great room as the tongues of flame leapt high, bathing the high paneled walls with a red wash and competing with the gesturing figure on the polished mahogany television console opposite.

The fire was Doc's only video competition, but there was much audio. The console faced a triple arc of choleric men who grunted at him, swore angrily, accosted him with unanswerable rhetorical questions and frequently commented that that was the last straw, they didn't have to listen to this commiecrat gobbledygook, they were leaving. No one left. The truth is that all were enjoying it — all except three in the front row. Judge Davies, Stuart Witty, and Clare Hewitt, the Republican chairman, were studying Doc's performance with professional eyes and silently giving him high marks. He was far more effective than they had expected.

Governor Blandford sat with them. The governor had followed the speech closely until he heard himself described as a son of the soil, smelling of barns; then he had beckoned urgently to a hovering waiter. The gesture had been repeated four times, and now he smelled only of cognac. In the astonishing interval of ten minutes he had drunk himself into a semi-coma. His head lolled, he belched frequently. The spectators in the rear thought he was jeering Doc, and they egged him on, but the judge, Witty, and Hewitt knew better. All three shared the same thought. Blandford would have to be watched every minute. He couldn't be trusted in public or alone anywhere.

The judge was in fine disarray. His vest was half unbuttoned, his string tie was twisted to one side, and below the ragged fringe of his mustache a ravaged, unlit cigar protruded at a reckless angle. Only his fine face was a mask. He knew a dozen men here were watching for his reaction, and he revealed nothing until Doc had finished denouncing the Bourbons of the state. Then he cocked his head toward Witty.

"Better make a note to talk to every Grange leader in the state tomorrow," he murmured. "Don't delegate it — do it yourself. This is strong medicine."

Hewitt whispered indignantly, "It's demagogic!"

"Oh bah," the judge grumbled. "It's quite within the rules."

"Write it down," Witty said to Hewitt. "I'll spend the morning on the phone." To the judge he said easily, "It *is* good, though I doubt it's good enough."

"Eh? No, no, of course not. It'll take more than this rooster crow to elect him. But he's still hurting you."

Like Newt Albert the judge was thinking of the lonely rural homesteads with the silvery R.F.D. boxes in front, the iron ranges in the kitchens, the seed catalogues in the parlors. The cities had changed mightily, and in another generation their swelling immigrant wards would seize political control, but as long as the new white-collar suburbs remained Republican the great keep of power remained in the homogeneous, Anglo-Saxon, Protestant counties, where family after family could be traced back to riflemen in the state regiments that had held the line of Hancock's corps at Gettysburg, and where first the G.A.R. and then the Grange had bloodied every Democratic candidate since 1866. It was curious, the judge mused; for nearly a century all state electoral verdicts had been echoes of the musketry on that red Pennsylvania field, yet the men who profited from them — the bilious hecklers in this room — were often descendants of merchants who had sent substitutes to the war. Jonathan Davies hadn't missed a day in court between Sumter and Appomattox. Isaac Hewitt had doubled his commission brokerage business the year of Antietam. And Ephraim Witty had been so tactless as to open his store the Monday after Lincoln's death, although, if legend were true, a line of disabled veterans in forage caps had picketed him until he closed.

The judge's reverie was interrupted by the hunchbacked retainer, who leaned across him to hand Witty a large brown envelope marked "Urgent." Witty broke the flap and drew out a *Star* first edition. Across the mast was Hallam Caulkin's blue-pencil scrawl: "Our new line. Suggest you follow through. Fore! H. C." A thick waxy arrow pointed to Al Swinton's story.

Witty read, grinned, and handed it to the judge.

"A little nostrum of our own," he whispered.

The judge squinted in the crimson firelight. So they couldn't even identify Vicksburg. *Magni nominis umbra.* He folded the paper and returned it. "This may restore *you,*" he said crisply, "but for me it's something of a complication. You forget; I have a responsibility. I'm a university trustee."

**

Behind his oafish manner Sam Theanapolis was a precise executive. Despite his distaste for the *Star* he had stationed a messenger in the lot where the paper's delivery trucks parked, and even as Hallam Caulkin had scribbled his message to Witty, Sam's runner had darted into a waiting taxi with an ink-fresh copy of the first edition. It arrived in the sponsor's booth only a few seconds after Witty's reached him.

Sam swore.

"It's starting," he said tightly. "The real slime's starting."

Newt grabbed the paper. He was slower to grasp the significance of the story. He scarcely thought of State as an educational institution. Contemptuous of anything that smacked of intellectualism, he took what he regarded as a hardheaded attitude toward that aspect of Doc's career. It was something better left unmentioned, of no real value to either side. He still couldn't regard it as a major issue, even though he conceded, as he finished the last biting paragraph, that it was a kick and might leave a little bruise.

"Mikel's that screwball with the bike clips?"

Sam nodded grimly. "I always knew he was cracked. He must really be ready for the couch to do this."

"Fire him."

"You can't just fire a professor," Sam said impatiently.

"They got a union or something?"

"Yeah. Sure." Sometimes Sam wondered about Newt. "It's a thing we got to live with, that's all."

"We'll live with it," Newt said indifferently. "It won't kill us."

He turned back to the studio. The painted book backs and second-hand loving cups on the other side of the booth window reassured him. They looked imposing, and that, he thought, was what counted. To Newt a university was a university, an absolute, like a Cadillac or a million dollars. He didn't distinguish between this one and that one. There were rivalries between them, but that was just part of the show — the mysterious campus pageant that he distrusted, respected, feared, and admired all at the same time. So a few kids flunked a test, he thought. What was that to John Q. beside today's football score?

"Forget it," he advised Sam. "Take the word of a wise old pol: it's nothing."

But on this Sam was the wise one. Newt knew ward politics, Grange politics, back-scratching, buck-at-the-poll-door politics. Sam knew public images. The voters had to have the right mental portrait of Doc, and Mikel's survey had blurred the oils, and that was bad.

"This is only the beginning," he said disconsolately, thrusting the newspaper down between his legs. "From here on in it's dirt."

**

"I predict a clean campaign," Doc was saying. "Hard-fought — yes. Cards on the table — yes, and face up, too. But I know Stuart Hathaway Plimpton Witty agrees with me that nothing's to be gained by gossiping like a bunch of corner loafers. I refuse to stoop to conquer, and I'm sure he feels the same."

The studio clock showed two minutes left. Newt signaled him. It was time for the payoff.

Doc frowned majestically. "I wish I could be as confident about his position on electioneering with taxpayers' money."

Only a handful of listeners knew what he was talking about, but they all sat up. Sam and Newt in the booth, Ham Markham and Nails Whipple in the Peabody faculty club, Hallam Caulkin behind his runway desk, and the men in the front row at the Clipper Club strained toward their screens, alert for the next line. Even the fuddled governor lurched forward, and as he steadied himself on a chair arm he heard his name again.

"In the twelve years Norm Blandford's been in the Statehouse the Republicans have taken over every department in the administration except mine. Maybe they think they own the government. I don't know, and I don't want to be a calamity howler, but, by Jupiter, sometimes they act that way. So I'm serving them notice, here and now. In my view, men whose salaries are paid by the public should work for the public and for *nobody else*. If they start using state employees to plump for Stuart Hathaway Plimpton Witty, I'm just going to have to fight fire with fire, and that's all there is to it."

It was Doc's last, deadly shot. He thanked them, blessed them, and bade them good night.

Stuart Witty leapt up. "Fire with fire! Now that *is* demagogic!"

Fire with fire: Newt had converted Doc to the argument that afternoon. It sounded reasonable, but as Witty indignantly told the judge — who nodded in vehement agreement — it was a false syllogism. Hallam Caulkin, hurriedly telephoning instructions to an editorial writer, compared it to Hitler's accusing countries he was about to invade of aggressive intentions. It was more complicated than that. Witty couldn't avoid using state employees. Every working Republican was on some departmental payroll. That was the way politics worked. If you won you passed out jobs, and if you wanted to win again your job-holders got out and hustled for you. Had Doc threatened to permit soliciting of votes by his Gideon staff there would have been little reaction. If that had been on his mind he wouldn't have even mentioned it, however; it would have been too trivial. He had other plans, and the speech had telegraphed them. He was preparing to mobilize, not his staff, but the university itself. It wasn't put that baldly; he didn't even admit it to himself; but there it was. The Republicans had been jarred by a sharp punch. Sometime within the week, they knew, Doc would accuse them of breaking faith and follow up with the roundhouse, the orders to State's hospital, farm agents, and extension services. They hadn't expected this. It wasn't even legal, since he was technically on leave, but his peculiar position as a state legend and empire-builder gave him the power, and there was now no doubt he intended to use it.

They could only wait helplessly and wonder when the blow would come.

It came on Tuesday.

THREE
Homecoming

TUESDAY MORNING Sam's office issued a release which tersely observed that, despite Doc's ultimatum, over five hundred Blandford appointees still held offices in Young Republican, Women's Republican, and Win-with-Witty Clubs. The release said that the Democratic State Central Committee was indignant, the university's board of trustees shocked, Doc himself saddened. One of his first acts as governor would be to present the legislature with a little Hatch Act outlawing this sort of thing. In the meanwhile, however, the administration had left him no alternative. He would have to consult his own interests.

He had been consulting them in his office since breakfast. Facing his desk, taking careful notes, were John Winkler and the directors of State's three chief off-campus services. Newt sat to one side with Jill and did not intervene, for Doc was indisputably in command. In faculty meetings he was sometimes at a loss; with Newt he was a fumbling apprentice; but he had built the services himself and drawn them up in battle formation for nearly a dozen legislative sessions. No one could out-general him here. He had invented this kind of warfare.

The directors, who had learned it from him, were coins struck from the same mint. They didn't look alike. Bill Shaw, the administrator of scholarships, was a slight, gentle man; Jake Russo, who directed agricultural services, had a pinched face and eyes gray as rain; Joe Massicotte, administrator of the medical school's Haven Square Hospital, was short and swarthy and volatile. But all three imitated Doc's iron handclasp. All had entered the office with his loping walk, wearing battered brown hats and carrying themselves with something of his rough rustic air. They were like junior executives paying quiet homage to the founder of the firm. Doc's new faculty might bait him behind his back; the loyalty of Shaw, Russo, and Massicotte was steadfast. There were no doubts among them, not even over the extraordinary orders he was giving them now.

"I expect you'll want to think hard about your outpatient clinics, Joe," he said as Jill tried frantically to catch up in her inexpert shorthand.

"Oh, sure. The accident room, too. We handled half of Birmingham's emergencies last year. Of course, most of the cases come from the Mechanics Street district," Massicotte said and added hesitantly, "which means a lot of bills are tough to collect."

Doc caught the hint. "As I recollect, your fees are paid on the spot."

"That's right. In Maternity we call it cash-and-carry." Massicotte's teeth flashed merrily. "Of course, if they happen to be a little short we don't call a cop. We just send them a statement the first of the month. Then, if they still ignore us, we turn them over to our retail credit people."

"Well, don't press them for awhile. Hold your outstanding bills until the second week in November. Don't write them off, now. You know what I mean."

Sam knew; so did Shaw when Doc suggested that all former scholarship holders be encouraged to support actively the party of their choice. Russo's role was more delicate. His county agents were more than agricultural advisers. They also had official roles as apple and egg graders, guardians of proper marketing procedures, and inspectors of livestock, seed, and drainage. The wrong kind of pressure from them would boomerang. It would be resented, and might even be illegal.

"I don't want any misguided enthusiasm from your people, Jake. No big sticks, no strong-arming." Doc thought a bit. "Still, there's no law that says enforcement officers must give up their rights as citizens. I suppose they can wear campaign buttons under their lapels if they want and tell people how they're going to vote if they're asked. Ordinarily I'd ask them to stay clear, but the way the other side's acting I think they can feel free."

Doc's eyes glinted. He was all business. Within a month he had reversed himself on the services because the month's events had persuaded him he couldn't win without them, and the need to win now eclipsed everything else. Since the first *Star* poll the desire for victory had been a cancer growing in him. After the second poll he had been ready for any pretext to break loose, and Newt had provided him with an ingenious solution. Clerks in the state's conservation bureau, roads commission, fiscal agencies, and health and welfare boards were contributing heavily to Witty, Newt had pointed out, exaggerating the size of their contributions and omitting the fact that no department was participating directly — that none, indeed, had the potential resources of the university. Until then Doc hadn't thought much about the traditional edge of a party in office. In a matter of minutes he had suppressed his misgivings and worked himself into a righteous fury. So he was being fouled. All right, he was no pansy. They'd find that out. If this was the kind of a campaign they wanted he could gouge and bite with the roughest of them.

Committed at last, he felt euphoric. His ruddy face glowed. He pointed at Winkler. "Who's using the community centers these days, John?"

Because the five former state teachers colleges were used to build up good will, they had been assigned to the university's public relations director. Winkler consulted a file and reported that center auditoriums had been reserved for meetings of assorted labor, lodge, veteran, and social groups.

"You're not thinking of canceling any of them?" he asked.

"Certainly not! But there's no reason we can't distribute a few pamphlets at their meetings. And maybe some of them would like to hear speakers from alumni groups on how my campus has grown and what it means to them. Turn those reservation schedules over to Jill. Jill!" She looked up hazily from her page of illegible hieroglyphics. "Make two copies of them," he told her. "Give Mr. Albert one set. The other will go to Mr. Theanapolis. I'll dictate an accompanying letter later."

By lunch he had finished giving orders. Only Winkler and Jill had questions.

"How do we handle the press?" Winkler asked. "They're going to be calling about this."

"Refer them to me."

"That'll mean daily interviews with Al Swinton."

"No, it won't." Doc winked. "It just means he'll *ask* for interviews. I'm afraid I'm going to be too busy to see that young man. He's had his last scoop from State." His face lengthened. He remembered Al's story on Mikel's survey. Since reading it he had been trying to find time to deal privately with Mikel, and he was about to ask Jill to make the appointment when she raised a hand. "Yes?"

"Do you want a transcription of my notes on this meeting?"

"Absolutely. We can't afford any misunderstandings. Everyone here should have a carbon."

"Oh," she said unhappily. And then: "What about Dr. Tate?"

Doc had completely forgotten Tate. Theoretically Shaw, Massicotte, and Russo were directly responsible to the provost now. Hang it all, he thought, the least I could have done was to ask him in.

"Yes, one for him," he said hurriedly, hoping Tate wouldn't be offended.

**

Sam Theanapolis had missed the morning conference because he had been told in advance what the outcome would be and was holed up in his Birmingham office, preparing for it. With the election only four weeks away Sam's day could be spent more profitably writing a leaflet for the new drive. Newt's headquarters had bales of handbills, but they were useless to the service directors because they listed the entire Democratic ticket, and even Newt realized that hospital orderlies and farm agents couldn't be that partisan. Only Doc could be advertised in the new literature, and his candidacy couldn't be mentioned directly. Instead Sam wrote "The Doc River Story," a lyrical panegyric with just enough college history in it to justify its distribution in university institutions. Nowhere did Sam say that the people of the state should be grateful to the heroic figure who had brought them so many blessings, but that was implicit; everyone understood. The leaflet was, indeed, the most effective piece of publicity ever produced by Sam Theanapolis Associates. After reading it Doc telephoned Sam and warmly told him so, and in Birmingham it was grudgingly praised by several of the firm's competitors. Sam himself was rather baffled. He had written it in a state of confusion. The decision to commit the services had amazed him. He wasn't at all sure he approved, and only his uncritical admiration of Doc prevented him from demurring. In fact that devotion was responsible for the pamphlet's triumph. Sam still had for Doc the shy, shiny-eyed adoration of the small boy following the neighborhood athlete home across the sandlot. Apart from his love for his family it was the purest and truest thing in his life. It was hero-worship; it struck a bright spark, and it made his tribute an immense success.

He finished correcting proofs late Tuesday afternoon and took them directly to his commercial printer. Rotary presses chattered off copies all that night, through Wednesday, and well into Thursday morning. By then thousand-copy bundles were being distributed to key points, broken into small lots, and stacked on tables in Haven Square waiting rooms, on community center racks, and in the back seats of the farm agents' coupes. Before the week end there were also a few posters, blown up from photographs of Doc, although that was the end of Sam's literature for the services. The leaflet had taken a heavy toll of their campaign chest, and Doc — to Newt's disappointment and Sam's relief — drew the line at the use of university contingency funds. It was a quibble really. University money, in the form of salaries, was being put to political use every day now, and in ways more telling than even Sam's encomium could be.

Until this year the state's Democrats had been restricted to one plan of attack. In election after election they had tried to amass so huge an urban majority that the counties couldn't stop it. Bitter figures showed that they were always buried. This time Doc's country background and Stuart Witty's glossy sophistication had suggested a fresh approach. The television speech had been a thrust in that direction. Paying Paul on the farm would be pointless if Peter in the city were robbed, however. Doc had to carry Birmingham by at least seventy thousand, which was where the hospital came in. In the seven years since its jagged concrete silhouette had altered the riverfront skyline it had become indispensable to the swarming tenements around the city gas works and the warehouse district. Even the *Star*, which knew the token clinic fees were made possible by big surcharges in the private wards, hadn't dared say so, for the hospital was sacred to the long lines of outpatients who gathered each morning in the cobblestoned plaza facing the entrance. The plaza was called Haven Square, and the hospital had been named after it. At the time Doc had liked that. Only now did he realize that the name suggested no connection with State. Thousands of cured patients had departed unaware that he had been their benefactor. Their ignorance was awkward, and Massicotte set out to remedy it.

He began by neutralizing the professional staff. Virtually all the doctors who practiced in Haven Square, including the medical school faculty, were rockribbed Republicans. They would balk at flagrant solicitation in the wards. At the same time Massicotte knew that they valued their hospital privileges and shrank from controversy.

Starting with the medical dean, he took them aside one by one, telling them they needn't be involved and reassuring them that no party labels would be mentioned. This, he insisted, was to be merely an information campaign. There were many arched brows, several disclaiming letters to the *Star*, but no resignations. Response from the staff was confined thereafter to occasional stony looks at the piles of leaflets — anything else, as Massicotte had shrewdly predicted, would have been beneath a physician's dignity — while the systematic distribution of literature was carried on throughout the hospital by orderlies who bypassed only the private wing, where most of the patients were in Republican income brackets anyhow. The following week the administrative force began mailings to everyone treated in the past year, to Haven Hospital Plan subscribers, and to all graduates of the nursing school. Posters of Doc in genial poses lined clinic corridors, gazed down encouragingly on mothers in labor, gave expectant fathers sympathetic glances, eyed VD victims reproachfully. Massicotte had neglected nothing. Sam, dropping in to make suggestions, could only pump his hand warmly. A tremor of excitement ran through Newt's downtown headquarters. Volunteer workers measured the quickening pulse in the slums and began predicting a city majority of a hundred thousand.

Jake Russo's task was very different. His farm agents, normally as rock-ribbed as Massicotte's doctors, were mugwumps this fall. A small kindness of Doc's was responsible. Each year he had made it a point to address their annual banquet, summing up football prospects in the season ahead. They felt a personal tie to him and would have bolted their party even if Russo hadn't suggested it. After leaving Gideon he summoned them by phone to the Walpole County community center for a council of war. Massicotte was trying to swell a Democratic tide; the trend in the counties would be the other way. Some townships hadn't had a local Democratic organization in sixty years, and the most Russo could do was hold Witty down. Any significant shift in upstate voting patterns would be a stunning contribution, however. If he could drive Witty's edge there below a hundred and thirty thousand, the returns from Birmingham, Pawnattuck, Dudley, and Rockton could wipe it out.

Russo's men deployed with caution. They concealed their I'm-for-Doc! buttons, as he had suggested, and circulated leaflets only when prospects wavered. There were plenty of waverers. Each agent knew 4-H leaders who enjoyed their summers in Gideon, rural women who depended on the university's home economics bulletins, voters indebted to the extension service. Because Russo's campaign was more unobtrusive than Massicotte's, it was slower to take hold. Yet every day more Blandford men became persuaded that Doc was one of them, a man above party, the right choice for dirt farmers. At harvest home suppers, swine-judging contests, and the big October county fairs where families milled around Ferris wheels and workhorse weight-drawing contests, Russo's agents baited their traps and stalked their prey all week end. Affable and unaffected under their slouch hats, withdrawing at the first sign of hostility, they provided the only real opposition field force to appear upstate since the Populist split of 1897. The Republicans were slow to react. They had never been seriously challenged here before. Then reports of defections began filtering down from the north, piling up on Clare Hewitt's desk, repeating again and again the startling news: for the first time this century the G.O.P. couldn't take the counties for granted.

John Winkler was working with Bill Shaw, the scholarship director. Winkler wrote every civic group that had signed up for a community center auditorium, inquiring whether it needed a speaker. The answers were predictable; speakers were always hard to find. Each morning's mail brought him anxious letters from legionnaires, P.T.A. presidents, and program chairmen who had long ago exhausted local talent. It just so happened they were looking for somebody to give a talk. Did he have any suggestions? He did; Shaw's mailing to former scholarship students had brought over a hundred replies from alumni who remembered him with gratitude. Shaw hadn't asked them for anything; he had merely inquired whether they could spare a few hours to help the university. The name of each interested alumnus was turned over to the civic group nearest his home, and he was asked to deliver a brief address on State. Shaw didn't tell them to mention Doc. He knew he didn't have to; each of them had lived four years in Gideon with the knowledge that Doc had wrung his scholarship money from the legislature. Because they were eager salesmen for his cause, all over the state audiences usually closed to politicians were hearing bright-eyed young alumni describe the gifts and charm of the man who had made their education possible. So earnest were the speakers, and so guileless, that many a rapt listener departed unaware that he had heard a new kind of campaign oratory. Only later, thumbing through his paper at home, would he remember that the paragon that fine young man had described down at the hall was a candidate — and, now that he thought about it, an attractive candidate — for governor.

Charlie Smathers's third *Star* poll, published that Saturday, showed Witty with fifty-eight per cent of the vote — a drop of two per cent, attributable to Doc's television performance. That was disturbing enough to Republicans — any loss of strength was an omen — but far worse were the new, uncounted straw ballots. A spot check revealed that the contributions of the services were hurting Witty everywhere. Another two weeks of this and Doc would be at his heels. And the election was over three weeks away. It began to look like a real race. The underdog was gaining, and the favorite, peering anxiously backward, felt a sharp pang of fear.

**

Hallam Caulkin had begun that week in a state of high excitement. His martial instincts were aroused. This was like being in the E.T.O., he told Marcus Gray, the *Star* publisher. More and more his bare office took on the aspects of a command post. Beside his situation map of the world he posted another, of the state, with flags in Birmingham and Gideon and pins in marginal districts. Each morning his editorial writers and news chiefs stood in a ragged rank before his desk while he briefed them on the day's developments, and after they had gone he would pace briskly back and forth, holding a brass pica rule like a swagger stick, planning ambushes. The Demmies were counterattacking in strength. Very well. He would seize the high ground and launch a by-the-book blitz that would clobber every last Democrat strongpoint.

But the war went badly. His intelligence was faulty, and his tactics inept.

Caulkin's knowledge of the enemy had come chiefly from Al Swinton. After the campaign button story and the Mikel survey Caulkin had had complete confidence in him. It was misplaced. Luck, which had been with Al, now deserted him. His only real source at State was Tate. The provost was still willing to cooperate, but he had little else to give. Because of Jill's unintelligible phonography her minutes of Doc's crucial meeting with the service directors were badly garbled. Tate handed over his carbon with an apologetic smile, and Al forwarded it to Caulkin, who crisply telegraphed back the truth, that it was worthless. Al fretted over that wire and fretted more when another followed, requesting that he solicit the acting president's opinion on the abuse of university services. That put Al in a difficult position. In his desire for Caulkin's unqualified praise he had neglected to tell him of Tate's defection. He had implied that the report had come to him through his own initiative, and now he was unable to protect his source. Dutifully he put the embarrassing question to Tate, who panicked and refused to talk to him, leaving Al without any campus contacts. In desperation Al conducted a student poll of his own, asking State undergraduates what they thought of Doc's exploitation of university facilities. The results were discouraging. None seemed to care. He falsified the figures, sent them off hopefully, and received a withering reply from Caulkin, who observed that he wanted information, not opinion, and that in any case Al's arithmetic had been wrong.

Lacking an efficient outpost in Gideon, Caulkin was dependent upon fragmentary stories from elsewhere. Word of Sam Massicotte's Haven Square electioneering reached the *Star* building quickly and was good for a page one splash, but Jake Russo's upstate maneuvers were more elusive. His agents talked only with acquaintances, who were close-lipped. It was even more difficult to explain what was happening in the community centers; there was no solid handle to grab. The *Star* had a cloudy picture. Diffuse reporting, moreover, was producing a diffuse editorial campaign. The general managing editor had planned what he called a series of small local offensives, denouncing in turn Doc's requests for money from the A List, academic standards at State, and the desecration of the Hospital. The whole lacked cohesion, and Charlie Smathers's figures documented its failure. Caulkin was stalemated. He brooded over his map, bombarded Al with messages, held daily telephone conferences with Stuart Witty, and looked in vain for the big issue, the break, the breakthrough.

His gloom elated the city room. Ham, arriving with the fourteenth installment of his series, heard nothing else there. Entering the general managing editor's office he risked a taunt.

"How's the battle?" he asked, tossing his story across the desk.

Caulkin eyed him sourly. "I thought you were staying in Gideon."

"I have to see my father-in-law. We're going to tie one on at the club."

"Don't be flip." He picked up the story. "What's this?"

"The stuff to give the troops. How the clapper of Peabody's Burmese bell was swiped in the fall of 1923 and mysteriously returned the next spring."

"Oh. Oh yes. That was in my time. I remember it."

"You would. You were one of the suspects."

Caulkin blinked. "I hope you didn't write that."

"I was tempted."

"Nothing was proved, you know."

"*I* know. But I'm not impressed. Nothing was proved against Consolidated Enterprises, either. Or didn't Frosty Warren tell you I knew that, too?"

Clearly Frosty hadn't; it came as a shock. Caulkin toyed nervously with his ruler, and Ham watched him narrowly. The general managing editor was Frosty twenty years from now — the mediocrity, promoted because of his connections, who would never understand how a real newspaperman worked. He had thought Ham had quit probing for the old scandal, had thought the past unfathomable because for him it would have been. His response was in character: first the quiver of surprise, then the fumbling review of possible answers, and finally the sullen silence. He sat immobile, his handsome flowered face heavy with disapproval.

Yet his combative instincts were genuine. When he struck he struck hard. Propping the ruler between open palms, he said, "What do you think of your former hero these days?"

"If you mean Doc, I'm still for him."

"You even condone his brainwashing of the sick, I suppose."

Ham was silent. Less than an hour before he had been pounding on Sam Theanapolis' desk, protesting the new direction of the campaign.

"He's putting on the most disgraceful performance in the history of state politics," Caulkin said cuttingly. "It was bad enough when we were just supporting his featherbed giveaways with our tax money."

"Anything that helps the poor is a giveaway to you," said Ham, flushing. "Those services were needed."

It was true. And that was why Doc's abuse of them hurt so. Doc had built well, and now he was burning what he had built.

"But this tops everything," Caulkin continued, ignoring him. "We're paying for his machine. That's what he's running on, you know — a featherbed machine." The phrase pleased him. He made a quick note of it, something for the editorial writers, and reached out, as though to rap Ham's knuckles. "Well, this time he's gone too far."

"He'll win," Ham said, without ardor.

"He'll lose," said Caulkin, without conviction.

"And meanwhile you want me to burrow deeper into the Peabody files."

"Well — with your attitude you can't be much help in the big show. Unless," he suggested feebly, "you'd like to do a little off-the-record birddogging around Democrat headquarters."

Ham stared, and Caulkin shrugged. Even he couldn't expect a foreign correspondent to be Al Swinton's leg man. The request itself was a slight. Coming in here had been a mistake, Ham thought. He should have left the installment with the secretary outside.

"Want to be remembered to the judge?" he asked, rising and stretching his long legs.

"Of course. And you might ask him when he'll be ready with his statement."

Ham knew of no statement. He looked inquiring. Before Caulkin could explain his secretary rapped and entered with a message. The judge had just called. He wanted Ham to meet him, not at the club, but in the Statehouse.

Caulkin expanded. "Five'll get you ten that means he's ready now. The statement, of course, will come from him as a State trustee."

Then Ham understood. He looked down glumly at his bell story, remembering a Burmese proverb: When two buffalo fight, the victim is the grass beneath them. If his father-in-law was coming out publicly against Doc he couldn't escape unbruised; he had recommended each to the other.

Five'll get you ten. Some gamble, he thought.

Heads you win.

Caulkin had resumed his military posture. "Carry on, Hiram," he said briskly. "And if the judge's declaration *is* ready, bring it in."

And tails I lose.

**

Judge Davies despised the secretarial practice of telephoning a man and leaving him to wait until the boss was free. In such cases his own solution was direct; he counted to seven slowly and then hung up. Others weren't so firm, however, and he had decided to handle this

Gideon call himself. If there was to be rudeness between them, it would have to come from Doc. The judge was determined to be correct.

He was not so correct with the operator. Ham, escorted into the governor's office by Clare Hewitt, heard his father-in-law before he saw him, the clipped voice high and strident with pique.

"Yes, yes, I'm aware that he's not on that extension. No, don't try again. Certainly I want to complete the call. Just ring seven-six-five, please. Eh? Hello? This is Roger Davies. I'm most anxious to reach Mr. River. Try extension what? Five-oh-four? Could you reach your operator? Mine seems to be a congenital — oh — ah — there you are, my dear. Five-oh-four, please."

Obviously this had been going on some time. The judge still wore his tweed topcoat, thrown open, and his soft gray hat, pushed back, but under the upturned brim his brow gleamed with perspiration. The operators were now negotiating formally. He shifted irritably in the revolving chair, shoved his rimless glasses down his nose, and peered myopically at Ham.

"Have a chair, Markham. I'm temporarily in the hands of lunatics." Then, furiously: "What? Not there, either? Then back we go to two-one-three. Yes, I'll wait. Till the other place freezes over."

Blandford was absent. Stuart Witty stood in a corner, flanked by shelves of law books and reading one. He looked, Ham thought, like his word picture in *Who's Who*. Dancy had told Ham of Witty's illicit appeal to women, and there were suggestions of that, too: athletic intensity, pride, restlessness; an elegant charm. And now he was preparing to charm Ham. He pounced over with the self-sell look of the eager candidate. "The name's Stu Witty," he said, deftly steering Ham to a wing chair. "I've looked forward to meeting you for some time." Glancing across the rosewood desk, he whispered musically, "Isn't it just like the judge to be baffled by modern communications? Though I suppose this time he can't be blamed really. We can hardly expect the opposition to be anything but slippery with us."

The judge heard that and disapproved. He didn't mind being called incompetent, but he disliked Witty's identifying him with the campaign; as a trustee he ought to be conspicuously neutral. The implication that he wasn't smarted because it was partly true. Not since his withdrawal from politics had he been so involved in an election. The leaders of his party, facing their first real threat in a generation, asked his advice daily, and it was hard to refuse them. Lacking an immediate family, the judge in his declining years had grown increasingly dependent upon the society of his own kind. The routine of his life threw him constantly with Witty and the members of the State Central Committee; he saw them everywhere — in his chambers, in his club, on the steps of St. Timothy's P. E. Church Sunday mornings. Had they asked for financial contributions he would have refused, but they hadn't. What they needed was guidance, and he found it impossible to turn away when they asked what he thought they ought to do next. He needed their companionship, he had to pay some price, and each encounter seemed casual enough at the time. Nevertheless he felt somewhat compromised. Witty, he thought, had been indiscreet to speak so to Ham. This setting was peculiar enough as it was — the governor away, himself in Blandford's chair, and the Republican candidate and his party chairman hovering around like figures in a palace intrigue. It looked shifty, sinister, conspiratorial.

Ironically, the judge had come to the Statehouse to avoid just that impression. After Sam had answered him evasively and Tate, in hiding since his last encounter with Al, had found it inconvenient to come to the phone, he had decided that the next proper step for a gubernatorial appointee was to seek out the governor. Accordingly he had left the message for Ham with Caulkin's secretary and taxied directly here — only to discover the office occupied by Witty and Hewitt, conferring. It was regrettable. But he wouldn't permit it to deter him. He was proceeding exactly as he would have had Blandford been there. Doc would be given a chance to meet his requests. Then, if they couldn't reach some understanding, there would have to be an open break.

The line was clicking. The operator had found someone who would talk to him.

"Hello!" he cried. "What's that? Jill who? Oh yes, of course!" He sighed his relief; he had found a friend. "Certainly I remember you, and with the greatest pleasure. I can't tell you how glad I am to hear your voice. You see, I've been trying to locate Mr. River, and it's taking an unconscionable amount of time. Can you put me through to him?"

He winced and held the receiver away from his ear. Jill's soprano was audible throughout the office. Oh dear, she was saying. This was, well, like embarrassing. She hoped the judge wouldn't think she was a droop, but she really couldn't do a single solitary thing. The party he was referring to was there — in the very next office if he wanted to know the truth — but she had orders, well you couldn't exactly say they were orders, but they were really, not to let the judge through. Yes, that was right. Those were what you might call her instructions, sort of. Probably she was an awful goofball to come right out and say so this way, but the judge had been nice to her and all and she couldn't bear to have him waste his real valuable time this way, calling hither and yon when there wasn't the remotest chance of his getting anything but egg on his face.

"Egg? Oh, I see. You're very thoughtful. Thank you." He hung up and looked hard at Ham. "You heard?"

"Real good. Like perfect."

"I'm gratified; I doubt I could have repeated it. However, I think we're both clear as to the sense."

He paused deliberately, lighting a cigar as Witty and Hewitt withdrew toward the bookshelves. They perceived that he wanted a few words alone with his son-in-law, and it was a virtue of their caste that they needed no cleared throat, no broad wink, no jerk of the head; they walked away and that was all. Or almost all; in the corner they couldn't resist oblique glances at Ham. Neither had met him before. Both had been amused, if faintly scandalized, by his book. They knew he had a local reputation quite independent of his successful marriage, and they wondered whether it were true that he was not only an alumnus of State but a devoted one. Hewitt looked upon Ham as something of a superior parvenu. He regarded him with the defensive arrogance that men of inherited wealth assume toward the self-made. Witty, the wiser of the two, respected Ham, though he couldn't see why Ham shouldn't shuck the loyalties of his youth. In Witty's experience such mavericks stayed clear of controversy. Their freedom from social obligations gave them, indeed, a unique advantage.

Ham shared that view. Instinctively he resisted involvement. Since returning from India he had been like a runner crossing a stretch of moor, trying to keep his eye on the far hill — his reunion with his wife and son — and tugging free whenever the fen sucked him down. Doc's snub of the judge disquieted him, but he resented his own feeling of responsibility.

"It's a damned shame, sir, though I don't think there's anything I can do about it."

"No, I suppose there isn't," the judge said thoughtfully. "Still, since you were present at the marriage I thought you'd be at least diverted by the crackup."

Despite Ham the fen gripped him. "You're going to resign?"

"No, I shan't file for divorce. It wouldn't be decent to quit so soon. I merely intend to complain to the neighbors."

"Caulkin told me you were going to make a statement."

"That's what I have in mind. A protest. A declaration of conscience."

"Isn't there some other way?"

"I see none. I've written Mr. Theanapolis, Dr. Tate, and Mr. River, requesting an extraordinary session of the university board, and I've tried to talk to all three. Plainly I'm being ignored. My pride will survive the jolt, but I'm a trustee. I have an obligation. Silence is properly construed as assent. I can't be quiet when the school's facilities are misused and" — he hesitated — "its standards maligned."

"Mikel's survey?"

He looked aside. "Yes."

"I can't understand why he let it get out."

"You had to print it, I suppose."

"Please. Don't blame me for everything in the *Star*. I take the rap only for my stories."

The judge straightened. "And you didn't write that?"

"Of course not! It was Al Swinton's — after the first edition it had his by-line on it."

"Yes, but Dr. Mikel thought . . ."

"Mikel thought what?"

". . . that the Star was protecting you. I had to be sure the account in the paper was correct, so I talked to him two days ago. Another interminable telephone call." He closed his eyes briefly, wearied by the memory of it. "Apparently he has been out of his office the past week, and he has an astonishing number of home addresses. In any event, when I finally reached him he verified the report. When I observed rather bluntly that it had damaged the university he snorted and said I had better talk to you about that."

"He thinks *I* did it?" Ham looked incredulous, then reproachful. "And apparently you thought so, too."

"He — ah — said that you had seen the survey."

"That's right."

"And in your calling you have to — ah — take information where you can find it."

"That's wrong. When something is shown to me in confidence I write nothing and tell no one."

The judge was embarrassed, Ham disturbed. The mire held him fast now. He had to talk to Mikel. And he had better see Doc, too.

"Suppose you delay your neighborhood complaint a bit. I'm driving back to Gideon tonight. The least I can do is get you some definite answer."

The judge pondered, and Witty, watching narrowly from the corner, decided to intervene. He counted on that statement. Crossing quickly to them, he joined the debate with Ham, citing, with his advocate's skill, the reasons why a delay would be pointless.

"The nub of the thing is that the survey is true," he said, holding one hand in a little cup, as though weighing evidence. "Does it make any difference how it reached print?"

"It does to me," Ham said grimly.

"Of course. But to the university? There it matters only that State graduates aren't properly educated."

"Careful. You're looking at one."

"A commendable example of self-education, I should say." Before Ham could reply Witty said, "Anyhow, the survey itself is a secondary matter. We are mainly concerned with the strange indoctrination State institutions are giving the voters. Have you seen what's going on at Haven Square Hospital?"

He paced the room on his short, powerful legs, now gesturing, now knitting his black brows, now inclining his beetled dome as he presented his arguments. Ham watched nervously, the judge gravely, Hewitt approvingly. It was an admirable plea. Nevertheless Witty erred in making it at all. He was not here as a lawyer. He was a candidate, and his rhetoric was a blind; he wanted the statement as propaganda. The judge couldn't yield to that kind of pressure.

"I'll wait," he said.

Now Hewitt came forward, remonstrating until Witty, who saw his mistake too late, waved him off. Hewitt subsided, but sulked. "At least we should have Blandford freeze university funds," he said.

"And starve the hospital?" The judge shook his head. "That would be most foolish, Mr. Howell."

"Hewitt, sir."

"It would also be of doubtful legality. No, gentlemen, subtler measures are required."

The judge was leaving with Ham when Witty called him back and unfolded a closely typed page of onion skin. "This arrived this morning."

The judge glanced at it impatiently, glanced away, and looked back sharply. The paper was a summary of confidential reports from county chairmen, assessing the party's upstate strength. Men who regularly delivered their districts by percentages in the eighties anticipated drops to the seventies, and the low seventies at that. All in all Witty averaged some ten points below Blandford's vote four years ago. And the crucial phase of the campaign still lay ahead. By November some of those estimates might drop into the sixties — too small a dike to hold back the flood of Doc's city majorities.

"Wait outside," the judge told Ham. "I'll be along directly." He carefully refolded the report and handed it back to Witty. "Alarming. But luckily you have a precedent."

Witty smiled weakly. "Not in my memory, sir."

"No, in mine. You're too young to remember what Theodore Roosevelt did to the party in 1912. It was brother against brother; every other farmer was a Bull Mooser. Yet Taft carried the state, by an eyelash. We brought him here — I believe an honorary degree from Peabody was the excuse — and sent him out in the fields to pick huckleberries. He didn't pick many, and he ate them, but he swayed enough hired men to turn the trick."

"You think we should bear down more heavily there?"

"If I were you I should."

Hewitt strolled over. "Why not show Blandford to the hicks?"

The judge coughed. "Please don't refer to our husbandmen by that term, Mr. Hewell. One of them might hear you, and then, if you'll excuse the vulgarism, it would be Kitty bar the gate."

"Blandford *does* bring them up stamping," Witty said.

The judge coughed again, delicately. "I'm afraid his excellency would stamp after the first jug of corn on the first farm in the first county."

"Oh no," Witty said, and Hewitt said, "Hadn't you heard? He's been on the wagon all week."

"I'm gratified. But the plan is still defective. Blandford would win votes for Blandford. And he's not running." He wagged a finger at Witty's Win-with-Witty pin. "*You*'re the candidate. I suggest you hail a John Deere tractor and ride north."

"I can't."

"Why not?"

"He has engagements in Pawnattuck," Hewitt said. "We're trying to counteract River's alliance with Lockwood Aircraft."

"Gentlemen, please," the judge implored them. "You're not *that* young. If we learned nothing else from the latter Roosevelt it was that Republicans never win the votes of idle men. In Pawnattuck you'd merely be advertising a weakness, while in the north you'd be picking up stragglers from your own colors."

Witty deliberated. "It's a point."

"Maybe we should send Blandford to Pawnattuck," Hewitt said irresolutely.

"Send him to Tanganyika if you like, but put a guard on him," the judge said. "The wagon, as you coarsely call it, is an unreliable vehicle. Buttermilk to vanilla extract — I know the type. And now you really must excuse me. I've kept Markham too long."

On the curving stairway Ham advised him to bundle up. "There's a raw wind out there."

"Bah. The East has thinned your blood," the judge grumbled, groping in his sleeve for a fugitive scarf. "Damned thing's caught in the lining. There!" He knotted it raffishly, like a Christmas card snowman's. "Rather fetching, eh?" They stepped outside and were nearly blown back.

"My God, Markham! You didn't warn me!"

"I did," Ham said firmly.

"Don't be difficult," the judge gasped, struggling through the mounting gale to a Yellow Cab. "You're as mulish as that young man back there."

"Our next chief executive? You should be more respectful, sir."

"Don't mean him." He snuggled against the cab's leather cushions and began lacerating an unlit cigar. "I mean the other fellow. What's-his-name. Howitt."

**

The exchange in the Statehouse had a curious aftermath. Ham's postponement of Judge Davies's public statement was brief. He shouldered his way into Doc's office the next day, but the moment he mentioned the survey he was told to skedaddle, and the following morning the *Star* devoted the top of its front page to the judge's declaration. It was a remarkable document, pithy and closely reasoned. In other circumstances it might have been telling. That day it went largely unread, however, for the state's attention was elsewhere, in Pawnattuck, where Governor Norman R. Blandford had publicly disgraced himself.

The stage for the disaster had been set even as the Yellow Cab crackled away over the capitol's pink granite drive. Witty and Hewitt had concluded that the judge's counsel was sound. Within the hour county chairmen were alerted. Frosty Warren arrived with a *Star* photographer, and by morning the Republican candidate was posing on stone walls, drinking cider, congratulating pink-cheeked 4-H award winners, and gingerly stroking perplexed livestock. Meanwhile there had been the problem of Pawnattuck. All very well for the judge to say they should forget about it, Hewitt had argued, but the fact remained that the party had made speaking commitments there, and a check for six hundred dollars had been sent to WASP-TV, the local television station. The Pawnattuck *Argus* had announced that Witty would deliver a thirty-minute address on the city's problems, which meant writing off the check wouldn't do. Despite Pawnattuck's heavy Democratic registration it had a respectable independent vote. The man on the fence would feel slighted, Hewitt had insisted. He had volunteered to handle everything, and Witty, to his subsquent sorrow, had agreed.

Blandford was the only Republican name big enough to substitute for the candidate. Had Hewitt left it at that, and confined him to the television appearance, he might have brought the thing off. But he grew ambitious. Arriving in the city at noon with the sober governor, he decided to go ahead with the entire schedule prepared for Witty. After lunch Blandford spent a strenuous afternoon denouncing socialized medicine at the medical society, Colonel Nasser at the Jewish War Veterans post, and automation at five union halls. It was the union halls that broke his spirit. At each he was greeted with a stony silence and jeered as he left. The hostility unnerved him. He toyed with his supper. By evening, when they were due at the studio, the last of his geniality had vanished. He was a sick old man, racked by a growing thirst. Outside the gale had grown worse; tottering up the WASP-TV steps he shuddered as though it were blowing right through him. A half-hour seemed a long time to talk, and he wondered where a fellow could wet his whistle.

At this critical moment Hewitt left him. The president of the Pawnattuck carpenter's local, an old John L. Lewis Republican, appeared on the windswept steps and begged a word. Hewitt couldn't refuse. After the disappointing receptions of the afternoon an endorsement from a union leader would be a bracing tonic, so he led this one into the sponsor's booth, leaving his ward with the station manager. It seemed safe. The program was less than an hour away, and the governor was in the manager's office. Hewitt could see the door from the sponsor's booth. He had checked inside; there were no other exits.

None were necessary. The stuff was there. The manager, an ebullient young man proud of his concealed bar for visiting celebrities, produced a bottle of Hennessy and suggested coyly that even a governor might like one for courage. The governor thought he had a point there. One for courage, he said, and maybe one for luck. He wrapped a gnarled hand around the bottle's neck, and, to the young man's dismay, declined to release it. Another host might have understood the situation — Blandford's drinking had been gossip among the well-informed for years — but the manager was new to the state. He was also awed by authority. A governor, he thought, ought to know his own limit. As a result Blandford entered the studio in a brandied daze. Hewitt saw it too late. He had been on the verge of an agreement with the carpenter's president, and when he looked through the plate glass and saw the telltale flush in the governor's cheeks there was less than a minute to go. He could only sit, frozen with horror, watching the sweep second hand of the studio clock arch toward catastrophe.

WASP-TV had a powerful transmitter. Its picture could be received in Rockton and Dudley and, if the weather was clear, in the suburbs of Birmingham. As an independent station it carried no network programs. Instead it ran old movies, and tonight the audience was unusually large because the regional television guide, published before Hewitt had bought his thirty minutes, listed a Marx Brothers comedy for this hour. The following morning countless coffee break wags told friends Governor Blandford was the fifth Marx brother — a cruel joke, but inevitable; he had been that bad. For the first few minutes he had tried to follow his script, leaning forward and squinting at the dancing words on the TelePrompTer; then he had sat back with a flabby smile and talked at random. None of it made much sense. He forgot names — forgot even Witty's — and seemed incapable of ending a sentence until, after a hideous silence during which he seemed lost in a private dream, he sat up indignantly and actually said that he hoped "None of you good people out there're under the impression I'm under the affluence of inkahol."

Hewitt found his feet then. He darted out, seized the stunned manager, and told him they couldn't finish — the station had to cut camera immediately and announce that the governor had suddenly been taken ill. The manager did that efficiently, though unfortunately the only canned program he could find to fill the hiatus was an old W. C. Fields short, which added to the uproar next day. Not everyone laughed, of course. Many were genuinely indignant, and indignation was feigned by all working for Doc's election. Nothing was published, but the story was told everywhere. It was, as Judge Davies vehemently declared next day in the Clipper Club, the most grievous single blow in the history of state politics. Overnight Blandford had transformed himself from a Witty asset to the worst possible liability.

Speaking of his statement on the university, the judge permitted himself a vulgarism. His punch, he said, had been pulled. Secretly he was content; he had written it to satisfy himself, not Witty, and the less political significance it had the happier he was. Naturally Witty was less detached. Photographs of his northern tour revealed the drop in his morale. More and more he looked like an unhappy dude rancher homesick for Birmingham pavements. His anxiety was contagious. In the *Star* halftones the other cider drinkers, the 4-H winners, and even the livestock looked worried. Of Witty's entourage only Frosty Warren, the paid optimist, remained cheerful. Each night he hit his portable harder, contriving an image of the exuberant candidate among worshipful admirers. " 'Mr. Depth' Flays 'Dr.' River Till Cows Come Home," the *Star*'s blackest Spartan declared; "New Depth Bomb—River using 'Maternity Ward Heelers,' " and "Witty Parity Expert, Says Grange Vet."

Caulkin was doing what he could, but nothing went right for him. Every day he came to the office determined to roll back the enemy, and every day he was caught off balance. First Blandford's performance had eclipsed the judge. Then the impact of Frosty's best feature—a description of Witty picking a prize Holstein—was completely destroyed when a deranged Dudley welder chose that very morning to take a swing at Doc, who, as even the *Star* was obliged to report, instantly flattened him. On Thursday the Pawnattuck union leader came through. Caulkin prepared to remake page one. He had scarcely finished his preliminary dummy when he was dealt the unkindest cut of his career; William Wallace Whipple, Dean Emeritus of Peabody College and Victor Lionel Hubbard Professor of Classics, announced his support of Doc. Caulkin couldn't bury it. With a heavy heart he decided to run it alongside the union leader's statement, and even that brought him some criticism in the Clipper Club; Nails Whipple might be dotty, he was told, but he didn't deserve to be paired with a labor goon.

It was through Whipple's declaration that Ham Markham finally found Harry Mikel. Since returning to Gideon Ham had vainly sought Mikel on both campuses and in every rooming house within five miles. He seemed to have vanished. Outside his grimy, littered office in the basement of Archer Chapel was a preposterous sign reading, "Doctor Is Out, Will Return at 4 A.M.," but the night watchman told Ham he didn't appear even then. The History Department secretary was uncommunicative. Graduate students said their meetings with Mikel had been canceled by mail; a substitute was handling his television lectures. Obviously he was lying up, nursing his wound. Tracing him was impossible. He wasn't a Blandford. Touring bars would be useless. If he was on a binge, it would be a unique binge. Later in the week Ham was confirmed; Mikel's peculiar tracks began to show up in the state's press. Outrageous letters appeared in the *Star*, the Rockton *Leader*, the Pawnattuck *Argus*, and the Dudley *Sentinel*, praising the memory of Sir Roger Casement, urging the castration of all males with I.Q.'s below 120, inquiring why lazy disabled veterans should draw pensions, and arguing that Abraham Lincoln had been an illegitimate child. The signatures were a giveaway: Norman Vincent Lowbelly, Mrs. Edith Pewke, Thais Straddle, Albert Loin. Mikel was away somewhere, scribbling and cackling. It was harmless; he had done it before; none of his colleagues on either faculty were concerned, with the probable exception of Whipple, who had also vanished. Ham suspected that Whipple also blamed him for the publication of the survey, and when he saw the story of his announcement in the *Star* he headed straight for his study. The old man would have to be at his desk today. Three generations of Peabody graduates would be telephoning him, fulminating, and it wasn't like him to dodge them.

He was in, and on the phone. And Mikel was with him.

They watched Ham enter in silence. Whipple sat cross-legged in his swivel chair, smoking and tut-tutting into the receiver. Mikel, also smoking, was sprawled beside him. His coxcomb was unrulier than ever, his skin scalier, his suit baggier. Whipple's file of *Slys* lay in his lap, completing, Ham thought, the picture of what Jill would call a D.O.M.

"Iscariot!" he hissed.

"Not at all," Ham said quietly, sitting on the desk.

"Ananias! Scapian! Mythomaniac!"

He tried to leer, but there was an afflicted look in his eyes; he had been hurt. Whipple, watching him narrowly, quickly finished his conversation and hung up. Immediately the telephone rang again. He lifted it from the hook, listened intently to several spluttered sentences, shut his caller off, and propped the receiver against a fat Greek dictionary, leaving the line open.

"Now then," he said crisply to Ham.

"Now then what?" Mikel cried, swiftly rolling a *Sly* into a bat and swatting his thigh. "Must we suffer further indignities at the hands of this oriental Hildy Johnson?"

Ham said evenly, "Which of you is the judge and which the jury?"

"Hah!" Mikel flailed the other thigh. "More sophistry! Having milked me, I suppose you now cadge legal terms from your ambulance-chasing relative."

Ham pictured the judge as a shyster and grinned. "Harry, you're too bad to be true."

They weren't amused. Mikel grimaced, and Whipple said icily, "Mr. Markham, I don't pretend to understand your profession. I'm sure you have your own concept of propriety."

"That's almost precisely what my ambulance-chasing relative said."

"You can scarcely expect us to endorse it, however."

Ham swung off the desk and strolled to the leaded window, his back to them. "No, I don't. I'd have thought you would have accused me to my face, however."

Mikel made an inelegant noise. Whipple said, "You were the only outsider to see that document, and it appeared in your paper. There was no need for a scene."

"So instead you withdrew into your professorial shells. You and Harry crawled off to some haunt, where he wrote childish letters to newspapers and tried to dissuade you from supporting Doc. You, I suppose, read Horace."

"Euripides," Whipple said uneasily.

"Probably he had the place bugged," Mikel said. "It would be in character."

Ham whirled. "Not even Doc accused me!"

"Adam didn't know you had seen it," Whipple said.

"He lacks our intellect," Mikel said and hesitated. Then, in a blurt: "In his usual doltish way he preferred to blame me."

"And you didn't deny it?"

"He didn't want to implicate you," Whipple said in a low voice.

"Harry noble? Oh, really!"

Whipple sat erect. The sunlight was in his eyes, but they were wide and steady. For the first time Ham understood why he was called Nails. Under his gracious manner he was sheet steel.

"Instead," he said slowly, "he let himself be relieved of his history chairmanship."

Ham was stunned. Mikel had been chairman of the department since its inception. There had been some mistake — Doc couldn't have done such a thing. Yet plainly he had.

"Harry now has the vague status of professor at large," Whipple said. "Adam is trying to drive him out."

Mikel hadn't moved. He sat slouched down, still gripping the rolled magazine, staring at the floor. Wit had momentarily deserted him.

"It was a pointless gesture," said Ham, his tongue like leather.

Whipple half rose. "See here —"

"Pointless because I didn't do it."

"What?"

Mikel stirred. "My dear Ham. Don't be brazen."

"I mentioned that survey to no one, Harry. Until my father-in-law told me of his call to you, I assumed you had released it."

"*I?*"

"Who else? Professor Whipple?"

"You should have known better!" Mikel snapped.

"And so should you."

Whipple held up his hands. "Please!" To Ham he said, "There is no chance of a mistake?"

"None. I discussed Harry's poll with no one, and I put nothing on paper. That was Swinton's story, first to last."

"It seems we have all been of little faith, then."

"It seems so."

A light was growing in Mikel's eyes. He bounded up, swung *Sly* in a great arc, and delivered a crashing blow on the desk edge, splitting the magazine in half.

"Tate!" he shouted.

Whipple was dubious. "But why?"

"Why does the asp strike? Why the adder? Poll *them* and you'll have the answer." Mikel pranced excitedly around the room, shredding the slick paper. "There was a reason, you can count on it."

"He has a copy?" Ham asked.

"He *had* one." Mikel drew up before the telephone, dialed the State exchange, and asked for Tate's secretary. "Ah! Mrs. Budd! Mikel here. I've misplaced the original of my infamous student survey. Absurd of me to fret, I suppose, but I want to be sure there's a carbon around. Do you still have the provost's? Yes, I'll wait." He bandied from foot to foot, tense with excitement. "Hello? Ah. I knew I was being foolish. Been there all along, I suppose. Oh? Oh? Indeed. No, I'll drop in sometime." He hung up with a crash and spun around. "Assurance made doubly sure!"

Whipple unhooked the receiver. "It didn't sound that way."

"The report was returned three days ago. Madam Budd wouldn't have missed it, but she crept into the office on her little cat feet just as Tate was slipping it back in the locked file. He told her he'd taken it home for study. Study!"

"You can't hang him for that," Ham said.

"*You* can't. *I* can."

"Doc won't even listen to you."

Mikel sneered. "He won't have the chance. Do you think I want another audience with that spavined Barbarossa?"

Disdain, cynicism, arrogance — these were typical of Mikel, and did not startle. But there was something else, something new. He cares, Ham thought. This time he really cares.

"I'll skewer him somehow. Believe me, I'll be that knave's Erinys. I'll grasp the hand of any useful ally. Indeed, your kinsman," he said, stabbing at Ham, "may be the very man I need. But I'll share no glory with him! This is going to be my personal *vindicta*. I'll swear it now on the Bible."

"Steady," Whipple said dryly.

Yet even he was excited. His eyes shone, his color was heightened — partly in response to Mikel, but also, Ham guessed, because Whipple himself had acquired a cause today. Out of conviction, perhaps, or perhaps from latent guilt over what Peabody had done to young Adam River long ago, he had left his monastic retreat and was publicly supporting Doc. Ham congratulated him for that after Mikel had left to call the judge. Whipple passed it off lightly, but a truer sign of his feeling came as Ham was preparing to follow Mikel. Whipple returned the receiver to its hook. A ring followed, and he snapped it up. "No, no," he said impatiently. "I certainly was not misquoted." He listened, reddened, and spluttered, "Look here, Hewitt, there may be alumni who are entitled to disparage my intelligence, but you aren't among them. Even in a class that was notorious for its lack of distinction you were conspicuous. Evidently the years have destroyed the little acumen you had. Good day."

So we are all committed, Ham thought later as he doggedly returned to his series in the musty Memorial Room down the hall. The most detached bystanders — the judge, Harry Mikel, Nails Whipple — were becoming participants, because the campaign had become more than politics. In the beginning it had been Newt Albert looking for a candidate. No struggle for power could be contained, however. The rods had been slipped from the pile, and in the building chain all causes had been joined, all issues linked, all men implicated.

But some were more implicated than others. He himself at least had a sanctuary here in the rusting past, he thought, reaching with a sigh for a heavy clasped volume bearing the tarnished gold leaf legend *Peabody Men in the Rebellion.* Remembering Mikel's survey he idly turned to a chapter headed "Vicksburg Invested." Ornate initial letters confronted him, and engravings of unlikely battle scenes.

Ham fought back a yawn. Another vortex. But not his.

He actually believed that then.

**

The election storm had an eye: Homecoming. Each year at the Wallace College game designated classes assembled in assigned sections of State's stadium. For two and a half hours they cheered violently, if needlessly — Wallace had never won — and then repaired to Fraternity Park for the evening. To them this autumn was no different from any other. Doc's class was among those back, but Sam persuaded Newt that approaching it would be a waste; they were already solid for him. If they hadn't been, it is doubtful that they could have been sold that week end, for nostalgia blinded the homecomers to everything else. Newsboys peddling that morning's *Star*, with Charlie Smathers's latest tabulation, showing Doc had forty-seven per cent of the week's straw vote, departed Gideon with fat bundles of unsold papers. Politics would have to wait until Monday. For the moment every tagged arrival was bent on what Sol Feinblatt called the annual found-and-lost week end; alumni began by finding old friends and generally ended by losing friends and selves in a sweet alcoholic dream of yesterday.

As early as the half there was an omen of which class would stray first. The poles bearing markers for '54, '49, '39, '34, '29, '24, '19, '14, '09, '04, and even '99 were proudly erect, but the '44 placard was listing badly. By the end of the third period it had vanished. The alumni secretary was content. It had had no business there anyway. Legally '44 scarcely existed. Only a handful of students had graduated that year. The others had been off in uniform, and when they returned and finished they were assigned to other classes. Nevertheless they were back in strength now, together for the first time since the war divided them — a little uncomfortable in the huge new stadium, a little unsure of one another's names, but loudly reminiscent, vehemently gay, and merrily drunk. By dusk the only abstainer among them was Ham Markham.

Somehow Ham didn't feel like celebrating. He declined a score of bottles in the stadium, ate well at the reunion banquet in the Gideon Arms, and reached Fraternity Park still sober. There, however, he felt the need of something. Over dinner he had learned that Tau Rho, the impoverished cooperative to which he had belonged, still existed. In the postwar frenzy of national affiliation Tau Rho had become the Sigma Chi house. It was now housed in a limestone mansion inhabited by tweedy young hosts who, in honor of Homecoming, had filled a great cut-glass tank with Fish House punch. Word of the punch had spread rapidly to other houses. The candlelit dining room was crammed with alumni, married undergraduates, students from other fraternities and their dates. Ham stood by the bowl, weary of familiar faces, dispirited, drinking alone. He felt like a beggar in the town house of a wealthy cousin. The cut glass looked expensive. The candelabras were sterling. The oriental rug underfoot was genuine, and the ghostly couples dancing under the dim blue light in the next room emitted pale little flashes of light, like bullion in a cave.

In a corner a fat boy was burning a five-dollar bill.

"Fabulous!" cried a girl in a golden sheath.

"In the groove!" said a man wearing a '44 tag.

With a start Ham saw that the man was Al Swinton. Al had no business here. Ham hurried over to expose him, but a growing crowd blocked the way; the boy had just ignited a ten-dollar bill.

"Hey, that's neat," said a red-faced army major, edging in.

"Burns better, don't you think?" asked the boy, looking around anxiously for approval.

"*Fabulous*!" the girl in gold shrilled.

"Yowzah," said the major. He beamed fatuously and on impulse shouted, "Hey-bob-a-ree-bob!"

"Boy, is *he* sloshed," a girl beside Ham murmured. "Why hello, Mr. Markham!"

It was Jill. Exquisite in a cobalt evening dress with subtle maternal lines, her waist was encircled from behind by the possessive arms of a grinning young drunk she identified as Jack.

"My husband. *Naturally*. He's stoned, too, as though you couldn't *see*." She nuzzled him affectionately. "And I can't even drink! Still, it *is* a super-blast. Don't you think so?"

"Yowzah." Ham glanced at the boy's expensive cinder. "But back in my day we had chaperones."

"Still do. *He*'s a chaperone."

"The arsonist?"

"The major — he's like R.O.T.C. Him and Hotflash Hatch came together, she's P.E., and Dr. Feinblatt brought Mrs. O'Donnell. We're legal as an eagle. Wow!"

The gasp was for Jack, who was running wise hands over the bosom of her formal smock. Uncomfortably Ham wished Jack wouldn't. He wondered whether the propinquity of University Village encouraged public affection, wondered where Kit, as chaperone, would draw the line. Good subject for discussion, he thought vaguely, beginning to feel the punch; ought to find her, talk things over. But the crowd had thickened. He stayed, fascinated by the crude spectacle in the corner — the major was holding a flickering Ronson to a twenty-dollar bill — and averted his eyes from Jack's restless hands.

Trudy Viggiantti was less prim. She weaved up, a dowdy, shrewish drunk, and crowed, "Glad to see *one* wife with her own husband. In case you haven't heard, *she*'s here, with *him*."

Trudy elaborated. Red had arrived with Daffy, who could barely stand.

"You're only sore because she got your apartment," said Jill, with a nervous glance at Ham.

Trudy didn't deny it. "Just the same, I got eyes." She rolled them in their rhinestone frames. "Daff's in no condition, believe me. And something fishy's going on. There's a real creep with them. He asked Daff for her autograph. Imagine! Naturally she was thrilled to do it. He's all dark glasses and a little dinky mustache. Looks like a phony preacher."

Geek Minton, Ham thought hazily. Probably Al brought him.

"Now Daff and Red are upstairs in a room. Alone." Trudy's eyes tightened. "One guess what they're doing."

"Smooching," Ham said.

Jack blinked, the girls stared.

"Like necking," he explained.

"They're balling," Trudy said flatly.

Ham looked grave. "Doesn't sound snazzy."

She eyed him suspiciously. "You a retread?" He displayed his '44 tag, and she set her lips. "I thought so. Well, stay away from me. Homecoming's always the same. Every D.O.M.'s got five pair of Roman hands."

"Mr. Markham's not like that," Jill protested.

Trudy sniffed. "Last year I got propositioned by two big Daddies. This year I brought protection." She opened her handbag and produced a rubber water pistol. "Anybody talks funny, I wet him down."

"Crazy!" Jack said admiringly.

"The craziest!" said Jill.

"Be careful," Ham said, for she was pointing it at him.

"Shoot first, ask questions later, that's my motto."

He backed away. "Well, don't use it promiscuously."

"I warned you," she said, and pulled the trigger.

Ham's cry diverted the group in the corner. They gaped at his streaming face, and the major cried again, "Hey-bob-a-ree-bob!"

**

Like Ham Major Wade was a victim of the punch. A malicious student had brought the chaperones a private bowl in their brightly lit little anteroom beyond the milling dancers, and he had fallen straight into the trap. Nor was he alone. At midnight, when Trudy squirted Ham, the only level head in the anteroom was Sol's. Kit had drained six cups, Hotflash nine. Hotflash was as unsteady as the major. She was also penniless. After he left they had switched from bridge to poker, and she had just lost all her change to Sol in an inept bluff.

"That cleans me," she said, rising massively. "Who's thirsty?"

Kit was. She swiveled around, her high cheeks smudged with a high flush, and offered her cup with a loose, graceless movement.

The bowl was empty.

"Bring you a shot," Hotflash said gruffly. "Got to look after my buddy anyway." She staggered out.

"Buddy?" Kit repeated, confused. "Does she mean the major?"

Sol nodded absently. "She was a WAC captain," he said, shuffling cards. "Want to switch to strip poker?"

She smiled demurely. "You know that's impossible."

It was literally impossible. Her black, high-waisted dress, with its hobble skirt and crepe bustle, was difficult enough when she was sober. She couldn't think how she would get it off at home. Making little arranging movements, she said, "You should've played it with her."

He peered after Hotflash. "Krisco? If I won I'd lose. She's got buttocks like volley balls."

Kit giggled. "That's not very nice."

"Neither is she. She's one of Tate's conspirators." He began a house of cards. "So's Dean Shoemaker, incidentally."

"That's ridiculous."

"No, I found out today. She's not in as deep as the captain, but she's committed. Nearly everybody is. They figure Tate's going to be boss, and they want their share of the pie — promotions, bigger budgets, research grants. Tate's encouraging it. The idea is that when the trustees start asking the faculty who the new president should be, they'll hear only one name. So we're all being approached."

"Even you?"

"Even lowly me. This afternoon I ran into Tate outside the stadium. Dean Elsie was with him. She put in a breathless word about the great new day about to dawn — that's how I know about her — and then he asked coyly how I'd like to be an assistant professor."

"Why, Sol, that's wonderful!"

"I'm not taking it." He added a final card. "I'm leaving here."

He studied the shaky edifice while she recovered.

"But — why? I thought you were for Tate."

"I thought so, too. Then he started taking over. I don't like what he's doing to this place. Suddenly everybody's an operator."

"Oh." She lowered her eyes.

"I don't mean you, Kit," he said gently. "You know how I feel about you."

She hadn't until then. Often before he had spoken of love, but always as a clown. Now that mask was down. She felt numb, and wondered how she had led him on. She didn't understand her own femininity, didn't realize that even now his declaration was challenging the flirt in her. Raising one hand, she arched it high to stroke her bun of hair. But her fingers were unsteady. She merely loosened the tortoise shell comb. Dark masses tumbled down her shoulders, giving her a wild, provocative look.

"Guess I'm a little high," she said huskily.

"As a kite," he said with a lightness he did not feel.

"Might as well really let my hair down."

She ran her fingers through it and tossed the comb aside, all unaware how deeply she was disturbing him. Her heart-shaped face was pallid, her eyes were muddy and swimming and dark. In Salem she would have been the first to be burned, Sol thought, feeling the fire kindle within. He wanted her; a part of his mind was plotting how to take her. Yet at the same time another part assured that nothing would happen. Sol lacked experience with women, but understood the diplomacy of sex. Even if seduction were possible here he knew it would destroy them both, and so he merely watched steadily and endured the pain within.

"You're lovely."

"Thank you," she said carelessly. And though she was kicking off her shoes she suggested, "Oughtn't we to go look for the others?"

"No. We oughtn't." He hadn't known his throat could be so dry.

"I wish you won't leave, Sol. Oh, I wish it so very much!"

Kit held out her hand and seized his, and he took it so eagerly the table shook and all the cards collapsed, though they were too intent; neither noticed.

**

Daffy had never been so drunk. Another girl would have been ill hours before, but her stomach was iron; though Red had switched her from punch to straight whiskey early in the evening, she was still conscious. Only she didn't understand. So many things were offbeat tonight, she thought. Like that mook that wanted all those funny little papers autographed. Who needed him? And what was she doing up *here?* Where was Red? Oh. There. Holding out another full glass. Glass, my ass; it's a Goddamned *vat*. Kee-*rist* I'm shook up. Never felt so whoopy in my life. But what the hell, might as well live it up, have a real ball. It's just I need a place to sit. There. That's what the lady wanted. Just curl up on this sofa and — oh, all right. If the boy's eager, he's eager. Only if he wants that he's gotta handle the buttons. *Mmm.* Nize. Now that really knocks me . . . *Ahhh,* better and better. That's it: buttons and buckles, belts and snaps, zippers and elastic and sli-i-ide 'em off. But why is it so bright in here? Why all those mad lights, is this a show? And why hand me a bottle, I already got this crazy glass. What's the story? Don't go 'way! *Help!*

"I'm right here, Daff," he whispered, panting a little.

She squinted up and saw him hanging over her, brawny in his taut T shirt, his face strangely driven. In desire Red was childlike. Now he was all efficiency. Casting around the little sitting room — he had rented it from a reluctant Sigma Chi sophomore for five dollars — he saw the green canvas girl's shorts he had left here this afternoon. He thrust her bare feet through them and yanked them up over her naked, straining loins.

Now what was this, she wondered stupidly. Undressing me, dressing me. Her eyes questioned him dumbly, like a sick pet's.

"There." He locked the zipper behind. "That's got it."

"Don't want that," she mumbled.

"I just like to see you in those," he breathed, backing away.

"Never knew you got your kicks funny ways." She held out the bottle. "Here. Take this."

"No, you keep it."

Red stepped swiftly to one side, and Geek, hidden behind a wooden Japanese screen on the other side of the room, deftly took his first shot. There was no flash; Daffy saw nothing. But Geek began to sweat. He had never been so close to anything this good. Most of his work had needed heavy retouching. The girls had been flabby here, scrawny there; their noses were usually wrong, their complexions always coarse. But no artist's brush could improve Daffy. Sprawled on the couch under the big State banner she was a *Sly* dream. Suppressing his desire, he studied her features with professional approval — her lithe legs, flat belly, strong pert breasts, sulky underlip, and cascading hair pale as a vision. Her sottishness blurred things somewhat. A thread of spittle hung from one corner of her lip, and her eyes were glassy. The spittle could be painted out, however, and her vacant expression was an asset; Geek had planned a spread showing State's head cheerleader celebrating a Titan victory. *Sly* closed two weeks before publication. If his prints reached New York tomorrow the story would make the November issue, which was due out the very day of the Hampshire game. It would be the triumph of Geek's career, and he had worked hard on the stage business; behind the couch were a pennant, a megaphone, a new majorette's baton, and shoulder pads. Red had been coached to pose her with each and then dart out of lens range. Later they would take her in her lingerie — a bonus, for another issue.

Red had been surprisingly malleable. Geek had bought him cheaply by shooting a single roll of Red in uniform. There was no chance the pictures would appear in *Sly* — Geek wasn't even authorized to take sports shots — but Red assumed all would be printed, and afterward he had followed the photographer's suggestions slavishly, planting the props, plying Daffy systematically, and persuading her to sign *Sly's* release papers, which he then witnessed. Now he was toiling over her, setting up tableaux. First the pennant was substituted for the glass. Geek's shutter clicked; then the megaphone replaced the pennant, the baton the megaphone. Finally the pads were laced on her naked shoulders. Daffy was helpless as wax. She sat in her stupor, listless, uncomprehending, responding only with a flaccid smile when he grinned over encouragingly. This must be some gag, she thought dully; some madball joke of Red's. He'd come to the point soon and they'd have a big laugh. She wished he'd hurry, though. If they weren't going to have sex she wanted some clothes on. It was getting cold in this crazy place. Abruptly she gave a convulsive shudder. Red glanced anxiously at the Japanese screen, and Geek gave him a sign. He had enough. They could switch to the lingerie. Daffy saw Red pick up her embroidered black Lastex pants and grunted in relief. Laboriously lowering the bottle to the floor, she reached behind her, loosened the zipper, and fumblingly drew the green shorts down her hips. The baton was poised suggestively in her other hand. Geek saw his chance; he steadied the camera and finished that roll with the most brilliant frame of his career.

**

Sam Theanapolis, Jr. was only a freshman pledge, but he was sober, so the Sigma Chi president had picked him as an emissary. He shouldered his pudgy frame across the rollicking dance floor to the threshold of the chaperone's anteroom and announced his delicate mission in a reedy voice.

"Major Wade just passed out."

Reluctantly Sol dropped Kit's hand and turned. "What about Hotfl — Miss Hatch?"

"She's stinko, too. And noisy."

"Put them to bed together," Sol muttered. The boy swallowed hard, and Sol said, "No, wait. I'll come along quietly." To Kit he said tenderly, "Can I get you anything?"

She looked around uncertainly. "Somebody was going to bring me some punch."

If they had been alone Sol would have suggesed that she had passed her limit. Young Sam was already volunteering to bring her a cup, however, and there was no tactful way to stop him. Moodily thrusting his hands in his pockets, Sol followed him across the floor, down a little hall, to the door where the fraternity president stood guard. Hotflash's deep baritone could be heard within, rumbling angrily.

"Miss Hatch wants to inspect the house," the president explained worriedly.

Sol shrugged. "You got something to hide?"

"Well, there's couples lying around. *You* know." Sol's face told him this was the wrong tack, so he dropped his voice and whispered, "I don't think she's in the right condition to go stamping around. She might hurt herself or something. And everybody would *see* her."

Sol nodded slightly. "Let me inside."

Inside was chaos. The major lay on his side in a deep armchair, snoring. Beside him stood Hotflash, rumpled and belligerent, denouncing two fidgeting students who stood before her, embarrassed but firm, like M.P.'s restraining a disorderly officer.

"Stand aside!" she barked. "I want to see every sack in this house, and I want to see it *now!* Anybody out of line goes on report in the morning. That includes you," she pointed, "and you. Give me your names."

She looked around for a pencil and paper and saw Sol.

"Hi, Cap," he said cheerfully.

"Come here, Feinblatt," she said, as though he were a reinforcement. "Talk to these people if you can. They won't listen to me."

"You want to check the premises?" he asked.

"Top to bottom. A real shortarm."

He studied the major thoughtfully. "How about your buddy?"

"Wade? He's had one too many. You know how it is." She winked with one whole side of her face.

"Yes, but do you want to leave him here? Alone?"

She frowned heavily. "Hadn't thought of that. You mean somebody might roll him?"

He nodded emphatically, moved up past the retreating boys, and led her to an adjacent chair, talking all the time about the defenseless major and silently hoping she would fall asleep. But Hotflash was tough. It occurred to him that she would be a hard woman to kill. Beefy, grim, stolid, she sat back glowering at the world and keeping Sol here. In the corner of his eye he could see the Sigma Chis conferring outside the doorway. Young Sam was off serving Kit. Anxiously Sol wondered whether she could handle another drink. After all, he thought, this would be her seventh.

Actually it was Kit's eighth. The seventh had been brought by Ham moments before. Ham hadn't meant it for her; he had been wandering by with his own refilled cup, and she had hailed him and reached for it.

"Oh really how nice!" She drained it with a swallow. Then young Sam arrived, and before he disappeared among the blue dancers Kit finished that one, too. She yawned languidly. "Didn't know you were here, Ham."

"It's my old house, Kit."

"Doesn't look the same," she said doubtfully.

He searched for something familiar and pointed to a love seat behind the door. "There's that. We used to have one of them."

"So you did!" She took two wobbly steps and collapsed on it. "But they don't dance the shag any more."

"No. No truckin', either."

"Ham, whatever did you do with that convertible raincoat?"

"Lost it. What happened to your saddle shoes?"

They were like classmates at the '44 reunion dinner, with this difference: once they had been closer than boys could be, and their nostalgia — of trivia, of dreams shared, of private jokes — was creating a dangerous intimacy. Kit forgot her son, Ham his family. To him Kit, lying back with her hair wild and her feet tucked under her, was nineteen again and again his. And she herself was thinking as a girl — a deception of liquor, but powerful and sinister, strong enough to raise the perilous little thoughts *Why not?* and *Who cares?* and *Now is now*, as though there could be no bitter to-morrow and after.

"It's been a long time since I've seen you unbuttoned, Kit."

"I do *feel* unbuttoned." She sighed. "Wish they'd play *Old Black Magic.*"

"Or *In the Mood.*"

"Feel in the mood, too." There was a significant little pause, dark eyes intent across the little distance, breath quickening. Trying to sound casual, she said mistily, "Why don't you shut that silly little door, Ham?" And: "Come over here." And: "Kiss me once, for old times."

Why not? he also thought. Just once for old times, the old black magic. He closed the door and crossed swiftly to her side.

But as he opened his taut arms to receive her she hiccupped.

"Oh!" She looked startled. "Excuse me!"

**

"Excuse me," young Sam said urgently, tugging at the sleeve of Red's topcoat. "Do you have a mo? Just a mo."

Young Sam was at the bottom of the campus pecking order, and Red looked down on him with all the severity he could summon. That wasn't much. Four of them were jammed on the stair landing — Red, Daffy, and Geek, descending, and young Sam, coming up.

"Later, kid," Red growled. "*Much* later."

"But this won't wait!"

"Look, crumb —"

"Remember you told us once, a bunch of us you told, any real good dirt you wanted quick? This is top drawer. I mean," he whis-pered, "Its about Mrs. O.D."

Red's exasperation vanished. He had to hear this. But the timing couldn't have been more inconvenient. Daffy was paralyzed, wholly supported by Geek's arm. They had chosen this back stairway be-cause she couldn't survive scrutiny. Red had dressed her inexpertly while Geek cleaned up his improvised studio, and under her camel's-hair jacket her clothes were wrinkled and twisted and caught around her waist. She was too insensible to take the most elemental pre-cautions; from time to time she would mumble disjointedly — slurred phrases, yet audible and damning.

"Thought you wanted to, you know," she said thickly to Red. "Didn't you bring a thing? A rubber job?"

Young Sam backed down the stairs, pretending not to have heard. Red said frantically to Geek, "We got to shut her up!"

"I'll take her home," Geek said quietly.

"Home? Like this? No, it's got to be the sorority. And you don't even know the way."

"Give me directions, I can handle her."

Geek didn't look able. He was encumbered with paraphernalia. The football pads were draped over his shoulders, giving him a gargoyle silhouette. His camera dangled from one arm, and he was carrying his flash bulb bag, from which protruded the megaphone, the pennant, and glittering baton. Red also should have been warned by his voice. It was feverish, clotted. He kept glancing down at Daffy's naked thighs, dimly visible under her open jacket, and though the hall was cold his face was streaked with sweat.

"All the sororities are together, aren't they?" he said persuasively. "I drove past there this morning."

Red hesitated and was lost. He said weakly, "She's in the last one."

So he abandoned her and ran down the stairs without even a glance backward to see Geek nuzzling her as he coaxed her down the steps, pressing against her and making strange little gestures under her jacket. Young Sam saw, and stared, but he was too daunted to speak; Red was already hurrying him down the corridor.

"So what's with Mrs. O'D.?" Red demanded.

Young Sam collected himself, then said in a rush, "All the chaperones got loaded except Feinblatt, and Hotflash and the major wandered off and conked out down the hall, meaning Feinblatt had to go play nurse and Mrs. O'Donnell was left alone soaking it up and looking ready, really *ready*, you get me?"

"No." Red wanted details.

"Well, she's like coming apart! At the, you know, seams! No shoes, hair down to her waist, and this bedroom look — well, if you saw it you'd *know*. I mean she gave it to me, and then she turned it on that Markham guy, and right after that they closed the door."

There was a dramatic pause. Red fingered the bridge of his nose.

"He still with her?"

"Oh, he's probably through. A thing like that, it's got to be quick with people around," said young Sam, the eighteen-year-old voice of experience. "I'll look if you want."

Red dismissed him. He could see for himself, and wanted no witnesses. Dressing Daffy had been a struggle. His desire had been deeply stirred. In her present coma she was too unresponsive for the kind of bout he wanted. Now, however, there was an alternative. For nearly a month the idea had been growing on him that Kit would be a diversion, a matchless test of his power. He meant to find out how far her admiration of him went.

But Ham was still inside. A hair of light outlined the closed door. There were voices.

Red sat impatiently on a straight chair beside the jamb, pretended to watch the few shadowy couples left on the dance floor, and eavesdropped. He had expected the rustles and murmurs of love and grew contemptuous when he heard none. Hambo doesn't have it any more, he thought, wrinkling his lip in a quiet sneer; he's too old; too soft.

**

One chaste embrace, then Ham and Kit had parted. Passion fled and left them confused. Their hands lay awkward in their laps. A silence grew. They sorted thoughts, wondering cloudily what they had been about to do, why they had turned back, which of them had resolved that. Neither realized that the first light brush of lips had decided them both, for reasons too complex for either to understand fully. One was habitual morality. Ham had never been unfaithful to his wife, and Kit was scarred by the two brief affairs of her youth. Decency was another check; this was no place for that. But the strongest rein was an undefined feeling that to make love now would be a compromise of what they had once had, a betrayal of something that had been right and true. It had been lost long ago. The fire was dead. But they could not trample the hearth.

Dissatisfied, yet resigned, they sat at peace.

Ham had spoken first. "Did you know Doc was a Peabody freshman once?"

It was an offering — the pride of his trade, a rare piece of news. To his astonishment she knew it.

"Spook told me once."

Spook again, again the tug at Ham's heart. "And Doc told him."

"Well — they talked about it just before Spook went overseas." She saw the hurt in his face and said impulsively, "Oh, Doc would've told you, too. It's just there were special reasons. I mean, Peabody meaning what it did to Spook — and — and — "

"And what?" he asked swiftly.

She was biting her lip. "I can't say, Ham. It's a thing I promised Spook. He never should've told me, but he did, and I gave him my word, and now . . ."

And now he could never release her from it. There was nothing Ham could say. Death absolved everything; he had to forgive Spook for returning to Gideon and sleeping with Kit, had to respect his last wishes. It wasn't fair, but there it was. To rebel would be another, grosser profaning of the past. Bewildered, Ham stood and walked slowly to the table. He was toying idly with the cards when Kit gave a start. She whispered, "What was that? Something creaked. Somebody's out there."

Ham grinned. "Be queer if there weren't. This is a party, Kit."

Still she was fearful. "Yes, and I'm a chaperone. It doesn't look right, us being here like this. Better open the door."

He did, and looked out carelessly, missing Red, who was gloating at him in the dark a few feet away. Returning to the table he propped two cards together and added a third.

"You didn't used to be so jumpy," he said. "You used to say you didn't give a damn what other people thought."

"I have to be careful now. Being careful's my job."

Four cards and he had the walls of a new card house. "Is Doc really that afraid of the Pope?"

Kit smoothed her skirt. "Dean Shoemaker thinks so. Anyway he *said* no divorced Catholics."

He looked at her with compassion. "So you wear black and pretend to be a widow."

"Yes." She studied her lap. "I live a lie. But at least my child has a home."

He fingered the fifth card, the roof, the ace of clubs. "You're worried about gossip," he said. "Have you thought what people might say about the boy?"

She glanced up quickly.

"You're a mother without a husband," he said deliberately. "You can't have any of the real signs of widowhood — the picture on the wall, the insurance, friends who knew you when he was alive, all that. Maybe you can get away with it, I don't know. But this is a nosy place." He palmed the ace. "Somebody just might get the idea you were never married."

"Ham!"

She looked so stricken that he hedged immediately. "Kit, I'm way off base. I'm sorry."

It was too late. Her eyes filled. "You mean they'll say Sean's a bastard."

"No, Kit!"

"Yes, and they will, too, they'll hurt him the same way I hurt Spook, and he'll think it's true the way Spook did. Oh God, the crazy wheel goes round and stops the same place. It's divine justice, but hard, so hard . . ."

Ham stared, dumfounded. She was sitting rigid, dabbing at wet eyes.

"Go 'way," she whimpered.

He dropped the card and turned wretchedly toward the door.

Red was there, scuffing the threshold.

"Phone for you, Hambo," he rasped.

Ham never thought to challenge the old dodge. He would have seized almost any excuse to leave gracefully, and he didn't even inquire of Red where the telephone was. Outside he asked young Sam, who was lurking among the dancers like a Peeping Tom. There was a booth in the front hall. Ham hurried there, but the receiver was on its cradle. He had been taken. Striding back past the big punch bowl he sensed the trouble before he saw it. Young Sam had fled. The couples there had stopped dancing. They were standing in a ragged semicircle under the blue light, facing the anteroom door, which was again closed. From within came a weird medley of sounds. Kit was crying faintly, making shrill little mews of fright; Red's voice was grating and growing louder in frustration.

Ham burst in. Kit was huddled against the end of the love seat. She had a stark, shut-off look. One hand shielded her breasts; the other was yanking her skirt back over her knees. Red crouched over her, his fingers plucking crudely at crepe hems and seams.

He twisted around and faced Ham floridly.

"*Out*side, Hambo. If I need your help I'll whistle."

Ham started forward; then Sol, who had been attracted by the babbling dancers, caught his arm from behind and whispered, "Get him away if you can. This is lousy for her."

Ham glared at Red. "Suppose we both go outside."

"You mean that like it sounds?" Red said defiantly.

And Ham said instantly, "I mean tomorrow you'll wake up with a fat lip."

They were both amazed, Ham by his own cheap theatrics, Red by what seemed to him almost an impertinence. No one had challenged him in years, and he thought of Ham as a setup. His viking eyes widened. He hulked up and flicked his thumb over his nose twice in an arrogant sparring salute while Ham measured him carefully. A real bruiser, he thought. Probably his right's like a weapon. *If* he lands it. For Ham felt no fear. Like Red he had never lost a fight, and though Red had a gym ring look about him, Ham had had been trained in a tougher school, on brick sidewalks under slum gaslights. His age was against him, but he still had the reach and the massive hands of an end. Once he slipped off this coat —

The coat stayed on. Red's mortifying failure with Kit demanded a blood sacrifice here, now. Without moving his feet he made a left fist and drove it at Ham's belt. Kit gasped; Sol protested; Ham sat on the anteroom floor with a thud.

Red jerked the thumb toward the door. "Now cut out."

"Oh, Ham," Kit moaned.

Ham didn't speak. He narrowed his eyes and rose, backing away with his elbows parallel in the odd cradling pose of the street fighter. He no longer felt cheap; instinct had smothered that, and as he shifted his shoulders for the lunge, Sol, who had also served time on asphalt playgrounds, cried impulsively, "Hey Red, your fly's open!"

Red should have known better. But no member of the faculty had ever spoken to him so. His eyes wavered just as Ham shuffled his feet and laced out with both balled fists whirling upward. Red only knew the Golden Gloves stance. He had never handled anything like this. Before he could set himself he was staggering back and back. His mouth began to bleed, and suddenly his nose was bleeding, too, gushing scarlet down his chin and on his shirt. He tottered wildly on his heels. Ham swayed; his right lashed out in a wide hook and smashed Red's working lips, and Red pitched up and over in an odd, swanlike arc. The crash was spectacular. One limp arm caught the empty little punch bowl, the other the leg of the table, and a shower of splintering glass, wet ice, and playing cards pelted him rudely.

He was unconscious.

Ham straightened, panting, and nursed his knuckles. Then he turned sheepishly to Kit. "Sorry again. I guess this really fouls things up. I just don't belong in this china shop."

A faint blush stained her cheeks. She said shakily, "Maybe not. But you're still a champ, Ham."

"A cham*peen*," Sol said with awe.

Ham looked at him dubiously. "Champeens don't need help."

"Well, in a way his fly *was* open," Sol said defensively.

They regarded the littered body, now stirring slightly.

"I thought he was such a nice boy," Kit said meekly.

"Making a pass at a chaperone's almost a capital offense," Ham said. "Even Doc would bounce him for it."

"Except that Doc won't know," Sol said rapidly.

"No, I simply can't get involved," said Kit, springing up. Awareness was returning to her, and sobriety. Snatching up her comb she rewound her long priestess hair into a neat hump, fastened it, and slipped on her shoes. Outside the dancers were still mumbling. She shut the door smartly. "There! *They*'ll talk, but at least we can shut out the newcomers."

Immediately the door flew open. It was a newcomer — Trudy Viggiantti, in a hooded coat and fluttering mittens.

"Mrs. O'Donnell, I got to talk to you quick. I — *ugh!*" She had seen Red. He looked like something in *Six Gun*. "Is he — is he — "

"He's all right," Kit said calmly, drawing her aside. "Just a bad fall, that's all. Now what's the matter?"

"Well." Trudy fanned her face, regaining composure. Then, with the many little wriggles and side glances of the gossip, she breathed, "I thought you ought to know. About a certain person in your house. I mean, she stays there sometimes. You know?"

"Affyday Ixday," Sol said *sotto voce*.

Trudy caught her lip in her teeth. "I don't want to get this person in any trouble, but I think for her own good somebody ought to do something. She's like in a jam."

"We've really got all we can manage here," Kit said wearily. To Sol she said, "Is he all right?"

"Coming around fine. I'm just afraid he's getting ideas again."

He was. He was awake and eying Ham's jaw beadily. Ham braced himself for another round, but before Red could struggle up

Trudy diverted him. He propped himself on his elbows and remained there, frozen, as she raced on.

"I was walking out through the parking lot with my husband when this creepish guy in green glasses and a square blue suit comes up to us. I'd seen him before. He's been letching around all evening. Well, now he's igglier than ever in shoulder pads. Honest! Football shoulder pads! He asks me real casual which way is Maiden Lane. Thinks he knows but wants to be sure. So I tell him and off he pads like something prowling back into the jungle, but it looks funny to me, so I pad right along after. Well!" Trudy leaned forward. The light from the dance floor, refracted in the rims of her elaborate glasses, glinted diabolically. "This certain person was leaning against a fender, and — I shouldn't say this, but I'm real worried about her — her jacket was all open, and her skirt was up to her neck, and her pants were, well, down. Not *off,* but *down,* if you get what I mean. I mean, there she *was!* In the *parking* lot!"

Kit's eyes flickered. "And then?"

"Then the creep slithers up and starts fooling around with her. He was in my way, but I could sort of figure what he was — sort of — doing."

Sol closed the door. "How?"

"I'm a married woman, Dr. Feinblatt!"

"Are they still there?" Kit asked stiffly.

"No! *That's* why I'm so worried. He shoved her inside and took off. Toward Maiden Lane! The Kat House!"

"Theta," Kit corrected her automatically.

Ham stepped over. "Is this the man you told me about earlier?"

Trudy nodded vehemently. "There's only one like him at Homecoming. I mean I *hope.*"

"He isn't even an alumnus," Ham said to Kit. "He's a gutter friend of Al Swinton of the *Star*. From what Al's told me, he *is* a letch. This could be ugly."

"I thought so!" Trudy cried.

Daffy's plight affected them variously. Ham and Sol were concerned; Kit thought that this might be her chance to get rid of her; Trudy wanted to regain her lost apartment. Red alone worried about Geek. All Geek's pictures would be in his car, including the sports roll. Trudy had started something, and obviously Kit was determined to finish it. Red rose painfully, picking debris from his clothes with his fingertips. He had to find a Sigma Chi with a car, and he had to be quick. Tiptoeing to the door, he slipped out unseen.

"Al was here a little while ago," Ham said. "He might come in handy. I'll have a look."

He searched. Al had left.

Returning, he found Kit buttoning her black wool coat. She was quite sober now, and she asked him to drive her home. "I've got to get to the house fast, and Sol has to stay here. We can't leave the dance without any chaperone at all."

Sol sighed. "I'll close up the joint. It's a man's job anyhow. Hotflash *and* the major are out, and at least one of them will want help to the vomitorium. Besides, I'll have to look after our wounded halfback here."

He turned and looked and looked.

It was then they missed Red.

**

If only she knew what was *going on*. If only things would start making *sense*. Man was driving so fast. *Whish, whoosh* around corners. And what happened to Red? It's all that shine, Daffy thought. All that rotgut. Makes my head whirly-twirly. Can't follow the score any more. Get lost, lost, lost. Switched, twitched, bewitched. Stewed, screwed, tattooed. Tripped, ripped. And stripped. I *am* stripped, she thought distractedly. So that's what he was doing when we stopped. Thought he was helping. *Said* he was. Some Helpful Harry *he* was. And on a cold night like this. He was nothing but a lowdown lowlife bastard.

She swiveled her wobbly head and tried to focus on him.

"Bah-stud," she said throatily. He didn't reply, and, lurching back against the cushions, she flapped at her goosepimpled flesh with palsied hands, trying to find some clothes.

There were none. They were all behind the cushions. She was entirely naked. Geek, impatient and inept, had stopped the car around the corner from the Sigma Chi house and tried to take her there. It was typical of his blundering approach, the reason he always ended by paying for love. His Thunderbird was too small; Daffy had been unmanageable. He had succeeded only in rousing her suspicions. She had inquired muzzily whether they had reached the house. Anxious to placate her, he had abandoned tentative plans for a College Inne detour and was hurrying toward the Theta House, where, in his ignorance of sororities, he thought he might find a deserted alcove and warm couch. Every minute his chances of subduing her diminished, for the car window on his side was open, he had neglected to turn on the heater, and in the dank night air she was rising, fathom by fathom, from the depths of drunkeness. Seducing Daffy required very little skill. She was almost wholly indifferent to the act of love. In liquor she was available to any man who simulated tenderness. Geek, however, was incapable even of that. He had forgotten the window and the heater because while obsessed with possessing her, he was blind to her needs. To him she was only an instrument for his own twisted compulsion. The crudest gesture of kindliness was beyond him, for he himself was his only friend, his only companion, his only lover. Emotionally he was isolated — and thus very like her.

Theta's gray clapboard hulk loomed. No alcove for Geek there; in Kit's absence the girls had brought dates inside, and every window downstairs was blazing. He squinted over the steering wheel. The house sat in an immense yard defined by a knee-high wall of hard, craggy stone. Within were parklike grounds; gardens and benches there were used by couples on warmer nights. Tonight was too chilly. But not for Geek. He passed the house and drew up in the shadowy dead end.

"This is it," he said, like a sergeant.

Daffy's face puckered in a tremendous frown. She was trying to concentrate. It was no good; her thoughts were jelly. He came around to her side and dragged her out, and she tried to squirm away, but she was all loose motion, and his thin hands were clamped tight under her flailing arms. Up the curb they lurched, and then over the low wall, a preposterous pair — Daffy a splendid shivering nude, Geek prim in his shiny double-breasted suit, with his black hair slicked back and his mustache neatly combed, with only the dangling shoulder pads betraying his inner fugue. His mind was working in starts. He was wholly unaware of the pads, and although he had turned the Thunderbird motor off he had left the lights on and the door open. As they floundered in shrubs he heard a clattering. He glanced back: the baton was rolling idly down the sidewalk.

"Hell with it," he muttered in his flat voice.

"Ouch," said Daffy.

Branches were scratching her; one willow switch whipped her across the face, and she whimpered. He was hurrying her across a lawn freckled with mosaics of fallen leaves, toward a long, initial-scarred bench under a squat oak. Her legs were rubbery; her head lolled back and she saw the moon, a day off the full. Across its mellow face a thin spume of cloud drifted slowly. In the yard the pale light gleamed on rocks, a bird bath, Daffy's wedding ring, Geek's tinted glasses. A wind was rising, and smelled of rain.

He dumped her on the bench like a hod.

"Whasis?" she moaned, struggling erect.

Geek sat alongside. "How about a little —" he hesitated "— a little fun." He hated really saying it.

"Huh?" Daffy stared and suddenly sneezed. She held out her hand. "Hankie."

He hadn't any. His fingers were crawling up her thigh; he was licking her shoulder.

"Fr-freezing," she said. Her teeth had begun to chatter.

His hands were rougher now. With growing comprehension she turned and looked directly at him. Despite his glasses and the darkness she saw the deeper night in his eyes.

"What you think you're doin'?"

"A little fun," he repeated in that drab monotone. "A little jazz."

"No. Don't."

"O.K.," he said tonelessly. "How much?"

It had to come to that. It always did, though not even Geek knew he really wanted it that way.

She looked blank. "Much what?"

"For gash." It was said. His hand darted in his shiny coat. He showed his wallet. "Twenty bucks?"

Disabled, numb, Daffy nevertheless revolted. This was crazy. *He* was crazy.

"No." She sneezed violently.

Geek heard brakes in the dead end.

"Thirty dollars." He threw himself on her. She sprawled flat, and he clawed at her swaying breasts. "Fifty, fifty dollars!"

He couldn't talk more. He was fumbling with his trousers as she thrashed and heaved, trying to wiggle free and press herself against the slatted bench back. She sneezed and sneezed again. Her nose was streaming.

"Oh I said no, I said no," she cried as the phlegm congested in her throat. "*Oh!*" For he had started. "*Ohhh!*"

She burst into a convulsion of sneezing, and Red, prodding bushes on the edge of the yard, heard her. "Over here!" he shouted to a slight, frightened boy in bifocals, and they came running. "Hey!" Red called ahead. "Hey, Daff! That you, Mr. Minton?"

Discovered, Geek recoiled and leapt up. Red, arriving only seconds later, found him bathed with perspiration but fully dressed, leaning helplessly over Daffy.

"What's the story, Mr. Minton? What's with Daff?"

Geek looked at him emptily.

Moving as though in great pain, Daffy sat up and cuffed her nose. Red gaped at her.

"For Christ's sake, where's her *clothes?*"

Geek drove his guilty hands into his pockets, and Red understood. How do you like this guy, he thought indignantly. Moves right in and tries to take over. But there was no time for words; the boy in bifocals was making urgent signs.

"Listen, we got to get out of here," Red told Geek.

No response. Geek looked away, his face deadly pale. Red shook him.

"They're coming! *Everybody!*"

He intended to startle him, to get him moving. But Geek, already in a dangerous mood, had a vision of a posse. He went straight into panic. Without a word he pivoted and fled to the street in a jerky, blundering sprint, his shoes rasping on the tussocky grass.

Red called, "Hey!" The Thunderbird motor was turning over. Red cupped his hand to his mouth. "Mr. Minton, *wait!*"

But Geek was gone in a blur of exhaust. All right, Red thought. At least the pictures were safe. Now all he had to do was get rid of Daff. Not here though; not now, with that teaser of a housemother howling down on them looking for scalps. They had to pull out, and fast. "Start the car," he told the boy. "This place is a trap." He touched his swelling nose and eyed Daffy with disgust. "And we both look like bait."

Her cold had abated for the moment, and she had risen unsteadily from the bench, but the marks of trouble were all over her — reddening welts from the willow and the slats, coloring bruises from Geek. She still prickled with gooseflesh; her eyes were watery and her own nose was raw.

"Come on, Godiva," he said, slipping an arm between her legs and lifting her easily to his thick shoulders. "I'll get you out of this some way." He strode toward the wall, thinking of himself as a Samaritan.

The boy had turned his old Mercury around and was racing the motor. His eyes were dancing with alarm. He had come because, like most students without campus status, he was awed by Red. Red hadn't told him what they were going to do, however, and now he knew he bitterly resented the risk.

"Let's go!" he whined as Red opened the door. He shrank from Daffy's nakedness. "Say, can't you dress her, or something?"

"Minton took off with her stuff," Red grunted, shoving her in.

"Well, can't you —"

"Shut up! Look!"

Headlights had appeared at the far end of Maiden Lane and were approaching swiftly. Red sprang in.

"The Village, and gas it!" he shouted.

The boy was motionless, trembling.

"Realgonesville, Ben, for Christ's sake!"

Then the Mercury hurtled from the curb, careened down the narrow street, and nearly sideswiped Ham's *Star* car.

Ham swore. "Goofy drivers tonight."

They had just dodged the red Thunderbird weaving on the wrong side of the road, though they hadn't known it was Geek's. Geek, they thought, must be in the Mercury with Daffy.

"Looks like we missed," he said.

"No!" Kit twisted around, peering at Mike's taillight as he braked for the turn, and said between her teeth, "There's room for a U-turn at the end."

Ham suppressed a protest; he too was caught up in the chase. Wrenching the wheel hard, he skidded on the unpaved apron beyond Theta and swerved around.

The rain was very near. Only a glimmer of moonlight was left, and that fading. Yet it was enough for Kit. In the gutter, out of the headlights' range, she saw a glitter and cried, "Wait a minute! I want to get something."

She was out and back in a breath, glowing with triumph. She had found Geek's lost baton wedged in a drain.

**

Emerging from Maiden Lane Ben swung north and opened up. *Fifty, fifty-five, sixty* read the speed clock, and still he drove the pedal deeper. Had there been a side street he would have taken it — anything to get lost — but the road ran smoothly in a great curve around the North Campus, unbroken by exits until it reached the fat fork between University Village and the Student Union. There were no other cars, and no buildings intervened to mask flight; the Department of Landscape Architecture had deliberately set halls well back from the road. Deception, therefore, was impossible. The glowing slits of the Mercury's rear lights were still visible when Ham passed the last of the sororities and turned left.

Ben looked up at his rear-view mirror. "They're coming!"

"Don't chicken out," Red muttered.

Yet he too was nervous. Like his pursuers he didn't know who was in the other car. He would have faced Kit arrogantly, would have met Ham swinging. The trouble was, they might have picked up Tate, or Yablonski, or a state cop. Red himself could brazen out almost anything, but he was thinking of Geek. Ben might talk, Geek might be picked up. If that roll of sports film were confiscated, Red's spot in *Sly,* his one chance for national publicity this fall, would be a broken dream.

The girl was enough for Ben. He had no friends in power. The fork rushed up to them, distorted by the first sweats of rain on the windshield, and he braked and drew over. Red wrenched around. Ham's lights were a mile away, two dilating yellow pins. In a minute he would be there.

"Last stop," Ben quavered.

"Look —"

"You look." He pointed to the huddled barracks of the Village, across the road. "You said here. O.K., we're here."

"But her place is a hundred yards!"

"That's right — a hundred yards I'll never get out of if I get in. We slipped out of one dead end. This time they'll be ready. And this end is *really* dead."

It was worse than Maiden Lane. Between the fork and the Village parking lot there was only a narrow dirt road strewn with stones. In the winter one stuck car would hold up a hundred. Ham had but to park and the Mercury would be bottled up.

"Either she gets out here or I tell everything I know," Ben said desperately.

That decided Red — that and Ham's lights, now the size of dimes. He flung open the door and tugged at Daffy.

"We home?" she asked, focusing on him. She hadn't understood their exchange, and the night outside was a maze to her.

"Home's up there," Red said, pointing grimly.

"But it's raining!" she cried, shrinking back.

He pushed her into the road. "Up *there*," he said again, savagely. "And haul it. See that car? It's after you, Daff, and it means biz."

"You come," she pleaded.

She was looking at him, Ben was looking at him. He had taken her out, fed her liquor, left her with Geek. Conscience stirred in him, but Ham's lights were flashing quarters, and he had had enough. He wanted to cut out.

"Can't do it," he said between his teeth, and dove into the car. "O.K., hike," he said to Ben, avoiding his eyes.

Gears rasped. The Mercury rocketed off. Daffy glanced after it, back at the approaching lights, and then hopped across the road, entwined in sheets of rain.

Kit had been peering past her slapping windshield wiper. "Why, she's *bare!*"

"I saw," Ham said in a low voice. He licked his skinned knuckles. "Saw Red, too."

"That *was* him, wasn't it. Oh, Ham!" she whispered, appalled but still implacable toward Daffy. Ham judged the boy, Kit the girl, but her judgment was harsher, because she was sterner with her own past.

Daffy was stumbling up the narrow road. The terror which had gripped Geek and Ben and touched Red was now upon her. She had lost all sense of presence; she looked like an animal. Crouching, waddling to keep her balance, she forced her flinching feet over the cruel stones. Her hair was matted in wet hanks, and she squinted fearfully over her shoulder to see the thing that was chasing her. She didn't know what it could be. Red hadn't told her. And that made it more terrible. She was like a child haunted by hobgoblins. Her heart was pounding, and in her fright she had strange fragmented memories of her stolid father thrusting her in his tarpaper tool shed and unbuckling his belt and coming at her. She hadn't understood why then and didn't now. But *something is after me, something is after me, something is after me* ran the keening chant in her head as she bounded up the road, through the parking lot, past the phone booth. Her cold was returning, her chest felt full of glue. And her feet were bleeding. And her left side hurt. It's a stitch, she thought frantically. I got a Charley; only a Charley makes you sore like this. Then she remembered Geek's groping fingers. Maybe *he* was after her, that crazy madball goof. *Oh what was that! Oh!*

She looked back with pitiful, cowed eyes and saw the headlights knifing through the rain, big and bright as moons.

**

Jill was rocking Daffy's baby in the Dix living room. Jerry had been trying to settle him all evening, and when he had heard Jill's voice passing outside he had called her in. She was glad to help. Her husband would be impossible in bed—Jack would never concede that liquor made him impotent—and as her own time drew near she enjoyed lavishing love on all infants. She told neighbors she was gaining experience, "being practical-like." In the blasé Village to admit the welling love of young motherhood would have been embarrassing, even bad taste. She needn't pretend with Jerry Dix, however. No one valued his opinions of Village society, so she could let herself go here and croon to the baby.

Jerry himself was on a stepladder, rolling Ceiling Flat White Super Kem-Tone on his new ceiling. He had been looking forward to the chore all week and had been working on it in snatches tonight while his son napped. To avoid spatters of paint he had donned a spectacular costume—a triangular hat fashioned from the front section of the morning *Star;* an old gray lab coat; army shoes. He didn't look at all himself, and Daffy, flinging open the door, didn't recognize him.

They stared. Even the baby looked stunned.

"Pardon," she panted, and turned to go.

"Daffy!" Jill breathed.

And Jerry echoed hoarsely, "*Daffy!*"

His first thought was that his wife had been raped. He crept down the little ladder and went to her with paint-flecked hands. He thought to comfort her. But she had had enough of hands; she drew back. Jill reacted intuitively. All this could only alarm the baby. Holding him against her heavy bosom, she went swiftly into the bedroom, leaving husband and wife facing in silence.

"Here." Jerry wriggled out of his lab coat and slipped it on her, then stepped back quickly. The rancid whisky was overpowering. He could smell it above the paint. "Why, you've been drinking!" he said in a shocked voice. "You've been drinking a whole *lot!*"

Daffy lurched to the maple sofa, strewn with newspapers, and collapsed on a Super Kem-Tone blob. She was trying to collect herself. She wanted to wrap the gray lab cloth around her, wanted to tell him to lock the door and turn out the lights, but she couldn't stop gasping. And then it was too late. The door was opening. Jerry backed away, bewildered, as Kit entered with a firm step. In her tightly buttoned black coat and fisted black hair she had a somber, inexorable look.

"Well, Daphne?" she said deliberately.

Ham had remained outside in the slackening rain. He felt this was an invasion. Daffy might have forfeited her rights, but her husband hadn't, and this, after all, was more his home than hers. There was something pathetic about the interrupted domestic task— Jerry's crude hat with the Spartan legend 'DOC' RIVER RAPPED BY WITTY on the side, the neat squares of other *Star* pages on the floor, the stepladder with its sheepskin roller and paint pan on top.

Kit stood quiet as a nun.

"I'm waiting," she said.

Daffy looked up dully. Then she sneezed.

Jerry touched his cowlick nervously. "You're Mrs. O'Donnell, aren't you? Could you please tell me what this is all about?"

Kit eyed him curiously. "That's what I'm trying to find out. It seems to be the latest lark of a cheap adulteress."

Daffy was impassive, but the word went through her husband like a cold blade. He touched his cowlick again, smearing it white. "You don't mean my *wife!*"

"She was like this"—Kit flicked at Daffy's nudity, visible under the parting lab coat—"on Theta grounds. A man just let her out of his car down the road."

"Oh, there's some mistake," he said, growing more agitated.

"Her mistake," she said ruthlessly.

"No, you just don't know Daffy, Mrs. O'Donnell. Sure, she likes to go up to the Theta house and help out—"

"Help out!" She laughed, a painful sound.

It piqued Jerry. "Well, she does! Daffy's trouble is, she can't say no."

"Yes," she said acidly.

"She lets those girls use her. Bringing her in to supper all the time so she can work, work, work on sorority stuff! You're the housemother, you ought to put your foot down."

"She sometimes comes to dinner. Never to work."

"All night, even!"

"What?"

"Three nights in a row once! Four in one week!"

Kit folded her hands before her. "Daphne has never spent a night at Theta."

He went dark at the mouth. "*Never?*"

"Not since I came back. Not this year."

Jerry had no reply. He turned his back to all of them and huddled over the stepladder, cleaning up with shaky hands. Kit ignored him, and Daffy's expression hadn't changed; she pretended to have heard nothing. In the bedroom, however, Jill was troubled for Jerry, and Ham, on the porch, felt almost as though he had been dealt a personal blow. He marveled at Kit. He had never seen this dark strength in her. Being a woman only made her more terrible, he thought. He could bloody Red's nose, but she struck with feline claws.

"You are no longer a Theta," she said to Daffy. "I am expelling you from the house now, and if you dare set foot in it again I shall call the police."

Daffy didn't reply. She lay limp, her arms at her side and her legs spread out, a soiled, forsaken doll.

"You might have the decency to cover yourself," Kit said sharply. "There's a man outside."

Daffy cleared her throat. Her lids fluttered, and suddenly her eyes were a flame of hate.

"Makes no never mind," she said.

Kit's clasped hands strained at each other. "Don't think this ends here. I intend to make a report."

"No never mind," Daffy repeated thickly.

Kit had said all she could. Staying now would only bring indignities. She looked around the chaotic room once, wrinkled her nose in ladylike distaste, and swept out past Ham. In the car she sat still, her head high. During the drive back she didn't speak once.

Jill also left, tactfully slipping out the back door. The baby was asleep. The Dixes were alone. Daffy's mind had begun to clear, and she waited, half in trepidation, half truculently, for Jerry's wrath. It didn't come. She had never understood her husband, and didn't see that in suffering, as in all else, he followed impulses foreign to her. Jerry's was a life of details. In details he took refuge now, carefully piling the stained newspapers in the corner, putting away the paint and ladder. He had always been attentive to her and remained so. She was ill; he brought her handkerchiefs and a robe. She was drunk; he made coffee. He was so methodical that her anxiety faded. She watched him for a while with her old air of tolerant contempt and then forgot him entirely. Her body was in disrepair, and she attended to it. She fetched lipstick and a hand mirror. Salves were applied to arm bruises. The welts, now blue and puckering, were veiled with her most expensive lingerie, and holding a comb and an electric hair dryer she sat by a space heater in the kitchen with her robe open, looking down in languid approval at red nylons and a pink, heavily embroidered slip. Her eyes were still dull with drink, her thoughts still fuzzy, yet her strong constitution was asserting itself. Delicate color was returning to her lovely cheeks. Apart from the cold she felt almost restored.

But Jerry's details were at an end. He had prolonged each little job, wondering all the time what course he should take, and now he appeared in faded flannel pajamas and sat opposite her.

He had rehearsed the question. It came out in a rush.

"Daffy, have you been having an affair?"

The comb paused. "Huh?"

"Because I want to be fair." He was determined to take a modern, sensible attitude. "If you want a divorce, you can have it."

She looked away and resumed combing. "Don't be silly."

"I'm not. I'm just saying that if you can't get over this man — and please don't tell me his name — I'll set aside."

"Oh honestly, Jerr," she said sulkily. "You're always *at* me. Always picking away, blowing little things up."

"This isn't a little thing."

"So we're going to have a fight."

"No. Just an intelligent talk."

She thought he was a fool. Intelligence and talk had nothing to do with it. At least that meatball on the Theta lawn had known what he wanted.

She crossed her legs warily. "You believe anything people say about me."

"I believe what I see. And I saw you come in tonight."

Back to that, she thought wearily. She tried to stare him down, but her eyes wavered. "Jerr, I —" She pouted and affected a broken cough. "I don't feel good."

"It'd be a miracle if you did, coming home intoxicated, in the rain, and — " The memory of her in that doorway was almost unbearable. He finished, "Like you were."

She lied recklessly: "It was a stunt!"

He blinked. "Without clothes?"

The clothes. She remembered her clothes. Oh God, I'll never see them again, she thought. She took rapid inventory: her camel's-hair jacket, her Angora sweater, her new loafers, best bra, pants she had been wearing tonight for the first time — all, all gone. She was furious. And because Jerry had always been the dumb victim of her anger, she turned on him.

"Yes, a stunt without clothes! A gag! Just some of the girls, that's all, and somebody fed me a mickey and stole my stuff. But a lot you care!"

"If it was a theft you should tell the police."

"You talk just like that bitchy widow! *Police.*" She spat it. "Wouldn't that be the greatest? A dozen coeds would get thrown out of State — innocent bystanders that just happened to be around. But *you* wouldn't mind. Oh, no; no feelings for anybody but your own sweet self."

"I suppose the coeds were sorority sisters."

She blundered. "Yes!"

"The ones you've been sleeping with when I'm alone."

Daffy dropped the comb and looked at him wildly. "O.K.! *O.K.!* So what if I do sneak out with some of the girls and have a little fun? Why not? Cooped up with a squalling kid, I got to have some kicks, I'd flip if I didn't. *You* never do anything for me. The only way we got a good apartment was I had to ask a friend."

His face whitened. She had scored. But the little triumph wasn't enough. Her eyes were filling; she couldn't forget her loss.

"Oh my coat!" she sobbed. "My sweater!"

She cried bitterly. And because it was a detail, a routine he knew, he reached out and comforted her. "We'll fix everything somehow, Daffy. It's just that you've got to tell me the truth."

"I did! I am!"

He didn't believe her. Yet he wanted to convince himself that there was some way to keep her and make things right, and he couldn't bear her crying.

"Do you have any witnesses?" he asked gently. "Not for me. I'm thinking of Mrs. O'Donnell's report."

"I'm not going to squeal on the other girls."

"I see." It didn't seem admirable to him.

"Oh, I never should've gone out tonight!" She wept, knowing how tears affected him. "You were right, Jerr! Only I get so *lonely!*"

It was true. She was lonelier than Jerry could have imagined. He had always thought of her as popular, himself as introverted. He had no idea how isolated she was within, and didn't realize that her visions of glory in the theater were pathetic substitutes for the warmth she should have felt with him and the child.

He did know how much her wardrobe meant to her, however. Trying to make peace, he said hesitantly, "Maybe I can get you some more clothes."

She wiped her nose wretchedly. "You can't."

"It's possible."

Jerry was thinking of budgets. If he took on another spare job he could meet the time payments. He knew it was a fantastic appeasement. Yet if it brought serenity . . .

"I'll do it if you stay home."

"Oh, I'm going to!" she said tragically. "I don't want to get hurt!"

Actually she had to stay. Dismissed from the sorority by Kit, exposed to her husband, she had to give up Red. After tonight it was a small concession. Her mind was too cloudy to grasp how completely Red had betrayed her — she had only shadowy memories of Geek's improvised studio, and hadn't seen the camera — but she knew he had introduced her to Geek, guessed he had left them together, and had been just sober enough to realize he was abandoning her on the road. If he would help her be Gridiron Queen, good. If not, not. She had another friend now anyhow. Mr. Bauer hadn't missed a Titanette rehearsal since they met. She would see him next Saturday.

By then she would have her new things. The thought was cheering. "I'm real sorry, Jerr," she whispered, stroking his pajama sleeve. "Starting now I'll behave. I mean it. I'm cured."

He heard her, heard the faint patter of rain outside and the baby turning in the crib, but his head was bowed. He wasn't aware of the dreamy smirk playing over her scarlet lips. Neither, for that matter, was she.

**

Mikel's Third Law, as he had christened it long ago, ran, "Whenever A learns a fact which tends to degrade B, A furtively informs C, provided C is in a position to enhance the general welfare of A." The Law was widely regarded as a prime example of his cynical wit, yet it had its applications. The day after Homecoming Trudy Viggiantti, Red Stacy, and Tom Yablonski, all of whom looked upon Mikel as a hopeless crackpot, followed it faithfully.

Trudy heard about Kit's successful pursuit of Daffy shortly after noon. Jill hadn't meant to spread the news, but it was too choice to keep from Jack, and an hour after she told him everyone in the Village knew. So much for Daffy, thought Trudy, looking around bitterly at her new, cramped quarters. Then she wondered. Suppose Mrs. O'Donnell didn't follow through? Worse: what if the Dixes were evicted and another family moved into the corner unit? Trudy might be stuck in this hateful hovel permanently. The solution, she decided, was to see that the investigation of Daffy kept its momentum—and to make sure she was given credit for it. Leaving her child with her husband, she borrowed a neighbor's car, drove out to the faculty housing development, and called on Dean Elsie Shoemaker.

Miss Shoemaker was recovering from one of her dreadful headaches. She received Trudy reluctantly and sat haggard through the story.

"So," she said at the end.

"Mrs. O'Donnell can give you the real dope, Dean."

"Yes."

"You going to call her?"

"Good afternoon, Trudy."

The idea, the dean thought indignantly, watching her secretary drive off. These girls grew more and more impertinent. Yet as the car disappeared she realized that she would have to call Kit after all. If only half of what Trudy had said were true there were still grounds for action.

Over the phone Kit explained that she was writing her report now.

"Can you tell me a little about it now?"

Kit described the chase, from her discovery of the baton to the exchange in Daffy's living room. "By then she'd thrown on a kind of smock. Before that she was running around without a stitch on."

"Oh *dear*."

The dean rubbed her forehead. She felt ill again. So *unsavory*, she thought; so *sordid*. Her course was unpleasant but clear. The provost had dismissed Daffy's College Inne adventure as a rumor. This was airtight, unimpeachable.

"Oh *my*."

And without further questions she scheduled a hearing for the following afternoon.

Monday morning Trudy gleefully typed notices and delivered them to Daffy, to Kit, and to Hotflash, Daffy's adviser. It was an established procedure, and part of it was to send carbons of all three to the provost of the University. Those carbons were to be Miss Shoemaker's alibi. She hoped to act without Tate this time. She counted on his being too busy to give the carbons more than passing attention, and thought that if he reproached her afterward for failing to inform him she could protest that she had. By then it would be too late for him to move. Daffy's name would have been removed from the rolls.

But Tate read his correspondence carefully these days. All his waking hours were spent plotting his succession to the presidency, and he was especially anxious not to offend the trustees. Both Red Stacy and Daffy Dix were sensitive names. Any move against Red would offend the board deeply, and if Daffy were disciplined she might implicate him. Even if she didn't, Tate would still lose, for she had acquired trustee status of her own. Paul Bauer often dropped into Administration Hall on insurance trips. Twice this month he had mentioned Daffy to Tate; last week he had confided that he had about persuaded his committee that she was eligible to be Gridiron Queen. Expel her now and Tate could forget about Bauer's vote.

So Trudy's carbons alarmed him. He dialed Miss Shoemaker's extension and asked how serious the charges were.

"I don't see how they could be worse," she said nervously.

He groped for a maxim. "Of course, punishment is the easy way out."

"Sometimes there isn't any other way," she said, and read him Kit's report.

"Circumstantial," he said weakly. "There may have been extenuating circumstances."

"Perhaps. But she won't explain them."

"Oh?"

"She told my secretary she didn't think she could come to the hearing." With heavy irony the dean added, "Apparently she has a cold."

"Really? I'm sorry to hear that. Well. Expect me there anyhow."

"You'll preside?"

"Why no, this is in your jurisdiction. I'll come as a friend of the court, so to speak."

He hung up scowling. That O'Donnell woman again. She left him very little room for maneuver. He paced his office most of the afternoon, drank three Manhattans before dinner, and was soaking in a hot bath when the Chairman of the Department of Physical Education arrived in his front hall to rescue him.

"Sorry to keep you waiting, Tom," Tate said, skipping down the stairs in a white terry cloth robe embroidered with cheerful mottoes. "You want to see me alone?"

Yablonski's face was grave. He glanced apologetically at Mrs. Tate. "If you don't mind."

"In the library, then," said Tate.

He had listened to Yablonski nearly ten minutes before he realized his luck.

"Red overheard all this?" he asked excitedly.

The coach nodded heavily. "Of course, not being a Catholic he didn't realize how important it was."

No, Tate thought cynically, but he knew *you* were one, and he had a pretty good idea how you'd take it. It was an astute move. Red had anticipated Kit's report. He didn't know whether or not he was mentioned — Tate guessed shrewdly that he should have been — so he was taking the precaution of discrediting her.

The coach rose awkwardly. "I don't want to get the woman in a jam — I don't even know her. It's just I figured you'd want to know."

"I'll be most discreet. And please thank Red for me." Tate's eyes glittered with his gratitude.

He arrived at the hearing late. Miss Shoemaker sat stiffly behind her Hepplewhite desk. Trudy, to one side, was intent on her Spiral notebook. Kit and Hotflash faced the dean on straight chairs. A third chair between them was vacant—Daffy had telephoned that her cold was worse.

"Oh, Dr. Tate!" Miss Shoemaker handed him a copy of Kit's report and indicated the empty place. "Would you like to come up here?"

He made for a reading chair beside Trudy. "This looks more comfortable." He winked broadly. "I don't have much padding, you know."

Only the dean tittered. Trudy was intent on her notes, and Kit and Hotflash had been arguing.

"It *must* be hers," Kit said, fingering Geek's baton.

"Maybe it is," Hotflash said, "but it wasn't issued here. We have a standard baton."

"I know she dropped it," Kit said worriedly.

Tate sank back and crossed his legs high. "Perhaps it was another girl."

"Not one of ours," Hotflash said. "Every Titanette gets the same equipment. If we started personalizing stuff they'd never quit nagging me. You know what women are like," she confided to Tate.

"Someone from the town?" he suggested tentatively.

"Impossible," Kit said. "And irrelevant, if you'll excuse me."

Tate's brow arched. "Irrelevant?"

"You see, we followed the car, saw her get out, and trailed her into the house. The whole thing's open and shut."

He laughed thinly. "You sound like bloodhounds! But how open and shut is it, really? Who, for example, is 'we'?"

"Ham Markham was driving me."

"Ah. The *Star* correspondent."

"He's a trained reporter, and he was there."

Miss Shoemaker gave the provost an addled glance. He had declined to preside, yet was assuming the brisk air of authority. She said uncertainly, "Perhaps we should have a statement from Mr. Markham."

"Unnecessary," Tate said. "I'm sure he'll back up everything Mrs. O'Donnell says."

His voice was biting. Kit frowned. "Of course. Because it's true."

Tate leafed through her report. "I believe you were a Sigma Chi chaperone Saturday night."

"Yes. So was Miss Hatch."

"I see. Miss Hatch, were you with Mrs. O'Donnell all evening?"

Hotflash looked preoccupied. She had been afraid of this. "No, a little before things broke up I went off with the other two — Wade and Feinblatt."

Kit eyed her with amused contempt. But the inaccuracies had just begun.

"How did that happen?"

"We were — inspecting the house."

"Really!" Tate folded his pallid hands. "And what did you see?"

Hotflash looked uneasy. "Nothing."

"I believe that," Kit said dryly.

"But this is extraordinary!" Tate cried. "Miss Hatch finds the house in order. Yet a few minutes later a student reports encountering Mrs. Dix in a compromising position — and in a condition which could scarcely have come upon her suddenly."

"That was me," Trudy said in a tiny voice.

"Eh?"

"I — I was the student. And it wasn't in the house, it was the parking lot."

Tate browbeat her, and Trudy, intimidated, began to hedge. Yes, it had been dark. Yes, Daffy had clothes on. Yes, there could have been a mistake. Trudy's evidence evaporated, and Tate returned to the greater threat, Kit.

"Why didn't Mrs. O'Donnell join your inspection, Miss Hatch?"

Hotflash shifted on the little chair. "I don't remember. She wanted to play cards, I think."

"With whom?"

"Oh — I guess it was Feinblatt."

Tate's eyes were round. "I thought Dr. Feinblatt was with you."

"He came along a few minutes later."

"And joined you."

"Yes."

"Leaving Mrs. O'Donnell alone."

"That's right."

"Why didn't you go?" he asked Kit wonderingly.

Kit was in a mood to crack heads — Tate's head, then Hotflash's. She couldn't blurt out that Hotflash and the major had passed out and still stay in Gideon. It just wasn't done.

"I don't see —"

"— what this has to do with the inquiry?" Tate studied his fingernails. "I'll tell you. It's my understanding that you weren't an entirely reliable witness Saturday night. I suggest that the reason you didn't accompany the other chaperones is that you'd had too much punch."

She flared, "That's not true!"

But there was truth in it, and Tate was an expert insinuator. Holding his glossy nails to the light he said, "I'm told that you let your hair down, removed your shoes, and curled up on a couch with this Mr. Markham."

The dean's hand flew to her throat. "Dr. Tate!"

"I'm also told that the door was closed." He looked hard. "Is that your idea of proper chaperoning?"

Kit was on her feet, her face fiery. She wasn't a Trudy, to be cowed by a word. The provost had crossed a forbidden line.

"Explain that!"

He spread his hands. "I'm asking *you* to explain it."

"If you're trying to say I did anything wrong in that room, it's a damned lie."

The dean rallied at last and waved Trudy out. "We'd better go into executive session."

"Precisely," said Tate. "I think we can excuse Miss Hatch, too."

Trudy left reluctantly, Hotflash with relief. Kit prowled up and down the room, restlessly rubbing her elbows, and when the latch clicked she whirled on Tate.

"When did you dream this up?"

"My dear Mrs. O'Donnell, I —" He looked around helplessly.

"In your tub this morning?"

It was a jugular thrust, and unpardonable. Tate's bath addiction had been campus gossip for years. The greenest instructor knew that he spent at least an hour each day reclining in steaming water, with his head supported by a sponge pillow, reading trivial paperback novels. Members of the Departments of English and Psychology had devoted long sessions to analyses of this quirk. Until today, however, no one had dared confronted him with it. The dean, unaware how deeply Kit herself had been hurt, gazed at her in horror.

The provost's face was an ugly red. "All right. A few minutes ago you called me a liar."

"I didn't. I merely —"

"We'll see who the liar is." He turned to Miss Shoemaker. "I want this woman's file."

The dean had seen the demand coming when Kit rose to challenge him and had awaited it with sick dread. Now she crossed forlornly to a corner cabinet and returned with a slim Manila folder. He riffled through it swiftly and paused.

"Divorced," he said shrilly. "So you admitted it after all."

The fight had gone out of Kit. She sat numbly. "It's not against the law."

"It is in your church."

"My church is more liberal than most people think."

"Unfortunately, what most people think is our law here."

"Then your law is illegal," she said desperately. "It's an intrusion into my private life."

"Housemothers have no private lives. Especially when it comes to religion."

Kit couldn't discuss her religion with him. She had no reply. He glared at the dean. "You knew this was forbidden."

"Well, irregular," she said feebly.

"*Forbidden!* Who were her references?" He thumbed through forms. "Mikel!" he snorted. "And Lutz." More thumbing. "Who was the third? Applications require three references, Dean!"

He was menacing Miss Shoemaker, and she knew it wasn't brag. The provost's power over her was absolute. On a dozen occasions he had terminated administrators' contracts without notice. She looked at Kit with pain and reproach.

"Don't tell him," Kit whispered. "I'll resign."

"That's insufficient," Tate said quickly, sensing something big. "Well, Dean?"

She sighed deeply. "It was Mrs. River."

The name ended the hearing. No one spoke again. Tate sat quiet for a full minute, weighing the folder, then strode out without a word. Miss Shoemaker was too distraught to say anything. He had broken her entirely. She wanted to be alone in her humiliation, and once it was certain that Tate had returned to his office, Kit left, too. They had adjourned with a tacit truce. Nothing was resolved. Everything was to be as it had been. Kit could keep Daffy out of the sorority, but Daffy would remain a student. Kit would also remain a housemother, for Tate had no intention of crossing Doc now, and in the absence of official action Trudy's Village gossip fell on inattentive ears. Even so, Kit was wretched. She knew that the meeting had been a disaster. Her secret was in hostile hands. She had mortally offended Tate; if he became president of State her dismissal would follow swiftly. That night after dinner she rocked Sean nearly an hour, clutching him to her bosom until he whimpered, and when her own bedtime struck she was long at prayer. She meant to be devout. But humility wasn't in her. Inside she seethed. She knelt by her bed with her thick black hair down her stiff back, her head tilted defiantly, her strong fingers telling the rosary with impatient jerks.

Kit was right: Tate couldn't forgive her. But he had put her out of his mind. Back at his desk he had confined himself to a single note — the next time he saw Bauer he would mention casually that he had seen Daffy through a minor scrape. The note went under his blotter with a sheaf of others, all equally calculated. The provost's campaign for office was by now as deliberate as Doc's. He was pressing every advantage, watching every angle, hedging every bet. Doc's stock seemed to be rising, so for the present Tate saw no more of Al Swinton. Nevertheless, still he had to consider the possibility of Doc's defeat; there was a lingering chance that he would have to deal with a Guelph, not a Ghibelline. He could find ways and ways to ruin Doc here after the election, but looking past them he saw that there still might be rival candidates for the presidency. Clearing the field in advance required careful planning, and the week after Homecoming he concentrated on that. As Sol Feinblatt had observed, Tate's first step had been to assure campus allegiance. The faculty and trustees were now as solidly behind him as they would ever be. That left only the appointment itself — the announcement by the new governor. *The announcement*. Tate's pulse hammered at the thought of it. But how could he make sure? Normally the governor would approve any recommendation from the board, yet he wondered. Suppose Witty *were* elected? Would he name a man of his own? The provost, like most academicians, was a registered Democrat. Maybe the Republicans had a sleeper. Maybe Judge Davies was one. He could have been planted on the board for just that reason.

Every evening Tate lay long in scalding baths, worrying.

There was one way to clinch things. He had four thousand dollars in the Birmingham Trust Company, and he had met Clare

Hewitt once at a Rotary luncheon. He decided to make a small investment with him. Friday morning after breakfast he telephoned the Republican chairman. He was driving down to the capital today, he said; he thought they might have a little talk. He explained that privately he admired Stuart Witty greatly, and he had something that might help him — something, he added coyly, to do with money. Hewitt hesitated. All his days were busy now. Yet Tate was close to Doc. He suggested they meet at the Clipper Club, and there, after drawing three hundred dollars from the bank, Tate joined him for lunch.

"My contribution," he said grandly, handing him the check.

The chairman was surprised. To Tate's confusion he seemed almost ungrateful. His party had all the money it needed. He had hoped Tate was bringing him a campaign issue — proof of mismanaged gate receipts, perhaps.

"Are you sure you want to do this?" he inquired, putting the check down. "We'll have to report it six months after the election, you know. Your chief won't like it."

Never before, not even to his wife, had the provost confided his ambition. Almost shyly he said, "By then I hope to be the chief myself."

Several moments passed in silence. Then Hewitt understood. And then he approved. The campaign contribution was nothing in itself, but Tate's commitment was very great. He would, Hewitt realized, make a pliant civil servant.

"Tell me. If you *were* chief, would you follow the pattern of the present administration?"

Tate grinned his monkey grin. "Hardly."

"You'd understand that in a state like this, with a fine private college, the public school should have a more modest share of the budget?"

"Certainly, certainly." Anything, anything.

Hewitt held out his hand and smiled. "Glad to have you with us, Dr. Tate."

So intent were they, and so deep was the rug, that neither noticed the light step of a passing member. They were still shaking hands, and the big check lay green on the starched linen, when the shadow flickered by.

"Good day, gentlemen," Judge Davies murmured softly and strolled on, unheard, unseen.

**

"Unquestionably it was money," said the judge. "My experience in these matters is vast."

Harry Mikel looked vinegary, Eric Lutz troubled, Dr. Budge mildly interested. They drew closer over the Gideon Arms table as the judge mouthed a fresh cigar.

"I think only one construction can be placed upon the exchange," he added.

"Skulduggery!" Mikel cried.

"Well." The judge pondered. "Certainly a union of interests."

He had decided that the meeting between Tate and Hewitt was not privileged. It had been in a public place — the judge actually thought of the club as public — and whatever they had been up to, he himself had been there in an unofficial capacity. He felt content. Reporting the encounter compensated somewhat for all the informal advice he had given Witty, and dinner here tonight had been superb. It was extraordinary, he mused, that Gideon should support so agreeable a chef.

"May I say that that was a capital claret?" he remarked in an aside to Mikel. "Each time we meet your taste is more remarkable."

Mikel did not sneer. Somehow the judge's presence curbed his crude exhibitionism. They had dined in the Gideon Arms twice before, alone, splitting the wine and dinner bills, and the two evenings were a bond between them. Outwardly it was an unlikely friendship — Mikel was so raffish, the judge so courtly — yet each was drawn by an awareness that the other was his own man. Both held integrity and intellect in reverence, each saw the fine steel in the other, and so they met as equals, as proud sovereigns meet.

They had met here first because Mikel had extended the invitation and had continued because in Gideon the judge felt vaguely in touch with the university. His public denunciation of Doc had made him a pariah with the rest of the trustees, but he still felt his responsibilities. Mikel, appreciative and sympathetic, had offered to introduce him to anyone he liked. The point of tonight's party had been to discuss reaccreditation. In that it had failed. Budge was reticent. The judge was the last man to request information under the table; he had merely thought he might acquire some idea of the team's progress. Even that was lacking, however. Budge honestly didn't know when the report would be ready, though he still expected to meet Doc's deadline. He had said that much, then stared deliberately over everyone's heads while Lutz and Mikel debated what the result would be. Mikel expected it to be negative; Lutz thought they might just pass. By coffee they had begun to repeat themselves, and the judge, abandoning hope of a joint opinion, had told his Clipper Club story.

"Not good," Lutz said, shaking his bullet head.

"But typical!" Mikel flashed. "Our provost is a paste jewel. He is consistent."

The judge blew into his mustache. "Am I to assume that if there were a change in Aggie's leadership — and some change seems likely — this Tate would be River's logical heir?"

Lutz nodded gloomily; Mikel muttered something about polluted blood. The judge smiled around his cigar.

"You would prefer another?"

"*Any* other." Mikel raised a fist. "It is a matter of personal honor! That hyena betrayed me!"

"So you have intimated." The judge made a smoke ring and watched it fade overhead. "Rather a grave charge."

"And he is crimson with guilt. No one else could have published that survey."

Lutz nodded heavily. "It is true. It had to be he. The rest of us did not even know it existed."

"He has all the instincts of an *agent provocateur*," said Mikel, propping a cigarette between bared teeth. "Reptilian, dissembling, a gifted liar — and hence, of course, almost impossible to expose."

They talked on: the others without direction, the judge purposely. He inquired about the university's administrative machinery and asked how copies of reports reached Tate; he questioned Mikel closely about the survey. And then he made a suggestion.

"There will be other — ah — confidential papers?"

"Inevitably." Mikel said sourly. "We have a silo of such documents."

Lutz indicated Budge with a continental bow. "Our colleague's report is an example."

"I am thinking particularly of that one," the judge said. "My interest in it is rather special, you see. I am the freshman on the board, and, at the moment, something of an Ishmael. If the team were critical, and its remarks went astray, I might be blamed. I should survive, of course, but my usefulness would be destroyed."

He looked directly at Budge. "I believe there will be a limited number of copies."

"One for each trustee and each officer of the administration."

"River and Tate?"

"I believe that's correct."

"Could you distinguish between them? Perhaps initial the back of each page unobtrusively?"

The request was out of character. Ham Markham would have been astonished, and people who had known the judge all their lives wouldn't have believed it. He rather shocked himself. He had never been a schemer, hadn't known it was in him. But then, he hadn't been directly involved in intrigue until now. Always before he had preserved a sense of distance from events. Even in his one foray as a political candidate he had been a man apart. Now that reserve was crumbling. He was becoming, as Ham had seen, a committed man.

Mikel sparkled. "What a splendid idea!"

The judge's lips curved slightly. "Well, Dr. Budge?"

Budge's heavy face was flushed. "It's never been done, sir."

He started to say more, then snapped his wide mouth shut. Everyone waited as he studied his fork, turning it over and squinting at each tine, as though searching for wisdom there. They guessed at his struggle. He was supposed to be entirely free of bias. Implicit in his mission was the shunning of factions; he should treat all Gideon alike. On the whole he had succeeded. His conduct had been bland, impersonal. But Budge had an original mind. He didn't like rule books. And privately, as the judge had guessed, he had formed strong opinions — the strongest of them a cold distaste for State's provost. The thought that he should unwittingly abet some low scheme of Tate's was unnerving.

In a harried baritone he asked him, "What makes you think anyone would let the report out?"

"Nothing. Very likely no one would. But should the findings indicate a weakness at Aggie —"

"Of course there's no sign that they will," Budge rasped, almost belligerently.

"I'm gratified."

"Or that they won't."

The judge nodded. "I understand perfectly. The point is that a prima-facie case has been made that Dr. Tate let slip one confidential item reflecting on the university. We have a precedent."

"What do you think?" Budge shot at Lutz.

Lutz thought all this most unfortunate. With his great respect for order he considered the setting of snares undignified. "Could not the copies be marked openly?" he inquired. "No one would dare be careless then."

Even Budge agreed this was naïve, and Mikel remarked acidly that it would be worse than nothing. Tate, if so warned, could simply make a copy.

"Nevertheless, you are suggesting an extreme step," muttered Budge, rubbing his jowl.

"*Fiat justitia, ruat caelum,*" Mikel said slyly.

"*Audentes fortuna juvat,*" murmured the judge, his lips curving more.

Over and over went Budge's fork.

Then: "Very well."

The judge closed his eyes. Mikel leered. Lutz looked resigned.

"But you must not mention this to me again." Budge added quickly "Only if there is trouble afterward. Only then."

"Very sensible," said the judge, calling for the dinner check. "And I pray there will be no occasion for trouble." He lifted the last of his claret. "May all your findings be acclamatory."

On that Budge remained mute. The judge couldn't dismiss it so lightly, however, and he slouched out moodily as Budge strolled ahead with Lutz. At the dining room entrance he decided to wait for Mikel, who had lingered to pay the bar bill.

"You really think it hopeless?" he asked, moving with him into the lobby.

"Oh, no. *This* approach is unlikely, but we'll get him one way or another." He added cheerfully, "I may cut his throat."

"I don't mean that. I'm thinking of accreditation."

Mikel grunted. "Don't think about it too much. It's a hideous prospect."

The judge said unhappily, "Oh well. Perhaps it would be best if Aggie did get bad marks. Something to shake things up, you know."

"Still brooding over my survey?" Mikel asked shrewdly.

"My dear fellow, it gives me nightmares. Especially that criminal thrust of yours about—" He whirled on a hovering waiter and blazed, "Why are you following me, young man?"

"The dinner check, sir," the young man said uncomfortably.

"What?"

"I think you put it in your pocket."

"Eh? Oh." His anger collapsed. "Quite so."

But he couldn't remember which pocket. He went through each meekly, producing a sheaf of unanswered correspondence, stubs — one, most awkwardly, an unpaid parking ticket — before Mikel leaned over and gleefully plucked the check from his vest. The judge covered his embarrassment by overtipping extravagently.

"And what was *my* crime?" Mikel taunted him.

"Crime? Oh, yes." Hurrying to rejoin the others, the judge said over his shoulder, "I meant your gibe about Vicksburg, of course."

**

Vicksburg also haunted Ham. For nearly a week *Peabody Men in the Rebellion* had lain open where he had left it. Hallam Caulkin had requested several stories on Peabody's endowment — turgid statistical accounts, obviously assigned as punishment for the unauthorized inquiry into Consolidated Enterprises — and it was late Monday afternoon before Ham could return to college history. He anticipated a treat. The early 1860's had a romantic aura for him; it was then the gaunt farmers of the northeast had hoisted their thick galluses and marched south to roll back the gray tide of insurrection. It had been the finest hour of the now dwindling Yankee race, and thinking of it Ham felt the fierce pride of blood. He also felt a personal sense of communion with the oval portraits of *Peabody Men*. In that war, as in his own, undergraduates had left books and classes to follow glory in an exotic land. They hadn't found glory; that promise had gone smash; yet in the open artless faces of their last college ambrotypes he saw the faith and innocence he himself had taken into the Marine Corps in his early twenties — the sanctity of young manhood, pure and honor-bright and doomed.

Dusk that Monday was one of those bleak October twilights when the sky over New England is streaked with red, and the sere ground has a barren look, and the first withered leaves twist free from blackened branches and dance wildly away on the harsh wind. There was a feeling of chill everywhere, even in the library. The waning sun flooded Ham's marble-topped table, bathing books and papers with a brick-colored glow, twinking on the fireplace brass and then receding into corners where forming pools of night spread their dark shapeless hulks. Below, the campus lights winked on. Ham didn't notice them. The long sullen gloaming crept up on him unawares. He left his lamp unlit and pored with strained eyes over stories of Peabody boys Following Freedom's Flag, sailing with David Porter past the Rebel batteries, marching with Grant through the low swamps and bayous of the Vicksburg oxbow. Union shells fell in Vicksburg; Vicksburg thundered back; Vicksburg grew silent; Vicksburg fell — and still Ham read on, peering hard now in the demented light.

A new chapter started at the bottom of a page: "Gettysburg and the Crisis." Ham turned the stiff paper and beheld a remarkable photograph.

It was the largest picture in the book, and filled an entire page. On the facing page a biography identified it as the graduation portrait of Isaac Lewis Bagby, '60, brevetted colonel at the age of twenty-three and awarded the Medal of Honor for gallantry in hand-to-hand fighting at Gettysburg's Highwater Mark. The citation was striking, but Ham was more struck by Isaac himself. The features in the picture suggested a distinct character. Other men in the book wore the flourishing mustaches of the period. Not Isaac; his thin mouth was closely shaved and crinkled by a mocking smile. Others were full-faced, sleek with youth; his cheeks were hollow and ascetic and his dark eyes slightly sunken. With his widow's peak and his high broad forehead his face had a mischievous, almost diabolical cast. There was reserve there, and irony — and loneliness.

Reserve, irony — loneliness . . .

Ham knew why the face drew him. Isaac had looked curiously like Spook. Strange, he thought, staring down at the long dead eyes. And yet he supposed it wasn't really. It was like the resemblance of a passing stranger to a celebrity, or to someone once beloved and now forever gone. Often on crowded streets Ham had skipped ahead to draw abreast of a girl whose boyish, pigeon-toed walk had reminded him of Kit Ryan's, or had watched breathlessly as a neat old man approached from the opposite direction with the stooped carriage of his father. It was only a sleight of fantasy. Nevertheless it could be startling. Slant a sardonic Chesterfield from Isaac Lewis Bagby's lips, or clench his face in that tight, scared expression Spook had always worn when he carried the ball, and the brevetted colonel of Gettysburg could have been Ham's lost roommate.

Conscious at last of the thickening murk, Ham reached for the lamp switch and then, abruptly, withdrew his hand. Light would destroy the illusion, and he liked it; in a gentle melancholy of remembrance he groped his way out into the last moments of daylight, into the grim engulfing cold.

Sol Feinblatt was supposed to meet him in the Gideon Arms taproom at six. This was the afternoon of the fiasco in Miss Shoemaker's office, however, and after her clash with Tate Kit had felt the need of company. She had considered trying to reach Ham, had decided she really preferred Sol, and had telephoned him instead. Sol was always ready to break a date for her. When Ham reached the taproom the bartender gave him the message — Dr. Feinblatt had been detained; he wouldn't be coming.

So Ham drank alone. Three Martinis heightened his nostalgia. Over coffee in Peabody's faculty club Ed Hardy, the bald retired coach, had offered to show him films of old State-Peabody games, and after the third drink Ham called him from the booth outside the ladies' powder room. Hardy was delighted. He suggested Ham come to his home after dinner; he had a projection room in his basement. It turned out to be a disappointing evening. Ham had never seen football movies taken by members of a coaching staff, and everything seemed drab. The showing was a tribute to Ham's triumph in the Peabody chapel, and something of a privilege; no outsider had ever seen these reels. Nevertheless he was stifling yawns at the end. The cameras had focused only on the flow of play. He rarely recognized Spook and could scarcely pick out himself. After the 1941 game he hinted he would rather see some of the older films of Doc. That was better; Doc's pillbox silhouette was unmistakable; his brawny shoulders loomed over everyone on the field. Even so, the footage on his ninety-three-yard run, the climax of his last game, was a botch. Peabody's photographers had been interested in the movement of the line. Once Doc passed scrimmage they had dollied away from him, and he had finished his tremendous, hurtling sprint offstage.

"He was the best we ever had," Ham said, blinking as the lights came on.

"I guess he was just about the best anybody ever had," said Hardy, bending over his projector. "Of course, that was before my time." He glanced up with a twinkle. "I remember *you*, though. You and Duschene. Want to see that long gainer he threw you in '42?"

Ham didn't. Some moments came but once, and he had had enough of memories for one day. Or so he thought. Ham might have escaped his prewar dreams that evening if Hardy, who deplored the end of football at Peabody, hadn't detained him with reminiscences while he rewound reels. The stories meant little to Ham; they were of a piece with the aimless chatter he had endured at Homecoming. But watching the film whirl backward — the punts returning crazily to the punters' toes and the scrimmages reforming — Ham found his mind going backward too. After his return to the College Inne it went right on spinning into the past, and as he prepared for bed it accelerated. He tried a sleeping pill. No luck; the faded photograph of Isaac Bagby had started him, and although his thoughts arched out in great circles touching on the war, his days as a fledgling reporter, and the early years of his marriage, the orbs grew smaller and tighter and finally closed in on the picture — not the actual ambrotype of Bagby, of whom he knew so little, but the superimposed, palimpsested image of Spook Duschene, who had once been closer to him than any man, dearer even than his father or the men who had died with him on Peleliu.

Spook and Ham had been more than roommates, classmates, teammates. They had grown up four blocks apart, wearing the same gamin uniform of corduroy knickers and cheap leatherette pilots' helmets, telling time from identical Mickey Mouse watches, competing together in marble tournaments and sharing the longest ash bat on the Birmingham Boys Club playground. Each had lost his father — Mrs. Duschene was a piecework seamstress; when Spook was killed in Belgium she sent Ham a crabbed, pathetic note FPO San Francisco — and both had grown into gangling adolescence with the desperate, bare-knuckle ambition of bright slum boys in the Thirties. By the autumn of 1940, when they hitchhiked to Gideon and entered State on working scholarships, Ham was taller and more loose-jointed. Spook slighter and quicker, but in their high-pocket pants, with their heads shaved in the Iroquois haircuts affected by Boys Club athletes, they were often taken for brothers. Neither had protested, and long before the war Ham had come to think of Spook as the brother he had never had.

And yet . . .

Brothers can be strangers. Spook hadn't protested, but unlike Ham he hadn't smiled at the confusion. Or rather, he *had* smiled — with that flouting little half-grin that wasn't a smile at all, that flickering scoff that was either a sign of arrogance or inner shyness. No one could be sure which; none was familiar enough to ask. Since his knicker days Spook had been that rare youth, the true loner. Others thought Ham knew him. Ham didn't. He knew and was wedded in friendship to one Spook, but there was another Spook, isolated and unapproachable, and this inner self shrank from real intimacy. Ham could go so far, no farther. If he persisted, if with the clumsy tactless probing of youth he kept trying to reach Spook's deepest yearnings and beliefs — then he met casual insolence, jeers, and, under the satirical grin, an arctic reserve.

"For Christ's sake, Ham, go beat the bishop."

Or, in a drawl:

"When you going to turn your collar around, Ham?"

Or, from the corner of his paper-thin, ever-tense lips:

"Button up, kid, you're hanging out."

In the next instant he would burst into that dirty, infectious laughter Ham could never resist. It wasn't faked, it was meant; Spook had drawn a line and the laugh was a handshake. They would race off to class or practice together, and within an hour Ham would have persuaded himself the ugly moment had been only a twisted fiction of his mind.

And yet . . .

It was no fiction. It was the most poignant aspect of a haunted boy. Spook was a loner, always alone, following his own lonesome trail, shaking off Ham or anyone who tailed him too far. It didn't make sense; it never had. Among Ham's earliest Mechanics Street memories was a fragmentary glimpse of Spook racing down the brick sidewalk on a second-hand tricycle, his face older than his age and his little mouth pain-torn, almost square as he fled from another child who had only wanted to play with him. Even at six he had passed up every Boys Club excursion, even the chance to see Doc's last game. Why? Ham never knew. In Gideon he would often vanish from the campus week ends. Where did he go? Another blank: Ham tried to follow once and Spook slipped away like a shadow. When war came he waited until Ham had enlisted in the Marine Corps, then joined the army. Ham was hurt and furious. They had always been together; why not now?

"Aw, who wants to be a bellhop?"

And:

"Don't you know war's a private affair?"

Then the laugh. The raw, broken-voice chuckle. The intimate you-and-me-know gloat: the handshake.

That last year, when they were waiting to be called up, was their finest together. Ham saw more of Spook then than he — meaning anyone — ever had. Both had always suffered from pregame tension, and working through Doc Spook wangled two beds in the college infirmary each Friday night through the autumn; in hiding from the rest of the campus they could doze and talk and dissipate anxieties in the wonderful bursts of convulsive, meaningless laughter only they understood. After the training season was over they sat up all night before exams, splitting bottles of cheap whiskey and quizzing each other in the still dawn. Afterward they were never tired: they had youth, animal vigor, energy without end. Yet even then Spook would from time to time retreat inexplicably into his hermit's pose. If Ham was baffled, outsiders were resentful. Especially during the football season Spook's cool detachment rankled with other students. As State's greatest halfback since Doc he was exempt from open criticism, but there were always a few muted catcalls when his turn came to step up at Friday evening rallies. Doc would stand on a crude platform by the mushrooming bonfire, calling out names of tomorrow's starting lineup while everyone waved torches. To be named was an ineffable distinction — now, nearly twenty years later, the ceremony still had an aura for Ham.

"Left end! Ham Markham, the lah-de-dah swamp Yankee with delusions of grandeur!"

Introductions were deliberately insulting. Everyone at the rally understood: Doc was telling the team what the big slicks across town thought of them. He was making them mad, getting them hungry.

"Fullback! Johnny Melotti, the big greaser!"

"Quarterback! Sy Epstein, the smart kike!"

"Right half! How do you say this hunky's name? Joe Rzegocki!"

Ten of them loved it. Ten darted up in their blue sweaters and stood at swaggering ease under the big red maple that stood south of the old practice field; ten breathed deep of the acrid wood smoke and lifted their eyes to the star-powdered sky and felt immortal.

"Left half — Spook Duschene, the famous Canuck."

Doc would mumble it, almost apologetically. He made it as mild as possible — in the circumstances saying nothing would have been a greater affront — for he knew how Spook felt. Everyone knew:

Spook showed them. He would idle out slowly with his scornful narrow smile and stand off to one side, the man apart. The rest of the varsity drank deep of glory, but he profaned the moment, murmuring sarcastically to Ham.

"East wind rising — I'll be chucking boomerangs."

Or:

"Looks like rain, Larry Kelly. You any good at water polo?"

Next day he would be brilliant, outmaneuvering ends with his erratic, dodging runs and dancing away from tacklers in the ten-second mazurkas that bought time for his long rainbows to Ham downfield. And then that night at the Tau Rho record dance he would withdraw again. He never brought a date. He would sit brooding by the corner turntable in a bedraggled beer jacket, changing records and cocking his ear to the speaker.

"Look over there," Kit Ryan would whisper to Ham as they danced past. "Old Stuck-up."

"Quiet type," he would whisper back uncomfortably.

"Carries himself like a gift. You know. Fragile. This side up."

"He likes the music, is all."

Spook could always tell you who was on the trombone, who on the tenor sax, when the strong beat was coming and why Goodman broke off the plaintive figures and built a quick fire under the soloist. He became the campus authority on jazz, because he was happier over there alone.

Over there alone, Ham thought bitterly, tossing on his noisy College Inne bed. Spook was over there forever now, forever alone in the secret earth. Spook Duschene, the famous Canuck. Himself a soloist to the end. Playing his quaint solitaire, smiling his derisive little smile, slipping quietly away from all of them in the roar and rubble of the Bulge. Breaking the insular pattern but once, with Kit, and then when Ham had gone and Gideon was almost deserted. Had that been the final senseless joke? Ham could almost hear Spook's oblique chuckle, mocking him across the years. Taunting him, and then dying away. Leaving him in anguish with the riddle of a lifetime. For now the puzzle was eternal. The solution was lost. The odd man had dropped out. He who laughed had laughed last.

**

And yet, *and yet* . . .

Nothing is ever destroyed really. Ham had built a career on that faith. Grieving in the College Inne that night he wavered from it, but it was sounder than he knew. A fact, a name, a fragment of the truth may be elusive; still they exist somewhere. There is always the telltale receipt lying in the safe deposit box, the yellowing parchment in the vault, the voucher in the dead file, the cardiogram, the snapshot, the laminated photostat —

Or the ambrotype.

It lay on the table where he had left it, sallow in the wintry morning light.

He studied it narrowly. The similarity had been stronger than he had thought. Those *were* Spook's eyes, that *was* his mouth. A relative, perhaps? Fantastic, he thought. And then he remembered that incoherent jumble of Kit's —". . . *Peabody meaning what it did to Spook* . . ." Still fantastic. If Peabody had become a select school in the twentieth century, in the nineteenth it had excluded all but the purest blood. Towns and streets had been named after the men who sent their sons there. Entire pages of the old leather-bound class albums were familiar to Ham — they read like the index of *Through Darkest Birmingham.* It was inconceivable that the son of a Mechanics Street seamstress could have had the remotest connection with an eminent member of the class of 1860. Besides, in those days Brahmins married Brahmins — always. Ham had been through all the social registers. There were no Duschenes there.

Curiously, however, there had been no Bagbys in *Through Darkest Birmingham,* either. Elite families never faded away. Yet this one seemed to have dropped out of sight. Where had it gone?

He strolled over to the elegant crank-operated windows and looked down on the ancient Peabody lawn. It was a busy time; classes were changing. Boys in topcoats and zipper jackets were crossing the walks between graystone buildings, stepping carelessly on the flat bronze plaques which had been inserted in the concrete to commemorate distinguished alumni. In the chapel steeple a discreet chime tinkled twice. The campus cleared, and Ham turned decisively the jutting, worn bindings of the *Alumni Directory* and *They Wore Green.*

No Duschenes, now or then. He was vindicated there.

But Bagbys —

There had been three Bagbys. All the entries were terse, and each was briefer than the last, but Ham, accustomed to Blue Books and thumbnail biographies, saw at a glance the story of achievement — and its dismal sequel.

Bagby, Isaac Lewis had been a great deal more than a war hero. He had also been a financier of remarkable skill. After Appomattox he had married a Henderson, one of the most baronial of state names, and in the next decade he had founded the Columbia Refining Company and Eagle Conduit, Inc., both of which were absorbed by Standard Oil in the 1880's. Apparently Bagby's price for getting out had been enormous. He had built a majestic estate on Hag's Hill outside Birmingham — the address was the giveaway; it had been split up and zoned commercial after World War I, but Ham knew something of its history — and had displayed his wealth in the countless little ways admired by dynasts of his generation. He had joined all the proper clubs: one, nautical and famous, suggested that he had owned a leviathan of a yacht. He had established offices in London and Paris and belonged to the New York Stock Exchange. In his last years he had become a major endower of his college, and he had made certain that his son would have all of what were then called the advantages.

Bagby, Lewis Henderson, must have been a sharp disappointment to him. Lewis was his only child. Apart from his graduation from Peabody in 1891 and a marriage to one of the respectable Sloanes, the boy did nothing to enhance the Bagby fortunes. Lewis in fact became a princely wastrel. By the time of his father's death in the first summer of the century he was sledding downhill, and after it he went right over the cliff. Once more cryptic addresses and dates revealed the cycle, the chief date being 1907, the year of the panic. Until then Lewis had been cutting his losses, closing the Paris office and (the boating club was omitted) selling the yacht. By 1908 it was evident that a cyclone had struck. The Bagby name had vanished from London, Lewis had resigned from the Stock Exchange, the other cherished club memberships had been forsaken, and all that was left was the Hag's Hill estate and — because Lewis had inherited Isaac's thin luck in bed — a single heir.

The entry for Bagby, Sloane Henderson was almost curt. He had been graduated in 1917. Instantly he had gone into seclusion — a polite term, in such sketches, for commitment to an institution. Breakdowns are always awkward for the writers of biographical abstracts, but this one was hideous. Young Sloane had withdrawn into his eyrie just six weeks after America declared war on Germany, and he had returned from it the month after the armistice. The implication — almost the only possible interpretation — was that his retreat had been from military service.

There were two other notations under Sloane's name, and they transfixed Ham.

The first reported that on April 1, 1921, he had married Thérèse Irene Duschene in Rockton.

The second recorded his death in Rockton on December 16, 1924. *December 16, 1924 . . .*

Ham felt giddy. Two men had died in Rockton that day — Shoes Lazzano and the well-dressed young man who shot Shoes and then himself. The well-dressed young *unidentified* man, he remembered, quietly closing the book. Unidentified by police, maybe. And by a stricken wife who wanted only to forget. And by a bankrupt father who decided his son's body would be less embarrassing in an unmarked grave. But not unidentified really. Sloane Bagby hadn't been a missing person. His death had been neatly entered in the Peabody archives. Maybe people hadn't talked about it, but a lot of them had known. Ham drummed his fingers on the green binding, remembering how Nails Whipple had hung back from discussing the Hi-Di-Hi crime. If the story had reached the anonymous author of this sketch, it would have filtered through the office of the college dean. And the dean might have heard unpublishable details — such as the history of the widow Bagby, née Duschene, and child.

He hesitated. It was absurd. But life was often absurd; he had seen lives joined by more grotesque coincidences. And the old nagging need to know was gnawing at him. He strode down the hall.

Whipple was in his study, correcting galley proofs. He carelessly waved Ham to a chair and then looked at him sharply.

"What's wrong?"

"You knew about Sloane Bagby."

The old man sat still. "I never should have admitted you to the Memorial Room."

"Why wasn't his name in Doc's folder?"

Whipple seemed to be looking through him. "Do you really think we would mention a thing like that in a memorandum?"

"It's in his obituary."

"Only the date. A date has no meaning."

"This one has plenty."

Whipple pivoted in his chair and deliberately picked up a proof.

Staring glassily at the long column of print he said, "I'm sorry, Mr. Markham. I can't discuss this matter."

"Even now?" Ham cried, exasperated. "It was thirty-five years ago!"

"Not for me." He was crouching over the galley, as though absorbed in it. "You see, Sloane was my first undergraduate protégé. I knew him very well."

"And did you know his wife?"

Whipple paused momentarily. "Poor creature," he murmured absently. Then, vehemently: "No, I never met her. And I really cannot tell you more."

"They may have had a son."

"No more, no more."

No more: he was through. Like Harry Mikel he had given his loyalty to an institution. The old scandal threatened it; the memory of the crime twisted his heart; time had healed nothing. And Ham understood. He himself was caught up in the dark events of other times, driven by the memory of an attachment cut short fifteen years before. In friendship he had given a part of his being, and he had to redeem it. He had to know what Spook's obsession had been, because it had lain between them, and had been shared, and he had a claim.

So the past touches us all.

And not with a dead hand either.

But he couldn't learn from Whipple. The old man had switched him out like a light. And Ham couldn't press him anyhow; he didn't have enough facts. He knew that Isaac Bagby had been a giant of a man, a hero, a titan. He knew Isaac's son Lewis had dissipated his fortune and fathered a degenerate who died squalidly some three years after marrying a girl named Duschene. What was that? Nothing. There were thousands of people named Duschene, and Ham didn't even remember Spook's mother's first name. Coincidence, a very ordinary coincidence, could explain Spook's birth a year after Sloane's marriage. The fancied resemblance between Isaac's features and Spook's was of course ludicrous, a parody of evidence. Ham was an expert investigator. If a stranger had approached him with that kind of proof he would have dismissed him with a word.

Because Ham was expert, however, he could check out his hunch. There were, for example, a dozen ways of finding out whether Sloane, following the Bagby tradition, had fathered an infant boy before his lapse into inversion. There were people and there were records. People weren't as reliable, and in this case they were few. According to *They Wore Green* Lewis Bagby had died in 1925. Relatives had never visited the Duschenes on Mechanics Street, and Spook, with characteristic reticence, hadn't mentioned a family. Still, there was one matchless witness. Spook's mother could clear up everything, and she wouldn't lie to Ham. He remembered Mrs. Duschene as slight, rather mousy, with a tender smile and a voice that admonished without scolding — an uncomplicated woman devoted to her only child. He hadn't seen her since before the war; hadn't, in fact, revisited the old neighborhood at all. He had grown away from it, and after his own mother's funeral there had been nothing there for Ham. It had become a dead space in his life, a flaw in the sound track of memory. Now that there was to be something there again he felt an undefinable sense of anticipation. If he had given a part of himself to Spook, he had given another part to the slum. Ham was a child of the Depression. And Mechanics Street was a mean, unswept Depression street.

He drove to Birmingham that morning. Caulkin had the backlog of statistical stories and wouldn't bother him for a week. The *Star* was caught up in the campaign anyway. Doc and Witty were entering the last lap now. Every day the headlines grew taller and fatter, and in each edition Ham's series was buried deeper in the second section. The excitement was contagious. Birmingham had an embattled look. Political billboards thickened on either side as Ham entered the capital; downtown he almost expected barricades. Then, at the corner of Carlisle and Mechanics Streets, he passed into limbo. The transition was startling. One moment you were in the shopping center, with smartly dressed women darting from store to busy store; the next moment you reached the traffic light, turned right, and entered the world of weary tenements and littered gutters and lone, hopeless figures trudging slowly from nowhere to nowhere.

The street had shrunk, as boyhood streets do. He passed his old home at 2507 before he realized which block he was in, and 2916, Spook's place, seemed a miniature of itself. Mechanics Street was one-way now — red signs warned of impounding — so he parked in an alley and walked back. Mrs. Duschene had lived in the third house above the alley, in the second floor rear. She didn't now. Ham knew that even before the squat, crabby young woman there told him; ascending the stairs he had missed the familiar baking odors, the hum of the Singer motor. No, the crabby woman snapped, she couldn't tell him a thing. She had lived here five years herself, and the last tenant had been a man — an AT truck driver. Maybe he could try Mrs. Raschi, upstairs; she'd lived here all her life. Ham was doubtful. He didn't recall Mrs. Raschi until he saw her, and then he remembered her as one of those vague, nondescript women who shuffle around in the background of every neighborhood, silent and unnoticed. But she had been there, all right. And she had kept her beady eyes open. Poor Mrs. Duschene, she moaned, wagging her head. Such a hard-working woman. Always had a nice word. And now —

Seven or eight years ago, Mrs. Raschi couldn't remember the exact date, Mrs. Duschene had been found by a neighbor, wandering toward the river and weeping to break your heart. The poor thing. Such a nice woman. Always had a good word. It just went to show. They had to put her away in Belton.

Belton was a state mental hospital two miles north of Birmingham — forbidding sandstone walls, barred windows, fecal smells. Ham found Spook's mother in a massive building crowded with senile women. The attendants were astonished; he was the first visitor she had ever had. Ham asked for her full name. They looked uncomfortable. No one knew; she had become a cipher to them. Finally one, young and obliging, volunteered to look in her dossier. He returned with dusty hands and the dreaded corroboration.

No. 32-21-47. Female. Thérèse Irene Duschene.

They brought her to him in a plain bare room with long wooden benches and walls of institutional buff, and despite that setting, despite her shapeless gray smock, he recognized her immediately. She was nearly sixty. Her cheeks were puffy. She had a strange, crestfallen air. Yet her hair hadn't turned; her smile was still gentle; and she was sewing, her quick fingers flicking over a bunch of cloth.

But the cloth was nothing. It was all sewn together. And her eyes were vacant. She didn't know Ham.

Patiently he tried to lead her back into her past. She seemed to have decided that he was a doctor, and she was trying to be helpful, yet none of his keys fitted the lock. No, she couldn't remember whether her father-in-law's name had been Lewis. She couldn't even confirm her own. Hag's Hill? Not a stir. Sloane Bagby? He thought he saw a quiver deep in her pupils, though couldn't be sure. Spook? She sewed a little faster, but her face didn't change. Everything seemed to have been swept under the shroud she had cast over her pre-institution life, and he was about to quit when he decided to try a final, wild shot.

"Mrs. Duschene, do you remember Shoes Lazzano?"

"Oh!"

She had driven the needle through her frail hand.

Ham hung back guiltily as the attendant led her, weeping, back into the ward. So now he knew. Jealousy had outlasted love. Somehow Shoes had reached her in a way no one else could. Her husband hadn't loved her; her son had been remote; but a man she had never met had struck cruelly at her womanliness, and she had never forgiven him, or forgotten him, or allowed the scar to heal.

Anyhow he knew. Or almost knew, he thought, driving back to the city. Records and routine checks would confirm the rest.

They did. And they did more. In tracing them he fell into the snare that awaits all researchers. He found the unexpected, the unwanted premium, the thorn that so often lies concealed beneath the bud, the barb on the hook, the hidden, crucifying nail. The white hunter falls into his own elephant pit; the sleuth handcuffs himself; the searcher finds more than he has sought. And once he finds it he cannot get rid of it. Because it sticks to him. Like Duco.

Ham had wanted to know. And in anguish he learned.

**

That night he slept in the judge's spare room, and next morning he was in Birmingham's city hall, riffling through old street directories. There wasn't much there. By 1920 the redevelopment of Hag's Hill had begun; only the manor house was left, occupied by Lewis and Sloane Bagby. Sloane was omitted from the 1921 listing. Apparently he hadn't brought his wife home after the wedding. Nor had she gone to her father-in-law after her husband's death — Lewis had lived alone on the hill until his death the following year. Poring over Birmingham marriage records would be pointless; the wedding hadn't been here. Ham's best bet was Spook's birth certificate. It should have been easy to find. He knew Spook's given name, George, and remembered his birthday, May 30 — Memorial

Day. But no George Bagby had been born in Birmingham on Memorial Day, 1922. There were no Bagbys at all that day. No Duschenes. Not even a George.

On impulse Ham called Gideon. The Statette in the Registrar's Office knew his name and was suspicious. Then he mentioned Jill and she thawed. Sure, she could look it up. Nothing easier. Half a mo.

"George E. Duschene '44," she read. "He never graduated."

"You don't have a birth certificate, do you? One of those copies?"

"Only this card, Mr. Markham. Gives his birthday, though — May 30, 1922."

"Thanks," he said dully.

"In Rockton."

"*Where?*"

"*You* know." She spelled it.

Of course, he thought, replacing the receiver. How blind could you be? Just because he remembered Spook as a child on Mechanics Street, he had assumed that he had been born here, when all the signs had pointed the other way. Sloane Bagby's wedding had been in Rockton. He had died beside a roadhouse just outside the city. Obviously the years between had been spent there — and obviously Mrs. Sloane Bagby had moved to Birmingham to escape everything that reminded her of them. But she hadn't gone near Hag's Hill. Ham admired her for that. No Lewis for her — or, more important, for her son. Lewis had ruined one boy. She wasn't giving him a crack at this one.

By early afternoon Ham was in Rockton. Everything was there, neatly filed and indexed. First the city hall marriage: Sloane Henderson Bagby to Thérèse Irene Duschene, 4/1/21. Then the clinching birth certificate: the birth of their son George in Rockton Memorial Hospital, 5/30/22. After that came voters' cards, commercial permits — Sloane had managed something called the Zenith Appliance Shop — and real estate records. The mortgage for their house on Rockton's Oak Street had been heavy; either Lewis Bagby had been down to his last securities or he had been boycotting the marriage. Ham wondered whether he had even attended the ceremony. He hadn't been among the witnesses. *Leader* files would tell. In a city the size of Rockton every marriage was an event. The story would also give a few details about Thérèse's early life, and Ham descended again into the grimy basement of the Rockton Public Library, turned on the bare overhead bulb, and opened the April, 1921 volume on the cement floor.

Bagby-Duschene Rites; Groom From Birmingham

The bride had been from Rockton — "a native of our Fireside City," the society editor had written, "educated at St. Sebastian's parochial school and the winner of many awards for her outstanding embroidery exhibits at the annual Franco-American Festival." In other words a mildly famous local Canuck. And future seamstress.

Lewis wasn't mentioned. Obviously the girl's background had appalled him. Probably he had shut himself up in his mansion and consigned his weak son to hell — where, in less than four years, Sloane had gone. But Lewis couldn't have stayed out of the picture entirely, Ham thought. Not in the last month of 1924 he couldn't. He must have reacted to his son's death with incredible speed. That was the only possible explanation for the most remarkable aspect of the short and shameful life of Sloane Bagby. Sloane had married a Rockton girl in Rockton's city hall, paid Rockton taxes, voted in Rockton elections, and managed a Rockton store. Yet Rockton police hadn't recognized his body. Rockton's newspaper had treated him as an anonymous stranger. The explanation, of course, was that his identity would have been highly inconvenient. To whom? To his wife? As though she cared that night — as though a young mother, distinguished only for her skillful embroidery, would have enough influence to smother the truth. To Peabody College? Obviously it had been jarred, Whipple still flinched from the disgrace. But even if colleges worked that way, they aren't kin and aren't notified that quickly. The smotherer had to have been Lewis. He would have had the pull. And that year, when he was busy with the delicate liquidation of his last Hag's Hill assets, he had the motive. The news of Sloane's suicide would have smashed the already cracking Bagby prestige. So Lewis had moved — to make the big fix.

Ham could picture the chaotic exchange of long-distance calls in the dark. Thérèse, hysterical, calling the father-in-law she scarcely knew. Lewis cutting her off. Lewis swiftly giving the operator the key numbers, ringing this politician, that mortician, calling the publisher of the *Leader* or a mutual friend if they weren't that close.

Ham had seen big wheels at work. He knew how it was done. No bribes were mentioned, but the wheel's voice assumed a certain mellowness when he mentioned undertaker's fees or campaign contributions, as he somehow managed to do. Money, of course, would have had nothing to do with bringing the *Leader* into line. There the play would have been straight class loyalty — the same sticky rally-round loyalty which later led to the mutilation of the *Star*'s microfilmed issue of that same date. Lewis might have been unpopular. He might have been poison to the rest of the Clipper Club. But when he ran up the Bagby flag everybody else with a respectable name to protect gave it a stiff, snappy salute.

One blank remained to be filled in. Ham checked Main 6-6119 and acquired the home address of Peter N. Healy.

Healy had just finished dressing. His red wrinkled face was still damp from his ablutions, and he had been sitting in his tidy little apartment a few blocks from the *Leader* building, reading the paper with the deliberate ritual of the old reporter and puffing on his first pipe of the day. When he saw Ham on the landing his mice eyes glittered with pleasure.

"Well, Mr. Markham, now this *is* glorious! Come right in and have some tea and tell a shut-in old man of your adventures hither and yon!"

"Hi-Di-Hi," Ham said. "I'm on the same adventure."

He perched on a rocker and accepted a cup embellished with a red floral design. The room was as he would have imagined it: ugly magenta wallpaper decorated with ornately framed pictures of Healy relatives and shelves of religious statues.

Healy leaned back in a Morris chair which might have been Ham's father's and smiled wistfully. "Ah, you grand fellows. Weeks on one story, and never a complaint from your office. How fine it must be to be a big-leaguer." He sipped and smacked his lips. "Now in my day it was four or five columns a night, one word after the other, as fast as I could punch them out."

"Maybe that's why you made mistakes."

"Aw!" He looked hurt. "I told you, it was your very own paper held back that license number from me."

"And who held back Sloane Bagby's name?"

The black eyes shifted twice. "Now who on earth could *he* have been?"

"He was that dead boy, Pete."

"The lad in the parking lot?"

"You remember. With his clothes so grand and his head so bloody."

Healy was examining the dregs of his cup. "You're a deep one, you are."

"Deeply interested, that's all. That boy's son was my college roommate."

"Ah?" The wizened brow arched. "So that's how you found out?" At the moment Ham didn't understand. He was watching the old Irishman's eyes. They darted from corner to corner, and Healy murmured, "Now isn't it remarkable how things turn out?"

"Sad, sad — the corruption and the sin."

"You mustn't mock me, now. I'm infirm."

"The mockery was of the facts."

"Aye, and you want them now. It's the vice of our profession, laddie. We're all sons of Lot's wife."

Ham sympathized with him. After all, Healy hadn't been a wheel himself; only a cog. "You were ordered to cut it out, weren't you?"

The eyes jumped around again, from photographs of Healys to replicas of the Virgin. "You're asking me off the record?"

"I won't write a word."

"Because the paper's still the only job I have."

"I told you. This is personal."

"Well, then — you got it right as rain. His name was Bagby, but I was told to give him no name at all. The desk said they'd chop it anyway. And I would've been fired."

"What about the police report?"

"No name there, either. More orders, I never knew from where. The chief would never talk about it, and I was in no position to ask, being nothing but a minion myself. The body was Bagby's, though — many and many's the time I'd watched him swish along the street with that pansy walk. Sloane Bagby, you're right. But he went into the cold, cruel ground as John Doe, and it's John Doe he's been ever since."

"There was a Mrs. Doe," Ham said softly.

"I know. Oh, I know," Healy sighed tremulously. "I went around to their house that very night, before the desk told me to lay off, you know, and there was the missus with a frowning sergeant standing by her like a guard, and the little tyke in her lap, and her bawling into the telephone — one of those old upright phones, with the cord all dangling. She wasn't fit to talk to me at all. I went off and that was the last I saw of the pitiful thing, the end of the whole benighted business." He crossed himself solemnly. "Till the boy came back, of course."

"The boy," Ham repeated uncomprehendingly.

"Your friend. Your college pal."

Until then Ham's trek through the paper jungle of documents and newspaper files had been a straight path, leading directly from here to there. Suddenly the trail had swerved. Dead ahead lay footprints — the tracks of a loner, tracks Ham knew.

"You mean Spook?" he asked, bewildered.

Healy, equally bewildered, shook his head. "No, young Bagby. Sloane's lad."

Ham's cup was rattling in his saucer. "Spook — George Duschene — it's the same."

"Duschene! That's the name he went by! From his mother, don't you know."

"He returned *here*?"

"Aye, like an avenging angel, and — " Healy looked suspicious. "Now weren't you telling me what a great friend he was of yours?"

"He was," Ham said, steadying the cup.

"And he never told you this?"

"No," Ham said slowly. "Never."

"Then how did you find out?"

"I found out," was all Ham could say.

Healy sucked in his cheeks. "You say he *was* your friend. How do I know this won't be used to hurt him now?"

It took a moment to put the words together. "Because there isn't any more of him to hurt. He was killed in the war."

"Ah!" said Healy, in one long breath.

"He was the last of his family."

"Hard, hard, terrible hard." Healy reflected. "Still, he died better than his father."

No argument there, Ham thought. Better than his grandfather, too, if it came to that. The only Bagby worthy of Spook had been that other soldier, that mighty defender of the Union, his great-grandfather.

"Killed in battle, was he?" Kealy asked curiously.

"A big battle."

"Not in a parachute jump?"

"No, around Bastogne."

"Because when he left here he looked like he didn't care how he hit the ground."

Ham stirred. "How did you know he was a paratrooper?"

"Why, he was in uniform! Tight-laced boots and little curly wings on his shirt. I followed the war, I could tell the boys apart," Healy said proudly.

"And when was this?" Ham asked quickly.

"Hard to say." Healy plucked at an ear. "It was the spring things were so bad around Cassino."

Sure, Ham thought; it had to have been then, that April when Spook came home for his only furlough. From letters Ham knew that he had spent some of it with his mother in Birmingham and some in Gideon; it was in Gideon that he had taken Kit to the College Inne. How strange, Ham thought fleetingly, that no spark of that jealousy, not a degree of that fever, remained in him. What was it Kit had said after the war when Ham had blazed out at her? *He needed me so*, and *He was on leave and hurt.* Hurt where? Not in combat; he hadn't been overseas yet. At the time Ham had been too angry for details, but now he saw a light. Spook had also been in Rockton that month. He could have been hurt here.

And even as Ham speculated, groping for bits and shreds, Healy was pasting them together.

"The reason I remember Cassino is, the chief had a boy over there. That was the reason he gave for letting young Bagby go. Said he couldn't bear to hold a soldier in a cell. Of course, us old-timers knew the real reason. The Police Department wasn't about to let that case be dusted off."

So Spook, like Doc, had been locked up by Rockton police. But why?

"The crime was serious. If the court had known, his bail would have been pegged at a grand. The chief was smart, though. He just locked him up as disorderly and let him go in the morning."

"But what was the offense?"

"Why, breaking sealed records!"

Ham's cup was rattling again. He had to put it on the floor. "The records of his father's case?"

"The very same! Somehow he had a hint of how his poor Dad had died, and he came to the courthouse to get the real story. If he'd asked for stuff on Sloane Bagby he'd have been sent away, because naturally there was no book under that name. Young Bagby had Shoes Lazzano's name, though. Just the name, mind you. He didn't know who Lazzano had been, or what him and his Dad had been doing together, though he did know the two of them had gone to their Maker together. Well, he got next to a young clerk and asked him could he see the Lazzano file. The clerk said sorry. He wanted to help, but couldn't do a thing, on account of the key witness in the case had been a technical juvenile."

"The truck driver," Ham said stonily.

"Say, that's right! Anyway, this clerk and young Bagby got to be great friends in an hour or so. Seemed natural enough. The courthouse is a slow place, this soldier had time on his hands, and they idled away the wearisome hours with contagious young laughter. You know how it is."

Ham knew. He knew.

"Well, all the time young Bagby's just buttering the clerk up. Getting the grand tour. Finding out what's kept where — especially where the sealed records are. Once he knows that he's as good as in free, because there's no lock on the records. The judge says they're not for the public, and that's it. At least, it always had been, till this lad in the tight-laced boots came along."

"So he went into the file," Ham almost whispered.

"He did exactly that. The clerk pops out to the lavatory, and when he pops back, there's the papers all over the floor. The whole kit and caboodle. Everything. Sloane Bagby's name's not actually there, of course, but the boy already knows his Dad died with Shoes, and there's the official dirt — the plain cold statement that they were perverts. And that his father did Shoes in and then blew his own brains out. Glory be! He's seen it all!"

"Including the driver's name." Ham was really whispering now.

"What? Yes, of course. Well, such a whoopin' and a hollerin' you never heard. If the chief magistrate hadn't been home with shingles he'd have heard it sure — *I* was out on the street, and *I* did. We all ran in and found the clerk yelling bloody murder, and there was tight-laced-boots sitting in a kind of trance, with documents every which ways. The chief grabbed him by the scruff of the neck, but young Bagby didn't move. He was dead weight. Limp as a rag. So the chief reached into his shirt and yanked out his dogtags for the docket. I told you that chief was smart. As soon as he saw the widow's maiden name he got the whole picture."

No, Ham thought numbly. Not the whole picture.

"Thanks for the tea," he said, blundering out.

"Now don't run off!"

But Ham had already left the Healy museum of family images and plaster saints and was headed for the courthouse.

Dockets were public, no charge. There was nothing in them Ham didn't know, but with the craftsman's urge to tighten all knots he checked the two obscure entries. In round police calligraphy they looked so very ordinary. The first read, "12-16-24 / Adam River / male / 19 / no certain address / driver / held for investigation." And the second, twenty volumes later: "4-17-44 / George E. Duschene / male / 21 / AUS / Cpl. / disorderly conduct." Showing how inaccurate records can be, Ham thought, pulling slowly away from the curb. Doc and Spook had been jailed on trivial, meaningless charges, when in fact each had reached the crisis of his youth here. In some ways they had been alike, restless young men trying to give form to their lives. But they hadn't left here alike. Doc's arrest had strengthened him. He had departed from this dingy mill town a confirmed social outlaw. After his expulsion from Peabody he was through pandering to the elite, ready to fight the rest of his life on the class lines they had drawn for him. While Spook —

Ham couldn't be sure about Spook. Not yet. He had to see Kit first, and maybe Doc. One thing was certain, though. Spook's discharge from Rockton Jail had been very different from Doc's. The truth about his father must have smashed the core of him. Ham thought of his own father, almost with tenderness. He had been an impostor, but a harmless impostor; if he had lied about himself, he had still dreamt the right dreams. Undeniably he had been weak. And Ham had turned away from the memory of that weakness and leaned on Doc. Yet how much harder he would have leaned, how much more desperate he would have been if he had learned that his father had been a Sloane Bagby . . .

And if he had then discovered that Doc had been a witness to that shame . . .

Oh God, he thought. *Oh God.*

**

Kit heard him out in silence. She sat stiffly erect in the tall wing-back chair beneath her sitting-room mirror, her sleek ankles neatly crossed and her hands folded quietly in her lap. She was in her most somber dress. A single shaft of autumnal sunlight winked on only two points of light, her wedding ring and her crucifix. At a glance she seemed serene: her face was a wan oval, and she was so very still. But her mouth was twisted.

He finished, and she clasped her hands, a slight sign of the anguish within.

She began with unexpected severity. "I suppose you feel sorry for his mother."

Ham nodded. "Among others."

"Women destroyed Spook," she said harshly.

"Sloane was a man. A male, anyway."

"Spook's mother did it," she insisted. "And I helped."

He waited.

"In fact, I started it."

Still he waited.

"You know what I was like in those days — a sweet face and a foul mouth. That was the thing about me then, I swore like a trooper. I thought it was so — so provocative."

And it was, he remembered. But he said nothing. He was waiting.

She took a deep breath.

"Spook spent the first day of his leave here. He was looking for somebody to talk to, someone he'd known. Mikel was away, Doc was off on a war bond tour, so he took me out. He told me I was last choice with that sarcastic smirk he had, and I was miffed. He'd always miffed me, the way he'd avoided girls. I told him so, and I called him a dirty bastard." She repeated it slowly, painfully: "A dirty bastard. I could see it hurt. I thought it was because he didn't like to hear a girl talk like that, and I was bitchy enough to twist the blade. I asked him was he afraid it was true. The horrible part is that he was. Always had been. Oh, he didn't tell me then. He just leered right back at me. But later in the week, when it all came out, he blurted out that I'd triggered things."

"Look, Kit, you're cutting yourself a big, greedy slice of blame. Slow down. Spook was always ridden."

"Never mind." It was coming in a torrent now. "He hitchhiked to Birmingham that same night and confronted his mother. Asked her why she hadn't any of his father's things. Wanted to know what his father had been, what he'd looked like. She acted like he wasn't even there. It was the same act she'd always pulled whenever he asked about his family, and it drove him crazy. She was caught in her own trap. She'd burned everything with the Bagby name on it — had even had her name and Spook's changed legally. Her only thought had been to shield Spook from what his father had been. What could she tell him?"

"Nothing."

But he thought of the little apartment at 2916 Mechanics Street, he pictured mother and son facing across the Singer machine, and he knew it wasn't that simple.

It was to Kit. She nodded grimly.

"She *should* have said nothing. His happiness depended on her keeping quiet. No matter how rough he got, she should have turned away."

"He could be pretty rough."

"Spook taunted her. He told me afterward it all came out of him at once — all the resentment from years of wondering and doubt. He asked her if she really knew who his father was. How many men there had been. How big a choice he had. Sizes and shapes of fathers. Religions. Races. Colors. If they'd been big spenders. What they'd smelt like. On and on. Till she cracked."

Ham thought of the second floor rear apartment, the blind rage, the cruelty, the things people do to those they love; he remembered the ruined old woman in the senile ward, and he knew Kit had it wrong. She was giving it to him as Spook had given it to her, flatly, lines without music, without the savage lyrical torment that must have been there to tear Spook's mother apart.

"She thought she was telling him just a little. She said his father was a member of a fine old family and had gone to Peabody. A lot of the rest she made up — that there had been an accident in Rockton, that she'd never talked about it because of the shock. But you can't fool around with something like that. You can't control it. And she made one big blunder. She couldn't hold back the other man's name."

"Shoes Lazzano," Ham said. And he remembered the convulsive jab of the needle, the cry of pain, the bright oozing bead of blood.

"She spat it out. It was all Spook needed. He found out the rest himself and came back here. Doc was home from his tour, and Spook went right to him, in the old gym. He had the goofy idea Doc had known who he really was all along. Doc hadn't, of course; hadn't had any way of knowing. But he knew after Spook told him. I don't know what Doc said. The first I heard about it was when one of the new girls in the house came fluttering in after lunch and yelped that there was a drunk soldier outside asking for me. It was Spook. He wasn't drunk, he was hysterical. We walked off in the fields, and I was trying to calm him down, and he choked it out a little at a time, in sobs and gasps. He kept saying he wasn't a bastard, he was worse."

Kit was kneading her knuckles.

"He thought he was like his father," she hissed.

Ham waited again.

"'You were right, I don't like girls,' he said over and over. 'I wouldn't be good, I don't have it.'"

Her knuckles were ridged, her lips pulled dryly at one another. She needed help.

"So you took him to the College Inne," Ham said gently.

She nodded tensely.

He wanted only to help her. "I think it was brave, Kit. And kind."

"It wasn't, it was cruel!" she cried.

Her fist flew to her mouth; her own voice had startled her. She said stridently, "Don't you see? He was — too upset. He couldn't — couldn't *do* anything."

Her face flamed crimson. It had been the most terrible afternoon of her life, and this was the first time she had told anyone. She finished in a mortified whisper, "It convinced him, absolutely convinced him he was right!"

There was nothing to say. How wise we pretended to be then, Ham thought, and how little we knew. He thought of all the bad collegiate jokes about sex and the desperation that lay beneath that flippancy. Doubtless Kit had been as terrified as Spook, as inhibited, and, in the end, as repelled. It had been pathetic, and in a way that had nothing to do with virtue it had also been wrong. Yet Ham still thought it brave of her. She had gone to the Inne with a boy she didn't love, as a ministration. She had risked being seen and had been seen, by the same fluttering sorority sister who had thought Spook drunk, and who had taken Ham aside the following year, when he returned to Gideon, and whispered all. Kit had lost much and gained nothing, and now in maturity she knew it. It had been a bad gamble. But somehow it deserved respect.

She rose with a quick, cramped movement. "That was all," she said under her breath. "I heard later he said good-by to Doc that night and left."

They moved slowly toward the door, stiff with strain. On the steps Kit made a rueful attempt to be bright. She stroked her hair and said lightly, "There weren't any skeletons in the Markham closet, were there?"

He shook his head. "No heroes, no merchant princes, no black sheep. Just stolid dirt farmers, one after the other — four pages of the family Bible."

She touched his hand. "I'm glad you had a family Bible, Ham."

"Sure," he said. "So am I." And he hurried off, wondering what had become of it.

**

Ham didn't feel equal to Doc now. He postponed his plan to visit the Mansion and in a fit of nervous energy wrote five *Star* articles painting nineteenth century Peabody student life against a backdrop of American social history. Caulkin was enthusiastic; despite of the campaign clamor the series was moved into the first section, and a small box on page one announced that the paper would publish it later in book form. Ham was secretly pleased, Peabody was elated. The campus had come to accept him as a kind of resident writer. In the faculty club he was treated as an honorary member; Ed Hardy, the retired coach, insisted he drive out for another evening of old State-Peabody films, and other, more stimulating evenings followed in the homes of younger professors. By the end of the week he had about decided not to see Doc at all.

And then Doc called on him.

Ham was in his Inne room, pecking out a letter to India. He scarcely looked up when Mrs. Prouty rapped on the door.

"Doc River's here!" she called excitedly. "He wants to see you!"

It seemed improbable. Doc had never been in the Inne in his life. Yet there he was, heaving up the stairs and waving two stiff fingers in greeting.

"Don't let me butt in," he said, tilting back his old hat. "I'm just passing by."

Ham closed the door. "I hope you weren't seen entering."

Doc's dimples were merry. "Why?"

"It's worth the election. Places like this are out-of-bounds for men with reputations."

"Oh, I never hold with that guff." He pounced on the bed; the springs shrieked. "Say, this bunk's a one-man-band, though. Why don't you move over to the Gideon Arms?"

"Witty owns it."

That pleased him. He shed his topcoat and chuckled. "You know I never knew that? Every day I learn something new. Maybe next week I'll learn I was happier ignorant."

Next week — a week from tomorrow — was the election. He didn't appear worried. His face was ruddy, his eyes glowed. He was enjoying the fight, and he was beginning to win rounds. The latest Smathers poll had him almost deadlocked with Witty. He looked hard to beat and obviously felt unbeatable.

Ham sat by his typewriter and fingered the space bar, wondering why he had come here. "Newt keeping you busy?"

"Busy's not the word, boy. I guess there just isn't a word for my life this month. It's talk, talk, talk. And then run, run, run. Why I'm only in town for three hours now — and I'm playing hooky at that. A man's got to get a little fresh air *some*times."

Fresh air my foot, Ham thought. This was business. He could feel it coming.

Doc looked around at flaking Venetian blinds, the stained reproduction on the wall. He adjusted his little glasses and said idly, "I talked with Kit Ryan a little bit yesterday."

Ham was wondering whether Kit had mentioned Spook — wondering how she could possibly have managed the details — when Doc looked at him sharply.

"Except that her name isn't Ryan any more. It's been O'Donnell for quite a spell."

Ham sighed. That was it, then. "So I heard."

"Seems everybody heard but me. Did you know she was a divorced woman?"

Ham said dryly, "That's not quite the same as a fancy woman."

"Well, no," said Doc, faltering a little, "but it breaks a rule I made."

"Maybe it's a bad rule, Coach."

"Maybe, maybe." He looked uncomfortable. "Sare thinks so, and I'm here to tell you there's been quite a ruckus about it."

The ruckus had been started by Kit herself. She had told Sarah the story of the meeting with Miss Shoemaker and Tate, and Sarah had moved with almost hysterical urgency. Her protective instincts were aroused. She was determined Kit shouldn't be harmed. In a flurry of activity she had brushed her coat, donned it, darted past the cook again, and swept down on the office of the dean and the provost. She insisted that the issue of Kit's divorce be faced immediately and announced that she was behind her. Doc, returning to Gideon, was met by an overwrought wife. She was demanding, literally demanding, that he support her and investigate the conduct of a Mrs. Daphne Dix.

Doc hadn't time for an investigation. He conferred hurriedly on the phone with Tate and agreed with his glib suggestion that they let things ride until after the vote. That didn't satisfy Sarah. She backed down some on the Dix case; she didn't doubt Kit, but the details were beyond anything in her limited experience, and she felt on slippery ground. About Kit herself she was quite clear, however. She wanted a decision, and now. Ordinarily Doc wouldn't have hesitated. He was firm about university regulations, and this one had political implications. Yet he couldn't refuse Sarah. He sensed that Kit's need was filling a void in his wife's life, that Kit, in her weakness, was giving Sarah something he, in his strength, couldn't match. Sarah's behavior was still erratic, but at least she had found a purpose in life. At least she was taking an interest. The return of the void, the drift, the emptiness in her eyes — the return of that tragic wasting of her spirit was unthinkable.

An hour ago he had called Tate back and declared Kit was an exception to the rule. He would put it in writing tonight.

But that wasn't really what he wanted to see Ham about. The call had brought him to the Inne. But not that part of it.

"I was jawing with my provost a little bit ago. You know, I left word with him that I wanted to know about any requests from *Star* reporters for stuff on State."

"I didn't know."

"Now don't misunderstand. It's just a sort of check. Some of those fellows want the darndest information. You can't imagine, Ham."

"Sure I can. I'm one of them."

"Yes." Doc shifted uneasily. "You are." He examined the white iron bedstead intently. "Fact is, that's why I dropped in. It's kind of silly, I know. Put it down to an old man's whim."

He seemed unable to go on. Ham, waiting once more, depressed his space bar twice.

"I wouldn't have thought twice," Doc said after the pause, "if you hadn't stumbled into that old business at the Hi-Di-Hi. Coming on top of that it did seem a little bit peculiar that you'd call from Birmingham and ask a girl about Spook's birth certificate."

So they were going to talk about Spook after all. Ham tapped the bar until the typewriter carriage reached the margin and stopped. The end, he thought. You can't go anywhere after that. Doc had been the end for Spook. Spook had left him only to recede into the gray blur of the army.

"He was born in Rockton," Ham said.

"That's right," Doc cleared his throat. "It's just that in my view it was a long way to call."

"Rockton," Ham repeated. "The same place his father died."

Dead silence. Doc gripped the mattress with fisted hands. "I told you to let it lay."

"Well, I didn't. I've been through everything, Coach, right down to Spook's arrest and his last night with you."

He looked up quickly. "How did you find out he came back here?"

Ham couldn't implicate Kit. He lied. "I saw his mother in Belton."

"So that's where she is," Doc said, unfeelingly. "I went down and visited her after he was killed. I kind of figured then she was headed for one of those places."

My God, Ham thought, didn't anyone pity the woman? Kit blamed her, Doc was callous; while on the other hand Spook loomed more and more as a tragic figure. They brooded over his death and seemed to share an irrational sense of guilt for it. Ham felt a little that way himself. The reason, he supposed, was that Spook, arrested on the verge of maturity, seemed endlessly promising. His unfinished life was like a projected arc on an imaginary graph, rocketing up and up. Of course, it might have turned out that way. It wasn't likely, but it was just possible, and that possibility, never to be tested, haunted the living, whose own arcs had climbed a little, wavered, and settled slowly into the depressing zigzags of reality. We all start big, Ham thought. We aim so high. And then we learn about gravity.

He remembered Isaac Bagby, the soaring exception.

"Spook didn't have much luck with his father and grandfather," he said, "but his great-grandfather was quite a man."

"I know," Doc said with surprising heat. "He told me."

"He found out from his mother?"

"Yes, and that's where she went wrong. He would have gotten over the fact that his father was a fairy. Sure, he was all stirred up about it. It had been a shock, and finding my name in the case didn't help one bit. He came up here thinking I knew all sorts of things. Started saying how he could never face me again, and on and on. But it would have passed." He hammered his knee. "I *know* it would have, if it hadn't been for that ancestor, that —" He groped.

"Isaac."

"Isaac, that was him. Spook got it fixed in his mind that this Isaac was someone he could hold on to and be proud of. That's all I heard that night. He'd give me that one-sided grin of his and say how his great-grandfather had been a bigger fellow than me, stronger and tougher and in top shape till the day he passed on. He didn't quit when he left here, either. I got a crazy letter from him in France. He was in some camp, waiting to go to the trenches."

The trenches, Ham thought. It was typical of Doc to think that World War II had been fought in trenches. Probably he had called GI's doughboys.

"Crazy in what way?"

"Oh, he was still pounding away at that one fool note. First thing he got home he wanted to change his name back to Bagby. Then he was going to dig out everything he could find on Isaac. Over and over the same note: Isaac, Isaac, Isaac."

Doc stared at the scarred floor. "Well, Isaac finally killed him."

"Look, Coach —"

"You think I'm imagining things?"

"No." Ham was thinking of Spook and Kit in the Inne that long ago April afternoon, perhaps on this very bed. "But when you come right down to it, a bullet killed Spook."

"It was a shell," Doc said flatly. "I know what I'm talking about. It took me six months after the war to track down the captain that wrote Spook's mother, but I found him out in Iowa, and we had a long gabble on the phone. He told me Spook got blown up going where he had no business to be. He'd started taking wild chances the day he came in and joined the outfit. After a while he began talking about leading a charge. He was only a corporal. Everybody thought he was loco. They'd have sent him to the rear if they'd had a rear. Finally they quit paying any attention to him. It didn't make any difference. He went right on. The morning he died — it was Christmas, Ham — he was out in a field of snow in no man's land, shouting to everybody to follow him. The shells came down and he didn't have any place to hide."

"No," Ham said under his breath. "He didn't."

"What?"

"In no man's land, I mean."

Probably Spook had been in front of a road block, out of defilade. No man's land would do, though. No man's land was just right.

Doc was fidgeting. "Don't you see? He was caught."

But not by Isaac, Ham thought.

"The point is, he still had that blamed ancestor in mind."

No. He had you.

Doc ran a finger under his collar. "Anyway, that's the long and short of it," he said unhappily, standing in the narrow space between bed and wall. "I guess you can see now why I can't have that old Hi-Di-Hi fuss brought up in the campaign. It just wouldn't do."

Ham watched him with compassion. Newt Albert had picked a more complex man than he knew. Some things were bigger to Doc than the election. He would rather lose than relive the indecencies of Rockton.

He had picked up his coat and was hesitating. "Maybe it seems a mite queer, me calling all the way out to Iowa just to satisfy my curiosity."

"Not at all." Ham pressed the margin release. "Spook was one of your boys."

"Well, that's right! That's right!" Doc thrust his arms into the topcoat sleeves aggressively.

In that shabby coat and wrinkled hat he looked needy. Ham wished he had something to give him.

"You were, too, Ham!" he was saying, fumbling with buttons. "You and Spook! I told Tom Yablonski once — for all Tom's record-smashing, you two were the best passing team State ever suited up."

Ham did have one thing. Maybe he should offer it now.

"I saw Peabody's movies of the '42 game the other night, Coach."

"Oh?" Doc took off his hat. He stood leaning a little, hat in hand. "They showed that last rainbow?"

Ham smiled wryly. "Not my grandstand catch. It was out of range, I guess. There was a good shot of Spook pitching, though."

Doc grinned. "That hippy dance of his!"

"And there's something else. You can see the line of scrimmage at the snap."

The grin disappeared. He said swiftly, "Don't tell me who jumped!"

He couldn't bear to know. After seventeen years of wondering which lineman had been at fault the prospect of truth was forbidding, even frightening. He clutched his brim and cowered.

"It wasn't anybody," Ham said.

Doc dropped the hat. It careened under the bed and vanished.

"Nobody was offside. We had a bad whistle, Coach."

It still hadn't reached him. "Ham, I know how you feel — I'm sure it looked that way to you —"

"No, it *was* that way. Both lines were hopped up and jittery, but nobody crossed. The ref was just cockeyed. Ed Hardy's known all the time. He told me he's been planning to say something sometime."

"Why didn't he say it then?" Doc cried.

"His alumni would've chased him. Never losing to State was a matter of pride with them — you know that. Hardy did change his records, though."

"So you won the big one after all," Doc said, almost reverently.

Ham said nothing.

"You and Spook."

Still Ham was silent, and Doc scrambled down to recover his hat. He reappeared beaming. "You understand what this means, boy?"

Ham shook his head, for he really didn't.

"It means State took the Percies!" Doc cried. "We had everything against us — no equipment, no real training, no fancy plays to speak of — and we still whipped them fair and square. I don't know when I've heard anything that set me up so much. Why, I feel like a new man."

"You look great," Ham said softly. And he did. He was glowing.

Outside a melodious horn sounded once. Ham stepped to the window and saw an immense Cadillac parked at the Union Street curb. The motor was running: a thin gray vapor whispered nervously from the exhaust pipe.

"Classy," he murmured, raising blind and sash for a better look.

Doc peered down over his shoulder. "Say, that toot was for me. I told Newt to pick me up here. Don't know why we have to ride around in a ritzy hearse, but he seems to think it helps."

He pumped Ham's hand and started down the stairs. On the landing he halted and hurried back. Ham hadn't moved; he looked up inquiringly.

"By Jupiter, do you know what I'm going to do?" Doc said warmly. "I'm going to have the trophy pavilion redesigned. Yes sir! I want a plaque — a bossy, brassy plaque — setting down the fact that on November 7, 1942 State beat Peabody, eighteen to fourteen."

"That sounds fine," Ham said quietly.

"What?"

"It sounds" — his voice caught — "just great."

"Oh." Doc had expected enthusiasm. "Well. Take care of yourself, boy." He started to say more and then whirled and was gone.

He remembered the day and the score, Ham thought, watching him step lightly into the limousine. It had meant that much to him. And now he thought it all resolved because it turned out that seven boys in muddy jerseys had known their place after all. Very easy. So simple. No strain.

Overhead the weather was making up. A livid sky had formed over the gaunt twin towers of St. Mary's Church, and a tang in the air suggested a snow flurry. Ham stood long by the open window, holding the soiled drape aside and feeling a weight grow in his chest. It was big and hard and black, like an anvil. For he remembered that day, too. But he knew the game, like Spook's youth, was frozen in time. Changing records wouldn't alter any of it. Nothing could recover that whistle. No plaque could restore that moment. No pavilion could correct a score, or recover a chance, or bring back a single breath. The past was irrevocable. The lost was lost forever.

FOUR

Live, from Gideon

GEEK MINTON made his deadline, and the November issue of *Sly*, containing his masterpiece, reached dealers the last day of October. Subscribers received their copies that Saturday morning.

The magazine's distribution was highly uneven. Urban circulation was enormous, especially on city newsstands and in novelty shops catering to adolescent boys, but in smaller communities druggists had found that stocking it was unwise. Women were offended, schools threatened boycotts, and policemen, under the prodding of respectable citizens, harassed dealers by insisting that display copies be stapled together or, occasionally, by outright confiscations. *Sly* scarcely existed in towns like Gideon. Subscriptions were available, but very expensive; the mails were closed to the publisher, and his part-time delivery agents fixed their own delivery rates. Outside Birmingham, Dudley, Pawnattuck, and Rockton, the only people in the state who saw the magazine regularly were traveling men, idiosyncratic bachelors, and boys with extravagant allowances and indifferent supervision at home.

A conspicuous exception was William Wallace Whipple, endowed professor of classics at Peabody College.

Whipple's distributor was a husky young Italian with a broken nose and icy blue eyes. Normally he was talkative. On his *Sly* job, however, he never asked questions. Each publication day he set out from Dudley in his father's pickup truck and followed a complicated five-hour route between seedy rural rooming houses and lonely farms, meeting every customer's eyes with the same lazy, expressionless stare. They paid for each issue in advance, but he had learned that if he grinned or winked or even shrugged they would quit him. The only way to keep his list intact was to pretend he hadn't the most remote idea what was in the plain brown paper envelopes he carried.

He dropped off Whipple's new copy shortly after nine o'clock. Entering the library, he was especially circumspect. Of all his customers this one was the strangest. The others were odd enough — pimpled kids, beefy hired men, and one buxom housekeeper with steel-rimmed glasses and steel-gray hair — but they at least received him with a fugitive air. Only Whipple carried out the delicate transaction in an office — and a library office at that — without the slightest sign of embarrassment. Sometimes the old man was actually cheerful. It made the boy's flesh creep. There were queers, he thought, tiptoeing down the hall. And then there were *real* queers.

He laid the envelope on the desk and held out a limp hand.

"That'll be two bucks for December, Mister."

"Mr. Whipple," Whipple said pleasantly.

"Sorry. Keep forgetting."

They held the same conversation every month.

Whipple thrust his lined yellow note pad aside and dealt out the bills. "Cold out?"

"Um," the boy said warily.

"I suppose I'll see you again after Thanksgiving."

"Um," said the boy and strode quickly out past the stacks, to his locked truck and expensive cargo.

Whipple sighed. He hadn't the faintest interest in the boy's opinion of him. Still, he wished they could talk. He would have liked to know more about the route, his fellow clients, the economics of distribution. A colleague at Iowa was investigating that aspect of popular culture, or subculture, as some sociologists in the Chicago Group called it. Whipple supposed he would just have to wait until those findings were verified and published.

He picked up his battered old ruler and slit the brown paper seam. *Sly*'s November cover was either whimsical or sadistic — he couldn't decide which. A naked blonde (all *Sly* cover girls seemed to be blondes, he reflected, making a note) was threatening a frightened turkey with a carving knife and fork. The blade was perilously close to the girl's breasts, which were pallid and ovoid and roughly the size of small watermelons. Whipple eyed them dubiously. No woman could grow such members. It must be a trick of some sort. He had observed similar distortions in the past, and he wished there were someone in the Group who could prepare a technical abstract on the technique. There had been some talk of approaching a journalism professor at Missouri, but nothing had come of it, journalism not being an accepted discipline.

Whipple's attitude toward the magazine was genuinely clinical. At Ham Markham's age, or even Doc's, he would have been aroused by the more imaginative girlie magazines. Not now; long ago he had passed into an inertia of desire. The excitement of the mind was excitement enough for him. He found some women interesting, but they were rarely young. The fatuous expressions of the fleshy models were to him dull, uninviting, and monotonously the same. He read subculture publications for data, not pleasure. He was was trying to test a general hypothesis: that Gresham's law was the most powerful social force in America; that democratic taste was destroying the values of the autocratic past. Unlike Harry Mikel, who agreed vehemently, Whipple was undismayed. The destruction, he insisted, was a phase, a transition. He even delighted in its excesses. The higher the flames leapt, the quicker new foundations could be dug.

Sly was only one of many indications that the fire burned bright. Data forwarded from Iowa had indicated that it was worth investigation, but in Whipple's forthcoming book, *After Henry Adams,* it would occupy no more than a footnote, or a paragraph at most. There was too much else to cover: the deterioration of such newspapers as the *Star*, the growth of digests, the crumbling standards of quality periodicals, and the descent of television, popular music, and paperback originals into chasms of bad taste. It was an enormous undertaking, even with the assistance of able associates, and sometimes he wondered whether he would finish it in his lifetime.

He turned the slick pages rapidly, looking for something new.

There was little. Nearly everything conformed to the stale formula he had observed six months ago. There was the usual sequence of a blonde undressing in a field, followed by two brunettes undressing each other, followed by the cover blonde, completely undressed and prostrate, regarding the camera with the pouting limpid expression of a Narcissus. Presumably the lens was her reflecting fountain, Whipple thought, and made another note. He leafed on. A youth in Jefferson City, Mo. had sent the editor a stark snapshot of his steady, which was reproduced in the correspondence column. Her bosom was forty inches; he had measured it. Whipple scribbled beside the letter, *manifestly a plant*. An article on a particularly vicious gang fight in Spanish Harlem described the invention of the Molotov cocktail. Whipple wrote, *bogus history*. The sports spread told drag racers that high premium gasolines were a waste of money unless their carburetors were properly adjusted. Whipple scrawled, *Don't they know that already?* He was nearing the end now. The editor always devoted the last two inside pages to the girl-of-the-month, and from the fare thus far Whipple guessed that she would be shown drunk. Every issue had at least one drunk girl. At the last meeting of the Group a Johns Hopkins psychiatrist had argued that this was a symptom of adolescent diffidence; lacking confidence in their charm, adolescents were attracted to helpless women. Nonsense, a Princeton anthropologist had replied; Anglo-Saxon folklore had always regarded alcohol as an aphrodisiac — see the porter's speech in *Macbeth*, II, iii. Whipple himself had concluded the discussion with a brilliant opinion. The significance of liquor, he said, was that society considered it a part of the vice syndrome. The rising generation, appalled by the world it was inheriting, was lashing out at all icons. Every girlie magazine feature, every telecast for the young, and virtually every paperback cover demonstrated this. Insobriety, indecency, licentiousness, drug addiction, theft, murder, foul play — these were the talismen of revolt, the fagots for the fire, and as long as they remained incendiary they would be in demand.

In all events, November's girl-of-the-month was dead drunk.

Nor was she acting. Whipple's study had sharpened his eye for contrivance. As a rule the smirking models with empty bottles were posing. This one was in an authentic stupor. She was also lovely — far lovelier than anyone who had appeared in the magazine before. Despite the limbo of age Whipple found her breathtaking. Momentarily his clinical manner vanished. As a scholar he could examine most material dispassionately. He was himself a product of the vanishing culture, however, and he felt affronted that such rare physical grace should be spoiled by such cheap devices. This girl needed no bottle, and needed even less the pennant, the megaphone, the crude football pads and the glittering baton which, in the largest picture, was poised over her yawning loins like a tense phallus. It was absurd, he thought indignantly. Beauty should stand alone. Why cloy it? Why fake a masturbation charade? Why try to make her a cheerleader?

Sly was a picture magazine; its prose was usually meaningless.

Some time lapsed before Whipple realized that she really was a cheerleader.

The improbable text read:

HERE'S CHEERS, STATESMEN!
Daff Quaffs in Game's Name

Only a real rectangular mook makes for the goal posts after the last ball's been kicked, according to pert, honey-haired Daffy Dix, who ought to know. Statuesque Daff (36-24-33) leads the shapely Janes that encourage the muscle-bound Johns that power the No. 1 eleven that lives in the State house ole Adam River bilt. She delightens the Titans Saturday P.M.'s, and whenever they conquer (as conquer they must) she ties on one big curly hair of last Saturday's dawg.

Right way to pick up your marbles, saysh thish mish, is to pour one ounce of All-American bottled-in-bond into a tall glash. Put the glash beshide th' baid sho relief will be only a shwallow away tomorrow A.M. Then tilt back your haid and shlowly empty the resht of th' jug between your lipsh. If a girlsh got lipsh like Daffsh, who'd mind being th' bottle? O.K., so shkip th' lipsh. Get down to *beeg* bishnish. Daffsh glad to oblige. It gets cold on that field. A shweater? Daff don't want nun. Liquor's quick, but shometimes a gal wants a *ma-a-a-an.*

Sho it's thish way. Heresh poor li'l Daff, crocked and uncorked, playin' with a li'l ole baton. Besht she could do. Wanna help? Nexsht time you're givin' witha *wheeeee* cheer thinka *weeeee* Daff wantin' a coupla armsh for them pink-and-juicy chramsh. Hic! 36-24-33! Hike!

Whipple's mouth moved mutely, as though lip-reading.

Extraordinary, he thought. Extra*ord*inary.

He groped for the telephone.

Mikel was in none of his haunts. At State's History Department a feminine voice remarked, with surprising bitterness, that it was just like Dr. Mikel to be out of town this afternoon, of all times.

The allusion baffled Whipple. He hung up and deliberated. For all his poring over public prints he remained a cloistered recluse, and was at a loss how to proceed. Someone must be told; that was clear. But what could be done? He couldn't imagine.

Adam. He would call Adam River.

He fumbled with his dial. The Statette at the university switchboard connected him with Jill, and from her he learned the significance of today, both afternoon and morning.

Oh no, she said breathlessly, Dr. River couldn't possibly be reached. It wasn't even *poss*ible. He was tied up this morning in a thingamabob, a whatsis — a trus*tee* meeting. With a visiting V.I.P. prof and all.

Whipple glanced at *Sly*'s date. November: of course: the V.I.P. would be Budge. More to himself than to her he murmured, "Re-accreditation."

"I really can't tell you," she said guardedly. She didn't know this Whipple character. He could be *any*body. "I mean, it's not my business."

He inquired when Doc would be free.

"Free?" she repeated, as though it were a new word. "Oh honestly, that's the sixty-four-thousand."

"Can you take my number?" he asked in exasperation. "And have him call me later?"

Even that was out. It would be a waste of time, she explained. The reason this meeting was today was this afternoon's game. *The* game. The *Hamp* game. In living *col*or.

Jill, warm by nature, grew confidential despite herself.

"It's all part of today's program. I mean on the top level. The big frogs are having a wingding. First comes this powwow with the prof, then lunch. Everybody's playing the violin around everybody else. You know. Brown-nosing."

Whipple winced. Of course, the child didn't know what she was saying.

"And after lunch," she said, "they all go over and watch the State bugger Hamp."

He flinched again, reached instinctively for his pencil, and made a hurried note.

"This is an emergency," he said desperately.

"Oh?"

He didn't dare say more, and she lost interest. She was very sorry, sincerely sorry, but she had her orders. If only he knew how many emergencies there were for Doc River these days. Some of them were real, too. Not that this one wasn't, but what with the election being three days off there were messages and calls every mo. A person couldn't keep them straight. Why, since she'd picked up the receiver just now probably three people had tried this line. That would be *av*erage. And of course Doc being in Gideon for the game made everything a zillion times worse. Going to the stadium might be good politics and all, but the complications! The funny little town-clerk-type candidates that wanted him here, there, everywhere this week end! They couldn't brown-nose Mr. Albert, so they tried direct.

Whipple considered asking for Tate. Even if everything Mikel had said about him were true, he couldn't ignore this. Jill, however, anticipated him.

"The whole administration's tied up today, Mister."

"Whipple," he said, less pleasantly than with the distributor.

"Well anyway, you might as well face it, it'll have to keep. You can try other extensions if you want, but I can tell you most of the secretaries will hang up without a wham-bam-thank-you-ma'am."

"Thank you," Whipple said, and set his lips, and hung up himself.

It was all most unfortunate, he thought, looking down sadly at the open magazine. It was deplorable, calamitous even, but he knew no one else to call. Apart from Mikel he hadn't met a member of the State faculty in years. There were no members of his discipline on the other side of town and scarcely any other professors with reputations worth mentioning. There was Mikel, of course. There was a physicist. And there was a promising botanist. That completed State's roll of the eminent, however, and men in physics and botany were far from his field and therefore strangers.

Nevertheless he had to do something, something, something . . .

He drummed his fingers on the page before him and noticed he was drumming Daffy's shoulder pads. Leaning forward, he examined her face. She was a trifle old for college, perhaps, and around her eyes there were little lines of wisdom he hadn't noticed before. Yet how exquisite she could be, he thought, drawing back his hand. Remove all those ridiculous gadgets, dress her in a proper gown, and she would be flowerlike, queenly. She was such a handsome young animal. After so many hundred wanton pictures he had thought his mind numb to flesh. It was refreshing to see how flawless the human body could be. Extraordinary, extraordinary. Not a wrinkle, not a single blemish had required retouching.

Whipple was almost right. *Sly*'s artist had made but one change. He had painted out Daffy's wedding band.

**

Budge was in charge. Sam Theanapolis sat in the chair of authority, and Tate's agenda controlled the order of events, but there was no doubt who was in command. After a season of discretion Budge had reached the end of his task. This was the day of judgment, and the real power was his.

He asserted it subtly. The proceedings had just begun, and he had said nothing. He seemed neither arrogant nor gay, despite his dark shirt and the sportively mismatched tweed jacket and slacks which suggested that he had blundered into a student's clothes closet. The trustees, in fact, couldn't see his face at all. Standing by the Colonial Room window with his back to them, his short sturdy legs braced far apart and his square hands clasped behind him, he might have been a truant board member who had grown weary of procedure and strolled over to take solace in the view.

Except for the report.

On the sill before him lay twelve mimeographed, stapled copies, neatly stacked and burnished by a patch of sun like a dramatic spotlight. Only Budge knew what was in them, and so they were his mace of authority. He had but to glance down at them and the room hushed. Tate's voice, reciting routine business, dwindled to a squeak. Doc stirred in his corner armchair. Sam looked heavier and older, Paul Bauer ran a quick tongue over his three gold teeth, and Judge Davies sat erect, vigilant. Budge ignored them all. He glanced away from the sun-glossed paper and looked up suddenly, as though diverted by something outside that he could see and they could not. It was a patent trick. He was playing with them, and they knew it, and they forgave him. For this was his hour; he had what they wanted.

Everyone was aware that his team had finished. Most of his colleagues had left last night. Beyond that, however, information about his inquiry was scant. Some, including Doc, who had returned to town less than an hour ago, had heard virtually nothing. The judge was the best informed. Ostracized by his fellow trustees, he still knew more than any of them about the team's deliberations, because Budge's men had continued to enjoy the hospitality of Lutz, who had confided in Mikel, who had told the judge all he heard. Yet there hadn't been much to tell. Budge had remained prudent. Lutz had learned very little. All he had been able to relay was that the team's departmental appraisals had been finished on Monday and that four entire days had been spent hammering out general conclusions. It seemed a long time, the judge mused, ripping a cigar from its cellophane sheath, though in itself it meant nothing. Professors were like lawyers, professional talkers. They dragged things out. Then he studied the broad tweedy back at the window and reflected that Budge was an exception. It was hard to imagine that dour block of a man permitting pointless digressions. *Quantum sufficit* and no nonsense; that was Budge, he thought. The judge leaned back, sniffing his cigar, wondering what those four days could have been about, and wishing that idiot Tate would stop his falsetto prattle.

Tate stopped. It dawned on him that he had no audience. His fluty voice trailed off in the middle of a sentence.

"So much for my minutiae," he trilled. "Shall we move on to the main business, Sam?"

The provost had no doubt that Budge had good news for them. He was anxious, but it was the anxiety of a child on Christmas morning. The gift under the teasing seals might be a surprise; nevertheless he was sure it would be pleasant. The invitation to the team members had, after all, been his suggestion. They had come to evaluate his work, and his faith in the outcome had never wavered. Academic reactionaries might frown on his work, but he had no doubt that men of eminence would approve the vision behind it. He folded his gaunt hands and restrained a grin.

Sam, only slightly less confident, cleared his throat formally. "Sounds O.K. to me." He glanced toward the armchair. "O.K. by you, Governor?"

Doc nodded solemnly. The room was suddenly quiet. Budge turned and the judge's heart sank. He had delivered too many verdicts himself not to recognize the sadness in that meaty face.

"You're ready for me?" Budge asked.

Sam cleared his throat again. "All set."

"You can question me after you've read the findings," Budge said and moved around like a newsboy, delivering the reports.

Doc and Tate had never sat on the bench and had therefore missed his elegaic air. Now, however, they had an unmistakable omen. They received their copies last, almost as an afterthought. A shadow crept into Tate's eyes. Doc looked mystified.

"As you see, the first section is procedural," Budge was saying. "The second gets down to cases, and the third" — his gravelly voice dropped — "is a summary."

Pages crackled. Everyone wanted the summary. And then, as intent eyes darted down the carefully numbered points and underscored sentences, they discovered that they didn't want it at all.

The judge had thought himself braced for the worst. Yet even he was stunned by the severity of the indictment. As he finished the first subsection of the summary, dealing with State's faculty, he understood why the team's sessions had been so long. Academic courtesy required that every critical conclusion be insulated by elaborate periphrases, and the report was all criticism. Stripped of its tactful passages it was terse and uncompromising; in parts it was almost savage. Budge's professors had been shocked at State's low salaries and the virtual absence of tenure. Even allowing for the silver cord of alma mater loyalty, it was astonishing to them that a man of Harry Osborne Mikel's stature had remained there. Little outside talent had been recruited, they noted, and in a deft backhand, employing the double negative customary in such documents, they concluded that academic conditions were "not entirely unrelated to the general mediocrity of the present faculty."

Across the room Doc hunched in his chair, tracing the lines with a blunt fingernail. At first he thought that there had been some fantastic error. The team had talked to the wrong people, poked in the wrong corners. He looked in vain for some mention of the achievements of his administration — the great new campus, the expanded curriculum and increased enrollment, the growing role of the university in the life of the state. It seemed incredible to him that they could have been so blind. Of course, he had expected some suggestions. He knew State wasn't perfect, not by a long sight. But these fellows weren't a bit constructive. They were negative, and downright picayunish. Why, most of the time they sounded like old Harry Mikel. If only they'd seen State twenty years ago! Rotting fire traps and cow barns and horseapples! But of course they didn't care about that. All they wanted to do was find fault. *General mediocrity*. The phrase stung. He turned the page swiftly, tearing it across, and indignantly began the second subsection, on the student body.

Sam had already finished it. He was a scanner by trade and was now running through it again, pondering implications. Like Doc he resented the team's disdain. It was all very well for them to point sternly at political scholarships and the emphasis on football, but he knew that things had to be that way; otherwise the legislature would turn its back and let the Gideon weeds grow. Like Doc he also thought of Mikel, who had made so many of these points before. He saw Mikel infrequently, however, and some of the most startling facts were unfamiliar to him. He had been chairman of the board for nearly a decade, yet only now was he fully comprehending that it was possible to enter the freshman class without a diploma, that nearly forty courses required no final examinations, and that there were fewer than three hundred seats suitable for study in the new library. Sam squirmed uneasily. As chief trustee he felt he should have been more adequately briefed, and as a father he was worried about his son. He wanted the best for young Sam. Until this morning he had never doubted that State was it. Now he had qualms. The business world grew more competitive every year. If State became known as a country club its diplomas would be of small value to junior executives. His bloated face puckered. He didn't blame Doc — he was incapable of blaming Doc for anything — and so he swiveled massively and glared at Tate.

Tate didn't see him. He was oblivious to everyone, studying the last subsection.

It reviewed the university administration, and it was the sharpest of the three. The team had abandoned tact here; it had been frankly outraged at the servile role assigned to the faculty. The Academic Council was variously described as "weak," "powerless," and "impotent"; the officers of the administration were "high-handed" and, in one place, "despotic." Had the report stopped there, it might have been interpreted as a rebuke of Doc, and Tate could have salvaged some pride. But it didn't stop. It went on to accuse the university provost of introducing into higher education "a secondary school ideology — and a discredited ideology at that."

At least they recognized the issue, Tate thought bitterly. At least they saw the master plan. It was small consolation to him. He had made a monumental blunder. Budge's evaluators, he saw, weren't big men after all. They lacked true insight; they were defenders of the vested intellectual interests. Education for living meant nothing to them. They would rather a student *be* than *do*, would rather graduate neurotic walking encyclopedias than healthy, well-adjusted young men and women capable of thinking for themsleves in the real-life situations of a modern world. It was a stunning blow. Tate hadn't expected stupidity and reaction from the team. Later, he knew, he would recover and be strengthened by the learning experience, but at the moment he felt fouled. He closed his eyes, rubbed the milky lids, and thought wistfully of his gleaming bathtub. He would have given almost anything if he could have crept there and convalesced in its healing waters.

Paul Bauer coughed, recalling him to dry reality.

"Excuse me," Bauer said to Budge. "I'm not quite clear about one thing. Right here at the end it says that State's recommended for probation."

The team chairman nodded silently.

"Well, what does that mean, exactly? Does the N.E.C.U. always follow recommendations like this?"

Budge wanted to be civil. He pretended to reflect and answered quietly, "I've never heard of a reversal."

"Well, does that mean —"

"It means that accreditation's been denied," Doc broke in hoarsely.

"Oh."

Bauer drew his lips flat over his shiny teeth. That made it final. The other members of the board exchanged stricken looks. Bauer had spoken for all of them; they hadn't understood either, and now they stirred with twitching little movements. plucking distractedly at their campaign buttons, lodge pins, regimental-stripe ties, and hard starched collars. When the flurry subsided they were all looking at Doc.

He took strength from that. His anger toward the team was ebbing; he realized it would be senseless to lash out at Budge. Still he seethed. He needed a target, and following Sam's hard stare he remembered that all this had been Tate's idea.

"I expect you all feel a little down in the dumps," he began, lifting his head and looking from trustee to trustee. "Well, I do too. I'm bound to admit I had my heart set on something a little different." He screwed up his eyes and growled, "I'd been led to believe we might even come out of this with a Phi Bete chapter."

Now he too was glaring at Tate. The provost saw the recriminations coming. He attempted a diversion.

"No one is more disappointed than I am," he said quickly. He drew a sharp breath and let it out on half a laugh. "But surely there must be a sunny side to the street." He leafed through his copy hurriedly. "We must have done a *few* things right."

Unfortunately for him the report disagreed. There was unqualified approval of the Agronomy and Poultry Husbandry Departments, but he couldn't use that; both had been established long before he came to Gideon. To his dismay the only other men mentioned with enthusiasm were professors who had repeatedly defied the administration in Academic Council meetings. There seemed to be no fragment, no crumb, no scrap of praise for him to grasp. The team had even condescended to pass on to him a piece of news about his own faculty. It observed that Solomon Feinblatt, the one poet of distinction in the English Department, had decided to accept an invitation from Carleton College next term. Tate set his thin lips. Ingrate, he thought waspishly. Feinblatt could have at least spared him this. Apparently there was no such thing as loyalty any more.

He riffled sheets furiously. "It can't be *all* bad."

Yet it was. There wasn't a phrase he could quote. His stark pate pinkened. "What about the medical school?"

"Our people from Hopkins think it could be improved," Budge said gruffly.

"And the School of Education?" Tate faltered, offering his pet.

Budge slew it without a flicker. "No."

Doc sat up with a restless movement. "It seems we've flunked everything, Dr. Tate. In my view this fiddle-faddle was nothing but your own —"

"Football!" Tate said wildly. He had to stop Doc. Already a plan was forming in his mind, but no plan could survive a public quarrel with Doc and its inevitable alienation of the trustees. "State's got the top squad in the country. What's the matter with that?"

He knew, and Budge knew he knew. The trustees didn't know — Bauer was again coughing for attention — but the team chairman had no intention of permitting this to degenerate into a wrangle over athletic scholarships. He merely remarked mildly that it was all in the report, and that ended that, for Doc declined the bait.

"*In my view*," he repeated, his lantern jaw lengthening dangerously, "this business is all the fault of one know-it-all wiseacre."

"He sounds sinister!" Tate cried, grinning desperately.

No one laughed. Doc had half risen. His eyes gleamed like water. He thought of the trust he had placed in his provost, and the enormity of the disaster, and he rumbled, "Incompetent is a better word."

Tate giggled, still trying to make a joke of it. "We're all ears!"

"By golly, I wish I had the ears of the whole state!" Doc thundered. "I'd like to tell the story of these monkeyshines on every TV from the Appalachians to the sea!"

It was the judge who saved Tate. He lit his cigar and drawled, "That's the very thing that mustn't be done."

Doc whirled. "How's that?"

"Not a whisper of this must go beyond that door."

"*I* know," Doc snapped. But he hesitated. He had lost his momentum.

"Not a syllable," the judge persisted. "Not an elementary human sound."

"Naturally. I told you that at our first meeting."

"And I agreed. I'm reminding you now of that agreement."

Doc sat back slackly, then nodded once. "Bull's-eye. I was just talking. You're right, of course. You've hit the nub of it."

The judge wrinkled his patrician nose. "The 'nub,' as you call it, is that Aggie is going to be placed on what is called probation — a flexible word, subject to various interpretations." He blinked at Budge. "I assume that the New England Association of Colleges and Universities will not inflict any — ah — penalties?"

The team chairman smiled slightly. "No penalties, sir."

"A consolation, gentlemen. We shall be free men. Now, then. Probation implies certain conditions — hurdles to be crossed, if you'll permit the banal metaphor."

Budge permitted it. He nodded benignly.

"They are set forth in this instrument?" the judge inquired.

"In detail."

"And I take it that once we've met those conditions we may emerge from the shadows."

"Completely."

"Then they shall be met, of course."

"Of course," Doc echoed. "We asked for this match, and we're going to win it."

The trustees considered the judge with new respect; he had calmed Doc, and this despite his use of the forbidden "Aggie." He didn't gloat. He was genuinely worried about the future of the report. He had seen the crafty look cross Tate's face, and Budge's promise in the Gideon Arms notwithstanding, he could find no marks on his copy.

He fenced with him, without success.

"Meanwhile we must all wear the gag," he said. "I take it the document does not exist outside this room?"

"One sealed copy has gone to the N.E.C.U. in Boston," Budge said. "The seal can't be broken until the quarterly meeting in January."

"I see. And there are no others?"

"None. The stencils have been burnt, and my colleagues destroyed their notes before leaving Gideon."

The judge looked at him sharply. He thought he saw a twinkle in Budge's eye, but couldn't be sure. He's heckling me, he thought. Very well. There was poetical justice in that. He himself had bullyragged a generation of Birmingham lawyers; now it was his turn to dance. He didn't mind, as long as Budge had carried out their bargain. But had he? Every copy here looked like every other copy. They weren't even numbered. If the *Star* printed even a rumor of the team's verdict before the election, everyone in this room would believe him responsible. Exasperated, he considered turning in his copy and decided against it; it would be beneath his dignity.

Sam meanwhile had taken up the judge's lecture on security. Convinced that Doc's greatest asset at the polls would be his reputation as a colorful but able administrator, Sam saw the report as potential dynamite. It could be the telling blow in a close campaign, the shattering election-eve disclosure that haunts the dreams of every political partisan. Sam thought that was what the judge had been driving at. He did him an injustice — the judge, as a scrupulous trustee, was bent only on protecting the university's name — and he compounded the injustice by wondering darkly whether this present fastidiousness might not be a screen to obscure the judge's own release of the report later. It was a low suspicion. But Sam was obsessed with the election. He betrayed it in a word.

"I think we can table this till next month, Governor."

Doc nodded heavily. "It wants deep thought."

The judge fired a final shot. Deliberately looking away from Tate's end of the room he added, "And complete freedom from public pressure."

He was himself unjust. Tate was aware of the report's power and wouldn't hesitate to use it in a crisis. For the moment, however, he had decided to hold his hand. Last week's *Star* poll had suggested that the race was becoming a battle to the wire, and today there had been no poll report at all. There was no point guessing what that meant. As long as the issue remained in doubt he had to be prepared to jump either way. The only sensible plan for him was to heal the breach with Doc, trim his sails, and await Tuesday's returns.

Healing the breach came first. Luckily he was in charge of the box seating this afternoon. He could assign himself to the chair beside Doc's, and with a little flattery, a little sophistry, a little eating of distasteful crow — yes, it could be done, he thought; given the right breaks he could shake Doc's kaleidoscope.

"Let's feed our faces!" he cried genially. At the vulgarism the judge's mouth crimped as though he had bitten on a bad tooth. Budge also looked distressed; he retreated into the hall, the bearer of bad news making his tactful departure. Elsewhere around the table, however, there was a contented rising and stretching. Tate himself stood and added slyly, "After lunch we can forget our troubles at the stadium."

He knew his man. Doc bounced up. "Gosh, I'd clean forgotten about the game!"

The judge then sacrificed most of his gains. He inquired blankly, "What game?"

They stared, Bauer with disbelief. Doc said, "Why, State and Hamp, of course."

"Eh?"

"In living color," said Sam.

"Live, from Gideon," said Tate.

"Oh. Yes. I see. Well, I'd like to attend, but unhappily I must return to the city before noon. I promised my chauffeur the afternoon."

Bowing with his quaint, old-world gallantry, he trudged out in a blue tobacco fog, the only trustee without a Doc button, the only one with a chauffeur — and the only man there indifferent to either. Smirks appeared behind his back and then vanished as the others saw Doc's dimpleless cheeks.

"Limousines," he muttered. "High-hatty manners and high-brow talk." He led Sam down the corridor, into the bright, winelike morning air. "Say, what do fellows like that *do* Saturday afternoons?"

Sam chuckled. "Oh, they hang around the Clipper Club. Maybe they shoot a little pool."

"Or play tiddlywinks," Doc snorted.

Tate, trailing them, whinnied appreciatively.

"Naturally they let the richest man win," Sam said.

"I bet," said Doc. "Then they can dun him for Witty's war chest."

Tate whinnied again.

"Newt don't think that money's going to do them any good, though," Sam said cheerfully. "I talked to him on the phone just before the meeting. He thinks Witty's had it."

"Oh?" Doc sucked his lip. "I heard from him at breakfast, and he was in a sweat over that straw vote being left out of the *Star*."

"That's just it. There's a story around Birmingham that they didn't print it because you're neck and neck, maybe even a little ahead."

"Well!" Doc stepped forward, then slowed. "Still, we shouldn't get overconfident. A lot can happen."

"Sure," Sam agreed. "Like this game. Hamp's good, and they're up."

It was the weekly shibboleth, repeated each Saturday to preserve the illusion of a contest. Hamp might be up, but they weren't good. None of the Titans' conference opponents were in their league any more, and Tom Yablonski would have drawn a forfeit before permitting the team to go on television in any pre-bowl game that wasn't a sure thing.

"We'll take them," Tate called aggressively. He remembered a minor triumph of his own and added, "We'll knock their eyes out with Bauer's Gridiron Queen, too. You've seen her, Governor. The head Titanette, Daffy Dix."

Doc pursed his lips. Dix. Daffy Dix . . . He'd heard that name recently. Before he could place the incident, however, Sam said thoughtfully, "It's going to be the biggest game we ever played."

Doc shook his head vehemently. "Those old Peabody games were the biggest."

"Well, it's the crucial one for you. John Q. will be glued to his set this afternoon, and he'll remember everything he saw when he goes into that booth Tuesday."

"The boys won't let him down," Tate called.

Doc hulked ahead, frowning to himself. He disliked this coupling of the squad and politics. Even the thought that a State victory would help his chances made him uncomfortable. He had conceded much to expediency these past few weeks, but always reluctantly, and he still believed it possible to play two roles at once: to campaign, and to remain aloof. The election was one thing, the game another. Each had its place, and he wanted each in its place.

**

The city room of the Birmingham *Star* was going through one of its periodic transformations. Balloting was still three days away, but the preparations for covering it had been under way all week. Bulletin board postings notified each reporter who could be spared Tuesday that he would be expected to visit two assigned precincts when the polls closed at 7 P.M. and phone in the results for the first election edition. A temporary switchboard had been set up by the city desk bull pen to handle these calls; a battery of IBM calculators waited nearby; and at the direction of Hallam Caulkin three leads, covering all eventualities, had been set in type.

BULLETIN!

Early city returns tonight foreshadowed a smashing state-wide victory for the G.O. Principles of Governor-Elect Stuart H. P. Witty as tallies from 80 barometric precincts heralded the repudiation of Adam R. River, vacationing president of the state university.

BULLETIN!

Inconclusive returns based on 80 weather-wise precincts indicated a photo-finish tonight in the electoral battle between Stuart H. P. ("Mr. Depth") Witty, the young Republican standard-bearer, and Adam R. ("Doc") River, the no-holds-barred choice of the Democrat Party and the state CIO-PAC.

BULLETIN!

Facing an uphill fight in the first election figures, Stuart H. P. Witty, leader of the state's Modern Republican movement, vowed tonight to continue his "better government and less spending" crusade while controversial Adam R. River took a seesaw edge on the strength of less than a hundred scattered precincts. Poll watchers reported an unusually large number of voter challenges and jammed machines.

Once these arrangements were complete the great block-long room had become virtually deserted. It was Saturday, a slow day. There were few advertisements and, consequently, little need for news stories to wrap around them. The general managing editor had retained a skeleton staff, nearly all of whom were idle. The sports editor, after sending most of his staff off to enjoy the game in Gideon, was handling the out-of-state wire with practiced ease. Caulkin himself sat beside the bull pen at what he called his "field desk," lazily editing political stories for the big Sunday editions, and the only man actually punching a typewriter in the calm after the lunch hour was Ham Markham.

Ham sat alone in the rear of the room under an isolated fluorescent lamp, exchanging occasional blank glances with passing copy boys. During his absence the day shift boys had become a noisome lot. They were here because they had left school and couldn't find better jobs; most had minor criminal records, and they wore startling clothes — bright green slacks with fitted cuffs; pointed purple suede shoes; crimson jackets with the white legend "Pythons" on the back. They seemed to spend a great deal of time in the men's room combing their hair. Ham had thought them harmless until he discovered that they were armed. He had called to one to sharpen a blunt pencil, and the boy had strolled over and casually whittled it down with a switchblade knife.

Since then Ham had ground his own pencils and carried his own copy. He gathered that the boys held their *Star* superiors in contempt, and he was right. He assumed that they looked upon him as a stodgy square, and was wrong. They had no use for reporters and editors, but a foreign correspondent was another matter. They admired him secretly, speculated on his adventures abroad, and argued among themselves over what he would do when his home assignment was finished. This afternoon one, a stringy youth, was leaning against the pneumatic tube that led to the composing room and eying him furtively. On his last trip to the morgue he had peered over his shoulder and discovered that he was writing a letter. After much grave thought he confided his conclusion to a fellow Python. He was pretty sure Ham was throwing a line to some piece in India.

Ham was. He was writing his wife.

*Star*light Roof
Birmingham
Game time

Dancy, dearest, dearest —

Brace yourself. I'm going to quit the paper. Now don't start packing; I'll be coming back to India, by Christmas for sure and probably in time for the ambassador's Thanksgiving party. It's just that I won't be taking the *Star*'s money any more. This trip has made a great many things clear to me. Among other things I've discovered that every year under Caulkin compromises something in me dearer (can you grasp this?) even than you. So yesterday I went down to New York and talked to a half dozen magazine editors and syndicate managers. In one day I picked up enough assignments to keep us going for a year. Oh, we may have to cut a few corners at first, but I'll be my own man, and I know you realize what *that* means to me.

I haven't told anyone here yet, but I've started on the usual travel list: renew passport, buy present for Hammy, weigh luggage, get new shots, BOAC timetable, American Express checks, etc. It'll be a happy parting. I'm fed up here. I've been wallowing in Yanqui creature comforts, but they don't mean a thing without you, Dance — I miss you from my Wildroot-softened hair to my Absorbine-Juniored toes — and I've had Caulkin.

He, I suspect, won't miss *me*. I can do a job, but I don't fit into his scheme of things. I'm not his fancy boy, I don't think nice thoughts, and I'm so absobloodylutely non-U. Item one: I wouldn't be found dead of VD on the Clipper Club membership list. (Your father understands that, but Caulkin never will.) Item two: I lack discretion. (Long after my Peabody series is forgotten, the memory of Consolidated Enterprises will rankle.) Item three: I'm hot for Doc.

Oh, I have mixed feelings. Even I have to admit that Doc's too naïve to be governor; he really belongs to Gideon, at State, straightening out the mess there. Yet I still want him to win Tuesday. Your father puts it down to class loyalty. I won't argue. If I'm voting with my heart, the heart has its own logic, and I do exult when the wind blows Doc's way, which it seems to be doing lately. I say *seems* advisedly. In this cockeyed campaign nothing is certain. The election special went off the track when hospital orderlies and agricultural agents started politicking, and now it's plowing up strange land. Nobody knows where it'll wind up. Charlie Smathers didn't make the paper today. The smart talk around town is that Doc had pulled ahead, but I got the real dope from Charlie himself. The poor guy's ready to commit hara-kiri with his ballpoint pen. According to his figures, *nobody's* going to win. Neither candidate has a majority, because the poll has suddenly turned up a big bloc of "Don't Knows."

A lot of them are supposed to drop off the fence today, because one of the most decisive factors in this zany business is a football game. The pros agree that if State wins today, Doc's half home. Don't ask me why. It has something to do with a bowl bid and the number of consecutive wins in the regional conference. Apparently every citizen will get a big charge if that redheaded halfback with the uncontrollable oestrus gyrates properly, which he's scheduled to start doing in about two minutes. I'll hear it on the sports editor's desk radio. Sam Theanapolis sent me a press box pass (I think he's still grieving because I lit into him about those orderlies and farm agents) but somehow I didn't feel up to the hour's drive. I don't share the victory fever. This kind of football has nothing to do with the football I knew. I just can't get used to the idea of a State squad holing up in an out-of-town health resort on the eve of a televised game to rest their tired blood. Believe it or not, that really happened last night, and to me it made them seem traitors to their class. Finally there's Spook. From the stands Red Stacy looks unbelievably like him. Watching the field is like being betrayed by the brother I never had.

City briefs . . . Sol Feinblatt (the poet) came to town last night with Kit Ryan (the housemother I used to know) to see a *Fair Lady* road show. Neither was touching ground, and I had the feeling they've set their sights for each other . . . The sports editor is now tuning to the game, thereby attracing an evil swarm of copy boys. One of those bland-voiced network announcers just finished a lineup rundown. Then he reminded us that State's annual Gridiron Queen pageant will be held at the half. I guess Red's vessel made it. Bland Voice says this will be the first married queen. The stars in their courses beam on the deserving . . . Caulkin just got a call. Maybe it's Stuart Witty. The Greatest Living American must be curious about that straw vote . . . Now B.V. is describing an innovation, a pregame prayer. Forty-three thousand fans have sunk to their knees on a signal from the P.A. system. Go ahead, cringe. *I'm* cringing —

Ham's cringe became a flinch. His desk telephone, inches from his ear, was ringing stridently.

"Mr. Markham?" It was the *Star* operator. She said apologetically, "I got a party for you. I didn't know whether to bother you, but Mr. Caulkin gave me this extension. He said you were on the post."

Ham stared balefully across the room. Caulkin knew perfectly well he was supposed to be off this afternoon. *On the post.* He wondered what Caulkin would do when he quit. Probably publish his name as A.W.O.L.

"Can I call you back?" He wanted to get this letter in the mail.

"Gee, I don't know. This man says it's real important. Name's Wimpole."

"*Whipple*," a far-off voice said testily.

Ham grinned. "It's O.K., Gloria. Dr. Whipple? I thought you and Mikel would be in reserved seats at the stadium."

"Don't chide me," the old man snapped. "If I knew where Harry really was, I wouldn't have disturbed you. I've been trying since before noon to raise some responsible person on the other side of town. They're all engaged."

"Well, it's a big day at State."

"Bigger than they know, I fear. They are in rather a nasty mess. I'd go over and try to corner Adam personally, but at my age such an expedition is out of the question. I remembered your devotion to State. It occurred to me you might be able to do something."

It was difficult to think of Whipple stumbling on a genuine crisis; he seemed too isolated, too removed from the streets and the real mud.

"I'll be glad to do what I can," said Ham, his tone unconsciously patronizing.

Whipple bridled. "It's not for me, young man! *I* don't need you. It's Adam! See here. Do you remember our discussion of that remarkable periodical *Sly?*"

"Sure. In fact, I meant to tell you — a few days later I ran into one of their photographers."

"In Gideon?" Whipple asked sharply.

"At the Gideon Arms. Later he crashed a Homecoming fraternity party. The last I heard of him he was taking a drunk cheerleader to a car, and —"

"Then that must have been the night!"

Ham felt a premonition. He drew the phone nearer. "What night?"

"I take it you haven't seen the current *Sly.*"

"No, I'm not the snappy type. I left the only copy I ever had in your office."

"You may recollect that I subscribe. I have the November issue on my desk now, opened at pages thirty and thirty-one. The article is entitled, 'Here's Cheers, Statesmen!' It is subtitled, 'Daff Quaffs in Games's Name.' "

Ham went cold. "Not Daffy Dix?"

"Yes, that's the name. The rest of the prose is almost illiterate, however. I simply cannot render it."

"But there are pictures?"

"Of course. It is a picture magazine, Mr. Markham. And the Dix illustrations, like the text, defy description. I think you fathom my meaning."

With blinding clarity Ham recalled it all: Geek prowling around the Sigma Chi house, Daffy helpless, Red slipping away from the chaperones' anteroom when Trudy reported seeing Daffy and Geek together. That evening had been more depraved than Kit had suspected. But why? Who was behind it? Who could win? Ham saw only losers. And the chief loser would be Doc.

He whispered, "This could be a hammer blow for Witty."

"That would be most distressing. But our Group's figures are reassuring. They suggest that *Sly* is hardly in the mass circulation category."

"Your Group never fought a tight campaign. Between now and Tuesday anything goes. If the Republicans get hold of this, people will be talking about it who never heard of girlie magazines, or even girlies. Doc has to move fast—"

Ham stopped short. He had just grasped the irony of *Sly*'s spread. Doc's only chance to anticipate Witty was today, in Gideon, before Daffy was crowned on television. And that would threaten a big Red Stacy win.

Yet it had to be done, for another reason.

"He has to," he repeated. "Election or no election, State can't wink at this."

"I thought you'd see that," Whipple said quietly. "That's why I simply had to speak to you."

Ham glanced up at the huge clock over the city desk. There was just time to reach Gideon by the half. "You were right. It couldn't be more urgent."

Already the two teams were lined up for the kickoff. The radio had switched listeners to the field. State's band was playing *The Star-Spangled Banner.*

**

Ham had closed his typewriter and was pocketing his letter to Dancy when he realized that he needed a copy of *Sly*. It would be pointless to approach Doc without evidence. He thought briefly of calling Whipple back and asking him to wait in his office. But the detour would take time. Perhaps there was a quicker way. He beckoned to the weedy boy at the composing room tube.

"You read *Sly?*" he asked bluntly. Ham knew he did. He had seen him taking it into the toilet.

The boy said guardedly, "I seen it around."

"Around where?"

"Oh, here, there. *Around.*"

"Look, relax. I don't care if you paper your bedroom with it," Ham said impatiently. The boy swallowed hard, and Ham realized that he had struck a truth. He said more easily, "I mean it, I *don't* care. I just want to know where I can buy it."

A stare, a swallow. "For *you,* Mr. Markham?"

"That's right. Now you tell me where."

A furtive glance toward the sports editor's surrounded desk. "Sancho, he's got the new one."

"That's the one I want. Which is Sancho?"

A stumbling retreat in pointed shoes. "I'll get him."

Sancho was the owner of the wicked knife. He was a short, swarthy youth, built for combat. As a senior Python he felt entitled to treat Ham as an equal, and he swaggered over indifferently. The stringy boy followed a respectful pace behind.

"Hi, Markham."

"Hi, Sancho," Ham said. Old pals already, he thought. Long time no see.

"Pinhead here says you're in the market for a meat book."

"A what? Oh, yes. I might be." It was like dealing with a bazaar *banya* in Delhi.

Suddenly Sancho grinned lasciviously. "Miss gettin' it regular, huh?"

Ham glared, and he felt as he had in the Sigma Chi anteroom with Red. He knew this was a cheap show for the benefit of the gobble-necked boy behind. But he hadn't time to take Sancho's knife away from him. "Listen, I'm in a hurry. You got the new *Sly* or not?"

"Got it right here." Sancho patted his jacket front, which rustled. "Paid four bits this morning at the Central News."

Ham dug in his pocket. "I'll give you four right now."

Sancho shook his grinning head. "I'm saving you a trip, Markham."

"O.K.," Ham conceded. The Central News Agency was six blocks away. "Six, then. Six bits."

The youth played craftily with his jacket collar. "A buck and you got a deal."

"All right," Ham said, snatching out his wallet. He flipped the magazine open to verify the issue and darkened as the big print of

Daffy flourishing the baton flashed into view. Sancho was watching and snickering. Slipping into his topcoat Ham asked carelessly, "You from Mechanics Street?"

The senior Python's face straightened. "Yeah, twenty-three hundred block. How'd you know?"

"I saw you around," Ham said over his shoulder, "about twenty years ago."

"How about that?" said Sancho, watching him stride out the back door of the city room.

"He must be flipping," the other boy said. "You wasn't even born then."

"Hey, Sancho!" a third boy called. "The colonel wants to talk to you and Pinhead."

Caulkin, ostensibly absorbed in editing, had watched the exchange with a growing sense of outrage. Familiarity between the copy boys and the staff was strictly forbidden. He would have to speak to Ham privately. In the meantime, however, he could settle these two.

"Front and center!" he barked.

They straggled up and assumed slouching, splay-footed postures before him. The copy children grew worse and worse, Caulkin thought, eying their bizarre clothes with distaste. He sympathized with the Personnel Department's problems, but did they have to recruit scum?

"Look like men!" And, to Pinhead, "Button that button."

"It don't button," Pinhead said. "It's for show."

"Well, your fly's not for show, is it? Zip it up!" He saw Sancho's grin re-emerging and said curtly, "Wipe that off! Goddamn it, I want a little discipline in this outfit. Weren't you people ever told not to bother reporters?"

"You mean Markham?" Sancho asked.

"*Mr.* Markham!"

"He sent for us," Sancho said sullenly.

"That's not the point." And then it struck him that perhaps it was. If Ham really had been fraternizing, he could throw the book at him. "What did he want? I said wipe it!"

The corners of Sancho's mouth were twitching again. "He bought *Sly* off of me."

"Bought what?"

"The new *Sly*. It's one of them meat mags."

"Meat?"

"You know." Sancho made suggestive sweeps of his hands.

"Yes, yes, of course," Caulkin said hurriedly. He didn't really know, but had heard of the girlie genre; Judge Davies had told a group at the Club how severely it was straining the First Amendment. And now the judge's son-in-law had acquired this filth from a boy. Caulkin's thick mustache bristled. "How much did he pay you?"

It wasn't worth a lie to Sancho. "One buck."

"And your investment was?"

"Four bits."

"I won't have peddling on the post." Caulkin held out his hand. "Give it to me."

Sancho dug into a pocket, his swarthiness deepening. The money was nothing, but the humiliation in front of Pinhead was insufferable. He had to show the flag.

"I told you it was Markham's idea," he growled mutinously.

"That's enough," said Caulkin, palming the coin.

"He just wanted to see that bareass cheerleader."

"I said that's enough!" said Caulkin, coloring himself. "Dismissed!"

Alone he brooded. The cheerleader reference meant nothing to him; nevertheless the incident was odd enough without it. He thought back. Relaying the *Star* operator to Ham's extension, he had noticed something familiar in the wispy voice on the far end of the line. Now he remembered: as an undergraduate he had heard that voice lecture on Horace for an entire year. So Nails Whipple had been anxious to reach Ham. The election was very near and a race to the wire, and Nails, like Ham, was supporting Doc. Caulkin wondered whether there could be a connection. Whatever Whipple had said had electrified Ham. Even from there Caulkin had seen him tense over his telephone. And then, immediately after, Ham had summoned a copy boy and bought a copy of a smutty magazine, paying twice its value. It didn't make sense. Caulkin shook his head, as though to shake off a whining gnat, and turned back to Frost Warren's Sunday story.

Five minutes later he pushed it aside and called the morgue. "Charlie? Caulkin here. I hope you've recovered from your disappointment about the poll." He purred soothingly, "Actually you should be flattered. The switchboard's been swamped with inquiries." An awkward pause. "By the bye. How would you go about locating a copy of a rather out-of-the-way journal?"

"Any special one, Colonel?"

Caulkin sidestepped him. It was bad enough that a junior officer like Markham had been indiscreet. If word got about that the general managing editor was collecting pornography, the whole building would titter for a month. "No, no. It simply occurred to me that I ought to know such things. You're not going to be with us forever, Charlie."

Charlie's alpaca coat rustled uneasily. "Gee, Colonel, don't say that."

A hearty chuckle. "We have to think of everything, you know."

"Well, we got pretty good relations with the city library."

"Suppose the library doesn't carry it?"

"Oh, they carry everything, sir," Charlie said earnestly.

Caulkin closed his eyes. He would have to give ground. "Suppose it was too popular for the library."

"Huh?"

"Something too — uncouth."

"Oh. Oh, I get you." Charlie got him. "Then we'd go to the Central News down the street."

Caulkin rattled on irrelevantly, covering his tracks, and then hung up. Ten minutes later he was entering the agency, ducking to protect his Homburg in the low doorway.

It was a tiny shop, crowded with paper. Shelves and revolving wire racks were piled or jammed with out-of-town newspapers, paperback books, television guides, and comic books. Instinctively Caulkin looked around for the *Star*. It lay ignominously between *Mad* and *Mad Strikes Back*. He was preparing a protest when he saw an "I'm for Doc!" poster overhead — directly, he noted with dry satisfaction, above a sheaf of New York *Posts*.

The proprietor appeared from the back of a Signet rack occupied entirely by Gold Medal originals. He was a grubby old man with a shapeless cap, a burlap smock, and knickers, and he studied Caulkin through large octagonal spectacles. "What's yours?"

"I'm — you might say I'm browsing," Caulkin said airily.

"O.K., Mac." The smocked back turned, revealing a mosaic of Doc pins. "Just remember that any stuff you look through, you pay for."

"Of course," Caulkin said quickly. Coarse-grained lout, he thought indignantly. Nevertheless he felt uncomfortable here. His office-home-church-club-links orbit never touched such places. The coming transaction would be trying. He had brought his dispatch case to mask the magazine after he left the store, but he would have to show it when he bought it, and he knew with painful certainty that the man would leer then.

At least he could find it for himself, he thought, peering at racks. At least he could spare himself that.

He couldn't, though. After ten minutes his mind was a blur of cover celebrities and gaudy, badly registered colors. He hadn't known there were this many publications in the world.

"See here," he said nervously. "Do you have a minute?" The big spectacles focused on him, and his discomfort grew. He cleared his throat. "I'm looking for a magazine called—" What the devil was it? Shy? Spry? "*Sly*."

The proprietor did leer. "It's right behind the Hartford *Courant*, Mac. I have to keep that nooky stuff hid. Sometimes respectable people come in."

Caulkin twitched. This was the ordeal. He found the copy, presented it, produced a five-dollar bill, was told it couldn't be broken, ransacked his pockets, and discovered Sancho's silver in his ticket pocket.

"You sure you don't want two copies?" said the man, rubbing the coin. "Most guys get two. That way you can cut 'em up, see, without spoiling what's on the back."

"One will do," Caulkin choked, and thrust the magazine in his dispatch case, and fled.

Back in the city room he was impossible. He ordered the copy children to square away their gear, reminded a rewrite man that crossword puzzling wasn't allowed on company time, and told the sports editor to switch off his radio. A half dozen men and boys had been huddled over it, listening to the scoreless game. They dispersed slowly, sulking.

After all that, Caulkin realized that he couldn't open his dispatch case here. He retired to his private office and locked the door. In less than a minute his cheeks were blazing. Like Ham and Whipple—like all *Sly* readers—he became wholly occupied by the pictures. Atrocious, he thought. Infamous, unspeakable. His tongue was dry, he felt sticky all over. Still he looked. He leafed through the issue once quickly, once slowly, and had started it the third time when he remembered why he had bought it. This time he read captions. And this time, at the end, he found the gold.

> . . . Statuesque Daff (36-24-33) leads the shapely Janes that encourage the muscle-bound Johns that power the No. 1 eleven that lives in the State house ole Adam River bilt. She delightens the Titans Saturday P.M.'s . . .

For a moment Caulkin looked cloudy. Ham had discovered this and hadn't told him. One of these days he was going to have to get rid of that young man. Then the full implications of the spread reached him. His face softened. Unless this was a fake it was a fantastic break, and it couldn't have been faked. Or could it? He called Smathers.

"What have you got on a girl named Dix? D-i-x. Dog-item-x ray. Call me back."

He toyed with a corner of the magazine, dog-earing it. Riley, the art editor, would be in. His hobby was aerial photography; he flew at dawn each clear Saturday and spent the afternoon in the *Star's* photo lab, developing plates. Caulkin dialed the photo lab extension. "Tell the fly boy to come out of his dark room. I want him upstairs."

He hung up the phone and it rang. "This is Charlie, Mr. Caulkin. About that girl. Is she by any chance a coed up in Gideon?"

"*Ah!* Yes."

"We got just one clip, dated last February. She was picked Rani — that's a sort of beauty queen, I guess — at State's Winter Carnival."

"Is there a cut?"

"It's mostly cut. There's just a short underline."

"Hold it out. I want to see her face. Anything besides her name underneath?"

"That's about all, except she's married."

"Married!" Better and better.

" 'Mrs. Daphne Dix,' " Charlie quoted, " 'the mother of a year-old son.' "

Caulkin was too enchanted to speak.

"It winds up, 'The coronation came too late in the evening to be witnessed by the infant, whose name is Charlie.' "

"Charlie," Caulkin mused. "It's a real coincidence, isn't it?"

"It sure is," Charlie said. "It's like a coincidence."

Now the general managing editor swung into action. He darted out his side door to the morgue, took a quick look at the features on the clip, and gloated when he saw that they matched *Sly*'s. The chief make-up man, a bulbous-nosed old man whom Caulkin knew only as Joe Blow, was then advised that the colonel would remake the all-star afternoon final himself; the desk was told that he was assuming personal command of all Sunday morning editions. He had alerted photoengraving and was instructing the number one rewrite man to stand by when he became aware of a dull thumping on the door leading to his secretary's office.

"Come in, Riley!" he called genially.

"Can't!" came the muffled complaint. Caulkin had forgotten to unlock it; he had to admit him.

Riley was a scar-faced, peppery little ex-pilot who was allowed great liberties at the *Star* because he had been a naval ace in the Solomons and, unlike Caulkin, had been decorated for bravery.

"So what's top secret?" he demanded.

"*Most* top secret — until the all-star."

"It better be good. I was cozy and warm in my dark little womb, listening to the game."

"State's losing?" Caulkin asked hopefully. He would have liked to have made a clean sweep of the afternoon.

"Nobody's losing. It's still tied up, goose eggs back to back. Hamp's surprising them, though. Stacy's had to make about five saving tackles from safety. *What's that?*"

He had just glimpsed *Sly*, open on the runway desk.

"That's the secret," said Caulkin, striding to it. He no longer felt embarrassed. He had a license now. "How do you like my cheerleader?"

Riley whistled. "Some headlights."

Caulkin stifled a rebuke. Riley, after all, was Navy. Fingering the page again, he said, "Do you think you can reproduce it?"

"In the *Star*?"

"On page one. I'd like to get all these shots, if possible. But I must have the one with the baton."

Riley eyed him with astonishment. "You blowing your stack, Colonel?"

Caulkin smiled indulgently. "I should explain. She's not really my cheerleader. She's State's."

Riley whistle again, long and low.

"Well?" asked Caulkin, dog-earing.

"I can do it if you stop tearing it up," the art director said, frowning. Caulkin withdrew his hand guiltily, and Riley said, "This is to shoot River down, right?"

"Can you think of better flak?"

"Well, it'll put a lot of holes in him. But what about us? How can you print those" — he swept his hand across Daffy's breasts "in a family paper?"

"I'm way ahead of you. Remember the art work for that piece we did on Belton? Inking black masks over the mental patients' faces so they couldn't be identified? We can do the same here — and explain it in the copy."

Riley chuckled coarsely. "I get it. Square little bra cups, like beauty spots."

"Roger," said Caulkin.

**

Daffy's costume bra was tight. Lashed to the unfamiliar corset, it was more confining than anything she had ever worn, tauter than even her shortest denim shorts. She didn't mind the bind, but in the hills of her childhood a large bosom had been considered a measure of beauty, and on the training table she had protested that she looked flatchested. Hotflash had replied with an impatient snort. Coed queens were supposed to look like maidens, the squat choreographer had grunted, lacing her into the 34 B cups; that was what the public wanted, and the public was paying the bill. If Daffy wanted to look like a Goddamm earth bitch off duty, O.K. But she wasn't going to blow the halftime show with a lot of loose skin.

Hotflash was no woman to cross today. She had been in a state of barely restrained rage all week. This annual pageant was the real measure of her job. For two months she had been honing her Titanettes, and every pinwheel, every group roll, had been built around Daffy, whom she had thought ineligible to be Gridiron Queen. Then Bauer's committee had upset everything.

"Any cow can sit on a float and look sexy," she had muttered furiously. "Taking Dix out of that line is like benching Stacy."

There was no appeal, however, and Hotflash, trouper that she was, had diligently shifted spots and coached the changed formation in her new dance routines, over which she had toiled as grimly as

Yablonski with his surprise plays. Humoring girls wasn't in her contract, though, so the strapless bra snaps had gone into the last reluctant notches; no apologies, nothing spared.

Daffy hadn't argued. She couldn't quarrel with anyone today. Since Monday, when Bauer had moistly taken her hand and led her under the revolving mobiles in the Student Union lobby and told her of the Athletic Committee decision, her lips had been curled in a constant smirk, and last night she had lain awake with her heart pounding like a metronome, drifting on a VistaVision cloud and seeing her future in wide-screen dimensions —her name in Variety, on Broadway marquees, in cigarette endorsements, in the brassy lights of L.A.; her husbands, each richer and more adoring than the last; her lovers handsome and reckless and defiant of convention. Red, she had concluded, would never do as a husband. He couldn't possibly afford her. But she felt a faint spark of loyalty, and she thought she might have a real affair with him later, in Las Vegas, perhaps, or Acapulco, or Sun Valley — in one of those lush resorts where the appearance of a train of lingerie trunks bearing the name of Daffy Dix (or Dixie Starr; she had about decided to switch to that) would signal the assembly of columnists and photographers and thousands of hysterical fans. Of course, she wouldn't have much time for Red: there would be foreign film commitments; then a TV series, The Dixie Starr Show; then a hoked-up flick, *The Dixie Starr Story.* Daffy trembled with anticipation. It was all so real. She could close her eyes and see everything as it would be described later in her biography, to be written by Gerold Frank.

It was the finest reverie she had ever known, and it had transfigured her. She stood in lonely splendor atop the huge, flower-decked float parked in the graded shadows of Gate C, awaiting the end of the first half. Tiers of red and yellow roses encompassed her feet; an arching parenthesis of wired gardenias enclosed her satin-sheathed figure and met, twining, overhead. Every blossom was exquisite, yet Daffy shamed the daintiest of them. She had never been more radiant. Her hair hung long, silken, and loose; her white gown was cut low, with a wide flaring skirt; her slippers were gold and glittered. After a wretched week her cold was now quite gone, her bruises healed. Even Hotflash had admitted grudgingly that she looked every inch a Gridiron Queen.

Below her the apparatus of the halftime performance lay in

jumbled snarls. On one side were three mobile television cameras, each with its coils of rubber tubing, through which technicians stepped deftly. On the other side was a low aluminum microphone and a canvas chair labeled "Director." Daffy had memorized the program. She knew that the instant the second period ended on the field the cameras would lead the Titanettes out and the microphone would become live so that Hotflash, sitting in the chair, could describe the intricate choreographic routines over the stadium's P.A. system.

And then —

And then the float would be rolled from the gate. Paul Bauer and John Winkler would meet it on the fifty-yard line. Winkler would hand a rhinestone diadem to Bauer, and he would mount the float steps for the coronation while the camera man, consulting Hotflash's charts, moved in for close-ups. Daffy ran it all through her mind for the hundredth time. Her heart thumped harder. She clutched a tin mace close and peered over the heads of the scrimmaging players to the Hamp bench, behind which Bauer was standing, talking to Winkler. Something flashed in Winkler's hand, and Daffy, who knew what the something was, closed her eyes again and took a deep breath of gardenia scent, mingled with rose.

Beside the float Hotflash was leading the Titanettes in physical jerks.

"Hup! Hup! Hup! Hup!"

The girls bounded in their turtlenecked sweaters and toreador pants, up, down, up, down, like marionettes.

"Ah-one, ah-two; ah-one, ah-two — "

"Any score?" said a hoarse voice under Daffy's feet.

Before she could reply Hotflash strode over, a menacing figure in a gray sweatsuit. "What was that?"

"Who's ahead?" asked the voice beneath the floor boards.

"Nobody," Hotflash said curtly, addressing the float. "And don't let me hear you again. This halftime show's going to cost sixteen thousand bucks for ten minutes live. I don't want you peons fouling everything up by breaking in on the audio, understand?" Without waiting for an answer she turned smartly back to the girls.

The voice belonged to Jill's husband Jack, who was one of ten students hired to propel the float. The air in their enclosure was rank. Any drifting fragrance from the roses above was lost in the contending smell of sweat. Clad only in shorts and sneakers, crouched over horizontal poles built into the frame, they looked like galley oarsmen standing by for the order to pull.

Jack, a Business Administration senior, was calculating rapidly. "So they're dishing out sixteen grand. We ought to get a bigger cut. At ten bucks a head we're being had."

"Like cattle," said an agronomist.

"Or whores."

"Did she call us peons?" asked an English major. "Proles would be better."

"Oh, I don't know," a haggard graduate student said cheerfully. "A dollar a minute's not bad."

The others jeered at him, but Jack fell silent; even in this fetid gloom he recognized Jerry Dix.

**

For the fifth time in the half State had missed a first down by inches, and young Sam Theanapolis was incensed. He blew a raspberry on his tuba and squealed, "O.K., ref, you can take out that glass eye now!"

"It's that backfield," growled a pimple-faced trumpeter. "The quarterback's chicken."

"Don't blame the backs," a bass drummer said. "We got about three plays, period. Yablonski's been living on that bucklateral cycle too long."

"No imagination," said the trumpeter. "No coaching."

Young Sam nodded vehemently, and on inspiration shouted, "What's new at Westinghouse? Switch us to Betty Furness!"

Several others took it up.

**

"It's so dull," Elsie Shoemaker told the deans' row. "They just keep kicking the ball back and forth. It does seem Red could break away once."

The dean of arts and sciences sniffed. "They're starting to heckle Tom Yablonski. If you ask me, he's got it coming."

"Our trouble is, we can't *see*," the dean of education said petulantly. He eyed the "S" Club seats enviously. "Over there they have a *view*."

**

In the "S" Club block a Department of Journalism photographer had just snapped Bill Shaw, Jake Russo, and Joe Massicotte cheering lustily. John Winkler had ordered the picture at Newt Albert's suggestion. It would be released to state media that evening, giving the lie to charges that the directors of the university's services were spending all their time campaigning for Doc.

**

Mabel Bauer was thrilled. After her disastrous performance in front of the Hillvilledale League of Women Voters she had thought Paul would give her a real dressing-down, but no, he had been sweet as pie lately, and here she was with the menfolks, on the fifty-yard line for the first time in her life, and in the president's box at that. Sooner or later the cameras would just have to turn this way. She hoped everyone in Hillvilledale Manor was watching.

"Oh dear," she sighed, as an incompleted forward pass bounced to the sideline. "I did so hope that one would be caught."

Tate whirled. "That was *their* pass," he said acidly.

"Oh?" She bit her lip. She just knew she should have kept quiet.

The provost felt out of sorts. The half was a greater disappointment to him than to most; he had expected the Titans to run up a big score, appeasing Doc and making a return to his good graces easier. Instead there had been nothing but this deadly stalemate.

"Hamp can't bottle us up forever, Governor," he said with strident cheer.

"They've made a good start," Sam Theanapolis said morosely. "Eight minutes till the break and we haven't been past their forty."

He saw the garlanded corner of the float in the shaded recess of Gate C and brightened a little. The queen's gown was by Sybyll Swanson, of Birmingham, New York, and Paris; the flowers themselves from Little Giant Florists, Inc. Sybyll Swanson and Little Giant were clients of Sam's, and Winkler had seen to it that both were mentioned in Hotflash's script.

Doc was leaning forward, his eyes riveted on the ball. "Hamp's sky-high," he said under his breath, "and we're plain namby-pamby."

"Tom will fire us up at the half," Tate said soothingly.

"He should have done it before the game," Doc said. "I hope he isn't losing interest."

**

In the Mansion Sarah was playing Russian Bank with Kit while Sol Feinblatt, in the corner of upstairs sitting room, showed Sean where was the church, what was the steeple, which was the door, and who were the people.

"I declare, that child's the limit," Sarah said. "I played that with him for a whole hour this morning. You'd think that would have been enough."

"Enough for him, maybe," Sol said. "I'm not tired of it yet."

"Well, you're spoiling him rotten," said Sarah and turned back to the cards.

Actually she wanted to be the one to spoil Sean; she was itching to hold him again. Kit understood. She finished the game with a flurry of dealing and jumped up, smoothing her tweed skirt.

"Take me for a walk, Sol. That boy's getting too fond of you. If you don't quit he'll start crying every minute you're away."

"That's the idea," said Sol.

She regarded him fondly, then took his hand. "*Outside.*"

Sarah was watching the leafless branches of the lawn elms. In a dead, dutiful voice she said, "You sure you two don't miss the game? The portable TV's downstairs. We could bring it up."

"No, we already saw a football game," Sol said. "Besides, television's bad for children."

She perked up. "That's right, I heard that!" And as they left she reached for Sean with greedy hands.

Newt Albert was in his library alcove, studying lists of poll watchers. Sol thrust his head in and shook his head gravely. "All work and no play."

Kit mimicked Doc's nasal intonation. "He just wants to get on."

"Run along, grasshoppers," Newt said lightly. "I'm busy with affairs of state."

"Affairs at State are none of your business," said Sol.

The extension beside Newt rang. "Sure, right here," he said. He listened idly, then intently, then openmouthed. "Oh *no!*"

"I bet he learned that in the movies," Sol said.

Newt snatched up a box of Cigarillos and fired one into his mouth. "Never mind how you happened to buy it. I buy it myself sometimes. But are you sure it's legit? How much of her can you see? And what about that thing between her legs?"

Kit pursed her lips. "Doesn't sound very nice."

"Not for a lady's ears," Sol said, and led her down the Mansion's front steps, hollowed by a hundred faculty receptions, into the clean air.

**

Down in Gate C Hotflash finished her jerks and sent the Titanettes out to rally the crowd's flagging spirit. They cartwheeled into position, pumped their arms three times to set the rhythm, and led the cheer:

Lean to the left! Lean to the right!
Stand up! Sit down!
Fight, fight, fight!

The band neither leaned nor stood. They sat listlessly, a panel of jaded experts.

"No gain again," the bass drummer observed peevishly. "It's that option play. So it worked the first time they tried it. You can only get one lemonade out of a lemon."

"Forget the score," said the trumpeter. "We're building character."

**

Al Swinton had a choice seat in the heated press box. It was wasted on him. That morning had brought a fifth of Jack Daniel's from Geek Minton, puzzling Al but pleasing him; he had opened it immediately after filing his Sunday copy and had left less than three inches in the Inne. It had begun to hit him at game time. *The Star-Spangled Banner* had been a struggle, and now the virescent field below was a blur to him, oddly shaped and swimming.

He tried to cope with the sportswriters on either side.

"See that Hamp fullback trap?" one cried. "It stops every slice."

"Every what?" Al asked thickly.

The other man grinned. "Get with it. I bet you're still looking for the old off-tackle drives of Jock Sutherland's day."

"That's right, that was *foot*ball," Al said sentimentally, wondering who Sutherland was.

"The handoff is to the T what the offtackle is to the singlewing."

"Right," said Al.

"It's State's power play," the man on the left said. "It should pulverize Hamp, but Stacy can't get past that Mason and Nixon line."

Al chuckled. "You got that wrong."

"Mason and Nixon," the man repeated. "Hamp's little tackles. They're sparking that packed ground defense. It's the key to the fort. That and desire."

"That double safety helps," said the man on the right.

"They don't pull many boo-boos on offense, either. Fakes, checks, chasers — very pretty."

Al gave up. He slumped against the collar of his topcoat and sank into a groggy trance, upon which the patter around him impinged like an obscure tribal chant.

". . . crossbucks into a 6-2-2-1 . . ."

". . . defensive halfs are sideblind . . ."

". . . personals are hitting, but what about the choices?"

". . . drags in the flat . . ."

". . . shotgun on the third . . ."

". . . T to the I . . ."

". . . slip-offs, bootlegs . . ."

". . . hooks . . . shovels . . . crosses . . ."

The chant faded, faded more, and died away altogether. Al was asleep, dreaming of gross by-lines.

**

The stadium faithful were growing restless. Unlike the sportswriters, they didn't admire the gallant stand of the light, white-jerseyed Hamp line. This wasn't what they had come to see, this marching and countermarching, this shadowboxing without score or glory. They had stake in something else, a cash stake. The honorary alumni had paid premium prices for their season tickets, and even the singles in the end zones had met scalper's rates. They had endured bone-shattering bus rides on the G.A.R. Highway, had bought pennants and souvenir programs, had prayed with the P.A. and obeyed the Titanettes' shrill pleas for noise, lustily caroling "Hit the Line"; "Cheer, Cheer"; "As State's Backs Go Tearing By"; and yet after all that they hadn't once been given the chance to sing their favorite fight song, reserved each year for touchdowns in this traditional game.

Here and there a wistful fan hummed it softly, to the tune of 'Boola-Boola':

Count the score, State,
Go for more, State,
Give a roar, State,
Smash up Hamp!

As the big minute hand crept upright on the illuminated scoreboard clock the crowd's mood darkened. In the beginning there was little noise. Programs were shredded and strewn over the descending rows of heads below, excessive drunkenness became apparent in the reserved sections, and there was some nasty sickness from drink. Here and there a bloodthirsty cry damned the officials on the field, but the most ominous sign of unrest was a dispirited silence. The only conspicuous enthusiasm in the stadium was directly behind the Hamp bench, where a tiny square of seats had been assigned to the visitors. The quiet elsewhere was inexplicable to them. It was a close game. Either side could win it. They couldn't understand the temper of the faithful, who had been led to expect a rout and who now squatted by the thousands in mass dissatisfaction, plucking at the handkerchiefs they had hoped to have waved long since. To the home fans this deadlock was confusing and exasperating. A tight battle with Navy was one thing, but Hamp! Little Hamp!

The frail old woman who had sat beside Ham at the season's opening game leaned forward.

"What's happening, officer?" she asked a man in the next row.

"You got me, lady," said the man, flattered to have been mistaken for a policeman. He had driven here straight from work and still wore the uniform of a Pawnattuck gas meter reader.

"You don't think those little boys could *beat* us?" she breathed.

"Naw, not us."

"I never saw State tied, even."

"Me neither."

Then an odd thing happened. The woman meant well. She disapproved of the apathy around her, and when Red Stacy stopped an end run at scrimmage she applauded politely. The gesture went astray, however. Applause was new to the stadium; spectators cheered, but never clapped, and a group of men near her misunderstood. They took this as a signal of protest and began clapping with a steady, monotonous beat which spread from section to section until the faithful, in their troubled faith, sounded like an enormous movie audience provoked because its screen had gone blank.

**

Tom Yablonski's ice-blue eyes grew icier. *Incentive,* he was thinking. *We need more incentive.*

Yablonski hadn't neglected incentive. He had been in the football business a long time, and he knew that solid player bait was as indispensable to a successful squad as hangdog discipline, personalized pre-season training critiques, and expert scouting. He had, indeed, been something of a pioneer in organizing player motivation. During his own student days boys had been rewarded after games by old grads observing time-honored rites, passing bills to halfbacks in handshakes or betting ends they couldn't jump over locker room benches. These makeshift arrangements persisted at State, but Yablonski frowned on them. They slighted linemen and blockers, without whom the stars would be dumped every time. For the season's big game he had therefore introduced a slush fund, to which alumni and other interested fans contributed and from which fees were distributed under a rigid system. The flashy backs weren't ignored. The first touchdown was still worth a fifty-dollar bill, and there were smaller payolas for later scores. But Yablonski's pool was a team pool. Anybody would earn a roll if he was hungry enough. A blocked punt brought forty dollars, an intercepted pass thirty; even a tackle behind the line of scrimmage was good for five. No, the coach thought, he couldn't reproach himself. He had given those apes out there the best incentives in collegiate sport.

And they were working. His spotters interphoned a steady stream of commendations for this guard, for that tackle; for the cogwheel precision of the sweeps and the low clean tackling of the line. The trouble was, the squad wasn't going anywhere. Both teams were right where they had started. The number slots on the scoreboard still showed double o's — as round and empty, thought Yablonski, as Orphan Annie's eyes. Of course, he knew what had happened. Every business has its hazards. The monkeys in white jerseys knew they had been counted out weeks ago, so with nothing to lose they had come to Gideon determined to upset the best regional record in the country. It was a scrappy try, and as a detached professional Yablonski gave it top marks. Not that he believed it would work. He had been tuning up Stacy for a year; the redhead, backed by the club, was an irresistible force, and there were no immovable objects in machine football. Still he scowled. It was small consolation now that Red, with the right pointers in the dressing room, could crack Hamp open in the third period. The coach had his reputation to consider. This was a network show. The halftime score would be announced at every other game in the country. If it was a scoreless score he'd be heckled mercilessly at a half dozen athletic directors' conferences next winter, whatever the final outcome. Moreover, the faceless mass up in the stadium was beginning to get out of hand. The coach was no rabbit ears, ready to flinch at the first whisper of criticism, but that repetitive applause, joined now by the stamping of feet, made his flesh crawl; it reminded him of the terrible forfeits other coaches had paid for failure. He needed a sop for the mob, a quick TD, and he couldn't get it by raising the incentive tribute, or by brooding, or by wringing the crying towel dry. Indeed, there was nothing he could do as long as Hamp had the ball and the freeze was on.

He clenched his face. A minute left.

Then Hamp punted out short, and Yablonski saw a light.

"Koski!"

A slab-sided substitute back raced up.

"Twenty on swing on three."

Koski didn't wave frantically for the referee's attention or catch his arm. The Yablonski System didn't produce giddy subs. Waving and arm-catching were signs of scrub eagerness, and Koski, although not in the first Titan unit, was no scrub. In high school he had been an all-Vermont choice two years running; he would have been the star of any other college squad in New England. Trotting out with easy, loping strides, he checked in and joined the forming huddle.

Inside it was like a coal mine. The rank facing the quarterback was grimy and streaked and gasping for air. They hadn't counted on this opposition. Their leather arm guards, new for this game, were scarred raw from savage blocks, yet their ground game still crawled, and the dirtiest, most mauled man there was their proud spearhead. Red was almost sobbing with frustration. He had expected to make a burning impression on pro scouts watching this channel, but Hamp's runt tackles had boxed him in all afternoon. He had quit snarling at them; between the last few plays he had been snarling at his own team.

"What happened to you?" he panted, glaring at the fullback. "You forget your pill or something? You can't con a spin if you don't move, for Christ's sake."

"Shove it," the fullback grunted.

"Up yours," Red flared.

The quarterback clapped his hands, calling for huddle silence, and looked quickly at Koski. "O.K., what is it?"

"Twenty on swing on three," Koski told him.

Red went tense. It was a way out. "The moon shot?"

"You heard him," the quarterback said. "Okay, break."

They moved swiftly into formation. Stacy and Koski crouched behind the quarterback. To Hamp the play seemed obvious. The Titans had been driving like moles, picking up a few yards at a time in a cloud of dust, Ohio State style, but with fifteen seconds and fifty yards to go they would have to try for the long bomb, and Stacy was their only passer.

Stacy was their only right-handed passer. Koski, Yablonski's sleeper, threw from his left.

"Hut-hut-hut-hut!"

Ham Markham came through the press gate, blinking in the sunlight, a heartbeat before the snap.

The pitchout went to Koski, and he and Stacy reversed, Red running downfield with the fullback and the ends while the line shifted left, a moving wall. The Hamp line wavered; their secondary and their double safety charged in. It looked like a delayed sweep, with the quarterback smashing in the corner. But Koski wasn't pivoting. He was prancing parallel to the line of scrimmage with a light, delicate movement, and his fingers were tightening on the leather seam.

Six seconds, seven seconds . . .

It was a rainbow after all. The safeties braked, too late; Red had his man beaten by three steps. He flew down the sideline, glancing over his shoulder like an outfielder waiting for the fly to come out of the stands. And here it came, soaring high among the roars of the faithful, spinning counterclockwise, arching up and out and down and dropping hawklike into Red's supplicating hands.

He took it on the Hamp five and bounded over.

The roar grew; handkerchiefs appeared. And then the faithful saw the red flag at scrimmage and heard the piping whistle. They were stunned. They leapt up, shaking knotted fists and screaming foul.

But Ham, who had seen the line play, knew there was no foul.

The exhausted Titans formed again. This time the defense was ready, and Koski's pass, deflected by a reddogging guard, bobbed erratically toward Gate C and landed ignominiously in the megaphone of a deft Titanette. The aroused stands, expecting another rainbow, shrieked in anguish.

But Ham could have told them there are no second chances.

**

Doc felt inspired. "I want to talk to the boys, Tom." He shouldered his way into the dressing room and peeled off his old topcoat. "I'll crank them up. I got a yarn that'll give them just the pepper they need."

The coach eyed him dubiously. Pinched on Yablonski's clipboard was a fat sheaf of notes from State's spotters, pinpointing Hamp's weaknesses. His line and backfield specialists were standing by with notes of their own; he had planned a brisk ten-minute lecture for the squad, and his towheaded freshman coach had been posted in the corridor and told to keep everyone out. Doc, of course, was an exception.

"Try to keep it short," Yablonski told him. "We got a lot to go over."

"Sure, sure, I know. Technical blah. I don't say it doesn't count. It does; it tells. But take it from an old sideliner, Tom — the main thing is spunk."

Tom didn't believe it, and though he stepped aside his hard face grew harder. He knew Doc's record and respected it. To him the old man had been one of the great little leaguers, the Jim Thorpe of New England. And afterward, he knew, Doc had turned out some rugged teams. But that had all been small time, amateur night stuff. Those had been primitive days. The best teams of that era would be laughed off the field today. The hell-fire-and-brimstone, one-for-the-Gipper school of coaching was as dead as the dropkick. Why couldn't these white elephants face it and crawl off to the graveyard?

Yablonski sank wearily to a narrow bench, wondering which tack it was going to be, hell-fire or Gipper.

It was the Gipper. Hat back, legs spread wide and arms akimbo, Doc was telling the story of Spook.

He regarded the boys fondly. He felt at home here among the

smell of rubbing alcohol and sweat. There was something poignant about their awkward sprawls. They lay on benches or training tables, or sat slope-shouldered on the buff concrete floor with their damp stained pads resting against locker doors, their mud-crusted eyes closed in fatigue, fighting for breath, each alone. Doc knew that loneliness. It stood out among the memories of his athletic youth — the feeling that there was no one but you, that you had to do it all by yourself, that no one in the world cared or would help. He knew it and he knew the need to fight it. He reminded them that they were a team. He told them that other boys had worn the Blue, and he described Spook's great pass, the penalty whistle, and Ham's discovery of the week before.

"Now, boys, there's a mighty important lesson there. I expect you're wondering which of you was offside a few minutes ago. Maybe you think you know. And maybe you're wrong — maybe nobody was. It happened once; could again. That squad long ago was shaken up bad afterward. I had young Tom here's job then, and I admit even I had some doubts about my boys. But the humbling fact is, I was wrong. They were all on the ball, all playing together, and after seventeen years it turns out they really won that big one. How? Why, by team play, of course."

He paused to let it sink in. Most of the lolling figures were listening attentively. Despite the cynicism bred by the Yablonski System they admired Doc. He was long past his prime, but a man still, and he had turned his own achievements in sport into a larger success. They didn't mind his sententiousness; they themselves were simple and uncomplicated, and he spoke to them.

The most dangerous exception was Red. None of this touched him. It's the old crap, he thought, fingering a thigh pad irritably; the old grabass. The bitter penalty had sandpapered his nerves, already raw. He felt the familiar gypsy urge to shock and defy. Suppose he told this gassy fossil to take a flying leap. What could anybody do about it? They needed thirty minutes more action out of him this afternoon, and that need was his power; flaunting it would be a shot in the arm after the bruises and failures of the first half.

"I'll let you in on a little secret." Doc looked knowing. "Team play's going to win another game I happen to be familiar with. What game?" he twinkled. "Why, this one, here, today. You're just the boys to make that *off*sides *on*sides. I don't say it'll be easy, of course. It'll take moxie and spirit blood-up-and-heads-down spirit — and, most of all, trust in each other."

Red yawned and made a show of picking his nose.

Several players looked at him with complicity. Yablonski shot him a warning glance as Doc, insensitive to the stirring around him, prepared to make his final point.

"How many of you read the Bible regular? Hold up your hands." No hands were raised. He laughed easily. "Well, I guess I don't crack the Book overmuch myself. But there's one verse I do remember, and I want to pass it along. It's something from St. Paul. You know, that old saint would've made a pretty fair coach He put it right neatly. 'Watch ye,' he said, 'Watch ye, stand fast in faith, quit you like men, be strong.' "

Doc waited for them to look up, but the only signs of life were the shifting of a taped leg and a long, whispering sigh. The initiative had passed from him with Red's yawn. The team was alert for their spearhead's next move. They knew him and knew it was coming.

"Quit you like men," Doc repeated forcefully.

"Oh balls," Red muttered.

Doc cupped his ear. "What's that?"

Someone snickered, and Red said audibly, "Up mine."

"Shut up, kid," Yablonski said sharply.

Red couldn't shut up. Every eye was on him. He was committed. "What's all this crap supposed to prove?" he demanded. "What's the point? We don't need our asses scratched. We'll deliver."

Doc misunderstood. He knew Red but slightly. They had talked together just twice before, after last year's freshman football banquet and just before the squad's departure for Camp TD last summer. The boy's overwrought, he thought, and no wonder. Tempers were always at hairtrigger during the half. Often in his coaching days he had come perilously close to provoking violence with his calculated racial insults and class gibes. He tried to withdraw with dignity.

"Do that," he said softly. "I want that." And in quiet reproach of Red's language he added, "But I want it done clean."

"Oh, go pound sand."

Doc's jaw lengthened. Yablonski rose, solid, intimidating. "Look, kid —"

"Look at this," Red breathed. He displayed his middle finger. "Does Daddy-O know what that means?"

Doc saw it. He stepped over, the softness in him gone. He said sternly, "Yes, I know, but I never thought—"

"You never thought. You never thought. Well, think. Because this," Red said, brandishing the thick finger, "is what'll clobber them Mason and Nixon clowns. Not sweet violets, but *this*"—he jerked it up and up—"is the secret weapon that's going to win your election for you."

"My *what?*"

"Oh, Christ, stop it. You think we don't dig this suction? Yablonski zeroed us in, man. We know you want us to get into Hamp so you can get into Witty. O.K., so we know, so cut the violins. We'll ram it home till they can taste it. We'll give you your new job by a frigging landslide, only scoff the shoveling. We're up to our ears, and we can't stand any more."

He hawked on the black vulcanite floor. In the silence it was deafening. There were no snickers now, no movements of cramped muscles. The coach was immobile. The players studied cleats, locker handles, motes of jersey dirt. Red glanced up slowly with a brutish grin, and Doc peered down blankly over his spectacles, and they saw themselves reflected, each in the eyes of the other. Doc didn't recognize himself. His features were distorted and unfamiliar. The strangeness of the image fascinated him, and he couldn't think what to say to it, and then he heard, as from a great distance, rising voices in the corridor.

"I've got to see Doc."

"I told you, your credentials don't mean anything here. Get up to the press box."

"You get out of my way."

Yablonski crossed to the door. In any other circumstance he would have been furious at the disturbance. Now it seemed a deliverance. He twisted the knob and instantly it sprang at him. The towheaded freshman coach had been backed against it; he staggered back, and Ham Markham, looming over him, stepped over the threshold.

"Well, look who's here," Red jeered. "The new shovel shift."

Doc looked, and his expression lightened. To him Ham's appearance now seemed almost marvelous. He couldn't decide how to cope with Red, and this was a way to sidestep him for the moment and return to his theme. Backing away he lifted his head and cried, "Boys, I was telling you about that bygone pass. Well. I want to introduce you to old number 88, the greatest end ever to lace on a State suit. I — "His voice droped. "What's wrong, boy?"

Ham's face was drawn. "Can you step outside?"

"Well — is it absolutely necessary?"

"Absolutely." To the freshman coach Ham said, "You stay in here. I'll watch your door."

"Thanks," the towhead said between his teeth. "I can handle it."

Yablonski took his arm. They had wasted too much time already. If Doc's visitor could get him out of the room, Yablonski would settle for that. Later he could pin Red's ears back. The kid needed a chewing out, no question about it; he was becoming a real threat to squad discipline. That was the trouble with glory boys. They got cocky and figured they could get away with murder. Well, Koski was coming along fine. Next season Stacy would either watch his step or be benched. But all that would have to wait. Right now there was a game to win, and whether they liked it or not, they couldn't take Hamp without the redhead; his signal was in every scoring play. Gripping the clipboard, Yablonski began reading his first spotter note aloud.

Outside in the long bleak corridor Ham was removing *Sly* from his topcoat.

Doc frowned at it. "Ham, I've given orders against that trash on this campus, and I appreciate your calling it to my attention, but couldn't you have brought it to me after the game?"

"I didn't get it in Gideon," Ham said, opening it to the last two pages. "I just brought it up from Birmingham."

"Then what's the fuss about? Of course, as governor I'll take state-wide action — a real clean-up-the-mind drive. It's hardly a proper campaign issue, though."

"It's not proper," Ham said under his breath, "but it may be an issue."

He held up the spread. Doc had been averting his eyes; he had looked through one issue a year ago, and that had been enough. At Ham's insistence he glanced down briefly. "Vile, vile," he said, blushing scarlet and looking away again. "But honestly, boy, I'll be jiggered if I can see what it has to do with me."

"Look again. Ever seen her before?"

Doc focused his Pickwickian glasses. "No, of course not." He leaned closer. "Why would I?" Closer, closer. Suddenly he shrank back. "*Why . . . that's . . .*"

"Daffy Dix, Coach. Head Titanette. Now read the fine print."

Doc's eyes darted down the column. Abruptly he grabbed the magazine.

"Boy, you've come in the nick of time!"

The nick of time, thought Ham. Doc never changed. Next he'd say there wasn't a moment to spare.

"There isn't a moment to spare!" he shouted. "Where's a phone?"

The shout could be heard in the dressing room. Yablonski turned to the freshman coach. "See if you can help him, Whitey," he said in an undertone. "Just keep him away from here."

Whitey had scarcely closed the door behind him when Doc caught his sleeve. "The phone?" he said hoarsely. "The nearest interphone — where is it?"

The freshman coach was startled. Doc knew as well as he. The same system which linked the Titan spotters with the bench also connected all stadium offices, dressing rooms, ticket windows, and gates, and obviously the closest receiver was in the room they had just left. Whitey started to remind him of that; then he remembered Yablonski's order and said, "There's one in the Mare's Nest, Doc."

"Oh, sure, of course."

The Mare's Nest was the women's dressing room, down the hall. Doc hadn't been there since the stadium was dedicated. Dismissing Whitey, he beckoned to Ham and strode with his high-kneed gait into the big vacant room. Among the lockers and wall radiators stood Hotflash's desk, an interphone on top. Doc snatched it up. Deep under the west end zone a line flashed on the central switchboard, always manned during games, and the Statette there came on immediately.

"This is Doc River," he said curtly. "Give me Paul Bauer."

The girl was efficient; she had before her a keyed stadium map showing the whereabouts of every personage at the game; she plugged a brass node in place, and the booth behind the Hamp bench rang.

John Winkler answered sourly. "What is it?"

"Give me Bauer."

"Oh, Doc. Gee, Paul's already on the sideline. I was just leaving. The Titanettes are marching off the field now — we're on next."

"Where's that Dix girl? The one Paul picked Queen."

"Over with Hotflash Hatch, Gate C! But they're —"

Doc had cut him off. He clicked the receiver, and the Statette came on again.

"Gate C, quick!"

If the phone there hadn't been inches from Hotflash's microphone she would have ignored it.

"This line's dead," she said curtly, and was about to leave the receiver dangling when she heard Doc's savage twang.

"Where's that queen, Miss Hatch?"

"On the float, Doc. Excuse me, I'll have to leave you now."

"By Jupiter, you listen to me. Get her off that thingamajig and send her down here."

"What? What?"

"Down in the Mare's Nest. *Pronto.*" He listened. "Hello?"

"I can't!" she wailed, almost femininely.

Hotflash was in an impossible position. Her microphone light had just winked on, and a dozen yards away the float was rolling into sunlight, trundled by the perspiring crew inside. Bauer and Winkler had reached their line of departure; the cameras were sliding in their dollies; the show was about to go on.

"We're on stage!" she wailed. Then, realizing her voice was live, she hastily swiveled in her canvas chair and whispered, "How long will it take?"

"I'll be brief," Doc said grimly.

"Yes, but how brief?"

He lost patience. "If she isn't here in two minutes, you're fired," he said, and slammed down the receiver.

Hotflash cut the mike's local switch and bounded up.

"Float, halt!" she yelped. It coasted to an erratic stop. "Dix!"

Daffy turned the fixed, brittle smile she had prepared for a nationwide audience. It was difficult to breathe in her corseting. She answered huskily, "Yes?"

"Get down to the dressing room on the double."

The smile evaporated, leaving the face of a bewildered child. She framed a question but couldn't find voice.

"Don't worry, I'll hold the house for you," Hotflash said gruffly. "I'll keep them happy somehow." She thought quickly. "The band can fill in." She turned to the phone, turned back. "But get hot, Dix! Doc River's waiting!"

Daffy swept up a handful of satin and vaulted down as Hotflash made the first of two rapid-fire phone calls, ordering the student bandmaster to march his men on the field double-quick. She worked fast. She had put through the second call, to the press box, alerting the chief camera man, before Daffy vanished into the stadium interior. Daffy's regal skirt was aloft in her fist; her gold sandals were flying. Behind her queenly train she left a breath of gardenia scent, a trace of rose.

**

Doc stood against a plain buff wall, a commanding figure. His huge hands were locked behind his back; from time to time he glanced imperiously at the dressing room clock. Ham, watching him from a perch on the desk, had the queer illusion that he was growing larger.

"I'm riled, boy. I'm blister mad."

"Sometimes that's good, Coach."

Slumped forward, with his knuckles braced on his knees, Ham appeared almost drowsy. In fact his most profound instincts were alert. He was a hunter, and he was ending the longest leg of his longest trek. Since summer he had stalked a web of spoors, some across the green breast of the new State campus, some through the canebrakes of the past. Now all the quarries were at bay. For all the tracks led, in the end, to Doc. Doc was the leader of every pack here, Doc notched the trails up and was king of the mountain. If there was strength in him, strength existed here; if not, then not. Whatever he was, the others were also, and among them, and intensely conscious of it, was Ham himself. Long ago he had invested in Doc blindly, intuitively, as a little boy commits his love with trusting hands into the hard rough hands of his father. Years later the boy may outgrow and outstrip his father; he may smile indulgently at the man who was his god, as Ham had often smiled at Doc these past months. None of that matters much. But if he loses respect for him, if he finds him dishonorable and despicable, then the faith in life which is the first of virtues has been dealt a crushing blow, and the little boy who still lurks shyly within him has been slain, and the love he gave, torn now and shattered, will swiftly perish.

So Ham waited, feeling the lip of the oak desk bite into his thighs, feeling the dampness gather in the hollows of his long body as the heat from the battery of wall radiators opposite crept under his topcoat and the sweatband of his hat, feeling the tension mount in Doc and feeling most of all the strain of his own toiling prayer.

After hanging up on Hotflash Doc had made one more call, to the president's box upstairs. He had wanted Tate. He had got Sam.

"A little trouble with the press, Governor," Sam had explained. "Some reporter's sick. I don't know, probably he's plastered. Anyway, we got to handle those things careful, and Winkler's down in the field, so Tate went up to take care of it. Where are you?"

"In the Mare's Nest."

"Hey, that's off-limits!"

"Not to me. Come to think of it, I want you here, too."

"Oh hell, Doc. I'm watching the show. Guess what! They decided to start with the band! My boy's out there, blowing his horn."

"Is Elsie Shoemaker near you?"

"Wait a sec. Yeah, she's up in the dean's row."

"Bring her with you. I mean it, now. *Move!*"

"O.K., O.K.. Don't get your bowels in an uproar."

Daffy had the advantages of youth, desperation, and nearly a full minute's start on Sam and the dean, but the float and the dressing rooms were at opposite ends of the stadium. Furthermore, she had to thread an involved interior route of tunnels and detours around gates, while they had but to descend a private flight of steps leading from the president's box. Thus they arrived in the bare corridor while she, racing headlong down vast echoing concrete conduits, was just approaching the fifty-yard line.

Miss Shoemaker rapped timidly and edged a pink, scandalized face around the jamb. "*Pssst!*" she whispered to Doc. "You're not supposed to be in here!" She saw Ham and gasped. "Oh dear. *Two* of you!"

"Never mind the hullabaloo," said Doc. "Where's Sam?"

He was right behind her. They entered nervously, the dean scrawny and birdlike in her severely tailored suit, Sam's Buddha belly swinging. Doc plucked *Sly* from his side pocket and flung it on the training table where Hotflash, two hours before, had struggled with Daffy's stays.

"Come here. Look at that."

They came, and looked, and recoiled.

"Aw Doc!" Sam protested, squirming with embarrassment.

The dean couldn't even protest. Obviously she had never seen anything like this before. Her face was the color of raw steak; she was cramming her unmanicured fingers in her mouth; her eyes were squeezed shut. Ham thought she was going to faint, and sprang forward to help.

Like Doc they hadn't recognized the face.

"That *slattern*," he told them fiercely, "that *trull*," he said, stabbing the page, "that *hooker* is the woman we're supposed to crown Gridiron Queen!"

Sam waddled closer. He asked on a rising scale, "It's Daffy Dix?"

Miss Shoemaker came back from the brink. One shock nullified the other. Her hand crept down her chin, her lips trembled.

"Dix?" Dix? Her lids fluttered open. "Why, it *is* Mrs. Dix!" she croaked. Her eyes bulged and bulged more. She was too guileless to see the implications of the largest picture, but it drew her all the same; something there was familiar. "Oh!" She remembered. "That's the baton!"

"What baton?" Doc snapped.

"The one at the hearing," she stammered. "It's — it's still in my office. Mrs. O'Donnell said she found it in a gutter. At Homecoming. When she said she and Mr. Markham saw Mrs. Dix — without any clothes on."

"She said it and we did," said Ham, studying *Sly* over her shoulder. "This job was done that night, at Sigma Chi."

"Aw Ham!" Sam pleaded now. "You know that's young Sam's frat." He leaned over the spread, looking for proof that Ham was wrong, and found proof he wasn't. "Oh no," he groaned, and pointed to the shadowy wall behind Daffy. To the right of the State banner, just visible, was a tiny chapter pennant.

"What was this hearing?" Doc demanded.

"Mrs. O'Donnell wanted the girl expelled," the dean said faintly. "We'd had hints, rumors — nothing we could prove."

Doc glowered. "But they were warnings."

"Yes — yes."

"You had a warning too," Ham reminded Doc gently. "I told you the campus gossip at the faculty reception."

Doc looked away. It was true, he thought miserably, it was true. And he had had more. Only last week Sare had asked him to investigate the girl. He hadn't had time for that then; he had left everything to Tate. *Tate* —

He whirled on the dean. "Did the provost know about the hearing?"

"Oh, he was there. In fact — " She bit her lip. She owed a great deal to Tate. But she had gone too far, and everything would come out now anyway. "In fact, that's why Mrs. Dix wasn't dropped."

"The provost overruled you?"

"He thought we were being ridiculous."

"I see." Doc's eyes flashed. "Sam! Bring me Dr. Tate."

Ham wished Harry Mikel were here, to hear the iron in Doc's tone and see Sam trudging out like an overweight *Six Gun* deputy sheriff leaving the town jail to fetch the sanctimonious rancher who, after years of successful connivance, has just been exposed as a rustler and a sneak and a pimp for Belle Starr.

Sam's resolute exit was spoiled. He had opened the door and was about to step out when Daffy, sprinting up at full tilt, crashed into him.

"*Oof!*" he gasped. "Beg pardon!" Then he saw who she was and stumped off without a word.

"Well, that does it!" she cried, and stamped a bare foot.

She was utterly disheveled. Back at Gate C she had removed her sparkling shoes and cradled them against her waist, each in a hand, and now her heels were raw from the cement floors. The bra and corset tortured her; her shoulders were heaving violently. Rivulets of sweat had ruined her makeup, her hair was matted against her forehead, and her lids were puffy with fatigue. Yet stars of hope still shone beneath them. She had carefully looped the train of her gown over one damp arm, and there it still lay, dusty and bedraggled but proudly aloft, cherished like an old flag.

They were watching her in silence. She fought for breath and poise, cast around, and recognized Ham.

"Oh hi," she panted. Then, tossing back her damp hair, she gave him her fixed, brittle, coast-to-coast smile.

**

The Titanettes had been thrown into the breach. State's band wasn't enough. The telecast demanded more, so the girls, who had been scheduled for a rest, were ordered to take the field. Snaprolling and flipflopping desperately, they had formed a wide semicircle in front of the bandmaster while Hotflash improvised into the mike.

"This bevy of luscious young all-American well-groomed highly trained coeds is virtually girl for girl the same award-winning ensemble that took top honors last summer in the women's matched drill tournament at the Boston Garden," she bayed nonstop. "Behind their flying jacknifes and human Immelmanns stands a picked band of ringing brasses and clear winds — the pipes, the flutes, the oboes, the trumpets, the clarinets, the trombones — with every bandsman the certified holder of an honorable mention certificate from the Madison Square East-West intercollegiate orchestration tourney semi-finals in June."

The lie almost gagged her. That frosh tuba player hadn't been with them then. She cocked an ear and listened, flinching, to the bleating notes of young Sam. *Oompah, oompah, oompah.* Fatso's off again, she thought furiously.

She glanced at her watch. The tyranny of time pressed harder and harder; if they didn't get this show on the road within the next three minutes there wouldn't *be* a road.

The band was approaching the end of "Semper Fidelis." They had been depending on hints from her, relayed via the P.A., and she crouched over the mike.

"Now the sixty-man-strong marching band will form a square and render an old favorite with a new twist, the ever-popular 'Stars and Stripes Forever.'"

Square was the word, she thought. If she had a tenth of Yablonski's recruiting fund she could build a real combine and give out with hit tunes, jivey stuff, but no, all she had was a gang of hopeless hacks, and these old turkeys were the best they could do.

Beyond the puffing band she could discern two indecisive figures — Bauer and Winkler, pacing the far sideline. They had expected their role in the coronation to be over by now, and hadn't an inkling of what was wrong. Circling the field to question Hotflash was impossible; the float might appear at any moment, and they would be needed where they were. They couldn't even telephone her. The switchboard Statette had closed the Gate C line the moment she began speaking over the P.A. If only she had been cut off a few seconds before, Hotflash thought. If only Doc hadn't got through. She couldn't imagine what was on his mind. He had sounded determined, but was it worth this? Was anything?

Time, time, time . . .

Time was running out. She could wait a little longer, but the band would have to carry on alone. The Titanettes had had it. Her expert eye read the signs. They were falling sloppily, their dives weren't clean. Better to cut losses and let the band drift than have overworked girls disgrace the Titanette name. She killed the mike temporarily and blew two sharp blasts on her whistle. The semicircle snapped to attention.

"Right by flank on the line!" she called, all throat.

They trotted to the gate, hup-hupping to themselves to keep in step. Once they had reached the obscurity of the shadows that discipline disappeared, though they were still a team; prostrate by the float they gasped together, in rhythm, like surf.

In the float itself Jack raised the voice of rebellion. "We want out!"

"Quiet, you," Hotflash snarled.

"Well, how much longer?"

"Not much. It can't be long now."

It couldn't. It really couldn't. A minute at most.

Time, time . . .

It was time to form an alternate plan. Dix hadn't returned, might never return, might be in a real jam. Maybe she'd murdered her husband, Hotflash thought whimsically. No, that was impossible, he was down there in that sweatbox. But she could have killed somebody else; she was a tough woman, and all woman. Secretly Hotflash admired Daffy, though that counted for nothing now. What was needed now was an understudy, a standby. Bauer wasn't here. She'd have to take over herself. She pondered. The girl would have to have class. They couldn't palm off a dog. Hotflash knew every figure on campus—her basic posture course was required of all coed freshmen—and she knew there were no candidates in the stands. No, the cream was here, in the shade. Narrowing her eyes, she appraised the collapsed forms around the float.

"Graham!"

A lithe brunette with dancing eyes skipped up. "You want me, Miss Hatch?"

Hotflash looked her over with a sailor's eye. Fine pointed breasts, she thought. And a hard, flat belly. Not as dainty as Dix, but maybe that was the tight toreadors; nobody looked innocent in them.

"The princess had to take off, Graham. You think you could take her spot in a pinch?"

A Cinderella look crept into the darting eyes. "And how!"

"In a pinch, now. Nothing's definite."

But this was the pinch. *Something* had to be definite, and soon. This couldn't go on another minute; the show was laying a chalk-white, king-sized egg.

The band, lacking P.A. instructions, had swung into "The Girl I Left Behind Me."

Oompah, oompah . . .

Time . . .

Hotflash wheeled and picked up the phone.

"Give me the Mare's Nest. I got to talk to Doc."

**

"Hi," Ham had answered Daffy, and his voice had broken a little with pity.

Doc had never really met Daffy before; he was observing her at close range for the first time. Vaguely he remembered now that she had been last year's Winter Rani. Strange, he reflected; once he had been on speaking terms, not only with every Rani, but with every girl in the student body. He had accepted his isolation from the mass of undergraduates as one of the penalties of State's greatness, never dreaming of implications as sharp and cruel as this. Nothing had ever hit him so hard. It was shattering because it was a blow at the code of ethics that lay at the heart of his very being, and thus a blow at State. Thus also it was unforgivable. Doc couldn't share Ham's pity. His face was stiff, expressionless. He meant to have vengeance.

Yet he had to be sure. He had to be fair. His message to Hotflash had been deliberately cryptic because he had to give the girl a chance to explain. That, too, was part of the code.

"Hi," she said to him, and then "Hi" to Miss Shoemaker, who still felt squeamish and was resting on a straight chair by the desk, her face slack and lowered. Hi's over, Daffy shifted uneasily from foot to scarred foot. "Excuse me," she said, uncertainly. "I got this real big thing, being queen and all. I mean, they're sort of waiting for me."

In a solemn tone that reminded Ham of the judge, Doc said, "Mrs. Dix, I want to ask you to tell me something."

"Sure, sure," she fretted. "It's just they're *wait*ing."

"What do you know about *Sly?*"

"*Sly?*" *Sly?* Once in Louisville a greasy pickup had taken her to his hotel room and shown her a copy in bed. She had leafed through it without much interest, knowing it was for him, not her, one of those crazy kicks some men needed to work themselves up; and she hadn't thought of it again until the official notice went up on the Realgonesville bulletin board. "I heard of it," she said cautiously, remembering that the notice, signed by Doc, had barred it from the campus. But what of it? It couldn't have anything to do with her. *She* wouldn't buy it. That Louisville greaseball? Gone long ago, to wherever jerks-of-all-trades went. "Somebody mentioned it once, that's all."

"Nothing else?"

"No. I just heard the name, see."

"Just the name."

"Uh-huh."

"Funny."

"Pardon?"

He pushed the magazine across the sloped surface of the training table, reversing it for her. "Please look at that."

"Sure, if it don't take, you know, too much time. I mean — "

"If you mean they're waiting, you already told me that," he said, his judicial air beginning to crumble. "All right, I understand. They'll wait."

She shrugged and inclined her head to see. Abruptly her little bow ended. She was like a motion picture film brought to a dead stop. One instant she was moving normally, the concert of a thousand tiny muscle actions blending into the smooth flow of life; an instant later she was a still photograph, as still as the *Sly* poses before her. It was all illusion. Calm without, she was chaotic within. Her mind was reeling blindly, in rapid succession taking up and discarding a series of fragmentary, unformed thoughts. She recognized herself first. Second she felt an odd, fleeting glow of pleasure — her picture had been published only once before, when she was picked Rani, and clearly this was something much bigger, a real deal. Apprehension followed: When had these been taken? Where? By whom? And then it began to hit her. She ran her dazed eye down the familiar lines and crooks of her own flesh. Why, she was practically stark naked! How had *that* happened? She saw the poised baton. *Oh no,* a sick voice within her whimpered. Not that, not *that*. It was too horrible, too dreadful, too horribly dreadfully *awful.*

Even Daffy knew it was awful, even she, who didn't understand why. Lacking any real standards of her own, she had always judged by the standards she had seen in others, a flexible attitude which permitted her to take whichever yardstick was convenient at the moment, but some things wouldn't fit any measure, and this was one. Cheap publicity, yes—a messy divorce, an arrest for disorderly conduct, or a term in the Lexington dope pen would pass if they helped build a romantic, star-crossed image. Sex, yes—almost all sex could be justified as love. But this, this, *this* was out. Out everywhere. With everybody. It made her look queer, and common, and tacky. That was it, she thought, remembering the word from her Southern childhood; it was just plain downright *tacky*.

Suddenly she remembered her father. She wondered whether anyone would show it to him, and guessed someone would, and felt the old gray chill of terror.

Like her father in the shed Doc was huge and threatening. He rumbled, "Seems you know *Sly* passing well."

She stirred, and as she raised her head Ham, watching from behind the dean's chair, noticed her sulky lower lip twitch slightly. Often in the back rooms of Birmingham police stations he had seen that twitching on the faces of suspects confronted by overwhelming evidence of guilt. It usually foreshadowed panic, irrationality, wild countercharges.

"I declare, I think it's just hateful of you to show me a thing like this," she whispered.

"Well, what can you tell us about it? How did it happen? Were you paid? It appears you'd been drinking hard liquor. Where'd you get it?"

"Just mean and hateful," she said, whispering always. "It's filth. Plain, low-down filth."

Doc's gaze was flint-like. "I'm waiting, Mrs. Dix. I mean to get to the bottom of this."

"I don't know what you're talking about." Her eyes shifted away from his, and she indicated the spread with a scarlet nail. "After all, it's not me."

Only Ham was unsurprised. He had heard more grotesque denials: men inventing twin brothers, accusing patrolmen of frame-ups, or pointing distractedly out the window and insisting that a passing stranger was the real culprit.

He said gently, "It can be proved, Daffy."

"How?" she challenged stridently.

Miss Shoemaker, startled by the enormity of the perjury, said tartly, "Your physical is on file here, Mrs. Dix. Every mark. Every measurement."

"It's somebody else," Daffy persisted, her voice rising unsteadily. "Somebody probably hundreds of miles away. Maybe not even in this country."

"Oh, she's in the U.S.A., all right," Doc said. He spread his gnarled fingers on the training table. "Not a hundred miles from here, either. Not a yard."

"Listen, I could sue! She just happens to look like me, is all!"

"Look again, young lady." He tapped the glossy reproduction of the State banner. "That picture was taken on this campus."

"In the Sigma Chi house," the dean said. "There's a pennant in the corner."

Daffy's eyes darted from Doc to her, back to Doc, over to Ham, and then away from all of them again. She was trying desperately to think, trying to cope with their questions and at the same time to place this insanity in the perspective of her life. Her pathetic evasion was deceiving no one; no evidence could be stronger than this. Yet Ham saw that her confusion was real. Since Whipple's call he had been puzzling over motives, and if there were none for the others, least of all was there one for Daffy. Doc had been in no mood to discuss the maneuvering that must have been behind this, but it had to come out, and it had to come out now.

"You were in Sigma Chi for Homecoming," he reminded her.

"I was not!" she cried, still ducking instinctively. Then she realized that was no good; half the campus had seen her there. Dimly sensing where this was leading her, yet still unaware of what had happened, she said sullenly, "Well, maybe I was. I forget. But so what? Lots of people were."

"I know. I was there, too. Do you recall what you wore to the party?"

"No." Then: "*Oh!*"

For suddenly she did recall. *The clothes.* The jacket, the sweater, the loafers — the best of her wardrobe, better than anything Jerry had been able to afford with his piddling little jobs since. Involuntarily she looked down at *Sly*. The borders of the pictures were indistinct; no one else could have made sense out of the smudges there. Nevertheless Daffy recognized them at a glance — a sleeve here, a hem there; the sheen of a new sole, the adjusted strap of her favorite bra. So *that's* when it had happened . . .

Ham was hurrying her. "Do you also remember an older man with a little pencil mustache? Skinny? Wore green glasses?"

Oh brother, Daffy thought wryly; do I ever. But she didn't reply. She didn't trust anyone here. It was safer to clam up, play it cool, and study the plumbing on the wall.

"Skinny," said Ham, spacing his words carefully, "was a *Sly* photographer."

Daffy forgot the plumbing. "He was? He was?" She fumbled at the magazine. "That creep did *this*?"

Doc's eyebrows went up. "Nobody told me one of those skunks was around here!"

"You were a threesome that night, weren't you?" Ham asked her swiftly. "There was you, and the photographer."

"I didn't know who he was," she moaned, dropping her mask completely.

"And then there was your date."

"What?" Doc demanded. "Who was he?"

Ham would have preferred to wait now. He wanted Daffy to work this out herself, and in her dilating face he saw the first flicker of understanding. It's coming, he thought. Coming slowly, but coming. Count ten and she'd have it.

Miss Shoemaker, however, couldn't contain herself. She had been running Kit's report through her mind, and she cried out, "It was that Stacy boy!"

There was no holding Doc now. He was through the door before Ham could draw breath, and in the corridor he almost ran down Newt Albert.

Newt had just added a link to the chain of Cigarillos begun in the Mansion library. He had been wandering around the subterranean tunnels and gate overpasses, looking for Doc, and he clutched at him, flattening the little cigar between his fingers.

"I got bad news, Governor. There's this magazine, I had a copy in your office once—"

"I've seen it," Doc said over his shoulder.

"Well, the new issue—"

"Seen that, too. I'm handling it now. The girl's down the hall."

The new stride carried Doc into the team's dressing room, where he did run down the freshman coach. Whitey had slipped inside to hear the briefing. He was standing directly in Doc's path, and before he could turn a mighty shoulder struck his back. In four years at Michigan State nobody had thrown such a block at him. He pitched over a bench, hit the floor inelegantly, and bounced.

"Hey!" he yipped, scrambling up.

Doc hadn't even seen him. Like an Old Testament patriarch, like Uncle Sam in a recruiting poster, he was pointing straight at Red.

"I want that man."

Yablonski had just wound things up. He felt confident and relaxed, and at first he didn't sense the urgency in Doc. "We all want him," he said, smiling one of his rare smiles. "And we're going to get him, the whole second half."

"Come here," Doc ordered Red.

Red rose, blinking. What was this crazy Dad up to now? He looked to Yablonski, who hesitated, seeing the fire in Doc's eyes now, and then nodded reluctantly. Probably the old man's still smarting from Red's lip, Yablonski thought. They'd better rub his back a little. But not for long. The team was due on the field now.

"Take 'em out," he told his backfield coach. "Get 'em loose, and we'll be right along." He slapped Red across the back of his pants. "Come on, kid."

Doc was already striding back, and they skipped until they caught up, Yablonski's basketball shoes lisping, Red's cleats clumping, and Newt Albert making no sound at all as he darted in the rear, puffing anxiously on his bent Cigarillo.

Inside the Mare's Nest the phone was ringing. Ham answered it and called out, "It's for you, Coach."

Yablonski responded instinctively, then dropped back as Doc bounded ahead. Red gaped. Coach? Dad? With that come-to-Jesus line? He followed *his* coach, the *real* coach, across the threshold, and he was just beginning to wonder what they were doing on the girl's side of the hall when he saw there were women here, too—old Dean Shoemaker and, of all people, old Daff. Must have been a quick halftime show, he thought. He glanced at her rumpled dress. Must have been rough, too.

"Hi," he said indifferently. "How was the big mo?"

There was no answering Hi. She seemed to be staring through him. He shrugged, sank to a bench, and resumed picking his nose.

"You got everything in shape?" Doc was asking the phone.

So that was the coach, Red thought contemptuously. O.K., Coach. Coach this.

"Let 'er rip," Doc said and hung up.

He turned to the room, counting heads, and they looked back diversely — Ham alert, the dean still mortified, Yablonski baffled, Newt worried, Daffy blank, Red surly. Everybody was there but the provost. Doc wondered how long to wait for him; then the door opened and Sam trudged in dejectedly.

"Tate's disappeared," he said, sitting beside Red.

"I'll see him alone later," Doc said crisply. He motioned Daffy to a facing bench and took up his station behind *Sly*, his hands braced on the table edge. "Stacy!" he ordered. "Step up here."

Red rose slowly, stretching his bull neck as though to free it from the battered jersey. It was an insolent gesture, and everyone but Daffy, deep in her trance, regarded him with dislike. Yablonski especially was provoked; he had a squad waiting for him. Stepping over, he shoved him forward. They drew up and, at Doc's mute nod, glanced down.

"Jesus!" Yablonski breathed.

Ham noticed that Red was their first relaxed witness. He inspected the pictures almost philosophically, and while Yablonski was still staring he went on to read the text.

"It's not very good English," he said, grinning crookedly.

So he *was* involved, Ham thought. But why?

"This happened at Homecoming," Doc said.

"No kidding?" Red said innocently.

"I'm told you were with Mrs. Dix that evening."

"Well, yeah, I saw her around."

"Let's nail this down," Ham said. "You saw plenty of people around Homecoming night. Me, for example."

Red rubbed his mouth thoughtfully. "That's a fact, Hambo, I did see you around."

"But you were *with* Daffy."

"Have it your way."

"And your chaperone was Geek Minton."

Red leered silently. Doc was about to pursue this, and Ham was wondering how they could break Red if they didn't even know what had incited him, when Yablonski, brooding over the spread, unintentionally provided a key.

"To think we wanted publicity," he murmured. "The *Star* blacked out the team, so we wanted publicity. Remember Winkler told us *Sly* had a man in New England?" he asked Red. "We even talked about the guy. But I never thought it would have anything to do with State."

"Winkler knew?" Doc asked sharply.

"Wrong tree, Doc," Sam said. "John wouldn't touch this with a barge pole."

Ham was watching Red's thumb. It had begun to creep along the edge of the magazine, lifting page corners.

"When was the last time you saw our public relations man?" Doc asked Daffy.

"When the Titanettes went to the Boston Garden," she said in a monotone, her eyes fixed on Red.

Sam was right, Ham thought; it was the wrong tree. Ham knew because he himself was beginning to see the right one. Branch by branch it was leafing for him; bit by bit he recalled this conversation, that incident. Red wanted to check the rest of *Sly*. To find what? Not nude pin-ups; he had everything he wanted in three dimensions. Well, what did he want that he didn't have? The long, tedious pillow talks Ham had overheard in the College Inne came back to him. Both Red and Daffy were bent on sudden fame. That was why she had set her heart on becoming Gridiron Queen, and why dazzling the faithful meant so much to him. Before the season Red's way had seemed clear. Then Doc's campaign had thrown up a block: no Titans were mentioned in the *Star*. Because of the *Star's* wire franchises, the block had knocked out out-of-state newspapers, leaving only magazines with sports sections. Really it left just *Sly*, the one magazine with a man on the spot. Probably Red had become available to Geek through Al Swinton, who had seen them both and had shown Geek Daffy's picture over drinks at the Gideon Arms. Geek's offer would have been gutter press routine — a sports feature in exchange for the girl. Ham knew that Geek hadn't kept the bargain; he had leafed through the issue while waiting for red lights during the drive up from Birmingham and had seen the story on drag racing. Even if Geek had, *Sly* was a poor substitute for a wire service. But Red, of course, wouldn't have known that. The printed word would have seemed enough to him. He had sold Daffy for counterfeit, and now his restless thumb was itching to throw open the sports page and see the glitter that wasn't there.

The wiggling thumb attracted Doc. "Stop that! I want this open where it is."

Red's hand jerked back. Ham remembered Trudy Viggiantti's drunken report by the Sigma Chi punch bowl and recognized the last telltale bud on the tree. He was ready now.

"Daffy's threatening to sue *Sly*," he began obliquely.

"Maybe she's got a case," Red said cagily. "I wouldn't know."

"She's got an airtight case if *Sly* doesn't have her permission." Ham paused. "In writing."

Doc snorted. "Seems to me you're cutting blocks with a razor, boy."

"In writing," Ham repeated. He paused again. "And witnessed."

"Still a quibble." Doc flicked a hand at the spread and said, "Any girl that gets to this pass is asking to have her name dipped in furniture polish."

"Maybe somebody helped her get there. Maybe that was the idea. The point is that *Sly's* lawyers wouldn't have allowed this out of the shop unless they had papers."

"Well, Mrs. Dix?" Doc asked crustily. "What about it?"

"I didn't sign anything," she said woodenly.

"No, but you gave that skinny ferret your autograph," Ham said. "You were seen. And Red was seen with you."

"Yes, what about that?" Doc asked Red. "What do you know about this camera bum?"

Yablonski, who had been absorbed in the photographs, looked up and saw the threat. He said uneasily, "Speak up, kid. You got nothing to hide."

"That's right," said Red, contriving to look hurt. "Man, I don't even know what's going on."

"All right, let's concentrate on Sigma Chi," Doc said. "Was there a photographer with you?"

"A photographer? No, I didn't see nobody like that."

"A ribby little fellow, then. You said dark glasses, didn't you, Ham?"

"Green glasses. And a mustache."

Red scratched his head, pretending to think. He brightened. "Oh, yeah. There *was* a mook like that hanging around. You mean he was from *Sly*?"

"You didn't know?" Doc asked suspiciously.

"Hell, no. There was lots of retreads around. Alumni. I figured he was one of them."

Ham stepped forward. "Didn't you think it strange when he asked for Daffy's autograph?"

"Autograph?" asked Red, parroting still. "Say, that's right, you're bringing a lot back to me. He *did* do that. No, it seemed on the level. I mean, Daff's like me. People are always edging up after games for this or that."

"It happens all the time," Yablonski said quickly.

"I don't know why," said Red. "They just do."

Ham moved toward the table. "So you weren't surprised when this louse asked you to sign under Daffy."

"Huh?"

A shot in the dark, but on target. Red had sagged lightly. It was time for Ham to bluff.

"Look, I can find out quick. We don't have to send a lawyer to New York. Everybody in my business is next to everybody else. I can put through a call to *Sly* in five minutes and they'll tell me whose name's on that sheet."

Red fell into the net. He thought Ham already had him. Yet he wasn't cowed. His hobo instincts quickened. Suppose they knew? What could they do? If a few Pawnattuck High TD's could square a rape charge, this Hamp game was worth some shook-up feelings. They had to have him, and everybody knew it, so why the hell didn't they put away their music? It wasn't like anybody was hurt for real. Daff had had her mo on the float; next half he'd give Doc and the voters theirs. Anyway, there was no point fencing now. Once they took the time to riffle through the rest of the issue they'd see the feature on him and guess at what the deal had been. He set his hands on swaggered hips.

"Remind me to bring you along for my next exam, cornball. You freshen up my memory real good."

"So you were the witness."

"I guess so. It was just another autograph, I thought." But why even play with them? "Sure, I signed."

"You did?"

The whisper, inaudible to Red, was Daffy's. During the grilling her eyes hadn't left his face. He was her one sure link to Homecoming, and she was struggling to recall details. Most of that night was an alcoholic swamp to her, trackless and meaningless, but there were a few islands. Red had brought Geek along; she knew that. There had been some jazz about his being a loyal fan — some noise that seemed a little offbeat at the time, because in the past Red had always cut birddoggers dead. She had said nothing, figuring the creep probably had a roll and Red was planning to get his. Then, just before the flooding tide of whiskey rose and drowned all thought, there had been someone murmuring something about write right here, it's just as a souvenir, that's the baby, that does it. Daffy's lids dropped. It was clearer now. *Thats the baby. That does it.* She could hear the coaxing in the murmur, and she knew who the murmurer had been. Red had told her what to do, and where to do it, and why. *That's the baby, that does it, that does it, that's the baby* hammered in her brain, over and over. It had done it, all right, she thought hysterically. It had loused everything up but good, and *he* was the baby, *he* was the —

She clenched her teeth. She mustn't flip. Her mind was still on the one note; after the half she'd scratch every trashy freckle out of that common, tacky face, but she had to keep the lid tight till Bauer had crowned her. Too much lay on the line to foul everything up now. The long wait, the sweaty run from Gate C, this Maidenform vise — they were all little investments backing the big commitment, and they were worth it. But how much longer was this going to take?

"Can we step it up?" Yablonski was even now asking Doc quietly.

Before Doc could reply the door opened and Whitey peered in. "You better hop," he said. "I just got the word. Hamp's made an official complaint, and the ref's threatening to walk off five yards against us for delaying the game."

Daffy gave a strangled little cry. She was on her feet, swaying, like a puppet dangled from unsteady wires. "How about the pageant? The float?" She held out a hand to Doc, a beggar's hand, cupped and trembling. "Please — I got to go. It's this thing I told you. Mr. Bauer and all. TV, live. You know — Gridiron Queen."

Red's nonchalance vanished. "You mean they haven't started the halftime show?"

"Oh, that's over," Whitey said carelessly and left.

"Another girl was crowned," Doc said. "I settled it on the telephone just now. Miss Hatch couldn't wait."

Daffy's movie had jammed again. She was a statue.

"You wouldn't have been eligible anyhow," Doc said grimly. He rapped a *Sly* page. "This automatically expels you from State."

Count down, thought Ham. Count ten, nine, eight, seven —

Daffy screamed.

"Now, see here!" Doc protested.

She didn't hear him, didn't see him. There was no one in the room for her but Red. She leaned toward him in a tense crouch, her face contorted and hideous.

"You bastard!"

"Stop that!" Doc snapped.

"You lowlife bastard!"

Red shuffled uncomfortably, his forked hands still on his hips. "Oh, Christ, Daff, it was just a gag."

"Part of a gag," Ham said to him swiftly. "He took some shots of you, too."

"This guy, he wanted a story, see —"

"— and you agreed to line up Daffy if another story was about you."

"No, it wasn't that way, but —" The hell with it. The hell with everything. "O.K., so it was. So what?"

Doc sucked in a breath. He was stricken, mute. His lips moved soundlessly. The others watched Daffy with shocked fascination. Her eyes were tiny, her tongue was flicking out like a snake. She moved nearer to Red, then nearer.

"You Goddamn son of a bitch!"

"Listen, I don't have to take this," he growled.

"You dirty —"

"Shut up!" he snarled. "You know what you can do with —"

"— dirty, stink-fingered bastard!"

"Excuse me," Miss Shoemaker whispered. She flounced toward a battleship-gray door labeled Women's Lavatory, hesitated, turned, and left them all for the corridor, her heels clicking nimbly.

Daffy had Red rattled. He had never seen such rage, and he tried to dampen it with derision. "Aw, go write a letter to your congressman."

"I should've kicked you out of bed!" she screeched.

He looked around in alarm and saw only intent, curiously pointed faces. Yablonski looked anxious, ready to intervene, but Doc motioned him back. He had to hear this.

"Listen, Daff," Red said desperately, "We can talk —"

"That's all you're good for. You can't hump worth a damn."

That kindled him. "Go down on this."

"Can't even give a woman a cheap thrill."

"Blow it."

"All them times you thought you grooved me! I never popped once, not once!"

He had caught fire. "You hillbilly whore!"

She grinned horribly. "The great lover!" she jeered, her voice like a fingernail skidding on slate. "The great stud!"

Red's face mottled. Now he too had tuned the others out. He saw only her, crouching catlike, creeping closer.

"You two-bit lay!"

Daffy was upon him. She straightened and held her face to his. "Know what you really are between the sheets? A clown! A frost! A cold screw!"

She spat in his face.

And then he hit her.

It wasn't a slap. His fist was knotted, and he drove straight up, hitting the point of her delicate chin while her tongue was still out. Her head snapped back; her teeth ground into her tongue with a rent like the sound of gristle tearing, and she staggered back, falling with a little stumble, choking and spitting blood. Yablonski pinned Red's arms from behind; Sam whipped out a handkerchief and knelt to nurse her; and Doc looked from one pair to the other, back and forth in disbelief.

Yablonski muttered, "You chuckleheaded —"

"Go ahead," Red rasped. "You think of anything she didn't say, you say it."

"That was great, golden boy," Ham said bitingly. "I'm glad to see you can knock somebody out."

"Now you start," Red said between his teeth.

"That's right, Bub. My turn. And this time I'll give you a real knuckle sandwich."

There was no fight. Red lurched forward, but Yablonski held him fast. Slowly Red's straining arms slackened. "I'm all right," he mumbled. "Let me go."

Yablonski did, though he held his hands poised, and Red stood alone, breathing hard and staring down at Daffy. She wasn't really out. Her eyes were dull but open, and she sat up with an effort, bracing herself on one arm as Sam wiped the scarlet froth from her swelling lips. Her gown was ruined. The bodice was scrawled with blood, and blots and stains smeared the length of the satin train.

"Better let me drive you," Sam said gently.

She stood, moaning, and propped her hand on his shoulder. "Money," she said thickly. "Sitter."

"I'll take care of the sitter," Sam said, helping her along. "We'll stop in the infirmary on the way."

The outer door was opened again, again by Whitey. He saw them coming through and started.

"We lost five?" Yablonski asked flatly.

"Five now." He held the door for Sam. "Five more if we don't kick off now."

"Then tell 'em to kick. Sub Koski for Stacy. I'll be right up."

Whitey withdrew, and Yablonski, satisfied that Red was quiet, led Doc to the battery of wall radiators. He said soothingly, "Now don't do anything hasty. Remember, the kid's just a kid."

Doc looked at him vacantly. "What's that?"

"Well, for a minute there I thought you were going to rupture something. You still look white."

Doc fumbled for his handkerchief, drew out his wallet instead, stared at it a moment, then shoved it back in his pocket. Color crept back into his cheeks.

"Are you talking about Red?"

"Sure. He's just a kid is all I'm saying."

"He's got his full growth," Doc said heavily.

"Yea, but you know kids."

"Stop calling him that! Are you taking his part?"

"No, no! Of course, I don't think he'd have blown up if it hadn't been for the tension. A tie game works everybody up." Yablonski added significantly, "And a lot rides on this one."

"You mean Tuesday?"

"Sure. Everybody knows it, for Christ's sake."

"I thought we'd heard enough foul talk here."

"O.K., O.K. But let's face it—you're in this deeper than me."

Doc remembered Red in the men's dressing room. So it was true. Tom *had* briefed them. The Titans were playing to win an election. He closed his eyes, then snapped them open.

"That girl's fast."

"Oh *she's* no good. You were right to give her the boot."

"It takes a rutting man to make a woman loose. The boy's no better than she is."

Ham could hear them. He stood a few feet away, his head bowed and his hands folded in mourning. He had just watched the brutal murder of a dream. Doc had always believed that youth, sport, and beauty were absolute values. He had enshrined them in his trophy pavilion and consecrated them in his heart; to him they had been incorruptible emblems of the good and the true. The dream hadn't been Doc's private creation, of course. Really it was an all-American vision. The delusion that the graceful were blameless had become as sacred as the flag, and trust in it died hard. Bill Tilden became a queer and Charles Van Doren a cheat; new heroes sprang up. Ingrid Bergman skidded, Diana Barrymore died drunk; there were corps of heroines left. The capacity to manufacture fresh symbols was infinite, a tribute to American know-how. And yet it wasn't evil. Lovely girls should after all be pure, and handsome men should be honorable; Ham felt a touch of envy for those who were so sure that they always were. But Doc was no longer among them. The grail had slipped from him. Daffy and Red had destroyed his faith, and smashed his idols, and cruelly taught him that beauty is not truth.

"Sure, I suppose he did sow a few wild oats," Yablonski was saying.

"Wild oats." Doc pondered. "I don't think he'd call them that. That wasn't the kind of language he was using."

"I'll make him pay for that. I'll ream him out good."

"That's closer to it," Doc said wryly. "No, Tom, it's too late to whale his backside or wash his mouth out with soap. There's only one thing to do with him."

"Well, I'll be dipped if *I* can guess it." Yablonski glanced at his watch in exasperation. At least one series of downs had passed and he didn't even know who had the ball.

Newt Albert padded over. So quiet had he been, so lost in his own deliberations, that Ham had forgotten he was there. Ham watched, faintly surprised, as Newt crossed to within earshot of Doc.

"He's out," Doc said nasally. "Same as her."

Yablonski started. "Out?"

Doc nodded. "Sauce for the goose, sauce for the gander."

"You can't!"

"I can't? Red!"

Red looked up, bearish, unrepentant. "You talking to me?"

"Turn in your suit and get out." Doc's voice was like a saw. "You're dropped from the university."

Red's hands shifted on uncertainly on his padded hips. "Huh?"

"I said get, get." Doc advanced on him, and now Ham was convinced that he had grown. His shoulders looked a yard wide. "You want me to spell it?"

"Don't," Yablonski pleaded, sidestepping over. "It'll ruin him."

"No, Tom. He's ruined already."

Yablonski searched frantically for an argument. "But it isn't fair — a kid like that, with a scholastic record like his."

In what? Ham wondered. In Elementary Tennis? Soccer Skills? Theory of Golf?

"G-E-T," Doc said to Red. And, like a rough cop: "Move along, now."

Red's mouth parted, closed, parted again and closed again. Abruptly he spun away with a halfback's pivot and stamped out. They could hear his cleats thumping awkwardly down the hall. The team room door opened, shut. Then silence.

"I can't win without him," Yablonski said in a dead voice.

"You can try," Doc said impassively and whacked his seat, as Yablonski had Red's.

Yablonski left, his sneakers squeaking harshly.

Newt stayed, champing on his dead Cigarillo. He was as disturbed as Yablonski, but craftier. No man recanted easily in the presence of others. He wanted Doc alone. Backing to the wall, he said softly, "I think you'd better reconsider that."

Doc shook his head decisively. "My mind's made up. You can jaw from now till the other place freezes over. You'll just be wasting good breath."

His nasal pitch was stronger, off-key, jarring. Newt saw that Ham was listening. "Come here a minute, Governor."

Doc came, frowning irritably. He came too close; he stood inches away, looming over Newt and forcing him closer to the pipes. "Well?"

"Simmer down a minute and listen. The coach says he can't lick Hamp without that redhead, right?"

"Maybe he can, maybe he can't. It doesn't make any difference."

"Oh, but that's just what it does. It makes a big difference — *the* difference. Look. As of this morning you were in. Well, maybe not quite in, but at least so close the *Star* didn't dare print that poll of theirs. So you got it practically made. Governor-elect! A Democratic governor, not in Mississippi, no; no, not even in Kentucky or Maryland, but right here, in the blackest Republican state in the union! It'll be a national story, Doc. Thruston Morton will have to go into hiding. Paul Butler will fly up to shake your hand. Your picture will be on every front page in the country."

Build it big, Newt thought. Make him taste it.

But Doc merely replied in his twang, "Maybe."

Newt's face fell. He had hoped for the beaming smile, the outthrust jaw, the dedicated shine in the eyes that were sure signs of capitol fever. It was as though Doc had been cured. But that was impossible. There was no cure, and Doc had had the bug since summer. He was just learning to play it smart, that was all, just learning control.

"My point exactly," said Newt, rallying quickly. "In fact, that's the very word I was about to use—maybe. Because you've been hurt bad today already. How bad I don't know. The *Star's* a hightoned outfit. Probably they won't see the magazine before Tuesday. I don't see how they'd dare feed that stuff to their family-type circulation anyway, even if they could get it through the mails. But that don't mean it won't be spread around. The word'll get passed. Witty's whisperers will see to that."

"Maybe," Doc repeated stolidly.

"Maybe, balls!" said Newt, nettled. "All right, all right, pardon my French," he added hastily, for Doc was inching up, bridling. "You got to get this thing in perspective, though."

"I have. That's right where I've got it."

Newt could feel the scorching radiator heat through his back. He lit his Cigarillo and made smoke rapidly, trying to drive Doc off. "By God, I never thought I'd have to teach a college president simple arithmetic."

"Political arithmetic isn't simple. Seems to me it's a kind of kinky algebra, full of X's and Y's that can stand for most anything."

Newt studied him. How did you handle a guy like this? If you had time you buttered him up, gave him a real grease job and pulled him along so gradually he didn't even know he was moving. But time was the one thing Newt didn't have now.

"X's and Y's," he said, thinking furiously all the while. "So that's algebra."

"Algebraic unknowns."

"Oh, sure, I remember." Newt was ready. He cocked his little cigar at a sharp angle. "Well, in this political algebra I'm the professor, and I know all the unknowns, A to Z. Take X, for instance. We just been talking about X. It's that *Sly* business, and it goes in Witty's column. It don't mean the election, now. It don't add up to that. I know a few number tricks. We can multiply a few fancy rumors of our own the next couple of days and probably pull through. But Y, now. Y is something else. Y is that game going on up there, and it's supposed to be on *your* side. I might as well tell you plain — I'd never have tapped you if Sam hadn't told me Hamp was a sure thing."

Doc stared down through the rich, coiling smoke. "Is that a fact?"

"It's a political fact. It's unknown Y — which I was told was known."

Doc pulled at his nose. "You should have given me this lecture before."

"Well, it's not too late," Newt said cheerfully, gaining a little confidence. "Forget the algebra a minute. Just add. Upstairs there's forty-three thousand people, most of them season ticket holders like me. We're honorary alumni, Doc. We paid for the privilege, and we want to see our boys on top. They ought to roll up the score, really, but the least they can do is take Hamp, so we can have a little fun swinging from the goal posts afterward and thinking about watching the big blue team down south New Year's Day. All right, there's forty-three thousand of us. *We all vote.* And we aren't the only voters looking for a win. Out in the state there's a million thirty-inch screens registering every shift and every huddle, and when those people aren't using a time-out to open a fresh beer or to run to the can during a commercial they're thinking about that New Year's bowl, too, and about the regional record, and about the millions and millions of other beer-drinkers and can-flushers tuned in all over the country who know these are the mighty Titans, the pride of this little state. So what if the Titans fall on their beefy butts? What if they lose? Why then, the pride falls flat on *its* butt, and all those TV fans here, all those disgruntled *voters* remember that the man responsible for the sorry flop is sucking around them asking them to pull their poll levers for him Tuesday. Tuesday, they think. We'll fix his clock Tuesday."

"Sucking around," Doc murmured.

Newt hesitated. Perhaps he had gone too far. "Well, it's a way of speaking."

"I like it. It fits. It's just what I've been doing."

Doc's face was expressionless. Newt looked at it doubtfully and cleared his throat. "Anyway, now you got the Y straight. Put the X and Y together on the same side and that equals Governor-Elect Stuart Hathaway Plimpton Witty. Understand?"

Doc nodded once in slow-motion.

"Then that's the lecture. Now the exam. You want to get elected, check?"

Doc nodded twice more. For he still did. He despised the yearning within him, but it was still there. Despite his calm air his heart had leapt when Newt had painted the picture of victory. The office meant so much. He remembered his childhood, when he was a hulking farm boy mocked for his awkward size. He remembered his Rockton jail nightmare and the way Peabody teams had whipped his squads autumn after autumn in the Thirties. He thought of all the digs and snubs he had suffered from the *Star* over the years, and how the election could bring both retribution for the past and promise too, a chance to give his kind of people security and dignity and self-respect.

"So far you got A-plus," said Newt, puffing. "Next question. You see why we got to beat Hamp?"

"I see it." It had been there a long time, but he was facing it for the first time.

"You're doing real good. Now. To win, that punk that slugged the girl will have to be in uniform and on the field. Right?"

"I wouldn't say that necessarily." The dream stirred in its grave. "There's such a thing as spirit."

"The old college try?" Newt shook his head. "Sorry, Doc. I got to flunk you there. Myself, I never even coached a checker team, but I can read a scoreboard, and the one I saw coming in here said nothing to nothing. That was with Red in there. Without him it's no dice. The boys'll lose the pot sure."

Doc flushed. Newt had never grasped how gambler's jargon annoyed him. "Don't make it sound like a game of chance!"

"My mistake. It's a game of no chance without Red."

"You think I should reinstate him, then."

"It's the only way."

"You want me to walk down that hall," Doc said, pointing a wavering finger, "and ask him to come back."

"If necessary. Sometimes you got to crawl in politics. That's another lecture, for later."

"Well, let me ask you a few things." Doc was so close Newt couldn't even raise his cigar. "You heard me dismiss that girl?"

"Sure. And it was the one smart thing you've done here. If the whispering campaign comes out in the open we'll at least have that."

"That's your only reason?"

"Only political reason."

"But you're more than a politician. You're a father, too. Don't you believe in morals?"

Newt faltered a little. "O.K., so you can't have tail running around with decent kids."

"You grant she's indecent."

"Ripe for the streets."

"And the boy?"

Newt's back stung. He tried to shift it, but Doc had him pinned. "Well, of course it's different for him." He didn't like this line at all. "A boy's got to raise a little hell."

"And sell the girl for a cheap story?"

"Well —"

"And then hit her?"

"Well, no." Even Newt had been shocked by that. "He shouldn't of done that."

"So you think I was right there, too."

"No!" Newt thought his back was on fire. Why did they always overheat dressing rooms? He struggled in vain; he was surrounded; Doc's great arms had swung out in a spreading motion. "That is, you would've been right, only we need him out there."

"We?"

"You. Me and the party, too, but you most of all."

"Then I should sacrifice State's standards for an election. Because that's what it would amount to. Every student on campus will know this story by night. Is that what you want me to do?"

"You got to, unless you'd rather be right."

"Be what?"

"Than governor."

Doc considered it. He liked the image of martyrdom as he had liked the image of triumph, yet he knew that what moved him now wasn't right or wrong. He had built here in Gideon, and whatever happened Tuesday he had to protect what he had built.

"I can't say I'd put it quite that way." The dream lay still. "But I guess *you'd* rather see me governor."

"You know it," Newt said fervently.

"Then all I can tell you is I'm obliged for the lesson." Doc stepped back decisively, turned, and saw Ham. "Why, hello, boy! I didn't know you were waiting. Want to join me for the second half?" He dimpled. "I got the best seats in the stadium, you know."

Still in his prayerful pose Ham said, "We better go right up, don't you think?"

"Golly, yes. I never missed so much of a State game. *I* don't plan any stops, do you?"

Ham's hands fell easily to his sides, and he winked. "I'd planned to step into a john, but maybe we could use the one right here."

Doc chuckled. "Why, boy, it's mental telepathy! I was thinking the very same thing. I never used a girls' room before. Wait'll I tell Sare!" And taking him by the arm he strode past the ranks of lockers, toward the heavy gray toilet door.

Newt stared after them stupidly. "Hey!" he called. They turned, faces bland. "You sending Red back in?"

"No, Newt. Can't be done." Doc's voice had lost its scraping tone. "Want me to withdraw from the race?" he asked calmly.

"Of course not!" Doc was all he had now, and the resilient optimism that had kept Newt active in the minority party all these lean years assured him that there was still a chance, they could still do it. Hell, anything could happen; the Titans might even be better without the redhead. He moved away from the blazing radiator. "I was just giving you advice, that's all."

"Then I take it X and Y aren't fatal," Doc said dourly. "Very well. I'll see you in my box after the game. I think we planned to visit Rockton for a spell tonight." He strode on.

"Wait a minute!" It was hard to let Doc go like this. He groped. Then, suddenly, "Say, what about Tate? Why not let him do a little sweating over Red?"

Doc paused, looking back. "He's going to sweat buckets when I get him on the carpet."

"I mean, he's acting president. Pull him in on this."

"I tried. I couldn't find him."

"Then pass the buck! Let things lay!"

Doc said steadily, "Some day I'll have to give *you* a lecture, Mr. Albert. I'll start by explaining what you really meant when you called me the man responsible here."

"Wait—"

"Sorry, I can't. I feel a call of nature."

Newt was still there, rubbing his seared shoulders, when they came out. They left without a glance, and after a deep sigh he left too, tossing his Cigarillo to the ebony vulcanite. It fell in a glowing parabola and lay between benches, smoldering.

The stub was still smoking—had, in fact, scarcely shrunk—when the hall door opened and a freckled, eager face peered in. Red had been lurking down the corridor, untaped and dressed, waiting for the voices to die away. He tiptoed over the threshold in square-toed sport shoes, fingering his jacket zipper anxiously. They had sounded upset, and he guessed they had been arguing about him. Great, he thought. Not that he gave a damn about picking up their crazy marbles. It was no skin off his ass. But there was a chance *Sly* had been forgotten in the quarrel. And it had been—it still lay on the table where Doc had left it. Red leered. Greater and greater. Daddy-O works up a sweat about coeds keeping their knees together and then leaves a book of meat art in their dressing room. Well, he had a little plan. Somewhere in Hotflash's desk would be a roll of trainer's tape; every dressing room had it. He'd take that magazine apart and plaster the walls with pin-ups the Titanettes would never forget.

But that wasn't why he had come. That wasn't why he wanted *Sly*. The pin-ups would come later; a quiet little celebration, a private blast. First he had to check that sports spread. He crushed Newt's Cigarillo underfoot, slipped over to the training table, and snatched up the copy. It was still open at "Here's Cheers, Statesmen!" Well, frig that. He flipped back to the cover, briefly admired the nude blonde pursuing the turkey, and turned to the contents page. A coy phrase under the mast played on the fact that *Sly* was a monthly. Red leered again. Not bad; the guy that wrote that must be real sharp. He ran briskly down the list of features: "Field Day for Peggy." "Tough Sheet." "Bare Facts." "Rumble Tips." Then the departments: Letters-to-the-Editor, Party-of-the-Month, and Sports Spotlight. That was it—Sports Spotlight, page twenty-two. Only one page? No, that would just be where it started. Man, it was a department; it would be good for two anyway.

He fumbled and found the folio number and reopened *Sly* on the table, his leer anticipatory now.

Sorry, wrong number. No — this was twenty-two, all right. Back to the contents. Yes, he'd had it right. Back to twenty-two. His grin was gone; he couldn't dope this out.

This was *sports?*

These were sports *cars*, for Christ's sake. Diagrams of carburetors. Gas tables. Pictures of every crazy hopped-up pile on the road — a Mercedes-Benz, an MGA-1600, a Jaguar, and an Austin-Healy-3000 on one page; Sprites and Triumphs at the top of the next; Sunbeams and Fiat Spiders below.

And that was it.

Maybe they had *two* sports stories. Maybe they'd had readers write in asking for less gash and more action stuff, so they'd switched things around a little. Made sense. Better check those features again.

His stubby fingers shaking, Red started at the cover and went through the entire issue page by page, remembering his poses with Geek and straining for a glimpse of one. There were none. The blonde undressed in her field alone; the stripping brunettes were intent on each other; the cover blonde gazed up adoringly at the camera. "Rumble Tips" — it was his last hope. He turned rapidly, wrinkling the paper. But there weren't any people in "Rumble Tips" at all. Just one photograph of a clenched fist holding a bottle of gasoline capped by a flaming wick.

And nothing else. Nothing else anywhere.

Red's eyes were slits. Under the jacket his chest swelled massively, and he braced his corrugated rubber soles on the vulcanite, and his powerful knuckles closed on *Sly's* glossy cover. He had forgotten the pin-ups entirely; he wasn't thinking, he was all hate. His hard, gripping hands parted. There was a rough splitting sound, and the blonde was torn from her turkey. He put the halves together and ripped them into quarters, ripped the quarters into eighths and tried to shred the eighths. He couldn't do it. The wad was thick, unmanageable; the staples were digging into his palms. Rigid, grimacing, his face a bunched polyp, he wrestled for a new hold, and the tin slivers tore his flesh, and he crouched over and heaved up in an abrupt, violent effort. The lumped paper slipped away from him. It flew up in a gay flutter, and he cried out, a gasp of pain: an open staple had sliced his hand across.

"Goddamn frigging son of a bitch," he sobbed, licking the wound. "Dirty, stink-fingered, asswipe . . ."

The sob died away in a bitter echo; he was running back to the team room for a bandage. Behind him *Sly's* shreds floated slowly to the floor like slick confetti, the last jagged fragments bright with blood.

**

The stadium thundered:

Hey Red! Big Red!
We want big Red!
Hey! Hey! Hey! Hey!
Hey! Hey! Hey! Hey!

"Can't have that," Hotflash said peppily. "Girls! Snap to."

The Titanettes, led by the new Gridiron Queen, scampered out and leveled their megaphones at the stands like cannon. Only one cheer was permitted inside the State thirty:

Hey, hey, whattayasay,
Let's go back the other *way!*

And one inside the twenty:

Hold that line!
Hold that line!

But the line wasn't held. Mason opened a hole for five yards; Nixon opened another, and a white jersey zigzagged into the end zone. The scoreboard flashed 6-0.

"*Boo!*" howled the faithful. "*Booooo!*"

Hamp faked the kick and ran. 8-0.

Boo, booooo, boooooo . . .

The old woman who had inadvertently started the abusive applause advertently flung her Doc pin on the field. The Pawnattuck gas meter reader shook his fist at the Titan bench.

"I don't get it," Bauer said to Winkler in a daze. They had remained on the sideline, paralyzed with horror by Hamp's lightning march.

"Something smells," said Winkler. "Why wasn't Yablonski here for the kick? The boys went five minutes without orders. He can't expect the quarterback to run the team."

The P.A. system crackled above the crowd's hisses: "Mr. Winkler, report to the president's box immediately."

"See you later," he said. "Doc must want some quickie release. Ten-to-one it's got something to do with that coronation snafu."

Bauer shook his head sadly. "That was a real letdown. You get a thing all arranged and then — blooey. Poor Mrs. Dix must've got sick." He puckered worriedly. "Hope it's nothing serious."

**

Daffy lay face down on an infirmary bed, weeping inconsolably. She had just discovered that she had lost a front tooth.

"How did it happen?" the R.N. in charge of the coed ward asked Sam.

He edged out. "Too long a story."

Yet a moment later he was telling Tate.

They met in the corridor between wards. Al Swinton had awakened and become violently sick in the press box, and a disgusted sport writer had advised Tate that the best cure for a hangover was Dexedrine. Maybe he could tap the squad's supply; otherwise it required a prescription. The provost had thanked him and driven Al straight to the duty physician. Al knew too much about Tate. In this condition he might talk irresponsibly.

"So you were here!" Sam accosted him. "I thought your man was just drunk."

"A stomach upset, scarcely more. Of course it *is* annoying."

"Listen, you're lucky," said Sam, and then told him.

"Doc *expelled* her?"

"On the spot. What would you have done?"

"That's not the point," Tate said prissily. "Any action should have been taken by me."

"Well, I looked for you."

"Doc should have waited till I was found."

"If I were you I wouldn't tee off on him," Sam said curtly. "You're on his list today. That accreditation report and now this — it's too much. I don't blame him, either. You had a tip about the girl. Why did you break up Dean Shoemaker's hearing?"

Tate's eyes darted at him like slim fish. So the dean had told them about that. Apparently she disliked her job.

"The evidence was insufficient."

"Yeah? Well, it's sufficient now, and Doc's biting nails. I'd lay low if I was you."

Tate considered a reply beneath him. He was tempted to withdraw, yet couldn't quite yet. The race of events might require a change in his plans. He had to know more.

"What did he do with Red Stacy?"

Sam gaped. He hadn't considered the possibility of Red's expulsion. But with Doc in this state —

"They got a TV here on the sun deck. I'll go see if he's playing." He hurried off, his great belly swaying.

Al appeared, haggard.

"How do you feel?" Tate inquired.

"My mouth tastes like a jock strap. The medic gave me a couple of orange pills and told me I'd pick up in a half hour. Cripes, that was a stupid thing to do," said Al, very low. He felt conscience-stricken. He had been on company time.

Tate heard Sam's returning tread. It was best Sam didn't know the identity of the sick reporter. Al's by-line had been on the Mikel survey story. There might be questions.

"Wait in the car. I'll be right along."

Al lurched out gloomily; Sam, even gloomier, barged in through the swinging door from the sun deck.

"Mason and Nixon," he moaned. "They sound like a vaudeville team. And what kills me is, they're both under two hundred pounds."

"We're behind?" Tate asked quickly.

"By two touchdowns and two big conversions." Sam shook his head incredulously.

"And Red?"

"Out. It figures, of course. But the fans don't like it." Nor did he. He plodded disconsolately toward the coed ward, mumbling that he wished he hadn't promised to take Daffy home, wondering aloud whether he could get back before the last period.

In Tate's car Al said, "You look like you could use a pill yourself. What's the matter?"

"Something on my mind," the provost muttered, cruising slowly down the infirmary drive. "There's an old saying about a tide in the affairs of men, you know." He wondered absently where it had come from. Anonymous, probably. "Anyway, it means a decision-making situation."

"Say, where are we going?" asked Al, for they were passing the stadium.

"I've got a story for you. You can telephone your paper from my house."

Tate hadn't yet decided to take his tide at the flood. Yet whatever happened in the confused days ahead, a *Star* man would make a useful ally. The scandal was bound to come out before the afternoon was over. He would risk nothing by telling it now.

"Red Stacy and the Head Titanette were expelled at the half. They were charged with misconduct."

"No kidding! You know, I kind of saw that coming." But he hadn't broken the story. He had seen it there in the Inne and hadn't been able to put his hands on it. Still, this was a consolation. "I'm much obliged. You handled it while I was conked out?"

"No." Tate accelerated. "Doc did it by himself."

Himself sensitive to slights, Al saw the wound in Tate. "You'd think he'd let you do your own job."

The provost glanced over gratefully and raised his brows in expressive pantomime.

"He must feel pretty cocky about this game, giving Stacy the toot."

"If he does it's unjustified," said Tate, decelerating for his driveway. "Hamp's sixteen points ahead."

The score had changed. Tate admitted himself — his wife, baffled by football, took the children to a Birmingham square dance Saturday afternoons — and turned on his downstairs television set a moment after Hamp's fullback had kicked a field goal from State's fifteen.

"It's good!" said the network announcer, shouting to make himself heard among the swelling boos. He chuckled tolerantly. "Looks like the fans are riding the officials."

A shower of empty beer cans had just fallen near the referee; he was fleeing upfield. Overhead the scoreboard read 19-0.

"If they win they ought to let Witty have the ball," Al said from the doorway.

Tate nodded reflectively. "The phone's in the library." He reflected more and added, "I may have another story for you later."

Al put the call through and sat back, searching for exact words. Grid Ace, Beauty Get State Ax, he thought. Skin Sin Rocks Doc. "Gloria? Give me the desk."

The desk gave him the general managing editor, who greeted him cordially. "Caulkin here, Al. I didn't think my message would reach you so soon."

"I got no message, Colonel. Got a good yarn, though. Two kids just got bounced here. One's that redheaded halfback —"

"I know, I know. River's public relations goon just called us. Something about the boy being implicated. It's a blackleg attempt to save face, of course. Too late; we'll print it, but inside. Now tell me — do you have *Sly?*"

"Who, me?" Al swallowed. He wondered how Caulkin could have heard about his subscription. Markham must have ratted, he thought resentfully.

"I mean the new one, with the pictures of the Dix girl." There was a silence, and Caulkin said irritably, "Now don't tell me you don't know *why* she was expelled."

Dimly Al began to understand why, and why Greek had sent him the whiskey. "Sure, sure," he improvised. "It's just I can't get the magazine. They don't sell it up here."

"So. I thought not. And I've anticipated your need. We've run the all-star off early — the first copy just came up." Al heard a creaking and knew he was leaning across the wide desk, reaching for the loaf of newsprint still damp from the press. "Circulation's sending a man to the College Inne with a dozen copies for you. You'll know why when you see page one." More creaking. "I want you to show it to every authority on the State campus and take down statements for the morning bulldog. Better get a few words from Nails Whipple at Peabody, too."

"They may be hard to find," said Al, who embarked on every assignment with a complete lack of confidence.

"Then draft Hiram." The creaking grew more strident. "I have reason to believe he's up there with you."

"I mean after the game. Especially if State goes on losing."

"They're *losing*? Actually *losing*? Damn! Why doesn't the staff keep me informed?" Then he remembered that he had ordered the sports editor's radio turned off and grumbled, "Well, it's good news any way it comes. Looks like our day, eh?" He was lunging over the desk now. "Ah!" He had made it. "*Damn!*"

"What's the matter, Colonel?"

"Ink all over my damned hand," Caulkin said furiously, and slammed down the receiver.

Tate sat before his set in a pensive attitude, elbow on knee, chin on fist. The Titans looked worse and worse.

"I just called a taxi," Al said. He explained that he would be back officially in his company car, with an all-star and a request for comment. "Orders," he said apologetically.

The provost nodded, and continued nodding to himself after Al had left. Of course the *Star* would want a statement from him. And this time he couldn't hide; this time silence would be regarded as a defense of Daffy's indefensible behavior. He watched a Titan punt, a long Hamp run, and a Titan tackle, and pondered his next step. Fuller and fuller grew the tide; he would be drowned in it unless he moved soon. Doc's chances of election declined with each play. The game and *Sly* were two heavy strikes against it. And even if Doc won, Tate seemed likely to be stuck as provost. Doc blamed him for the Budge disaster, and Sam had made it clear that he also held him accountable for the dean's failure to expel Daffy after Homecoming. If Doc lost, however, Tate had a powerful friend in Clare Hewitt. Then it would be necessary only to make sure that Doc's position here was untenable. Force Doc to resign and the job would be his; vacillate and he would be stranded here forever, growing forlorn and flaccid with failure. That was the issue, thought Tate. To *do*, to *go*, to *act* — those were his felt needs.

The game was becoming a rout. By the closing minutes of the fourth period the score was Hamp 35, State 0, and the officials had stopped play twice, once to clear debris from the field and again to request that the crowd refrain from jeering when the Hamp quarterback was calling signals. The request was ignored; if anything, the uproar grew. The announcer reported that Doc River had instructed the Titan bench to accompany visiting players to the dressing room. Otherwise the mob might attack them after the game.

At the final whistle Hamp substitutes had driven the demoralized Titan line back to their goal line and were threatening to cross it again. The camera cut to the 35-0 scoreboard, cut to a field now black with milling people, cut erratically to the sky, as though jostled; then the stadium picture dissolved completely and was replaced by successive images of a collie eating Burgerbits, a girl wearing Playtex Living Gloves, a loaf of Tip-Top Bread whispering that it was fresher, and a man drinking beer by a waterfall and singing a catchy jingle about it. Tate switched the set off. The waterfall reminded him; he hadn't bathed since morning.

He was about to mount the stairs when his phone rang. It was Doc, calling from the stadium. Tate steeled himself.

"Sam send word he'd seen you. I've been calling high and low. What're you doing at home?"

"I — my patient wanted to lie down."

"Could've done that at the infirmary. Maybe if we'd had fewer stick-in-the-muds and a little more support here we might've taken this one."

Tate was tempted to point out that the stadium had been packed. Doc didn't sound in the mood for reason, however, so he merely murmured his regrets.

"Well, it's done now, and that's that. What I want to know from you is, why wasn't that Dix woman expelled?"

"I understand you took care of that," Tate said edgily.

"Right! And Stacy, too! But you should've done it after Homecoming."

"It's rather a long story — "

"Never mind. I haven't got time to chew the rag now. My car's waiting. You just better sharpen a pencil and get to work on a report, mister. And I don't want any nice-Nellie fiddle-faddle. I want *facts*."

Bang. He had hung up.

Intolerable, Tate thought hotly. Treating me like a slavey. Well, the worm was about to turn. But first he needed a hot tub.

Again he was delayed. His bell chimed. Al was back.

"You got to see this to believe it," said Al, awed, and thrust out a folded paper.

Al could scarcely believe it himself. Daffy and the rampant baton occupied four columns from the mast to the fold, and despite black paches over the tips of her breasts it was the most provocative picture Al had ever seen, in *Sly* or elsewhere. His feelings were mixed. He was proud of Geek's achievement, yet somehow he wished the *Star* hadn't rephotographed it. His neighbors knew he had been assigned to Gideon. Some of them might not understand.

Tate studied the paper intently. So Sam hadn't been exaggerating. Really, it was too bad of Paul Bauer to have picked this girl. If Bauer hadn't taken a fancy to her Tate might never have crossed swords with that detestable O'Donnell woman. Suppose Doc told the trustees about Dean Shoemaker's hearing? It could be difficult, most difficult.

The story was headed:

Coed, Protégé of Doc River,
Strips for Drunken Poses;
Civic Leaders Frame Protests

The provost saw a sign. If Doc was to be beaten, as clearly he must be now, the faster his bandwagon coasted downgrade the better. Tate could give it a neat shove and at the same time obscure the awkward part he had played in the dean's office.

He laid the paper aside and lit a cigarette.

"I mentioned the possibility of another story. As it happens, there are two others. One of them touches on this. It's yours if you shield me. Doc made an agreement with certain Birmingham legislators, prompted, I believe, by some turmoil at C.C.N.Y. He promised them he wouldn't hire any Catholics with secular divorces. Well, he broke his word. He made an exception; sent me a memo to that effect. The woman's name is Mrs. Catherine Ryan O'Donnell. She's been housemother this year at the Theta sorority—which, it turns out, is the Dix girl's sorority."

"No crap!"

"Ah—please remember: I mustn't be mentioned."

"Don't worry, I never heard of you."

"In fact, you'd better act as though someone had given you a vague tip, someone not really reliable. You might call her up to verify it. But you'd better think of some way to stop her from cutting you off. I warn you—she has a vixen's temper."

"I know a few dodges. Listen, this is the nuts," Al said enthusiastically. He visualized a juicy insert; perhaps even a sidebar, with a by-line. "What's the other story?"

Tate smiled velvetly. "Don't be greedy. I'll have to see how you handle this one first. Would you like to use the telephone here? I'll just run upstairs, wash up, and prepare a meaningless little statement for you."

Al, easily discouraged, nearly gave up when the Theta cook told him Mrs. O'Donnell hadn't returned. Then he thought how the religious angle would tickle Caulkin and asked where she could be reached. The Mansion, Mrs. Santo said promptly. *Si*—Doc River's house, on the hill.

Kit was just returning from her long walk with Sol. Her color was gay; her eyes sparkled. He shuffled behind her in a clumsy little dance and caught her around the waist.

"Not here!" she cried. "Besides, the telephone's ringing." She darted into the Mansion library while he pretended to mope. "Hello?"

"I would like to speak to Mrs. Catherine Ryan O'Donnell, please," Al said formally.

"Who's that?" asked Sol, resuming his shuffle.

She covered the mouthpiece. "A man, for me." She made a face. "He has the most divine manners."

"Unlike certain persons you could name."

She stuck out her tongue.

"Hello? Hello?" said Al, worrying again.

"I'm sorry. This is Mrs. O'Donnell."

"Oh. Well. Ah—I represent the Society of Jesus."

"Did he say Jesus?" Sol whispered, seizing her from behind.

"Don't!" She cut her eyes back merrily. "You *mustn't!*"

"I figured he'd be calling," said Sol, and let her go.

"I can't hear you," Al complained solemnly, wondering what was so funny.

"Excuse me. Some interference." She sobered and brushed her hair back. "I'm sorry, Father. Did you say you were a Jesuit?"

"Yeah. I wanted to talk to you about this husband of yours."

"You—*what?*" Kit breathed, "What's happened to him?"

"Huh? Oh, he's all right," Al said peevishly, wondering whether Tate could have been given a bum steer. "The thing is, you're divorced, aren't you?"

"Oh. Oh. Oh yes."

Sol was prowling around behind her again. She waved him off and whispered, "Something's funny."

"Not Jesus?" He grinned. "Maybe a Black and Tan."

"No, Sol, funny peculiar. I mean *really* peculiar."

He saw she was pale and subsided. Outside on the lawn there was a confused, indistinct babble—many voices, coming closer. He peered out, meantime listening absently to the crackling on the phone.

"We're kind of worried about you," Al said.

"I — I've worried too."

Her voice was faint. Al asked her to repeat it and then said, "Well, you should worry. It's a big thing."

"Father Logan has been a great help," said Kit, humble still.

"Who?"

"You don't know Father Logan?"

"Oh, sure. The Society of Jesus is pretty small, Mrs. O'Donnell." Al exulted. She had admitted it. He decided to try for more. "Now. I heard a man's voice a minute ago. Who's he?"

"I beg your pardon?"

Kit's color was coming back, and with it came suspicion. Jesuits didn't behave this way. And the Society wasn't that small. And Father Logan wasn't one of them — he was the local priest.

"What did you say your name was, Father?"

"I didn't say. I'm asking about that man."

"I think you should tell me."

Al slipped. "*You* tell *me,* sister."

She covered the mouthpiece and turned trembling to Sol. "It's some kind of trick."

He turned from the growing medley outside and seized the phone.

"Who's speaking?" he demanded.

Al had nothing to lose now. Besides, Caulkin had a rule about reporters identifying themselves in telephone interviews. He said loudly, "Swinton, of the *Star.*"

Kit heard him and gasped; Al heard her and smirked. Then the babbling on the other end became audible to him, and just before the receiver there was replaced the voices were joined by the brittle sound of glass breaking. A Frosty Warren would have wondered what it meant; a Ham Markham would have guessed; but Al merely shrugged and put through his call to Caulkin, gloating over his shabby spoils.

Upstairs in the rear of the house the householder also gloated. His bath was drawn and steaming. Dropping his motto-scribbled robe to the tile floor he stood naked a moment, smiling down absently and sucking the last of his Marlboro. The cigarette was incongruous. Tate's pallid figure, almost completely devoid of hair, suggested that of a deprived child. Only the long, knobby feet were adult, and at the moment they were concealed by the folds of the robe. His flesh had a delicate, unmanly texture; his ribs were conspicuous; his loins were shriveled and small. He didn't look old enough to smoke.

Abruptly he dropped the stub into the toilet, where it spluttered, darkened, and began to come apart. Like Doc, Tate thought, fastidiously flushing it away. Doc too was beginning to break up, and within the week he would vanish also. No university president could survive the publication of a report like Budge's; resignation would be almost automatic. Of course, releasing it was an extreme step. It would mean a few rough years for State. And it was particularly unfortunate that the evaluators had singled out Tate himself for criticism. But there he felt he could count on the trustees' short memories and their distaste for fine print. As for the damage to the university — well, he was a young man; he had plenty of time to rebuild. Could the leak be traced to him? he wondered. It seemed doubtful; he was a far less likely source than, say, that old Republican judge. In any event, Witty would be deeply obligated to him after this week end. The first chance he had he would drive down to Birmingham and tell Clare Hewitt just how obligated Witty was.

He stepped gingerly into the scalding water. How marvelously things worked out, he thought. All autumn the flag of his hopes had fluttered indifferently, now rising a trifle, now hanging limp. This morning it had been sliding down the lanyard, furled, vanquished. Yet how quickly that had changed! Scarcely six hours later he had as much as plucked the flower of safety from the nettles or thorns or whatever it was that old slogan said safety had to be plucked from. His standard stood out bravely in a rising wind, glory ran at his stirrups, the presidency would be his. Sighing tremulously, he sank down to wallow. The water crept up his thin legs, tinting them lobster red. It reached the wrinkled sack of his scrotum, and he gave an emasculate little giggle.

**

The trouble on the Mansion lawn had started in the stadium parking lot. The rabble on the field had looked ugly, but had been quickly dispersed by the game's routine state police detail, which, though small, was led by a determined lieutenant who had mounted the Hamp bench and shouted out that his men would use gas grenades at the first sign of violence. He had then fired a pistol shot in the air and ordered the arrest of a few obvious trouble-makers. That quieted the others. They filed toward the exits, muttering but under control, and if they had been driven directly to the G.A.R. Highway that might have been the end of it. Unfortunately the shot had been heard outside. The bus drivers were on edge. The sullen mood of the first arrivals on the lot frightened them; they saw the dark masses boiling out of the gates, and a dozen of them panicked, leaving with most of their seats empty. The result was a transportation snarl. As dusk thickened on the stadium grounds the last bus meshed gears and rolled away leaving some five hundred people stranded, and the only consolation the dispatcher could offer was that he had radioed his Birmingham office for help. Some of those abandoned merely groaned and settled down to keep vigil; some wandered off to telephone relatives, but a hard core of nearly a hundred and fifty decided to cut loose. They were all men, mostly leather-jacketed, motorcycle-booted young laborers from cities. They wanted solace for their anguish over the Titan loss, and there was just enough liquor in them to make Sam Theanapolis bitterly regret next morning his failure to screen honorary alumni.

Until today the disgruntled mob had been proud of that status, though they knew little of the campus and drifted about aimlessly, like surly D.P.'s, once they were beyond the lot. Then two of them, burly and menacing, cornered a passing student. He gave them directions to Yablonski's house and the Mansion, and after passing bottles around and arguing briefly they split into twin posses bent on vengeance. The Mansion demonstration became the best known of the two, for despite Al Swinton it made the *Star*. Among the fans stuck on the lot was one of the sports editor's cub reporters; he had become separated from his friends in the post-game turmoil and had decided to buy a bus ticket. Bored and shivering, he trailed the hill posse and later phoned everything to the desk. His story, terse and graphic, shamed Al. It told how the men had begun by waving handkerchiefs at the porch; how someone had thrown a Zippo lighter through a window; how Sol, and then Kit, had come out and tried to quiet them; and how the ringleaders' refusal to believe that Doc wasn't inside brought Sarah River, who appeared in the doorway, wan and dazed, unmoving while a drunken lout lurched toward her — remaining quiet even when Sol, with surprising speed, knocked the lout down, shoved her and Kit inside, and locked the door. The men on the lawn had wavered for a few minutes after that and then stumbled off, jeering, leaving only the diligent cub. After a decent interval he had knocked politely at the back door and taken the names of the beseiged from the bewildered cook. Caulkin struck out all but Sarah's. He couldn't very well make a heroine of Mrs. O'Donnell with that Swinton story in column six, he genially explained to the desk, and as for Feinblatt — well, if a man named Solomon Feinblatt wanted to be a hero in the *Star* he could go fight Arabs in Israel.

The smashing of the window and the threat against Doc's wife ran nearly two columns. Yet Tom Yablonski's ordeal, though ignored, was at least as bitter. Yablonski was home. He was reading to his little daughter before supper when the second posse reached his door with a crude effigy fashioned of laundry stolen from a neighbor's clothesline. Fired and thrown among his shrubs, it kindled a mound of dry leaves, and when he came out to stamp on the flames he was stoned. The stones stung; the sting to his pride was greater; but though he was a match for any three of the mob he held back, for he knew that if he waded into them and was struck down from behind his wife and daughter would be left defenseless. So he set his jaw. And ducked showers of driveway gravel. And put out this fire and another, more serious, under his dining room sill, without once acknowledging his tormentors or even glancing up. He hoped to outwait them, and he did, but it was long past suppertime, and his daughter was weeping uncontrollably before the hulking shadows receded into the night.

That was all for the Mansion and the Yablonskis, but not all for Gideon. The worst lay just ahead. The two dissatisfied posses rejoined in the stunted orchard east of the Student Union, and there someone remembered seeing the package store on the Common. Delegations were sent, like infantrymen filling canteens for a company. The mob drank deeply and grew uglier. There was talk of cracking a few young eggheads, of getting even — with whom no one said, or knew, or much cared. Exchanging hoarse shouts of encouragement the men split into smaller groups and roamed campus and town, looking for fights. By now the state police, alerted by Sol, had sent four squad cars to reinforce Gideon's lone constable. Singly and in pairs the stragglers were picked up, but it was a slow business — at a distance the prowlers were indistinguishable from strolling students — and a series of nasty scuffles continued through the evening, reaching a peak in the hour after the moon rose and tapering off shortly before midnight, when the last drunks were locked up. Both State and Peabody boys were drawn into brawls. A Peabody senior, the son of a Rockton manufacturer, was stripped and robbed of a wallet containing a hundred dollars. Young Sam, who had dropped into Blandford Library after the game, was tripped as he came out, and his tuba bent. Two fraternities were looted at State, one of them the Sigma Chi house, and after the man who had pitched the Zippo into the Mansion found a crumpled copy of Caulkin's all-star outside the College Inne, where Al Swinton had dropped it, three drunks burst into the Kappa Kappa Gamma living room. The housemother kept her head. She telephoned the constable's office; a police car raced up just as the third man was leaving. He was the gas meter reader from Pawnattuck, and he was handcuffed and led away. Behind him the girls chattered excitedly. One, a journalism major, later wrote a sardonic ballad about the incident to the tune of "Aura Lea." She gave the intruders the droll name by which they were known thereafter in Gideon: the Mau Maus.

These were undergraduate incidents. A graduate student, an alumnus, a resident of the Inne, and a member of the State faculty were also accosted by free-swinging men offering to take anybody on. The graduate student was Jerry Dix. Trudy Viggiantti, another journalism major, was doing a term paper on *Star* editions; a glance at today's final and she took it straight to him. One glance was enough for Jerry, too. The baby belonged with grandparents now. He wrapped little Charlie in a blanket and telephoned for a taxi, and while he was waiting outside the Village booth three leather jackets lurched out of the dark. The baby didn't save Jerry. In fact, Jerry scarcely saved him. They were shoved together against the booth; Jerry was kicked in the groin; and when the taxi drew up five minutes later he could scarcely walk to it.

Sam, the alumnus, was lucky. He had been in the infirmary all this time, talking first to the R.N. and then to the staff psychologist, who examined Daffy for over two hours and concluded that her trouble was far graver than anyone had thought. She was deeply disturbed; they would have to transfer her to Belton in the morning for psychiatric diagnosis. Sam had walked slowly to his car and was behind the wheel, fumbling with the keys, when an empty gin bottle ricocheted off his hood. He turned on his high beam lights. Five crouched figures were advancing unsteadily. Ordinarily Sam would have opened the door and asked for an explanation, but not tonight; none of the weaving men was as frustrated as he. He gunned ahead and roared down on them, and one, leaping aside, sprained an ankle. The others carried him to the infirmary.

Al Swinton was the Inne resident. After dictating the facts about Kit to the desk, Al had enjoyed a leisurely Manhattan with the cleansed provost. He had agreed to meet him in the Acme Diner the following morning and had then departed happily in his *Star* car with Tate's bland statement. Everything seemed to be coming Al's way. Acquiring other statements turned out to be even more difficult than he had thought, however. The all-star had a searing effect on professors and administrators. They started, flushed, and asked him to leave. Eric Lutz didn't say a word; he walked straight back into his laboratory and slammed the door. Nails Whipple was bitter. Al found Whipple leaving the Peabody Library, and the old man remarked curtly over his shoulder that if the files of the college physician still contained a nude photograph of Hallam Caulkin he would be delighted to release it for publication. Back at State Al saw lights in Administration Hall. Stumbling around, trying doors, he discovered Miss Shoemaker. She was stuffing Geek's baton in a trash can; before he could display an all-star she gave a feeble little cry and bounded inside the building, flipping the lock behind her. Al turned away, fuming. Enough was enough. Nobody could say he hadn't tried. He'd have to draft Ham after all. But Al, having disregarded the tinkling on the Mansion phone, was unaware of the Mau Mau. He walked off openly and fearlessly, and danger came to him in the form of a flat-faced youth who stepped out from behind a bush and swung wildly. Al dodged, ran, fell over the trash can, and was kicked in the mouth. He lay long without moving. Twice he called timidly for help; then, realizing he was alone, he crept painfully to his car and drove to the infirmary. The doctor there didn't recognize him. He mistook him for one of the troublemakers and left him until the sprained ankle was bandaged. By then Al's exploring tongue had discovered his injury. He had lost a rear molar.

The faculty member escaped peculiarly. A dozen of the drunkest toughs were lounging in front of St. Mary's Church, bragging and displayed skinned knuckles. One of them saw a single light approaching — a motorcycle, he thought, maybe a cat from the Birmingham Pythons; but no: it was coming along the sidewalk.

"Hey, look, a bike!" he crowed. "Let's knock him ass over elbows."

"Aw, let him alone," said a second man. "It's only a kid."

"Yeah, let him peddle his papers," said a third.

"Sure, the squares want to see them *Star* knockers," said a fourth.

Dirty laughter. Then amazement, then panic. The cyclist was trying to ride them down.

"Look out, kid!"

"Vermin!" snarled the approaching figure.

They scattered, shouting, "Hey!" "For Christ's sake!" "He's like crazy!"

"Cannon off the right into the pocket," snapped the figure, whizzing past. They had a fleeting glimpse of a snowy forelock, stitched lips, a green bookbag, and tattered, driving sneakers.

"Kid hell," one panted. "That was a frigging ghoul."

"Hah!" the figure hooted and vanished into gloom.

So much for Gideon: an ankle, a tooth, a window, a Peabody wallet; a jailed reader of gas meters, a crippled Village cuckold, two score contusions and abrasions for police reports; a dented horn for young Sam, a dented hood for his father. Elsewhere in the state the reaction to Saturday's events was slower but more profound. That evening was quiet. Doc spoke uneventfully in Rockton. Few of his audience had seen *Sly*; fewer still had seen the all-star, which was chiefly a Birmingham edition for late street sales. Caulkin's first plan had been to blanket Dudley, Rockton, and Pawnattuck with this afternoon final, but the defeat of the Titans, the report of the campus rioting, and the emergence of Daffy's housemother changed all that. He needed time to wield his brass pica rule, to plan effects. The delay was all to the good, he decided; Sunday circulation was the week's largest. He would shoot the works in the morning. He did precisely that: everything was spread on Sunday's page one with shotgun effect. Only Gideon news went out front — integration news, space news, Summit news was buried or spiked. Even so the page had a crammed look. There was scarcely room for Today's Laff. The baton picture had been reduced to two columns and shared the display with three thick headlines. On the far right was the *Star*'s first big local sports story since a Rhodes scholar from Peabody had stroked Oxford against Cambridge five years before:

Hamp Whips Bewildered State

And beside that,

Throng Storms River's House

And beside that,

Naked Girlie Is 'Doc's' Coed
(Other pictures, page 18)

Nestled beneath this was Al's poison:

Her Housemother Laughs;
Reveals Own Marital Past
By Alvin Swinton

An index opposite the weather ear summarized other political news:

Witty outlines four-point program . . . . page 3
"Mr. Depth" laughs with kiddies . . . . page 5
Halfback, cheerleader leave State . . . . page 21
Pics arouse clerics . . . . page 2

The church support was impressive. Five clergymen, including the rector of St. Timothy's P.E., had written deploring sermons and provided the *Star* with carbons. The most powerful religious medicine, however, was in Al's story. It wasn't explicit; it was all between the lines. The *Star's* libel lawyer had passed the rest of the edition with some reluctance, but had drawn the line at Kit. Any frank discussion of her Catholicity would, he said, be indefensible. The general managing editor had therefore turned reporter. He had picked up Father Logan's name from Al's dictated notes and called him in Gideon, and the priest, innocent of the press, thinking he was speaking in confidence, believing that Caulkin was writing a feature about student weddings, acknowledged in a sad aside that not all the coeds he had married had turned out as he had hoped. Caulkin probed carefully, and Kit's name slipped out. It was enough. A Ryan bride and an O'Donnell groom in a church called St. Mary's meant only one faith. The *Star* needn't say it; every Catholic reader would say it to himself—Doc River had entrusted the morals of the young girls to a wanton who had forsaken grace, and as he sowed so had he reaped a Daffy Dix.

The Sunday *Star* was a packet of ignited matches deliberately tossed into a firework pyramid. That morning, as boys flung it on porches and churchgoers picked it up in corner drugstores, the first pinwheels began to turn. By noon they were spinning furiously in hundreds of thousands of urban homes, and everything that had been said before in the campaign, everything Doc had done in his life, every political promise and commitment was forgotten in the scream of skyrockets and flaring Roman Candles. Caulkin had been disappointed by Al's failure to send a sheaf of statements from Gideon; now he had enough statements to fill a week of editions. The *Star* switchboard was jammed. Everyone wanted to go on record. Orderlies in Haven Square hospital defaced the posters they had put up and reported it. State alumni speakers canceled talks and called in to explain why. A Mrs. Hernando Fernandez, a member of the Democratic State Central Committee and the leader of the Women-for-Doc movement, said she would withdraw from the campaign within the next twenty-four hours unless she were given an explanation, which, she added, had better be good. Sam's Citizen's Committee was decimated. Two members quit outright, and five others spent the afternoon in his home, demanding immediate action.

Action had in fact already been taken, by Kit herself. A trembling Theta had brought her the Sunday paper at breakfast. Within twenty minutes Kit had written and delivered her resignation to Miss Shoemaker. She wasn't contrite. She was defiant. Al's brutal call and the cruel story had worked a dramatic change in her; the fierce pride of which she had always been ashamed, and which she had repressed, now rose up and smothered her feelings of guilt, and she curtly informed the embarrassed dean — whose own shocked study of the *Star* she had interrupted — that from here she would taxi directly to the Acme Diner, interrupt Sol Feinblatt's Sunday ritual of ham and eggs, and ask him to take her, her child, and her baggage into his apartment. People could think the worst. They would be right. Any future communications for her could be addressed care of Sol. She herself would communicate with no one, for she was determined not to bring any more pain to her only other friend in Gideon, Sarah River. That pointedly excluded Miss Shoemaker, who straightway went to bed with a sick headache. Yet this was no hour for weakness. The dean had hardly touched her lavender-scented pillow when duty roused her. Crutching her throbbing brow on one shaking hand, she made arrangements to chaperone the Theta house herself that night and then groggily dialed the provost and, as an afterthought, John Winkler. Each was given a hurried account, with hazy references to Sol; Miss Shoemaker couldn't discuss Kit's trip to the diner just now. Tate, himself just back from the Acme, snickered vindictively. Winkler alerted Sam, who immediately took the news to the *Star*, where the general managing editor quietly scheduled it for page twenty-eight of the Monday edition.

Meanwhile the fever mounted in the city wards. Others than Catholics were incensed: Protestants mourned the loss of puritan bedrock, Jews the passing of family authority. Their resentment was real, though its inspiration wasn't as lofty as it seemed. The linking of Kit's story and Daffy's had provided a convenient blind. It permitted people to behave as though they were guided by the ancient star of righteousness, when the star which really led them was secular and mundane, illumined by neon. They thought of themselves as followers of eternal law. Really they were parishioners of society. Their prayers were said to gods of here and now; their candles and novenas were offered to the ultimate idol of getting ahead. They wanted the badges and insignia of position: a chromed car with right silhouette, a home on the right street, a Bendix, living color. The rub was that this wasn't enough. They also hungered for the sense of exultation which had once shone down from the now darkened altars of the past. Society had given them a substitute: since childhood they had been conditioned to live vicariously, and they identified with celebrities seen only in blushing Eastmancolor or on electronic screens, or heard on LP stereo. Most of these quasi-religious celebrities were national, but local pride remained strong; the people had heavy emotional investments in the fortunes of New Englanders who had made what was everywhere known as the big time. The State-Hamp game had been big time, like the Sox or the Celts. It was as though they had been out on that field themselves, determined to show the nation what their state could do. Thus Daffy's shame was their shame, and thus, because the faith of the stadium faithful was universal, the fall of the Titans had inflicted a communal wound. Few grasped that; none spoke of it. But many a split-level wife felt she herself had been disgraced in *Sly*, and many a husband who denounced Kit across the table was grieving secretly for the lost bowl bid.

Because Newt Albert understood some of this, because he anticipated the search for scapegoats, he had redrafted his plans for the closing days of the campaign before leaving Gideon Saturday. Doc would continue his stumping tour and return to Birmingham Monday night for a state-wide election eve telecast; Newt himself would spend the next two days in the capital, stalking Witty with the long knives of the political guerrilla. Newt didn't discuss his tactics with Doc. He hadn't time to argue, and things would be difficult enough as it was. Whatever he did, most of the voters would blame Doc for what had happened at State. Yet he could make a few telling counter moves. He had no hope of competing with Witty's costly expedient of telephoning of thousands of short, recorded, last-minute appeals to individual voters, but he could spend the last of his party treasury on newspaper ads and repetitive thirty-second television spots accusing the Republicans of a cheap smear. He could charge Blandford with cutting State's Department of Physical Education budget — a clever lie, since it would bring the governor back into the public eye and remind everyone of his performance on Pawnattuck's WASP-TV. Finally, the party's precinct men could be told to pass the word that Stuart Witty was a philanderer. That was not a lie. Witty was too discreet to be flagrant, but Newt, whose business it was to uncover such things, knew that he had violated the Mann Act three times and therefore wouldn't dare sue. The rumor had a serious flaw; Witty didn't look the part. Nevertheless it was worth a plunge, and Newt decided for it. He worked all that night, and when the hour struck for early mass — though not ordinarily churchgoers, the Alberts always attended services before elections — he had begun to feel sanguine. Then the first blow fell. Newt opened his morning paper. The exposure of Kit was wholly unexpected. He felt fouled; it was hard to believe that Doc could have been so stupid. He sent his wife to church alone and spent the entire day on the defensive, calming Mrs. Hernando Fernandez, calming some thirty other rebellious organization workers, repeating to every caller that this was just another smear and revising his ads and spots to say so. It wasn't too late, he reassured Sam, who called gloomily after leaving the *Star*. Hold the fort: help was coming: this was the darkness before the dawn. He sounded convincing and had convinced himself, though in a stupor of exhaustion he wondered that night why this had happened, what had gone wrong, how he could have been caught in such a goof. Newt was a man of the age. His star was neon too. It would never have occurred to him to challenge the established truth.

Meanwhile the second blow was being prepared in Caulkin's office that Sunday evening.

This one was beyond Newt's understanding. He had seen the importance of the Titans, the significance of Daffy, but there was another aspect to the general interest in the university, particularly important in the lower middle class and spreading down. These voters weren't satisfied with status for themselves. They wanted to equip their children, too. Doc had made that possible; anyone could be graduated from State and move into circles which had been closed to his parents. The splendor of "the college man"—the golden magic of the degree, even though conferred for a skill which would have been taught in a trade school a generation before—dazzled the families who had been sending their sons and daughters to Gideon since the war, and tomorrow, the day before the election, they were going to be told that the shimmer was false, the gold brass.

Caulkin needed no shotgun now. He had only one story. Slashing at a yellow ruled pad with a thick broker's pencil, he wrote the headline while Al Swinton watched excitedly.

ALL STATE DEGREES WORTHLESS, SAYS U.S. BOARD
OF TOP SCHOLARS; 30,000 CAREERS IN JEOPARDY

The text of the report was to be published inside. With it there would be two statements. The first, from Stuart Witty, regretted the findings and promised corrective action as the first order of business after his inaugural. On the whole it was temperate and statesmanlike; Witty knew when to speak softly. The second statement was from Judge Davies, and it was the most intemperate the judge had ever written. After announcing that he was asking the chairman of the university's trustees to call an emergency session tomorrow, he accused the paper of purloining a privileged record and exploiting it for political advantage, which, he said, was "far more dastardly than the pathetic and ludicrous pornography that soiled the breakfast tables of *Star* subscribers today. It is a politician's cliché to say that a matter will not rest," he concluded, "but I vow I shall not rest until this despicable matter is settled to my satisfaction."

Caulkin hadn't counted on that, and he hated printing it, but once he had read Al's story to the judge over the telephone and ask for comment he was obliged to follow through. The judge was no man to treat lightly. He could make life wretched for Caulkin in the club and in St. Timothy's vestry meetings — could even reach him here in the office, since he was one of the few men on intimate terms with Marcus Gray, the publisher. Every word the judge wrote must therefore go in, though an editor's note could be appended, stiffly observing that the *Star* followed, had always followed and always would follow the heritage of John Peter Zenger, pointing the truth without fear or favor in the belief that the people had a right to know.

It was a great day for Al. Caulkin had scrawled his by-line under the head and was specifying the type: fourteen-point Spartan capitals.

"Of course, this is also worth a raise," said Caulkin, patting his mustache.

"Cripes, I only picked it up from — "

"Not a word!" Caulkin raised his hand. "You must protect your source, even from me. If I know, I can tell."

He meant that. The judge's threat had been ominous. He might badger old Gray into ordering a disclosure of details, which would be tragic for the *Star;* a paper that couldn't keep a confidence wasn't worth the price of newsprint. In fact, it might not be a bad idea to get Al off the scene for a few months. Then there would be nobody to talk.

"I'm citing you in my monthly report, Al. This will all go in your service jacket, and we might even put another bar on your shoulder. How would you like a tour of duty as foreign correspondent?"

"Cripes!"

"Naturally it would be temporary. You'd be brevetted, so to speak. Let's see — " He turned and examined the pins on his map. You couldn't send a man like Swinton to Europe. He didn't speak any foreign languages; barely spoke his own, when you came right down to it. Still — the publisher was a bug about the French Foreign Legion. He collected books about legionnaires, got their magazine. Maybe a Beau Geste series would be just the thing. He turned back. "How would you like the Sahara Desert?"

Al's face fell, and he said once more, with feeling, "Cripes."

"Can't talk like that overseas."

"No, Colonel." The Sahara, Al thought dismally. It was like a joke. He ran his bruised tongue over the place where his tooth had been.

"And you're not going yet," Caulkin said decisively. He was looking down at the story under the by-line. There was one glaring hole in it. Al hadn't any comment from Doc. "I want you to see River."

"Oh, he won't talk to me," said Al, thwarted at the outset as always.

"Well *try!* And another thing. Where's Hiram Markham?"

So now he was responsible for Ham. Some citation, some bar. "I guess he's in Gideon. I saw his company car parked down by the stadium. But he didn't sleep in the Inne."

"Wait a minute, I've an idea. Tell Hiram I want *him* to interview River. He's a State graduate — a natural for this thing. Besides, he's been goldbricking lately. You can tell him that, too."

But Al couldn't find Ham.

Nor, more remarkably, could he find Doc.

**

They were together in Walpole County. The trip wasn't a flight, as Al insinuated when he phoned the desk next morning. Doc had planned a week ago to barnstorm the farm areas in a final swing before the last telecast, and Ham, at loose ends after Saturday's game, had asked if he might tag along. Doc had been deeply pleased. He had whacked his hands together and declared that nothing would suit him better. It was just the thing to chirk an old codger up. Jake Russo was going to meet them after the gabble in Rockton, and afterward they'd just leave that swanky limousine behind, pile into Jake's pickup truck, and strike out for the north country, where a man could be as rough as oak bark and plain as a granny knot and nobody'd care a mite.

Next day there had been a hitch. One of Jake's farm agents had met them outside a general store with an armful of Sunday *Stars*. He had been driving from town to town, buying them up, and he thought Doc should see why. After reading the story about Sarah Doc's first impulse had been to cancel everything and return to her. Jake suggested the telephone would be quicker. Ten minutes later Doc emerged the store booth, chuckling.

"By Jupiter, she's got her sass back. I swear it sounds like the tussle did her good. She says she'd got a bucket of dish water fixed to dump on the first man that sticks his nose in the door, including me. She won't have any fuss made over her, and that's that. I think she was tickled I called, though." He paused and added soberly, "She wants me to do something about Kit."

"If I know Kit, she's got a bucket of her own," said Ham. "She'll crown the first person who mentions divorce to her."

Jake looked up grayly from the front page. "There's going to be trouble over this in the towns."

"Maybe," said Doc.

And that was all he said. The stories of the lost game, Daffy's baton, and the attack on the Mansion cried danger, yet apparently his only concern had been his wife. As he climbed back into the truck Jake and the agent exchanged confused looks. Couldn't he read the signs? Ham was less surprised. This was of a pattern with Doc's responses to crises — the mindless lull came first, then the spasm of decision. By evening he would be ready to speak. And he was. The lull endured through an afternoon of handshaking over rural mailboxes and farm porches, but that night, as they prepared to retire in the agent's house, he drained a glass of buttermilk and set it down with a thump.

"I expect Newt's waiting to hear from me," he said, examining the lees. "Well, he can just wait. I'm on my own for the first time since summer, and I like it. Maybe I'm losing the race. I allow there's considerable reason for thinking so. But at least I'm losing on my own. It's a sight better than wearing somebody else's bib and tucker, boys, and who knows? Maybe it's the only way a fellow like me can win."

His voice was light, almost cheerful. He hadn't given up, Ham saw; he was merely repeating his play of thirty years ago, when he had run ninety-three yards through the Peabody team without blockers, carrying two defensive backs over the goal line with him. There was only one day of the campaign left, a few more hands to pump and a final speech, and every moment of it was going to be Doc's. His — his alone. No Newt, no Titans were going to screen the goal from him. He could run his own interference, and who knew? Maybe he could do it. Experience denied it, but experience is cold, and Ham's heart was warm with affection as Doc stood, stretched, and lumbered off to bed with his pitching, furrow-to-furrow farmer's stride.

They were up Monday at dawn. Outside the rutted ground was brittle with frost; behind the house a barn door creaked as the stiff wind shifted. They hurried out to the pickup truck, their breaths paling on the crisp autumn air, and drove away under a clear sky penciled on the horizon by a few light clouds.

"Snow," said Doc, squinting through the windshield.

"Maybe you're wrong," said Ham, wondering which to hope for. It was inconceivable that Doc could carry the upstate vote, but he might hold it as no Democrat before him had. These counties were beyond the circulation sphere of the daily *Star;* Russo's men had been touching base here every day for a month.

"He's got the best storm eye in New England," Jake said. "If he says it's coming, it'll come. Not today, and maybe not tonight. But tomorrow certain."

Afterward Ham remembered that day as the end of the pilgrimage into the past he had begun the morning Nails Whipple slid Doc's dusty Peabody folder across the desk to him. These were Doc's people, and this was the home of his youth, here in this curious, scarcely altered land of another time, where there were still women named Hannah and Mercy and Abigail, and men named Caleb and Levi and Silas who carried huge old pocket watches wound by keys and tucked their napkins in their collars and buttered their bread a slice at a time; where there were still Franklin stoves, and pine sledges greased for winter, and barns fragrant with the scent of herbs and crushed hay, and vast cellars stocked with home canning and cider and black strap. Doc was of all this, as Ham could never be. Ham had the Yankee frame, but he had grown up in exile, and the people knew it when he spoke. When Doc spoke at the parlor teas Jake had carefully arranged — when he poured half his cup into the saucer to cool and leaned forward — there was a kindling, a fusion of spirit, as though passwords were being exchanged in some obscure rite.

"By Mighty, I believe . . ."

"This Witty's out to cinch and hog-tie . . ."

"Now I don't set much store by . . ."

". . . flummery . . ."

". . . larruping . . ."

". . . gumption."

They transferred cars three times, twice to the pickups of other agents, and finally, after a twilight cider rally, to the limousine.

"Now how did *that* get there?" Doc said, eying it unhappily as they drew up at a dim crossroads.

Jake said apologetically, "I used the phone a way back."

Doc snorted and sank disconsolately into the deep cushions, then patted the seat alongside. "Come in, Ham. Keep me company while I think about this cussed speech."

"You had a good day, Coach."

"Well, I did, and that's a fact."

Ham hesitated. "I thought we might visit your house. We were in the neighborhood, weren't we?"

Doc turned with a little half smile. "I'll tell you about that a little later."

He closed his eyes and concentrated on the imminent telecast. Ham thought his question had been forgotten, but as they entered Birmingham Doc turned again, again with a faint twinkle.

"You wanted to know about the homestead. I'll let you in on a secret. There isn't any; hasn't been for twenty-five years. I was the last River to work a hoe, and the truth is I made a mess of it. Right after I got out of State times turned hard up north. I went back and struggled with the dirt every whichways for three hungry years, but it was no good. My folks died, and when old Dean Aaron offered me the job as coach I gave up and let the bank have the place. I guess nobody in the county remembers." He looked out the window. "The bank took over a passel of places in '32."

Vaguely Ham remembered his father talking of mass foreclosures, sheriffs battling pitchforks, milk spilt on highways. "Then it wasn't your fault."

"Oh, I was a bust behind a plow, all right." He smiled. "I expect it's the only fact about me your high-hat friends at the *Star* never published."

"You wouldn't recognize it if they did," Ham said bitterly. "Caulkin would turn it into a farmer's daughter Laff."

A newsboy flashed by holding a Monday all-star aloft. Doc pressed his face against the window. "Looks like they know something I don't. All I could catch was 'State Trustees Meeting,'" he said, sitting back. "Well, I'll find out at the station. Sam will be in the sponsor's booth." He closed his eyes. "Sam and Newt and a whole conbobberation of politicians."

Ham was still thinking of Caulkin. Yesterday's edition had made his position impossible. He saw the brownstone *Star* front looming ahead and wondered whether the colonel was still there.

"Let me out at this corner." He sprang to the pavement and held the door ajar. "I hope you sweep the state tomorrow, Coach."

Doc reached out and pumped his hand solemnly. "Thanks, boy."

"Incidentally, I'm walking out on my job here."

"Oh?" And then instinctively, out of a Depression memory: "You got another?"

Ham grinned. "I've had a hundred offers."

"You know, I believe it. You're a smart fellow, Ham. Just between the two of us, you're a lot smarter than me," Doc said, and though Ham couldn't see his face in the darkness of the limousine, his voice sounded humble.

The general managing editor hadn't left; he was pacing the city room, switching his tweedy thighs with his brass ruler. He saw Ham at the same moment Ham saw the morning headline.

"So Al unearthed you," Caulkin called, crossing the room with a full thirty-inch stride. "Did you see River?"

"Just left him," Ham murmured, looking down the column under Al's huge by-line. "We had a long talk."

"Oh?"

"He thinks it looks like snow."

"What? It's not forecast. Was that all? Put that paper away!"

Ham dropped a page at a time; they slithered across the floor, offending Caulkin's sense of order. "Police up!" he snapped at a passing copy boy. "What's the matter with you, Hiram?"

Ham looked blank. "I've just been reading how my career's in jeopardy."

"Yes, well, that's why I wanted you."

"To do a piece on how I slaved in Doc's diploma mill?"

"Certainly not. By George, your post here *is* going to be jeopardized if you don't get cracking!"

Ham clicked his heels. "But my enlistment has expired."

"Of course, it's too late for a River interview now, so I'll use you on number one rewrite starting at noon tomorrow. I need a couple of fast hands on a typewriter."

"And I'm not shipping over."

"Have you been drinking? You'll handle the main election story with me. Naturally your name will go on it."

"In fact, I might even turn traitor."

Caulkin sniffed and smelt cider. "You're *drunk*." Traitor reminded him: "By the bye, your father-in-law's been trying to find you, too. He's over at the club. I'll have the desk phone that you're on your way. Give him my compliments and assure him there are no hard feelings here about his statement on the report. And remember — report to me at twelve sharp. *Sober*."

Swish went the swaggering ruler, and he was gone. It was so like Caulkin, Ham thought, to decide that whoever said what he didn't want to hear must be addled. Well, he had been told, anyway. Would it be necessary to tell him again? No: a letter would do.

Then, hailing a cab below, Ham had second thoughts. A letter might do, but would be dull. Perhaps there was another way which would impress itself upon Caulkin indelibly. Ham's eyes wrinked with the lines of the schemer. He would report tomorrow, all right, at twelve sharp, and he would be dead sober.

The judge too was scheming. In the Clipper Club foyer he crooked his finger artfully. "I suggest we retire to the dining room, Markham. The other members have finished; we can be alone there."

Tapping a nervous fingernail against the stem of a tumbler, he described his dilemma and asked for certain information about Ham's bootlegging investigation.

"Well —" Ham hesitated and then gave it.

"I suspected something of the sort," said the judge. He explained his plan.

"Sounds fine." Ham glanced at his rumpled suit and smiled. "You're not as whimsical as you seem, sir."

"Eh?" The judge fumbled for a cigar, shedding dark brown flakes on the club's best Italian cutwork tablecloth. "The point is that it's *not* fine. Mikel's cooperation is still essential. I spoke to him today; he's decided to be difficult."

"Oh, not Mikel," Ham said dryly.

"He was childishly secretive — wouldn't even tell me whether he'd located Budge. After all, *I'm* going to be in the room with the board. *He* will be in the hall. We should have a better understanding, and I'm rather at a loss how to proceed. I fancied you might help me there, too. I couldn't trace Dr. Lutz, and I know literally no one else close to him. Mikel has great respect for you. Do you think you could intercept him outside the meeting? It's to be at Aggie, at two tomorrow afternoon."

"I have to be in the city room." He had to be. Everything he had heard here strengthened that.

"Hmm. I doubt Mr. Theanapolis would change the time for me. All this has put me under a scowling cloud; my hand is thought to be against everyone. Do you suppose we could see Mikel tonight?"

Ham struggled with a yawn. He had been traveling since Saturday.

"I'll do what I can, but I can't promise much. He lives all over Gideon, you know."

"Then we'd better start now."

They were waiting at the cloak room counter when Stuart Witty came out of the library.

"Not campaigning?" Ham asked.

"About to," said Witty, doffing a black velvet smoking jacket and donning a respectable Republican cloth coat. "I'm on Channel 5 in an hour. St. George is on now, trying to slay all the dragons that have risen up over the week end."

He minced off, chuckling. Ham edged into the library. Some thirty men in dinner clothes stood between the fumed oak walls, sipping brandy and watching the television console. Ham stepped toward it. He was appalled at the change in Doc. An hour ago he had been cheerful, ready to race to the wire. Now the face on the screen was ashen, stricken. He had seen Budge's report in the *Star*. He had seen his dream in tar and feathers, and he hadn't much fight left.

"So the tumult and the shouting dies," he was saying nasally, "and the captains and the kings depart."

And that, thought Ham, is what he had been preparing in the limousine. He looked at the false book backs and tinny trophy cups behind Doc and tried to smile. He couldn't; the smile wasn't there, and when a man near the fire grinned openly, Ham glared.

"I guess you're pretty sick of me," Doc said.

"And how," the grinning man said over his cognac, and Ham moved closer to him.

"Well, I'm pretty sick of myself. I'm not at all sure I was cut out for this politics business — maybe it's not good politics to say so, but I guess that only proves my point. Just the same, I've done what I could with it, and if in the fullness of time you decide tomorrow you'd like me to have a stab at being governor, why, I'll give it the best I know how. That seems fair enough. A fellow may promise more, but he can't *do* more."

"Oh Christ," the man by the fire said. "How long do we have to wait for Stu?"

Ham studied him coolly. He was his own age, a slim Jaycee type with fair, thinning hair, a yellow toothbrush mustache, and a standard old family tuxedo — singlebreasted, herringbone, worn with pommeled cotillion pumps.

"However, that's neither here, there, nor the other place," Doc went on. "It's something I'll handle if, as, and when I win." His voice began to rise. "What I want to discuss right now hasn't anything to do with politics — leastways it shouldn't, and didn't, till the *Star* brought it up."

The Jaycee giggled. "I thought he was going to say '*brung* it up.'"

But the other club members were quiet. They realized Doc wasn't preparing to ask for votes. He was going to give, and it was going to hurt.

"I'm talking about your state university. It *is* yours, of course, every lick and brick of it, though I hope you won't mind if I say that in a way it's mine, too. I can't even begin to tell you the battles I've gone through for it. I allow you've heard some of the yelling and hollering, and I expect you know who was gouging and kneeing and rabbit-punching me most. It was the *Star*, first to last. The *Star* never wanted State to be more than it was when I started — a little six-bit, two-by-four school for dirt farmers who didn't care if they ever climbed out of their dell. The high-and-mightys that run the papers were dead set against any change. They were bound and determined that the most of us were going to go right on saying 'Please,' and 'May I,' and 'Thank you' to the few of them — the silk-stockinged, silk-hatted few that had taken their veils at Peabody nunnery."

"Oh-oh," said the Jaycee. "He slipped that time. Nunnery's just the one word he shouldn't have used."

Ham took two midget steps sideways. Their coats touched.

"Their lordships still feel that way," Doc said, and his voice, which had grown strong and biting, began to fall again. "They mean to have their flowers drive out our weeds, and they won't stick at anything till the job's done. I hope you'll tussle with them just as hard as I have. I hope you'll go after them hammer and tongs and never show the white feather. I hope and pray you won't let this setback we just had make you lose heart, because if you do you'll be losers, and I learned a long time ago that when you lock horns with those fellows and lose you can't be a good loser. It can't *be* or *feel* or *do* good. You've lost — that's the size of it — you've just plain lost."

" 'Them' fellows," mocked the Jaycee. "He just should have said 'them.' "

Ham bowed his head. He knew now what was coming, and his eyes stung, and forcing them open he stared down wretchedly at shoetops — his heavy brown Church's brogans, bought for Delhi tramps, and the Jaycee's patent leather pumps.

"But we have had the setback," said Doc, very low. "There's no whitewash that can hide the fact; we've been hurt, and the fault's mine. I don't know how it happened — I guess if I did it wouldn't have happened at all. The main thing is that here we are. Where do we go? Well, I see today's *Star* has one suggestion. One of those thoroughbred cocker spaniel editorial writers that never signs his name says I've lost the confidence of the people and ought to quit State. I'd like to spat with him. There's nothing I enjoy more than cruelty to that particular kind of animal. But this once I'm obliged to give the devil his due. I won't do the university a mite of good by staying, and it looks like I might do a sight of harm. So whoever that faceless, lispy-tongued *Star* scribbler is, I'd like to strike his hand right now and tell him, and all of you, that no matter how you make up your minds tomorrow, I've made up mine tonight. I'm writing my resignation from State before I wash up and go to bed. The trustees are meeting tomorrow, and it'll be submitted to them then. It'll be accepted, too." Doc's hollowing dimples were faint shadows under the klieg lights. "They never say no to me. I don't allow it."

There was a pause. The Jaycee smirked. "Poor Daddy," he said. "He's going to miss Peaches Dix."

Ham raised a broganed foot and stamped hard on a shiny pump.

"*Ai!*" shrieked the Jaycee, hopping jerkily.

Heads turned. Ham moved swiftly toward the hall. The judge stood in the doorway, blinking over his rimless glasses.

"What's the matter with that man, Markham?"

"He brung it on himself," Ham said.
"Eh?"
"He's been drinking. He's *drunk*."

**

Doc didn't attend the Colonial Room meeting. He was in his office, cleaning out his desk, and after his resignation had been approved there was an awkward silence.

Sam broke it gruffly. "I wish he'd change his mind."

"It's too late," Paul Bauer said tragically.

"If only he'd waited till tomorrow!" said Tate, joining in unscrupulously.

"That was the idea," Sam growled. "He's got us boxed in."

Tate sighed. "I suppose you're right. We could hardly ask a man to *not* leave when he may *have* to leave the very next day."

"That's right, he's still got a chance," said Sam, glowering down the table. Something was goading him. "Everybody been to the polls?"

Heads bobbed. Everyone had. Stunned by the defeat and scandal which had defiled State's name since their last meeting, the trustees were still loyal to Doc. He had given them their place in the Civitan-G.P.-small business sun, and if the sun was dark now, it was Doc who had taught them never to say die. They weren't quitters, and they weren't fair weather friends. They wore their Doc pins proudly and looked defiant.

The inevitable exception was Judge Davies.

Sam eyed his bare, custom-tailored lapel. "I guess *you* pulled the Republican lever."

This was no time to fight for the secret ballot. "I've been voting the straight ticket since I reached my majority," the judge said mildly. "It may be a bad habit, but I'm afraid it's unbreakable."

"Is slipping stuff to newspapers another habit?"

"Eh?"

"I got to hand it to you, you're one smooth operator," Sam said bitterly. "All that stuff the other day about the need for us to wear gags. And then pasting the *Star* and demanding this meeting. Pretty smooth. Pretty smart. But it don't fool me."

"I meant every word of it," the judge said quietly. "I regard the release of that document as outrageous."

"It has certainly shaken up the students," Tate chimed in. "The registrar is swamped with applications for transfer." He didn't add that one of them was from young Sam. He was determined to offend no one here.

"I told Doc this was no time to have a Witty man on the board," Sam fumed. "We took a viper to our breast, and now we know it."

"You're saying *he* gave them the report?" asked Bauer, open-mouthed.

"I'm saying he sold us out."

"Extraordinary charge," the judge said under his breath.

"It had to be you! Only the people that were in this room Saturday had copies."

"One went to Boston," Tate put in, demurely walking the fence.

"It was sealed," Sam said curtly.

Tate persisted. "Perhaps the stencils —"

"The stencils were destroyed. Look at the minutes of the last meeting. It's all there, thanks to our foxy friend here."

"I am not a fox, and I am not a viper," the judge said tremulously. "I am a member of the bar, and I remind you that I'm entitled to a fair hearing."

"You knew that report was loaded. You knew it would blow a hole in Doc's campaign big enough for Witty's Cadillac to drive through."

The judge puckered. "I believe Mr. Witty's machine is something called a Jaguar."

"All right! There you are! Nobody else here would know that. And nobody else wants to see that Jag parked in front of the Statehouse the next four years."

"That's your proof?" the judge inquired, sounding very consonant.

"No. That's *your* motive. The proof is that I was in the *Star* building at ten o'clock this morning, trying to get a few dinky paragraphs in, and I almost ran into you sneaking out of Hallam Caulkin's office with a dispatch case under your arm."

The judge started. He didn't know he had been seen. He blurted out, "It wasn't Caulkin's office."

"He admits it!" Bauer whispered.

"Oh dear," said Tate.

"What were you doing there?" Sam demanded.

"See here —" But it was no time for dignity, either. "I shall come to that presently."

"You were getting your copy back, weren't you?"

"Of course not."

"Then it's still there?"

"Its in proper hands."

"Proper blueblood hands, you mean."

"Oh *dear,*" said the provost, and bit his cheeks to keep from laughing. It was too delicious. The judge was such a clumsy victim of circumstance; Tate's own copy, the sinning copy, had been returned Sunday night and was here in his portfolio. It occurred to him that that might be worth pointing out. "I propose that we search ourselves," he said silkily. "How many reports have we here?"

He produced his. The trustees, aware of the meeting's implications, had brought theirs. The exception, once more, was the judge.

"Mine has been in the custody of the chief clerk of the State Supreme Court since an hour after I left our meeting Saturday," he said stiffly.

Tate decided it was time to jump off the fence. He whispered to Sam, "The clerk works for him, of course."

"Sure, it's a fix," Sam said aloud. "We all know that, and he knows we know it. He doesn't even dare look at us."

The judge's pale eyes were intent on an unlit cigar trembling in his fingers. He appeared the picture of guilt, and was in fact uneasy. The time had arrived for him to present witnesses, yet he didn't even know their names. Last night he and Ham had tracked Mikel to a local lair, in vain; Mikel had merely laughed roguishly and assured them he would be outside the Colonial Room at two o'clock with everything required. The judge had waited in the hall until the last possible moment, but when Archer's chimes struck twice the only outsider in the hall had been Al Swinton, soliciting interviews from trustees and being rebuffed. The judge was in the position of a magician who must produce a rabbit from a hat and doesn't know whether the rabbit is really there. He wasn't entirely unprepared; he had come with a few tricks of his own. Mikel's role, however, was vital. It was all very vexing. What would a good magician do? Even Houdini had to bluff sometimes, he supposed.

"Gentlemen, you slight my intelligence. Don't you suppose I saw this accusation coming?" He met Tate's eyes. "Did you honestly think I would come here with nothing to refute it?"

Tate smiled. He had thought that and still did. To him the

judge was a fusty old man with many affectations and no real core of sense.

"Refute, then," Sam challenged.

"Excuse me." The judge walked to the door and opened it a crack. Al was still outside, dozing on a bench. Across the corridor a figure lurked in a doorway. It was Mikel, puffing on a Camel with an inch of ash. The judge took a deep breath. "Mr. Chariman, do I have your consent to bring Dr. Mikel in here?"

"Oh God, why?"

"He has — some data."

"It can't do any harm," Tate said fruitily. Mikel, after all, was just another fogy. "Judge Davies should be given every chance to clear this up."

"All right, but I warned you," Sam said.

Mikel entered, bookbag swinging, and struck an attitude. "*Sauve qui peut!*"

"See?" said Sam. "The rest will be in Latin, too."

Mikel rolled his eyes and primped. Though no one much noticed, he had dressed carefully for this performance. He had bathed, shaved, put on a clean checkered shirt, and bought a new pair of Keds. His business here could have been safely left to the judge, but he had sworn an oath of vengeance, and he intended to redeem it personally.

"I wish to bring two other people in," he announced.

Sam groaned. "This is a *board* meeting, for God's sakes." He propped his fleshy cheeks on his hands. "O.K., O.K."

Mikel went to the door. "Mr. Swinton?"

"Huh?"

Al rubbed his eyes. Reconciled to the Sahara, he had been dreaming of houris and dervishes. His passport was due tomorrow; Thursday he would be in Washington, acquiring visas.

"Please step in here a moment," Mikel purred. Al did, and Mikel said sharply, "Now tell the board why you met W. Denton Tate in the Acme Diner Sunday morning."

"What?" said Al.

"*What!*" said Tate.

Mikel returned to the hall. "Dr. Feinblatt!" Sol crossed from the doorway opposite, and Mikel threw a withered arm over his shoulders. "I encountered a friend of Dr. Feinblatt's near my lodgings yesterday, and she disclosed the most remarkable titbit."

"I saw the provost in the Acme with a man Sunday," Sol said. "He was giving him some papers."

"Rubbish!" Tate croaked.

"Tut-tut," said Mikel. "You must have patience; the titbit is about to grow even tastier. Today Dr. Feinblatt recognized the man in this building."

"That's him," said Sol, pointing to Al.

"Listen, I'm just a reporter!" Al protested.

"Ah, you're too modest." Mikel wagged a reproving finger. "You are reporter of the hour. We shan't soon forget your gripping account of our failure to pass Budge's final exam."

"There must be some mistake," Tate said rapidly.

"A phrase, a phrase," Mikel murmured.

Tate was thinking fast. It had seemed inconceivable that a faculty member should frequent a cheap highway diner. Now he had to lash out with the only weapon he had, Miss Shoemaker's sketchy report on Kit.

"I appeal to Judge Davies," he shrilled.

"Eh?"

A tiny twitch appeared in Tate's right cheek, a nervous parody of a wink.

"The judge knows the rules of evidence. He can tell you the character of a witness is an issue. This man Feinblatt is dismissed from the university."

Sol grinned. "I object. You can't fire me. I've quit already."

"Overruled. You had to quit. Your conduct has become disgraceful." Tate faced the board. "Allow me to identify the feminine friend Harry Mikel met by his lodgings. I have reason to know that she has been sharing Feinblatt's bed the past two nights."

Sol darkened. Mikel clapped him gleefully on the back. "Go on — punch him in the nose."

"Her name is Catherine Ryan O'Donnell," said Tate.

Trustees named Manning and Boyle were on their feet, and Bauer, up before either of them, was baring his three gold teeth. He stammered, "Why — she's the woman who led that poor Southern girl astray!"

"Hit him, too!" Mikel's eyes had a lunatic glint. "Him first, then the Hibernians!"

The judge intervened. Mikel's impish irresponsibility was endangering everything. "I think we can excuse Mr. Swinton and Dr. Feinblatt now. Thank you, gentlemen," he said, prodding them out. "Thank you very much, just go along."

"I hope I won't have to defend myself against the lies of any more men like that," Tate said caustically.

"No," said the judge, closing the door. "No more like that, and no lies. Dr. Mikel, would you sit there? In the corner, that's fine. Now." He turned on Tate, his mustache bristling. "The man you must defend yourself against is me."

Tate's twitch worsened. "Really, this is too much!"

"It is," said the judge, biting off words, "but we are going to hear it all."

Sam was bewildered. One minute he had exposed a Witty plot, the next minute the plotter had taken the gavel from him. "Say, you haven't even told us what you were doing with Caulkin."

"It was Marcus Gray, not Caulkin. I went over Caulkin's head to find out how that Swinton wretch had laid his hands on a privileged record."

Tate felt safe here. "Well?"

He was safe. "I learned nothing."

"Nothing?" asked Sam, exasperated.

"Not at the *Star*. Gray summoned Caulkin, who insisted Swinton couldn't be reached."

"So you struck out."

"Ah — not quite. You spoke a moment ago of motive. Of course you were right; Budge's instrument, once published, became a political weapon. It occurred to me that it might be enlightening to learn whether I really would be the only member of this gathering interested, as you put in, in seeing Mr. Witty's foreign machine parked beneath the capitol spire." He paused deliberately, as before passing sentence. "I drove to Republican headquarters in the Hotel Birmingham and learned that the provost of this university has contributed three hundred dollars to the party's campaign."

Sam's face went angular, like an object seen through water. "Is that right, Tate?"

Again the twitch, and then again. Tate couldn't believe Hewitt had betrayed him. "Who told you that?"

The judge wasn't quite ready to talk about his brief, sharp interview with Hewitt and Witty. He felt sure Mikel had another shot to fire, and he sidestepped adroitly. "It was simple, really. I happened to see you handing a check to a Republican functionary in the Clipper Club. I've been active in the party for a half century. All files are open to me."

The trustees swore softly, Sam heavily; Tate tried to control his cheek, and Mikel hissed "Rasputin!"

"Everything was quite legal," Tate insisted stridently. "It's slanderous to suggest that one man's free choice of a candidate had anything to do with the report."

Mikel rose, as the judge had expected. "My ups." He rooted in his green bag and drew out a battered Monday *Star*. "Remarkable how cheap the printed word has become," he said, turning to the page with the text of the report. "Indeed, it's so abundant it's rarely read. Ah! Here we are." He flung the opened paper on the table. "How many of you took the time to compare this with the version Budge gave you?"

"Version?" the judge echoed.

"Version?" Tate re-echoed.

"I see none did. Well, there were *two* versions," said Mikel, rubbing his hands. "As a low professor I wasn't privy to either, but my fellow proletarian Lutz gave me the unlisted number of Budge's Illinois laboratory. Yesterday I called Urbana to inform him of this startling turn of events."

"Admit it, you were trying to snoop," Tate said with desperate sarcasm.

"Trying successfully."

"I suppose you charged the call to the History Department."

"No, to you. I'm no longer history chairman, and your office happened to be vacant. It will appear on your next monthly statement. Rather expensive, I'm afraid. You see, Budge startled *me*. I'd never have dreamt an academician could be so cunning, though I suppose it's the only way we dons can survive the new barbarism. Allow me to read you a poignant passage, so appropriate to this moment of truth." He leaned over the *Star*. "'The university provost,'" he read, "'has introduced into higher education a secondary school ideology — and a discredited ideology at that.'"

"I'm familiar with that," Tate snapped.

"*You* are. I am addressing the group. Can anyone else find it in his report?" Pages fluttered. Mikel raised a dramatic hand. "I'll save you the trouble. It's not there. Budge inserted it in only one copy — the provost's."

So Budge had kept faith after all, the judge thought wonderingly. He had found a device far more effective than the initialing of pages, and he had taken the time to cut twin stencils because during his brief Gideon stay he had cultivated a cold hatred for Tate. Remarkable. Extraordinary. What an odious little man the provost must be.

Tate twitched and twitched. His mouth worked and he whimpered, "That was unprofessional of him!"

Mikel sank back to his armchair, cackling bitterly.

Paul Bauer had continued to search his report. He was slow — as an undergraduate he had been failed twice by Mikel. But he was dogged — he had returned the third semester and passed with a low mark. He glanced up now, his eyes widening.

"Tate did it!"

"C-plus," Mikel caroled.

"Goddamn," Sam whispered.

The Hibernian named Manning asked, "But why?"

"It's rather obvious," Mikel drawled. "I think we can assume that he counted on Witty ordaining him here."

Now the judge was ready.

"We needn't assume," he said. "We know. I spoke to the Republican chairman. He and the provost had reached an informal understanding."

Bauer's teeth flashed. "To make Tate president?"

"I'd quit," said Manning.

"I'd quit," said Boyle.

"I'd quit after the assasination," said Sam, lowering at Tate.

"All unnecessary," the judge quavered. "Witty has repudiated Hewitt. I have his assurance in writing. You see, the files also disclosed that the provost is a registered Democrat."

That would hold them. The truth was more complex. In the dispatch case he had been carrying this morning was a photostat of the Consolidated Enterprises charter, obtained after last night's talk with Ham. The judge had been polite to Witty. He hadn't raised his voice. He hadn't threatened him directly. But he had made himself quite clear — unless Witty signed the repudiation immediately he would be exposed as a former bootlegger who had allowed Doc River to take his place in the dock.

Tate pushed back his chair and squirmed up. His bald skull gleamed with sweat, and there was a horrible cadence to his twitches his cheek was jerking regularly every half second in violent, convulsive spasms.

"This is the most outrageous . . . I've never been submitted . . . I assure you this matter . . . this libel . . . all I've done . . . won't put up another minute with —"

But they didn't seem to be listening. He swallowed, seized his portfolio, and stumbled into the hall.

"All right, all right!" he bawled. "I resign!"

"*Whipeye!*" Mikel howled after him.

The stumbles, the bawl, the howl reverberated down the long corridor. Outside the Colonial Room Al and Sol stared after the fleeing figure; inside the board sat stock still. Then Manning said slowly, "So we don't have *any* president."

"Oh, you'll find someone," Mikel said acidly. "Somebody from the Ford Foundation. Some major general."

"After the report it'll be tough to really get the best," said Sam.

They were contemplating that when heavy steps pounded in the hall. It was Doc, in shirtsleeves, his hands grimy with the dust of housecleaning.

"Say, what's the matter with Tate?" he demanded.

The trustees avoided his eyes.

"Well, *some*thing is! He just came busting past my office, making the air blue. There were students around."

"A ribald," Mikel said.

Sam cuffed his forehead. "I'll tell you about it in a little bit, Doc."

"Looked washed out, too," Doc said worriedly.

"He bathes often," said Mikel.

"No, poorly. Off his feed."

Mikel nodded. "Distemper."

Sam lingered as the other trustees filed through the door, shaking Doc's hands and assuring him that they had voted. They oozed confidence; only the Republican among them noticed that nobody had called him Governor. The judge pottered off toward the parking lot exit, musing over that, and as he stepped outside the building he realized with a sense of wonder that although everyone in the Colonial Room had been within a few feet of its three double windows, no one had glanced out at the campus. His old Packard wore a thickening crust of white. It had been snowing for an hour.

**

7:03 P.M.

The polls had closed three minutes ago.

Ham sat in the *Star* bull pen, absently fingering the question mark key of a Remington typewriter.

Electricity was all around him. He himself wore heavy headphones plugged to a private six-line switchboard box — six switches, six tiny colored light bulbs, all his. Another, much larger switchboard stood against the nearest wall. Girls holding black crayon pencils and tally sheets hunched over the control panels there; other girls toyed with the nearby battery of adding machines, and opposite the desk were two gigantic television sets, mounted on tripods and sprouting rabbit ears.

At the moment no current flowed — it would be at least ten minutes before the first returns began to trickle in — but when it began Ham would become its transformer. Caulkin, at his field desk, was on a distant perimeter; Ham sat on ground zero. He was the number one rewrite man, the bull pen bull's-eye. The number two and number three men would feed him notes from either side. The girls would slip columns of figures under his elbows. Reporters watching the television sets would bring notes here, and here, over the private switchboard box, would come calls from veteran *Star* men on the outside.

7:05

Since voting in the morning Ham had been writing steadily for the afternoon *Star*. This was his first real break. He bit into a sandwich, sipped from a carton of black coffee, and sat back yawning.

Lucky all those wires are insulated, he thought. All day Caulkin had been bellowing at copy boys to police up the place, but the desk remained a tumbled mass of litter. Yards of yellow wire copy hung to the floor; stacks of retouched art mingled with stacks of morgue envelopes; advance proofs of Today's Laff obscured advanced proofs of George Sokolsky; inky new editions had been dumped on obsolete old. Ham lidded his eyes and surveyed the headlines of election day trivia, the last jabs at the punchdrunk voter:

Million and Half Voters Choose New Governor Today. Record High Vote Seen; Independents Hold Balance. Govs to be Picked in

Other States. State Trustees in Grim Gideon Meet. Election Interest Improves Health of Leukemia Victim. Wittys Vote Early in City. "Doc" Says Did His Best, Expresses Confidence. Mrs. Witty Chats with Friends. Witty's Daughter Waits Hopefully at His Side. Young Witty Watches from Korean Outpost. Titans in Listless Practice. Unopposed Seats Give G.O.P. Legislative Edge. Sodality Flays "Doc." Low Level of Demmie Campaign Bewailed. Blandford Calls Witty "Take-Charge Guy." Calls Budget Cut "Supreme Aim." Calls on Party Stalwarts in Hard-to-Figure Election. For the Verdict read the morning *Star!*

And be grateful for a free press, thought Ham. He stretched and glanced through a half-dozen staccato messages known to the office as FYI's; all bore his initials and were skewered on a spike beside his typewriter carriage. The top FYI was from Al Swinton. It had been dictated less than an hour ago; even when in the presence of an event Al was slow to perceive its meaning.

HM de AS — W. Denton Tate resigned as State provost this PM. Executive session stormy. No more dope immediately available.

Ham smiled faintly. There was plenty more dope, and he had it all. After returning to Birmingham Judge Davies had telephoned him the details from his chambers. Mikel Seen Take-Charge Guy, Ham thought. Board Flays Joyboy "Educator." Tate Upended in Hard-to-Find Doublecross.

There were two other messages from Al, one from Frosty Warren, and one, laconic, from the rewrite man handling weather.

HM de AS — Doc switching plans. Will stick in Gideon tonight and hear returns in manse. Albert and Sam the Greek to handle Dem show in Birm'm.

HM de AS — Albert predict. Sees Doc winding up w. plurality of 40,000. Doc to come out of Birm'm w. 80,000 margin, pick up another 20,000 Rock'n, Dud'y, and Pawn'k.

Counties to cut this by 60,000. In capital Albert claims 1st 6 districts, though 6th could be wobbly.

HM de FW — Hewitt predict. Witty overall state plurality to be 100,000 as follows. Will lose Birm'm only by 35,000; Rock'n, Pawn'k, Dud'y by 5,000 each. To carry counties by 150,000. Is sure Witty can carry 6th,

7th, 8th districts Birm'm, maybe even 5th. For y'r pvt. eye: Hewitt coy on State sex-&-God issue etc. Says *Star* raised it, *Star* can figure it.

HM de JH — Weather Bureau so sorry. Snow after all. I'll insert skinback in all-star weather ear. Maybe 5 inches starting early PM. Could discourage upstate cornfed vote.

Beyond the FYI spike lay an all-star flipped open to a page of photographs — photographs of candidates, of voting machines, of closed bars; and two large shots of party headquarters. It struck Ham that the headquarters pictures really belonged in a political science primer. They told so much more than Caulkin intended. There was the elegant lobby of the Hotel Birmingham, now decorated with potted palms, tricolor bunting, American and state flags, clusters of gas balloons bunched against the ceiling, and smiling posters of Mr. Depth. In the column alongside was the drab lobby of the Yankee Inne, no relation to Gideon's College Inne, though both might have been under the same management; the Yankee was the cheapest hotel in Birmingham, only a block from Mechanics Street, and despite the ribbons of colored paper entwined in the lone glass chandelier and the brave "I'm for Doc!" banner hung across the reception desk it suggested hurried lunch-hour adulteries, pot-bellied house detectives, foul invitations scribbled on toilet walls. The Democrats must really be strapped to hire it, Ham thought. No wonder Doc decided to leave it to Newt and Sam and the party hacks.

Ham patted his shirt pocket. Inside was a cable from India, delivered that morning. In Rockton Saturday night he had decided to wire Dancy that he was leaving the paper, and her reply was — DARLING DARLING WONDERFUL IDEA BED WARM ONLY HURRY SIGNED YOU BETTER KNOW WHO. Well, he was hurrying. It was just that he had a few knots left to tie. He opened his top drawer a crack and peered in. A diaper of light fell on a brief story, properly slugged, edited, and headed. He had come to the office an hour early to write it. It bore every sign of having passed the desk of the general managing editor, though Caulkin had no idea that it existed. If he saw it he'd probably declare martial law, Ham thought, smiling inwardly. Thirty minutes from now the first election edition would be closing; the desk, the city room, in fact the entire building would be in chaos, and a man who knew the *Star* and knew when to be where could get almost anything in the paper.

7:06

A green light flashed on Ham's board. He flicked the switch.

"Mr. Markham, this is Gloria. I got this personal call for you — a Mrs. Feinblatt, she says. Do you want it?"

"Yes, *yes*." He struck the Remington exclamation mark. "Kit?"

"Ham?" she said tentatively.

"You and Sol really married?"

"Well, not exactly. I didn't dare use my real name. O'Donnell's a little iffy these days, you know. Right now Sol and I are sort of common law."

There was a scuffle at the other end, and he came on jovially. "She likes it this way, but I don't. We're getting a license at the first stop."

Another scuffle, then Kit. "He means we're at the station, going west. He has a job, and Sean and I are camp followers." She was breathing quickly, though whether from happiness or anxiety Ham couldn't tell. "I wanted to say good-by."

"Oh."

"This is probably forever."

"Oh." He felt a husk in his throat.

"I mean, I probably won't see you again."

"No." No: never again the raven hair, the slanting lashes, the valiant shoulders, the shuffling, pigeon-toed walk. He closed his eyes and saw saddle shoes. "What are you wearing?"

"Wearing? Oh." She understood. "Rags mostly. We're not very prosperous at the moment. In fact, we look like Okies or something — Yankee Okies, all snow and slush. Sean's sleeping on a bench, and my bags are leaking ratty unmentionables. But at least I threw those damned eyeglasses away. And I'll be spiffy once I can get to some stores. I've got a shopping list. Spiked heels, some of those heavenly Mexican skirts — *you* know."

"Yes." Yes: a few years of the full flower of her mature beauty were left, and she would cultivate them for Sol. Her breath was a breath of happiness after all. And suddenly there were two breaths there — Kit and Sol were facing the receiver together, cheek to cheek, both talking at once, speaking in a rush to their first friend in three harrowing days.

"You hear about Tate fouling out?" Sol asked. "Good. I watched it. Very nice." He turned away briefly. "Listen, our train's leaving in a few minutes." Already he was the solid married man. "Probably we're keeping you anyway, Frankenstein. This *is* the big day for your word machine, isn't it?"

"Not yet. We're just tinkering now, stripping paragraphs down. I've got things all over the floor. Nouns. Prepositions. Clichés."

"Keep your nose to the you-know-what," Sol chuckled.

His breath was gone, Kit's lingered. But she couldn't think what to say. Nor could Ham. And yet, though an undercurrent of noise around him signaled the first city returns, he couldn't bear to hang up. It was as though the breaking of this last tie with his youth would instantly bring him great old age, like the girl he had seen wrinkle up and turn gray in *Lost Horizon* at the Bijou Theatre on Mechanics Street that many years ago.

"End of the line, Ham."

"I guess so. Happy?"

"As a clam. Good-by, dear," she said softly.

"Good-by, Kit." Good-by, 1943. "Dear, I—" But the line was dead. He cut the switch and sat back, and he did feel older.

The noise was growing, a muffled clamor. Lights flashed on the big board. Telephones jangled. On the television sets commentators appeared, chalking numbers on blackboards. The chaos had begun.

Two slips appeared at Ham's elbow. Seventh District, 21st ward, 302d precinct—Witty, 497; River 53. Second District, 5th ward, 81st precinct—River 393; Witty 123.

It was a set piece. The Republicans hadn't lost the 21st ward since 1936, and then to Lemke. And the 5th ward was so incorrigibly Democratic that Hewitt hadn't even bothered to rent its peeling billboards; Witty posters would have been defaced or torn down overnight. Still, 123 votes . . . Ham reached behind his typewriter and consulted a chart Charlie Smathers had prepared that afternoon at his request. In the last election the 81st precinct had given Blandford just 87—Blandford, the most popular governor in a generation. Was this an omen? Probably not; there were no reliable omens this early. But there should have been over four hundred Doc voters on that slip.

Caulkin was on his feet. This first rash of returns was important to him. He had picked eighty precincts, a fifth of the city; every available man had been sent out to cover them and telephone the figures before the 7:30 deadline. It was a typical Caulkin operation. Passes from the Board of Election Supervisors had been issued, neatly clipped to detailed instruction sheets. Each man was told to drive to precinct A, call *Star* extension B, ask for clerk C, and dictate results D; drive next to precinct E, call extension F, and give figures G to H. A fine M1A1 plan, thought Ham, watching Caulkin hovering over the nervous girls. There was just one trouble with it. Caulkin was completely ignorant of the voting patterns within the city. He didn't know which were the key precincts. He had been too proud to ask Ham, say, or even Smathers, and the consequence would be a hodgepodge of numbers, some significant, some meaningless.

The big switchboard was ablaze. It was 7:19. They had a running total now, and a deft feminine hand slid it toward Ham.

River (D) 24,430
Witty (R) 15,280

Again, the expected. A tenth of the city in, and apparently it was anybody's guess how big a shield Doc would carry out of the city. And yet . . . maybe all the guessers were wrong. Ham checked his bundle of slips hurriedly. God, what a Blimp that Caulkin was. He'd picked every tight little Democratic island downtown and slighted the suburbs badly. The story wasn't in the total. It was on Smathers's chart. Witty was outrunning Blandford. Of course, it could be a fluke. Let it be, he prayed; let it be a wild, monstrous freak, because if Birmingham had abandoned Doc it was all over but the crying.

Two more slips, these from the 13th ward. Caulkin had stumbled on something here. An appendix of Ham's book had been devoted to the ward. It was the city in microcosm — the typical census tract, with the average number of rooms per dwelling unit, the median income per family, the mean incidence of children, electrical appliances, crime, and disease. Its voting pattern was a norm, and tonight it was going Republican three-to-two.

Ham removed his earphones and shouted at the girl. "Are you sure these are right?"

She stiffened. "We repeat every digit, Mr. Markham. Mr. Caulkin's orders."

Another clerk brought digits from the 3rd ward. There was no active Democratic organization there, nor any need for one; this was lower Mechanics Street, the pit of the slum. Ham almost dropped the paper. The 35th and 36th precincts gave Witty 420, Doc 418.

It was impossible.

Witty was carrying the city.

Ham crossed to the switchboard and tapped Caulkin's back. "Have you seen these?"

"What? Oh. Looks close, eh? Say, shouldn't you be writing? We've got sixty precincts in."

"And Witty in with them. If this holds he'll take Birmingham."

Caulkin stared.

"You think I like it? Listen, I wish I could eat this damned paper. Come over here." Ham showed him the chart. "Blandford never laid a glove on anybody in the 3d."

Caulkin burbled, "A weathervane, eh?"

"Pointing to a landslide," said Ham. He averted his face and half sobbed a vile phrase.

Caulkin didn't hear it. The clamor had become an uproar. A blizzard of slips had fallen on Ham's desk, and a new total lay on top.

River (D)	. . . . .	33,760
Witty (R)	. . . . .	33,280

"We're still trailing," Caulkin said doubtfully.

"Oh, for Christ's sakes!" Ham exploded. "Can't you see that's because you loused up the precincts? If you didn't have a Sherman tank for a brain we'd have a real trend here."

"That'll do!" Caulkin said turgidly, then hesitated. "All right, Hiram. Write it as you see it. I'll take care of the bulletins on the stone."

Ham snatched up the earphones. "Gloria? Hold the boys off for fifteen minutes. I've got to screw some prepositions into some clichés."

"Mr. *Mark*ham!"

7:24

River (D)	. . . . .	43,290
Witty (R)	. . . . .	42,980

7:29

The sheer mass of figures was taking over.

Witty (R)	. . . . .	51,320
River (D)	. . . . .	50,130

7:30
Ham's typewriter machine-gunned the last sentence of the first edition. He tossed the page to a copy boy and sat back, feigning exhaustion. Actually he was closer to rage than fatigue — the coming mortification of Doc would be his mortification too — but this was no time to crack up; he had been waiting all day for this hectic moment, when the composing room downstairs would be a tumult of yammering linotypes, hot lead, and yelling make-up men. The general managing editor's elation made it easier. Caulkin checked Ham's story hurriedly, tossed it back to the boy, and bounded toward the corridor. He couldn't wait to tell the publisher the news.

7:31
Ham opened the drawer and was rolling the hidden story there into a tight cylinder when his eye fell on a Laff proof. It would be so easy; a few strokes of a pencil to give the inane feature some point. Well, why not? He groped for his pencil, wiggled it, inserted the altered proof in the cylinder, and strode over to the pneumatic tube. Story and proof were slipped into a leather cartridge; the cartridge cap was snapped in place. A sigh of compressed air: it hurtled down. So much for John Peter Zenger. Then it occurred to him that even a harried make-up man might glance twice and call Caulkin. He strolled toward the unoccupied field desk.

7:32
Caulkin's phone did ring.

Ham held the receiver away from his mouth. "Hah?"

"This is Joe Blow, Colonel."

"Uh-huh."

The make-up chief sounded perplexed. "About this Markham bulletin."

"Mmm."

"It's O.K.?"

"Uh-huh."

"Oh. The new Laff, too?"

"Huh?"

"We get them on mats, you know. You sure you want to reset?"

"Uh-huh."

"I don't think I get the joke."

You will, Ham thought, and said, "Um."

"I guess that don't matter, though."

"Uh."

Ham could go on grunting forever. The pressure was off him. Joe, however, was still locked in his deadline vise. He couldn't have read much more than the head and the first paragraph of the story before calling. There was no time for him to do more now. The clock on the composing room wall would be jerking off the last half-seconds, and Ham knew Joe's eyes were riveted on it.

"Well, we got to close now, Colonel."

"Mmm."

"Just wanted to check."

"Uh-huh."

Caulkin came back as Ham was turning away.

"Looking for me?"

"I wondered whether we'd made an election bet."

"No, worse luck." Caulkin snapped his fingers in an exaggerated gesture. "I could have taken you into camp, couldn't I? Not," he crooned, "that I believe in hard feelings."

"Gee."

"Doc's bid was quite in line, perfectly proper in a democracy. Every dog's entitled to one bite." So much for magnanimity. "By the bye, how's the score coming?"

"Search me. Going upward and onward, I guess."

"Well, find it! Get cracking! Tell the civilians!"

The new total was big. Police stations had begun their relay of the unofficial count over leased phones; 183 precincts were in. The gap was widening — 107,568 to 102,468. Witty was going to carry the capital by over 10,000 votes, and he had taken early leads in Rockton, Pawnattuck, and Dudley. No one had dreamt of such a surge. Thousands of Democrats in every neighborhood were splitting their tickets, taking everyone on the slate but Doc. Normally elections weren't decided for two hours. This one was already over. Manipulating his six switches, watching the tiny lights brighten, die, and brighten again as he mechanically took notes from the staff men outside, Ham saw a bleak future: Doc broken; the Democratic organization crushed; and Witty, sleek in triumph, thinking not of the state but of the excitement, the glory, and the restless wives in Washington. Witty, the managerial brain. The man of the G.O. People. Spineless, slick, on the make.

Cool and successful.

The iceman cometh.

Get cracking, tell the civilians . . .

Caulkin was preparing to tell them himself. At his field desk he was jubilantly writing the headline for the second edition:

WITTY LEAD MOUNTS, SOLID WARDS CRACK
PUZZLED DEMMIES WATCH HIS MARGIN GROW
G.O.P. CLAIMS 'TIDAL WAVE' OF VICTORY

Ham rose to fetch a fresh wad of paper and saw that last line, scrawled in big block letters. It was the first he'd heard of Republican crowing. But of course Caulkin had sources of his own. Doubtless he had talked to Witty and Hewitt from the publisher's office. The feudal clan of the wealthy needn't deal with underlings just yet. Later, after they had toasted each other with Tiffany goblets and savored the expensive bouquet of triumph, Frosty Warren would be summoned to the butler's pantry and handed a prepared statement. But gentlemen shouldn't be hasty. And it wouldn't do to cavort openly in the lobby of the Hotel Birmingham. One mustn't make a spectacle of oneself, even if one had graciously condescended to stand for office. After all, what the next governor of the state was up to was nobody's business but his and the clan's.

8:14

Witty (R) 370,759
River (D) 351,253

Outwardly Ham was detached. Reflexes told him which questions to ask of reporters, which calculations to make, what inferences to draw. Like a windup toy he swung the Remington carriage back and back, drumming off sentences, cranking out finished sheets, cranking in clean. Yet his mind was in Gideon. Somewhere in the old-fashioned scrollsaw Mansion Doc's huge shoulders were bowed in suffering. It wasn't the first time, Ham thought. This was the day of his greatest play all over again. The Peabody students were alumni now; they didn't carry Harold Lloyd pennants or wear raccoon coats any more, but they were the same jeering topers, and Doc was the same codfish upstart who had been caught trying to change his ready-made clothes into tailor-made. Tonight was the rerun of an old melodrama. But it would be the last run. The patsy was finished. This time he had nothing left. He had lost his home, his money, and his vision of youth, and in the end he had lost them because his own team wore splayed-out helmets and jerseys with sickly blue stars on the shoulders and thick rings around their socks, like Mamie's in Moon Mullins.

8:29

Witty (R)	. . . . .	414,873
River (D)	. . . . .	390,522

Lost, ignominiously lost. Oh God, Ham thought, when would it end?

It was lost, but not ignominiously, and the rout ended five minutes later, when Doc carried his first county. Conway County, in the northwest corner of the state, had always been among the last to report. At the last election it had approved machines, however, and the county commissioner had just sent his tabulation over the state police teletype net. It was final: River, 31,023; Witty, 30,685.

Ham knocked off a quick insert, handed it to a boy, and peered intently at the chart. Four years ago Blanchard had swept Conway.

Caulkin hurried over, the insert fluttering in his hand. "What does this mean?"

"Every dog's entitled to one bite," Ham murmured, still peering.

"Those people are supposed to be Republicans!"

"And the city's supposed to be Democratic. Wait a minute." Two more county slips were being thrust at him. "Bits and pieces," he said, reading them. "Nothing complete. Interesting, just the same. Doc's sweeping Gideon. Witty's ahead by a hair in Leeds, trailing by a hair in Walpole." Back to the chart. "The big thing, though, is that the farm vote's down everywhere."

"Snow."

Ham nodded and sank back limply. "Maybe if the hicks had come out in force Doc could have made a fight of it. I don't know. But this way you can relax. These city majorities are unbeatable."

"Snow," Caulkin repeated softly. "An act of God."

"Sure. A High-Church Episcopalian God."

"Don't be profane."

"Don't bother me."

Caulkin marched off indignantly, and Ham called the Clipper Club. The judge, he knew, wouldn't be in the Hotel Birmingham tonight. He was still very much a State trustee. As a man of honor he would keep a dozen city blocks between himself and the elaborate suites of the party elite. Nevertheless, he had the shrewdest political mind in the state, and he also had his own grapevine — old friends in county courthouses who would be only too glad to give him a running count over the phone. He was talking to them now; an unctuous club steward explained that he was on another line. By the time he was free Ham had a thick batch of upstate slips, and they compared figures.

"It's extraordinary, Markham." The judge coughed a high, precise cough. He had created his own cigar-smoke-filled room at the club. "Altogether it's the most remarkable development since T.R. raised havoc here in 1912. Imagine a Democrat leading in half the counties!"

"He can't win, can he, sir?" Ham knew. He wanted only to be told.

"Ah — no. To be vulgar, he may as well throw in the towel. Still, Witty's in rather an awkward position. He can scarcely claim a mandate, you know. Oh, his plurality will be impressive, but he will have been elected by mugwumps. The ugly issues of the past few days brought him the support of a mob" — to the judge, with his respect for party discipline, any switch voter was a member of the mob — "while his own organization was falling apart. I rather expect he'll be a one-term governor. You see, the farmers have always formed the hard Republican core. Banally speaking, they've propped us up. Now *they*'re mugwumps, too," he concluded sadly.

"Looks like a rebellion."

"Precisely. Daniel Shays all over again."

Red and blue lights were winking rapidly on Ham's box. He had two urgent calls waiting.

"I've got to break off. Will you be there all evening?"

"Eh? Oh, certainly. An old war horse, you know."

"Could you spare your Packard? I'd like to run up to State."

"Of course. Delighted. I'll send it right over. It's an eccentric machine, though. Better let Franklin drive you."

"I'll tell you tomorrow why I couldn't use a *Star* car," Ham said and turned to the switches, wondering whether it were true, as Dancy had once told him, that her father had rechristened his chauffeur on November 9, 1932.

"Take the blue," he told the number two man. "I'll take red."

The red light was Frosty.

"Got a Witty statement," he said breathlessly.

"From the butler's pantry?"

"What? Listen, this is good stuff. Long as the Bible, but the front office will love it. It's, you know, statesmanlike. Can you make any of it in the two-star?"

It was exactly 9:00 P.M. The second edition was about to close. Wet copies of the first would be up from the press room in five minutes.

"I'll try," Ham lied.

Caulkin called over, "You men have anything else coming?"

Number two had been having operator problems. His connection had just been restored. Ham replied, "A must here," and to Frosty, "O.K., shoot."

Frosty said:

"This is in quotes. 'I would be less than candid if I did not acknowledge that my deepest feelings tonight are those of humility. To assume the leadership of this mighty state is no light task, nor indeed do I take it lightly.' "

Ham typed:

"Died, suddenly — a dream, beloved of Adam R. River, in the first week of November, A loyal and devoted friend of long standing, its passing darkens the shadow cast by the loss of a son in World War II. An estranged daughter is making a new home in the West. A second son will mourn in the East. Condolences are extended to any other survivors in their bereavement. Interment: strictly private."

Frosty continued:

" 'Especially am I cognizant of my responsibilities at this crucial hour when the free world is locked in mortal struggle with the forces of godless Communism.' "

Number two banged down his phone and shouted, "That's it! Newt Albert says Doc's conceded."

Ham typed slowly:

"We shall all miss the aid and comfort of the deceased."

He looked up from his keyboard. The news of Doc's capitulation had brought Caulkin to his feet. The general managing editor looked like pictures of George Patton after the Bulge. His legs were braced far apart, his hands were on his hips, his expression was proud, arrogant, cock-a-hoop.

"Copy wallah!" Ham snapped. "Take this to the colonel."

He laid his earphones on the desk and listened solemnly to Frosty's muffled recital as Caulkin approved number two's brief insert, took the other page from the copy boy, glanced at it, glanced again, and lowered it uncertainly.

"Hiram!"

"On the double," said Ham, leaving the mumbling headphones.

"What the hell is this? It looks like a paid obit."

"It is an obit. I'm paying for it myself."

"I know, but —" He was muddled. This was his moment of conquest. He hadn't counted on the element of surprise. "You know we don't take notices at edition time."

"I've been away."

"And it sounds crazy anyway!"

"It's poetry."

"Poetry! In the *Star*?"

Overhead the city desk clock read 9:05. The room was relaxing; number two was heading for the cafeteria. A copy boy in a brilliant Python jacket appeared carrying a dozen first editions. Ham plucked one and handed it to Caulkin.

"In the *Star*," he said.

"By George, you're not making sense," Caulkin said angrily, hurling the obituary into his wastebasket.

"*Requiescat*," said Ham.

He waited. Caulkin scanned the top of the front page quickly, checking the layout, the headlines, the box with results from his eighty selected precincts. Everything was in order, Or almost in order. His eye darted to the lead story, set two columns wide. There, just between the headline and Ham's by-line, were two paragraphs in boldface.

Bulletin!

Hiram A. Markham, *Star* foreign correspondent and author of *Through Darkest Birmingham*, disclosed tonight that he had submitted his resignation to this newspaper. "More in anger than in sorrow," Mr. Markham said, "I take leave of a publication which has abused its privileged role to maul a man and maim an educational institution. This is no sacrifice for me. I'm not a lackey. I refuse to be a thinking man's filter. And I don't belong to the *Star* class in my own right. The management of the paper has always known that this last was important. Now I know it, too."

Mr. Markham was a protégé of the recently discredited president of the state university. A member of a family with no social standing and, indeed, no clear antecedents, Mr. Markham is a member of no desirable organizations. He made his remarkable charge of *Star* misconduct to Hallam Caulkin, the general managing editor of the newspaper, who, it was noted, was awarded the Bronze Star for excellence in keeping combat records during the North African campaign in 1943.

Caulkin's face turned putty-colored, then mulatto.

"You see, I was making sense," Ham said. "And I am paying."

"Joe Blow!" Caulkin shouted into his phone. "I want a stop-press!"

"With the election bulldog?" Ham inquired mildly.

Caulkin's hand drooped and he followed it. The first election edition was really an extra. If he delayed it there might as well be none.

"As you were, Joe." He looked faintly nauseated. "But kill that lead-all bulletin before the two-star." He replaced the receiver clumsily.

"You didn't resign," he said indistinctly.

"Oh yes. Your secretary has the envelope."

"Well —" Caulkin fumbled. He still didn't see the ramifications of what Ham had done. "You might have been decent about it!"

"I might have, but I wasn't. After all, some allowance must be made for my background. It's all there." He tapped the story. "I thought it quite fair."

Glimmer by glimmer, the radiance of Witty's victory was receding from Caulkin, and now he grasped the bulletin's implications. This wasn't merely something between him and Ham. In the next hour thousands of people would read those two paragraphs — would read, and laugh, and tell others, who would also laugh and ask everyone they met if he had heard the one about the *Star*. By morning the story would be lore. It would be repeated at every election, a timeless joke. And Caulkin was its butt. His friends would snicker behind his back. His wife would ask if it were really true that he had been decorated for being an efficient military clerk. Charlie Smathers would slyly record that it was. Marcus Gray would be furious.

"You may go," he said thickly.

"To Gideon," said Ham, and executed an about-face.

He stopped at the desk for his coat. The earphones were still squawking.

"You're coming through fine," he said, leaning over the mouthpiece.

"How's everything in the office?" asked Frosty, who was getting husky.

"Million and Half Voters Chose New Governor," Ham said. "Colonel Watches from Chairborne Outpost."

"I'm about half through. Jesus, it's endless. They ought to get a dozen editorials out of it, though." He resumed: "'The source of my moderate-progressive inspiration has always been the market place of ideas,'" and Ham listened gravely until Caulkin, who had been following him with an agate-eyed stare, lost his temper.

"*Move out*!" he bellowed across the startled desk.

"Just saddling up," Ham said, and slipped on his coat, and strolled away.

Caulkin flung himself into activity. He issued a spate of commands, directing a copy boy to confiscate all city room copies of the edition and store them on his desk — at least there would be no laughter *here* — and leaving orders that when the number two rewrite man returned he would become number one. All this took a full minute. Then he remembered that Ham said something about going to Gideon. Going how? He hadn't a car. By George, he wouldn't have the cheek to —

"Give me the *Star* garage. Hello? Caulkin here. Get this straight. Hiram Markham is no longer on the staff. He's not to be given a car under any circumstances. Do you understand? *No car for Markham*."

"He don't need one," the garage attendant said. "A big limousine just picked him up outside."

"A what? Oh. Oh, very well. Carry on."

He didn't hang up immediately. He had been looking at the top paper on his desk. The bottom fold was showing, and Today's Laff was conspicuous.

LOSER (D): When will you hold your next election?
WINNER (R): Tonight, at the crub.

"Joe Blow!" He clutched the receiver rigidly. "Joe! Is that Laff in the two-star? *What*? Well, kill it in the three! Melt it down! Yes! No, we don't need *any* Laff! By George, I want a full report . . ."

And across the room by Ham's vacant chair, Frosty droned on in a hoarse monotone:

"New paragraph. And the last, thank God. 'I trust and on the whole I believe that the sturdy farmers of this great agricultural state will speedily repledge their allegiance to our justly named G.O.P.' Got that, Ham? 'Our *Gee Oh Pee.*' Hello, Ham? Hello? Hello? *Hey*!"

**

Jill admitted Ham to the Mansion.

"Hi. Did I keep you waiting? I did, didn't I. Poor man, and it's so nasty out and all. It's just I've gotten so *tubby*, I can't get *around*."

Ham stamped snow on the mat and shed his coat. "You've been here all evening?"

"Yes. I guess it's the end of my job," she said sadly. "I mean, what with Doc getting the flushogram and everything."

"Flushogram?"

"The jilt."

"I see." Jill was always instructive.

"All those *droops*," she said crossly. "Honestly, I'd give anything if *I* was old enough to vote."

Of course, that was absurd, Ham thought. The Jills of the world never bothered with causes; they believed only in the life within them. And that was their strength. There was something indestructible about Jill, a strenuous, irrepressible vitality. He missed it in himself tonight, and envied her.

"Where's Doc?"

"He went out by himself a few minutes ago. Looking a little oddballish, and no wonder. *Mrs.* River's in her room. Want to see her?"

Ham hesitated, then nodded. She showed him upstairs, bounding awkwardly ahead.

Sarah was knitting. "Sakes alive! It's Ham Markham, or I miss my guess!"

He looked at her sharply. He had been reluctant to come up because he had thought she would be more stricken than Doc. She wasn't: her color was high, her eyes cheerful.

"You set right there and visit with me. Wait downstairs, Jill—you can't tell, we might have lots of callers." After Jill had gone she whispered, "A nice girl, but into everything." She folded her hands. "Now we can talk in peace."

Ham was taken aback. Her serenity was so unexpected. "I just wanted to say how sorry I am."

"Tell *Doc* that," Sarah said tartly. "*I'm* not sorry, not the littlest bit. Believe you me, it's all for the best. He'd have been wretched with those men. I told both Sam and that Mr. Albert so last time they phoned."

"But he doesn't even have State any more," Ham said helplessly.

"No. And maybe that's a blessing, too. He'll just *have* to rest now."

And that, Ham saw, was what Sarah had always wanted. There

were women who could find themselves only by comforting men who had lost their way, and she was one of them. When Doc had been on the crest there had been no place for her. Now he had been toppled, and she could lead him into the quiet shade and make him lean on her.

"He's outdoors this very minute. Can you imagine? In weather like this? But you know him — he has to walk things off. Fasten your overshoes, I told him. Bundle up warm. And after all that bless me if he didn't forget his scarf. I had to run out the door and fetch him back."

"Where will you live?" Ham asked despairingly, for he was a man, and couldn't sympathize.

"Oh tut, that's nothing to fret about. He might stay in Gideon. That coach, Yab — Yab —"

"Yablonski."

"Polish. Well, Doc said today he's leaving here, so that'll be open. And if it doesn't work out, there's always the farm."

Ham shook his head in bewilderment. "He lost that in the Depression."

"Lost *his*," she said craftily. "*My* place is still in Conway County."

So that was Sarah's solution. Doc would either go back to the bottom rung of the coaching ladder or retire on her slim dowry. Somehow neither sounded like him. Yet it would have to be one or the other. He was naked now. He would have to take whatever clothes there were.

Ham stood. This had been more painful than he had expected.

"It's hard to think of State without Doc," he said, his voice catching.

"Hard for him, too." She puckered slightly. "You won't believe it — he spent the whole blessed dinner hour worrying about who the new president's going to be."

"Well, the trustees are bound to ask for his opinion."

"Are they?" She looked surprised. "I expect you're right. Anyway, he took all that time to settle on two names. Let me see." She pinched the bridge of her nose. "They rhyme, like a limerick. Oh yes — Budge and judge."

Ham took a tight breath. Budge? Not likely: he had told all Gideon how much he disliked administration. The judge? That was more likely. He felt strongly about State now. He just might be available.

And if he wanted it, it would be his. Witty, weak in the party, wouldn't dare snub a Republican elder. It would be the best possible appointment. The judge would make a superb president — even though the board, Ham thought laconically, might cringe to hear the head of the university call it Aggie.

He pressed her hand.

"Racing off so soon?"

"I thought I might find Doc."

She mused. "Yes, you do that. A little company is the best cure for what ails him. He's feeling out of sorts, you know," she said, with the first trace of compassion. "Right up till the last minute he believed he was going to win. After supper I thought he was going to catch fire, he was so fidgety. He went into the library, and he didn't speak a word to me. He was talking on the phone, scribbling numbers, watching the portable television and I don't know what-all. It's a mercy it didn't take long for the truth to come out. That room's a sight as it is. Once he'd told Mr. Albert he was giving up, he left, and I started to tidy up. Well, I picked up just one paper. Only one. After I'd read it *I* gave up, too." She smiled wistfully, the smile of a mother who had discovered her son wearing his father's hat. "It was an *acceptance* statement! I guess he'd written it sometime during the day. It did beat all, though. Such flowery language you never heard."

"Good-by, Mrs. River."

"You mind his scarf's tied tight."

"I'll mind." He edged away.

"Not that it'll help him much. It's one of that store kind. No more warmth than a dishrag. Now *this*" — she held up her knitting — "will keep him cosy as a stove."

Downstairs Ham found Jill in the library, twisting the television knob.

"Not a thing but news, news, news," she complained. "I mean, the election *is* over."

". . . which places the Witty plurality at forty thousand," said a sonorous commentator.

"Yes, it's over," said Ham, his voice dirty with strain.

There was something pathetic in the room's disorder. Crumpled pages lay strewn on the alcove floor, and here and there the corner of a sheet revealed a sum done hurriedly, a frantic subtraction — the wild, stabbed arithmetic of a loser watching the embers of his hope turn gray and die. Ham didn't look for the draft of Doc's acceptance. Even Sarah hadn't been entitled to read that. A man's love letters to himself were for himself alone.

He asked Jill which way Doc had gone.

"I haven't the remotest. He could be most anywhere. I mean, he just took off. Is it snowing again? If it isn't, you might trail him."

It wasn't, and that was what Ham did. Sliding in beside the judge's chauffeur he directed him along the drive, down which the Packard proceeded slowly, like a police car stalking a vagrant. At the turning they saw steps, big, scalloped pits on Ham's side, headed down toward the campus. Some fresh snow had fallen — since early afternoon the storm had been intermittent — but not enough to cover Doc's prints. He had cut heedlessly through drifts, as though in defiance of Sarah, and he had walked with the unswerving direction of a man who knows where he is going.

Ham opened his door. "I'm getting out, Franklin."

"Want me to wait here, Mr. Markham?"

"No, over by the big gate. I'll meet you there."

Doc's tracks led down the steep Mansion hill path. Ham stood alone a moment on the crest, studying them and shivering and listening to the receding crunch of the whitewall tires. Below him State glittered and shimmered like a snowscape in a fable. It was late, cold; Blandford Library had closed, and the students had fled to their rooms, leaving a fleecy, fairylike, Christmas card campus, silent but for the sounds of night and illuminated only by isolated shafts of light fanning out from the great Georgian halls and the colonial lantern posts which marked the crisscrossed ways between Student Union and University Village, Fraternity Park and Maiden Lane, stadium and Athletic Dorm. How magnificent it is, thought Ham. How exquisite — and how fragile. The delicate, sparkling umbrellas in the elm tops would melt tomorrow with the dawn's warm breath; the jeweled icicles that stitched the eaves of Archer Chapel would last only a little longer, and then the plain below would be mutilated by plows, soiled by boots. Snow is so splendid at first fall, he thought, and it tarnishes so quickly. Like beauty, like youth; like all that Doc had held inviolable it either disappears without a trace or is swiftly transformed into such a travesty of the glory we knew yesterday that we resent *it,* blame *it,* and wish it had never been.

He picked his way down the hill, ruefully, for it was bitter on the slope. Clouds of icy silt slid off the sumac boughs and stung his cheeks; his ears ached; his chest trembled. The snow was higher than his brogan tops, and his feet would have been wet long before he reached bottom if he hadn't stepped carefully in Doc's steps. He was following him once more, though this time not into strange country, for Doc had veered toward one of the few untouched relics of the old campus. The cratered file left by his overshoes vanished into a dark, familiar grove of canoe birches east of the stadium. Ham's breath quickened. Since the war the clearing beyond the trees had been known only as the Titan's practice field. Yet once it had been so much more. For fifty years State teams had fought to check Peabody on that battered ground, and Ham's first and last memories of it were of splendor in failure — of Doc's mighty solo and of his own stumbling catch on the two-yard line. Time had run out then as it had run out tonight, disqualification and penalties dashing the underdog hope. Doc's truest instincts had led him here now; his real trophy pavilion was Aggie Field.

It began to snow again. Gently at first the tender feathery flakes drifted down from the black void overhead. Abruptly the air thickened; Doc's craters began to fill. Ham turned up his collar, and as he passed the silvery trunk of the first birch he heard, as from a great distance, the chimes of Archer's glockenspiel.

Fair and fairly shall thou always
Be beloved, great
Blue and true through later gray days
Sainted symbol, State!

It was cold in the chapel. The chimer's fingers were numb. In slow measure the strains of the alma mater tolled across Gideon, a dirge, largo; a taps:

Ever, always, our eternal
Shrine and temple be
Never shall we leave thy altar
— Loyal, faithful, we!

Oh Coach, *why?* thought Ham in sudden anguish; why always the forfeit? Why can't the favorite lose once? Yet there was no need to ask Doc. Ham knew — shielding his eyes from the white, blinding gusts and listening to the pilfered melody echoing in the copse he knew: all Doc's life he had failed because he had confused sheen and substance. Even as he had distrusted the tailoring and accent and mannerisms of the Brahmin caste he had secretly coveted them; he had believed that he could make State a Cornell by borrowing Cornell's anthem, a Peabody by copying Peabody's gate. He had thought he could offer everyone in the state the lush ivy tradition if he transplanted the ivy here and used it to clothe the frivolities of a Tate — ice cream workshops and child development laboratories, mobiles and electric eyes, courses in life insurance, in television continuity, in airline hostess techniques. Now that Budge had exposed the fraud it was a shabby thing, but in its heyday it had been dazzling. The public had trusted the placebic curricula while the ivy flourished in alien soil, growing taller and stronger and more abundant until its leaves turned a brilliant Metrocolor green — the shade of arsenic, though few saw that, or noticed that the vine was corrupting the very qualities Doc in his innocence had believed incorruptible. Then, with learning defiled and purity besmirched, it had flowered hideously in Red Stacy and Daffy Dix. They were its final issue. In them evil reached its ultimate blossom, and Doc in horror had hacked them down, and in rage the deceived stadium faithful had turned on him. Now all he had left was stalk, and even that wasn't his any more. Tate had seen to that, although Tate had been only an instrument, really; the forfeit, the original sin, had been Doc's, and Doc alone had lost the struggle.

Ham was staggering in the grove. It had grown so since he was last here. Only a little light penetrated the branches, a frail beam from a single lantern post, the last sentinel of the new campus, and the storm had mounted; Doc's tracks were becoming indistinct. The snow found Ham's socks at last and dampened them unpleasantly. A fresh deluge, a chill sensation on his neck. Wind, bleak chill; treacherous stones underneath. He plunged on. His watch strap caught on a stem; he stopped to free it and loosened a dollop of snow above, which frosted his hair, face, throat. More stones, a stiffening wind. He ran afoul of tangled shrubs, and being unsure of himself he blundered this way and that, this way and that, until he tottered past the last birch bole and emerged, frozen and harassed, into the open.

Here he felt surer. He had known this place so well. Before him stretched a gray gloom, hazy and flickering and serried, yet he saw landmarks. The ghostly silhouette of a giant oak loomed on his right; he was near the west end zone, within a few yards of the scuffed patch of grass, now shrouded by the wind-wrinkled snow, where seventeen years before he had juggled and held Spook's pass. This was the north border, the visitor's side. On the south horizon there was a slight rise; down there lay the goal they had defended in that final period, there Doc had lurched with the Peabody safety men on his back in Ham's childhood. A line of spaced maples defined the boundaries of the home team side, and crouching and squinting he made out Doc's trail, a twin line of blurred hollows crinkling the immaculate surface of the twenty-yard line and cutting diagonally toward the center of the maple rank. Ham blinked—there was a dim movement across the field. It was repeated, repeated again, lost, seen, lost and seen again. The wind slackened, and between the sweeping flurries he glimpsed a misty figure, swinging arms in unison. The stance was unmistakable. It was Doc.

Doc stood apart in time, a few feet from where the State bench wasn't, looking over to where the Peabody fans weren't, his overshoes braced on an invisible sideline. Were bench, fans, sideline there for him? It was impossible to tell, but they were for Ham; he could distinguish the grid of lime markers, could discern the throaty cheers, could detect above the iron cold the rancid scent of sweat. A field, a scrimmage, conflict; he saw them clearly on the screen of memory, evoking images of the vivid autumns when he, like the snow, had been fresh and young, and Doc had made all issues one issue, as hard and sharp as an ice crystal:

—*Left end! Ham Markham, the lah-de-dah swamp Yankee!*

—*Fullback! Johnny Melotti, the big greaser!*

—*Quarterback! Sy Epstein, the smart kike!*

—*Right Half! How do you say this hunky's name? Joe Rzegocki!*

And how do you say it now, when the banner is fallen and the distinction between caste and caste is bleared, when the apotheosis of the Thirties has been betrayed because you had to try to cross the scrimmage barricade and steal the mandarin signals? Do you change Rzegocki to Rogers and put him in a back pew at St. Timothy's and pin a big Witty button on his narrow new lapel? That was in Ham's heart, but he couldn't ask it, even in thought. Above ideas, people; more than the issue, the man—he lived by that, and so he had no reproaches for Doc, only a sense of desolation that the hero had been crushed, and tears within that in the end the game had turned out to be just a game. A lost game. Forfeited now and forever. Dying on a harsh last whistle. Leaving the swamp Yankee and the greaser and the kike and the hunky to straggle off in a broken crocodile of defeat.

The swinging arms over there stopped swinging. Doc turned away and moved slowly downfield into deepening murk. Ham knelt on one knee, head in hand. He couldn't shout after him. He had nothing to say.

Yet was Doc's vision dead? Had he really failed? Red said so, Daffy did, Tate did, and Budge confirmed them. Nevertheless Ham wondered. He wanted so much more. And presently he saw more. The past had been slain, that was certain. But perhaps it was well dead; in malice there was only more malice. The new campus would remain. And that was a gain; for all the *Star*'s sneers about bricks and mortar there was no teaching in a pasture. Perhaps Doc had done all one man could do. Perhaps his career had been political after all, a rebellious rising that carried the wave just so far and left it to its own momentum. If his empire had been a stultifying parody of learning, if he had consecrated the wrong idols, he had also broken a sacred precedent, which was the real reason the *Star* hated him so. His yearning for a democracy of the mind had brought intellectual chaos, a collapse of standards; but he had given the disinherited their great chance. That wasn't mean, that wasn't small. Peabody, Ham remembered, had been almost fifty years old before students were allowed to major in anything except religion. In another generation, possibly within a decade, card-carrying educators like Tate would be cast beyond the gate. Standards would come, and with them would come the values, not of Haves or of Have-nots, not of Ins or Outs, but of a new society making its own laws, its own manners, its own truth. Ham rose slowly. Clearer and clearer the paradox became: in disaster triumph, from the ashes the phoenix, Doc the vanquished yet the sower of the seed which would in time bring a finer, fairer flowering.

"You won!" he cried exultantly across the smoke-colored waste.

But Doc hadn't heard. Oblivious, he retreated down the far side, to the old ten-yard line, to the five, to the buried end zone. The twinkling rays of the one lantern, deflected by birches, shone feebly on his bowed shoulders. He was going, he was going, and he hadn't heard.

"You won!" Ham cried again, and cupped his hands to his face. "You *won!*"

But the sifting snow foiled him. The swirling snow baffled sound. The hurrying snow fell in a dense curtain, and Doc was going, and Doc was gone, and Ham stood alone under a sky barren of stars calling desperately, calling brokenly, calling vainly to the night.